FIRE OF THE FOREBEARS

HERITOR'S HELM BOOK ONE

L.A. BUCK

REDHEARTH

This book is a work of fiction. Names, characters, places, and incidents are the product of the author's imagination or are used fictitiously. Any resemblance to actual events, locales, or persons—living or dead—is coincidental.

Copyright © 2022 by L.A. Buck. All rights reserved.
Cover illustration by Erik Taberman.
Cover design by Maria Pangilinan.
Edited by Emma O'Connell.
Proofread by Ellie Owen.

Outside of reviews, no portion of this book may be reproduced in any form without written permission from the publisher or author, except as permitted by U.S. copyright law. If you would like permission to use material from this book (other than for review purposes) please contact Labuckauthor@gmail.com.

ISBNs: 979-8-9853265-1-2 (trade paperback), 979-8-9853265-2-9 (ebook), 979-8-9853265-6-7 (hardback)

For a digital and interactive copy of the map, visit my website: https://labuckauthor.com/

*"A CHILD OF SCYTHE AND SWORD
THIS SONG THE BLACK BIRD SINGS
RIGHT BY ÌSENDORÁL RESTORED
VICTORY THE AUTUMN BRINGS
ONE FLAME FROM THE SHADOWS
WILL LIGHT ONE THOUSAND MORE
A GALLANT HEART OVERFLOWS
TAKING BACK WHAT WAS BEFORE"*

Contents

Map	VIII
	IX
Part One	1
1. Claws	2
2. Bound by the Law	10
3. Láefe L'Fonfyr	21
4. A Grey World	29
5. Gift-Giving	38
6. Harvest	44
7. Six	54
8. Travail	58
9. Prisoner of War	64
10. Fool's Leap	74
11. Of Beasts and Monsters	83
12. Homecoming	89
Part Two	93
13. Two Paths Diverge	94
14. Ìsendorál	110
15. Twelve	120

16. Sword-Bearer	122
17. The Toll	130
18. Davka'vara	135
19. The Crowfoot's Tale	145
20. Domvik	151
21. Half Truths	159
22. The Long Ride	167
23. Flickering In Firelight	181
24. Not Without Consequences	189
25. By Way Of The River	199
26. The Council of Nansûr	208
27. Bellicosity	217
28. A Good Man	228
Part Three	235
29. Lingering Enigma	236
30. Bargaining	244
31. Reciprocity	250
32. Shadow of Shalford Tower	255
33. Backtracking	268
34. Patchwork	274
35. Rih Hill	287
36. Under Cover of Darkness	300
37. Ghosts	307
38. The Withering Tree	314
39. Errant Thoughts	323
40. Veracity	332
41. The Reckoning	340

42. Mortal Severance	354
43. Juncture	367
Part Four	373
44. Traitor Among Renegades	374
45. Bounden	385
46. Repercussions	393
47. Duty and Dereliction	397
48. Invocations	408
49. Banished Tears	415
50. Arbitration	423
51. Among the Fallen	436
52. Pretense	451
53. Fire	460
54. As the Stones Settle	484
55. Alone	493
56. First Impressions	498
57. By the Power	505
58. Will and Prophecy	514
A Note from the Author	523
Glossary	525
Want to Read More?	527
About the Author	529
Find me Online!	530

Avaron

Kedar

Eigen Mountains

Wynhire Waste

Fool's Leap
Compound

Everard River

Tarr Fiann

Davka'vara

Feldland Plains

Gulf of Mrok

Arléant

Saligen Mountains

Salkrov

Rivmere Forest

Lake Merholm

Lovaria

- Rohgen Mountains
- Shalford
- Dol
- Laroe
- Rih Hill
- Beaduras River
- Drida
- Edras
- Deorwynn Forest
- U'Dal Plains
- Ciridian Bay
- Lynavir

PART ONE

ERSTWHILE

Chapter One

CLAWS

Leafy branches snatched at her cloak and sleeves but Kura ran anyway, heart pounding, through the thickest part of the forest. She knew she ought to be afraid. She had been the first time, probably the second, but now excitement sent the blood coursing through her veins. That, and foolish hope.

She threw a glance over her shoulder, scanning the sun-speckled undergrowth to make sure none of the other farmhands had followed. They'd be crazy to try—there were simple rules for surviving the Wynshire and this broke most of them—but it didn't take guts to ask where she had gone. If they pressed her, she'd have to make up *another* story, her unsatisfied neighbors would talk, and slowly but surely word of this would reach her family.

Somehow, only the fear of disappointing them stuck with her.

The distant gurgle of the Everard River echoed in the ravine, but Kura turned uphill toward a group of fir trees that stood among a ring of boulders. She leapt over the nearest stone, hands and feet sliding across the damp moss, and dropped into the basin to wait in the cool shadows. Birds called in the distance and the afternoon breeze whispered through the branches, but no footsteps followed hers.

Pulling a leather parcel from her baggy pants pocket, Kura rose and secured the package within the half-rotted trunk standing in the heart of the grove. She slunk back into the shadows, then hauled herself into the nearest tree. It wasn't easy climbing the evergreens—she was always left covered in sap—but she kept her feet close to the trunk as she trod the spindly stairs to her customary perch, as near the top as she dared go.

Now, she waited.

She steadied her breath as she swept an unruly lock of auburn hair behind her ear. Her contact had told her not to wait, but she didn't give serious thought to obeying him. There was always *someone* watching whatever moved in the Wynshire, and while most would just keep watching, she couldn't trust the more curious to keep their paws on their own business.

Twigs snapped, then a grizzly bear's muzzle pushed through the underbrush. Kura stiffened. She'd expected a squirrel, or maybe one of the badgers that lived on the hill, but not a bear. The beast lumbered into the basin and rose on two legs, its wet, black nose wrinkling as it sniffed the air. A man, shrouded in a mottled green cloak, struggled to keep his seat on the creature's back.

"Down, boy!" the man said.

"I'm not a dog," the bear grumbled, but he begrudgingly dropped to all fours. Sunlight flashed off a chunk of onyx decorating the leather strap on one furry limb—the mark of the Northern Sleuth. But what was he doing this far west?

"Of course you're not a dog." The man laughed nervously and slid off the beast's back. "I wouldn't dare imply anything like that."

Kura clenched and unclenched her fist around the hilt of her sword. They couldn't be king's men—at least, the bear couldn't. Could he? Whoever they were, they shouldn't be here.

The man stretched, then sighed as he glanced around the grove. "So, where is it?"

The bear huffed and jerked his nose toward the hollow trunk.

Chewing her inner lip, Kura pushed aside one of the pine branches to watch as the man pulled the parcel from the trunk. She breathed a frustrated sigh. Maybe she could scare them off.

She dropped from the tree and landed with a grunt on the needle-covered ground below. The bear snarled and pulled back as the man shouted in surprise.

Kura rested her hand on her sword hilt and fought to keep her voice steady. "Who are you?"

The bear scoffed. "I thought I smelled a human, but I guess it was only you, child." He bared his thick, yellow teeth in what might have been a grin. "How many springs have you seen? Nine, I'd say, by the looks of you."

Kura frowned. "I've seen twenty."

"My mistake, then. You humans are all so tiny."

"Hey now," the man said, raising his arms as he stepped between Kura and the bear. "We're all friends here, right? Let's be nice."

Kura met his gaze. A brown scarf hid all but his dark eyes, his black skin, and a few strands of thick, black hair, but he had a stocky build—most likely from muscle, though it was hard to tell under his cloak. His voice marked him as her elder, but not by much.

"You recognize this?" the man asked.

Kura flinched as his hand drifted toward his broadsword, but he reached into a pouch on his belt and produced an opaque crystal suspended from a hemp cord.

Surprised, Kura let go of her sword hilt. She reached behind her shirt collar and produced a similar stone from around her neck. "What happened to the last guy?"

The man shook his head. "Lost him in a skirmish with a royal patrol a week ago."

"Oh." She hadn't exchanged more than a few sentences with the fellow, but it still felt like she should have more to say. "I'm sorry."

The bear snorted. "You aren't supposed to recognize us, and we're not supposed to recognize you." He extended a massive claw toward the parcel in the man's hand. "Might I assume you've forgotten what this is supposed to be as well?"

Kura forced herself to look the bear in the eye but couldn't help taking a step back. "I marked on your map all the places I've noticed any creature activity. As always, though, it's just been nostkynna, like you. I've never seen saja here."

"Good enough." The bear sighed, though it sounded more like a growl. "We should depart. No doubt this idling will lead to the death of us as it is."

Kura frowned again. "I wasn't followed."

"The edges of the world are not your refuge, girl. A darkness moves in this land."

"Darker than the Wynshire at night?" She laughed, shaking her head. "Don't worry about me, I'm used to it."

The bear measured her with unblinking eyes. "Perhaps you shouldn't be."

"Alright," the man muttered, and gave the bear a pat on the shoulder. "Stop terrorizing the locals. Let's go."

"Wait—" Kura froze when the bear swung back to look at her. "I apologize if I'm being blunt, but the other guy promised to secure safe passage for six to a home in the mainstates in exchange for my information."

Another growl rumbled deep in the bear's throat. "Is that all you care about? Your own skin?"

Kura bit back a scowl. "I want to see Dradge gone as much as anyone, but you can't fault me for putting my family first."

The man nodded. "We'll do what we can, I'm sure."

Kura studied his face. His tone was too placating for her to trust him to follow through, but what else was she supposed to do? "Thank you."

The bear turned back toward the forest, and he and his cloaked companion disappeared among the trees, the gentle sway of low-hanging branches the only remainder of their passage.

"Goodbye, then," she muttered.

A cool fall breeze whistled through the grove, making the shadows dance on the boulders and dry leaves flutter to the ground with a muffled crunch. Kura slipped her thumbs behind her belt and strolled back the way she had come so urgently before.

How many months had she been doing this now? At least seven—three more would make it a year—but she and her family weren't a day closer to leaving this godsforsaken place. She kicked half-heartedly at the bed of leaves.

At least I'm trying to—

A branch creaked above, and Kura stopped. She surveyed the trees, hardly allowing herself a breath. After a dozen heartbeats she caught a glimpse of a sleek, tan form leaping from branch to branch. A cougar, headed toward the fields.

The cat paused, the tree limb bending under its weight, his pale eyes locking with Kura's. He bared his fangs, stuck out his tongue to jeer at her, then leapt to the next branch.

Kura muttered a curse and took off at a sprint. *Those cats are getting bold.*

With mere animals the solution was simple—loud noises, more people, some strategically placed campfires at night—but nothing was that easy with a nostkynna. Much more than talking animals, their intellect made them most akin to a human. Kura only hoped she wouldn't have to kill this one. As she'd learned with the wolves, that made future negotiation difficult.

The cougar wove casually through the treetops, pausing at times to watch birds scatter or grin at Kura below, but she ran through briars and tangled branches to keep her trajectory straight—and pulled ahead. She burst into the sunlit cornfield and tore through tall, brittle stalks until she reached the wheat. She'd left the others here; the man was swinging a scythe to fell more of the harvest while two women followed behind him, gathering the cut stalks into bundles.

"Cougar!" Kura shouted, and each face shot up to meet hers. They hesitated, the women holding Kura's gaze as the man looked to the trees. "Leave the stuff, go get help!"

One woman pointed toward the field. "The goats—"

"I know, I'll get them, go!" Kura charged through the field, doing her best to keep from trampling the crop. She pressed her index fingers under her tongue and let out a sharp whistle.

A speckled, long-eared face peeked out from among the stalks.

"Cougar!" Kura shouted. The goat stared at her, and a few more shaggy heads emerged from the wheat beyond it. "Cougar!"

With a piercing yowl, the cat leapt from the trees and landed at the edge of the cleared field. One goat bleated, then ran for the footpath between the crops, and the rest of the herd followed. Kura leapt onto the path after them, skidding to a stop as she drew her sword.

The cougar sauntered alongside the rows of corn, baring a toothy grin. "Hello, *human*." He spat out the last word like a curse. "What a pretty claw you have. A pity it's only one."

Kura raised her weapon, her hands steady despite her pounding heart. "No farther!"

The cougar laughed, then sat back on his haunches to raise one of his front legs. "These are real claws, squatter." Five barbs shot out from the cat's paw. "If you didn't taste so terrible I might have already given you a closer look."

Kura didn't move. "This is our field. The wolves respect that now, the bears get a tribute, the foxes and the raccoons—"

"Is that what you think?" The cat crept forward again, lean muscle rippling beneath his thin coat as his tail twitched. "That you can bully and barter your way to safety with all of us?"

Kura took a hesitant step away. Someone should have been here by now to back her up.

The cat pounced, his claws aimed at her chest. She lunged to the side, slashing the beast across the face with her sword. He howled and skidded across the dusty path, but was airborne again in an instant. Kura tried to raise her sword, but the cat drove his claws into her shoulders and knocked her to the ground.

His howl filled her ears. In a wild panic, Kura flung the weight of teeth and fur off her and scrambled to her feet. The creature lay on the ground, writhing, as blood soaked his side and turned his pink tongue red. With a grimace, Kura drove her sword through his eye, and the creature stilled.

"Kura!"

She glanced up from the carcass, letting out a breath. Her brother, Faron, a longbow in his hand and a quiver full of arrows rattling on his belt, ran toward her from across the field.

"About time!"

Faron greeted her with his usual unamused frown. "You alright?"

Kura nodded. Faron was three years her junior, although now his lanky frame made him at least a head taller. Like her, he had a square face with strong features, although he sported fewer freckles on his white skin, and the long hair tied back behind his head was a deep brown.

"Wait." Concern sprang into his eyes, and he pointed at her shoulder. "Kura, it scratched you—"

"Hey." Kura batted his hand away, then ran her fingers over the claw-marks in her quilted doublet. The cat had torn through several layers of her makeshift gambeson, but hadn't reached her skin. "I told you I'd make you some of this if you want."

Faron shook his head absently and prodded the carcass with the end of his bow. "Is he dead?"

"He's dead." Kura let those words linger as she forced herself to look at the cat. It didn't always feel like it, but killing a nostkynna was essentially the same as killing a human. She tried not to let herself forget that. "I gave him a chance to leave."

Faron slung the bow over his shoulder. "Looks like one of the Treefall pride."

Kura frowned at the beast's bloody shoulder, which bore his clan mark: a deep white scar in the simple shape of a tree. "Another one of them was lurking around here last week. Killed two of the goats."

"Did you try and chase that one off on your own, too?"

Kura flashed him an innocent smile. "I follow the rules, Faron. Negotiate, present terms, then fight."

Faron watched her with a skeptical frown, then sighed. "Well, come on. Let's get rid of this."

Kura cleaned her sword off in the grass before slipping it back into its scabbard, then joined Faron in picking up one of the cougar's rear paws to drag the carcass toward the forest.

"You know," Faron said, "Father would kill me if something happened to you while he was gone."

"Right back at you, little brother."

Faron stifled a groan. He no longer appreciated that distinction, and Kura knew it, but it didn't change the truth.

It still startled her sometimes when she caught a clear glimpse of the fingers missing on his left hand or noticed for the hundredth time the impaired movement of that arm. She tried to forget that day had ever happened—mostly she did—but it remained the moment she'd become the oldest, and she would always carry the weight of that responsibility.

Faron dropped the cougar's paw as they came to the edge of the forest. "Here's good enough."

Kura did the same, examining the trees above. "I suppose we ought to bury him?"

"Of course." Faron stepped forward to clear away a patch of brush. "How would you like it if someone killed you and just tossed your body in the woods to be eaten by the animals?"

Kura half-heartedly picked up some fallen branches. "I meant maybe we should leave him out, as a warning or something."

Faron chuckled, as though it was supposed to be a joke.

"Dradge's soldiers do that, to men. He sticks their heads on pikes and everything."

Faron gave her a discerning look. "To Avaronian citizens?"

"No, Lovarian scouts. But that's kind of the point. It's to scare away trespassers. And for all we know, he'd do the same to us out here." Faron didn't reply, and Kura gave a sigh of defeat. "Well, are you going to give him a eulogy? Father always says something."

Faron shot her a sideways glance, but straightened and folded his hands respectfully before him. "All transgressions are forgiven, *tasona*, and may your spirit find peace."

Kura nodded thoughtfully. "Tasona?"

"I think that's their word for cougar."

She shrugged. "Good enough. I guess I'll go find a shovel."

Chapter Two

Bound by the Law

Most considered the city of Edras to be the crown jewel of Avaron, but Triston had his reservations. The castle Avtalyon was a jewel, maybe, but while most rooftops still sparkled in the sunrise, the city growing around it better paralleled uncut stone.

Rows of short, neglected log cabins lined the alleyway where he pulled his horse to a stop. A line of soldiers, dressed in chain mail overlaid with a tunic bearing a black bird overlaying a red, pointed cross—the mark of the king—waited behind a makeshift wall of wooden crates stretching across the town square. A similar barricade lay at the other edge of the courtyard, behind which several common folk cowered, hurling both insults and the occasional stone.

This was a single misstep from becoming a riot.

Triston dismounted and left his grey mare in what he hoped would be the safety of the alley, then strode toward the group of soldiers.

The nearest man turned, leaping to his feet as he slapped his right fist over his heart in salute. "Prince Triston, sir! I—I didn't know you were coming, sir."

"I didn't know I was either. This was supposed to be routine." Triston looked up as another shout—possibly his name—rose from among the commoners. He turned away, then nearly grinned as he found the old soldier still standing at attention. A shorter man, his rugged appearance contradicted his grandfatherly air. It was a good thing one of the younger captains wasn't in charge of this. "At ease, Garan."

The soldier relaxed his stance, then flinched as a stone struck the nearest crate. The commoners cheered, and Garan met Triston's gaze. "I'm not sure you should be here, sir. We were thinkin' about goin' in with the batons."

"What happened?"

Garan looked down at his polished boots as he slipped a hand under his helmet to scratch the back of his neck. "We came to fulfill three draft orders, sir. The first two fellers came easy enough, but this last one, well... his momma riled up the whole block."

Triston sighed deeply. In the past, any man called to serve had come at the asking—out of loyalty or fear, he didn't know—but lately a draft notice was as likely to start a war as compel a trained man to fight in one. Not that there was a true war going on anymore, but that was beside the point.

Another soldier jogged to Garan's side. "We've got fifteen—Triston, sir!" He grinned and came to a salute, right fist over his heart. "What are you doing here?"

"Hey, Mory." Triston returned the salute. "How's the baby?"

"Oh, she's doing great, sir. She said her first word yesterday."

"Already? What was it?"

Mory stifled a laugh. "I don't know I should be repeating it."

Garan cleared this throat. "Sir, you want us going in with the batons?"

Triston glanced across the courtyard. He glimpsed one larger woman and two men brave enough to peek out from behind their barricade; they couldn't be armed with more than the stones they'd already thrown. The rest of their fellow would-be rioters scrambled away, back to the presumed safety of their stoops and doorways.

He nodded toward the shield Mory had slung over his back. "Can I borrow that?"

Mory shrugged, then handed him the shield—it was a light wood, circular, and rimmed with a strip of hardened steel. "What you got in mind, sir?"

Triston attempted a smile as he strapped the shield on his arm. "Well, if this doesn't work, just have your batons ready."

He jumped up onto one of the wooden crates that made the soldiers' barricade. The commoners on the other side shouted to one another—panicked attempts at cooperation or commands, like a shield line breaking to a cavalry charge—and the woman hurled a stone at Triston's head.

"Hey!" He knocked the stone aside with the shield. "Can I just talk with all of you, or what?"

The woman growled. "I ain't got nothin' I want to say to you!"

Triston stepped down into the open space between the barricades. Both of the men ducked behind their crates, but the woman stood her ground.

"Well," Triston said, holding his shield at the ready, "I have something to say to you."

The woman laughed, and Triston was close enough now to see the glaze in her eyes. She was drunk. "Just scram, you little whelp! You might be happy traipsing all over for your daddy, but my boy ain't dying for any whims of his." She scowled and spit on the street. "The rebel king, ha! Look where it got the lot of us!"

Her companions behind the barricade rallied at this, and one of them threw another stone at Triston; it went wide and clattered to the cobblestones. The rebel king. Triston had of course heard that title before, though it used to be spoken with pride. It wasn't entirely accurate. His father's rise to power had been a military coup, not a rebellion.

Triston stepped as close to their barricade as he dared. "You know anyone who's gone through the year fifteen training is eligible to be called up. It's a random process."

The woman muttered something and balled her large hands into fists.

"And don't go thinking I've got a pass. I've been in the service since I was eleven, I didn't have a choice." Although, had he been able to choose, Triston wasn't sure he'd change anything.

"Ha!" The woman jabbed her finger at his face. He fought the urge to duck behind his shield before he realized her hand was empty. "Your daddy's gonna keep you safe, keep you dayrides from any real fightin'!"

Triston held back a grin. Her claim was decidedly untrue—his father had too much respect for him to do anything of the sort—but there was no use explaining that here. "Well, then, how about I keep your boy with me? He'll go where I go."

The woman eyed him, suspicious. "You'd do that?"

"Sure, I'd do that. What's he trained in so far?"

The woman shuffled her grubby boots and grumbled something under her breath. "Crossbow."

"Perfect. I can always use another man with a bow." Fortunately, that was true.

The woman let out a strained sigh, and her angry facade cracked. "Darrow?"

Her shaky voice hung in the air as a young man peeked up from behind the crate. Triston drew in a breath. *Damn, am I that old?* The requested recruit was supposed to be sixteen—only five years his junior—but the soldier that stood before him wasn't much more than a boy.

The woman wrapped her arms around her son, her bulky frame enveloping his wiry one. "You come back, you hear me?"

The boy nodded, his voice muffled against her arm. "Yes, ma'am."

Soldiers came forward then led the boy over his barricade. The woman watched them go, tears streaming down her cheeks—until she fixed her gaze on Triston. She scowled. "Don't think this changes anythin'. Your mother would be ashamed of you."

Triston winced involuntarily. This woman had no right to judge what his mother would think, but somehow the words still stung. He managed a cordial nod. "Afternoon, ma'am."

The two other men came up to the woman's side, whispering in her ear and patting her on the shoulder, but Triston walked back to his own barricade. He wanted to be relieved—he was relieved—but the fact he'd had to do this at all diminished the victory. He climbed back over one of the soldier's crates, and Mory met him with a grin.

"Well done, sir!"

Triston nodded, trying to appear grateful, and handed the man his shield. "That went as well as expected, I guess."

"Are you kidding? Sir, last time..."

Mory didn't have to finish; Triston already knew. Last time four civilians and a soldier had died, and three more civilians had been seriously wounded. Last time, he'd realized the whispers of rebellion were something more than rumors. Last time, he'd resolved it'd be *the* last time anything like it happened in Edras again. Of course, ensuring that was another challenge entirely.

Garan saluted. "Thank you, sir. I hadn't wanted to go in with the batons, sir, but I didn't know what else to do, rightly."

"It's alright, Garan." Triston squinted at the sun hanging over the crooked, thatched rooftops. "What time is it?"

Mory shaded his eyes with his hand. "Almost eleven?"

Triston muttered a curse under his breath and jogged toward his horse. "I'm going to be late!"

Brushing the dirt from her hands, Kura lagged behind Faron as they followed the path through rows of carrots, turnips, and potatoes. It'd taken the better part of an hour, but they'd dug a sizeable hole and given the nostkynna a proper burial. The other farmhands had been so startled they'd packed up the harvested wheat and fled for the walls hours before sunset, and Kura welcomed an excuse to return to the compound early.

She'd always wanted to name the place. The other villages all had names, but her family had never agreed on what to call it, and now she could only think of foul names to give it anyway. The compound itself was neither large nor picturesque, but it was at least formidable. Tall logs—thick, pointed at the top—had been sunk in the ground to make a wall. Only one doorway granted passage in or out, a front gate in which two men could stand shoulder to shoulder.

Currently, a crowd of both goats and humans was gathered in the clearing outside the walls, all huddled around a small handcart propped beside the open gate.

Faron slowed his pace, and Kura nearly ran into him.

"What's going on?" he asked.

Kura shook her head, still inspecting the group. "I don't..."

A man stepped up onto the handcart, waving his arms as he tried to talk over the rest of the crowd. Kura stared at him in surprise. "Father?"

Spiridon was a tall man with broad shoulders and straight auburn hair that reached his neck. Everyone said Faron would look just like him if Faron ever grew the same brown, bushy beard. He stopped talking as he noticed Kura and Faron standing off to the side, and he gave them a tired wave.

Kura ran toward him, pushing her way through the crowd as a smile spread across her face. "We didn't expect you back so soon! What—" Fear caught in her chest as she noticed the two oblong shapes covered in bloodstained blankets on the ground at the base of the cart. "What happened? Where's Elli?"

Her father climbed down from the cart. "I sent her home, she's fine."

"For how long, huh?" A man forced his way to the front of the crowd. It was the Murderer—he had a name, but most were better known by their crime, and his scarred and wrinkled face was a hard one to forget. He stuck a fat finger in Spiridon's chest. "It's you who said we'd stay safe here!"

Spiridon shook his head. "I didn't promise that, only hoped. But I was a fool to think I could find peace for myself while the rest of the country withers away."

"Father..." Kura's frown deepened, but the rest of the crowd spoke over her.

"It was you who insisted on going to market!" a woman, the Horse Thief, shouted over the rest.

"We didn't have trouble at market, love," her husband said. "It was afterward. There were soldiers in the Waste..."

The crowd returned to their fury, all crowding close to shout their questions.

Kura caught hold of her father's arm. "There were soldiers?"

Spiridon sighed. "A few. We ran and they didn't follow, but archers shot the Drunk and the Thief. We weren't able to do anything for them."

Kura stole a glance at the bloodstained blankets, trying not to imagine the grey faces underneath. "What were soldiers doing in the Wynshire?"

"They burned down the compound east of here." Spiridon spoke calmly, as if the soldiers had ever braved these woods before. "They executed every family there for taking part in the rebellion. I suspect they were approached by that same man as we were a while back, only they didn't send him away."

A new fear caught in Kura's chest this time, and she hoped it didn't show on her face.

"And who's to say the soldiers'll stop there?" the Murderer shouted, drawing everyone's attention. "It's time to move on, unless we all want to end up dead like these folks."

A murmur of conversation rippled through the crowd.

Kura turned to them in disbelief. "We can't just run!"

"Kura—" Spiridon started, but she leapt into the handcart.

"This is our home! It's not much, but we've worked hard for what we have. They already drove us out of the mainstates. You're going to let them drive us off here, too? We know the land, and we have the advantage. We can put archers along the walls and pikemen near the—"

"Of course you'd say that!" the Horse Thief said. "You're the Soldier's daughter!"

The crowd murmured in agreement.

"Kura, come on," Spiridon said, catching her by the wrist. Reluctantly, she let him drag her down from the cart, but words of protest still echoed in her mind.

"That's it," the Murderer said, pushing his way toward the open gate. "I'm gathering my things, and I'm heading for Lovaria in the morning."

"They won't welcome you," Spiridon said with a shake of his head. "And you won't make it over the mountains before winter."

The man scowled. "Whatever you say, deserter. You were a coward then—who's to say you're not the coward now too?"

Faron pushed toward the man. "Hey!"

"Faron." Spiridon caught his son by the shoulder.

The Murderer met Faron's gaze with a crooked grin. He threw his hand over his head as he turned to the rest of the crowd. "Any of the rest of you are welcome to join me!"

The crowd broke apart, most with apathetic shrugs, to debate among their own families, but Kura stepped closer to her father's side.

"They can't go," she whispered harshly. "The harvest isn't finished, we need—"

"We can't stop them." Spiridon sighed. "Families come and go like this every year. We'll make do, we always have."

"Are you all leaving, then?" a soft, high-pitched voice said at Kura's side. It was one of the goats. Large horns curled atop her shaggy head, lending her height enough to reach Kura's chest.

"Not all of us," Spiridon said.

The goat shook her head, the motion flapping her long ears and the wattles nestled into the fur below her jaw. "The others said it was a mistake to make our home with you. Perhaps they were right after all. Humans have no place among nostkynna."

"Yes we do," Kura said. "Think of all the good things your herd has had these past few months: a safe place to stay out of the rain, large open fields to pick weeds from, not to mention protection from the wolves and cougars."

The goat tilted her head. "That is true." She flicked her tail. "I suppose we can't leave now. The other nostkynna would think so little of us for having taken your charity."

Faron nodded cordially. "You're welcome to go or stay as you please. But we do hope you choose to stay."

The goat chewed her cud leisurely, and strolled away. "We shall see…"

Spiridon nodded toward the gates. "Come on, your mother is waiting."

Faron followed at his side, and Kura reluctantly tagged along behind. She still wanted to argue, but she didn't know what to say. Her father never changed his mind, and no one listened to the daughter of a deserter.

They passed through the gates into the compound, several others from the crowd following. It was not a large space, and the family cabins packed between the walls made it smaller still. Most were old and run-down, although a few were better crafted.

A short overhang jutted from the right wall, forming the goats' shelter—their home was a long, two-walled shed filled with hay, and every one of them said it was better living than they'd ever had. Spiridon stuck to the center path, walking Kura and Faron past the clay hearth in the heart of the compound.

"Spiridon?" Kura's mother's voice carried over the other conversations in the courtyard as she stepped into the doorway of their family cabin.

Jisela was a taller woman, skinny to the point of seeming frail—although she was far from it—with narrow shoulders and wide hips. Her flowing brown hair was tied back in a messy bun. She had Rowley—a young, auburn-haired baby—swaddled and strapped to her back, his face just visible over her shoulder.

"Kura!" Elli's voice rang in the doorway as she barreled past her mother. Kura dropped down on one knee, and the girl threw her arms around Kura's neck.

"Hey, Elli." Kura held her in a hug before letting go. Although she'd soon turn seven, Elli's round baby cheeks hadn't yet softened to match their mother's features. But she did have their mother's brown hair, alongside Kura's freckled cheeks and bright hazel eyes.

"You promised to float bark boats with me when I got back."

Kura laughed. "Not now, but soon. How was your first trip to Tarr Fianin?"

"I saw a man at the market—he juggled fire!" Her smile faded. "But on the way back something bad happened and Father won't let me see it."

Kura nodded, tousling Elli's hair. "I know." Haltingly, she rose to her feet. Her parents were already talking about the same thing, her mother's face twisting in shock and fear.

"Are we leaving too, then?"

Spiridon tilted his head. "Do you want to?"

Jisela huffed. "I am tired of running from this war."

Quiet amusement broke through his stern expression. "You speak as though it's already begun."

"King Hilderic started it, and even though they killed him it hasn't ended yet." Jisela frowned, balling her hands into fists. "When I can go to the tavern and tell my stories again, the Forebears' tales again, without getting vegetables thrown at me or the king's men threatening to haul me away, then the war will be over."

Spiridon smiled faintly, taking her hand in his. "You still have hope it will ever be over?"

Jisela nodded. "Come, everyone." She reached out for Faron's hand. "I'll recite the *andojé*."

Kura frowned. "Shouldn't we talk about—?"

"Shh!" Faron hissed as he came to stand beside their mother.

With a sigh, Kura took Elli's and Faron's hands as they formed their lopsided circle outside their cabin. She cringed as she glanced over her shoulder. The other cast-outs were starting to stare, their judgmental frowns all reeking of the same word: fanatics.

"Essence of light, illuminate us," Jisela began.

In droning voices, the family responded. "Illuminate us."

Kura sighed again, the all-too-familiar words falling short of her lips.

Jisela continued. "Essence of strength, protect us."

"Protect us." Kura mumbled along this time, glancing back at the curious eyes watching them from the courtyard.

"Essence of all, move in us."

"Move in us." Kura looked at her mother, ashamed of her own frustration. Jisela was so sincere; she was always so sincere.

Jisela breathed in deeply. "*Láefe l'fonfyr.*"

The rest of the family nodded, each squeezing the other's hand. "We hope in the promise."

Jisela opened her eyes and released her grip on Faron's and Spiridon's hands, then looked to each of them with a smile. "Even in times like these the Essence moves with us. We just have to hold on to our own, until the time comes."

Kura fought the urge to scoff. "You're still talking about the fonfyr?"

"I believe in the fonfyr," Elli said proudly.

Jisela leaned over and smoothed her daughter's unruly hair. "I do too, Elli. And your father believes, and your brother, and your sister, and so many, many other parents and brothers and sisters before you. The fonfyr led our people to this land, protected us and brought us together, and one day the Essence—the *Elaedoni*—will call him again. To be a judge and captain among men."

"How many more generations are we to wait, Mother?"

Jisela gave her a small, stubborn frown. "As many as we have to. The world moves as the Essence intends."

Kura clamped her mouth shut and turned toward their family cabin. She knew it would be a mistake to speak up here, but still fought to keep from voicing her thoughts.

It's about time we stopped waiting for some mystical movement of the Essence to save us, and just saved ourselves.

Chapter Three
Láefe L'fonfyr

Triston took the stairs two by two, fumbling with the bundle of parchments under his arm as he tucked in his shirt.

The castle Avtalyon was a haphazard collection of towers built by different kings in different times, growing with the pine trees on the rocky mountain that jutted from the center of Edras. This tower, both the shortest and the most central, served only two purposes: greeting guests in the throne room below or entertaining debate in the council chambers above.

A voice echoed from the end of the stairwell. "Hey!"

Triston turned back. "Dylen?"

Dylen flashed a wide grin and jogged to catch up. He was tall and sturdily built, with a thick braid holding back his frizzy black hair, his dark skin a contrast to his untucked white shirt. "Am I not late, then?"

Triston continued up the stairs. "Depends on what you're here for."

"The council meeting?"

"Then you're late." Triston eyed him curiously. "Why are you going, anyway?"

"I have to argue for my father."

"Ah."

Dylen stopped in the hallway and let out a deep sigh. "Look, you know I wouldn't be siding against you today if I had any say about it."

"Oh, I know. Out of curiosity, whose side would you take?"

Dylen held up his mangled folder. "You ask that like you think I've read through any of this stuff."

Triston smirked. "I guess I've won already then, haven't I?"

Dylen laughed and pushed open the council room door. "Don't expect me to take it easy on you."

Narrow windows lined the edge of the stone wall nearest the ceiling, and bright rectangles of sunlight fell on the opposite floor. An oblong mahogany table nearly filled the space, though only the three nearest ornate chairs were occupied.

Triston's father sat at the head, his elbow leaning on the table and his temple resting against his hand. He met Triston's gaze, then pushed himself to sit up properly. "There you are." Dradge was dressed in his typical worn leather jerkin and cotton shirt, but he had at least tossed on a silver-hemmed green cape. "Alright, now we can start this thing."

Dylen made his way to an empty chair on the opposite side of the table. Triston took his seat beside his father, giving a nod to Lord Therburn, seated beside him, and Seren, who stood at the chair across from him.

Seren gave him an exasperated smile. "We were about to begin without you, actually." Seren was older than Dradge, though his short brown hair held only a hint of white and his grey eyes glinted with persistent youth. He was on the shorter side with a slender build and a thin, intelligent face, with a well-trimmed beard that hid any wrinkles around his lips.

Triston shrugged in apology, then slid his bundle of parchment across the table. "My evidence, as you requested."

Seren sighed and took his seat. "We'll get to that. Now, Lord Therburn, I believe you were in the middle of saying something?"

The man cleared his throat and folded his hands across his wide belly. "I suppose I was just getting to it. It's only that..." He cleared his throat again and fiddled with his bushy white beard. "I'll just come out and say it. The people are unsettled."

Dradge laughed softly, although his tone and expression were devoid of mirth. "Is that all?"

"Well..." Therburn gave an apologetic nod. "They were happy for a while, after you cut the income and the harvest taxes, but with what they have to pay the guilds just to buy or sell or trade anything... and that's on top of the fact that many've been housing and feeding soldiers on and off for much of the year. Those that have hope asked I speak to you. The others..."

"The others?" Seren said.

Therburn glanced toward him, then back down at his hands. "They won't stop talking about the rebellion."

"Then we shall crush them!" Dylen pounded his fist on the table. The rest of the council jumped, and Triston pressed a hand against his mouth to hide his laughter.

Seren rubbed his temples. "Master Vanderlee, where is your father?"

"Inspecting one of the mines out in the Rivmere." Dylen straightened in his seat and seemed to be fighting back a grin. "Was that not what he would have said?"

Seren smothered a sigh, but Dradge laughed.

"You've got the right spirit, I think, but too much enthusiasm." Dradge leaned back in his chair, interlocking his hands behind his head as he propped his feet up on the table. "Don't worry, a few hundred more of these meetings and I'm sure you'll get a feel for it."

"Dradge, come on." Seren rose and pushed the king's boots back onto the floor. "I would have thought you'd have a little more enthusiasm yourself."

Triston shifted uncomfortably as a heavy silence settled over the room. Everyone had apparently picked up on what Seren had left unsaid: *considering the rebels killed your wife.*

Triston was only a boy when it happened. They'd been at some feast—wasn't anything special, as far as he could remember. There had been a commotion, his mother had run to the safety of his father's arms, and the assassin had caught her instead. A simple mistake that shattered the happy, comfortable world he'd thought he knew.

He'd run the night over and over again in his mind for months—years—afterwards, trying to make some sense out of his own fear, his own horror. Even now he could picture it more clearly than he'd like, but for him it was a distant memory. His father still bore the scar; on his skin, at least, it was one of many.

Dradge sighed and sat forward in his seat. "Alright, Therburn. Continue."

The old man scratched uncomfortably at his jaw. "I don't know I have much more to say, sir. I was just hoping you might be willing to cut some trade taxes, or move troops—"

"That can't be done," Seren interjected.

Therburn retreated into his seat, but Dradge frowned. "And why not?"

"Well..." Seren reached for a stack of papers on the table before him. "I was going to save this," he said, sending a meaningful glance in Triston's direction, "as it really speaks to why we can't end the draft, either."

Triston frowned, knowing the expression had to match his father's. "Alright then, present your argument."

"The Fidelis are moving with the rebels."

Triston leaned back in surprise. The Fidelis were unnaturally powerful men and women who could control the elements, the weather, the very ground they walked on. They had played a hand in the coup that placed his father on the throne, but the last real sighting of one had been the cloaked figure who had driven a shard of ice through his mother's back. Or so everyone said.

Fidelis are holy men," his mother had told him, more than once. She was Láefe, she would have been the last to believe these rumors, and so he never quite believed them either. But his father did, and the Fidelis had suffered dearly for it.

Dradge smiled grimly. "They've come to taunt the dog again, have they?"

"My king," Therburn said. "The Fidelis denied having anything to do with Lyara's death. They may not have backed you after the coup, but that does not mean they don't respect your rule—"

Seren laughed. "Does it not?" He rummaged through his stack of papers and pulled out a single parchment. "This is an eyewitness account from a merchant in the Feldlands. Men and women from the rebellion are extorting supplies from the locals with displays of their unnatural abilities."

Therburn's expression darkened. "I had not heard of this."

"But," Seren said, "by your own admission you have heard the rumblings of rebellion. That's why we have troops in the Feldlands in the first place. We've just driven off a whole roaming gang of Fidelis—although what do they call themselves?"

Therburn's lip twitched in the semblance of a sneer. "Kins."

"Right, of course." Seren nodded. "And even though they're all more contentious than a Lovarian, you let them continue to roam free."

Therburn scowled. "I did not take this position to tell the people of my region how to live their lives. I'm here to keep you all from overstepping—" He caught himself and sent a look of apology in Dradge's direction. "I'm sorry, but I do not believe my people would side with the rebellion without what they feel is a good reason."

Dradge leaned back, his green eyes distant. "I've tried, Therburn. I really have. I let them alone and they kill my wife. I beat them down and they rise ever stronger the next time."

Triston studied his father's face with sympathy, but the councilman laughed, forced and uncomfortable.

"We are who we are, sir. It's not in any Avaronian's blood to take things easily."

Dradge grunted, his eyes fixed on the empty corner beyond him as though he were only half listening. "Hilderic was a coward. I watched those centaurs press in from the west and those nostkynna move in from the north—raiding villages, killing women and children. One month I waited for him to send us out. In two more months I'd taken his throne and done it myself." He managed a hint of a smile and absently ran his fingers along the grain of the polished table. "Sometimes I think those were the only two months I knew what I was doing."

"Dradge," Seren said dismissively—almost scoldingly. "This is only temporary. We just need—"

"Temporary?" Dradge laughed and pointed toward the side wall. "Pretty sure I've heard that line from you before."

Triston glanced at the wall. In the center of the grey stone hung, mounted on an engraved wooden placard, a lone broadsword. Jewels covered the hilt and ancient, flowing letters glistened in the mirrored steel blade. As a boy he'd found it incredibly fascinating, and even as a man he had to admit he felt some lingering sense of curiosity whenever the weapon caught his gaze. He'd asked, but his mother had never explained exactly what it was—just that it was a lie, and that there was a real one out there somewhere. She'd always seemed, oddly enough, both proud and ashamed of the decoration.

Seren sighed, and Triston figured if it hadn't been uncouth the man would have rolled his eyes. "I thought we gathered here to discuss the present, not rehash the past, but if I must, I will reiterate. I had that sword forged because we needed the Fidelis to back us against Hilderic, and you were plenty grateful for it at the time."

Therburn scoffed. "I suppose all of this is just, then. Serves us right for meddling in prophecy."

"Ah yes," Seren said with a smirk, "our lone Láefe hanging on to the old legends."

"They aren't legends. They're our history."

"My friend, prophecy is a stepping-stone to be either used or forgotten. History does not write itself. It is written by those daring few willing to stand on the shoulders of their ancestors instead of in their shadows."

"That may be," Therburn grumbled, "but are we standing on their shoulders or trampling them?"

Dylen laughed, then stopped as though to consider what his father would have done.

Seren's grin didn't waver. "Are you ashamed of where you are, Lord Therburn, or only how you got there?"

"Alright." Triston sighed, offering Seren an attempt at a smile. "I seem to recall someone complaining about how this conversation was fixated on the past?"

Seren lifted his open hands. "Do continue."

"Well..." Triston straightened in his seat. "Lord Therburn mentioned the trade taxes. I don't think I've spoken to anyone who didn't have a complaint about that. But here in the cities—Edras especially—they're upset about the draft." Triston glanced at his father and motioned to the bundle of parchment he'd brought with him. "Those are all accounts of mistreatment of Edras folk at the hands of our local troops, several of which I witnessed for myself. I can only imagine what's going on beyond the borders of this city. Talk of rebellion is spreading for a reason. Let's take away that reason."

Seren looked down at Triston's papers, nodding slowly. "We may not be at war now, on that you are correct, but out of Lovaria—"

"Ah." Dradge waved his hand. "Seren, I've had enough of the rumors. What's next, more stories about shadow-men? Are you my strategist or my nursemaid? The pass through the Rohgens will be snow-filled within the month. Even if I believed Lovaria planned to move against us, they still couldn't do it until spring."

Seren opened his mouth to speak, then sighed. "How do you plan to quell this rebellion without troop numbers?"

Triston tried to maintain a pleasant expression. "Who says we need to quell anything? The people are just upset, that's all. They're still reasonable, so I say reason with them. And that's usually more effective when not done at the point of a sword."

"Oh," Dylen muttered, and fumbled with his papers. He cleared his throat, then began to read in a monotone. "It is imperative that we maintain our resources in the event of invasion and/or civil unrest. A king, uh..." He glanced up at Triston. "Or a prince too, I guess, must be wise enough to discern a people's best interest despite their better wishes and his good intentions. I—er, General Lavern—trusts that our crown is endowed with just such wisdom."

Dradge chuckled. "Wise now, am I? That man certainly has a way with words..."

Seren rose from his seat. "I propose a compromise." He pulled a thick parchment from his stack, then unrolled it across the table. It was a map of Avaron, simple in style and brightly colored; he pointed to the dark bundle of trees to the far west. "The unrest may very well be dealt with in other ways, but the rebellion has already taken root. Here, in the Wynshire."

"The Waste?" Triston laughed. "What's out there besides trees and angry nostkynna?"

"Scouts say criminals have built entire villages now, and these folks regularly stop in border towns to trade without proper clearance and without paying taxes. Troops intercepted a few of them venturing out of the Wynshire and into the Feldlands on our assignments last month, and they were carrying all sorts of information intended for the rebellion."

Therburn grunted. "You have proof?"

Seren rested a hand on his stack of papers. "Always. If those 'angry nostkynna', as you put it, Triston, aren't working with the rebellion themselves, then they're at least building a haven for the lawless. A criminal with anything less than a death sentence is going to find shelter in a more amicable part of the country. These people are nothing but trouble."

"So," Triston said, "we clear out the Waste, crippling the rebellion, then you'll approve the end of the draft?"

Seren nodded, but looked to Dradge.

Dradge shrugged. "Sounds like a plan to me. Or a good *compromise,* as you said." He waved a hand in Seren's direction. "I sign off on all the funds and those forms you always come back asking me about. Just be reasonable, please? Anyone who surrenders peacefully enough deserves a hearing on the king's bench."

Seren raised an eyebrow. "Are you allocating the funds for that, too?"

"Yes," Dradge said with an exasperated laugh. "I swore an oath that I would never let myself become the tyrant I had overthrown. I still mean to keep it."

Dylen chewed his lip as he shuffled through his stack of papers. "Is this something the rest of the council has to vote to approve? Am I able to vote for my father?"

"Yes to your first question, Master Vanderlee," Seren said, "and no to your second. Fortunately..." He pulled another parchment from his collection. "Lady Rigan, Lady Tanith, and Lord Hamlyn have already signed their approval for this arrangement."

Triston shook his head. "You had this planned from the beginning, didn't you?"

"I come prepared, Triston." Seren grinned. "Don't worry, I will one day teach you my ways."

Dradge laughed. "Seren, you've been working on me for twenty-three years. How long until you give up?"

Seren shook his head, still smiling. "Oh, I'll never give up on you."

Chapter Four

A Grey World

Lady Rigan hosted the banquet that night on one of her larger boats in the bay. A council member, or some aspiring socialite from Edras, held such a get-together once a month, as long as the weather was warm and the rest of the country remained relatively peaceful. Tonight the orange sunset clung to the horizon, casting little more light than the strings of paper lanterns hanging from the mast over the upper deck and creating a stunning backdrop to the festivities.

As a boy, Triston had spent nights like this stuffing himself with food and running around, creating trouble with his friends. As he grew older, however, the expectations placed upon him had begun to change—although he did still try to enjoy the food.

The rest of the guests had already eaten their meal, and the servants were clearing the tables from the upper deck to make room for dancing. Triston meandered toward the stern, plate in hand as he pushed through the crowd. He was set on a second helping of the herb-baked potatoes—the crops had fared poorly in the late summer rains that had hovered around Edras, but Lady Rigan benefited greatly from her oversight of the shipping routes.

"Prince Triston?"

The woman's voice sounded from behind him, and he cringed, a half a scoop of potatoes already on his plate. Triston set his food down and turned, trying to force a smile. "Lady Albree."

She was a mirror image of Lady Rigan—pale, oval face and hip-length brown hair—except that she was shorter, and somehow even skinnier. She demurely folded her gloved hands against her chest.

"I was hoping you might give me the honor of the first dance?"

Triston stiffened, that grin frozen on his face. She'd asked him for the first dance last month, and the month before that—his one placating 'yes', ages ago, had only redoubled her efforts. He didn't want to insult her or crush her spirits, but how could he explain he wasn't interested in a girl who seemed like she'd snap under the slightest bit of pressure? Although the thought of denying her came easier after he had noticed the way her mother urged her forward, and he'd come to understand the hungry look in Albree's eyes: she was after something far more expensive than a dance.

"I..."

A few loud giggles came from behind Albree, and Triston glanced over her shoulder to find other noble ladies gathered behind their friend, whispering to one another.

"Isn't he just adorable?" the nearest said, a little too loudly. The others nodded in agreement and continued their gossip more quietly.

Triston's smile faltered and he looked down, rubbing the back of his neck. He figured the ladies meant it as a compliment, but he had a hard time taking it that way when he'd heard them use that same phrase to describe a new pair of shoes, or a ratty stray dog.

Then, among that small crowd, he spotted a friendly face.

"I'm sorry, Albree." Triston took a step past her. "I've already promised my first dance to Lady Madilene."

Madi moved away from the group of women, tauntingly holding Triston's gaze. "Is that so?"

She was tall and well proportioned, her flowing gown well suited to her long legs. Triston, Madi, and Dylen had all been born the same year. Before the councils and the parties, many nights of innocent mischief had forged friendships that had lasted into adult years.

Albree struggled to hide her scowl. "I see."

Triston nodded, forcing the grimace that should have been a smile back to his face. "Maybe next time." He took Madi by the hand and led her out onto the center deck as Albree huddled in among the other girls to join in on their whispering.

Madi gave him a mischievous grin. "You shouldn't have said that."

Triston sighed, then placed his hand on her hip as the string music began to play. "I know."

They danced, each step slow and dispassionate, as the other couples gathered in around them.

"So, why *are* you dancing with me, Triston?"

"Because, Madilene, you're the only girl here who won't take it as a marriage proposal."

"Oh, come on, you've got to loosen up a little. Have fun, enjoy the sport of it!"

Triston's grin faded slightly. "What if I don't enjoy this sport?"

"Oh, silly—everything about this life is a sport, so you'd better learn to enjoy it." She pursed her lips. "Ah, I know what it is. You're still shy."

"I am not."

"Yes, you are. Remember when you tried to ask Tilly Riholt to dance at the Iverset winter ball and you hardly got three words out before—?"

Triston laughed. "You know I was twelve, right? And anyway, isn't she married now?"

"To Gy Inegram, one of the captains. You two were a terrible match, anyway. But it was hilarious!"

Triston shook his head. "Have you still got my matches planned out for me?"

"Oh, I try." Madi tossed her head to throw her curling brown locks over her shoulder. "But I've hit a bit of a snag after that Lovarian girl came into the picture."

"Jerese? I met her once, last year, and she hardly spoke a word to me. Wouldn't even look me in the eye."

"Oh, I know. She plays the game even more poorly than you do—which I used to think was impossible, by the way. But that's the smart match." Her grin faded, and her eyes grew distant. "Reuniting sister countries separated for two hundred years... They might even put you in a tapestry for it."

Triston rolled his eyes. "My life's dream."

Madi looked up, her sharp gaze staring straight through him. "Alright then, Prince, what is your life's dream?"

Triston grinned, although it faded the longer his thoughts ran without settling on an answer. "I'll have to get back to you on that."

The song came to a gradual end, and the crowd answered it with soft applause. Triston stepped back, giving Madi a gallant bow, and she rolled her eyes.

"Alright, what's going on here?" Dylen's voice carried over the crowd—it usually did. He shoved his way through the dispersing dancers and came to a stop at Triston's side, a frown on his face but a smile in his eyes.

"Dylen." Madi pouted, taking hold of his hand. "You missed the first song!"

Dylen latched on to her arm and held it up, pointing to the tightly fitted gold band encircling her wrist. "Do you see this? I paid a hell of a lot of money for it, and since I'm wearing the matching one right here, I don't know how you got the idea in your head that you ought to be dancing with my woman."

Triston held up his hands. "You got me."

Madi wrapped her arm around Dylen's. "The Beloc girl was after him again and he panicked."

Dylen laughed, glancing from her to Triston. "Is that right?"

"It was a calculated decision," Triston said.

Dylen laughed again, even louder. "Man, you better check your arithmetic."

The band began to play again, smoothly transitioning into another slow tune. Triston took a step back. "Well, you two have fun. I'm going to get myself some more food."

Madi gave him the slightest shake of her head, then pulled Dylen farther out onto the dance floor.

Dylen met Triston's gaze. "Save me some."

"No promises."

Triston weaved his way through the crowd and back to the food table. Unfortunately, he found that Lady Rigan's wait staff had already cleared it away, leaving only the keg of that year's hops brew. Mildly disappointed, Triston poured himself a mug. He took a sip as he made his way aimlessly along the edge of the ship, watching the dancers in amusement.

He used to love dancing, before his age and standing had brought to it a certain, uncomfortable weight. His mother had been quite a dancer—that was all anyone said, anyway. His father never danced, or at least not in a long time. Triston thought he remembered his parents dancing together, but these days his father hung at the edges of the party—as he was now, a mug in one hand as he laughed with Seren or anyone else who might want to listen to another of his old stories.

"Enjoying yourself this evening?" Lady Rigan asked, stopping at Triston's side.

He quickly swallowed the gulp he had just taken from his mug. "Yes, ma'am. You have been a fine host, as always."

The woman didn't blink. "You're alone, I see."

Triston stiffened. "Just enjoying a sip of beer. A very good brew this year."

"Mm." Rigan gathered her skirt about her and took a step past him. "Well, thank you."

The loud clack of her shoes against the wood of the deck faded into the murmur of the crowd.

"Well," Dradge called out, and Triston turned to find his father and Seren watching him from the chairs near the ship's railing. "What did you do this time, boy?"

Triston shook his head with a sigh and made his way to the nearest empty seat. "I don't know."

Seren grinned at him, mischievously. "Do you want to?"

"No. No thank you."

Both men laughed.

Dradge took a drink from his mug. "Hey," he said, smacking Seren on the shoulder. "What do you know, anyway? You're a terrible dancer, and you only really talked to that one woman—what was her name?"

Seren wagged his finger. "First of all, I am a fine dancer, just not to doltish music like this. And second of all, her name was Sela, and we only called things off because I went to university at Drosala and she wouldn't come with me."

"Well, I always did think that book learning stole the last of your good sense."

Seren smirked. "That's exactly what I'd expect to hear from the man who ran off after the first semester to join the army."

Dradge laughed, then raised his mug as if in a toast before taking another gulp. "I don't think my father ever forgave me for that."

Metal boots thumped across the upper deck, and a soldier came to a salute beside Seren's chair. "Lord Seren, sir?" It was Colmac, one of Seren's captains. There was a time when the man didn't command anyone—he used to just give his advice as a royal strategist—but over the years, as troop numbers grew, that had necessarily changed. "You asked me to inform you once any of the prisoners had spoken?"

"Oh, yes." Seren took a quick swig from his mug before setting it aside.

Dradge frowned. "What are you talking about?"

"From the little skirmish along the western border," Seren explained. "We managed to catch a few."

Dradge sighed, his face darkening. "Don't you ever just want to give it a rest?"

Seren gave him a sideways glance, as though the question meant nothing. "What'd they say, soldier?"

"Only one spoke, sir," Colmac said. "But he gave us a list of his informants in those border towns and within the Waste."

Seren rose from his seat. "Excellent."

"Now where are you off to?" Dradge grumbled.

"I've got to plan a trip across the country." Seren nodded toward Triston. "You said you wanted to go on the next one, didn't you?"

Triston shrugged. "I think I did."

"Very well. I won't tear you away from the festivities, but we can catch up tomorrow?"

"Alright."

Seren nodded, holding Triston's gaze for a moment, then met Dradge's. "Enjoy the rest of the night, gentlemen."

Triston watched as Seren made his way toward the bow of the ship, Colmac tagging at his heels like a well-trained dog.

Dradge smacked Triston's shoulder. "What's the matter? You've been talking for months about taking another trip to see the country, but now that you've got the chance you want to back out?"

Triston traced a finger along his mug. He had hoped he wasn't so transparent. "It's just this rebellion."

"What of it?"

Triston sighed and glanced toward the darkening horizon. "Do you ever get the sense that, I don't know, you're on the wrong side?"

"What?" Dradge laughed.

Triston grinned slightly. "Have you met any of these so-called rebels? They're regular people, Father. Everyday people."

"What else do you think rebellions are made of?"

"I don't know. But when I see how they live, while I live like this, I'm not so sure I can fault what they're fighting for."

Dradge nodded thoughtfully and took a slow sip from his mug. "This isn't where I ever imagined I'd find myself. I suppose I've adjusted to this life, but it was a struggle for me, and looking back I won't ever say I got it all right." He stared aimlessly at the dancing crowd. "When I was a younger man it all seemed so much clearer... This is a grey world, Triston. That's what I've come to see over the years. But you have a good heart: follow it."

Triston nodded, though he fought to appear appreciative. *And why should my heart know the way?*

Sunset fell, as it did in autumn, long before anyone was ready for it. After they had all completed their evening chores, Kura climbed the ladder into the loft as her mother's melodic voice carried up from the ground floor, where she was telling yet another of the forbears' tales to Elli.

"...from the rubble there rose first a hand which grasped a sword, and then Gallian emerged, unscathed. He faced the monster and lifted the sword Ìsendorál to the sky. Lightning flashed in the clouds and became one with the shimmering red blade. Gallian pointed his weapon at the beast and said, 'You, who have meddled in the darkness, become one with it as the light beholds your doom...'"

Kura crawled across the loft to push open the shutters on the far window, revealing a red-orange glow that lit the sky like fire from behind the sharp peaks of the Eigen Mountains. She poked her head out of the window, then, turning, grasped the beam above her and hauled herself onto the thatched roof of the cabin. From here, her mother's story was little more than an excited murmur.

A cool evening breeze swayed the trees and pushed her loose hair back from her face, which Kura tied back with a strip of cloth before stretching out on the roof, her head resting against her hands. The air echoed with the nocturnal chatter of the brush, filling her ears with a disjointed song, but her mother's tale continued to echo in her mind.

She wanted to deny it, but Kura knew that a part of her—however deep within—*wanted* those stories to be true. Not so long ago, she herself had been that starry-eyed child at her mother's knee, listening to the forebears' tales as if the whole world was opening up for her young eyes to behold. She sighed again as her gaze fell upon the silhouetted mass that was the surrounding forest. A person could wish their life away waiting for a miracle.

Fire, a dancing red flash of light, sprang up from beyond the walls.

Kura sat up, her mind racing, and then remembered that a group had ventured beyond the walls to—with the proper ceremonies—bury the bodies of the two dead men. She settled back on the roof, shaking her head. Cast-outs typically had sense enough to give up their hopeful delusions after a few weeks in the Wynshire, but most Avaronians were practicing Svaldans, and there were always a stubborn few hanging around the compound.

The Svaldan gods had a number of rules for burying someone: the body had to be at least one hundred paces from a dwelling place lest the dead linger among the living; proper herbs had to be sprinkled with the burial dirt; the appropriate talismans had to be made and then burned to ensure safe passage into the afterlife. The best of humanity went to Aldorra, a place of honor among the gods, the worst went to Hell, and the rest reunited with family in some in-between place. Brennsumar, they called it—although Kura's mother called it all nonsense, and in the end Kura called it none of her business.

Benger's buried somewhere out there.

She clenched her eyes shut, wrinkling her nose. That was a thought she didn't need, and it was probably untrue anyway. Her older brother had likely never received a burial.

Kura turned away from the fire as she shoved that memory back into the darkest corners of her heart, where it belonged. This was the Wynshire. Creatures killed people every year; that year it had just happened to be Benger. That was what she told herself, anyway, and after a while it became familiar enough to be a comfort.

A blood-chilling howl overcame the other sounds of the night, and another answered from the other side of the ravine. The other side. Had she still been Elli's age that howl would've kept her awake tonight, her mind fixed on the stories travelers told about the man-eating beasts, half horse, half man, that ruled that side of the Everard River. Now—after Kura had heard hundreds of stories and never seen one centaur—she had good reason to doubt. But a certain fact remained.

No one who crossed the ravine ever came back.

Rowley's crying broke Kura from her thoughts, though he fell silent before long; a family member must have tended to him. What would his life be like?

Kura resettled against the roof. They would survive; they always did. Her father would be up at sunrise tomorrow, ready to work the fields, no matter how many families left for Lovaria in the morning. Nothing ever fazed him, and her mother tried her best to be the same. But they couldn't stay here forever.

Lovaria would never welcome them—Kura took her father at his word on that. And besides, why should they leave Avaron? The mainstates were supposed to be lovely places, if a person had the proper papers to mark them as free citizens. The man with the rebellion had said he would look into getting the passage her previous contact had promised for her and her family. That meant far more than her mother's legends ever would. It was tangible, it was probable, and she could make it happen.

She *would* make it happen.

Chapter Five

Gift-Giving

Horses' hooves thundered against the dry pathway as the company of soldiers passed through the open gates to the city. Triston sat taller in the saddle to keep from breathing the dust that drifted around him. For all this day of traveling, he'd been looking forward to reaching Shalford. Most excursions stopped here before venturing beyond the Helm River, to stock up on supplies at one of the bustling open-air markets.

As his mare carried him into the town, however, the atmosphere washed over Triston along with the chill in the autumn breeze. Men, the few that milled about, all looked up from their tasks with wary glances. Women clung to their children, then ran to the sides of the street and ducked into alleyways. Shalford had been growing—thriving—the last Triston had seen it, but now the rows of stone houses were mostly empty and veered on the edge of disrepair.

Seren halted the company in the center courtyard at the base of the tower. The stone building, thatched roof atop the fourth story, dwarfed all others in the city; Triston pulled his horse to a stop in the structure's shadow. Townsfolk gathered around the soldiers, keeping a moderate space between them, to watch with wide eyes.

"We've already given ya all we have!" a gruff man hollered from the back of the crowd, before the others shut him up.

Triston dismounted, his frown deepening. He caught the eye of the woman standing closest to him and nodded in the man's direction. "What was he talking about?"

The woman gasped and stared at the ground, pulling her daughter closer.

"Where is your fire?" the girl called out.

Triston laughed. "What?"

"Shh!" the girl's mother hissed, dragging her daughter back.

"Your fire!" the girl repeated, tugging against her mother's arm. "The ones who came before carried fire."

Triston held the girl's gaze, then glanced to the nearest faces around her, but he didn't know what to say. Every one of these people was absolutely terrified. He took hold of his horse's reins and dragged the animal behind him as he pushed through the crowd. "Seren!"

The man climbed down from the saddle of his stocky white gelding and turned toward him.

"What happened here?"

Seren shrugged. "The Fidelis. They come and they take—food, animals, men, whatever they want."

"That's impossible. This is a garrison outpost."

Seren laughed, bitterly. "And what are soldiers supposed to do against men who hold the power of the elements in their hands?"

Triston hesitated. It was one thing to hear those words in the council chambers...

Seren placed a hand on Triston's shoulder. "It's because of towns like this that we're making our trip in the first place. We're only watering the horses here, and then we'll be back on our way."

With the sun setting behind the distant Rohgen Mountains, Triston and the rest of his company set up camp in a clearing close to the Beaduras River. Most of the men laughed and talked among themselves, but Triston pitched his tent in silence. The same gaunt and fear-filled faces had lined the street to meet him in every town, each of them watching the troops pass as though life—bad as it was—would be better without him in it.

Three years ago he'd traveled to Lynavir on the southern coastline; two years ago he and his father had gone on a hunting excursion in the Feldland plains. Even a mere four months ago he'd overseen the construction of a new garrison tower in Lâroe. This land—these sad and broken people—was not the Avaron he recognized.

And I thought this was going to be a vacation.

Triston tightened the last guy line on his tent, then made his way to the fire to stir his tin of mash. He'd brought that boy from Edras, Darrow, on this trip—along with Mory and several other good men he knew had been itching for a change of scenery. Now he wondered if that had really been in anyone's best interest.

He tapped his spoon clean on the edge of the tin, then straightened. It would be alright. After all, they were only after a handful of rebel informants.

In the trees beyond, pounding hooves mingled with low voices before the ghostly outline of Seren's gelding emerged from the darkness, two other captains in tow. The man halted at the edge of camp, then dismounted and handed his reins to one of the men who followed beside him. He strode toward Triston's fire, brow creased and head down.

Triston nodded in his direction. "What took you so long?"

Seren glanced up, then sighed and took a seat on a log beside the fire across from Triston. "Just making a thorough sweep of the area."

Triston retrieved his tray of mash, then sat back, cross-legged, on the ground. "Find anything interesting?"

"Nothing to report." Seren scanned the campground. "Looks like everyone's got their tents set up properly. Any trouble?"

Triston shook his head, blowing steam from his spoonful of mash.

Seren jerked his chin toward the tin in Triston's hands. "You really going to eat that?"

"Mmhm." Triston forced a dramatically wide smile as he cleaned his spoon. "I love mash—I'm going to eat me every drop of it. If you want some, I think there's dry mix left over there..."

"Absolutely not." The hint of a grin crept into Seren's eyes. "You want to know why?"

"I doubt it."

"In the very first year, when our forebears crossed the sea, it is said there were seven ships, not six. The seventh belonged to a house called Falere. The other houses packed stores full of a variety of foods from their homeland, but can you guess what Falere chose?"

"Do enlighten me."

"Mash." Seren pointed to the tin in Triston's hand. "Just like that. Portable, yes? And easy to store? Perhaps not. It is said that every son and daughter, mother and cousin, of Falere went mad due to tainted rations. They steered their ship into a storm and were never seen or heard from again."

Triston nodded, feigning interest, as he scooped another spoonful of mash into his mouth. "Fascinating."

Seren laughed, half to himself, and reached into the large satchel slung over his shoulder. "Well, that's why I always pack my own rations." He produced a misshapen white bundle of cloth, then unfolded it to reveal a quarter loaf of bread and a hunk of salted pork. "Here," he said, tearing off a bit of the pork and tossing it over. "I'll share."

Triston caught the meat, although he nearly spilled his mash in the process. He wouldn't bother explaining it to Seren, but he deliberately didn't pack his own rations, if only to maintain some comradery with the enlisted men. He wouldn't refuse salted pork, though.

"Oh." Seren reached back into his satchel. "Your father wanted me to give this to you yesterday."

Triston set aside his tin before catching this next bundle. "What is it?"

Seren shrugged, taking a bite of his bread.

Triston pulled the twine off the oblong sack, then unwrapped the burlap to find a small note. *"Dear Triston, Happy Birthday."*

Triston smiled to himself. His father never forgot his birthday, but he always had to wait until the end of the day to open his gifts. That was his mother's rule: she had had to wait until sunset to meet her gift on his true birthday, so Triston had to do the same on every one after.

"It wasn't your birthday yesterday, was it?" Seren asked, a look of dread coming over him as though he already knew the answer.

"It's alright, I didn't remember either." He set the note aside and unwrapped the rest of the bundle. Inside was a short dagger, skillfully crafted with an embossed leather sheath and the glint of precious stones in the handle. He drew the weapon and inspected it, the shimmering silver blade reflecting the image of his own light blue eyes, marked orange by the firelight.

"Very nice," Seren said as he looked up from his meal.

Triston nodded as he secured the dagger and scabbard on his belt.

"You know," Seren began, after a moment, "I almost thought you weren't going to accompany me on this."

Triston met his gaze.

"I know we disagreed on this whole business with the rebellion. And the draft. But..." Seren glanced at his meal. "I hope you know I had no intention of ill will—"

"Oh, of course not," Triston said with a laugh. "And, for the record, we still disagree. But what made you bring that up?"

Seren shook his head, tearing off another piece of cured pork. "No particular reason. Just... reminiscing, I guess." He peered up at the dark, cloud-mottled sky. "Nights like this, they always make me think of Redfaern."

Triston glanced at the sky and shrugged.

When he was a boy the story of Redfaern had spread with the force of a legend, but he'd come to hate the word. It was on the road to Redfaern Pass where he'd first killed a man—and saved Seren's life—but while his father, and nearly everyone else, had spent the next month congratulating him on his bravery, Triston had spent most of those nights awake, trying to forget what it felt like to plunge a blade through a man's stomach. Of course, by now he had forgotten. Repetition had a way of pushing things from memory.

"So," Seren said, breaking the silence, "why did you decide to join me?"

Triston hesitated. Did he really have a good answer? "I was always going to—I just had questions about this rebellion." He glanced across the fire. "How do you reconcile the fact we're setting out to oppress the very same people we're supposed to guide and protect?"

Seren laughed—not unkindly, but in a way that said he'd never considered the question. "Triston, stop trying to think with your heart! The heart is fickle and bullheaded."

Triston returned the grin. "Wait a minute now—I believe someone told me the Svaldans actually consider the heart to house both thoughts *and* emotions, making it the home for the soul. In that case, I believe you just insulted me."

"Yes, well, I didn't expect you to take my bit of trivia to have any serious application. And last I checked, you were not a Svaldan."

Triston laughed. "No, I'm not."

Seren raised an eyebrow. "Láefe, then?"

"No! No, of course not. You think I spend my free time whispering to the spirits of the world, or whatever it is they do?"

He shrugged. "I know your mother did. Your father as well, for a time. The Láefe actually believe every living thing is equally infused with spirit—with soul—and they place a variety of rules on the handling of all parts of the body. Some will not eat meat, for example."

"Hmm." Triston found his attention wandering to the slight rustling of the leaves in the forest beyond his campfire. "You're trying to convert me to something, is that it?"

Seren laughed. "The truth is in all things, Triston. You just have to know how to look for it."

Chapter Six

Harvest

The whining hum of the summer's last insects hung in the air as Kura paused to wipe the sweat from her brow, a half-husked corn cob in hand.

"Kura!" Elli sat cross-legged at Kura's side and looked up to give her a scolding frown. "Don't stop now, or they're going to beat us!"

Kura grinned and tore the rest of the husk from the cob. "Yes, ma'am." Harvest games were as much a part of fall as the harvest itself. The Burglar's kids, the reigning champions, were their competition this round.

Faron leaned in closer to both of them as he grabbed another ear of corn. "They're way behind."

Kura gave a cursory glance over their pile of corn and had to nod in agreement. The mound was nearly as tall as Elli. Whatever part of her was still a child at heart stirred with excitement; they might actually win this year.

A short, sharp scream pierced the air. That alone wasn't any cause for alarm—those Gambler's kids were always making a ruckus—but another followed, and the bustle of conversation within the compound walls fell to a murmur. Kura froze, part of the way through husking a cob, as dread twisted in her gut.

"What was that?" Elli asked.

Kura rose from her seat, the corn cob falling from her hand as she took a step forward, her eyes glued to the open gate. She couldn't bring herself to even think the words.

One of the farmhands charged into the compound, breathless.

"Soldiers!" Raw panic lent his voice volume enough to echo through the compound. "Soldiers!"

Faron rose to his feet, Elli let out a cry, and the compound broke into a frenzy. Kura stood there, dumbfounded, as shock prickled down her spine. After all these years, hearing the words didn't feel real.

A child began to sob, but two men ran forward to shove the gate closed. Still, the dull pounding of horses' hooves echoed from the other side.

Kura shook herself and grabbed both of her siblings by the arm.

"Ow!" Elli whined.

"Hey," Faron said in frustration. "What's—"

"Come on!" It came out more intense than Kura intended, but she didn't loosen her grip as she dragged her siblings toward their cabin.

Jisela stood in the doorway, eyes wide with panic, chewing her fingernails, Rowley crying in her arms. She caught Kura's gaze and smiled in relief. "There you are."

"Where's Father?"

"Here," Spiridon replied, forcing his way through the crowd to Kura's side.

Anxiety broke through Jisela's facade of calm. "What's going on?"

"Soldiers, thirty or more, coming this way."

"We can barricade the gate." Kura pointed over her shoulder. "Then put archers on the walls and—"

"No," Spiridon said tersely. "The other families are already scattering. We're leaving."

"But, Father, we'll never—"

"No," Spiridon snapped, his expression fearfully stern. "Gather whatever you can carry. Now."

Every fiber in Kura's being demanded she protest, but somehow she heeded her father's words—practically ransacking their home, gathering up whatever useful thing crossed her path. In little time, the family returned to the front step of the house. Kura had her cloak, her gambeson, and her sword, while the rest of them stood similarly laden with weapons, clothes, and bundles of food.

"Go." Spiridon ushered them out the door to join the people streaming toward the wall.

Jisela didn't hesitate, urging Faron and Elli along with her, but as Kura stepped to follow, Spiridon placed his hand on her shoulder.

"Look at me." His face was stern, his brow creased with worry, but only love shone in his eyes. "Whatever I tell you to do, just do it, alright?"

Kura swallowed, then nodded and glanced at her feet. "Yes, sir."

A sense of purpose had lowered the crowd's initial panic to a fevered anxiety, leaving an eerie silence as each family—their faces ashen, their arms burdened with a few meager possessions—made their way across the compound toward the back wall.

"Kura..." Elli whispered, the one word both a question and a cry.

Kura took her hand. "Stay close to me. We're going to be fine."

In the back of the compound, a trapdoor led under the walls and into the woods beyond. Years of work in the rocky soil had produced a tunnel large enough for a person to crawl through. With the gate shut, it was the only means of escape.

Shouts carried from beyond the compound walls—men's voices, many in number. The walls shuddered as something crashed against the gates. Kura studied the latch and had to consciously keep herself from squeezing Elli's hand. How long could that hold?

She turned to her father. "Archers along the wall—"

"Keep moving!" he called, far too distracted to even notice that Kura had spoken.

The few families gathered around the tunnel entrance pushed and jostled themselves to the front of the line, and just that easily, panic and anger merged. Spiridon held his family back from the commotion and ushered the others forward. "Go on!"

Again, the soldiers crashed against the gate, but the walls still held. Kura stood with her teeth clenched, her fist repeatedly closing around her sword hilt. *We should be doing something!*

One soldier's voice rose above the rest. "...have been found guilty of treason, of aiding in rebellion and supporting acts of sedition against His Majesty King Dradge..."

Aiding in rebellion... Kura's stomach lurched. Thoughts tumbled through her mind, but they stopped short of her tongue as she turned to her father in horror.

"Go!" Spiridon motioned toward the tunnel entrance as the last of the other families made their way below.

But, but...

"Help Mother with Rowley," Faron said to his father. "Kura and I can take up the rear."

Spiridon took both Jisela's hands to lower her into the tunnel, but Kura couldn't move.

Gods, it was me! How—how did they find out?

Elli pulled on her arm. "Kura, come on!"

Numb, Kura helped her little sister into the tunnel, but she had to steal one last glance over the compound before she followed. It was in disarray, mundane tasks left half-done, without a living soul to be seen. A ghost town, which moments ago had been teaming with life.

Tearing herself away, Kura leapt into the tunnel, then pulled the trapdoor shut. Muffled voices carried in the clammy darkness and she pressed after them, crawling on her stomach toward the dim sunlight on the other side.

"Hey!" She grimaced as someone—probably Faron—shoved their muddy boot in her face. She smacked the foot out of her way. "Watch it!"

Someone shouted something at the end of the tunnel. Steel clashed with steel. Jisela screamed, then the door slammed shut, leaving Kura in total darkness.

"What's happening?" Faron called out. Elli began to cry.

"Let me through." Kura pushed her way past her siblings to the front of the tunnel, her hands shaking. "Father? Mother?"

There was no reply.

Kura felt along the dirt walls until her hands brushed against the wooden trapdoor above her. Carefully, she lifted it a few fingerbreadths.

A horse's hoof crashed to the ground before her face, making her flinch. Soldiers, some on horseback, some on foot, swarmed in the forest, rounding up whomever they could catch. Her mother had fallen to her knees a few strides from the tunnel; she cradled Rowley in her arms as a soldier pointed a sword at the back of her neck.

"Please, leave us alone, we've done nothing!"

At her mother's side, a second soldier drove a knee into her father's back to pin him face-down in the leaves.

Rage surged in Kura's chest, and she reached for her sword.

"What's going on?" The slit of light from the open trapdoor fell across Faron's face, illuminating his eyes. He was afraid.

Kura opened her mouth to explain, but she didn't know what she should say.

"Where are they coming from?" one of the soldiers called out.

"I don't know," a second said as he secured the knot on the rope binding Spiridon's hands behind his back.

Spiridon shook himself from the soldier's grip and dashed awkwardly into the forest, away from the trapdoor. "Run!" The second soldier kicked him in the back, knocking him to the ground before he could get far. Grunting, he pushed himself up to keep shouting at nothing in the empty forest. "Run, all of you!"

"Try that way," the second soldier said, pointing over Spiridon's shoulder in the direction he'd yelled.

Tears welled up in Kura's eyes, and she let the trapdoor fall shut before Faron and Elli saw her cry. "Follow me."

Silently, the three of them made their way back through the tunnel, Kura pushing her way past them again to take the lead. What had seemed like such a long journey moments ago now passed in an instant. Kura threw back the trapdoor and climbed out of the tunnel.

"Come on." She offered her hand first to Elli, then to Faron to haul them out of the tunnel.

"We..." Elli took a breath. "We left Mother and Father and Rowley."

"I know." The words caught in Kura's throat, but she didn't know what else to say. *Father, I've done what you told me.*

A crash sounded at the gate, followed by creaking wood.

"Back to the house!" Kura pointed across the courtyard to their empty cabin. "Hide in the loft and wait for me."

Elli immediately jogged toward the cabin, and Faron took a step after her, but when Kura didn't follow he stopped. "What about you?"

"Just... wait for me."

Faron stared at her, and Kura was certain he was going to argue. Another crash came from the gate, making both of them jump.

"Come on!" Elli grabbed Faron by the hand and pulled him toward the house.

Faron held his ground for a moment, then slipped his bow and quiver from his shoulder and tossed it to Kura. "Here."

Kura caught it, then met his gaze. Faron only nodded, and somehow that said enough. She yanked the bow—already strung—from the quiver, hooked the quiver onto her belt, then took off toward the walls.

Some large object smashed against the gate, splintering the wood and knocking the posts out of their bases. The soldiers had yet to break through, but their dark figures flickered in the sunlight beyond the crumbling slats. Kura pulled several arrows from the quiver and placed them in her bow hand, then scaled the wall.

Flinging her leg over the wall to maintain balance, she nocked an arrow and pulled the string back to her cheek. Several soldiers hoisted the fallen log they were using as a battering ram. She targeted the nearest man and loosed her arrow.

The man cried out as it pierced his neck, and with startled shouts the other soldiers forgot the battering ram. Heart pounding but breath steady, Kura loosed the remaining arrows in her hand. One shot through a man's arm—he screamed and dropped his sword. Another ricocheted off a man's chestplate. Another sank into a shoulder, another a thigh.

"There, on the wall!" One of the soldiers raised a crossbow.

Kura flung her leg back over the wall and let herself drop as the bolt thudded into the wood where she had been sitting. She slid down the inside of the wall, then hit the ground hard. The shouts on the opposite side of the wall shifted from surprise to anger.

"Get this gate down!"

Kura snatched up the remaining arrows in her quiver; there were only three. She nocked one on the string as she pressed her back against the wall, taking deep, intentional breaths to calm her nerves as she waited for the first man to come through the gate.

One more hit from the battering ram, and the splintered wood gave way. Shattered logs fell to the ground, only to be crushed by the fallen tree and then trampled underfoot as the first of the soldiers charged into the compound.

Kura waited until she could see each man's neck—the weak point in their armor, between their chestplate and helmet—before she loosed her arrows. Her first shot sank fletching-deep into the man's throat and he stumbled, giving a garbled cry as he clutched at his bleeding wound. The next two men pressed forward, unfazed. Kura's hands shook, and her last two shots ricocheted off their metal armor.

With a grunt, she tossed the bow and quiver aside and fell back against the wall, drawing her sword. The wreckage of the gate secluded her for only a moment longer. One soldier stepped beyond the splintered wood and Kura leapt forward, thrusting her sword below and past his chestplate before he brought his weapon in to guard. Her blade sank into his gut until it reached bone, and she found her eyes locked with his.

They were earnest eyes, innocently questioning *why*, as she pulled her blade from his stomach.

He crumpled into a heap at Kura's feet and all she could do was stare at him, her thoughts silenced by a multitude of questions. Silver flashed in the corner of her eye and then he was gone—the man's face, the questions, all of it—and she spun around, blocking the next soldier's strike. They exchanged blows, parrying back and forth in short, quick hits as Kura forced him back through the gaping opening in the wall.

The soldier caught his foot on the discarded battering ram and fell. Kura lunged, intending to drive her blade through his throat, but the man rolled to the side, smacking her sword away with his metal vambrace. He scrambled to his feet, snatching up his fallen weapon, and thrust it at her chest. She jumped to the side, swinging her own blade through the man's wrist.

The soldier let out an agonized cry as his fist—still clutching his hilt—fell to the ground.

"Hey!"

Kura froze. She'd ventured past the relative safety of the wall—the fields lay beyond, teeming with soldiers. Two riders cantered toward her, rallying more men to their call. The first, a young man with black hair, sat tall in the saddle of a mare that might as well have belonged to the King of Avaron himself, while the second raised a crossbow.

Kura sheathed her sword and bolted.

She knew it was foolish the moment she took the first step, but she wouldn't lead them back to Faron and Elli, and she couldn't just stay standing. Horses' hooves pounded behind her and she cringed when the crossbow snapped, sending a bolt over her shoulder, but she didn't stop. She might lose them in the trees.

Branches whipped against her cheeks and briars snagged and tore at her trousers, but Kura kept to the underbrush as she charged downhill. It was a path those horses couldn't easily follow. The trees passed by her in a blur; she focused on the bright patch of open sunlight beyond the boughs as she chased the gurgling of the Everard River. The horses would probably spook here by the ravine, then she could circle back—

She screamed as a crossbow bolt tore through her shoulder. The force threw her forward, and she stumbled to her hands and knees in the leaves beside the cliff. Her breath came in gasps as her own panicked heartbeats pounded in her ears, but the searing pain made it impossible to think. The soldiers stood high on the ridge above her. The dark-haired one said something—she couldn't hear him over the pain—and nudged his grey mare forward as the other soldier reloaded his crossbow.

Fighting back tears, Kura grasped her bleeding shoulder. She couldn't run any longer, she couldn't fight; there were soldiers before her and the ravine behind. The soldiers promised death, but the steep slope to the river below offered a chance at escape.

With a shriek through gritted teeth, she pushed herself over the edge.

Sharp rocks and sticks jabbed into her back and sides and Kura clenched her jaw, holding back another scream, as the world around her flashed between warm sunlight and cool shadows. She tumbled farther and farther into the ravine as the soldiers shouted from somewhere above.

Finally, it came to a stop.

The first thing she noticed was that pounding of her own pulse in her ears. She tried to sit up, grimacing as the effort jarred her injured shoulder and aggravated her bruised back and limbs. It took a moment for her eyes to adjust to the shadows, but with a strange sense of relief she found herself on her back in the bottom of the Everard Ravine.

"Hello?" The man's voice came from above and echoed in the ravine.

Kura scooted back against the cliff, biting down on her own cloak to distract herself from the pain that shot through her each time she moved.

"Hello?" The voice came again, dismissive this time.

Shadowy figures shifted against the opposite side of the ravine. They muttered to one another in low voices, and one knelt down as though he intended to follow her into the ravine. Then, one at a time, the shadows disappeared.

Kura breathed a sigh of relief and let her head fall back against the rocky cliffside. That relief didn't last long. With a groan, she forced herself to sit up, whimpering as she pressed a hand against her shoulder.

Stupid, stupid, stupid!

She grasped at the side of the cliff, but her left arm was too weak to move, and the wet, pebble-strewn dirt slipped between her fingers.

A stick cracked and she spun around, heart pounding, and peered into the shadows. More than a stone's throw separated her from the other side, and the Everard River churned through the center. Nothing grew in the cold shadows; only a few tufts of grass and an old, scraggly tree filled the space between her and the river. She waited, trying to quiet her gasps for breath, to hear what had made the sound.

Nothing moved, and there came no sound but the river.

She sighed, then winced as even that movement jostled the arrow. Her gambeson must have blunted some of the blow, but it hadn't been enough—fletching stuck out of her shoulder blade, while the steel point protruded through her chest. She jerked her hand away, her own blood drying on her fingertips.

Don't pull it out. She had to repeat that to herself as she fought the urge to do it anyway. Her mother had taught her enough to know it would be better left in place until... until what? She had no guarantee anyone would come for her. Not now, and especially not here.

She gritted her teeth and with slow, deliberate motions pulled her dagger from its sheath on her belt to cut a few strips of cloth from her cloak. As gently as she could manage, she wrapped the makeshift bandages around her wounds.

An owl's screech drew her attention to the other side of the ravine—the opposite edge of the Everard, from which no man had ever returned. She shuddered, studying the shadowy figures of trees that populated that forbidden ridge. She would be safe enough here, right? After all, she hadn't crossed the ravine. She'd only rest a minute. Just until she was sure the soldiers had cleared out.

Yet unease settled in her gut as she placed her hand on the hilt of her sword. How would she climb to the top of the ravine with one good arm?

Kura clenched her fists. She'd figure something out. She always did.

Chapter Seven

Six

Triston grimaced as he wound a bandage over the gash on his arm. Briar bushes—the entire forest was filled with them. The cut wasn't too deep, but somehow those damn thorns had made it through his chain mail and quilted gambeson.

He sighed and scanned the campground with a frown. He, Seren, and the rest of the company had finally been able to provide medical attention to the injured men and secure the group of prisoners.

Six. That was the number of holes they'd dug—the number of bodies they'd leave behind in this wasteland, the number of families that would spend the next week mourning when they returned home. And that one cast-out had killed all of them. Seren wasn't pleased about leaving someone unaccounted for, but Triston was almost glad she'd fallen in that ravine.

This miserable place could have her.

He and his company were lucky to have found this clearing in the dense forest in which to cram their rows of white tents. The prisoners had to spend the night among the trees at the edge of camp.

"Well, what is it we have here?"

Triston dropped his bandages in surprise and scrambled to his feet. The red sunset cast long shadows through the trees, and it took him a moment to place the voice. He was looking for a man, but out of the forest slunk a large cat.

The animal met his gaze with a snarl—or maybe it was supposed to be a grin. "Where did you all come from?"

Triston stepped back, placing his tent between himself and the cat as he drew his sword. "That's far enough."

The cat laughed as it sauntered along the edge of the clearing. "You're awfully bold to try giving me commands, two-foot."

Triston followed the animal's movements with the point of his sword. The last time he'd seen a nostkynna, he'd been maybe ten years old, and it had been part of a performer's troop. "Are you traveling through? You should know this area isn't safe."

The cat stopped, its yellow eyes locking with Triston's. "Isn't safe?" Lazily, it sat down, its thin tail curling around its legs as it let out a yowling laugh. "Of course it isn't safe!"

Triston adjusted his grip on his sword.

The cat slowly licked its lips. "Still, you silver-chests have been far more agreeable than the squatters. How long are you staying this time?"

"We're—we're not staying."

The cat's ear twitched it and rose up on all fours. "I thought as much." There were markings on the animal's flank—maybe an old wound, but while the cuts must have been deep, the scar seemed intentional, as it roughly formed a tree. "I shall find my supper elsewhere tonight. And I will tell the rest to do the same, as long as you swear to take the squatters with you and be gone by morning."

Triston nodded. He wasn't sure if he should agree to anything, but he already had every intention of striking out for Avtalyon by the time the sun rose, anyway.

The cat flashed him a grin before it leapt into the forest and disappeared among the autumn leaves, as silently and as suddenly as it had come.

Triston lowered his sword. He'd heard tales of the Wynshire Waste—everyone had; the stories traveled quickly after dinner when the beer had been served—but he had never really believed them. Who would believe them? The beasts became larger and more fantastical with every rendition.

He stared into the shadow-crossed forest for a while longer, frowning as he measured those rumors with a more critical eye. Nostkynna, wandering free? What kind of place was this?

Shouts carried from the other side of the clearing. Triston muttered under his breath, shoved his sword back into its scabbard, and took off at a run through the tents. The commotion came into view as he stepped in among the trees. One of the prisoners had broken from the group and shoved toward the clearing, even as two soldiers fought to hold him back.

Triston threw his weight into the fight, pushing with the soldiers until the man fell backward onto the ground, still shouting.

"You're sentencing us to death!" The man was tall, had he been standing, and while he was not young, he'd been the most belligerent of the group since the beginning. "No one is safe in this forest at night, no one!"

The prisoners beyond the man voiced agreement, and several leapt to their feet and threw themselves against the ropes that bound their wrists and ankles to the nearby trees. The soldiers closed in around the group, their swords bared.

Triston and the soldier beside him hauled the man to his feet, but he continued to struggle against their grip. "You don't understand!"

Riders merged in from each side, Seren leading the group. He leapt from the saddle, drawing his sword. "What is this?"

The man yanked his arm from Triston's grip and dashed forward, but the second soldier dropped him with a solid punch to his nose.

"Hey—" Triston started, but the soldier didn't give another blow. The man struggled to sit up, pressing his hand against his face as blood seeped into his auburn beard.

"This one again?" Seren sighed. He nodded to the soldier beside him. "Get him up."

The two soldiers dragged the man to his feet once more, steadying him as he held on to his bleeding nose.

Seren looked him over with a disgusted frown. "Your papers."

A cold rage burned in the prisoner's eyes, and then he spit a mouthful of blood in Seren's face. Seren jumped back and the two soldiers shouted, pulling the man away.

Seren raised his sword with a scowl. "I ought to make an example of—"

"Hold on." Triston intercepted Seren's arm, and he reluctantly stepped back. Triston nodded toward one of the soldiers beside him. "What did you confiscate from this man during the search?"

The soldier stepped back to pass the request down the line, and after a moment another man jogged up carrying a satchel stuffed to the brim with papers, concealable weapons, small trinkets, and other personal belongings. He rummaged through it to produce a folded parchment, stained and crumpled, which he held out toward Triston.

Seren snatched it from his hand. "Thank you," he muttered, still wiping his face on his sleeve. His grey eyes glided across the page, then looked up at the man in surprise. "You are Spiridon, son of Emerick?" He smirked. "I always remember the name of a deserter. I think fifty firri was the most I offered for your head. You remember a Sergeant Merric? He has your job now."

The man said nothing, didn't even look Seren in the eye.

Seren turned back to Triston with a half-smile. "I believe we have found our rebel."

"I am no rebel," the man said quietly, his voice a rumbling whisper in his throat. "But I should have been."

Seren's smile faded. "Explain."

The man hesitated, but his rage didn't cool. "I know what you've done to those boys. I saw them at Tjrim Rock. At Lamok Falls. At Orhl. I saw what they did with my own eyes, or just days after. Before the dark creatures could cover it up."

Seren laughed. "A conspiracy theorist as well?" He casually motioned toward the rest of the prisoners. "Put him back in line."

The two soldiers dragged the man with them, and he didn't resist.

Seren muttered a string of curses under his breath as he tried to wipe the red splatter from his shirt. Triston watched him with a trace of a laugh, but the amusement didn't last. "You know, we might not want to stay here tonight."

Seren raised an eyebrow.

"I came across this talking cat, and it—"

"A talking cat? What did it say?"

Triston rubbed the back of his neck. "Well, ah, it wants us out of here by sunrise."

"You're right. We're heading out now."

Chapter Eight

TRAVAIL

The snap of a twig woke Kura from a shallow sleep.
She blinked, fighting the weight of her own eyelids, as she wondered if she'd really fallen asleep or just passed out. She hadn't moved from her place beside the cliff, and sat with her cloak wrapped tight around her in a feeble effort to stay warm. The ravine was empty, with the river before her and the trees high above. No noise followed the first, and she leaned back, relatively certain she was—for better or for worse—alone.

With that little nap, she'd squandered the remaining sunlight. Now she was beyond the clearing, in the Wynshire, at night. She didn't want to be afraid, but relentless, anxious thoughts ate away at her resolve and she found herself gripping the hilt of her sheathed sword like it was some sort of talisman that could ward off the evil lurking in the darkness.

What about Faron and Elli?

A shock of fear coursed through her. They would be alright in the compound, wouldn't they? But the gate was in pieces, and what if they wandered off to find her? What if the soldiers found them first? Kura let out a desperate sigh, frustration rising over her fear. None of this should have happened. They should have been safe here—at least, safe from the soldiers. Dradge had always left them alone before.

She blinked and tried to fight back the swell of tears. *It's my fault.* Her father had sent that man from the rebellion away because he'd worried this would happen, but she had played the informant behind his back because she had been sure nothing like it ever could—not in the Wynshire. She squeezed her eyes shut, spilling hot tears down her cheeks, as a sob racked her chest.

All of it—this horrible, irrevocable mess—all of it was her fault.

Kura looked up, through tears, at the stars. She had to fix this, somehow, but she didn't know where to begin. Desperation mixed with the fear in her heart, stirring something deep within the very marrow of her bones.

"Essence of all things," she shouted at the sky, "if you have ever loved me, spare me and my family from the fate that I have woven for us!"

Her voice resonated in the still silence of the ravine. A light breeze rustled through the trees far above her, and a spiral of dry leaves fell to the forest floor below. The cold wind made her shiver, and jolt the arrow stuck in her shoulder.

With a sigh, she let her head fall back on the cliff behind her. She didn't know why she'd expected anything to happen, anyway.

She might survive here until morning. Most of the animals and nostkynna stayed away from the ravine. Once the sun rose, she would make her way upstream. The cliff was less steep there; she could probably climb it and trace her way back to the compound before noon.

Pebbles rattled as they tumbled down the opposite cliff face. Kura shot up, her fear re-kindled. She thought she glimpsed something moving, beside the river—there, silhouettes outlined in the moonlight.

Wolves.

Kura struggled to her feet. The change in elevation made her vision shift dizzily, and she leaned back against the cliff to maintain her balance. The dark figures crept toward her, their tails raised and their ears lowered.

"What's this...?" the nearest wolf rumbled. Its long snout and tongue broke the softer consonants, but Kura had long ago learned to understand their pattern of speech. "A woman-child out alone in our forest?"

Several silhouettes followed the first, their paws crunching against the bed of dry leaves that covered the floor of the ravine. Kura counted four more—that made five wolves total, probably an entire pack.

"We could smell your blood and your fear from a hundred paces," a second wolf said, its eyes glinting silver in the darkness. It stepped closer. "You'll be our best catch of the night, I think."

"I'm sorry," Kura said, fighting to keep her voice from shaking, as she gripped the hilt of her sheathed sword. "I didn't mean to be here. My people have an agreement with Agafy that—"

"This isn't the farm, woman-child," the first wolf said, teeth flashing in the moonlight. "And Agafy is not alpha here any longer."

"What do you mean? We have an agreement. We leave you alone, Agafy and his pack leaves—"

"The saja move!" the first wolf snarled. "Saja-brothers fear no child of man!"

Kura drew her sword. It was an effort to simply keep her arm raised, and her head spun as she fought to draw each breath.

"It has been long since saja-brothers tasted man-flesh," the second wolf mused.

"Stay back!" Kura shouted, her voice cracking. "Stay back!"

The wolves laughed, the sound rippling through the pack in a low, shared growl. The nearest animal darted at Kura's ankle, teeth bared. She slashed at the wolf's shoulder, but it pulled out of her reach.

"Yes, a challenger!" The wolves laughed again and began to circle her, yipping to one another in some excited argument. Another darted forward, evaded Kura's blade, then latched onto her ankle and pulled her foot out from under her.

Kura fell back against the cliff side, crying out at the impact to her shoulder. A mix of pain and darkness swirled in her mind, but the wolves' paws crunched the leaves at her sides—their breath brushed hot and humid against her face. She lashed out, swinging her sword with reckless abandon, her shaking limbs fueled only by an innate desire to survive.

A scream sounded from the other side of the ravine, and the wolves pulled back.

Kura threw her eyes open, gasping for breath, and stared into the darkness. Several tall figures sloshed through the river, but their dark shadows blurred together. They were riders—they had to be soldiers. Her heart sank, and it took all her strength to even keep the grip on her sword.

The wolves barked nervously to one another. "I thought we'd lost them."

"They are persistent, like flies."

One of the rider's horses whinnied—that had been the scream. The wolves bolted and the riders thundered after them, giving chase upstream.

Kura gripped the hillside behind her and dragged herself to her feet. Her legs shook beneath her and she fell against the stones. She needed to run, but the pain in her shoulder throbbed with each beat of her heart and it took all her willpower to keep from passing out.

Something moved in the ravine. The soldiers.

"Get back!" Kura called out, weakly, and raised the weapon she somehow still held.

One horse snorted and stomped its hoof, but they came no closer. Their dark silhouettes danced before her eyes, then—as if by some magic—one rider suddenly held a light.

Kura's mind told her it was a lantern. The wooden frame certainly had a lantern's shape, but the light in the center seemed to emanate from a fist-sized, marbled stone which pulsated as it glowed.

The rider with the light muttered something, but only gibberish reached her ears. He held his lantern out as his horse stepped toward her. Kura's eyes widened as she stared at his face. Where was the horse's head? She blinked hard to try to clear her mind. She wasn't sure if she should laugh or be utterly terrified.

The rider with the lantern turned over his shoulder, whispering in his gibberish with the rest of his group. And gradually, she came to understand. These were not riders.

Their lower halves were horses—large, stocky animals, from what she could see in the mix of light and shadow—but their upper halves were human, broad-shouldered humans with simple cloth shirts and olive-colored skin. And big horse's ears.

Centaurs.

One of them stepped forward and pointed his massive pike at Kura's neck.

"You have one minute to explain why I should let you live." The creature spoke slowly, his words weighted by a heavy accent. Kura struggled to comprehend him at first, and even when she did understand, she couldn't get her muddled mind to focus on anything but the large white scar that notched his lip and ran the length of his face.

He pressed the rusted blade against her neck. "Don't make me ask again."

Kura dropped her sword.

The one with the lantern muttered something scoldingly and brushed aside the scarred one's pike. He held his lantern closer to Kura's face, his eyes widening as his gaze fell on her shoulder.

"Little one, what happened here?" He spoke more quickly, his accent light. Both time and weather had wrinkled his long, narrow face and his ragged, shoulder-length hair bore a curious white streak. But his amber eyes—unblinking and almost yellow, like a wolf's—held hers with such intensity that she was compelled to say something.

"I..." Her hand found its way to her injured shoulder, and she drew in a breath as she glanced down at it. The lantern's light glistened in the blood that had soaked through her bandages and stained the whole left side of her shirt.

The creatures whispered among themselves. They obviously weren't happy, but the one with the light handed his lantern to another and stepped toward her with empty hands outstretched. "We can help you."

Kura didn't believe that, but even all the strength she had wasn't enough to fend off the strong arms that picked her gently off her feet. Then the light vanished and she began to move, her face pressed against a rough bit of cloth that smelled of sweat and dirt. She swayed with the galloping of a horse's gait, darkness surrounding her, and the ache in her shoulder overcame all else.

Centaurs, in Avaron? She laughed, either aloud or in her head. *Not in a hundred years. Not in a thousand years!*

She found herself seated on the floor of a small domed hut, the space lit by a large, glowing stone that closely resembled the one she had seen before. There were many of those creatures here—towering over her, casting dark shadows across her face. They motioned to her as they whispered amongst themselves, one holding in his hands what appeared to be bandages, and a second several small knives and a rope.

Normally Kura might have been alarmed, but the pain made her groggy and everything felt detached, even dreamlike. So she watched, the scene fading in and out of light and darkness, as she tried to remember why she needed to stay awake.

A centaur girl gingerly propped up Kura's sagging frame.

"This will ease the pain," she said as she pressed a mug of steaming liquid to Kura's lips.

Hardly knowing what she was doing, Kura swallowed some of the drink. It had a sweet, honey-like taste initially and a bitter aftertaste. Horrible. But the girl offered her a few more sips and Kura took them.

The room was so warm and soft... She let her eyes fall shut.

Chapter Nine

Prisoner of War

Kura awoke with a gasp.

The world around her was dim and heavy, and she sat up, wincing as that movement sent a familiar shock of pain through her shoulder. She was lying on a bundle of blankets at the edge of a round room. Alone.

The room itself was taller than it was wide. Thin saplings, bent and lashed together, created the domed ceiling. Large, overlapping strips of bark formed the walls, while the door was nothing more than a thick piece of cloth, which flapped in a breeze. She squinted as each of its movements sent a flash of blinding sunlight across her face.

Faron. Elli.

She threw back the rough blanket that covered her legs, then stopped short. The arrow had been removed from her shoulder—bloodstained bandages had been left in its place... and there was a chain clamped to her ankle and fixed to a stake beside her.

Kura tugged at the latch on the shackle. She had some vague memory of centaurs, but—centaurs? She shook her head, trying to clear the lingering fog. *Weren't there soldiers?*

Voices, low and muffled, sounded outside near the doorway and she froze. One belonged to a man and the other a woman, but she couldn't make out what they said. Kura turned her attention instead to the stake, a part of her threatening to become frantic, but the bit of wood was sunk deep into the ground. Definitely frantic now, she grabbed hold of the chain with both hands and gave a sharp pull. The force jerked her shoulder, and she bit back a cry.

A flash of sunlight filled the room, followed by a long, dark shadow that enveloped Kura as it stretched across the dirt floor. She stared up at that towering figure, her eyes wide and her fists clenched in fear. It *was* a centaur.

In fact, it was *the* centaur, the girl who had given her that terrible drink. Her horse's half was thin; she had gangly long legs, and her fur was a burnt red speckled with white.

"Oh, you're awake!"

Kura pulled back as the centaur stepped toward her, and recoiled as the girl dropped to her knees.

"It's alright, I've brought you some breakfast."

Terrified, Kura stared at the girl. She couldn't have been more than Faron's age, probably, with olive skin, narrow, angular eyes, and thick black hair pulled back in a large braid. A human face, except for the horse's ears. And teeth.

She gave a bright smile and held out a tray of food. "I wasn't sure what you'd want to eat, so I brought a little of everything. My name's N'hadia."

Kura stared at the tray. There was a soup bowl full of an amber liquid that smelled faintly of grass, a few green and yellow fried patties that resembled a fall field, and several other mugs and plates full of similar, unappetizing plant-based dishes.

"You're, um..." Kura faltered. She was speechless, but her mouth was trying to say something anyway. Was this what had happened to all those others who had disappeared crossing the ravine? Centaurs bound their wounds, fattened them up, then ate them?

"Are you feeling alright?" The centaur girl watched Kura's face with the most innocent look of concern. "I was so worried for you when they brought you in last night. I've always been told that humans are not as strong as the Cenóri, but Konik is a good physician, he—"

"N'hadia!" boomed a voice at the door.

Both Kura and N'hadia jumped. A male centaur stood in the doorway, his towering figure dwarfing both of them. Abundant white splotches overlaid his black horse's half, and his human half was bare, his olive skin marked almost entirely by black tattoos that were as intricate as they were abstract. Kura cringed and met his gaze. He was the scarred one—the one who'd threatened her with the pike.

The centaur muttered something in his own language, and N'hadia hung her head. "You." He jabbed a large index finger in Kura's direction. "Come with me."

He tossed N'hadia a small key. Obediently, the centaur girl undid the chain from Kura's ankle.

Kura saw her chance and took it. She burst through the door with all the strength she could muster. N'hadia and the other centaur shouted behind her, but louder than that came the pounding of her own heart and the voiceless call of freedom.

The sunlight still made her squint, but she was in a village—a strange village of bark huts, and a few curious centaurs who yelled at her. Kura sprinted for the trees. Her shoulder ached with each movement, but she kept her legs powering beneath her.

Effortlessly, N'hadia and another centaur overtook her. Strong hands shoved her from behind and she toppled to the ground. She tumbled across the hard dirt, every joint aching. Voices murmured around her. Kura rolled onto her back, blinking through dust as she looked up at the centaurs towering above.

"Please"—she forced the words out between gasps—"I've worked the fields all my life. I'll be tough—very tough. And I doubt you'd even get half a pot of stew out of me. Not worth the time it would take to butcher me, I'd expect—though of course I don't have a taste for man-flesh—but I've processed my share of wild game and I—"

"What?" one centaur laughed. "Little one, what is this about stew and man-flesh?"

Kura stopped, her mouth hanging open, as she peered through the thinning cloud of dust to study the centaur's face. She recognized this one, too—he was the one with the white stripe in his hair, the one with the lantern the night before. He leaned down and gently pulled Kura to her feet. She still fought for air, and her legs shook under her own weight, but the centaur kept a grip on her arm to steady her.

"You..." Kura drew in a deep breath. "You *are* planning on eating me, aren't you?"

In horror, N'hadia covered her mouth with her hands.

"Goodness, child," another centaur said with an angered swish of his tail. "Our meals are all plant-based! Haven't you ever spent any time around horses? Did you see any of them eating men?"

"There—there was an old gelding in the next settlement over..." Kura swallowed. "And he would nip fingers sometimes..."

The one with the white stripe laughed earnestly.

"Barbaric," the scarred one muttered. "But what should I expect?" He caught hold of Kura's injured arm. "Move."

Kura sucked in a breath through clenched teeth, clutching at her shoulder as the centaur dragged her forward.

"Brant," the one with the white stripe growled.

The other centaur grunted but did loosen his grip on Kura's arm. She walked as quickly as she could, her shaking legs making her stumble, as the group of centaurs moved beside her and led her into the center of the village. A few curious eyes peered out from among the huts—mostly men and women, but also a few children that appeared to be about N'hadia's age. For such a large village, there were few villagers, in only three distinct generations: the young like N'hadia, the middle-aged like the scarred one, and the old like the one with the white stripe.

"Here," Brant grumbled, shoving Kura toward the door of the nearest hut.

This house, still round, was at least four times the size of any other building in the village. Perhaps these centaurs didn't want to eat her, but they certainly wanted *something*.

Bracing herself, Kura pushed the door flap aside.

While the hut she'd left had been dim, here natural light shone through open flaps in the domed ceiling. One centaur was already waiting, near the wall—an older woman with black striped tattoos leading from her eyes and down her cheeks. They were her only markings, a complement to the fin of black feathers that adorned her head and a contrast with the shock of white hair hanging past her waist.

Brant took hold of Kura's arm again and dragged her toward the stake in the center of the room. A short metal chain hung from the wood, and Kura flinched as the centaur locked a cold shackle around her wrist.

"So you don't get any more ideas about running off."

Kura fixed her eyes on her shoes. How many had stood where she did now? The smooth, packed dirt at her feet said the number had not been small.

The rest of the centaurs filed into the room, murmuring in their own language as they formed a circle around the stake. Most hung back in the shadowy corners of the long hall, but the striped centaur took a stand beside Brant. Hesitantly, Kura turned back toward the door. N'hadia was talking with another centaur—her father, most likely, considering their similar features. He scolded her softly, then left her outside the hut, the flap door falling shut behind him as he filled the last empty place in the circle.

"We have come to seek the truth," the striped centaur said, motioning toward the white-haired woman on the other side of the room. "May the eastern wind guide and the sunlight bring us clarity."

The woman nodded solemnly and removed the bundle from her back. It contained only two things: a tall, thin table with a cloth top, which she unfolded before her, and a small pouch. This she cupped reverently in her hands and whispered to it words Kura didn't understand.

"So," N'hadia's father began with a frown, "I thought your kind had finally learned to keep to the clearings at night. What were you doing in the ravine?"

Kura looked him in the eye. What should she even say? "I—I apologize for trespassing." She lifted her hand, and the chain rattled dully. "Unshackle me, and I will gladly return home and never bother any of you again."

"Home?" Brant repeated with a laugh. His smile was even more disturbing than his scowl. "We extend to you the same two choices our ancestors have given your kind for generations: subservience, or death."

Kura glanced at the other faces surrounding her. They all seemed to be in agreement.

The old woman shook the pouch in her hands, the soft jingle of the items within drawing the other centaurs' attention. "The Temper will discern for us the truth."

She unceremoniously dumped the contents of her pouch onto the small folding table before her. It was a collection of trinkets—bits of bone, colorful beads, twigs, feathers, and other small items. The woman inspected the table, her frown deepening, and she shook her head. "The black stone touches the bone of man. In her heart lies deceit."

"What?" Kura exclaimed, as a murmur of disapproving voices filled the hut.

N'hadia's father gave her a discerning look. "Are you *forreada*?"

"What... what's a *forreada*?"

"They are grey creatures, like all of us," the striped one said, as though that explained anything, "who have promised themselves to the darkness."

"Well, I am not that!"

The old woman gathered up her trinkets, then cast them again on the table. "The bone of man stands alone. She tells the truth."

Brant scoffed. "She's a soldier, then. One of the ones running with the saja."

Kura laughed under her breath. "Are you all looking for those things, too?"

"What do you know about the saja?" N'hadia's father asked.

Kura turned, startled to see such seriousness in the faces watching her. "Well," she started, mentally running through the stories her mother had told her, "they're nostkynna who gave themselves to the Crux—the *Myrk'aviet*—and became terrible, twisted monsters. But Gallian drove them over the mountains and they haven't been seen since." She was still confronted with four intent stares. A grin tugged at her lips. "They're a myth."

N'hadia's father snorted. "A myth?" He swished his tail. "Is all of your race as foolish as this? A myth?"

"Piotr," the striped one scolded.

Piotr sighed, before turning back to Kura. "Are you a soldier?"

"No. I would rather die than fight beside a king's man."

The old woman again tossed her handful of trinkets. "Oh," she said in surprise, holding up a large, golden feather. "The wing feather of the eastern flicker lies across the bone of man and the blood ruby. She speaks the truth now, but it will not always be so."

Murmurs again rippled through the group, and Kura stared at the old woman in disbelief. "How can you...?"

"You doubt?" The woman remained perturbingly calm. "You can't feel it, can you? You and your kind are deaf to the soft voice in the wind, hardened to the chill that lingers in the air despite the sunrise. With every passing day, it grows colder as the Crux tightens its grip. You won't feel it until it's crushed us all entirely."

"Autumn is almost here," Kura replied stiffly. "And so the cold weather is coming down from the mountains. I haven't seen any Crux, or Essence for that matter, but I have seen plenty of sunrises."

The old woman lifted her chin, studying Kura with a haughty sense of validation.

"Little one," the striped one began, a spark of mischief in his amber eyes. "You can't see it with your eyes, so you know it must not be there? What about the wind, or the heat, or the cold? These too you cannot see, and yet if someone said they were not there you would think them a fool."

Kura glanced at her feet. She understood his point well enough, but that didn't change anything. "Are you Láefe, then?"

Each of the centaurs gave an exclamation of surprise, anger, or both.

"What more do we need to hear?" Brant said. He took another step toward her, scowling. "Trofast sent you to spy on us, has he?"

Kura moved back, placing the stake between her and the centaur. "Who's Trofast?"

Brant snorted. "Konik?"

The striped one sighed deeply, then pulled a small object from his belt. Kura's hand instinctively went to her neck, but it was bare. He had her necklace—the one the rebellion had given her.

"Little one, you recognize this?" The look in Konik's eye said he already knew the answer.

"Don't lie to us, child," Piotr said. "We all know there is only one place in Avaron to mine a stone such as this."

Kura shook her head slightly. "I still don't know who Trofast is."

The old woman looked up from her table. "She speaks the truth."

"Explain the medallion, then," Piotr said. "Is it a family heirloom? Did you trade for it? Did you steal it?"

Kura hesitated, glancing from the centaur's stern face to the old woman's casting table. She was very tempted to lie, but she feared being caught in a deception only a little more than being caught in the truth. "It's a rebel token, one I wore in the hopes of escaping this godsforsaken wasteland, before the royal army came and destroyed everything I ever knew." She let out a desperate breath, emotion catching in the back of her throat—but she wouldn't cry, not here and now. "I promise you, I want no part of your lands or your people or your anything. I just want to go home."

Brant didn't waver. "Don't we all?"

The jingling of the old woman's trinkets filled the room. "She speaks the truth."

"I don't care what the casting shows." Brant scowled. "Trofast would have rid of every one of us if he had the chance."

Konik shifted his stance uncomfortably. "He is still my brother."

"For whatever difference that makes," Piotr muttered. "Still, this human seems to know nothing at all. I see no reason for us not to keep her for now. N'hadia can watch her in the meantime."

The rest of the centaurs gave varying responses of agreement, and a few turned toward the door. Kura watched them, dumbfounded. That was it?

"Wait!" she shouted, then cringed as each set of eyes turned back to look at her in disapproval. These were dangerous creatures; too quickly she had forgotten that. "What are you going to do with me?"

The group of centaurs shared a few sideways glances, then Konik nodded toward the old woman. She cast her handful of trinkets.

"Destiny, of chance and choices..." She pushed aside a piece of bark to reveal a sparkling red stone. "Hidden underneath, but smoldering like fire." In one hand she picked up a broken piece of a steel blade; in the other she raised the golden feather. "Danger, that is what I see in you. The potential for great danger."

Kura held the woman's gaze, brow furrowed. She spoke nonsense —like those fortune tellers, the Pokalfr, in Tarr Fianin—only, this woman had nothing to gain. She wasn't getting paid.

Brant grunted and managed a wry grin. "Big words, for such a little thing." He glanced back, his expression hardening as he looked to Konik. "Perhaps we'll make use of her after all."

Konik frowned and motioned toward the door, and silently the group of centaurs filed out of the tent. While Kura saw their faces, she could almost imagine they were human. Not now. The old woman was the last to leave, as she deliberately returned her things to her pouch before following after the others.

N'hadia brushed past the woman in the doorway, trotting toward Kura with an excited whinny. "So, we're keeping you!" She grinned like a child who'd been gifted a new pet.

Kura tried to return the smile, but the best she managed was a grimace.

N'hadia's face fell as she saw the shackle on Kura's wrist. "Oh."

Kura sighed, jiggling the latch. "N'hadia, could you get me out of here, please? I have to get back home."

N'hadia shook her head reluctantly. "I can't." She stood there, silently, and simply stared.

Kura frowned. Was she an amusing toy, or was the girl actually considering letting her go? "What in the world could I possibly do to any of you?"

"You're a prisoner of war! It wouldn't do to be letting you go free before the battle's won."

Kura blinked. "A prisoner of what war?"

"What war?" N'hadia gave her a woeful look. "It's *the* war—the Reconquest. Your kind started it. You came from over the sea—you try to control the Temper and you take what is not yours." N'hadia snorted. "Do you think we would live here if we had a choice? Your king drove us to this place."

Kura grinned wryly. "I wouldn't be here if it wasn't for Dradge, either. He's no king of mine."

N'hadia eyed her curiously, then shrugged. "Don't worry. They are old grudges—they sway some of us but not me." She glanced down at Kura's shoulder. "How is your wound? You shouldn't have been running like that earlier."

Before Kura could answer, N'hadia pulled away the shoulder of the loose cotton shirt, then peeled back the layer of bandages. Kura stiffened in anticipation of the pain, but it was nothing compared to the night before. She looked down, and her eyes widened.

A dark, purplish bruise rimmed the wound itself, but while she had been expecting to see some grisly red gash where the arrow had pierced her, she found instead only a thin, raised line of skin knotted together with a very fine thread and caked with a layer of dried blood. "How...?"

"Cenóri are skilled physicians, although it is good you were not wounded in the leg. We are not familiar with *your* kind." N'hadia turned toward the door. "Stay here, I will get some fresh bandages."

Kura opened her mouth to speak, but N'hadia had already turned and left, the door flapping as the centaur girl's hoofbeats disappeared into the distance. She sighed and pulled her shirt back over her shoulder.

She was alive—far more alive than if she'd been left to fend for herself in that ravine—and she tried to focus on that, rather than the nagging voice telling her she had to run. But she didn't want Faron and Elli staying another night alone in the compound.

Assuming they'd survived the first one.

Chapter Ten

Fool's Leap

The moons, one new and the other almost full, hung low in the northern sky, casting a silver light on the company of centaurs as they trotted to a halt in the village courtyard, pulling their prisoner behind them.

Kura's feet ached from the hours of walking, but she was at least grateful that the centaurs—for most of the trip—had slowed their pace to match hers... though they didn't seem to share her need for breaks. With a sigh of relief, she collapsed to sit in the dust as the others spread out to search the huts. Those sagging, birch-bark structures would have been lucky to cast shade on a sunny day, much less keep someone dry in the rain.

North, always north. After concluding their council meeting, they'd taken her on this relentless trek north. Every step farther from home poked at the knot of anxiety in her gut, but she couldn't be too far away yet.

The centaurs muttered to one another in their own tongue, then without a word Brant stomped over to her. He latched on to the chain that bound her wrist, dragged her to her feet and into the nearest hut, and secured the chain to a beam.

Kura chewed her lip, studying his dark silhouette with a scowl. "I am not your enemy."

He stopped in the open doorway, the moonlight highlighting his stocky frame as he turned back. "Why should I believe that?"

"I hate Dradge as much as you do, and I can use a sword. Let me prove it."

Brant held her gaze for a long moment in silence, then snorted, and with a swish of his tail walked away to rejoin the others. His shadow faded into the darkness, and Kura muttered a curse under her breath. It had been worth the try.

Centaurs' voices rumbled outside, muffled by the dilapidated walls. There seemed to be some sort of debate, possibly a prayer, and then with a shout they rode away, hooves pounding dully on the dry ground. They were off to fight some battle, as well as Kura could figure based on the polearms, broadswords, and bows they carried.

She waited, the silence overcome by the buzz of insects and the call of a few night birds. With a grunt, she tugged at her chain again, not yet convinced the effort was futile.

"What are you doing?"

Kura jumped. N'hadia stood in the doorway, her face bathed in the soft, white light of the strange lantern she held up in her hand. Kura opened her mouth to explain, but the words didn't come.

The centaur girl smiled. "You'll never get it off like that. Come on, I still have the key."

N'hadia knelt down at her side to undo the shackle. Kura watched her, confused, but not about to protest. "You didn't go with them?"

"My father says I'm too young to fight." She caught Kura's gaze as though commiserating with a kindred spirit. "Twenty-five years—since birth—he's trained me and yet I'm still too young."

Kura pulled back in surprise. N'hadia was twenty-five? She would have guessed fifteen, at most.

"But he never said I was too young to watch." She rose to her feet with an awkward lurch, as horses do, then extended her hand to Kura. "Now, you must promise not to run away," she said very seriously as she pulled Kura up. "I don't even want to think about what my father would say if he caught me doing this."

Kura nodded, feeling incredibly guilty for the part of her that was inclined to run anyway. "I promise."

N'hadia laughed excitedly, then pulled a bundle from her back and tossed it into Kura's empty arms. "Here, your things. The elders must have taken your sword. We do not often come across foraged weapons, and so some see them as quite valuable."

Kura untangled the bundle. It was her brown cloak, scratched and tattered from her chase through the forest, and her gambeson vest.

Her shoulder ached reflexively as she ran a hand over the massive bloodstain on the left side.

N'hadia's ears lowered. "I didn't get the chance to mend it."

Kura shook her head, even as she had to press a finger through the tear the arrow had left behind. "That's alright. Thank you."

"Well..." N'hadia's smile returned quickly. "Stick close to me." She reached toward the glowing, marbled stone.

Kura couldn't help but stare. "What is that?"

"*Lenêre* stone," N'hadia answered simply. "A light found only in dark places. Your kind may say they have the stronger magic, but no man knows the world as truly as a Cenóri does."

She placed her hand on the stone and the light flickered out entirely, leaving her black outline backlit by a dark blue sky. Kura stood, blinking in the darkness, unsure how much she should trust her own eyes.

The centaur girl reared up, then trotted for the tree line. "Come on!"

Kura pulled her gambeson over her head, tossed her cloak over her shoulders, then broke into a sprint to catch up with N'hadia. The centaur girl kept to the shadows, hardly making a sound as she hurried across the village clearing and into the forest beyond.

Kura looked back at the village with a frown. She wanted to ask for a weapon, but under the circumstances she couldn't bring herself to do it. N'hadia was putting far too much misplaced trust in her as it was. Still, she kept stealing guilty glances into the surrounding woods, wondering where they were along the ravine and how far a walk it would be to get back home.

A distant firelight shining between the tree trunks broke through the darkness, bringing both Kura and N'hadia to a stop. Voices echoed beyond the light, carrying along with the pounding of metal on wood.

"Come on!" N'hadia whispered, motioning for Kura to follow.

Against Kura's better judgement, they crept forward side by side, the light brightening and the voices growing in volume. A loud crash sounded from the clearing beyond, and both Kura and N'hadia ducked behind nearby trees.

The clearing was more mud than grass, with gnarled stumps scattered throughout a bare patch cut back from the edge of the ravine. Torches bathed the area in a dim, flickering light. And... there was a *bridge*. It was a crude structure—nothing more than a few rough logs laid across the span of the river to connect the two ledges—but it was more ambitious than any cast-out attempt Kura had seen. *Is it the Lovarians?*

Workers, mostly men but a few women, stalked about the clearing. They wore cotton shirts and those intricate quilted gambesons soldiers wore under their plate armor. A few were shorter, scraggly-looking fellows wearing muddy cloaks and fur-trimmed leather jerkins. One of them shouted, then the rest pulled back as a massive, freshly hewn tree toppled into the clearing.

One of the scraggly workers turned in Kura's direction, and as he tossed off his cloak she gasped. This was no man.

He certainly had a human shape—at least, he walked upright under his cloak—but his face and limbs were those of a wolf, some terrible corrupted wolf. Short, twisted horns protruded from his head, curling down around his pointed ears, and haphazard white stripes marked his shaggy wolf's fur. Kura might have called him a nostkynna, if he hadn't been wearing so many clothes—baggy trousers covered his legs and worn leather wrapped his feet, lending the illusion of shoes.

The men continued to mill about the clearing while the wolf-thing picked up an ax and began to hack branches off the felled tree. Looking around, Kura drew in a breath. There were far more creatures here than humans. They were all twisted things—strange, gnarled animals with wicked horns. Some wore clothes, some didn't. At a glance they looked like large cats, or bears, or even prey animals such as deer or goats, but the firelight offered glimpses of what they really were.

Saja. The word echoed in Kura's mind, no matter how hard she ignored it. But saja weren't real, she knew that—every sensible person knew that.

Shouts rang out from the other side of the clearing, along with the clash of metal on metal. Centaurs charged from the forest with staffs and pikes and spears to fall upon the unsuspecting monsters. The clearing filled with the screams of excited horses, angry creatures, and dying men. The centaurs had the advantage of surprise, and they pressed it, forcing the group back from the fallen tree and toward the edge of the ravine, but the men and monsters had them vastly outnumbered.

Several loud twangs sounded at Kura's side. She turned, startled, to find N'hadia standing in the open space between their respective tree trunks, her bow in one hand and several arrows in the other as she expertly shot into the clearing.

"N'hadia!" Kura hissed, not entirely sure what she meant to say.

"Stay there!" N'hadia advanced farther into the clearing, her bowstring twanging again and again. Kura watched, impressed, as beast after beast fell with arrow fletching in its right eye. Why didn't they let her fight?

A pack of those monsters dropped onto all fours and, with yips and snarls, charged toward the forest—toward N'hadia.

Kura ducked behind the tree. "N'hadia!"

The centaur girl didn't move; she didn't even flinch. Two of those creatures fell, tumbling over their own feet as they howled in pain, but more came after them. Kura bit back a curse and pressed herself behind the tree trunk. *I need a sword!*

She heard another snarl, then a yelp. The creatures had reached her. Panicked, Kura jumped, latched on to of the branches above her head, and hauled herself into the tree. The creatures converged on N'hadia in the clearing, snapping at her flanks even as she spun wildly, kicking at them with her back legs and striking them with her bow.

Kura ground her teeth. She couldn't stay here and watch the monsters tear the girl apart.

"You saw a human in here?"

Kura froze as a soldier, on horseback and flanked by one of the wolf creatures, circled the other side of the tree.

"Yes," the creature growled.

"Well, I don't see anyone."

The soldier's metal sword hilt glinted in the firelight, and Kura was struck with the semblance of a plan.

"That's no surprise," the wolf-creature said. "Coming from you." Kura crept down to one of the lower branches, above the soldier. "You can't see worth scat in the dark, can't smell hardly at all, can't even hunt as well as a pup without your—"

"Oh, do shut up."

Kura crouched down, secluded by the clinging fall leaves, as she adjusted her grip on the branch.

"I don't know why the lot of you are even—"

She swung down, kicking the soldier in the back. He tumbled to the ground with a shout as Kura's momentum carried her forward, and she landed awkwardly on the horse's bare rump. The animal began to turn and kick, but she caught hold of the saddle and pulled herself into the seat. Her injured shoulder throbbed, but she didn't have time to notice. She sank her feet into the stirrups, gathered the reins into her hands and yanked the horse around to face the wolf-thing.

She meant to grab the soldier's sword.

The beast growled, fur bristling and bared teeth glistening in the firelight. Kura drove her heels into the horse's sides and the animal bolted forward, trampling the creature under its hooves. She grinned slightly, then yanked the reins to the side, and she and her stolen horse burst out of the forest at a full gallop. She'd been taught to ride by a nostkynna stallion who had wandered through years ago—she was rusty, but trained by the best.

Kura didn't know what she planned to do next, but it didn't really matter. Before she could feel the proper fear, her horse closed the distance between her and the mass of creatures that had surrounded N'hadia. The nearest beasts fell beneath the horse's flashing hooves, but not many of them were unaware enough to die that way. Growling, the rest pulled back.

"You alright?" Kura asked, yanking the horse to a stop at N'hadia's side. The girl nodded, breathing heavily and pressing her hand over a bleeding wound on her arm.

A low chant rose from the clearing, an eerie sound rising in pitch and intensity. Nervousness churned in Kura's gut, until she realized the song belonged to the centaur company—and then she remembered they weren't exactly her allies, and the nervousness returned.

N'hadia flashed Kura a grin and nodded toward the clearing, where her people fought among the horde of monsters. "Come on!"

The girl snatched up a discarded spear. The soldiers and creatures withdrew a few paces to reform their line, then tried to force the centaur company back into the forest beyond. Alone, N'hadia charged that enemy line from behind, felling anything that crossed her path.

The centaur girl's foolish bravery was strangely inspiring, but that nagging voice in the back of Kura's mind spoke louder. This was her chance to slip away.

She turned her horse toward the ravine, guilt eating at her even as she drove the animal forward. Over her shoulder, she watched the centaurs and the beasts clash, adjusting her seat in the saddle. This wasn't her fight—and besides, she didn't even have a sword.

A loud, familiar shout rose over the rest of the noise. Brant broke from the line and charged toward her, his pike in hand. Kura yanked back on the reins; here she was, sneaking away from the battle—on a soldier's horse, no less.

"Wait!" she shouted, raising her open hands.

Brant flung his pike at her head. Kura ducked, and the large blade passed over to sink into the soft ground behind her. The centaur muttered something and charged at a gallop.

"Stop!" Kura pulled her horse back, swinging the animal around the pike sticking out of the ground. She wrenched the weapon from the mud and gathered it up with both hands. It was much too big, but certainly better than nothing.

She had no intention of killing or even fighting Brant if she could avoid it, but he did not seem to share that sentiment. The bridge was only a few strides away. She shouldered the pike, yanked the reins to the side, and drove her horse to a canter.

Brant's footfalls thundered behind her along with the creatures' angry cries, but Kura pressed forward, her sights set on that bridge. Her horse leapt onto it and the two of them charged across the ravine, the horse's metal shoes clattering against the rough-hewn logs. The dark, glittering Everard River churned far below, and for just that moment she dared to look down.

The horse sailed over the bridge's end and landed with a jarring lurch on the other side of the ravine. Kura stole a glance over her shoulder. Brant stood at the opposite end of the bridge, shaking his fist and shouting what could only be curses, but he seemed unwilling to cross. A wolf-thing snapped at his leg and he swung back into the fight.

With a pang of remorse, Kura considered turning back, at least for N'hadia. She resettled herself in the saddle, directing her horse downstream. Faron and Elli were her first priority, and after all—what else was she supposed to do? If those creatures didn't kill her, Brant would.

For a long while, she drove her horse at a canter, keeping the river in earshot—while minding the edge of the ravine—just so she'd have a point of reference in the darkness. Gradually, however, the weight of that pike on her shoulder overcame her urgency, and with the moons' light drifting through the leaves above, she finally pulled her horse to a stop in a dense part of the forest. She dismounted, then tied the horse's reins to an overhead branch.

"Hey, buddy." She stroked the horse's neck. "I think we can both use a break."

The horse flicked one ear, its head hanging low as it shifted its weight off one of its rear legs. Kura took a seat on the ground beneath a nearby tree and placed the pike across her lap. Her injured shoulder was throbbing again; the silence made it impossible to ignore. She gritted her teeth as she gingerly inspected the wound, but found she'd only broken a few stitches.

Struggling with the massive staff, Kura turned her attention to the pike. She tugged at the binding that held the dull blade to the shaft, and with considerable effort snapped a few of the strands, wiggling the blade loose. "It's a sword!"

Pale moonlight glinted dully on the rusted metal. Dry, rotted leather wrapped the hilt, and a small metal guard separated the base from the blade. Light caught in uneven intervals along the fuller, illuminating small notches that looked more like strange letters than scratches or nicks. Curious, she ran her fingers along the flat of the blade. Was it mud, or—?

A branch rustled in the forest overhead. Fear coursed through her veins as she scanned the tree line, and a raspy, guttural squawk emanated from the darkness.

It was a bird—nothing more than a black silhouette framed by a starlit sky. Just a bird. Kura laughed at herself, shaking her head, and turned back to the sword.

The weapon had not been treated kindly, but it was far better than the pike. She used some of the longer bits of the cords which had held the blade to the pike shaft to make a sling, then got to her feet, slipping the strap over her head and under one arm.

She and her horse had rested long enough. It was time to get home.

Chapter Eleven

Of Beasts and Monsters

Triston woke to the clang of the camp warning bell. He scrambled to his feet, throwing his chestplate over his head, then darted out of his tent, sheathed sword in hand. A coolness had settled in the valley along with a thin layer of fog, which shrouded the conclave of white tents, but wasn't thick enough to hide the other soldiers scrambling into formation around him. He ran toward the guard's post at the edge of camp, buckling his sword around his waist as his loose armor slapped against his torso.

"What's happening?"

The guard jumped at the sound of Triston's voice, and only stopped ringing the bell after Triston placed a hand on it.

"I..." The man's voice cracked, and he pointed toward the forest. "I saw—something..."

Triston scanned the dense forest, all the while debating just how this jumpy soldier ought to be disciplined. But he realized he heard, over the sounds of the men gathering behind him, the pounding of hooves.

"There!" the guard shouted, pointing into the thick of the trees. Triston saw it, too: a lone dark figure, taller than it was wide, an imminently approaching spot of black among the trees and the fog.

"Form up!" Triston called out, glancing over his shoulder at the rest of his company as he took a step back to join them. He drew his sword. "Bows at the ready!"

The figure let out a scream—something like the mix of a man's shout and a horse's whinny—and quickened its pace. A shiver ran down Triston's spine, and he involuntarily tightened his grip on his sword as he kept his heartbeat steady. This was no ordinary horse and rider.

"Loose!"

A barrage of arrows snapped free from the crossbows behind Triston as soon as he gave the command. The figure grunted as it stumbled, but didn't slow its charge. The fog obscured it until the beast was well in range.

It was a horse, on its lower half anyway, but its upper half was a man—a burly man with bare olive skin stained red by the arrow wounds in his chest. Triston held the thing's gaze. The animalistic rage in his narrow amber eyes looked eerily out of place in such a human face.

"Loose!"

The crossbowmen released a second barrage. The thing screamed, more in anger than pain, then collapsed into a heap in the dry leaves. Its chest heaved for air, its horse's legs thrashed at the sky, and then it lay still. A wavering calm bristled down Triston's spine as muffled silence settled in the woods.

"We're clear."

"What is it?" the guard at Triston's side whispered.

The soldiers broke formation, most of them stepping back as a few moved cautiously forward, muttering the same question.

Triston shook his head, but didn't take his eyes off the forest. *Why was there only one?* "Hold on," he called out, and the men brave enough to venture forward stopped immediately.

Triston crept toward the carcass, holding his sword before him as he watched the body for movement. Its face certainly looked like a man's, aside from the horse's ears. Triston put a foot on the thing's shoulder and pushed. The heavy body crumpled over, its limp arms sprawling out against the ground as its vacant eyes stared aimlessly at the sky.

What did I just kill?

Voices, and hoofbeats, carried from the forest beyond him, and Triston jumped back, raising his sword. "At the ready!"

The soldiers scrambled back into position, raising their crossbows and drawing their swords. A sharp horn blast shook the leaves, and Triston straightened, more confused than concerned now—it was the call of non-aggression one camp of soldiers would give the next.

"Stand down!" a voice shouted from among the trees.

Triston smothered a growl of frustration. "Seren?"

The man's white horse emerged from the mist, with the rider following soon after. "Stand down—it's all taken care of, stand down."

"What is this?" Triston lowered his sword and jogged to Seren's side. "You said you were going ahead to scout a trail the prisoners could manage on foot."

"Triston—"

"And what is that?" Triston pointed his sword at the carcass in the leaves. "What were you doing, chasing it?"

Seren gave a heavy sigh as he climbed down from the saddle. "Keep the men back in camp," he said in a low voice, his expression serious. "There was a bit of a situation, but it's under control."

Shouts carried from deeper in the forest, drawing everyone's attention.

"It's alright," Seren called, waving his hand dismissively as he stepped toward the camp. "As you were."

Triston pushed past him and through the trees with long strides to find a company of soldiers—fifteen men on horseback, at least—hiding in the periphery outside his camp. Their familiar red cloaks shone like embers even in the dim morning light, and the embroidered tunics overlaying their chain mail marked them as far more than enlisted men.

"Triston, wait—" Seren shouted after him, but the nearest rider turned back, his eyes widening slightly as they met Triston's.

Triston frowned. "Colmac? What is this?"

"They're a scouting company," Seren explained quickly, stepping between Triston and Colmac's horse. "They were patrolling the western border."

"Under whose orders?"

Seren stiffened. "Mine."

"You—"

A scream emanated from the center of the company of soldiers. Triston recognized the sound now: it was from one of those creatures. The riders tightened their circle, many brandishing spears, which they jabbed toward the center of the herd.

Triston gritted his teeth and forced himself past Colmac's horse. "Hold your positions!"

"Triston, leave it—" Seren tried to catch his arm, but Triston pulled out of his grip. The company of soldiers hesitated, with many an eye glancing between Triston and Seren, but in the end they raised their spears and pulled back.

Triston suspected what he'd find, but what he saw stopped him in his tracks. A dozen of those creatures stood before him. They were shackled together like a mass of slaves, each with their hands tied to their neck, which was bound to the next creature, and then the next, making a long chain. Rope hobbled their hooves and left each with only the flexibility to walk.

Dumbfounded, Triston found his gaze jumping from face to face. There were men, women, and children—as human in the eye as they were animal in the body, aside from the large horse's ears and teeth. Very few didn't bear some cut or bruise, and they were splattered with mud and dried blood.

The nearest one laughed, its face twisting into an unnerving grin. "Take your time, pretty boy, take it all in."

Triston looked the centaur in the eye, transfixed by both the scar running across its face and the fact that it had just spoken. He turned back to Seren.

"They speak?"

Seren shrugged. "Sometimes."

"They jumped the morning patrol," Colmac said, folding his reins over in his hands. "It's honestly a bit of a miracle we came out of it in one piece."

Triston frowned. "You've seen these things before?"

"Well, sir, in the Waste—"

"Call me a 'thing' again, boy!" the one with the scar shouted, straining against its ropes. "I'll give that word some meaning!"

Triston glanced back at the creature. He'd heard of centaurs, the same way he'd heard of the forebears or any of those other old stories, but he never really thought he'd see one—at least not in Avaron. His father had made sure of that long before he had even been born.

He nodded to the creature. "Where are you from?"

The centaur laughed. "You find your courage, little man, and that is what you ask me?" It spit on the ground, then muttered something in its own tongue—a language surprisingly fluid and delicate for such a brutish creature.

"Why did you attack my soldiers?"

The one with the scar only scowled.

"They are *forreada*!" a girl's voice shouted from among the centaurs. "They are saja-friends, they—"

"That's enough," Seren called out. He placed a hand on Triston's shoulder. "They lie," he whispered, turning Triston away from the company to lean closer to his ear. "They're as crafty as they are temperamental."

Triston stared the man down. "So you've fought these before? When?"

Seren glanced down at his boots. "Only once before, last month."

"There were no patrols authorized last month, and there are no patrols authorized now. Are you scheduling these behind my father's back?"

"Yes." Seren gave a heavy sigh. "Yes, Triston, I authorized this without consulting your father."

Triston wasn't sure whether he should be surprised or angry, but Seren calmly held his gaze.

"You want to know why? Because for the last three years I've been asking for his permission—and I've been denied. Just rumors, he calls them. Same as my reports on shadow-men. Look at them," Seren said, motioning toward the group of centaurs, "and tell me they're just rumors."

Triston looked up at those many faces towering above him. He shook his head slowly. Of course he couldn't, and he'd seen the number of arrows it had taken to drop the first one, running alone and unarmed. "What are you going to do with them?"

"I have a facility."

Triston leaned back, leery, waiting for him to continue.

Seren sighed. "Look, I don't mean to be keeping things from you, or your father. But this needs to be done—and *now*."

"I'm sure if you brought it up with the council—"

"The council? Triston, the best you'll ever get a group of five people to agree on consistently is petty compromises. What we need is decisive action. Your father still has the power to act without the council—"

"But he's choosing not to, because it isn't a king's place to meddle in the lives and decisions of his people."

"Meddle in their decisions?" Seren shook his head. "The common man is foolish and ill-tempered, and you know it. Left to their own devices, they'd be at each other's throats within the month—preoccupied with petty grievances while creatures like these only grow in strength and numbers. Is that what you want Avaron to be?"

Triston stiffened. "It isn't your place to be—"

"You're right." Seren took a step back, raising his open hands at his sides. "You're right. This is not my place. But what's your place, Triston? Because I think you're meant to be more than a soldier following orders. These are your decisions to make now, too. Don't let your father make them for you."

Triston scowled and rested his arm on the sword hilt hanging at his side. Seren didn't always win arguments, but he was a master of confounding the issue.

"Sir," Colmac said. "We did encounter a minor complication..."

Seren frowned. "Explain."

"There was a girl, a peasant or a cast-out, fighting along with the rest of them, until she stole a horse and ran south."

Seren glanced over at Triston. "Didn't you chase a cast-out over the ravine?"

"Yeah. But there's no way she survived."

Seren grunted. "Well, evidence would seem to indicate the contrary. Tarr Fianin is south of here, and that would be a suitable town for a fugitive to seek refuge." He flashed a grin. "It looks like you'll get to enjoy the scenic route after all."

Triston snorted. "I don't think I want to anymore."

Chapter Twelve

Homecoming

The night passed at an agonizing pace, despite her stolen charger's speed. In the darkness, Kura followed the river, guided by the sound of rushing water echoing in the ravine. As twilight gradually gave way to a red sunrise peeking over the treetops behind her, she found the thin trapper's trail which led to the compound.

In the distance, dark against the blue morning sky, a thin trail of smoke drifted above the trees. *A cooking fire?* she dared to hope—but why would Faron and Elli build one so big?

Bouncing in the saddle, she slowed her horse to a trot as they emerged from the forest into the open fields. Wheat and corn swayed in the breeze, their soft rustle the only sound to carry over the repetitive clop of the charger's hooves against the dirt path. A few small brown birds and a larger black one were picking at the corn; they all flew away, squawking, as Kura rode past.

"Hello?" she called out, then bit her tongue. If there were still soldiers lurking around, they had surely heard that, but there was no reply.

The horse trotted up to the compound walls, and Kura pulled him to a stop. The splintered gates hung in disrepair, as though they hadn't been touched since she'd left them. She dismounted and crept toward the walls. Dark blood stained several places on the path, and with a shudder she remembered that had been her doing.

"Hello?" she called out again, stepping over discarded bits of wood as she led her horse around the wreckage. "Faron? Elli?"

Silence.

Kura wandered into the compound, the horse tagging along obediently behind her. She glanced from house to house, peering into open windows, thinking she'd see Faron or Elli's face appear any minute. They didn't show.

At the back of the compound, she found the source of the smoke. The entire wall lay scattered, still smoldering with the flame that had scorched her family cabin and the one beside it. She sprinted to the door and paused, hands shaking and heart pounding, before she wrenched what remained off its hinges. "Faron! Elli!"

The house had been torn apart, the table and chairs thrown aside and their few belongings scattered across the floor. She searched both rooms, still calling her siblings' names as she shoved aside anything that got in her way. There was no answer. There were no bodies.

They were just... gone.

Kura collapsed into a nearby chair. *Gone.* That was better than dead, but somehow her heart didn't believe what she couldn't see. Sunlight streamed through the hole burned in the thatched roof, granting her glimpses of the clear blue sky.

"The other cabins." She leapt from her seat and ran out the door to tear through each of the remaining homes in the compound. She found each house empty. Finally, she stumbled out of the last cabin, tears catching in her throat as her legs crumpled. She fell to her knees in the dirt.

Tears welled up in her eyes, blurring the image of her family cabin before her. Faron and Elli were either dead or had been taken away by the king's soldiers, and she wasn't sure which was worse. She balled her shaking hands into fists and clenched her eyes shut, hot tears streaming down her cheeks.

This is my fault.

The old sword slipped from her shoulder and landed hilt-first in the dirt with a thump. Frustrated, she tore the uncomfortable thing off and tossed it to the ground. The sunrise behind her caught in the dull shimmer of the blade, illuminating it with fiery red as it clattered to a rest among the leaves. Kura stared at the fallen weapon, the breeze drying the tears on her cheeks.

She wasn't dead yet.

Drawing in a breath, she wiped her tears with her sleeve, and picked herself up. If her family were alive, she'd save them. If they were dead, she'd bury them.

She had to know, even if it meant traveling to the ends of the world—she had to *know*.

That wasn't much comfort, but it was something and she clung to it. Crossing the courtyard, she retrieved her sword, then headed back to her family cabin to scrape up some supplies.

She would make this right. Somehow.

PART TWO
ENIGMA

Chapter Thirteen

Two Paths Diverge

The evening sun burned hot on Kura's back as she pulled her horse to a stop among the slender trunks of a thinning forest.

A wide clearing of tall, dry weeds filled the space between her and the walls of Tarr Fianin, though from her vantage point on the hill she could see into the heart of the city. It was a collection of short log cabins packed together around an open town square. Mountains rose on all sides, pinning the lopsided town in the basin of the valley.

Tar Fianin was the first hint of civilization outside the Wynshire, the farthest east she had ever been, and it seemed like the sort of place a company of soldiers would have to stop at on their way back to Edras. She'd visited the city once before—at about Elli's age—when her father had brought her on his annual trip to the market. Mostly, she remembered hanging on to his hand.

Of course, he wouldn't be at her side this time. No one would.

Kura spurred her horse to a trot, guiding him with a nudge of the reins to the footpath that led from the forest to the city walls. A short line of farmhands—men and women dressed in worn cloaks thrown over threadbare pants and tunics—waited outside the gates, murmuring to one another, but conversation fell to silence as Kura pulled her charger to a stop behind them.

"Oh." The man at the end of the line chuckled nervously and jerked his chin at her horse. "I thought you were a king's man, ridin' in on an animal like that."

She laughed. "No, not me."

The man squinted at her, then at her horse again. "Where did you get that animal? It's a fine beast, although you've been drivin' him too hard."

The second man in line slugged him in the arm. "Shut up."

"Hey," the first man grumbled. "I was just makin' conversation."

The second man glanced back with a scowl. "You better have papers, missy, or this is the end of your trip."

Papers!

Her birth wasn't documented; she had never had papers. Only her father did, and he usually kept them stored away in the walls of their cabin until he was heading to the market. Frantic, Kura rummaged through the saddlebags, keeping her horse moving in line. She pulled out a small bundle of parchments, the top one embossed in the corner with the king's seal. She recognized the word *name*, but not much else.

"Next," the guard at the gate called out.

Kura straightened in her seat.

"Papers," the guard said. She was tall, her head reaching almost to Kura's shoulders, a dark brown cloak shrouding her face and figure. Kura placed the folded bit of parchment in the guard's gloved palm. She glanced up at Kura, then back down at the papers, and then up at Kura again, this time her head cocked to the side.

"You're Rodlin of Deane? Soldier to the king?"

"Yes, ma'am," Kura said with what she hoped was a casual grin.

The guard frowned, most of her face concealed beneath the shadow of her hood. "Your horse certainly looks the part. But 'Rodlin'...?"

"Rodlin is the name of the firstborn of my family line for seven generations. I had the misfortune of being a firstborn daughter."

The guard looked down at document again, then shrugged. "Well, it all looks official." She handed the papers back. "Have a good stay in Tarr Fianin, Lady Rodlin Deane."

"Thank you," Kura said, smiling in relief. She stuffed the papers back into the saddlebag, then urged her horse on through the gate.

An assorted group wandered the muddy street between two rows of lopsided, thatch-roofed cabins. Most were human—gruff mountain folk, or even rougher locals carrying bundles of animal skins or leading mules that pulled carts of corn or potatoes or wheat. A lone Lovarian trader served as striking contrast to the rest, thanks to his layers of brightly colored jackets. Occasionally a nostkynna wandered among them: small creatures such as squirrels or badgers, each wearing a simple hat or cloak to distinguish themselves from their unwelcomed lookalikes.

Kura thought she'd stand out—a dusty young woman on a royal charger—but that concern proved unfounded.

"Hey, move it!"

She glanced over her shoulder, expecting that raspy voice to belong to an old woman, but a short black bear waddled toward her, pulling a rickety cart of shriveled wildflowers.

The bear peeked out from under her patchwork head-covering, pulling her greying muzzle back into a snarl. "What, are you lost or something?"

"Sorry," Kura said, nudging her horse over to the side.

"Bah," the bear grumbled, then trudged along, pulling her little cart of dead flowers behind her. Kura watched her go, no longer wondering why her younger self had been so afraid in this town.

A lukewarm, soggy breeze meandered through the city, carrying the scent of baking bread, wood smoke, and something quite unpleasant. Kura hesitated, glancing down the nearby alleyways, her attention drawn to the clatter of dry leaves as the wind pushed them around the corner. In her head, the plan had been simple: come to Tar Fianin, find the soldiers. Too simple.

The majority of the crowd flowed further into the city, following the main road. She nudged her horse into the mass of travelers, and in the center of the town square she found what everyone had come for: the open-air market. Booths and tables lined the streets and salesmen pressed into the crowd, hawking their wares with varying success. A man in the heart of the commotion stood on a wooden crate, juggling torches as the people cheered and tossed him the occasional coin.

Kura directed her horse to the side of the road as she watched him. This was as good a place to start as any.

She dismounted and led her horse behind her as she walked up to the nearest booth. It more closely resembled a mound of forgotten tools and cooking supplies than a storefront, but she could hear someone rummaging through the pile of utensils behind the counter.

"Um, hello?"

A rain of forks and spoons clattered to the ground, then a raccoon popped up from behind the counter. "Hello!" He flashed a smile and adjusted his wide-brimmed hat. "If you're looking for something, I have it, or I can get it. What do you need?"

Kura held back a grin as she glanced at the trinkets piled around her. All stolen, likely as not. "Actually, I'm just wondering if you've seen any troops—"

"Oop!" The raccoon held up one of his tiny, clawed fingers. "Nothin' is free here, I've got my livin' to make." He scrambled across the countertop on all four paws. "How about this?" He picked up a frying pan, then smacked it against the countertop. "Sturdy. Seven firri."

Kura stifled a laugh and took a step away from the booth. "Um, not what I'm looking for right now. Thanks anyway."

The raccoon sat back on his haunches and shouted after her. "Five firri?"

A woman at the next booth didn't let Kura get three words out before trying to fit her for a new cloak. The next man, selling shoes, wasn't much better. Finally, Kura did start buying things with the silver coins she found in her stolen horse's saddlebags, but she ended up with half a loaf of bread, an old apple, and a necklace before someone had any answers to her questions.

"Soldiers?" The girl—she couldn't be much older than Elli—scraped a medallion with a small, curved knife.

"Yes."

"Well, I did see one. He came into town a week or two ago, alone, and he never left. Everyone says he's trouble and that I shouldn't talk to him."

Kura bit out a blemish from her apple and spit it on the ground. "Where can I find him?"

"I just saw him walking toward the Dancing Drake inn," the girl said, securing the medallion on a hemp cord. "It's in the back corner of the city." She pointed over Kura's shoulder. "Along one of the smaller roads."

The man behind the girl leaned back from the bundle of cloth he'd cut for another customer. "Don't be talking to strangers."

"Yes, Father." The girl waited until her father looked away before holding up the necklace with a smile. "I'll put this on you." She climbed up to kneel on the table, reaching Kura's eye level, then tied the medallion around her neck. "It's a flicker. It will bring you luck."

Kura took the medallion in her hand, nodding. It was crudely done, but the shape resembled a large bird.

"They say Tácnere takes the form of a flicker and visits us sometimes."

"Tácnere?" There were so many Svaldan gods; Kura never could keep them all straight.

"Yes, the guardian." The girl weighed her with a curious look, but seemed happy to explain. "They say he gave his life to drive out the dark creatures before our forebears settled here."

"Oh, Gallian."

The girl tilted her head. "I don't know who that is."

Her father rose and placed a hand on his daughter's shoulder. "False stories," he said with a frown as he held Kura's gaze. "The Láefe are not welcomed here."

"Oh, sorry, I'm actually not—"

"Please, leave now," the man continued, holding his daughter at his side.

"Father—"

"Do you want to bring the king's soldiers upon us?"

Slowly, the girl looked down and shook her head.

Kura fished a silver coin out of her stolen pouch and placed it on the table, then climbed back into the saddle and nudged her horse into the crowd. She stole a glance back at the booth before the mass of people merged in between, and she could see the father scolding the girl.

She sighed, not sure if she should be frustrated or embarrassed. She wasn't trying to cause trouble. Her family all faced scorn for her mother's convictions, but it was another thing to bear those scowls alone.

Guiding her horse off the main road, she continued down an alley that seemed to take her roughly in the direction the girl had indicated. At least she'd finally learned something useful. One soldier was far fewer than she'd set out to find, but he had to know something.

Triston stretched his back as he adjusted his seat in the saddle. He'd been waiting at the edge of the forest, prisoners corralled into a ring in the clearing, for over an hour. That couldn't be a good sign. Seren had insisted that he had to enter Tar Fianin alone to scout for that missing rebel girl—without his horse, as anything more might mark him as a king's man. Which was probably true.

He still could've let me come with him. The man pretended he knew how to handle himself in a fight—he fooled most people—but Triston had witnessed first-hand why Seren had risen through the ranks as a strategist and not in a role more reliant on athleticism.

Voices echoed from the city gates. The gate itself had been shut sometime around when the sun had sunk below the ridge, but now it creaked open as two figures leapt out into the road. Sunlight flashed gold on their bare sword blades, and the clash of metal reverberated between the trees and city walls. The first figure Triston didn't recognize, but the second—stumbling through a series of obnoxiously formal sword stances—was undoubtedly Seren.

Triston drove his heels into his horse's sides, reaching the city walls in a matter of seconds. He drew his sword, leapt from the saddle, and ran to meet the man at the gates. "Hey!"

Seren tripped over his own feet to wind up sprawled in the dirt, but the cloaked man paused and looked up. Triston lunged into the fight, beating back the man's strikes.

The cloaked figure pulled away and lowered his weapon. He was tall and thin, with a face shrouded in the shadow cast by his hood. The uniform certainly wasn't regulation, but the guard attempted a salute before pointing his sword at Seren. "This man is no longer welcomed here."

Triston didn't lower his blade. "Why?"

The man looked Triston up and down, then reluctantly sheathed his weapon. "Unwarranted snoopery."

Triston quirked a grin. "Is that the technical term now?"

The guard bowed stiffly at the waist. "You'll have to forgive me if I'm not familiar with the official jargon, sir. Simple country folk and all that. But those are the town rules, which I understand I have limited sovereignty to enforce." He stepped back behind the walls and slammed the gate shut.

Triston chuckled under his breath, then shoved his sword back into its scabbard and offered Seren his hand.

"I had it handled," Seren muttered as Triston hauled him to his feet.

"I'm sure you did."

Seren brushed the dust from his tunic, then bent over to retrieve his fallen sword.

"You know, this is why I wanted to come with you," Triston said.

Seren grumbled something and sheathed his blade.

Triston shook his head, still grinning, and retrieved his horse's reins. "So, what'd you do?"

"Asked a few decent questions from a few indecent people." Seren started toward the forest. Triston followed, pulling his horse along at his side.

"What about the cast-out?"

Seren huffed. "Everyone says they haven't seen her."

"Maybe she didn't stop here. Or maybe she was never here at all—I mean, how would someone get out of that ravine?"

Seren grunted, his eyes distant. "Somehow, she did. And these people may very well have seen her, they're just not inclined to say so. It was a mistake to let towns post their own guards."

Triston glanced over his shoulder at the city walls. He knew what Seren was thinking about: how many soldiers it would take to man the gates, and how quickly he could have troops rearranged to replace those guards. Large cities had reserve troops designated to patrol the streets and people there were grateful for it, but sending troops out here? To folk like this that might as well be an act of war. These outskirt towns were always more loyal to each other than to their country. Their neighbor did more for them than the crown ever could.

"So, are we moving on?"

"No," Seren said with an exasperated laugh. "She's in there, I'd bet on it. They're hiding her—I know it."

Triston sighed. "Well, what do you want to do? We've already squandered the opportunity to try my idea—knocking on the gate and simply *asking*, like any decent person would. And we don't have enough men for a siege."

"We do if we can intercept Colmac's company, join our prisoners with his, and enlist some of those more seasoned fighting men to our ranks."

Triston frowned. "That was supposed to be a joke. You know these towns are unpredictable. A siege is most effective when we have numbers large enough to scare them into submission without fighting. Even with Colmac's men we won't be close to that."

"Ah," Seren said with a grin, "so you have been paying attention to some of your studies. These townsfolk are easily spooked. We can set campfires in the forest and obscure our numbers."

Triston rubbed his eyes. "What's the urgency here? If this one girl really is so important, we can come back—"

Shouts rang out from the forest. The company scattered, pulling from the shadows of the forest as flashes of black rained from the tree line. Archers. Triston leapt into the saddle and drove his horse forward, leaving Seren behind.

"Shields, form up!"

The men fell into place, forming a line on either side of Triston, facing the forest. Several riders holding shields pushed to the front, raising their guards before the rest of the company.

"Loose at will!"

From the back of the line, the crossbowmen let loose, their black darts flying into the trees. A cloaked figure fell to the forest floor, then scrambled to its feet, limping back as several others sprang down from the trees. They were tall men, few in number, all dressed in dark, natural colors with their faces shrouded beneath the shadow of their hoods. One casualty and they were already retreating?

A shield man broke formation to charge after the fleeing archers.

"Hold the line!" Triston shouted, and the man fell back into place. He watched the forest skeptically as the last figure disappeared among the trees. A small scouting party, by the looks of it, and there was no telling how many more men awaited them in the shadows. They dressed too much like the town guard.

Triston caught the attention of the captain beside him. "Keep watch."

Seren jogged up beside Triston's horse. "So, you agree with me now?"

Triston frowned. A siege was still a bad idea, but he couldn't deny that there remained here some pressing threat. "I guess I can't say I don't."

The farther Kura ventured from the town square, the emptier the streets became.

She stood in the stirrups to adjust her seat and took the chance to scan the alleyways behind her. The streets narrowed so that two horses couldn't pass side by side, and the few dilapidated cabins that still looked livable had boards covering their windows. That once faint stench grew stronger here, and Kura kept a sleeve pressed against her nose.

The wind picked up, tossing her hair across her face. It carried the distant scent of rain, rattled loose shutters, and rapped a cabin's shop sign against the wall. Weather had worn the placard smooth, but it displayed a few hand-carved words—'The Dancing Drake', Kura assumed, based on what the little girl had told her—along with the faded green image of a winged serpent.

She eased her horse to a walk as they approached the building. It was a story taller than the rest around it, but wasn't in much better repair. Voices rumbled somewhere within, and laughter carried out onto the street through broken slats in the closed shutters. Her father always set up his own tent in the marketplace rather than stay in the inn, and until this moment she had always assumed he was being frugal.

The inn door flew open, and a figure tumbled out into the street.

"And stay out!" the burly man in the doorway shouted, kicking at the man's legs. The scrawny fellow scrambled to his knees, splattering himself in mud as he struggled to untangle himself from his tattered red cloak.

"Please!" he shrieked once his head was finally free. He wasn't much older than Kura—thirty at most—but his pale face housed bloodshot eyes and his brown stubble couldn't hide his sunken cheeks. "I'll—I'll pay for it! Here!" He tore at his empty pockets, turning them inside out.

The big man spat at his feet. "You think I'd waste my best whiskey on a king's man?" He glanced at the bottle of amber liquid in his hand before glaring at the soldier. "I catch you here again, I'll beat your face in."

The soldier stared, sitting in the mud with his mouth open and his eyes wide, as the big man turned toward the door. "No, wait, don't—!"

"I'll buy the drink," Kura called out, spurring her horse toward the inn.

Both the tall man and the soldier turned to look at her in confusion. Kura dismounted, her boots splashing in the mud, and tried to smile at the big man.

"That." She motioned toward the bottle in his hand. "I'll buy it."

The man first looked at her, then her horse, with a skeptical frown.

Kura pulled three silver coins out of her pouch and held them out on her open palm. "Is this enough?"

The big man blinked. "Sure." He held Kura's gaze for a long moment, his brow furrowed, but finally took the coins then slapped the bottle into her hand. "Enjoy the company." He pushed his way back into the inn, muttering under his breath as the door slammed shut.

A tense silence settled over the street, broken only by the sloshing of Kura's boots as she walked to the soldier's side. She held the bottle out to him. "Here."

The soldier peered through his mess of stringy hair. "Do I know you?"

She shook her head.

"You're with the royal police, aren't you?" He scrambled back, his hands sliding in the mud. "You've come to take me in, you've found me, I—"

"No, I'm not with anyone."

The man stared at her, his chest heaving. Finally, he stretched out a shaking hand to snatch the bottle. He tore the cork from the top and took large gulps of the amber drink. Kura grimaced; this was a broken man, the poorest excuse for a soldier she could find. She sighed. He was still something.

Haltingly, the soldier lowered the bottle. He stared at her, a glint in his eye like that of a savage dog leering at a passerby who'd interrupted his devouring of a carcass. "What do you want?"

She crouched down so they were eye-to-eye. "Have any troops passed through here recently?"

"Have they?" the soldier shrieked. He laughed, in a wild panic, breathless and two octaves too high. "No self-respecting royal soldier would ever frequent a hell-hole like this!" He took another long swig from the bottle, dribbling some down his chin.

Kura looked him over in disgust. "What... what happened to you?"

"What happened?" he whispered. His unblinking eyes locked with hers, and she fought the urge to look away. "I've tried to forget. The gods know I've tried! The others crawled their way out of hell, but left me behind..."

"What if there were troops near here, coming out of the Wynshire, maybe with prisoners? Where would they go?"

The soldier scoffed. "They'd take the main road straight back to Avtalyon as fast as their horses could carry them, same as any man with half his senses." His eyes grew distant. "That's what I should have done—run for it when I had the chance. Hell, I never should have left home at all!"

"How do I find the main road?"

"What?" The soldier looked at her like she was crazy. "The main road out of town is where it begins, and it ends at the gates of Edras."

"Thanks," she muttered. "If they did have prisoners, would they take them to Avtalyon or somewhere else?"

"Prisoners?" He gave an incredulous laugh. "The royal army does not take prisoners! Death, swift and bloody or not at all—that is what comes to those to disobey... those who disagree... those who desert." He gripped that bottle with all the strength he had and took several long gulps.

Kura rose, trying to fight back the tears that stung her eyes. Even a crazy man knew what she refused to accept: the royal army didn't take prisoners. Her family was dead. She climbed back into the saddle, fists clenching the reins.

No. Rage smoldered in her heart, and she kindled that rather than face the tears. They weren't dead. Not until she saw the bodies for herself.

She squeezed her horse between her knees and the charger took off like a shot, leaving the soldier behind in the mud. If she didn't find her family in Edras, then she'd keep looking until it killed her. That was preferable to living the rest of her life wondering about their fate, knowing only that whatever had happened to them was her fault.

When they neared the rear gates, she pulled back on the reins. The empty road stretched out before her, the long shadows of patchy trees breaking up the sloping fields between her and the distant mountains. The sun would set in less than an hour, but everyone said the lands beyond the Wynshire were safe to travel at night. At this point, she felt brazen enough to risk it.

A guard stepped from the shadows into the open gateway. "Stop there."

Kura didn't move, but gathered up the slack in her reins. She recognized this voice and the tattered brown cloak: it was the same woman who had been at the front gates. "Is there a problem? I still have my papers—"

"Off the horse," the guard continued, her voice stern. "Over this way."

Kura yanked the reins to the side, driving her heels into her horse's ribs, and they fled down the street. The guard shouted something, but Kura nudged her charger into the nearest alley, then the next one, his hooves splattering mud over them both. These were footpaths—not made for horses—and they had to leap over stoops as townsfolk shouted obscenities and dove out of the way.

A blanket hung out to dry on a rope stretched between two of the houses. Kura yanked back on the reins, her mount protesting as he slid to a stop. She leapt from the saddle and dragged him behind the blanket, into the narrow passage. They could wait here for the guard to pass, then make a run for the gates and—

"Hello, stranger."

Kura spun around, reaching for her sword. This wasn't an empty alleyway. Paper lanterns hung from ropes suspended between roofs and abstract tapestries colored what would otherwise be log walls. A woman in a deep blue cloak sat hunched in one of two chairs beside a wooden folding table set with food.

"I... Is this your...?" Kura glanced between the woman and the colorful blanket that made the far wall. A soft murmur of voices and the wavery tune of a stringed instrument carried, muffled, from somewhere beyond it. Of course. The Pokalfr—Svaldan spiritualists. "I'm sorry, I didn't mean—"

The woman laughed, the sound a grating cackle that somehow still seemed jovial. "Lost, are you?" She rose from her seat, outstretching a thin hand, but only wispy locks of grey hair escaped the shadow of her hood. "Come, come. Strangers are always welcomed here."

Kura took a wavering step toward her. Traveling groups like these could, apparently, be found in any trading town throughout Avaron and Lovaria alike. They were Svaldans dedicated to one particular god or another—fortune-tellers and petty merchants by trade—and all she really knew was that her father never let her near them.

"Sit, sit." The woman tottered back to her seat. "If you stay, at least sit."

Reluctantly, Kura took a seat—but didn't let go of her horse's reins. "I'm sorry, I..." The table had been set with two steaming mugs of dark liquid, two plates with a slab of meat, two halves of a loaf of bread. "Were you expecting someone?"

"Yes, yes!" Her voice was almost as grating as her laugh. "Eat up, now."

Kura laughed, hesitantly. "I really need—"

"To leave so soon? The guards will find you, but not if you stay here."

Kura rose to her feet, eyes fixed on the shadow that was the woman's face. "I know, but—"

"Eat. They are there now. Leave and they will catch you."

Kura turned toward the street. Footsteps sloshed through the mud and voices carried, but she couldn't hear what they said.

"Eat," the woman said again, more a command than an invitation.

Kura sighed, then picked up the bread to nibble on the crust. It was dark and bitter—like rye she'd sampled from Lovarian traders—but the outer edges were soaked in salt. She coughed as she tried to swallow.

"Drink," the woman said, standing to pick up the mug.

Gagging, Kura took it and sucked one gulp of the steaming liquid. It tasted like boiled dirt, with an overwhelming overtone of some odd spice, and she could only swish it around in her mouth before spewing it onto the ground.

The woman cackled. "Not like a mother's cooking, is it, child? Or is it just that you are so far from home?"

Kura wiped her mouth on the back of her hand, trying to find the woman's eyes under her hood. "What do you know about it?"

"I know a little, child. I always know a little, never a lot. Come, come." She scooted closer. "Give me your hand."

Cautiously, Kura placed her open palm in the woman's outstretched hands. Her skin was charcoal black and peppered with coarse red hair.

"Yes..." the woman murmured as she slid her ragged nail across Kura's palm. "Destiny... that is a word men use to lift the burden of their own choices."

Kura shivered as a chill ran down her spine.

The woman latched onto her hand and turned her shadowy face up to meet her gaze. "Maker of kings, slayer of the gods, an ember smolders in your soul. Ignite it, and you will engulf the world. Smother it, and you will have peace."

Kura wanted to speak, wanted to say *something*, but in that moment she saw the woman's hideous face. Her bright eyes shone with a yellow sheen, her short nose sat scrunched into her face, her wide lips parted to reveal white teeth, sharp and grinning. She was wrinkled beyond old age, a creature once human—perhaps still human.

"Two paths diverge; you must choose."

"I..."

"Two paths diverge; you must choose."

"But I don't want—"

"You must choose!"

"Then I choose peace!" Kura blurted out. "Who wouldn't choose peace?"

The woman grinned, then let go of Kura's hand, and shadows overtook her face again. "Peace, yes. We all search for it, but who finds it? Remember your promise, child."

"I didn't..." Kura sighed and shut her mouth. This wasn't a discussion worth having.

"Now you must stay," the woman said, standing, as she retrieved another piece of bread.

"What?"

"Stay," the woman repeated, more forcefully this time. "Your peace is here—the guards will find you out there. Foul creatures they are, quite different from you. And me."

Kura hesitated, glancing at the blanket separating her from the alley. She didn't hear any movement—and guards or no guards, this was about the last place she wanted to stay.

"I..." She faltered, catching her horse's reins again as she stepped away from the table.

"I see," the woman said softly, a trembling calm in her voice. "Go, then." She waved a limp hand toward the alley.

"Alright." Kura pulled her horse along behind her.

"Remember your promise." Amusement tinged the woman's voice. "Remember what you have chosen."

"Right."

Kura brushed aside the blanket and, after glancing up and down the alley for guards, stepped into the street. There was something *wrong* with that woman. The few townsfolk meandering in the alley shot her nasty looks, but she walked past the houses, leading her horse between her and the rest of the street, as she debated how she could best blend in.

"You're not very good at this, are you?"

Kura jumped, then turned to find a hooded figure leaning, arms folded, against the doorframe in the shadows of the nearby house. It was that same guard.

Nudging her horse back, Kura reached for her sword. "What do you want?"

The guard sighed, then pushed herself upright and turned down the alley. "Just follow me."

"Why?"

The guard paused. "Fine. Don't. I'll let the soldiers have you."

"Aren't you one of them?"

The woman grinned, her teeth reflecting the dim light at odd angles. "You can head to the gates and ask them."

Kura took a step after the woman, leading her horse along behind. "There are soldiers at the gates?"

The guard simply nodded and kept walking.

"They have any prisoners with them?"

The woman muttered something under her breath. "Just—come on."

Chapter Fourteen

ÎSENDORÁL

Kura paused beside the post to which she'd tied her horse. The guard hadn't spoken another word, but simply led her through winding back alleyways until they'd reached this ramshackle guard house built into the wall beside the north gate. An unnerving quiet had settled over the town, and the flickering glow of many campfires lit up the greying evening beyond the city.

The guard climbed the short wooden staircase, heavy boots creaking each step, then pushed open the door. "You coming?"

Kura sighed and begrudgingly followed her up the stairs. This was foolish. Every instinct told her to run, but she couldn't bring herself to do it. These strange guards surely knew more than that drunk at the Dancing Drake, and even if they did hand her over to the soldiers outside, that'd certainly be a more expedient end than her planned cross-country trip.

Two more cloaked figures sat in chairs at a small table in the guardhouse, but the rest of it more resembled a storage chest or a root cellar than an official outpost. Worn gambesons and metal armor sat on cluttered shelves, and various bundles of drying herbs hung from the exposed rafters. The guard nudged Kura farther into the room, then shut and barred the door behind them.

The seated figure nearest the door rose and stepped to the side, but it was the other man who spoke.

"Rodlin of Deane." He looked up from a pile of old books, the light of the lantern beside him reflecting yellow in his eyes. "That's not your real name, is it?"

Kura hesitated. "Of course it is."

"Hmm." He nodded, and absently shut the book highest on his pile. "I guess you're not the worst liar I've ever met. So..." He leaned back in his chair. "*Rodlin*. Why's the Prince of Avaron asking for your head?" The lantern light illuminated the grin his hood had kept in shadow.

Kura stifled a cry and drew her sword. This wasn't a man. Those were wolf's eyes, and a wolf's face. Like... like those *things* out by Fool's Leap.

The guard behind her snarled as soon as Kura's sword left its scabbard, but the first only rose to his feet.

"Hey, it's alright." He pulled back his hood, and his toothy grin didn't fade. He had the shoulders and shape of a man but a wolf's snout, fur and ears—an unholy blend of human and animal that belonged too well in the shadows. "If we wanted to eat you, we would have."

The other two guards slowly lowered their hoods as well. They were monsters, all of them. The other man seemed to be some kind of bear, right down to the claws that poked through the fingers of his gloves. The woman was a wolf, with flowing silver hair tied back in a hasty braid and many scars in the fur on her face and muzzle.

Kura tightened her grip on her sword. "Are you... saja?"

The woman bared her teeth, but the wolf-man only laughed. "Oh, possibly. If you think one choice defines a lifetime." Kura didn't lower her sword, and he sighed. "I'm Skellor." He motioned to the woman. "Pening you've met, and that's Faeng. We call ourselves *Varian*." He stepped forward and pushed the tip of Kura's sword away. "We—ah!" He pulled back, swinging his hand as though he'd just touched a hot pan, and muttered something under his breath.

Both Pening and Faeng stepped as far out of Kura's reach as they could manage. Faeng said something in a low, guttural tongue. Skellor answered him, then fixed his attention on Kura. "Where did you get that sword?"

Kura eyed all of them, curiosity fighting against her caution. They were scared of it? "I'm not sure that's any of your business."

Skellor waved his hand dismissively. "Oh, come on, Rodlin." He nodded toward the far corner. "Faeng, Pening, go stand over there. Make our guest a little more comfortable. And here..." He shoved half of his books onto the floor to clear a space on the table. "Maybe place your blade there? I swear I only want to look at it. From a distance."

Hesitantly, Kura did as Skellor asked, although she didn't let go of the hilt. His yellow eyes fixed on the rusted sword as he guardedly circled the table corner.

"There weren't many blades like these made, because of course it's not easy to temper steel in the blood of a living saja. By now I thought they'd all been broken down for arrowheads and whatever else you idiots thought were more useful at the time..."

Faeng said something again in his own language, but this time Kura recognized one word: 'Ìsendorál'. Where had she heard that before?

A light sprang into Skellor's eyes and he rummaged through his pile of books, recklessly thumbing pages and tossing each one aside when he apparently didn't find what he was looking for. "Ah!" He flipped open one large, leather-bound volume and slapped it down beside the blade. "Recognize this?"

Kura prepared to explain that she hadn't learned to read much after Elli had torn up their one learning book years ago, but the page Skellor pointed to contained only a string of symbols. She glanced between the book and the blade. The first symbol, a flowing set of lines that somewhat resembled a head of wheat or the wing of a bird, oddly enough seemed to match the rust-caked engraving in the fuller of her sword.

"Weapons like these were made in the beginning of your history, when your ancestors' quest to conquer this continent left them fighting saja most often, and of course it takes more than plain old arrows and steel to beat those things back. All blood-quenched swords were marked with the sigil of whichever of your forebears' houses had them made," Skellor said. "Rodlin, guess who this one belonged to."

Kura shrugged.

"Well, judging by this text here..." Skellor looked down at the page again, then shook his head in disbelief. "This sword belonged to Gallian."

"Gallian?" Kura said. "Forebear, 'first king of Avaron' Gallian?"

"To put it mildly. Aren't you aware of your own prophecies? It's said on the night Gallian died, every seer in the whole of this country—Fidelis and Svaldan alike—awoke from sleep compelled to scrawl the same words." He turned the book toward him to read from the next page.

"A child of scythe and sword
This song the black bird sings
Right by Ìsendorál restored
Victory the autumn brings
One flame from the shadows
Will light one thousand more
A gallant heart overflows
Taking back what was before."

Ìsendorál. Her mother's legends. Kura lifted the blade, trying to figure out how much respect it deserved. Her mother would be *ecstatic* to see this—any Láefe would be. A thing like this was supposed to be a herald of better days, the first step in the fulfilment of the promise of peace her forebears had crossed the ocean looking for—the remnant of an age of heroes for which her years in the Wynshire had taught her not to hope.

"You really believe those old stories?"

Pening bared her teeth. "You brought it here. Are you telling me you can't believe what you hold in your own hand?"

"I can see I found an old rusty sword, yes, but I stopped believing in children's stories a long time ago."

Pening snarled, but Skellor caught her by the shoulder. He muttered something in their own tongue, then looked to Kura. "Where'd you come by this?"

Was there any point in lying? "Centaurs had it, in the wilds beyond the Wynshire."

"Of course," Faeng mused quietly. "All the Cenóri's foraged weapons are recycled, and where else have we not gone in search of it already?"

Skellor crooked a grin. "You're Wynshire folk, are you? Certainly explains the attitude."

Kura couldn't tell whether he meant that as an insult or a compliment.

Faeng stepped toward the blade as though transfixed by it. "Do you realize what this would mean for the rebellion?"

Skellor laughed. "Folks around here have come to appreciate us, but I'm not sure even this would be reason enough for Trofast to see us."

Pening crossed her arms. "We don't even know if it's real."

"It's a genuine blood-quenched sword at least," Skellor said. "You can poke it yourself if you'd like."

Pening stared at the blade with more than a little apprehension. "Let Trofast figure it out. We can find someone else to take it, maybe one of the townsfolk here. Most of *them* still have half their sense."

A pensive growl rumbled in Faeng's throat. "And separate the sword from the sword-bearer?"

The Varian each shared a glance between them, then their gazes settled on Kura.

"Well?" Skellor asked. "How about it, Rodlin? Would you betray your king?"

A grin tugged at Kura's lips, but she didn't trust the desperation in their eyes. "What do you mean by 'sword-bearer'?"

"We could take that," Skellor said, motioning to the blade, "bundle it up real good and keep it from touching our skin, then dump it on the rebellion's doorstep, but that'd be no better than leaving them a sack of rocks. A sword's just a hunk of steel unless it's got someone to wield it. Even that sword. And, well, Rodlin, you found it."

Kura began to laugh, but they continued to stare. "...You're serious about this?"

Pening narrowed her eyes and Skellor shrugged, but none of them spoke.

Cautiously, Kura looked down at the sword in her hand. Her instinct said to shove this blade back in its sheath and continue on her way, but guilt pooled in the pit of her stomach as she imagined her mother watching. She'd believe in this. She wouldn't look at Kura the same way the Varian did—wasn't the fonfyr supposed to be Fidelis, at least, of all things?—but her mother would believe in it with everything she had.

She shook her head and tossed the sword onto the table. "Just keep it. I have my own business I need to attend to. You said something about soldiers at the gates?"

Faeng whispered in his own language as Pening scoffed, but Skellor narrowed his eyes at her. "Yeah, what of it?"

"Do they have prisoners?"

"They had some," Skellor said. "Centaurs, and a few humans I think. But they sent them on ahead hours ago. They're gone."

Hope shot through Kura's chest, tinged with frustration. "They're gone?"

Skellor nodded and his expression softened, as though he somehow understood.

"Where were they headed?"

"East," Skellor said. "But that's just the start of your problems. There's a battalion of soldiers outside those gates, asking for you. And the townsfolk here will give you up. It might take a day or two, but when it comes down to it, you're one person, and a stranger at that."

Kura growled and ran a hand over her face. She shouldn't have stopped here at all.

"I'll tell you what, maybe we can strike a deal."

She looked up, and Skellor grinned at her. He picked up a book, then used it to poke the sword. "You promise to keep this, and we'll get you out."

Kura scoffed, but she glanced from Skellor to Faeng to Pening and found each of them deathly serious. "What is it you expect to get out of this?"

Skellor shrugged. "Probably nothing. Come on, Rodlin—we have a deal or not?"

Kura looked down at that sword. Ìsendorál. The Varian hoped for an impossibility, but Kura didn't see any downsides for her in this arrangement. She picked up the hilt, then slipped the blade back into the scabbard at her hip. "We have a deal."

She expected Skellor to lead her to a tunnel or a gate, but instead she followed him—her seated in the saddle, him loping along on all fours—down a narrow alley toward the edge of Tarr Fianin. There, in the dark along the wall, stood a small group of Varian. Each was dressed in mismatched pieces of steel and leather armor with a weapon—either a sword, spear, or bow—in their hand.

"Skellor," Kura said, "what is this?"

He straightened to stand on his hind legs. "Soldiers've taken up places at the gates and around the walls, so when I give the word, we'll bring down a section here and break the siege lines for you to get through. When you do, don't stop. Keep off major roads and get as far away from here as you can."

"But..." Kura whispered. "They're going to..."

"Die?" Skellor stared her down, as if taunting her to continue.

Kura had to look away. "This is ridiculous. You don't even know me."

He gave a wry smile. "I've never been one to live life slowly. Besides..." He jerked his chin toward the sword hanging at her side. "Either you're the fonfyr, or you're not. This is the most promising thing I've seen in a generation, and I'm willing to take the bet."

"I'd seriously advise against that."

Skellor's smile only widened. "You don't have to agree with me, Rodlin. And maybe you can't see the world the way we do. But if you respect what we're trying to do, then let us believe." He held her gaze a moment longer before nodding. "There's a rebellion gathering at a place called Nansûr. Very few know of it, although I've heard it's somewhere along the Beauduras. If you're meant to find it, you will. Can you navigate by the stars, Rodlin?"

"Yes, but—"

"From here, then." Skellor glanced up at the sky, where thin clouds formed a sheer veil over greying starlight. "Just follow the eye of the sea-serpent constellation—Cenestre, I think you call it. You understand that?"

"Yeah," Kura said with a bit of a laugh. "And my name's Kura."

"What?"

"My name's Kura."

Skellor studied her, then laughed. "Well, Kura, I swear to you now, if that sword is what I think it is, we'll be there fighting at the side of whoever draws it. To death or victory."

Kura didn't know what to say to that, but she still didn't look away. Audacious hope burned in his eyes, and it somehow reminded her of her mother. She got that same look whenever she told one of her old stories.

Pening jogged to Skellor's side, shouldering a spear. "Saja've been spotted moving towards this side of the city."

Skellor muttered a curse. "Where from?"

"The north, as best as I can figure."

Pening stepped closer to Skellor. "Do they know about the sword?"

Skellor gave a slow growl and tilted his head to the side. "Pening will be your escort."

Kura looked at Pening in surprise, but the Varian only shrugged.

Skellor jogged toward the rest of the group. "On my mark!"

Kura watched him go, shaking her head and biting back the words she didn't know how to say. This wasn't right. She'd be a fool to spurn the help, but if she hadn't been carrying this old sword they probably wouldn't care about her at all.

Skellor's howl—a piercing, mournful sound—broke the stillness of the night and carried over the clatter of soldier's armor outside the city walls. A shiver ran down Kura's spine as the sound faded into silence, then the Varian leapt into motion.

A narrow section of the wall fell with an ominous thump. Soldiers, their chestplates and horses' bridles reflecting distant torchlight, scattered into the forest as the beasts broke through their ranks.

"Let's go!" Pening shouted, sprinting toward the opening.

Pulling her sword from its scabbard, Kura launched her horse forward at a gallop. She passed through the wall and the sounds of battle washed over her—howls and shrieks and growls, punctuated by the occasional human cry. She wrinkled her nose. It was just like home.

A rider charged from the darkness, sword drawn. Kura swung her horse around to meet his strike, but Pening loosed her spear. The shaft sank into the soldier's chest.

"Go!" Pening shouted, making a run for the opening the fallen rider had left in the siege line. Kura didn't hesitate. Her charger crossed the field in a few strides to reach the tree line, and even as branches tore at her face she pushed forward, the Varian somehow matching her pace.

Then Pening snarled. "Saja!"

Kura's horse reared up, striking with shining hooves at the silhouettes shifting in the night. She clung to the saddle as some misshapen beast screamed and veered off into the forest. Pening charged, drawing a dagger, and leapt into the darkness after something that resembled a large cat. Kura's horse dropped back down and she swung it to the side, slashing at any irregular shadow or thin branch that came too close.

A massive deer with glistening fangs and antlers, barely lit by distant firelight from the city, burst through the underbrush. Kura's charger juked and she managed to rake her blade across the beast's side as it rushed past. It lumbered into the forest, whimpering, and didn't return.

Kura shouted in surprise as a shadow landed on her shoulder—it was a cat, half the size of a cougar. Panicked, she jabbed her sword at its face. The blade met flesh, but the beast bared its teeth then sank its massive fangs into her sword arm.

A spear whooshed past her face. The cat howled in pain as the shaft flung it back and pinned it to a nearby tree.

"Go!" Pening shouted.

Grasping her bleeding arm, Kura spun her horse around. Several wolf-like shapes slunk from the shadows and tore at the Varian's legs. She drew a dagger and slashed at any in reach.

"What are you doing?" she shouted. "Go!"

Kura circled back, nudging her charger to canter through the swarming monsters. Pening snarled at her and snapped at her ankles.

"Hey! I'm—"

"If they catch you, this will all be for nothing!" Pening dropped down on all fours, eyes gleaming with an animalistic rage. Blood splattered what was left of her trousers and tunic. The monster within had devoured her human facade. "Make this worth it. You probably can."

Pening nipped at the charger's hocks. The horse leapt forward, Kura scrambling to regain control, and with a howl the Varian ran —the opposite direction, into the waiting line of saja.

Tears stinging her eyes, Kura drove her heels into her charger's ribs. Screams echoed from the city behind her. She tried to block them out—she tried to focus only on the dim forest before her, but it felt like hours before the sounds of battle finally faded away. Even then she pressed on, almost in a daze. She couldn't get Pening's ghoulish face out of her mind.

Eventually, Kura pulled her horse to a stop in a moonlit patch of silent forest. Her arm throbbed where that cat had bitten her, and she harvested a few more bandages from her cloak to dress her wounds. A clear, cloudless sky hung above her, every star shining like bright points of silver in the dark of the night. Her father had taught her navigation—as much as he could get her to remember. The dim star peeping up over the horizon was called the Cornerstone, and if she traveled due right of it she'd intersect the road to Avtalyon.

Above the Cornerstone and to the left was Cenestre. Her eye shone brightest in the sky, and after a while Kura caught herself still staring at it. She hadn't asked for this. And yet the Varian's sacrifice was not something she could brush aside. She owed them something now—far more than she wanted. Kura sighed, then shook herself and nudged her horse to the right at a slow walk.

She had a responsibility to her family, too. And they certainly took priority over any stupid old sword.

Chapter Fifteen

TWELVE

The sunrise cast a sickly yellow glow over the city, bringing light to a scene of carnage better left in darkness. Triston stood in the center, droplets of rain cascading down his cloak, and grimaced as he surveyed the billowing tendrils of smoke and steam that emanated from the charred clearing. It was a bitter dawn—one he'd been dreading.

Twelve. There were twelve men unaccounted for after the last night's battle.

So far they'd found seven, all of whom had died within the city after it'd been breached. Now, with the first of the morning light, Triston picked his way east of Tarr Fianin's walls—or, more accurately, what remained of the walls. Several townsfolk were already attempting to replace the damaged logs, and they sent embittered glances in Triston's direction. At the moment, he didn't care.

Carcasses, stiff from death's embrace, littered the clearing. A few were men—far fewer than Triston had first believed. During the battle he'd been unable to tell, but now he saw plainly the faces of his enemies: they were monsters, beasts that walked like men but wore the faces of animals. Perhaps this was clearest in death, their features twisted into unnerving snarls, their fur splattered in blood and matted by the rain.

He hadn't believed it before, but he knew it now: the Wynshire was a dangerous place, and they never should have come.

Among the drab garb of the dead there shone a patch of bright red—a soldier's cloak, the color undampened by the rain. Triston crossed the field to kneel at the dead man's side. It was Mory, face pale, lifeless eyes staring up at the sunrise. Triston carefully pulled the man's wet cloak over his body.

"Triston." Seren's voice broke the stillness. He maneuvered around the debris like a mother crossing a cluttered playroom to tell her child to pick up his toys. "I thought I would find you here."

The anger that had been brewing in Triston's chest threatened to boil over, and he clenched his teeth as he rose to his feet. He didn't want a conversation, not now and not from him.

"Come on," Seren said gently. "You can let the captains do this."

Triston closed his fist around the sword hilt at his side. Of course Seren would say that; a strategist delegated the burden while a military man shouldered it. "How do you explain these?" He motioned toward one of the dead creatures as he looked Seren in the eye. "Is it saja? Not seen in Avaron for generations?"

"They're not saja." Seren's apparent confidence set Triston's teeth on edge. "They're dangerous, though. And worse yet multiply in Lovaria even as we—"

"Stop. Just... stop." Triston shook his head, and he couldn't help but stare at the red cloak covering Mory's body by his feet.

"It's not your fault."

Triston laughed bitterly. "Not my fault? What did I tell you yesterday? I said these towns were unpredictable. I said we needed more men."

"And you were right." Seren's tone was somewhere between consoling and placating. "I should have listened. But I still outrank you: the siege was my decision."

"But it was the wrong decision, and I knew it. I shouldn't have let my men follow you."

Seren's eyes narrowed slightly. "What do you mean to suggest?"

Triston sighed. *Did I really just say that?* He ran his fingers through his wet hair. Yes, he'd said it. And he didn't want to take it back. "I don't know what I mean."

Seren nodded slowly. "You had best find out."

Chapter Sixteen

Sword-Bearer

The light drizzle turned into respectable rain, and it drove Kura off her course in search of shelter. Any number of the large, leafy trees towering above her would have been shade enough for her, but eventually she found a short outcropping of rock under which both she and her charger could hide.

"Looks like we'll be taking a rest here for a while," she said wearily to the horse as she patted its neck. The animal snorted and stomped its rear hoof. Kura chuckled. "Well, I still need a break."

She rummaged through the saddlebags until she found the half loaf of bread she'd packed, then with a contented sigh took a seat on the dusty ground to eat. This was the second night she'd ridden through with little sleep, and it was finally taking its toll. At this rate she might reach Avtalyon in a week, if she got lucky and didn't come across any other soldiers along the way.

Large raindrops splattered against the drying leaves of the autumn trees. Kura shivered as a chill settled across the forest, then winced as that movement sharpened the throbbing ache in her forearm. She'd become accustomed to the dull pain in her shoulder from the arrow wound, but this saja bite felt worse than it had yesterday. She popped the last bit of the bread into her mouth, then pulled back her makeshift bandages to inspect the wound.

"Gods..."

On her skin were the shallow indents of teeth, as red and raw as if she'd just been bitten, their edges rimmed by a deep purple bruise. Her arm had swollen to about twice its normal size, which would explain why it was so painful to move her right hand.

With a grimace, Kura re-wrapped the bandages around her wound. What did her mother use to reduce swelling? Some green-leafed plant that grew farther up in the mountains. She might be able to purchase it in the next town.

Leaves rustled in the forest. Kura flinched, her attention fixed on the mist-shrouded trees before her. *Saja?*

More rustling followed, then a squirrel popped up from under a pile of leaves. Kura let out a sigh of relief, but the sense didn't linger. Saja—that had been her first thought, when just a few days before she'd been confident they didn't exist at all. The question remained: had she been the fool then, or was she the fool now?

"Well, buddy," she muttered as she hauled herself to her feet, "we should move on."

Her horse simply stood with his neck relaxed, his ears flicked back to listen, one rear hoof casually upturned. He perked up as she climbed back into the saddle, and Kura nudged him to an easy trot through the dwindling rain. They'd probably near the main road by evening—though they'd never walk it, of course—and then from there...

An image flashed in her mind. A desolate place, dark and grey and barren, devoid of trees but covered in a crackled, grassy plain that stretched to the horizon. That was where she should go, after they found the road.

What sort of place was that? She'd never seen it before in her life, and she most certainly didn't want to go there. Kura rubbed her dry eyes. "Next town we come across, we're finding ourselves a place to stay for the night."

It couldn't have been much past noon, but with the grey cover of clouds Kura wasn't sure. She did know she was tired, far more tired than she'd ever been, and her whole body ached. The damp fall air felt like the dead of winter; the rain had nearly soaked through her clothes, but even after she loosened her shirt and threw back her hood, she was still both too hot and too cold.

This was more than a lack of sleep.

Her right arm had swollen so much she struggled to control her fingers. She recalled the gleam of the saja's fangs in the darkness, and realized now how much they reminded her of a snake.

She had to focus to stay in the saddle, and after what seemed like hours spent swaying on her horse's back, she suddenly noticed she had no idea where she was or where she was going. This wasn't the road; it was just a patch of thin trees. With a heavy sigh, Kura pulled her horse to a stop, then slipped out of the saddle. Her legs crumpled beneath her as her feet hit the ground, and she fell to her hands and knees on the wet leaves.

With a groan, she pushed herself to her feet and stumbled the few steps to a nearby tree. She collapsed at the base, gasping for breath as if she had just run a great distance, and let the horse's reins slip from her hand. This was the edge of the forest. A wide field of golden grass, swaying in the breeze, stretched beyond the trees.

"Good," Kura murmured as she shut her eyes and rested her head against the tree trunk. She was traveling the right way, if she wanted to reach... that grey place with the broken ground. Whatever that strange place was. The place she was supposed to go to.

The horse nuzzled her face with its nose. Weakly, she tried to push it away.

"I'm only resting a minute... just a minute..."

The horse whickered nervously, then snorted. With some effort, she forced her eyes open. The charger was staring into the forest, gaze trained on... nothing. He stood frozen, ears perked and shoulders stiff, then turned and bolted for the field beyond the trees.

"Hey!" Kura shoved herself to her feet, stumbling, but the horse kept running. Legs trembling, she chased him into the field. Dead grass snagged on her trousers and crunched under her feet; the horse more than outpaced her. "Stop!"

Her next step found nothing but air. The tall grass had concealed the wide cracks in the field. She tried to pull back, but momentum carried her over the edge and into the dark fissure. She grasped for the ledge—her hands scraped uselessly against dirt and stone—and landed in a heap on the dusty ground.

Groaning, Kura forced herself to sit up. Her muscles ached, but it didn't feel as though she'd broken anything. Where was she?

Stone spires—tall and jagged—reached toward the clouded sky like bare tree trunks, like fingers, like the skeletons of dead mountains. The stones were at her back, at her sides, stretching on above her and beyond her as far as she could see, their distant edges shrouded in a growing grey mist. A cold, moaning wind rushed between the spires, whipping her hair back from her face. She was chilled to the bone already, but her saja bite burned like fire.

She tried to stand, panicking as she gripped the rocky wall behind her. She didn't belong here; she didn't want to be here.

A fire sprang up near her feet. She jumped back, but it was only a campfire, its logs contained by a ring of small stones. How...?

"Hello, darling."

Kura spun around. A woman stood on the opposite side of the fire.

She was short, with thick arms, broad shoulders, and a stance that exuded a casual confidence. She wore strange brigandine armor, intricately detailed and brightly decorated. For a moment Kura thought she must have been Lovarian, but her clothes, while similar in style, were far older. An unruly mess of blonde dreadlocks hung to her hips and framed her thin face, and her bright blue eyes contrasted with her pallid skin.

Fear seized Kura's heart, although she wasn't sure why. "Who are you?"

The woman smiled. She almost seemed friendly; she was the only one in this forsaken place to understand it. Pain shot through Kura's arm and she cried out, grasping her saja wound. Her own pulse beat beneath her hand.

"The more you resist, the more it will hurt."

Kura locked eyes with the woman, her voice a whispered breath. "What?"

The woman's blood-red lips twisted into a wide grin. "Have they really taught you nothing? There was a time when men quaked in fear at the sight of me."

Kura grit her teeth against the pain. "Am I dead?"

"Oh no, pet, you are very much alive." The woman lifted a slender hand, and the campfire fell to mere coals; the searing heat leapt into Kura's veins. She screamed.

"Give me the sword, girl." The woman seemed so calm, but her simple command carried the force of a storm.

Kura shook her head, limbs trembling.

"The sword!" the woman repeated, flinging up her hand.

Fire surged through Kura's veins, fracturing her natural wall of stubbornness, and she clamped down on another scream. What did she care about the sword?

The pain vanished. Kura fell onto her hands and knees in the dirt, coughing as she drew in ragged breaths. A bird called overhead.

Just a bird? Of all things? She almost laughed.

The fog swirling among the spires receded to reveal a scraggly dead tree a short distance away, with a bird perched on the top branch. It was the size and color of a raven, except for the spots of white—like stars in a dark sky—scattered across its chest. The bird gave another call, the sound a harsh chatter, and flapped its wings to reveal the golden feathers on its underside. It was a flicker.

The woman hissed. "Out of so many, you come for her?"

Kura struggled to her knees, but her limbs didn't support her own weight. The woman turned back to her, brushing aside her displeasure with a grin. "Go on. Fight."

Kura tried to stand, but her feet slid on the dry dirt.

"Fight with all the strength you have."

Kura fell back, chest heaving for air. The woman held a staff, a long wooden pole that held a single-edged blade—one straight and the other curved—at each end.

"That way my victory will be all the more sweet."

With a shout, Kura ripped her sword from its scabbard and met the woman's advance. That rusted blade clashed with the sharpened staff, the impact reverberating through the stone spires as a flash of white sparks lit up the darkness. For just that moment the woman's face was illuminated, and for just that moment her smile faltered.

Strength surged in Kura's limbs and she leapt to her feet, thrusting her sword at the woman's chest. The woman stepped back, knocking her attack aside. Fatigue and anger clouded Kura's vision, but she pressed forward—slashing wildly, striking at any opening in her opponent's guard. The woman continued to retreat, swinging her weapon with strong, fluid motions that met each of Kura's thrusts with apparent ease.

The sword caught in the weapon's curved blade. The woman twisted her staff and wrenched the sword from Kura's fingers, sending it with a clatter into the obscuring fog. Kura froze, her breath catching, as the woman's eyes met hers. The irises were as blue as any others, but the rest—the rest that should be white—was a deep black, blacker than the night, as black as the emptiness in the sky.

The woman swept Kura's feet out from under her with the curved blade, then spun her staff to drive the other end through Kura's chest.

Kura flinched, gagging. It was like a hot weight had settled on her heart, and it took her a moment to even notice she was screaming. Her stomach heaved and she coughed up the metallic taste of blood. As hard as she tried, she couldn't breathe.

The woman laughed, the sound soft and innocent. "Despair, pet. It's all you have left."

Her cold fingers latched onto Kura's face, and suddenly Kura was somewhere else. It was a village of simple log cabins, engulfed in fire, with women and children running and screaming around her. The mangled body of a dead man lay at her feet, and his blood was on her hands.

But they weren't her hands. They were the woman's.

"I once almost conquered the world," the woman whispered, her voice echoing in Kura's head. "So many of your kind helped me do it."

The vision changed: it was another village, a different body at her feet, bright red blood splattered across the white snow and on different hands. Kura tried to run, tried to scream—tried to do anything—but she was a prisoner in her own mind, helpless to do nothing but watch carnage and destruction wrought by her own hands.

She clenched her eyes shut. This wasn't real. It couldn't be.

Those cold fingers pulled back from her face. She was lying in the dirt in a puddle of her own blood, staring up at the towering stone spires. The woman still knelt at her side.

"Oh, I relish this moment..." She gave her weapon a sharp twist, which sent a spasm of pain through Kura's body. She wasn't sure if she cried out loud or just in her head. "I'll watch as the light fades from your eyes, and then you'll either be damned, or you'll be mine. It's funny... when given the slightest bit of persuasion, most follow me in the end."

"I'll never," Kura choked out, warm blood trickling down the side of her mouth.

"You will or you'll die, darling," the woman cooed, her hot breath tickling Kura's ear. "And you aren't ready for that."

Each attempt to breathe brought pain instead of air, and Kura gagged on her own blood. The woman rose leisurely, leaning on her staff as she looked down with a beguiling smile.

"Take your time. The decades have taught me patience." She took a step into the fog, the mist curling around her, and her red lips twisted into a grin as she bent to retrieve Kura's lost sword.

The woman held up the rusted blade, then cringed. Fear sprang into her eyes, the blade flashed red, and suddenly the world was overthrown with light.

Kura awoke with a jolt, face down in the dirt.

A soft silence and calm, grey darkness surrounded her. She scrambled to her knees, sandy pebbles sticking to her cheek as she frantically felt her chest for injury. Her heart pounded beneath her hands, as strong and healthy as ever. It was night, that blueish twilight just after sunset, but she saw well enough to realize she was seated in a grassy clearing beside the forest.

Had it all been a dream?

That cold forest of stone was nowhere to be seen, but just out of her reach glowed the embers of a dying fire. A loud snort at Kura's side made her jump. It was her horse, lying down a little way from the fire, his ear lazily twitching and his eyes half-closed. His saddle and tack lay in a pile beside him.

Mystified, Kura scooted closer to the charger to lean up against his warm back. While her seat was not particularly comfortable, it was a great comfort to be close to another living thing. Her gaze drifted up toward the cloudy night sky, and she rubbed her arm. The burning pain in the saja bite was gone. She flexed her fingers —to be sure she still could—then ran her hand across the back of her arm. The scratches were still there, but they felt like the mild cuts they should have always been.

If it hadn't been a dream, what was it? Hallucinations?

She drank in the overbearing silence of the night, tracing her fingers along the engraving of the necklace hanging around her neck. She didn't know what to believe, but for the moment it was quite enough for her to sit there staring at the cloudy sky, fighting to get her hands to quit shaking.

Gradually the grey clouds moved aside, revealing a blazon of stars and—Kura drew in a breath. Rising in the distance, above the far mountain range, was a single, red moon. All her life two moons had graced the Avaronian night, one smaller than the other. Tonight there was only one alone, large and bright and red, the color of blood and fire.

Something deep within Kura's heart stirred, and she couldn't take her eyes off that one moon. She didn't understand what it meant—she didn't understand what any of it meant—but she knew it meant something. And something great at that.

A glint of red in the tall grass caught Kura's eye. Slowly, she rose and approached the object. It was the old sword, cast from her hand just as the woman had sent it clattering into the fog. Her fingers encircled that leather-wrapped hilt and she lifted the weapon until the blade was a black silhouette in front of the red moon.

No, it had not been a dream.

Kura slipped the sword back into the scabbard at her hip, then returned to her horse, heart still pounding. She wasn't sure what to believe about the prophecy or the fonfyr, but she could now be certain about one thing: this was not just some rusty old sword.

Chapter Seventeen

The Toll

"Will that be all, sir?" The city guard spoke slowly, as if that were the key to appearing pleasant.

Triston nodded affably. "As soon as Lord Seren's company joins us, we'll be on our way."

He took a step beyond the Tarr Fianin gateway to look over the company of soldiers who waited along the road. He'd insisted on staying to repair the damage their ill-conceived siege had inflicted, and thankfully Seren hadn't argued too much. However, the townsfolk didn't seem to appreciate the effort.

The guard frowned beneath his mustache. "Well, there was something my captain wanted."

Triston looked the man in the eye. This guard—an older, skinny man with a wiry grey beard—was the only member of his company to have made much conversation, and to walk about with his hood thrown back.

The man gave a shout, stepping back into the city as he waved a hand toward one of the narrow alleyways.

Three figures emerged from among the rows of houses. Two were cloaked city guards, and between them they dragged another man. This fellow stumbled like a drunkard and the unkempt brown hair that fell across his face made him look like a vagrant, but his cloak—while threadbare and mud-stained—hinted at what he probably was: a soldier. He was muttering something, but stopped as the tall, cloaked guard shoved him before Triston.

The hooded captain grunted, his voice low and his face shrouded in the shadow of his cloak. "We would appreciate it if you left with what was yours."

Triston peered into that shadow, searching for the man's gaze.

"Sir!" The deserter leapt into a clumsy salute. "I..." His eyes fluttered between Triston's face and where Triston rested a hand on his sword hilt. "I didn't desert, sir, honestly I didn't—in fact..." The light of hope sprang into the man's wild eyes. "In fact, I have something to tell you, sir."

Triston nodded, making a minimal effort to hold back his frown. "You have my permission to sp—"

"Triston!" Seren's voice carried across the open roadway. Colmac and two other captains followed at his heels.

The deserter shrieked and leapt behind Triston as Seren jogged to a stop beside him. "You! Not you, I—"

Triston pried the deserter's fingers from his arm. "Get a hold of yourself, man!" He glanced back at Seren with a sigh. "You know him?"

Colmac stepped forward. "I do, sir. He was in my company, part of the western patrol before he deserted."

Seren shoved past his captains to stare Triston down. "What has he told you? The man is unstable."

The deserter laughed fearfully, his features twisted into a terrifying grin.

Triston shrugged. "Nothing."

"He deserves to be hanged," Seren muttered, catching hold of the man's arm.

The deserter screamed, and feebly attempted to wrestle his limb free from Seren's grip. "Please, I wasn't going to say anything, I—"

The hooded guard leaned toward Seren's shoulder to speak over the deserter's noise. "That is of course your business. Let's see you and yours out of here, hmm?"

Seren scowled. "I'll see to it that your kind have no place in this town, or any town like it. The guards will be soldiers, good king's men with—"

"Seren," Triston said. Begrudgingly, the man turned back. "We've caused enough trouble here already, haven't we?"

Seren huffed, but remained silent.

"Good day, gentlemen," the hooded guard said, with a stiff—though cordial—bow in Triston's direction. Both he and his hooded follower turned away, and he motioned for the first guard to follow them. The man gave Triston a hasty salute, then ran off after his comrades.

Seren grunted, muttering something under his breath, before he caught Colmac's attention. "Bring him."

Triston sighed deeply and made his way through the city gates with Seren and the soldiers following behind. Seren knew more about this man than he was letting on, but Triston didn't have the patience right now to play the game and ask any of the right questions. The only things Seren *readily* shared were useless trivia or farfetched rumors.

"Damn you!" the deserter shrieked, dragging his feet as Colmac pulled him forward. "May the gods damn you all!"

Triston gave Seren a sideways glance. "Do all your secret patrolmen lose it like this? What's he seen, the centaurs?"

"They are a fearfully powerful race."

"I won't go back to the Waste!" The deserter's voice carried across the quiet street, drawing the curious eyes of the rest of the company waiting in the roadway. "I won't do it!"

"We're not going back!" Colmac snapped.

The deserter stopped in his tracks with a smile of relief. "You're leaving it, then?" He laughed. "You're leaving! Then—then I know something. Someone was looking for you, in the city."

Both Triston and Seren turned back.

Seren caught hold of the man's sleeve. "Explain."

The deserter flinched, then swallowed. "It—it was a girl. She was asking about prisoners from the Wynshire. She had to force the information out of me, but I sent her to Avtalyon."

Seren frowned. "Is that all?"

"No." The man's eyes darted between Seren's face and Triston's. "She, she was this tall..." He held his hand higher than his own head. "With brown or red hair, and—and she had a soldier's horse."

Seren smirked at him—which was about as close as a man of his stature came to saying 'I told you so'. "Would you recognize her if you saw her again?"

"Oh yes, sir, definitely, sir."

"Well, this hasn't been a total waste, then. Triston, I will take this man"—the deserter shrieked but Seren continued—"and maybe one or two others, and follow after this rebel. Colmac can show you to my facility, where you will take the prisoners—"

"Your facility? You're seriously going to try to make those beasts my responsibility?"

Seren hesitated. He looked as though he meant to say yes, but of course he knew that was the wrong answer.

Triston held his gaze sternly. "You put them under my charge, and I'm setting them free. I'm not about to throw myself blindly into your business."

"Triston—"

"No. Perhaps I would have foolishly done it had you asked me yesterday, but not now, not after all of this."

Seren sighed. "Someone must still bring in the rebel informant."

Colmac shouted something, and the deserter screamed. Both Triston and Seren looked up as the captain leapt back, the deserter's limp body crumpling to the ground. Triston muttered a curse and ran to his side, Seren following.

Triston rolled the deserter onto his back. Blood covered his tunic, colored the dagger that fell from his hand, and streamed from the gaping gash in his neck.

Instinctively, Triston pressed his hands over the man's bleeding wound, even as he glared up at Colmac. "What—?"

"Sir, he—he took my weapon..." There was such an honest look of shock on the soldier's face that Triston was inclined to believe him.

Hot blood poured through his fingers and the deserter reached up, grasping his baggy sleeve. The man tried to speak, his mouth opening and closing as voiceless air escaped his chest, spurting blood through the gash in his neck. His face twisted in desperate horror, and Triston could only watch with a sinking sense of dismay as life faded from the man's eyes.

He leaned back, the deserter's blood drying on his hands.

"He..." Colmac started as he stared—dumbfounded—at the body at his feet. "He said he'd rather die than return with us..."

Triston rose, haltingly. "Colmac, tend to the body. Have it brought back to Edras with us." This end didn't entitle the soldier to be buried with honor where he'd fallen, but this poor soul still deserved *a* burial.

The soldier saluted and hurried toward the company.

Triston looked down at the blood on his hands, contemplated wiping it on his riding pants, then finally sighed and met Seren's gaze again. "That man was going to tell me something, before you walked up. And now he's dead."

Seren's brows rose in innocent surprise. "Are you accusing me of something?"

"Am I?" Triston grinned wryly. "Gods, what reason could I have for that thought to even enter my mind?"

Seren eyed him. "Triston, as I said, it wasn't my intention to keep things from you. But everything is already in motion. I can't stop it—and I can't guarantee where we'll all land when the dust settles. But... I promise I will tell you everything, when the time is right."

"I know you will. You're going to take those centaurs to your *facility,* then bring the rest of the prisoners along and I'll meet you in Avtalyon. You're going to explain all of this to my father."

Chapter Eighteen

Davka'vara

Kura jerked awake as she nearly tumbled from the saddle. It'd taken all night—a night she had spent cringing at the distant, rustling wind, unable to shake the feeling that the woman's black eyes were watching her in the darkness—but she'd followed the Cornerstone out of the forest she knew and onto this unholy, flat land. Her horse plodded dutifully along the narrow path, which wove across the plains toward the distant, snow-capped mountains, but even with the bright sun hanging over the horizon, she struggled to keep from falling asleep.

She probably should've made camp to rest, but she had never settled on the right time. In the warm sunlight she felt foolish, being so afraid of a phantom, but in the darkness it had been an entirely different thing.

Maybe her fears weren't unfounded. The stories she'd heard about these plains said they were a territory dominated by either ruthless, nomadic gangs or territorial cattle ranchers. None of those sounded like pleasant company.

The sorry trickle of water that ran beside the road finally turned into a respectable creek, and once she stumbled upon a lone copse of trees, Kura decided to take a rest. She directed her horse into the shadow of the largest tree—which, given its gangly branches, wasn't saying much—then slipped from the saddle. Stiff legs made her first few steps difficult, but she gratefully collapsed at the side of the creek.

Kura cupped cool water in her hands to take a long drink, then splashed some on her face. She sighed and wiped her cheeks dry on her sleeve. What was she doing? She was running, scared—like a child—from a nightmare. She frowned and ran her hand over the sword hilt at her side.

Maybe if she brought the rebellion their special sword, they would be willing to find her family?

It seemed too much to hope, but if the sword meant as much to the rebellion as it did to the Varian... She shook her head. That kind of thinking had gotten her involved with the rebellion and caused this mess in the first place.

A low rumble, like thunder, carried across the plains. She glanced first at the sky—it was cloudless—then back toward the road. A red-tinged cloud of dust grew in the distance, the amorphous shape broken only by the occasional flash of silver in the churning mass of black figures at the base.

What is that? She rose to her feet and caught hold of her horse's reins. She considered trying to outrun it, but how far would she have to go? She'd been traveling toward those mountains all day and they didn't appear to be any closer.

The rumble grew to a roar of pounding hooves, and the ground—the very air itself—began to tremble with the sound. It was a herd of buffalo, the dust no longer obscuring their dark, shaggy bodies. Wild eyes sat low and wide in their long faces, and their short, curved horns glistened in the sunlight. Riders, mounted on horseback, ran on either side of the herd. They seemed to be directing the stampede directly toward the creek.

Kura climbed back into the saddle—her muscles protesting—while her horse shifted nervously beneath her. Two riders charged past without so much as a glance in her direction and cut the herd off, urging it to the side before they reached the copse of trees. The cows bellowed, pressing against each other as most of them turned away from the riders, but a few stragglers broke from the line and continued toward Kura.

One rider pulled away from the herd, his little brown mare galloping to try to catch the runaways. Kura's horse snorted as the cattle neared them, but the rider's gaze fell on Kura. He pulled his horse to a stop as the buffalo charged past both of them.

Her eyes met his green. He was scrawny, with tan skin darkened by the autumn sun, and he couldn't have been any older than Kura herself. He had brown, greasy hair tied behind his head, and the scraggly start of a beard on his cheeks. The smoldering end of a hand-rolled cigarette hung from the side of his mouth, and he stared Kura in confusion before a dimpled grin spread across his face.

"Well, hey there."

Kura froze somewhere between a smile and a frown. His mismatched, worn clothing showed he was some kind of renegade, and she wasn't sure how to tell the wanderers apart from the ones that liked to rob people.

Angry shouts rose over the pounding of hooves, and both Kura and the stranger turned back. Two other riders had broken from the herd—these men were dressed in simple cotton garb, not the long leather cape the young man wore, and that would seem to mark them as ranchers.

"Oh shit, they think you're one of us. Run!"

Kura hesitated to follow him. She didn't want to get involved in this.

The nearest continued to shout something unpleasant as the furthest raised a longbow, an arrow nocked and string set. She dug her heels into her charger's sides and the horse darted forward, closing the distance between her and the stranger in a few strides. An arrow whistled past her horse's flank, followed by a second, which passed over the stranger's head. He laughed, the cigarette butt falling from his mouth.

"Dodge!" he shouted, and his horse juked to the left.

Kura nudged her horse to the right and glanced over her shoulder. The nearer rancher pulled back and veered off after the herd, but the farther—the one with the longbow—kept his course. He raised a fist and shouted something—probably obscenities, but she couldn't hear him over the pounding of the buffalo's hooves.

The friendly stranger let out a sharp whistle. He waved his arm over his head, then motioned to the three stray cows he and Kura were still driving before them.

Kura looked at him in disbelief. *He seriously wants me to help steal these animals?*

Two more arrows sailed past her, sinking into the dirt between her and the stranger, and that made her decision easy. The stranger whistled again, let go of the reins to bring his hands together in the shape of a triangle, and pointed ahead. Not far in the distance rose a large, straight outcropping of rock. A narrow passage pierced the center, leading from the lower plains on which they now traveled to the plateau above.

Kura spurred her horse forward to cut the buffalo off from the side. Bellowing in fear, the animals turned away from her and toward that passage. The stranger pulled back, cattle charging past him, then spurred his mount forward until he and Kura were again riding side by side, trailing the stray cows.

The shaggy beasts snorted, but with Kura on one side and the stranger on the other, they settled into single file and ran into the shadow of the passageway. Kura yanked back on the reins, falling into line after the stranger as he darted in behind the cows.

The rocky path curved steeply uphill, and after few lurching gallops Kura and her horse emerged into the sunlight to the sound of cheers. Many other riders were waiting on the plateau, and they charged forward to form a circle around the three stolen buffalo and drove them in a tighter and tighter loop until the animals stopped running.

"Well done!" the stranger said, riding up beside Kura with a wide grin. He paused to catch his breath before extending his hand. "Aethan."

Kura reached across her saddle to shake his hand, swallowing to settle her own breathing. "Kura."

One of the other riders broke from the company circling the cattle. He was wide-boned but scrawny, tall and dark-skinned, and wore what was fine armor compared to the attire of the rest of his crew. A large, white gash left only one of his dark eyes functional, and his weather-beaten face curved into a crooked smile as he set his sights on Kura. "And what do we have here?"

"She's with me," Aethan said, urging his horse to step between Kura and the newcomer. "And just passing through. Got mistaken as one of us."

"Mistaken?" the man said, looking up and down Kura's figure. "Can't be. I seen what she brought in here." He edged his horse forward until he could give Kura's hand a fervent shake. "A pleasure, ma'am."

Kura nodded, as cordially as she could.

"A well-bred beast there," a soft voice said. It was the man's horse —a stocky, brown mare that gave a sort of grin as she shook her mane, her large eyes fixed on Kura's charger.

The man laughed. "Don't mind her, she's an animal."

Kura fought to keep her smile. This man and his nostkynna were friendly in all the wrong ways. "I've actually got to be moving—"

"Nonsense! You help rustle the cattle, you help in eating the spoils!" The man pounded his fist against his chest. "That's the one platitude I've always lived by. The Crowfoot rule, for scavengers who earned their keep."

Kura grinned—or at least she tried to, but surely by now it'd twisted into something less pleasant. In the field beyond, other men had already dispatched one buffalo and several women were skinning the hide and removing the internal organs. She glanced over at Aethan, the only one in this group she had half a mind to trust.

He laughed. "Don't worry, you don't have to stay long. Let me show you to the watering hole. Your horse would appreciate that, I think."

Kura shrugged. That much at least was true.

"Come on," Aethan said, motioning with his hand as he turned his horse out toward the rolling plains beyond.

Kura encouraged her horse to follow his, but looked back at the other man. He was still watching her with that same crooked smile. He caught her staring, and she turned away.

"You from one of the other kins?" Aethan asked, his stocky brown mare walking at a near trot to match the strides of Kura's charger.

"No. What kins?"

"I didn't think you were, although you ride well enough. Where are you from?"

"The Wynshire," Kura replied, not seeing a reason to lie.

"The Waste, really? So folks do live out there after all?"

"We used to, anyway."

"Ah." Aethan's smile faded and he glanced toward the horizon. "They say there's peace to be found somewhere. Not here of course," he added with a quiet laugh. "But somewhere." He met Kura's gaze. "Where you headed?"

"East." She wasn't about to tell the whole truth. "Edras, maybe."

"Really?" Aethan studied her with an incredulous grin, and Kura couldn't tell if he believed her or not. "Well, then you made the wrong turn about a quarter day's ride back that way." He motioned over his shoulder. "The main road keeps heading east. That one you were on heads north towards the mountains."

"Oh." She didn't remember making any turns, but she didn't know for certain what she'd done the night before.

"The watering hole is just over here."

They crested the top of the rise, and Kura caught a glimpse of the village. It was nestled in the wide, flat space between the low-rising hills, and seemed to have been built with reckless abandon. The dwellings were small and ramshackle, just tents with old blankets for walls and bundles of dried grass for roofs. Smoke trailed up from the cooking fires scattered amongst the structures, and only some of them were tended by older men and women who walked with a hunch in their back and a hesitance in their step. There were no children.

"Welcome to Davka'vara," Aethan said, his eyes distant. "The finest caste camp this side of the Beaduras, and home to the kins of Rakingr."

"Kins of Rakingr?"

He shrugged. "We're all the kin of somebody on the plains—you're born that way, you're made that way, or you're driven off." His hand came to rest on the hilt of the sword that hung at his side. "In Rakingr you're made that way."

"And what about the ranchers?"

"They'd get rid of us if they got the chance. Not that I blame them, but most of us only take what we need."

Those working in the village looked up as Aethan and Kura approached. The women curtsied with their loose-fitting skirts and the men—frail, boyish-faced—bowed at the waist as they passed by. Kura tried to nod or smile, to do something to assure them she was not the royalty they'd apparently mistaken her for, but none looked up at her.

Aethan dismounted and led his horse the rest of the way to the watering hole on foot, and Kura followed his lead. The watering hole itself was a short stone basin, and she frowned at the cloudy water contained within. Her horse didn't seem to mind it.

"Afternoon, Serika," Aethan said cordially as one woman walked to the basin.

She glanced up, startled, and nearly dropped the clay jar she was carrying on her shoulder. She was a shorter woman, skinny too, although her baggy dress largely hid her frame. Her skin was a golden tan, which highlighted the brightness of her eyes, and while she was clearly older than Kura, it wasn't by many years. A halting smile crossed her face as Aethan spoke, and she leaned over to scoop some water into her jar.

The three of them stood in silence as Kura's horse slurped its fill from the pool.

"Well," Kura began, gathering her reins, "thank you for your hospitality."

Serika looked up, her blue eyes peering through her curly black hair with a look of surprise. "Baza invited you to dinner..."

Kura glanced over at her. The woman spoke so softly she hadn't been sure at first if Serika was even addressing her. "Baza's that man with the one eye?"

Aethan nodded. "But you don't have to—"

"You don't want to overstay your welcome," Serika continued, a bit louder, "but you don't want to spurn it either. You won't find anyone more ruthless or more loyal than a Rakingr."

Kura laughed, trying to hide her frustration. "I'm sorry, but I really have to—"

A horn blasted on the other side of the camp, and every eye turned to look.

"Shit," Aethan muttered. "I thought they'd give up by now."

Kura looked back. A thin cloud of dust rose from the plains beyond the village, and traveling before it was a band of orange-cloaked figures on horseback.

Aethan leapt into his saddle, then with a shout, drew his sword and charged.

"The Kivgova want to claim our territories," Serika called out, her voice trembling, as she ducked behind the stone wall of the watering hole. "They've been following our camp for months."

The Kivgova let out a cry and barreled into the village, hooves thundering and weapons flashing. The villagers screamed and ran as the remaining members of Rakingr—those who had helped steal the cattle—drove their horses to meet the advancing enemy line.

Kura swung onto her charger's back, gathering the reins with one hand and clenching her sword hilt with the other. It wasn't her place to be taking sides, but she didn't feel right standing idle—not when someone had drawn blades on people who were unarmed.

Two Kivgova riders veered for the watering hole. They were shorter figures, either young or scrawny, with faces shrouded in orange scarfs. One held a spear and the other a curved Lovarian saber, which he pointed in her direction. Kura grimaced, drew her sword, and drove her horse to a gallop to meet them.

Her sword glanced at an odd angle off the Kivgova's blade, but the fighter was slow to take advantage. She pulled back, then struck at the neck of his saber and sent the weapon flying. He yanked on the reins, his horse's hooves sliding on the dry grass, and fell behind.

A scream pierced the air. The first rider had reached the watering hole and pulled Serika onto his saddle. Angry now, Kura drove her horse forward, only open plains between her and the first rider. He slung Serika over his horse's back, then flicked his reins and made a break for the fields beyond the village.

The man's shaggy horse was fast, but Kura's charger proved faster. She cut him off, edging him toward the village as she thrust her blade at his neck. The man ducked under the weapon and leapt from the saddle. He rolled once when he hit the ground, then popped up onto his feet and ran off after his disarmed comrade.

Kura watched him run, not sure if she should be impressed at his agility or disgusted by his cowardice.

Serika continued to scream. The woman was draped like a sack across the now riderless horse's saddle, and the horse was barreling toward the plains. Kura drove her heels into her charger's sides and closed the gap between her and Serika in a few thundering strides. Bracing her feet in the stirrups, she reached out and latched onto the horse's reins. She pulled back—both on the abandoned horse and on her own—and gradually brought the loose animal to a stop beside hers.

Serika slid off the horse's back, gasping for breath. Kura leapt from the saddle, lowering her sword as she crouched down at Serika's side. "You alright?"

The woman nodded, wiping the tears from her cheeks as she met Kura's gaze. A sudden fear filled her eyes, and she gripped Kura's arms with all her might.

"I was wrong, I didn't realize, you—fly from here. Fly while you have the chance!"

"Hey." Kura tried to smile, and placed a hand on Serika's shoulder. "It's alright."

Hooves pounded in from the open plains, and Kura sprang to her feet, raising her sword.

"You two good?" It was Aethan, bringing his stocky brown mare to a halt beside Serika. "The Kivgova have been..." Then his eyes fell on Ìsendorál and widened in utter astonishment.

He recognized the sword. The sounds around Kura faded under the pounding of her heart. How did he know? What would he do? What should *she* do?

"Serika!" a voice boomed behind them. Baza charged in atop a large, black-and-white speckled stallion. The horse Kura had spoken to earlier ran in the field beyond them, rounding up several of the other abandoned Kivgova horses.

Serika scrambled to her feet and bowed her head, folding her hands before her. "I am here, husband."

Baza grinned, a shock of white against his dark face. He nodded in Kura's direction. "Well done, Crowfoot."

Kura tried to return the smile, but unease dominated her thoughts. He was starting to look at her the way his horse had looked at hers.

"I made no mistake inviting you to stick around." Baza laughed, as if that were some sort of joke. "Come, you *must* stay for dinner now."

Kura hesitated, then nodded graciously as she slipped her sword back into his scabbard. "Thank you, I would be honored."

Every bit of that sentence was a lie, but she could see the blood splattered on his clothing and the gleam in his eye. Baza was not a man to be crossed. At least, not to his face.

"Come, Serika," he commanded, and Serika obeyed.

Kura turned away, unease settling into the rhythm of her pounding heart as she climbed back into the saddle. When she glanced up, Aethan was still staring at her. His mouth hung open as though he meant to say something, but he hadn't spoken a word.

"Come, Aethan!" Baza shouted, wrapping his arms around Serika as she settled into her seat before him in the saddle.

Aethan flinched. "What?"

"Get your ass moving. We're packing up!"

Chapter Nineteen

The Crowfoot's Tale

Cold rain fell with a gentle patter over the camp, and at last Kura took a seat by the fire under the dry overhang of a tent.

It'd taken the rest of the evening and into the night, but the kins of Rakingr had packed up their village, moved it, and set it up again in the jagged mountains at the edge of the plains. Having grown up at the base of the Eigens, Kura laughed at the thought of calling these hills *mountains*, but as she worked alongside the plains dwellers, she found herself using their terminology anyway.

"Thanks for your help out there," Aethan said as he took a seat on the ground beside Kura's stool. She simply nodded.

After his initial shock at seeing Ìsendorál, he'd moved on as if nothing had happened. She was content to leave it this way, although there remained that nagging doubt in the back of her mind, overshadowing her thoughts like a dark cloud. Maybe she *should* ask him what he knew—clearly it was more than she did—but this wasn't the simplest subject to broach with a stranger.

"What are you going to call this place now?" she asked instead, shaking the beading water from her cloak.

Aethan looked at her quizzically, then laughed. "Oh, it's still Davka'vara. The name means 'wayward refuge'."

A boisterous laugh shattered the relative calm of the tent as Baza entered, flanked by several of the other men and followed by a few women. He grinned and motioned to the empty crates and spaces around the fire. "Dinner is served, gentlemen."

Still immersed in their previous conversations, the men gradually —and loudly—took their seats around the fire. But they weren't actually all men. Some were tall, burly women, dressed in the same loose-fitting armor and speaking with the same boorish ferocity as the other men in camp.

"So he looks up at me all defiant-like, right," a woman continued as she took the seat beside Kura. "And he's all, 'Don't kill me, my family can pay ransom'. And I'm thinkin' to myself, no way—if they could you wouldn't be wearin' that jacket." The others laughed, and she took a swig from her mug.

A figure at Kura's side placed a plate of food in her lap. It was Serika. She and several others—the short, skinny men and women who'd bowed to her in the village earlier—moved silently around the tent, giving trays of hot food to the rest of the gang.

"Thank you," Kura said, meeting Serika's gaze. Serika started to return the smile, but she saw one of the others watching her and regained her submissive demeanor.

"And so," the burly woman said, taking a bite out of the chunk of meat on her knife, "he's like, he knows I don't believe him. So he gets that look in his eyes, you know what I mean, and he starts prayin'. And I'm thinkin', man, if there was really an Arakt out there he would have saved you already."

The others laughed, but Kura shifted her seat to look the woman in the eyes. "It's rather bold for you to say that, considering he was suffering at your hands."

Conversation fell to a low murmur, and Kura stiffened as each resentful glare fixed on her. *Idiot! Why'd you open your mouth?*

The woman scowled. "Don't tell me you're one of those Svaldans. Some others said you're a follower of Tácnere."

"I'm not a follower of Tácnere, or any of those other gods."

"Oh, then don't say you're a *Láefe*," the woman said with a laugh, and a few others chuckled as well. "I didn't think there was any of those fools left."

One of the other men spoke up. "You have to admit she's got a point." The accusatory stares of the rest of the group turned on him, and he shrugged. "Just sayin'."

Baza laughed, his voice shaking the tent. "That's rich coming from you, Sygus, considering the things we've all seen you do."

Sygus retreated back to his meal. "Hey, I ain't proud of all I've done. But it don't mean my mother didn't try an' raise me right."

He nodded in Baza's direction. "What would you do if you met him, tonight? Be it Tácnere, or Arakt, or whoever. What would you do?"

"Bah." Baza wrinkled his nose, and leaned over to spit on the dirt floor. "I'd ask him how he dared to make a world like this." The tent grew quiet, and Baza straightened. "The rest of them out there, they say the gods'll damn us for what we've done, and they say our kind deserve it. Well, there ain't a damn one of us who ain't already been through hell and back. And for what? The gods made it this way."

Kura picked half-heartedly at the food on her plate. Some of the other cast-outs had had the same fear, and she'd always thought it nonsense. But that had been before last night. "What if you met the Crux?"

Baza hesitated, then laughed. "What do you mean, Crowfoot?"

"You know, the *Myrk'aviet*—the force of evil, the opposite of the gods. What would you do if you saw her, or it?"

Baza grinned at the faces around him. "With company like this, I don't know we need a Crux. What would you do, girl?"

"Well..." What had she done? She'd fought with all the strength she had, and she'd lost. "I guess I'd hope that there's a good god or something out there, because sometimes we can't get this world right on our own."

Silence hung in the air, then Baza broke it with roaring laughter as he raised his mug. "I say fuck the world. I've got everything I want right here."

The rest of the crew laughed with him and downed their drinks while Kura shrugged and turned back to her meal. She felt Aethan's gaze fixed on her, but when she looked up, he glanced away.

She grinned. "What?"

"Nothing." He returned the grin. "I just agree with you, that's all."

Kura stared at her empty plate, grateful for at least one friendly face among the gang. But she had already stayed here far longer than she'd intended. Giving Baza a cordial nod, she rose from her seat. "Thank you for your hospitality."

"Oh, you can't go," he said, a bit too quickly, and Kura frowned. Baza laughed. "I mean, you must stay the night. I think we owe you that much. And besides, these mountains are hard for even the best of us to travel in the dark and the rain."

Kura sighed. The darkness didn't bother her, but she had forgotten about the rain. She forced a smile. "Well, thank you. I'll stay the night and head out in the morning."

"Splendid!" Baza clapped his hands. "Serika!"

"I'll show her to an open tent," Aethan said, rising from his seat.

Baza looked him over with a scowl, then shrugged. "Do what you like, *domvik*."

Aethan stiffened at that last word, but nodded anyway. "Come on," he said, and motioned for Kura to follow him outside.

She stepped into the cold rain and shivered. Maybe that tent had been more welcoming than she'd thought. She pulled her hood over her head, her breath hanging in a white cloud before her face.

"It's just this way," Aethan said.

Weak torches, set on stakes and sputtering in the light, misty rain, provided enough light for them to pick their way along the small, rocky path in the hillside. Aethan exchanged pleasantries with the few strangers they passed, but the murmur of voices and scuffle of feet gradually gave way to the pattering rain and the encompassing blackness of night beyond the camp.

Kura slowed, tucking her hair behind her ear, as they approached what was perhaps the most ramshackle tent of all. It was a short dome, with a willow-wood frame and a patchworked cloth cover. She chuckled. "You think this thing will keep out the rain?"

"No, this a Pokalfr house. It's not being used now."

Pokalfr—of course. Kura had seen one of these tents before, in Tarr Fianin as a girl. A man wearing a bit of patchworked cloth around his waist had been attempting to entice wanderers-by inside a similar tent—a hot house—promising them an encounter with the gods. Kura's father had shooed her away, but occasionally another cast-out would enter the tent and return to the group with a story about some strange spiritual experience.

"You want me to stay here?"

"No, no." Aethan continued around the tent, chewing his lip as he scanned the village behind them, then crouched in the shadows beside the tent.

"What are you doing?"

"Where did you get the sword?" The words came at barely a whisper, his expression full of hope, desperation, and disbelief.

Kura crouched down at his side, then hesitated; against her better judgement she was inclined to tell the truth. "I—I just found it."

Aethan's expression didn't change. "So you do know what it is."

Possibly.

"But you're not Fidelis."

Kura laughed, despite herself. Unlike the Varian, he was asking moderately sensible questions. "Of course I'm not. And I'm not the fonfyr, either, so don't go getting that idea."

"But how..." Aethan searched her face, looking for the elusive point of fact that would put the pieces into place. He wanted to believe her. In this ruthless village of cynics and skeptics, it seemed he wanted to believe all of it. "You really are heading for Avtalyon."

"If I have to."

"What, do you want to die?" Aethan tried to hold back a derisive laugh, but mostly failed. "Stealing a soldier's horse doesn't make you a one-woman army."

Kura frowned at him through the darkness.

"Sorry." He shook his head, breaking from her gaze. "I'm sorry. But you have to know you won't find what you're looking for. Not that way."

Kura sighed deeply. She wanted to keep glaring at him, except he was probably right.

"But that sword..." he said. "There's a place called Nansûr, it—"

"Oh, I know."

Aethan hesitated, studying her with pensive curiosity instead of awe. "If it's Dradge you want, then that has to be the best way to get at him."

She laughed softly. Old stories couldn't save anyone; the rebellion had already brought her enough trouble as it was, and yet she could almost feel that woman staring at her in the stillness of the night. She'd killed those monsters outside Tarr Fianin herself, and Pening...

Kura sighed and ran a hand across her face. "Let's have this conversation in the morning."

"We can't. You need to leave, tonight."

Kura waited for him to explain.

"I'm sure you've noticed how it is around here—the strong conquer, and the weak serve." Aethan hung his head. "I'm sorry I got you caught in any of it. If the Kivgova hadn't shown up, I would have sent you away hours ago. A lawless place like this easily becomes a refuge for criminals, and it has."

"Then why are you here?"

He crooked a smile. "What makes you think I'm any better than they are?"

It was a fair question, but looking at him, for some reason, she hadn't been compelled to ask it. "Baza said I'd need a guide to get out of the mountains. You up for it?"

"I can't go to Nansûr."

"Why not?"

Aethan sighed and raked his fingers through his hair. "I can take you as far as the Beaduras."

Kura shrugged, then grinned. "That's good enough for me."

Chapter Twenty

Domvik

Dark figures of beasts and men flickered in the firelight, their amorphous shapes dwarfed by the trees that shrouded them in shadow. They shifted in silence, deathly silence, unclear in face and purpose, but then shattered into clarity with a piercing scream.

The centaur screamed. More animal than man, he screamed, and the sound curdled the marrow of Kura's bones. His arms folded against his chest, his legs coiled like a dying spider's. Foam gurgled from his mouth, dark eyes rolled back into his head, and his twitching form churned amongst the muddy leaves in the clearing.

It was Brant.

"He's dead." The man stood beside the corpse as it fell still, studying it, one arm folded across his chest and the other hand raised to his chin. His patient grey eyes shone silver in the moonlight.

"Well, I told you it wasn't going to work." It was a woman—it was *the* woman, with the strange leather armor and the glowing black-blue eyes. She stood beside the grey-eyed man, peering down at Brant's body with what looked like the start of an amused smile.

Kura tried to run, tried to slip into the shadows before she was noticed, but she wasn't here—she was watching from above, and yet at the same time she saw through the woman's eyes. She *was* the woman.

The grey-eyed man scowled at her. "Yes, you've always been so encouraging."

"Darling," she laughed, "it's a matter of history. Their kind is incorruptible—they hear both the Essence and the Crux and yet they can use neither. They are *infuriating*. I would prefer that you killed them all."

"It may come to that. But they would be such powerful weapons, could they be controlled..."

"There are always alternatives."

The grey-eyed man shot her a sour look. "Don't you start on that again. You asked for an army, and I've built you one made of the finest soldiers Avaron has ever seen."

"Oh, so you *do* have kind things to say about your king."

He winced, as though wounded.

Domvik, she mused. *He is weak. And I once had such high hopes for him.*

"You enjoy all of this a little too much, I think."

"Darling, I have to find some way to entertain myself. I've only been waiting on you for the last thirteen years." She ran her slender hand along his shoulder. "I thought you had vision, I thought you deserved everything he—"

"Don't touch me."

"As you wish," she said, tracing her fingers along his arm before stepping back out of his reach. "Keep playing your games in the shadows. But you have let this get out of hand, and you know it."

He shook his head. "I'll explain everything to him, and he will understand, in time. I'm only waiting for the proper moment."

"The proper moment?" She laughed, the sound musical yet grating. "You've already waited, what, one lifetime? And I've waited seven! The course to what must be has already been set. You took your first steps long before he was born, and there is no turning back. If you lack the temerity to do what you must, then I will do it for you."

Anger flashed in his grey eyes. She respected that, and had to fight back a grin as he glared down at her, pressing himself into her space. "Don't you even think about letting one of your beasts touch him! I found *you*, remember? Without me, you would still be rotting away in that cave—you'd be nothing. Your blade is sworn to *me*."

She smiled, sweetly. She had made him that promise. She'd given it to men before, and she would give it again. "Of course, darling."

With a jolt, Kura found herself awake, Aethan's hand on her shoulder.

"You good?"

She rubbed her eyes, then sat up. The sunlight was a harsh glare, the morning air cool, and her old arrow wound stiff from how she'd slept on the ground in the clearing. "Yeah, I'm fine. Just a weird dream."

Aethan held her gaze as though he wasn't convinced. "Alright," he said finally, and rose to his feet. "I've got the camp about packed up if you're ready to go."

Kura glanced around her. Both her charger and Aethan's fuzzy brown mare were saddled, and the only evidence they'd camped there last night was the fact that she still sat on the ground, half-wrapped in her cloak. She clambered to her feet. "You should have woken me up sooner!"

Aethan grinned and hauled himself onto his horse. "It'll be your turn tomorrow."

Kura shook the grass and pebbles from her cloak before tossing it over her shoulders, then climbed back into the saddle. "I'm holding you to that."

It'd taken most of the night, but Aethan had led her out of the hills and back onto the sprawling plains. They'd stumbled across this small grove of trees to sleep under, but gentle rolling hills—covered in swaying grass and bright white and purple wildflowers—stretched off toward the horizon in every direction.

"These are the Feldlands," Aethan said casually, spurring his little horse to a smooth trot at Kura's side. "If you traveled southeast," he added, pointing to his right, "you'd reach the Au'dal Plains. The horse folk live there."

"Horse folk? Like the centaurs?"

"No." Aethan laughed, then squinted at her as though trying to figure out how seriously she meant that question. "They're regular folk who raise horses—the best horses in Avaron. They probably bred that animal you've got there."

Kura glanced down at her charger as she failed to keep her cheeks from flushing with heat. Of course that had been a stupid question. But after everything she'd seen since leaving the Wynshire...

"Back there," Aethan pointed over his shoulder, "you can still see the Eigens. But that's where you're headed." He nodded toward the tall, snowcapped peaks rising in the distance beyond them. "The Rohgen Mountains. Avtalyon is nestled in among them somewhere."

Kura grinned. "'Somewhere?' You don't sound like a very experienced guide."

"Nope, you'd be my first client, actually. I've only seen the mountains from a distance. These plains raised me, and it's about time I left them behind."

His words sounded so familiar. A few days ago Kura would have said the same thing about the Wynshire. She'd still say the same thing about the Wynshire.

A herd of pronghorns frolicked across a nearby rise—prey animals, frolicking, without a predator in sight. What in this peaceful country would be enough to drive a man like Aethan away?

"You ever see a place full of tall stones, like a dead mountain or some sort of stone forest?"

Aethan nodded. "I've never seen it, but I've heard about it. Throgog, city of the stone trees. Legend says many saja lived there, with Vahleda, the Grey Lady."

Kura swallowed. "Vahleda?"

"Sure. She's one of our forebears who bound herself to the Crux, becoming one of the first vojaks. She was the first to die, too, in the war of the covenant. They say she killed herself, before Gallian and his forces reached Throgog and buried the place forever."

Kura shuddered, clenching her white-knuckled fists around her reins as she fought to keep her expression calm. "Was she a rather short woman, with deathly pale skin, long, kind of messy, stringy hair—"

"I don't know," Aethan said with a laugh, catching her eye curiously. "I wasn't around two hundred years ago. Though..." He shrugged. "I have had folks tell me they've seen her. A grey lady, like an apparition, wandering the plains on especially dark nights. Svaldans think she's Yadgul, god of the mountains. In my opinion, they've just been drinking too much wine."

Kura nodded thoughtfully, then forced a smile as she realized Aethan's joke. Too much wine. So foolishly—and desperately—she had hoped he'd have some sort of explanation for what she'd seen.

She rubbed her dry eyes. Maybe she was going crazy. At this point that seemed entirely possible.

"Well, shit," Aethan muttered. He stared down the road behind them in resignation. "We're going to have company."

Kura jumped and glanced back. "Soldiers?"

A thin cloud of red dust rose from the distant road, but it wasn't enough to obscure the dark figures of the riders cantering toward them.

"Baza's gang, I'd say." Aethan flashed a grin. "Just stick to the road. It's the first rule of the vagrant: strangers will assume you belong until you act like you don't."

"And if they aren't strangers?"

Aethan shrugged, his smile fading. "Then don't hold back from that man anything he thinks is worth fighting over."

Kura mulled over Aethan's words as they settled into an uncomfortable silence. He probably knew what he was talking about, but she still would've made a break for it if there'd been any decent hill or boulder to hide behind.

"Hallo!" The loud voice—Baza's voice—carried over the plains.

Kura was tempted to be relieved, but then she turned back. The entire gang was there: Baza and eleven of his tall, broad-shouldered men and women, each armed with bows, swords, and clubs—which at least currently hung from their belts and saddles.

"Hello, Baza," Aethan said with a surprisingly friendly grin. "What brings you out traveling this morning?"

Baza laughed, but true joviality was missing from his dark eye as he halted his horse a fair distance away. "I've lost something, and I've come back to find it."

Aethan urged his horse forward a few steps, placing himself between Kura and the group. "Oh? And what is it you've lost? I've been out traveling this morning, too, and maybe I've seen it."

"I'm sure you have." Baza grimaced, then spat on the ground. "None of this had to involve you, boy, and it still don't."

"I told you I wouldn't be a part of your harem-building, Baza."

Baza laughed, this time in amusement. "Is that what I'm doing, eh?" He glanced at the followers around him, who began to chuckle as well. "I thought I was offering a refuge for homeless prairie rats like you. I thought you would be grateful!"

Kura nudged her horse forward to stand beside Aethan's. "He's free to come and go as he pleases, just as I am."

Baza's black eye fixed on her, and she held his gaze.

"There are rules on these plains, girl. When someone offers you hospitality, you don't spurn it." Baza's eyes flicked toward Aethan. "But that ain't what I'm here for. Not yet, anyway." He gave a sharp whistle, and the group parted as the stocky, brown horse emerged from among the rest, her neck arched in pride.

Kura cringed. Serika sat in the saddle, hands bound and tied, and there was a fist-sized bruise on her cheek.

"Tell us what you heard, woman," Baza commanded.

Serika hesitated, her hands shaking, and didn't look up. "I…" She spoke quietly, too quietly for Kura to understand.

"Speak up!" Baza shouted.

"I heard them making plans to escape," Serika blurted out, on the verge of tears. "To join the rebellion."

Baza scowled. "Join the rebellion…" He stared at Aethan. "Sygus, what's my one rule?"

The chubby-faced man beside Baza looked up. "Oh, uh, it's don't have nothin' to do with the rebellion, sir."

"Mm-hm. And why is that?"

"'Cause, um, it ends badly, sir. Brings in the king's soldiers."

Baza nodded. "I was young and foolish, once, like you. But I learned my lesson, as hard as it was." He pinned his one eye on the faces around him. "We have our freedom here, don't we? But one slip-up and we'll lose it, huh? You remember what happened to the Blackembers, don't you?"

Anger flashed across Aethan's face, and he clenched his jaw.

"The rest here said I was a fool to bring you in. They said I ought to have killed you like they did the rest of them, but I didn't listen. How did you repay me, boy?"

"Fuck you, Baza."

"How did you repay me?"

"That's enough!" Kura shouted. Every angry eye in the gang turned on her, but she pushed back against the pounding of her heart and kept her voice steady. "Is all this really what you want? To live in squalor, to fight and bleed for it, under Dradge's thumb until the day you die? That isn't freedom."

Baza growled and reached for his sword. Kura pulled back on the reins, prepared to draw her own weapon, and with a whoop the group cheered them on.

"Stop!" Aethan spurred his horse forward between Baza and Kura. For a moment all attention was on him, and he unbuckled the sword at his hip and tossed it into Sygus's open hands. "I renounce my kinship."

Baza's eyes widened. "Is that all this family is to you, boy? A trinket, tossed aside for what?" He motioned toward Kura, and laughed. "For her?"

"What does it matter?" Aethan said. "I'm no longer any kin of yours. There's nothing left here to fight over."

Baza watched Aethan for a long moment, then grinned. "This will be the end of you. Secession is permanent."

"It better be."

Baza looked over at Kura, his smile fading, and gathered up his reins. "I see either of you again, I'll kill you." He gave a shout then cantered away, the rest of his gang thundering along behind him.

Kura watched the riders fade into the distance, the rising cloud of red dust gradually enveloping their dark figures. "You just..."

"I know." Aethan turned his horse back down the road. "I should have done it a long time ago."

With a lingering quiet, the morning turned into afternoon, dragged along by the monotonous thud-thud of the horses' hooves against the packed dirt road. Aethan said very little, and Kura could tell he was hurting—or was at least momentarily and bitterly contemplative—but she didn't know him well enough to have a real idea what to say.

They passed only the occasional clump of scraggly trees, flock of songbirds, or distant herd of shaggy buffalo, but no matter how long they traveled, the mountain range in the distance came no closer. Finally, Kura could no longer stand the pressing silence, and she asked the question that sat foremost in her mind.

"Who are the Blackembers?"

She winced. That was the wrong question.

Aethan glanced across the short distance between their horses. "They were just another kin." He let the silence linger, then sighed. "My true kin. Although not really by blood, either."

"I'm sorry. You don't have to tell me."

He squinted at the sunlit horizon. "It's no secret. Our commander believed in the revolution, and I suppose the rest of us did too. We started ambushing soldiers traveling through the plains, stealing shipments of food and weapons bound for the western border. Dradge did not take kindly to that, of course, and one visit from the royal army left all but me…"

"I'm sorry."

Aethan shrugged. "What are you, then? Some sort of rebel scout?"

Kura hesitated.

"And hey," Aethan said, a gleam of mischief in his green eyes, "I think I've earned myself a little bit of truth here."

She held his gaze, a grin spreading across her face. Fair enough. And so she told him the truth. She wasn't a rebel scout now, but she had been. No, she still wasn't Fidelis.

"What about what I said yesterday, about taking the sword to Nansûr?"

Kura let out a deep sigh. For some reason, she saw Baza's face—him and the rest of his gang viciously clinging to whatever little they thought they had—and it felt too familiar. "I suppose I ought to."

Aethan perked up some at hearing that, but cocked his head at her all the same. "You know where it is?"

She tried not to grin as Skellor's instructions echoed in her mind. *If you're meant to find it you will.* "I'll know it when I see it."

"I see." There was a knowing edge to Aethan's smile. "Let me assure you I do in fact know how to get to the Beaduras."

Chapter Twenty-One

Half Truths

"Are we going to be moving on, sir?" Merric's voice echoed in Triston's ears.

Triston sighed, gritting his teeth as if that could drown the little man out, and continued to stare down the crossroads. There were no markings, no unique set of footprints to discern from the mass of cloven hoofprints—nothing to distinguish one path from the other beyond just the slightest bend in the right path and the slightest narrowing in the left. Their destinations made all the difference.

The left would take him into the mountains, while the right was the main road—the road he was supposed to follow, the road the girl had supposedly taken.

"Sir?"

Triston gathered up his loose reins, squeezing his horse between his knees, and then he and his small troop were simply trotting down the main road—the rightward path.

If he'd been able to bring just the boy, Darrow, with him as he'd wanted, the decision would not have been so difficult. He would have veered left, found a warm meal and soft bed by the end of the day at the outpost along the Amdais River, then procured a boat and arrived back in Edras in under two days. Then he could start searching for the answers to legitimate issues, instead of wasting resources hunting down one wayward rebel.

But Seren had insisted that two of his captains—Colmac and Merric—accompany him. As babysitters, likely as not, but they certainly jumped at his every command as though they intended to follow him alone.

Merric nudged his horse beside Triston's. "It is an honor to finally have the chance to serve with you, sir," he called out over the hoofbeats. "Everyone says it's a chance to learn a thing or two."

Triston nodded and struggled to give even a cordial smile. At least Colmac knew when to keep quiet. He didn't trust either captain, and couldn't figure out why Seren did. He'd always given the man the benefit of the doubt—Seren was an accomplished strategist, after all, advisor to the king, and he was good at what he did. One would be hard-pressed to find a project in Avaron that *didn't* have the man's knowledge or approval. And that had never bothered Triston before.

Maybe it was one thing to look at a tapestry, and another entirely to be a thread in it.

"They say that rebel's following the main road, huh, sir?"

"Yup." Triston didn't bother meeting Merric's gaze. "And the sooner we find her, the sooner we all get to go home."

The evening sun burned bright behind the long, thin clouds that hung over the mountains, but a creeping chill settled over the plains. With a sigh of relief, Kura dropped from the saddle and let her charger run to the water source Aethan had been promising them for more than an hour. It was just a shallow creek a little ways off from the main road, but her horse slurped it greedily.

Rolling up her sleeves, Kura knelt on the bank beside her horse to take a drink herself.

"What happened to your arm?" Aethan asked, wiping the water from his chin.

Kura glanced down at the bloodstained bandage lashed around her forearm, which had been covered by her sleeve. "It was... a saja, I guess?" It felt uncomfortable saying that out loud. "It had these fangs, like a snake."

Aethan frowned, dejected. "Kura, you really don't have to lie to me."

"I'm not lying to you. It's what I thought I saw, anyway. It *was* dark. It's dead now, though."

Aethan rose to his feet, a seriousness about him that threatened to make her nervous, and motioned to her arm. "Let me see it."

Reluctantly, she removed the bandages. The saja's bite marks were deep, but they'd knitted over and no longer had such a disturbing purple hue. Gingerly, Aethan ran his rough fingers across the wound, shaking his head in amazement.

"You should be dead." He grasped her wrist and turned her arm over, rubbing the smooth underside of her forearm. "And you said you're not Fidelis?"

"Of course I'm not," Kura said with a laugh as she pulled her hand out of his grasp. "What are you talking about?"

Aethan raked his hand through his hair. "Kura, that cat was a helry. Vahleda's pet, if you'll believe the legends. Most saja are nostkynna who have sold their soul for enhanced strength, that sort of thing. But helries are more than that." He shook his head in disbelief. "They aren't even supposed to exist anymore. Their bite is tainted, filled with a venom that plays on the mind to attack the will. You either die, or become a vassal of the Crux. A vojak."

"Oh." On some level she knew she should be terrified, but to hear that explanation—any explanation—was a comfort. It made sense, as much as it didn't make sense at all.

"'Oh'?" Aethan repeated with a laugh. "How did you do it? How'd you get out? A human can only become a vojak if they're willing, but that poison is supposed to *make* you willing, or kill you if you aren't."

"I..." She fully intended to share the story, but she couldn't speak. To put it into words would make it too real, would dredge up the questions she didn't know how to ask.

"I'm so sorry," Aethan said suddenly, and he placed his hand on her shoulder. "I can't even imagine—I shouldn't have asked. I'm sorry." He turned back to his horse and pulled out half a loaf of bread. "Here." He ripped the bread in two and shoved one piece into her open hand. "We can take a rest for a while."

She chuckled to herself as she watched Aethan take a seat on the riverbank. It was as if she'd suddenly become a wounded little bird in his eyes—something delicate, something that needed tending to. But her legs were stiff from the saddle, and she wasn't about to argue with him. "How do you know so much about these helry things?"

Aethan's expression remained far more serious than her tone. "I knew a man who was bitten by one. He survived, and spent three weeks under the control of the Crux before he broke free."

Kura shuddered. "He became a vojak?"

Aethan nodded. "He hardly ever talked about it, but he said it was like having your will stripped away and the Crux put in its place..."

Kura swallowed, the bread dry in her mouth. "How do you know I'm not a vojak?"

Aethan laughed, easily, as if the question had never even entered his mind. "You're not a vojak."

Kura looked down at the bread in her hands. Her mother had never said much about vojaks—*too scary for children,* she'd whisper, and then tell some other story. "The man you knew... how did he survive?"

Aethan met her gaze with a bit of a smile, but there wasn't joy behind the look; he was searching her face for something—some sort of assurance he could answer honestly. Finally he sighed, tossed the last of his bread into his mouth, and leaned back against the grassy hill behind them. "He was Fidelis."

Kura laughed, despite herself. "You knew a Fidelis?"

He gave her a sideways glance. "Some of the Blackembers were Fidelis."

Kura studied him, uncertain. Under normal circumstances she would have accused him of being a poor liar, but after all she'd seen —of Aethan and of everything else—she had sense enough to at least stay open-minded.

"My mother talked about them," she offered. "I think she believed they would come back someday."

"You remember the Fidelis fondly?"

"Sure. I mean, weren't they supposed to be the greatest of our forebears? The powerful warriors who braved the sea and forged our country? Able to hold fire in their hands, shake the ground, control the rain—stuff like that?"

"Oh yes—it's just... where I grew up, the Fidelis were not remembered in anything more than the occasional curse. Svaldan superstition and the royal army made sure of that."

Kura nodded and traced her finger along her necklace. "We didn't tell those sorts of tales in the Wynshire."

"No?"

"We had plenty of *real* monster stories to scare the children with, we didn't need to go making up our own."

"So, you really don't believe in any of it?"

"Well, I've never seen them."

"And you've seen everything?"

She grinned. "No."

Aethan nodded toward the sword hanging at her side. "How about that, then? The Forebears' prophecy. Do you believe in it?"

"Well…" Kura wanted to say no—it would be easiest to say no. And she certainly couldn't say yes.

Monsters of legend and a few strange dreams weren't enough to totally shake her grip on reality. To believe in something like the fonfyr… well, would it really be so different from her Svaldan neighbors burning talismans and performing rituals for gods they'd never met? Not that Gallian had been a god; just a warrior, seafarer, Fidelis, peacekeeper, king of the New World—the next closest thing. But still, she'd seen that woman with her own eyes.

Kura rubbed absently at her chest where that phantom blade had run her through. There was an undeniable possibility that reality held more than she understood. And, most troubling of all, that childish part of her still *wanted* it to.

Aethan laughed. "If you have to think for that long, then the answer has to be no."

"I didn't use to believe it," she said carefully. "But I guess I don't know what to believe anymore."

He grinned. There was a look in those green eyes that seemed to say he understood more than just what she'd said. "Life has a way of doing that to you, doesn't it?"

"If you kick it hard enough."

Dark clouds had settled over the purple-orange sunset by the time Kura and Aethan pulled off the path for the night. The Rohgen mountain range loomed in the near distance and Kura could almost feel those tall green trees calling to her, beckoning her out of the nakedness of the plains and into the safe blanket of the forest.

In the meantime, she would have to content herself with the small grove of scraggly fir trees that grew beside the trickling stream. With the horses tethered and happily grazing along the river-bank, Kura hauled their tack back to the camp and placed her and Aethan's bundles at the base of a tree before taking a seat on the soft, needle-covered ground.

Leaning against the tree trunk, she breathed out and let her eyes fall shut. A faintly sweet, cherry smell wafted in the air, and she opened her eyes to see Aethan lighting a cigarette over the fire. He took a quick puff, rolling the smoke around in his mouth before exhaling.

"You really like that stuff?"

Aethan shrugged, then grinned. "A man picks up a lot of bad habits living this life. He can't be expected to drop them all at once." He reclined on the tree behind him, taking a few more drags on the cigarette, then picked up the long, straight stick he'd set on the ground beside him.

"What are you doing with that?"

Aethan pulled a dagger from his belt and placed the stick across his lap. "I'm going to do my best to turn this into a fighting staff." With long strokes, he shaved off some of the smooth bark. "This is a soft wood so I don't know how well it's going to turn out, but I don't have my sword anymore, so..."

Something chattered in the open plain, and Kura jumped.

Aethan laughed, not unkindly. "That's a grass owl. They're not much bigger than my hand."

Kura tried to return the smile, but found herself studying the darkness anyway.

"Is this the farthest you've ever been from home?" he asked.

"Is it that obvious?"

Aethan shrugged and turned back to his staff.

When no sound followed the first, Kura resettled against the tree trunk and let her attention drift toward the sky. Sleep called to her, but the stars shone through the thin branches, innumerable spots of light blurred by thin and distant clouds, and it was strangely captivating. She recognized most of the constellations but they seemed shifted, like a painting set crooked in its old frame. She was so incredibly removed from all she knew, and yet she wasn't certain that was a bad thing.

"Right there is my favorite," Aethan said, pointing up through the trees to a bright clump of stars to Kura's left. It was a jumbled mess of three lopsided triangles joined by several strings of dimmer stars.

"What is it?"

"You can't tell?" Aethan said with mock disbelief. "It's Eordemer, the drake of the night sky."

Kura squinted at the constellation. "It looks nothing like a dragon."

"It's said that, at the beginning of time, all the constellations really did look like something. But on its first rising, the sun shot across the sky, splitting the moon in two and sending ripples through the stars. You can still see the trail the sun left behind."

Kura had heard this story before—her mother had told it more than once—but she glanced up at the night sky anyway, tracing the dense section of stars with her eyes as they meandered from horizon to horizon, a lopsided path of light in the darkness. "First client or not, you would still make a great guide. How do you know all of this?"

"Oh, I can be a good listener sometimes. They say that one day all the constellations will reform into new shapes, and the moons will become whole, and the *Elaedoni* will move on Ehlis again as it did in the beginning."

Kura nodded, thoughtfully. "I saw a single moon. Two nights ago."

"I saw it too." He glanced up at the sky as though he was going to continue, but in the end turned back to carving his staff.

The loud pop of an ember in the fire joined the chanting of the crickets, and Kura gave a contented sigh. "I think I'm going to turn in."

For a moment Aethan didn't respond, but he glanced up. "Sure, I can take first watch."

She shifted her cloak around her shoulders to use as a blanket and undid the belt buckle that held the sword around her waist. Aethan watched as she placed the scabbard on the ground beside her.

"Do you, um..." He just kept staring at that scabbard. "Do you mind if I...?"

Kura shrugged. "Sure." She drew the sword and then handed it to him hilt first.

Aethan reached for it, then froze, like he'd never wielded a sword before. Gingerly, he took the hilt and held it out to inspect the blade. The Varian had evaluated the sword with academic curiosity and seen it as something of circumstantial value, but the look in Aethan's green eyes was some sort of reverence.

"I never thought I'd..." He traced his finger along the sigil at the base of the fuller, then laughed, sheepishly, as his cheeks turned a shade of red. "I'm sorry." He quickly handed the sword back to her. "Thank you."

Kura just returned the blade to its scabbard, Aethan watching until she'd set it aside.

"You're not what I expected," he said.

She snorted. "I told you, I only found that thing."

"I know." He nodded and looked away, but his expression didn't change.

"What were you expecting?"

Aethan shaved another length of bark from his staff, then absently shook his head.

Kura grinned. She already knew what he must have expected: a gallant hero, a Fidelis, someone grand enough to carve a place for themselves in history beside Gallian and their forebears. Someone far more than a fugitive sword-thief. "The fonfyr's disappointed you that much already?"

He laughed, but didn't meet her gaze as his cheeks turned red again. "I didn't say that."

Chapter Twenty-Two

The Long Ride

Dim light permeated the heavy curtains, failing to drive the darkness from the room. Yet the darkness was... comforting, somehow. A brief respite—a stipulation for solitude—unpleasant in its own right, but altogether welcomed.

The door slammed open, Kura flinched, and for that instant the space filled with light. She scrambled for cover, but there was none—she needed none. She was just watching; she wasn't really here.

She glimpsed embroidered chairs, richly colored tapestries, and sparkling silver decorations before a man stormed in, the light banished by the door that fell shut behind him. He held his fists clenched, and his footfalls against the stone floor echoed as he threw himself down in one of the chairs.

The man didn't speak to her, but his soft mutterings overcame the stillness. Were those... tears?

Kura stiffened as the woman—Vahleda, the Grey Lady, an apparition—appeared at his side, her figure flickering like a hazy shadow. Not this woman. Not again. But just as before, there was nowhere to go. She *was* the woman; she saw what she saw. She had every right to be wherever she wanted.

She folded her arms across her chest and peered down at the man's hunched figure. "Well?"

Silence was his first reply—he sat motionless, his head resting in his hand, as though she hadn't spoken. Finally he looked up, the muted daylight catching in his grey eyes. Gods, he *was* crying.

Rage surged through her, but she didn't let it show. "Childish tears for a childhood friend?"

Anger sprang like a spark of fire in his eyes. "Damn you, woman." He spoke softly, through clenched teeth. "Damn you! Why didn't you let me take the *atgár*?"

"You understood why. We couldn't risk you being implicated—"

The grey-eyed man threw himself to his feet. "I would have killed the right person!"

She paused, emotion fading. There was no reason to be so agitated; this was a minor setback.

He violently wiped the tears from his face, then stomped to the window and yanked back the curtain. Daylight chased the darkness, lengthening the shadows in the room behind him. In the distance, beyond the unsymmetrical stone towers that rose among the narrow pine trees, a bell clanged—slowly, repeatedly, mournfully.

The man sagged against the windowsill, his shoulders slumped, as emotion snagged his voice. "Gods, he loved her."

The queen. That fool he hired must have killed the queen instead of the king. She shrugged. "This is nothing that can't be remedied."

The grey-eyed man laughed—a bitter sound borne of anger, not mirth. "You don't understand, do you? Dradge would have been *happy* to die for her, a thousand times over if he had to."

She pursed her lips. "A missed opportunity, was it?"

The man's laugh caught in his throat, and he beheld her in disbelief. "Can you not feel?" The question was a whisper. "Is that what it's done to you? Can you not remember what it's like to have a heart? To be human?" He sank to the ground at the base of the window, shaking his head as he continued to mutter under his breath.

Feel. Perhaps she could remember—images of faces, the smell of springtime, the touch of warm lips against hers—but they were in the past, foolish pursuits long ago cast aside by the eternal purpose of the nezjir. "We can send someone else."

"No." The man had run his fingers through his hair, and he sat there with his elbow propped against his knee and his head in his hand. "No. We'll find another way."

She bristled. "What?"

He stared her down, teeth clenched. "We will find another way!" He sighed, anger's strength leaking from him as he sank back against the wall. "The boy saw it all... seven years old and he watched his mother die." He stared aimlessly at the ceiling. "I held him in my arms, afterward. I told him it would be alright. I told him… gods, what could I tell him? If his father had died, I could have filled that gap, but now…"

She folded her arms again, frustration sinking to bitterness. This was the man she'd make king? *Domvik.* She hesitated even to think that word to describe one she had once held in such high regard, but it was the truth now. He was weak. Well, once he'd dried his tears perhaps he could still be useful.

Kura cringed, blinking awake in a cold sweat. The surge of color and emotions from the dream lingered, and for some time all she did was lie there, wrapped in her cloak. It had to have been a dream, right? She told herself so—if only to keep from facing the ramifications of any other answer—but it had felt so *real*.

Vahleda's presence made as much sense as it ever had, but why would she dream about Dradge? His wife had been murdered when she was a kid; her mother still teared up talking about it sometimes, although that might just have been because rumors said a Fidelis had done it, and the king had slaughtered them in retaliation.

She pushed herself to sit up against the tree trunk at her back. It was that grey time just before dawn, and a light drizzle mingled with the fog that crawled across the plains, although the small grove of trees kept her, Aethan, and their horses mostly dry. She wasn't sure how long Aethan's first watch was supposed to have lasted, but he'd never woken her—he was curled up at the base of another tree, sound asleep. He looked so innocent, with his face peeking out from under his cloak, that she had to laugh.

The sound of the trickling creek drew her attention to the water, and as she looked beyond it, her smile faded.

"Aethan, get up." She leaned over and shook his shoulder.

"What?" He sat up, fumbling with his blanket. "What is it?"

Kura pointed across the creek. A group of riders, their figures a black mass against the grey fog, edged closer with each passing second.

Aethan scrubbed the sleep from his eyes. "Soldiers?"

"I don't know." Kura climbed to her feet and offered him her hand. "I'd rather not find out."

Without another word, they gathered up what was left in their camp, saddled the horses, and set out in the rain, following the creek. Only a stretch of barren plains separated them from the forest now, and once they crossed it, they might be able to disappear among the shadows of the towering pines.

Kura goaded her horse to a gallop, the cold raindrops pelting her face, and stole a glance over her shoulder. The group had emerged from the fog; each rider wore the telltale red cloak of a royal soldier. In a minute or two they'd reach the grove of trees she and Aethan had left behind and spot them for sure—if they hadn't already.

"There!" Aethan pointed toward a break in the forest.

The thick branches hung low, but the creek—just a trickle now—dropped off the edge of the plateau and into the only opening among the trees. He directed his fuzzy mare toward that opening, and Kura followed his lead, riding at his side for a few thundering footfalls before passing him.

The soldiers shouted something, their words lost to falling rain and pounding horses' hooves, and Kura didn't glance back until an arrow whooshed past her charger's flank. The two nearest soldiers had crossbows and they were aiming at the horses.

Kura coaxed a burst of speed from her charger, while Aethan's little mare powered along behind them. The horse's jarring pace threw her back and forth in the saddle and the roaring wind made her eyes water, but in a dozen strides they reached the forest.

Kura braced her feet in the stirrups, fighting the urge to pull back on the reins. The break in the trees was actually a short waterfall.

Her horse leapt over the edge, throwing her forward in the saddle, and they landed with a lurch in the pebbled creek bed. She scrambled to keep her seat, but her horse maintained its pace, its hooves splashing in the shallow water. A shale cliff lined both sides of the creek, trapping her in the basin for as far as she could see, but at least her path was clear and the overhanging trees kept out the rain.

Aethan's fuzzy mare came to a stop at the edge of the waterfall. He goaded the animal forward, but it wouldn't budge. Kura yanked back on the reins, her horse grunting as its hooves slid across the pebbled ground.

Aethan waved her forward. "Go on!"

"No, we—"

He pulled away, driving his horse along the forest's edge and out of sight. She muttered a curse under her breath as she urged her mount back to a run. The group of soldiers—there looked to be four in total—galloped in from the field, one splitting away to chase after Aethan as the next paused at the edge of the waterfall.

She smiled grimly. He was too afraid to follow. Then she noticed the movement on the top of the cliff—the remaining two soldiers rode the ledges above her, one on each side. Their lean horses powered along the cliff's edge, raining pebbles into the creek below as thin branches tore at the riders' red cloaks.

One horse leapt from the ledge.

Kura yanked back on the reins, her charger crying in anger as it fought for footing on the wet ground. She watched, wide-eyed, as the soldier's horse sailed over her head and landed on the creek bed before her. Her charger screamed, the soldier's mount snapped at her, and they slammed together.

It was a massive tangle of fur, skin, and metal. Kura cried out as her leg was pinned between the two horses, but she drew her sword and slashed in the soldier's direction. The blow glanced off his chestplate and he pulled back, unsheathing his own weapon. She drove forward, thrusting her blade at the soldier's neck. He parried her first stroke but was too slow to meet the second, and he screamed as she shoved her blade through the seams in his armor and into his ribs.

The man fell from the saddle and, with a clatter, collapsed face-first in the creek.

Kura gathered up her reins, squinting as sunlight glinted off polished metal. It was the second soldier, still perched on the cliff above—and he had a crossbow aimed at her chest. She launched her horse forward. The snap of a bowstring echoed in the ravine.

The charger screamed. It tried to keep its pace, but only wheezed and stumbled. She leapt from the saddle, then tucked into a lopsided roll as she hit the ground hard. Shoulder stiff and shirt wet, she grimaced against the pain and jumped to her feet in the middle of the creek. Her horse lay on the ground at her side, an arrow sunk into the red stain on its chest. It was dead, but still twitching.

She turned away. *I liked that horse.*

Hooves splashed farther up the creek. So, one soldier had followed her after all. Sunlight caught in Kura's red blade where it'd fallen just out of her reach, and she flinched as, on the ridge above her, the soldier's crossbow snapped back into the loaded position. She dove for her sword, and an arrow glanced off the river stone at her feet.

"Hold." The soldier's voice, calm and commanding, carried through the ravine.

Kura stepped back into a defensive stance. The soldier strode toward her, leaving his horse behind. He stood half a head taller than she was, with a red cloak draped over his broad shoulders, but he couldn't have been much older. Dark, curling hair fell to his neck, framing a strong jaw and icy blue eyes. His expression was a mask—he might have been heartless, focused, or bored, Kura couldn't tell which—and the silver sword he held in one hand, while exquisite in its craftsmanship, was unmarked along the blade, as though it had seen either great care or little use.

She recognized him; he was one of the soldiers who'd chased her over the ravine in the Wynshire. The bastard hadn't managed to kill her before, so he'd followed her halfway across the world to finish the job?

He held her gaze. "You have been charged with insurrection, fleeing His Majesty's—"

Kura charged the man with a fury built up over a lifetime. Her bruised leg protested and her body ached from being thrown, but she hardly noticed. That rusty blade flashed before her, relentless like fire—but instead of flesh, it was met by silver. The soldier jumped to the side, redirecting her strike, and let her own momentum carry her past him.

Stumbling, she muttered under her breath, then whirled around to face him again. He stepped toward her, blade poised, and she lunged, strokes more calculated this time. Sweat beaded on her temple and her breath quickened, but she tempered her movements, driving the soldier toward the cliff.

Still, there was a hint of a smile in his eyes—the same sort of casual amusement a master swordsman might show a child playing knight with a wooden stick—and he parried her strokes with ease. He didn't attack, and he didn't pay more than half a mind to his footwork.

She was being played with.

Kura grit her teeth and jumped at him, aiming for the man's neck. His sword flashed, knocking hers aside, then slipped past her defense to poke her shoulder—just enough to pierce her gambeson, not much farther. She leapt out of his range, shocked her shoulder wasn't stinging; the blow could—and should—have been much worse.

The soldier circled away from the cliff face, adjusting his grip on his sword. Then he lunged, landing strike after strike on her defenses. She backed up, struggling to maintain a solid guard, and somehow did. She leaned into his strikes, catching his blade against hers, and kicked his exposed chestplate. The soldier stumbled back, and Kura jumped out of his reach.

He regained his footing, genuinely laughing. "You're good!" He circled her slowly, minding her range. "You've got an unconventional style, but some of the best blade and footwork I've come across in a long time. Where did you train?"

She hesitated. He seemed so... earnest? Her eyes narrowed. He thought this was a game.

"Triston," the crossbowman called out from the top of the ravine. "What are you doing?"

The man before her sent an annoyed glance in the crossbowman's direction.

Triston. Kura knew that name. Everyone in Avaron knew that name. Triston, son of Dradge, heir to the throne of Avaron—and the best swordsman in the eastern states. Fear prickled down her spine. She'd challenged the Prince of Avaron? She let out a long breath.

There was no undoing her choice now. She'd either kill the king's son or be killed by him.

She darted forward, striking at Triston's guard. They charged each other in a flurry of blows and counter-blows until she slipped her blade past his defenses, slashing him across the arm. Triston cried out, more in surprise than in pain, and withdrew.

Kura stepped back, tense, as she readied herself for the counterattack, then froze. She saw it in the set of his jaw: the game was over.

She tightened her grip and resettled her stance, ready to fight with all the strength left in the life she was about to lose, but then the prince was in front of her, his silver blade flashing. Stumbling back, she attempted a block, but he struck at her sword—steel ringing with sickening clarity—and twisted the hilt from her grip.

In horror, Kura watched as her blade tumbled through the air and landed with a muffled splash in the creek. Triston stepped forward, and she could only stare—wide-eyed, mouth hanging open—at her fallen weapon as she sank to her knees in the water. The prince placed his cold blade on her shoulder and she cringed, pressing her eyes shut.

"You've beaten me," she mumbled through clenched teeth. "Just—get it over with."

"I'd be satisfied if you'd come peaceably."

Dumbfounded, she met Triston's gaze. He was smiling, as though they were old friends who'd just finished a sparring match. This was a trick. It had to be.

His smile faltered. "Unless of course you want to lose your head. I suppose that can be arranged."

She let out a breath, looking away. "Alright. I'll come peaceably."

Triston lowered his sword, then took her by the arm and helped her to her feet. "Are you hurt?"

It took her a moment to realize he was staring at the dark bloodstains in her gambeson from her old arrow wound. The wound itself ached, like it always did. "No."

Hooves clattered in the ravine, and Kura looked up as another soldier rode along the creek bed, Aethan and his little mare in tow. At first she was relieved to see him alive and unharmed, and then she realized that he was bound and tied to his saddle. They were both prisoners.

The crossbowman eased his horse down a less steep section of the ravine. "Well, sir, I think you've..." His gaze fell on the body of the soldier Kura had killed, still lying face-down in the water where it'd fallen.

He let out a wordless cry—Kura's heart caught in her chest—then leapt from the saddle and ran to his comrade.

Triston kept a firm grip on Kura's wrist and dragged her along as he jogged to the soldier's side. He knelt beside the body to check it for signs of life, though surely he knew he wouldn't find any. "I'm sorry, Colmac."

The soldier leapt to his feet and pointed at Kura, who stepped back. "She deserves death for this. You know that."

Triston's face darkened. "I told the both of you to just follow her along the ridge, to not engage."

Rage sprang into Colmac's eyes, and Triston nudged Kura a few steps away.

"I'm done waiting, *sir*. Either fulfill your duty, or I stop holding them back."

Triston's expression didn't change, and when he spoke his voice was fearfully calm. "Captain, to attention."

Colmac shoved Triston in the chest. The prince stumbled one step but regained his footing within a second, his fists raised and ready for a fight. The soldier ran to his horse and swung himself into the saddle.

"Colmac!" Triston drew his sword. "You swore an oath! Until death or release, I swear to uphold the king's justice—"

"The king's justice?" Colmac laughed. "Justice is the tool of the righteous, dealt to the deserving." He urged his horse a way downstream, then began to speak, his voice low and his words garbled.

A wolf's howl sounded from the direction of the plains.

"Gods..." Aethan murmured, his wide eyes fixed on the retreating soldier. "He's calling—"

Saja slunk from the trees and to the edge of the ridge, snarling as their many yellow eyes flashed in the dim sunlight. The rain that had been pattering the branches high above the creek burst through the tree cover, but the beasts didn't care. They were cougars, wolves, goats, and foxes, each larger than they should have been, their fur shaggy and discolored and their heads marked with grotesque, curling horns.

Kura shivered, her heartbeat quickening in fear. She hadn't seen the creatures in daylight before, and now she wished she never had. They were a shadow of what they should have been, a twisted perversion of the creatures she knew and recognized.

Darting forward, she snatched up her fallen sword as the saja descended into the ravine. What was she supposed to do, one girl staring down a pack of monsters? She charged the nearest beast with a shout.

A wolf howled, a cat hissed, and a goat jumped forward and butted her in the side, knocking her to the ground. She lashed out, wildly striking anything that came into reach, and scrambled to her feet. Her leg ached but the saja pulled back—some of them growling, most of them bloody, all of them watching her dull red blade in aversion.

Aethan's shouts carried over the rumbling howls—he was still tied in the saddle. The monsters had surrounded his horse and were nipping at the animal's legs, trying to tear him from his seat. Brandishing her bloodied blade, Kura ran toward him. The saja pulled back, hissing as they eyed Ìsendorál.

He tried to point. "Behind you!"

Kura swung back and met the saja's leap mid-stroke. The animal howled as the blade struck it across the face, and when it hit the ground it retreated, nursing its vengeance as it circled with the others beyond Kura's reach.

Triston and the other soldier had charged downstream after that Colmac, and despite the chaos, Kura laughed. She sliced through Aethan's bonds. "Let's go!"

A deafening roar shook the ravine. She turned, her soaked cloak clinging to her shoulders and wet hair sticking to her face.

It was a saja shaped like a bear: a horned creature covered in scars, far larger than any regular bear she'd ever seen—and regular bears were large enough. As it lumbered toward them, even the other saja whimpered and pulled back.

Kura's first instinct was to run, but where? She was in the bottom of a ravine, soldiers in one direction and a monster bear in the other. The saja stood on its hind legs, its greying muzzle tilted toward the distant sky, and let out another roar. Aethan's horse whinnied, bucking in fear. It knocked Kura back and threw Aethan to the ground.

He pushed himself to his feet. "Get down!"

Kura took a few steps back, her gaze flicking from the saja to Aethan's face. "What?"

"I said get down!" He didn't even look at her, but strode *toward* the bear.

"Aethan!" Was he crazy? Kura hesitated, the cold rain soaking through to her scalp as she adjusted her grip on her hilt. What did she think she was going to do with this sword against that monster?

The rain stopped falling.

She froze, her eyes wide. It hadn't stopped *raining,* but the rain had stopped *falling.* All around her hung small drops of water that glistened gold in the rising sun. Aethan stood in the center, his teeth clenched and his arms shaking. The saja bear stopped, watching him. Then, with a shout, Aethan threw his hands out from his sides.

The rain moved—not down, as it should, but shot horizontally in all directions. Kura dropped to the ground, crying out as a droplet grazed her arm. Saja howled and screamed, and she huddled behind her dead horse, covering her head with her hands.

Then it was over.

Kura lifted her head. A gentle, natural rain fell again on the battlefield and pattered against her cloak. Twisted saja carcasses lay along the cliff and in the creek—even the bear. Some of them still writhed in the throes of death, and each was pierced with dozens of small red spots—like miniature arrow wounds but without the arrow. Farther downstream the saja yelped, their bristled fur falling flat against their backs, and they scampered up the sides of the ravine to disappear into the forest.

They were afraid.

Aethan stood in the middle of the carnage. He swayed, then collapsed onto the pile of dead saja at his feet.

"Aethan!" Kura jumped to her feet and ran to his side. She sheathed her sword and knelt down beside him to gently roll him over onto his back.

He groaned, and weakly managed to sit up. "Oh, I'm alright." His face, arms, and shoulders were marked with shallow bites and scratches, but none seemed life-threatening.

"What... you...?"

Aethan gave a weary grin. "Would you believe the Fidelis never left?"

Kura opened her mouth to say something, but the words didn't come.

"Damn it." His eyes were fixed on her arm. "I'm so sorry, I tried to control it, but I..."

Kura glanced down. That raindrop had sliced across her upper arm—the cut smooth and superficial, as if from the brush of a sharp blade—but it wasn't high on her list of priorities at the moment.

Aethan wrapped his hands around her forearm and began murmuring something under his breath.

"Aethan..."

A comforting warmth radiated from his hands, chasing away the pain. Then he pulled away, and Kura looked over her arm in disbelief. Blood stained the tear in her sleeve where she'd been hit, but the wound underneath had disappeared. Only a scar remained.

"How did you...?"

Aethan laughed and sank back against the saja carcasses behind him. "The Essence moves by its own intentions."

She nodded at the gash on his leg. "What about you?"

He shook his head, still gasping for breath as his eyes fell shut. "I can't spend my own life to save it." He gave what he must have meant to be a reassuring smile. "I'll be fine."

Kura rose to her feet, then gingerly tried to help Aethan to his. His limbs shook and he struggled to stand; she had to put her arm under his shoulders to steady him.

"What the hell was that?" Triston's voice carried over the patter of the rain.

Kura turned, drawing her sword.

The prince's white shirtsleeves were marked with red gashes. With one hand he led his horse by the reins, while in the other was clenched his bloodied sword. One soldier—a young boy with wide eyes—followed at his side, still seated on his mount, clutching a crossbow with shaking hands like a child might cling to his favorite blanket.

Aethan laughed weakly. "That," he said, motioning to the dead saja bear lying in the creek a ways behind them, "is the biggest fucking saja I've ever seen. Although I figured you'd know, since a subordinate of yours is the one who called it. Still, I killed it for you. You're welcome."

Triston's eyes narrowed and he stopped a fair distance away. "I was talking about the rain."

The four of them stood there, studying one another, as raindrops plinked into the creek.

Triston broke the silence. "You Fidelis?"

Aethan only smirked.

"Are you planning on poking me full of holes, too? Because I have half a mind to kill you right now."

Aethan's smile faded, and he sagged against Kura's shoulders. "No." The cocky strength leaked from his voice. "No, I'm not poking anything else full of holes today."

Triston relaxed slightly, then glanced in the other soldier's direction. "Go get the horses." The boy nodded and did as he was told, and Triston continued forward cautiously.

Kura stiffened, her shaking hand clenched around her sword hilt.

"Please." Triston stopped, one lunge out of her reach. "I'd rather not have to hurt you."

If she couldn't beat him before, she certainly had no chance now. She gritted her teeth and let her sword drop into the creek.

Aethan pushed himself out of her grip, then sank to his knees at her side. Triston watched them, suspicious, but eventually sheathed his sword, pulled a length of rope from his belt, and stepped forward to bind Kura's hands together. He confiscated her weapon and scabbard, and bound Aethan's hands together as well.

When the young soldier returned with the horses, Triston forced Aethan back onto his shaggy mare, and then Kura up into the saddle of the horse that had belonged to the soldier she'd killed. He tied her bound hands to the saddle horn. "Keep them close, Darrow."

"Yes, sir." The soldier glanced downstream. "Are... are we going to leave Captain Merric's body here, sir?"

Triston shook his head, brows furrowed. "Colmac and those *things* took it with them." He tied the ends of her reins to one side of his saddle, then Aethan's to the other side, before mounting his horse. "Come on, you take up the rear."

And with that they were off, Triston's dappled grey mare dragging Kura's new mount and Aethan's poor little horse along beside it while Darrow tagged along behind. The raw adrenaline from the fight was fading, but the rage burning in Kura's heart kept her from really feeling the pain in her limbs. Clenching her shaking fists, she fixed her glare on the back of Triston's head.

She hated him. She hated his father. She hated every man who bore on their tunic that black bird and red pointed cross—the mark of the king. This one might have let her live, but he and his company hadn't been so kind to her village, or her family. Kura pressed her eyes shut before the tears escaped. This wasn't the time to cry.

The group meandered out of the ravine and to the banks of a wide river—the Beaduras, most likely. Straight pine trees towered overhead, and Triston led them into the clearing beside the water to continue downstream unhindered.

Kura sighed and made half an effort to tame her fruitless anger. She wasn't dead yet, despite her efforts toward the contrary. And this soldier could very well take her directly past Nansûr, or to her family. Maybe.

In any case, it was going to be a long ride.

Chapter Twenty-Three

Flickering in Firelight

Triston leaned over the fire, stirring yet another tin of that goopy, inedible mash.

He had thought that after securing his prisoner and making a good evening's ride east he would be able to find some sense of peace. Even the greying sunset brought relief from the rain, and cheery stars peeked out from behind the thinning clouds. However, as he took a seat beside the fire—Darrow on his left, his two prisoners on his right—he found himself only more uneasy.

Colmac had deserted. That weighed on him most, maybe because the sudden appearance of monsters long lost to the annals of history was a bit difficult to accept. The one thing he'd always respected about his father's soldiers was their discipline, their loyalty. His father had devoted less oversight to the army in the years since his mother had died, and until now Triston had seen that as a prudent delegation of the burden of kingship. But Colmac wasn't one of his father's men—he was Seren's. Though a brilliant strategist, Seren had never been an inspiring figure. That fact might have finally shown itself out in the field.

This—all of this—reeked of something darker, something deeper, and Triston didn't want to let his mind wander in that direction. Seren, despite his lack of any personal front-line experience, had offered to oversee the garrison in this time of relative peace. Dradge had never asked for it, and only agreed in recent years. Triston smothered a frustrated growl.

When he finally made it back home, Seren had better have answers.

The female prisoner coughed, a deep, wet sound that heralded some kind of illness. Kura—that was her name, wasn't it? Her auburn hair was wet and tangled, her face scratched and dirty, her clothes threadbare and covered in blood, mud, and burrs. He'd been imagining this rebel informant as some sort of spinster, but this woman wasn't any older than he was. She was underfed, but built broad and sturdy—shapely, in her own way. In her eyes shone ferocity, determination—*nobility*, if he dared use that word under these circumstances. But she was certainly the farthest thing from a noblewoman he'd ever met.

She hated him; the bitter glances she stole in his direction whenever she thought he wasn't looking made that painfully clear. And, strangely enough, Triston found he couldn't blame her. He'd wanted to hate her, too, for those of his men she'd killed. But then he had seen how she fought: fearlessly, dangerously, feeding on the primal hope of mere survival.

As though she were in a battle of life and death, and he was death.

Slipping his cloak from his shoulders, Triston rose to his feet and crossed the distance between him and the prisoner. "Here." He extended the cloak toward her. "You look cold."

Kura peered up at him—jaw clenched, lips nearly blue, quivering arms folded against her chest—and anger flashed in her eyes. "I'm not."

Triston stood there, the cloak in his hand, with a sort of wonder. She was so stubborn—stubborn enough to survive... and kill herself in the process. He glanced toward the second prisoner who sat beside her. The Fidelis.

Triston scolded himself for discounting that fact, but looking at the man it was easy to do. He was on the shorter side and scrawny, his hair greasy and disheveled, and his tall cotton boots and leather cloak marked him as nothing more than a Feldlander. A criminal? Yes. Belligerent? Probably. A threat to anyone other than a rival gang? No.

The Feldlander met Triston's gaze, then shrugged, his expression saying enough. *Too little, too late.*

Numb, Triston returned to his seat by the fire. He'd set out on this trip—like a bright-eyed fool—because that was what his father wanted. He'd followed Seren's lead because that was what Seren wanted. Anger swelled in his chest. Was that all he was, a witless puppet?

Darrow's timid voice broke the silence. "Sir?"

"What?"

The young soldier's eyes widened. "I—I think the mash is done, sir."

It was more than done. "Thank you," Triston said, making an extra effort to sound amicable, if only to apologize for snapping. He retrieved the meal and silently divided it among the others. The Fidelis—what was his name, anyway?—gratefully received his bowl and began eating before it had a chance to cool. Kura hardly looked at him as he walked by, and he set the bowl by her feet before returning to his seat by the fire.

Triston let his mash cool then ate in silence, numbly shoveling glops of that grainy mush into his mouth as Colmac's betrayal played over again in his mind. Had he missed the warning signs? What were Colmac and those beasts planning on doing? And those were the easy questions—the tougher ones led him back to Seren, back to the road that'd end in treason, back to the path he wasn't sure he dared to take.

If only there was a way to shut himself up.

Triston glanced at the forest, and for a second his eyes met Kura's. She seemed to be staring aimlessly at the dark forest beyond their camp, but he watched her discreetly and saw that she kept looking at his saddle, behind him, where he'd stuffed her sword.

He chuckled grimly. She was going to try to escape, and he had half a mind to let her. But he hadn't gone through all this trouble just to set her free. Triston placed his bowl aside and retrieved two lengths of rope from his saddlebag before returning to his prisoners.

"It's just a precaution," he said as he knelt down beside Kura. He'd left her hands tied, and now lashed a second rope to those bonds so he could secure her to something solid. He couldn't bring himself to look her in the eye—her hands were frigid—but she watched him with a scowl.

"You treat the others like this?" Her voice came at a near whisper and it shook—with anger, not from the cold. "Or did you just kill them straight off, without all the games?"

"What?"

"The Wynshire. The village. You were there, I saw you."

Triston nodded. There was no use denying it. "We arrested twenty-nine people in the Wynshire. They're passing through Shalford, and I expect they'll be arriving in Avtalyon in about a day for their hearing. Ideally you'll join them, but don't count on this journey taking any less than two days."

Shock flashed across her face. "They're—they're alive?"

This whole time, she thought...? No wonder she hated him. Triston's heart broke, and under very different circumstances he might have up and hugged her right there. "Yes—gods, yes, they're alive. I had no idea you didn't know."

Kura pulled away from him, pressing her knees to her chest and her bound hands to her face. She was trying to hide her tears but he saw them anyway, streaming down her dirty cheeks, and her shoulders shook with muffled sobs. He didn't know what to do; he stood there like an idiot—the other end of her restraints in his grip—as the Feldlander placed his hand on her shoulder.

Sickened with himself and thoroughly embarrassed, Triston finished tying the other end of Kura's rope to the small tree beside his seat. He wasn't going to even glance her way again, but her voice rose over the crackling of the fire.

"I did it."

Bracing himself, Triston met her gaze.

She smeared the tears across her cheeks but didn't look away. "I was the rebel contact, none of them knew anything about it, I—"

"Stop."

Amazingly, she fell silent.

Triston drew in a breath. "You don't know what you're doing. They can't convict you without a confession or two witnesses. I can't say for sure what you'll get for killing soldiers, but if we had no real reason for raiding your village that's something in your favor."

"But I..." And then her eyes widened in understanding.

Triston gave her his best attempt at a smile, and was certain he failed miserably. "You're delirious," he said, kicking the bowl of mash at her feet, "with hunger and cold. And I don't exactly remember what it was you just said."

In silence he bound the Feldlander's—the Fidelis's—hands together and secured the other end of that rope to the tree, too. Then, with a sigh, he retook his seat beside Darrow. The quivering harmony of the night encircled the camp with the darkness, but Triston resigned himself to his familiar, sour thoughts as his focus settled on the flickering fire.

After some time, the Feldlander spoke first. "What do you want with her?"

Triston glanced up absently. Kura had curled up at the base of the tree and appeared to be asleep.

Nothing. That answer came readily, but he realized how foolish that would sound aloud. "She's been charged with inciting rebellion, killing royal soldiers, and fleeing His Majesty's royal forces."

"And what are my charges?"

Triston shrugged. "The same."

He nodded, slowly, and fished a cigarette from his pocket. "Isn't death the penalty for any of that?"

"No. Every Avaronian citizen is entitled to a hearing before the king's bench."

The Feldlander laughed and began chewing on the unlit cigarette stub. "Well, fuck me. Since when?"

"Since always."

"You better tell that to your soldiers."

Triston frowned. "What was your name again?"

"Aethan."

"Well, Aethan." Triston leaned forward. "A lot of men in my position would have killed you out of fear, out of spite, or maybe out of plain old good sense. I didn't, but don't make me change my mind."

Aethan nodded again and sank back against the tree trunk. He didn't look particularly agreeable, but at least he'd given up that smug grin. "Understood."

A soft groan broke the momentary silence. Triston winced when he realized it was coming from Kura, her body shuddering in the cold even as she slept. Drawing in a breath, he rose to his feet with his cloak in his hands, and felt Aethan's gaze on him as he crossed by the fire to gently drape the cloth over Kura's shivering form. She didn't wake up.

"This is a dangerous line you're walking," Aethan said, watching him through narrowed eyes. "You think you're safe, you think you're above it all, but one misstep and you'll end up at the bottom with the rest of us."

Triston didn't look away. "Doesn't make a difference to me whether I'm walking or climbing."

In a groggy daze, Kura found herself awake.

Her limbs were stiff and sore, but she wasn't shivering. She was draped with a cloak—a certain red cloak, the color bright even in the waning firelight. She sat up, fully awake now, and her initial urge was to cast the wretched thing from her as if it were a snake. But the night air was so cold, and she realized she wasn't nearly as warm as she'd thought.

Huddling into a ball, she leaned against the tree at her back. She flinched when she noticed Triston lounging beside a tree on the opposite side of the bed of embers... except he was asleep, his head hanging down to his chest. She suppressed a sigh of relief. It seemed he was supposed to be taking watch, but at the moment she was the only one awake—Aethan's soft snores mingled with the light chirping of the night creatures, and the soldier Darrow was curled up beside the fire.

Kura coughed, softly, and looked in vain for the stars hidden somewhere behind the clouds. *My family's alive.* Her limbs ached with new and old bruises, but somehow that one thought made her discount all of it. That was, if she could trust the word of the Prince of Avaron. She watched his sleeping form with a scowl. Every instinct advised her against it, but that deep—possibly foolish—hope burned in her chest anyway.

Something moved in the trees, and Kura froze.

In the branches, a stone's throw away, blinked a pair of eyes—bright and round as the moons, which glowed a sort of red-tinged yellow in the light of the flickering embers. Saja eyes. They were fixed on Triston.

Kura reached for the sword she ought to have had on her hip, then hesitated as a terrible thought crossed her mind. That saja wasn't after her, not yet, and if Triston was dead she would be free. *Ridiculous.* The saja would kill her, Aethan—all of them. And yet she watched—motionless, quieting her breath—as the wolf-like monster slunk through the darkness.

Disgust settled in her gut. No matter what that saja wanted, she would have no part in it.

She leapt to her feet and flung the red cloak into the embers. The saja snarled and jumped from the branches, but the smoldering cloth burst into flame. She flung the burning material in the monster's direction. "Go away!"

Triston woke with a cry and scrambled to his feet. The ropes binding Kura's wrists to the tree went taut and held her back, but with a shout she continued to swing the flaming cloth at the saja.

"What are you—?" Triston started, angry, then froze as the saja bared its fangs and stuck out his tongue before scampering off into the darkness, its bristled tail disappearing among the silhouettes of the trees.

Kura beat the cloak against the wet grass to put out the fire. Triston ran to her side, stomping the flames into pungent tendrils of smoke.

Darrow latched onto his crossbow with shaking hands. "What happened?"

"Saja?" Aethan asked at the same time.

Kura collapsed to her knees, coughing and struggling to catch her breath. She felt sick, like she'd caught the winter cough. She hardly ever caught the winter cough.

Triston placed a hand on her shoulder as he dropped to a knee by her side. "You alright?"

Kura nodded, forcing strength to her voice. "I'm fine." She laughed, mostly to herself. "Sorry about your cloak."

Triston gave half a grin as he picked up the half-charred cloth from the ground. He shook dirt and twigs loose then wrapped it around Kura's shoulders. "You can keep it."

Kura met his gaze.

She still hated him—at least, she still *wanted* to hate him—but those light blue eyes shone in the firelight, and for the first time she simply saw him as he was. That was uncomfortable; it was easier to hate—but the image burned in her mind. This was not the Prince of Avaron she'd imagined.

"We've got to get moving," Aethan said. "The saja will be back. They always come back."

Triston frowned, then sighed. "You're probably right." He pulled a dagger from his belt and cut Kura's bonds with one swift stroke. She watched him—surprised, but not about to argue—and accepted the hand he offered to help her to her feet.

"We'll be traveling at night, sir?" Darrow asked, his voice quivering.

Triston nodded. "Take heart, soldier! There's four of us."

Chapter Twenty-Four

Not Without Consequences

Kura breathed in the sweet morning air. Dim sunlight peeked over the golden plains, beating back the dark of night, and it was a surprising comfort. They'd spent the night traveling, her wrapped tightly in that singed cloak, her horse plodding along behind Triston while Darrow dragged Aethan and his mare along in the rear.

They hadn't seen another saja since the one she had scared away, but that didn't prove reassuring. Kura made a habit of studying the spaces between the trees, only able to imagine what waited in the shadows. She didn't have a weapon anymore, but she'd torn a few strips of cloth from Triston's cloak and bound them around her forearms. At least when a saja went for her neck, she could give it something less vital to chew on.

"Hey," Aethan called out. "Do you guys eat breakfast or what?"

Triston turned back, his expression distant. He gave a slight nod, then led his grey mare through the thin line of trees between them and the river to stop along the rocky bank. Kura's horse halted beside his, and Aethan and Darrow filled in the space beside her.

Kura coughed as she dismounted, and with stiff limbs took a seat on a large rock a few steps from her horse. Triston, out of what was probably foolish charity, had left her and Aethan's hands unbound since spotting the saja, and she'd been idly contemplating making a run for it the next time the group came to a break. Now, however, it was quite enough to fight the urge to fall asleep.

She was sick; there was no denying that any longer. And maybe she shouldn't be surprised—she'd spent the last few nights on the road, in the rain, with meager meals and precious little sleep.

Aethan flashed her a weary smile, then took a seat on the ground beside her. With the dark bags under his eyes, he looked worse than she felt.

Triston moved silently through the group, passing out a strip of dried beef to each of them. Kura ate her meal in similar silence, deliberately chewing each dry bite as she watched Triston out of the corner of her eye. She couldn't read him; his stoic expression masked anything that might linger in his heart or run through his mind. That was, of course, assuming he was thinking or feeling anything. Kura expected he was—there was a spark of something intangible in his eyes—but he was still Dradge's son, and a soldier at that.

Finally, he wandered downstream to water his horse, and Kura nodded in Aethan's direction. "Sorry I got you mixed up in all this."

Aethan shrugged, taking another bite of his bit of meat. "I made the choice. I don't regret it."

Kura smiled, but couldn't hold his gaze. How should she take that? She still regretted her *own* choices that had led them here. "So you're really a Fidelis?"

"I used to be, anyways."

"Used to be? I saw what you did yesterday."

He chuckled. "This is what you haven't seen." He pulled up his sleeve, and Kura's eyes widened. All along the underside of his forearm a thin, blackish-purple bruise ran downwards in a fractal pattern, resembling some strange imprint of lightning as it followed his veins.

"That looks awful!"

"It feels awful," Aethan said as he pushed his sleeve back over his arm. "But it's what I get for trying to bend the Essence—the *Elaedoni*—to my own will."

Kura gave him a curious look.

"Well, it's been at least several months now since I last did any of my invocations..." He sighed, running his fingers through his hair. "I guess I can say it like this: the *Elaedoni* is a river, and it's moving in one direction. If a Fidelis wants to draft an element, he's got to first find the stream, then figure out how it's flowing, and then he has to get himself moving in the same direction. We can go against the current, for a time, but not without consequences."

"I thought the Essence was supposed to be, you know, a good spirit."

"Oh, for sure. The Essence is the material expression of the immaterial good—the good that creates us, sustains us. It is good—it is *the* good."

Kura frowned, glancing down at Aethan's arm again. "How can you say that after what it's done to you?"

Aethan laughed. "The Essence didn't do that to me, I did. I tried to swim against the current. I can try and bend the *Elaedoni* to my will, and maybe I could for a time, but in the end the strain would kill me."

"See, that doesn't sound very good."

"Maybe not, but no one said I had to try and draft. I *chose* to. What comes from that... well, I knew what I was doing."

Kura nodded thoughtfully. "My mother believes in it—the Essence, I mean. There was never a Fidelis in all of her family line or my father's, but she believes in it anyway."

Aethan looked at her, curious. "She's Láefe, then? I've heard there were once many, back when anyone remembered how the Fidelis died to drive out the dark creatures and make this land worth settling." He shrugged. "But then of course there was the Centaurs' Reconquest, Svaldans are always superstitious, and the royal army has managed to kill most of the rest of us and sully our legacy along the way. The order is dead."

"Well, you're still here."

Aethan gave a small, though grateful, smile. "Officially, though, I'm not Fidelis—I'm *elyir*. Means something like 'tainted'. My father was Fidelis, but my mother was of common blood."

"What difference does that make?"

"Beats me. The Fidelis trait either passes on clearly, or not at all. But there are all sorts of politics involved, and only those directly descended from one of the six founding Fidelis houses are permitted to be trained. My mentor, Féderyc, trained me anyway—in secret—until the damned abbot elect found out and kicked him out of the order." Anger flashed across Aethan's face. "He never should've been in the Feldlands, he was a better man than that. But when his order wouldn't support him and the rebellion worked too slowly, he took matters into his own hands. He formed the

Blackembers, gave us lost kids something to believe in..." He drew in a shuddering breath but didn't look up. "I watched him die. I had a choice: charge in and fight with him, or run and save my own fucking skin. I ran."

Emotion caught in Kura's chest. She had no idea what to say.

He shook his head, still staring at the ground. "I was going to stay the winter in Baza's camp, then keep running... head over the mountains for Kedar and if I didn't make it, then—then maybe that would be alright because I don't deserve..."

"We're heading out in three minutes," Triston said, making both Kura and Aethan jump. He stood close by, his face betraying no emotion as he leaned against his horse's shoulder.

Kura stood and offered Aethan her hand. He stared at her, his eyes red but his expression hopeful. He took her hand, and she pulled him to his feet.

Seated in the saddle, Kura didn't even try to stifle her yawn. It was nearing noon—probably; she caught glimpses of the sun through small breaks in the towering evergreens—but it felt as though they'd been traveling for days. Triston had tried to break up the monotony with bursts of walking and trotting, but when Aethan's little mare couldn't keep up he switched to walking beside the horses for long stretches with the occasional break to ride.

Kura's horse screamed and lurched to the ground.

She tumbled from the saddle and scrambled to her hands and knees in a panic. The horse continued to scream, thrashing about as its wide eyes rolled toward the sky. Kura crawled forward, hands out and ready to do—*something*, but the animal's chest had fallen into a hole. The pit had been dug in a section of loose soil, covered with a thin layer of dirt and branches, and filled with crude wooden spikes. Several glistened red with the horse's blood.

A blur of slobber, teeth, and fur knocked Kura to the ground. She threw her arms up over her face, goading the creature to chomp down on her padded sleeves, then caught it by the neck and rolled over, pinning it to the ground. The saja squirmed, clawing at her as it struggled under her weight, but Kura pressed her knee into the creature's gut and hurled a few solid punches, cracking a rib under her fist.

"Get down!" Aethan's voice mingled with the pounding of horse's hooves, and Kura ducked as he swung a branch over her head to smash a second saja in the face. She scrambled to her feet, coughing and trying to catch her breath, as both wounded saja pulled back, whimpering.

Aethan charged forward with a shout, swinging that branch as though it were a formidable weapon. The saja lunged away, snarling, as even his fuzzy brown mare leapt into the fight—her ears pinned against her neck—and kicked in the nearest saja's direction.

Kura clenched her fists. *I need a sword!*

"Hey!" Triston's voice carried over the fray as though he were a general directing an army. Maybe he thought he was. He drove his horse toward Kura, reins and bloody sword in one hand so he could lean over in the saddle and extend the crook of his arm.

Saja nipping at her heels, Kura grabbed hold of the prince's elbow and swung herself into the saddle behind him. The charger lurched to a gallop as she latched on to the saddle seat to keep from slipping off the animal's back. Aethan and Darrow followed closely behind, saja flanking them on one side and driving them toward the river.

"Hello again, darling."

The voice echoed in the valley. Triston's horse reared up, whinnying in fear; Kura's grip failed and she tumbled to the ground. Saja pressed in but she scrambled to her feet. The horse bucked and pulled back as Triston tried to wrestle it under control.

A woman stood beside the river. A grey cloak shrouded her shadowy figure, thick blonde hair fell in dreadlocks beneath her hood, and her blood-red lips twisted into a smile. *Vahleda.*

Pain shot through Kura's arm and she bit back a cry. Her saja-bite burned, feeling swollen under her hand. She swallowed back nausea, but her legs buckled and she collapsed onto one knee.

"*You are a feisty one, aren't you?*"

With a splash, Triston landed in the river beside her. He scrambled to his feet, muttering curses under his breath as he caught hold of his horse's reins. Saja pressed forward, cutting them off from Aethan and Darrow, and pushed them farther into the river. The nearest beast lunged, snapping at Kura's feet. She jumped back, sloshing her ankles in the icy river water—beside Triston's horse. She tore her sword from the sheath stuffed beneath the stirrups.

"Ah," Vahleda purred, "*there it is.*"

The nearest saja snarled, but Kura swung around and met its advance. She caught the first across the face—it yelped and fell back—and she pressed on against a second, then a third. The beasts circled her an armsbreadth away, the reflection of that red blade flashing in their wide, yellow eyes.

"Why run, darling?" Vahleda's voice was everywhere and nowhere. She stood in the center of the pack, the saja passing through her as though she were a cloud of smoke. "*I'll find you. I'll always find you.*"

Kura charged the nearest saja, severing its head from its body, and just kept hacking at any that stepped into her range as she pushed her way toward the apparition. The woman only grinned.

With a shout, Kura swung her blade through Vahleda's neck. The image rippled, like a reflection on water, but the woman didn't move; her smile didn't falter.

What? Kura froze, then tried again, slashing through Vahleda's midsection with the same result. A wolf sank its teeth into her calf. She cursed and struck at its neck, but the monsters edged in on all sides. She'd let them draw her out.

A thin stream of water swirled around Kura's feet, driving through each of the saja. It was like a whip and a spear at once, and in a matter of heartbeats it brought death to the entire pack. The stream trembled, then fell in a puddle at her feet with the writhing carcasses of the dead saja. The pain in her arm vanished. Vahleda was nowhere to be seen.

Kura let out a breath.

Aethan drove his horse toward her, waving his hand in frustration, even though he slumped over in the saddle.

"Come on!" Triston shouted, leading his horse by the reins to her side.

Kura returned her sword to its sheath under the stirrups and, ignoring the pain in her leg, climbed into the saddle. Triston vaulted up behind her and she stiffened. Uncomfortable was too tame a word to describe riding so close to the Prince of Avaron—with his arms draped over hers to hold the reins—but under the circumstances it couldn't be helped.

Triston's mare lurched to a gallop. The horse's stride pitched her back and forth, and Kura couldn't secure her seat on the awkward front of the saddle. She scrambled to grab hold of the horse's mane but the animal stumbled, jerking her to the side.

Triston wrapped a strong arm around her waist and pulled her back into her seat. "Grip with your knees! We're almost there."

Almost where? Kura glanced forward and spotted a thin trail of smoke rising from the forest not far beyond them. A few more pounding footfalls and she caught sight of the source—a small city, built on the edge of the river, with tall log walls surrounding it on all sides.

Frantically, Kura turned back. Darrow and Aethan were falling behind, and the few lean saja who'd kept the pursuit had pulled into formation behind Aethan's little mare.

She reached for the reins. "We've got to go back!"

"They'll make it!" Triston pulled her hands away and wrapped his arm around hers, holding her back.

"Let go! We've got to—"

Several sharp whistles sounded overhead as small, black darts shot across the sky. The nearest saja fell, arrow fletching in their skulls. Archers stood along the city walls, each of them dressed in the bright red cloak of the royal army. Triston directed his horse toward the open gates, and the animal gave them another burst of speed. Arrows continued to fly, and saja's howls rang out in the forest.

Triston pulled back on the reins as his horse carried them through the gates. The mare's hooves slid on the muddy streets, but they came to a jarring stop before they ran into one of the nearby log cabins. Darrow came charging in after them and veered to the left, followed by Aethan, whose tired little horse came to an abrupt halt beside Triston. As soon as the fuzzy mare's rump cleared the wall, two soldiers slammed the gate closed.

Kura breathed a sigh of relief, which turned into a fit of coughing. The soldiers from the city pressed forward, asking questions, which Triston answered, but Darrow's cry overcame all of it. Blood stained one side of his white tunic, and—was he missing a hand? Triston leapt from the saddle, but Kura had to turn away. It reminded her too much of the night Faron had almost lost his arm, the night her older brother, Benger...

She caught Aethan's gaze as he nudged his mare to stand beside her. He was pale and struggling to catch his breath, but she found herself whispering the question anyway. "Can you do anything?"

Aethan looked down at his trembling hands, then turned back to the young soldier. "I... I can try."

Triston ran to Darrow's side and carefully helped the boy from his horse. Darrow was gritting his teeth to try not to cry—either out of shock or a sense of pride—but tears stained his cheeks anyway, and he swayed under his own weight.

Triston motioned for one of the sentries and slipped an arm under the boy's shoulders. "Where are you hurt?"

Darrow bit back a cry and motioned with a mangled hand to the other side of his neck.

Triston nearly cursed aloud. Some monster had taken a bite out of the boy's flesh; blood soaked his tunic and spurted in rivulets on pace with the heartbeat. He lowered Darrow to the ground, then drew a dagger and cut the binding straps of the boy's plate armor to toss it aside. When the sentry returned with bandages, Triston took and pressed a handful of the cloth against Darrow's wound. "Is there a medic here?"

The sentry shook his head. "I'm sorry, sir. There's only the few of us."

Darrow stifled a cry. "I—my mother, I can't—"

"Steady, soldier." Triston tried not to grimace at the blood soaking through the bandages. "You're going to be fine."

One of the other sentries barked a command. Triston glanced back to find the Feldlander trying to force his way toward him through two armed guards. "Watch that one!"

Aethan sighed and held up his empty hands—both were trembling—as the soldiers reached for their swords. "I just want to help."

Triston frowned. He'd heard many rumors about Fidelis' capabilities, and he wasn't inclined to believe most of them. But maybe that didn't matter. "Bring him."

"Hey!" Aethan exclaimed as the two sentries grabbed him by the arms, dragged him over, then shoved him to his knees at Triston's side. The Feldlander shook himself free of their grip and shot a glare at the nearest soldier. "Nary a charity unspurned, eh?"

Darrow winced as Aethan placed his hands over the wound, but Triston cautiously pulled back to watch. The Feldlander clenched his eyes shut and began muttering under his breath in some other language—the New Tongue by the sound of it, though Triston had never learned more than a few words.

The other soldiers cried out in surprise when Aethan's hands began to glow. Triston fought the urge himself, fascinated. A soft blue glow—the shade of moonlight filtered through the clouds—emanated from Aethan's veins. Then the glow flickered. He winced, biting back a cry, and Darrow screamed.

Triston shoved the Feldlander away from the young soldier. The sentries drew their swords and moved in but Aethan only sat there, panting to catch his breath, then pounded his fist against the dirt. "Fuck!"

Darrow whimpered and tugged at the bandages pressed against his neck. Triston pulled them back and, to his surprise, found the wound changed. Some parts were as red and raw as they had been, but others formed the semblance of a scab or looked to be scars decades old. Though astounding, it was a job half-done, and poorly done at that.

The sentries hauled Aethan to his feet, shoving his arms behind his back to bind his wrists. The Feldlander didn't resist—maybe he couldn't; he just stared with vacant eyes at the young soldier lying on the ground.

Darrow grasped at Triston's sleeve. "Don't…"

Triston pressed the blood-soaked bandages against the wound.

The boy took in a shuddering breath and blinked, slowly. "Don't let me…" He swallowed, his gaze drifting. "Don't…" Darrow's head fell back, and he didn't move again.

Triston held that bandage in place anyway, his arms refusing to move. The blood on his hands felt too familiar. He wanted to wipe it off but couldn't bring himself to do it.

He'd seen plenty of men die, but in the back of his mind he'd always known those lives had been lost for the greater cause—for someone else's cause. His father had directed troop movements. Seren had made that mess in Tarr Fianin. But here... Triston forced himself to look into the boy's dead eyes before closing them, to remember that face no matter how much it hurt.

Here, he had no one to blame but himself.

Chapter Twenty-Five
By Way of the River

The riverboat was a rickety old thing and at the first sight of it, bobbing innocently on the clear blue water of the Beaduras, Kura knew she hated it.

Somehow she hated it more than the ropes digging into her wrists, more than the soldier who carried her slung over his back and tossed her into the bottom of that boat like a sack of grain.

If growing up beside the Everard had taught her anything, it was that rivers were dangerous things. Every year some fool brave enough to wade into those waters died in them, and she knew better than to pretend that anything—even a boat—would be safe. These soldiers, however, did not seem to share her concerns.

One of them—a middle-aged man who jumped at any command given by either his captain or his prince—tossed Aethan, who'd been similarly bound, into the bottom of the boat beside Kura, then climbed into the vessel himself. Kura's stomach lurched as the boat pitched under the man's weight. It would sink, and she'd still have her hands bound.

Triston—his eyes distant, face stern—climbed into the boat last. The silver-eyed old captain came to a salute on the docks beside him.

"Forgive me, sir, but I must again recommend against this."

Triston offered the semblance of a grin. "Duly noted, Garan. But it's probably just looters snagging boats again. I'm sure I can handle it."

The captain's expression didn't change. "Understood, sir. But these are strange times."

Triston nodded thoughtfully, and saluted, right fist over his heart. The soldier returned the gesture, then pushed the boat from the docks. In an attempt to peek over the edge, Kura squirmed atop the sack of Triston's things that had been tossed into the boat before her. She didn't get far and she couldn't see much, but the roof of the small dock house passed overhead, followed soon after by a section of wall, which overhung the river as they drifted out onto open waters.

Aethan hadn't said a word or even moved since settling into his place near the bow. He stared aimlessly, face ashen and eyes dark-rimmed. He'd taken the young soldier's death hard. The entire company had—a few old soldiers had struggled to hide tears as they gave the boy a warrior's burial on the battlefield—but Kura didn't know what to make of her own emotions. The boy had been a king's man, after all, and yet he could've been her brother.

Something whistled near the shore, then an arrow sank into the side of the boat.

"Get down!" Triston jumped into the bottom of the boat, and the soldier at the front did the same.

Kura crouched, but tried to steal a glance at the shoreline. After all, anyone shooting at royal soldiers would likely be a friend of hers. Setting sunlight burned bright in the spaces between the trees, illuminating the empty water's edge. No arrow followed the first.

Guardedly, Triston returned to his seat in the rear by the rudder. He wrenched the arrow from the rail beside him with a frown. "There's something wrapped around the shaft." He unrolled a scrap of paper, then glanced up at Kura. He looked away as soon as their eyes met, then rose from his seat, drew a dagger from his belt, and cut both Kura's and Aethan's bonds.

"Here." He tossed the scrap of paper onto her lap. "It's addressed to you."

Confused, Kura unrolled the parchment. She couldn't understand what it said, but she recognized the symbol drawn in red ink at the top corner: it was the first of the symbols inlaid on her sword. Gallian's sigil. "I... can't read it."

Aethan leaned closer to her, still rubbing his wrists. "Dear Kura of Wynshire, as you can see I could have killed the king's boy a second time, but I will follow your lead and not do so at this time. I pray to the gods you know what you're doing. Meet me at the withering tree at your earliest convenience. Cordially, Skellor." He shot her a sideways glance. "What's all this about?"

"The Varian..." Kura began, then looked over at Triston as she remembered whose company she still kept. Follow *her* lead...? She drew in a breath. That saja she'd chased away in the woods last night—it must have been a Varian. That would explain why there had been only one.

"The Varian?" Aethan laughed in disbelief. "Kura, what on Ehlis were you doing with the Varian?"

She blinked. "They helped me escape Tarr Fianin."

"Is that what those were?" Triston asked. He glanced between them, eyes narrowed; he'd been listening absently since giving her the letter, but it seemed this piqued his interest. "I thought they were saja."

Aethan grunted. "Most would agree with you, actually."

That comment settled the group into an uncomfortable silence. Kura absently rubbed the paper between her fingers, then folded it and shoved it into her pants pocket. It had never occurred to her that Aethan didn't know—or wouldn't trust—the Varian.

She peered over her shoulder, studying the shoreline, searching the sunlit spaces between the trees for whoever had shot that arrow. She didn't find anyone. For a moment she seriously considered jumping over the edge of the boat and trying to swim to shore, but the spike of fear in her chest kept her planted in her seat. She probably wouldn't get far, trying to run through the woods, soaking wet—especially with this cough. And that was assuming she could make it to the shore in the first place.

For a moment she dared to hope the Varian had another rescue attempt planned, but there was a finality to Skellor's letter. They were done plotting; escape was on her, now. She was surprised—and maybe a bit unnerved—to learn they'd been watching over her at all. Kura sighed and folded her arms across her chest. She wasn't ready to give up on the idea of escape entirely, but the more sensible part of her whispered that she'd have to accept the fact that should've been apparent days ago: she was stuck here.

The boat drifted in silence, carried by the current and guided by Triston's rudder. Finally, Aethan scoffed and glanced sidelong at Triston. "You boat much?"

"Yes, actually. Why?"

Aethan scowled and sank lower in his seat. "Oh, I was merely inquiring whether I should expect the king to hang me in a few days, or the river to drown me tonight."

For the first time that day, Kura saw Triston truly smile. "I wasn't going to say anything, but you are looking a little green. Here." He held up his hand. "Rub your thumb on your arm three finger's widths down from your wrist. My mother showed me that—she grew up by the sea. It works for some people."

Aethan frowned skeptically, but did start massaging his arm.

Kura pulled her singed cloak around her shoulders and settled back against the edge of the boat as well as she could. Surely she wouldn't see dry land again until they reached Avtalyon.

Under the circumstances, that could not come soon enough.

"Sir!" The soldier's shout wrenched Kura from a shallow sleep.

She jerked upright, her stomach churning as the boat lurched. The sun hung low behind the mountains, lighting the tall evergreens with a soft red glow.

The soldier pointed over the front bow. "There's something up ahead!"

All eyes turned to look. The river directly before them was smooth, but farther downstream a stretch of stones protruded from roiling, glistening water—and it spanned the entire width of the river.

"Rapids," Triston mused in a voice that was entirely too calm. "But we've had enough rain this year, there's no reason for the river to be so shallow..." He motioned for the sack of his things in the bottom of the boat beside Kura. "Get a good grip on anything you want to keep. If you fall out, swim or float to shore—don't stand up."

Numb, Kura handed him the sack. "I can't swim."

"It's alright. If I say lean, lean with me, and we can probably keep the boat from flipping." Fear twisted in Kura's stomach. Triston must have seen it on her face, as he gave her a semblance of a smile. "Don't worry, if you fall out I can catch you."

She gripped the bench seat beside her with shaking hands. Coming from someone else, that might have been comforting.

Aethan nodded in Triston's direction. "You've done this before?"

"No." The Prince of Avaron nearly grinned. "I've always wanted to."

The boat lurched forward as the current tugged it to the side, and Kura found that she hadn't quite been gripping her seat as hard as she could.

I'm going to die.

It was odd for this to be the first time that thought crossed her mind, but she felt the sickeningly precarious movement of that stupid boat in the pit of her stomach and knew the truth. This damned river would be the end of her.

Triston threw the rudder to the side, whipping the rear of the boat around to set it straight in the current. The river caught hold and the vessel rocked dangerously. Kura held her breath, and if she'd remembered her mother's *andojé* she might have said it.

"Rock!" the soldier shouted just before something crashed into them. Waters raged, timbers splintered, and the impact threw Kura to her knees at the bottom of the boat. She scrambled to her seat, the boat spinning as a wave of ice-cold water splashed across her face.

"Lean left!" Triston's voice echoed over the commotion as the left side of the vessel tilted into the air. Somehow, Kura found herself throwing her weight against the frame of the boat along with the others. The hull sunk back toward the waters, even as the current tossed it forward.

The vessel swung around, the bow dipped beneath the river, and the soldier at the front disappeared in the spray of water illumined gold by the sunset.

It's gone too far—Kura screamed internally—*it's gone too far!*

Triston might have shouted, Aethan and the soldier might have tried to throw themselves up against the side, but in the end it didn't matter. The boat listed, the uncontrollable mass of dark water churned below, and then she was in the river.

A flash of cold came first, then nothing over the roar of the water. She caught a gasp of air, a gulp of water. She flailed wildly, the river bashing her off rocks or logs or whatever else the current buried. The force plastered her up against a rock, tossing her head free. Screaming, she gasped in a mixture of air and water before she was sucked down again. Flashes of light hinted at which way was up or down, but she couldn't fight the river—no one could fight the river.

Suddenly, a strong arm wrapped around her waist. She burst out into the air—that cool breeze warm compared to the river—and fell, her fists clenching gritty soil. She coughed, water spewing from her lungs as raw panic pounded with the heartbeat in her ears.

"You alright?"

Kura rolled onto her side, still coughing. Triston was kneeling beside her. He was soaked; his baggy shirt clung to his arms and streaks of his long black hair stuck to his cheek, but he held her gaze with a genuine sense of concern.

He'd done it. He'd really saved her from the river. She sat up, trying to thank him, but the effort sent her coughing again.

He chuckled and slapped her a few times on the back. "When you said you couldn't swim, you weren't exaggerating."

The setting sun on the other side of the river shone bright in the scraggly undergrowth on the shoreline, and flashed red like fire on the churning river. The soldier jogged from Triston's side to meet Aethan at the riverside.

Aethan laughed and brushed back the mess of wet brown hair from his face as the soldier latched on to his other arm. "Ever vigilant, are we?"

Triston slipped the sack from his shoulder. "We ought to make camp here and get dried off." He glanced into the thick forest around them, then rummaged through his rucksack and tossed Kura her sheathed sword. She almost didn't catch it, thanks to her cold, shaking hands, then could only stare at him in disbelief.

He grinned. "I think I'd rather have *you* kill me than have one of those creatures do it."

Without another word to her, he had the soldier corral Kura and Aethan to a seat on a driftwood log, then went about himself gathering dry branches to build a fire. The sun dipped behind the trees, painting the forest on a harsh canvas of light and shadow. Kura kept her arms pressed against her chest, but she was soaked to the bone and nothing brought her any comfort until Triston finally lit that fire. Even then the warmth struggled to permeate her wet clothes, although she at least managed to massage feeling back into her fingers.

The soldier shifted in his seat. "Where does this leave us, sir?"

"Walking." Triston sighed, then shaded his eyes as he glanced at the horizon. "Shalford's probably closest?"

"Or Dol, sir. Either ought to have horses to lend us. We should be in Avtalyon by tomorrow afternoon."

Kura shivered and tightened her grip on her sword. Triston never should have given it to her. The temptation to draw it was palpable, almost strong enough to make her forget the cold, her trembling limbs, and the fact that she had no idea where she was. But the Prince of Avaron would not let her go without a fight. And if nothing else, she knew she wouldn't kill him.

Maybe she *should* go to Avtalyon. That was where her family was, right? Even the thought of it set her heart pounding. But what would come after that? They'd each be hanged as likely as not, or meet some other unfortunate end. Perhaps seeking the rebellion at Nansûr had been the right trajectory all along.

"Well," a man's voice called out, "look what we've got here now."

Kura leapt to her feet, drawing her sword, as Triston and the soldier did the same.

A man emerged from the forest, a broadsword in one hand and a torch in the other. He was in his early thirties, maybe—older than Kura, but younger than her father. His thin, curly beard tempered the youthful bent of his face.

With a shout, the soldier charged. Two shots whistled from the forest and the soldier fell, an arrow sticking from his neck and temple. Kura cringed, tightening her grip on her sword, and Triston stepped forward with something akin to a snarl.

"Stand down—"

Two more figures emerged from the shadows of the trees. A centaur with a chestnut-colored horse's half nocked another arrow on his longbow. A black-and-tan dog—it might have been a wolf—trailed along at the first man's heels.

The dog flashed the man a toothy grin. "I thought they'd given up on the shipments. But hey, more loot for us."

"Don't move." The centaur's bowstring creaked as he pulled it back to his cheek and trained his arrow on Triston. "Toss that over here."

Reluctantly, Triston obeyed. His sword landed with a thunk in the soil at the centaur's hooves.

Kura blinked and lowered her weapon. A centaur, this far from the Wynshire? "Are you—?"

"And that goes for you too, missy," the centaur said, shifting his aim to Kura's chest.

"You don't underst—"

"Drop the sword!"

With a heavy sigh, Kura tossed her blade onto the ground next to Triston's.

"Well, I'll be..." the man murmured. He pointed at Triston with a gloved hand. "I know who you are." He flashed a smile then bowed dramatically, his loose dreadlocks falling over his shoulders. "Your majesty." He straightened and glanced over the rest of the group with more than a hint of disappointment. "This is it?" His dark eyes fell on Kura, and he frowned. "Wait, don't I know you too?"

Kura hesitated. He didn't look familiar, although there was something about his voice...

The man snapped his fingers. "Yeah, no way! You're the Everard contact."

"What?"

"Yeah, you are! I met you just a couple days ago. You remember, I came with Rusket the bear."

Gods, that seemed like a lifetime ago. "I never saw your face."

"Renard..." The centaur nodded toward Triston with a frown. The man looked over and his smile faded.

"Aw..." He gave a heavy sigh and met Kura's gaze in disappointment. "You sold us out, did you? Is that what happened out in the Waste?"

"No, I wouldn't—"

"They all say that," the centaur said, training his arrow on Kura's chest again. "I say we shoot them now and be done with it."

Renard shrugged. "The girl deserves to tell her side of the story."

"I'll just shoot the rest of them, then," the centaur agreed, turning his bow back toward Triston.

"Hey, we can at least ransom him." Renard turned to study Aethan. "Nope, don't know you."

Another figure pushed her way to the front of the group. Though shorter than the rest, the deep purple cloak shrouding her petite figure gave her an elegant air that was more than out of place in this company. She hesitated beside the body of the dead soldier, but with a shudder pressed forward to point at Kura's discarded sword. "Look!"

Renard squinted at the weapon. "What?"

"Her sword!"

Curious, Renard picked up the blade, and his eyes grew wide. "Oh, Trofast is going to want to see this." He turned back toward his group. "Let's go, guys. Pack up what you can salvage."

"But I don't thi—" the centaur began, his bow still trained on Triston.

"No—stop!" Renard waved his arm in the line of fire. "No shooting anybody else."

The centaur frowned, but sighed and lowered his weapon.

"They oughta be blindfolded," the dog said, leaning toward Renard in what she likely intended to be a whisper.

Renard nodded. "Do it."

The centaur pulled scraps of cloth from the pouch on his belt, but Kura held up her hands and stepped back. "Wait, just listen for a second—"

The centaur grunted. "Save it. Come peaceably, and I might not throw you back in the river."

Kura let out a frustrated sigh. Peaceably. Right.

Chapter Twenty-Six

The Council of Nansûr

Kura gasped in a breath of cool, musty air as someone yanked the burlap sack off her head and shoved her from behind. She stumbled through a set of iron bars and fell to her knees on the dusty floor. Both Aethan and Triston had been prodded into the holding cell before her—Aethan crawled to the side, away from the door, while the Prince of Avaron kept his balance and leveled an annoyed glance at their captors—though except for the bars on one side, the space more resembled a cave.

"Hey, be careful will ya?" Renard muttered to someone.

Kura pushed herself to her feet, stifling a cough as she met his gaze. That centaur still stood at his side, a torch on the hallway wall emphasizing the creases in his face as he frowned. Renard gave her an apologetic shrug and the centaur slammed the cell door closed.

"Hey!" Kura lunged to catch hold of the cold metal bars. "I was sent here—"

"Save it," the centaur said with a swish of his tail. "We've seen your kind before, and we'll see them again. Pray you leave here with your life."

Renard rolled his eyes. "Ignore him. His people have a flair for the dramatic. This is just a precaution."

A large shadow shifted at the far end of the hallway, followed by a deep, echoing growl. Kura stiffened as a bear lumbered into the torchlight. It wasn't just any bear—it was Rusket, the nostkynna she'd met in the Wynshire.

She watched Renard follow the centaur down the hallway, then shuddered as she forced herself to look the bear in the eye. "I didn't betray you. I would never—"

"I know." The bear sank lazily onto his haunches. He spoke through clenched teeth, attention fixed on anything but her. "The last man assigned to contact you in the Waste was one of several captured by royal soldiers a few weeks ago. I'm sure he or one of the others gave you up."

Kura wanted to relax, but the beast's acrid tone made that difficult. "I've been trying to find this place for days, actually. Maybe we can strike some kind of—"

Rusket snarled. "Enough, child. I lend no ear to bargaining. If we see the same cause worthy, then perhaps you will fight at my side. Beyond that I have no care for you."

Kura could only stare into the bear's dark eyes, mouth agape, as she tried to channel her growing rage into coherent thoughts. "I sacrificed *everything* for your cause."

"Everything?" Rusket tilted his head. "While you yet draw breath?" Kura started to speak, but the bear rose on all fours and shoved his snout as near to her face as the bars allowed. "There are more lives to lose than just the ones you happen to love."

He turned away and retook his seat with a huff, but Kura glared at his back. Everything he said was so wrong, but she couldn't shape her anger into words.

"This was a mistake," Aethan whispered to himself. Triston stood beside the bars, leaning against the cave wall with his arms folded as he casually surveyed their surroundings, but Aethan sat in the corner, his knees pressed to his chest. "This was a mistake. *L'cenóri n'obleri gemeye.*"

"What are you saying?"

His wide eyes met hers. He was terrified. "You don't know, do you? Though... why should you?" He drew in a shuddering breath. "You can't tell them what I am."

Baffled, Kura nodded.

A door clanged at the end of the long hallway. She spun around as an old centaur emerged from the darkness, two men at his flanks like paupers lagging behind their king. Scars marred the blue-roan fur on his horse's half and intricate black tattoos covered his lean human torso. Rusket lowered his gaze as the centaur approached, then stepped aside.

The centaur casually chewed a stalk of grass as he stopped before those iron bars, and Kura balked when his dark eyes came to rest on her. Something about him was familiar—not that she'd met him before, but that sharp, cleanshaven face framed by wiry black hair reminded her of someone else: Konik, the leader of the centaurs in the Wynshire.

"So." He shifted the stalk of grass to the other side of his mouth. "You are the one who found the sword."

"Uh, yes, sir."

He snorted. "I was envisioning someone quite different." He jerked his chin toward Triston and Aethan. "Who are your friends?"

"Oh, well, they're..." Kura began, then realized she didn't know where she was going. "The first is not my friend. I, um, was his prisoner until I became yours."

The centaur chuckled, though his expression didn't change. His focus lingered on Aethan, who rose apprehensively to his feet. "And him?"

"He's, uh, my guide across the Feldland plains."

"Hmm." The centaur motioned toward the bars, and one man beside him stepped forward to unlock the cell door. "Well, come on." He beckoned to Kura as he turned down the hallway.

She took a step to follow but paused in the threshold, glancing back to catch Aethan's eye. He almost reached for her—his expression screamed for her to stay—but she couldn't be sure if his fear was for her or for himself. She shrugged and did her best to give him a reassuring smile.

Rusket slammed the bars shut behind her.

Setting her jaw, Kura followed the centaur into the dim hallway, leaving all the others behind. He didn't even give her a second glance. They walked past a flickering torch and into the shadows, toward an open archway leading into another hallway just as long and narrow as the first. Kura drew in a startled breath. That wasn't a torch—it was a flame, but it was no torch. The fire itself emanated from a nick in the wall, as though it were burning the stone or the air.

The centaur managed the ghost of a smile when he caught her staring. "It's fitting a child of man should be so fascinated by that, when a lenêre stone would be twice as bright and half as dangerous."

Kura met his gaze but found herself unable to hold it. He sounded amused, but in his eyes she saw nothing but indomitable restraint, a veritable fence through which no emotion dared to slip. He nodded toward the end of the hallway, and like a dog tailing its master she did as directed.

Silently, the centaur led her down several winding hallways, each resembling the last, until a soft white light replaced the fire-lit darkness. It resembled sunlight, but the light itself emanated from glowing veins of stone which wove across the cave walls, just another layer in the mountainside.

Lenêre stone, the same as N'hadia had had back in the Wynshire. Kura traced her finger along the glow as she walked. There was no heat, only light. The vein wandered along the wall, then disappeared in the light of the room at the end of the hall. A murmur of conversation echoed past the open doors, but it fell to silence as soon as the centaur stepped through the archway. Hesitantly, Kura followed.

A domed ceiling—every handbreadth painted with colorful abstract patterns—overhung a massive, half-circle stone table. The veins of lenêre stone wound around the room like misshapen spider's webs, rendering the room as bright as a summer's day. The bench seats were largely empty, and as the centaur made his way to the head of the table, most of those seated around it put aside their food and papers and rose to their feet.

"Trofast!" Renard exclaimed, looking up with his mouth half full of some sort of stew. "Damn it, just when I thought you were going to be late."

The centaur frowned. "I'm sure you'll be able to fill your stomach later."

Trofast. Kura peered up at the beast-man with new appreciation. The centaurs in the Wynshire had feared his name, and the Varian hadn't seemed too friendly with him either. She stole a glance at the others as she tried to keep her freezing hands from shaking. There were two men, including Renard, and then the dog and the girl she'd met by the river.

The group retook their seats and Trofast fixed his piercing gaze on Kura. "Your name."

"Kura of Wynshire."

"With what intention do you stand before us today?"

Kura glanced from face to face, as if in those expectant stares she'd get a clue of what answer they were looking for. She let out a breath. "By complete accident, I came to find the sword Ìsendorál. I've brought it here to you, so you can find someone to wield it."

A heavy-set man in flowing blue and gold robes frowned. "You make no claim to it?"

"No, I do not."

Trofast inspected her with what might have been a wry smile. "Two men came to me with a sword like this, though not this one I think, and neither of them managed to wield it. Still, the last purported sword-bearer lives on today. Perhaps you've heard of him? He is Dradge, son of Rhowan, King of Avaron."

Kura burst out laughing despite herself, but stopped as she found herself the only one. "That can't..."

Trofast gingerly lifted the sword, still housed in the battered old sheath, from the table before him. "You stole this?"

"No sir, I..." Kura started, then hesitated as she recalled the exact circumstances. "I just needed a sword. I didn't know what it was. This has all been some strange twist of fate..."

Trofast grunted. "I do not believe in fate, nor do I trust in circumstance. Something has brought you here, Kura of Wynshire, but whether it is for good or ill I do not know."

The dog shook her head and hopped up to brace her front paws on the table, her rear paws resting on the bench seat. "She reeks of saja blood, Trofast. If that's the kind of enemy she keeps, then she's well on her way to being a friend of ours."

"Grenja, if only it were so simple." Trofast drew the sword from its scabbard. The lenêre stone's light reflected dully in the rusted blade, and his eyes narrowed as they fell on Gallian's sigil near the hilt. "Child, do you know why I bear these marks on my skin?"

The intricate patterns on his body aligned with white gashes, not to cover the scars but accent them, decorate each with the impressions of vines, flowers, or other shapes—placing them in prominence.

Kura shook her head, and as hard as she tried, she couldn't hold his gaze. "No, sir."

"Each commemorates a wound that I received in defense of my people. A mark of honor, as such a pursuit deserves fitting recognition." He ran a finger across Ìsendorál's fuller. "I tell you this for two reasons: the first is so that you understand the price I am willing to pay in order to defend those I love and what I believe, and the second to show you this." Trofast lowered the weapon and lifted his right arm. A white gash, far more grievous than any of the other scars, ran across his ribs. It had not been decorated. "This I received at the hands of the last ones who came to me bearing a sword of this name, and while it did not take my life, it has taken any idle trust others may have afforded you before now."

Kura nodded respectfully. "I understand, sir." She held his gaze this time, even as she had to press her cold arms against her chest to keep from shaking. "But I hope you understand that I too bear scars, although you may not see them, and I earned them by bringing this sword to you."

Trofast nodded, thoughtfully, and laid the bare blade on the table. "What is it you want, then? Money?"

"No, sir. I only hoped you might be able to—"

The centaur laughed, but his ears were pinned against his neck. "So you do want something. That is just as well. Your kind has a saying: a horse without a driver carries his cart into the ditch. Though I must point out that a poor driver produces the same result. Whether you intend to hold the reins or not, I'm afraid we must ask you to try. But I promise, no matter the end, you will be justly rewarded."

Kura studied Trofast's face, a lump forming in the pit of her stomach. She couldn't be sure if he intended to wish or well or to threaten her, but either way he meant what he said. "What do you want to ask me, sir?"

Trofast nodded to the man in the colorful robes. With his immaculately clean hands and oiled brown hair tied behind his head, he looked like a scholar among soldiers. However, his angular green eyes were stern and as they scrutinized her.

"When were you born?"

Kura blinked. "I'm twenty—"

"I didn't ask how old you are, I asked when you were born. In what season?"

She tried to hold back a frown. "Fall."

"Your trade?"

"Uh... farming. I guess."

His eyebrow twitched. "And what about your parents?"

"My father was a soldier and my mother was a bard."

"Lovarian soldier?"

"No." Kura shook her head fervently. "In Dradge's army. Before I was born, though."

The man clenched his jaw and looked down at the table before him. "Thank you."

A wide grin broke across Renard's face. "She passed your test, didn't she, Erryl? What did I tell you, huh? What did I tell you?"

The man scowled but didn't reply.

What test? Anxiety shot through her veins. The forebears' prophecy—Skellor had recited the thing to her only days before. All those lines about autumn, scythes and swords, of black birds and Ìsendorál... The fonfyr was Fidelis, a hero of epic proportions, more than anyone—much less an unlucky sword-thief—could possibly dream of being. "Look, I'm not the fonfyr, I already told you—"

"And we heard you, child," Trofast said softly. He picked up the sword, then handed it hilt-first to the girl in the purple cloak seated beside him. "Test her."

The girl rose, pulling back her hood to release curling black hair. She had dark skin, a shade lighter than Renard's, and a round, innocent face. She reverently took the sword into her hands, and her bright green eyes met Kura's for only a moment as she held out the weapon.

"Careful, Idris," Erryl muttered.

Kura frowned in his direction, but the girl didn't pay him any mind. She placed the hilt in Kura's hand, then took a deep breath and stepped back.

"I'm going to say some words. Can you repeat them for me?"

There's no getting out of this now, is there? Kura sighed. "Alright." She grasped the sword hilt with both hands and stepped into a simple guard stance.

Idris took a shuddering breath, then began to speak. "*Ettere fonfyr dar les deamyur.*"

"*Etterie fonfyr dare less...*"

Idris laughed quietly, a smile piercing her solemn expression. "Sorry, I'll try again. *Ettere fonfyr.*"

"*Ettere fonfyr...*"

Kura did her best to repeat the words. They were strange and flowing, the vowels softer and the cadence slower than Ristaer. As the final syllables rolled off her tongue, energy surged through her veins. It was as though she'd been hit by a wave of water, but instead of knocking her aside, the force became part of her.

The sword burst into flames.

Kura screamed and threw the weapon to the ground. She turned to the others in panic, but they were staring at the sword. Bewildered, she looked down. The blade was no longer on fire, and it was also no longer chipped and rusted. The fuller shone with a line of swirling, engraved letters that burned red like fire, and the blade itself glistened like gold.

"My god..." Renard murmured.

No one seemed to have anything more to add.

As they all watched, rust grew on the blade again, creeping like ice from the hilt, up the fuller, and towards the point. The edge itself seemed to remain sharp and the steel still glistened with a mute gold beneath the marred surface, but apparently the transformation wasn't strong enough to last.

Idris covered her hands with her cloak, then gingerly retrieved the sword from the dusty cave floor. Kura cringed as the girl held the hilt toward her again. *All this time, I've been carrying that?*

"Again," Trofast said, his face stern.

Grimacing, Kura wrapped her cold fingers around the hilt. Idris recited those strange words and Kura again tried her best to repeat them, her heartbeat increasing with every passing second. She kept her attention fixed on that blade, and gradually everyone and everything else faded into the periphery.

Red light flickered in the lettering by the hilt. It swept up the fuller, intensifying as each letter illuminated, until the blade burst into flame. Kura's first impulse was to toss it away again, but against her better judgment she held on. The flames danced before her eyes, as bright and natural as any fire she'd ever seen, but what was it burning? The blade continued to shine, as gold as the autumn sunrise shimmering on calm waters.

Then she felt it: a strain, not just in her muscles but every part of her, as if she were running—sprinting, winded, and with all her strength—up the steepest mountain, although she hadn't taken a step since the blade had caught fire. She gasped for breath, her limbs shook, and the flame on the blade flickered.

The next thing she knew, she was sprawled on the council room floor.

Several voices filled Kura's ears, but she hardly heard them. She rolled onto her side, her chest heaving, and forced her eyes open. The world was a blur of light and darkness, but she blinked a few times, hard, and the hazy image of Idris's face came into focus. The girl was kneeling over her, saying something to the rest of the council.

Kura tried to sit up, but even Idris's slender arm was enough to hold her down.

"It's alright," the girl said with a tight smile, her voice oscillating in panic. "You'll be alright."

Kura doubled her efforts and forced herself to a seated position.

"Hey, kid, take it easy." It was Renard on her other side with a look of sympathy, supporting her with his arm. "Can you stand?" He offered her his hand and she took it, but even with his help she used all her strength to get back to her feet.

"Tend to her, Idris," Trofast said. Something had changed in his expression—it wasn't sympathy, but maybe close to it.

"No." Kura feebly tried to force herself out of Renard's grip. "I won't go, not without my friends."

Trofast's eyes narrowed. "So now you do call Dradge's son your friend?"

Kura paused. She hadn't meant it like that, but what else was she supposed to say? "If I must, to have him treated decently."

Trofast held her gaze, then nodded. "Alright." He turned to Erryl. "See to the both of them as well, and return here on the hour."

Chapter Twenty-Seven

Bellicosity

Kura's head dropped to her chest, startling her awake. She drew in a deep breath and snuggled deeper into the thick, warm blanket draped over her shoulders. Idris and Renard, with an armed escort, had brought her to this rickety old chair in a small, dimly lit room and then promptly left—although someone stood guard in the hallway beside the open door.

That would have bothered her a few days ago, but now she was just grateful for the quiet and the chance to catch up on some sleep. The fire on that blade had burned away any energy she'd had left, and it felt like she'd need to nap for a week to get it back.

Some soft sound caught her attention. Kura blinked and found Idris standing at her side, holding a steaming mug. The girl smiled shyly and held out the drink. "It should help with the fatigue, and your cough."

"Thank you." Kura took the mug and straightened in her seat. *How long was she standing there, waiting for me to notice?* Carefully, she sipped the scalding liquid. Warmth shot through her as she swallowed, but the flavor was both bitter and sweet, like honey mixed with some horrible spice that didn't blend with the others. She grimaced and took another sip.

"I'll get you something to eat." Idris shuffled to the other side of the room, where wooden shelves stood beside the tapestry on the wall, and returned with a few slices of brown bread on a plate. Kura nodded in thanks and took two of them.

"This is her?"

Idris jumped, nearly dropping the plate, as a woman in a worn cloak and muddy knee-high boots stepped through the doorway.

Grey peppered the stringy brown hair she'd tied behind her head and wrinkles collected around her lips as she frowned, but she stood tall and her piercing green, angular eyes surveyed the room with a bearing that rivaled Trofast's.

"Erryl sent me," the woman continued, shaking the cloak off her shoulders to hang it on a hook beside the wall. Her tunic and trousers were threadbare and mud-stained, though the embroidery on the sleeves sparkled with a hint of silver. "Because of course we can't expect him to get up off his ass, even in times like this."

Idris nodded respectfully and set the bread aside to come to a sort of attention at the woman's flank. Kura hesitated mid-bite as the woman leered over her. Trofast had seemed to look through her, past her facades and into her heart, but this woman looked *beyond* her, as if there was nothing to find behind the facade in the first place.

"Well," she scoffed, "she's not even elyir."

Idris nodded again. "Yes, Prior Devna, but—"

The woman snapped her fingers. "Stand up."

Kura scowled, but Devna didn't blink. Sighing, Kura shoved the pieces of bread into her mouth to hold them, then forced herself to stand on wobbly knees. Idris jumped forward to steady her, but Devna shooed her away.

"Malnourished." She prodded at Kura's arms. "Overworked." She gripped her chin, tilting her face to inspect it. "I probably wouldn't find a drop of highborn blood in your family line even if I traced it back to the ancestors your ancestors left on the other side of the ocean."

Kura pulled herself out of the woman's grip, still scowling, and took a bite from her bread. "If it's a destrier you're after, you'd better look elsewhere."

Devna laughed, her smile sharp like a cat baring its teeth. "Who put you up to this? That bastard Cynwrig?"

"She's—" Idris shuddered, then straightened her shoulders. "She's here of her own volition."

Devna gave the girl a sideways glance, but seemed satisfied with her explanation. She shook her head, then turned to grab her cloak by the door. "At least patch her up, would you? We can keep our puppet in one piece a bit longer."

Kura sank to her seat with a huff as the woman strode into the hallway. "Who was that?"

"Devna of the fifth branch, prior elect, of House Randre." Idris muttered something under her breath as she gently pulled the blanket over Kura's shoulders. "I apologize, she's like that with everyone."

"That's alright," Kura mumbled, shoving her last bite of bread into her mouth.

Idris crossed the room, picked a small jar off the shelf, then returned to Kura's side. "I can help you, like she said, if you want."

Kura watched the girl with growing wonder. Her small stature and meek demeanor made her easy to dismiss, but she had Aethan's same bright green eyes and a certain poise when she spoke. "You're Fidelis, aren't you?"

Idris nodded, shyly meeting Kura's gaze for a moment. "I am of the seventh branch, born of House Singan and House Appris. Are you familiar with draft healing? I noticed you are traveling with an elyir."

I didn't sell you out, Aethan! "Um... I'm not familiar with it, no."

Idris nodded. "Can I ask you to remove your tunic?"

Muscles protesting, Kura slipped her gambeson over her head and set the soggy jacket aside. She shivered as the cool air met her damp shirt, and that reminded her of the old arrow wound in her shoulder. Her shirt was just as torn and stained as the gambeson, but fresh blood marked the wound.

Idris drew in a sharp breath and pulled a stool up beside Kura's chair. "Can I ask you to move your shirt?"

Kura tugged her baggy shirt over her shoulder to expose the wound. The bruise's color had shifted to a pale yellow-green, but the past few days had not been conducive to the healing process. Several of the stitches had popped loose; the scab's edges were raw and weeping, and she had to wonder how it didn't hurt more than it already did.

The girl winced as she inspected the wound. "The Cenóri tended to you?" She almost sounded surprised.

Kura nodded.

From her pocket, Idris produced a small knife, pointed blade curved like a seamstress's thread-cutter, and a pair of tweezers.

"Will you allow me to remove the stitches?"

Kura simply nodded again, and eventually had to look away as Idris delicately broke each stitch with her knife and removed it with her tweezers. The girl was incredibly gentle, but Kura could still feel each strand slide out of her skin.

Finally, Idris set her tools aside. She picked up a clay jar beside Kura's chair leg, removed the lid to scoop out a handful of salve, then spread the oily substance over her hands. It filled the room with the faint scent of peppermint. "Some things serve as a conduit for the Essence's movement," she explained, catching Kura's stare.

"Like the sword?"

Idris grinned, as if Kura had said something funny. "Ìsendorál is the original conduit. With it the very first Fidelis, Gallian, drafted fire from the sky and brought an end to the darkness that had reigned on this land for generations before. Hence its name, ìsen, which is used to describe the force of the water flowing in a fast river, and dorále, which means lightning." She hesitated, her hands hovering before Kura's shoulder. "This might hurt a little."

Kura stiffened as Idris's hands made contact with her skin, but the salve was warm and it didn't hurt as much as she was expecting.

Idris closed her eyes and began to speak quietly in that same flowing language she'd had Kura recite earlier. A subtle green light flicked in her hands, following her veins, and gradually a warmth seeped into Kura's shoulder. She set her jaw and tried not to fidget. It didn't hurt, but it wasn't pleasant—like a stiff muscle stretched a hair too far. And it itched.

Finally, Idris opened her eyes and leaned back, releasing Kura's shoulder. Only a jagged white scar remained. Grinning, Kura traced it with her fingers; even that didn't hurt. It should have belonged to an injury received years ago, not days. "How…?"

"The healing process quickens your own body's abilities. It's nothing you wouldn't have done on your own with enough time. It's fortunate the wound was several days old. I would not have been able to heal it entirely if it were fresh, as I can only do so much at one time." Idris motioned to Kura's arm. "I can still tend to that as well, if you'd like."

Kura rolled up her sleeve and held out the saja bite. The toothmarks themselves were fading, but deep purple bruises still marred most of her forearm. Idris rubbed more salve onto her hands, grasped Kura's arm, then began whispering again in her strange tongue.

Every muscle in Kura's arm contracted. She grimaced against the pain, her fingers spasming out of control. Idris yelped and pulled back.

Kura rubbed her arm as the muscles settled. The bruises were as dark as ever, and if anything, the bite felt worse.

"You denied her..." Idris stared, eyes wide. "You didn't believe in any of it, and you still denied her..."

Kura frowned, waiting for an explanation, but Idris picked up the jar with shaking hands and jumped up to return it to the shelf. Pressing her arms against her chest, Kura sank into her seat as she massaged her hand. She should have known better than to let the girl mess with that helry bite.

"I—I'm sorry," Idris started, still facing the shelves. "It scared me, is all. I wasn't expecting..." She turned, shaking hands at her side, but couldn't look her in the eye. "There is a gift that runs in House Appris. Well"—she laughed bitterly and began pacing along the wall—"a gift is what they call it, but my mother calls it a useful burden and I call it a curse. The *Elaedoni* is always, is timeless, and so sometimes, when I touch something, I see what has been, what may be, or what will be." She paused, twirling her finger through her hair. "I saw you find the sword when I touched it. Trofast asked me to do it before he brought you in. He already knew everything, because I'd told him, but he asked you anyway because he thought you'd lie. They all thought you'd lie, but I knew you wouldn't. Not about this."

Kura studied the girl with growing appreciation. Her appearance commanded no presence, but maybe it should. "Why did they think I'd lie?"

Idris met her gaze quizzically. "You laughed when Trofast told you. King Dradge made a false sword and used the lore of the prophecy to trick the Fidelis into fighting alongside him against Hilderic. Our last abbot elect, Cynwrig of the fifth branch, born of houses Gallian and Randre, helped him make that sword. But the sword you brought us... well, you saw it for yourself."

Kura swallowed. "...What exactly did I see?"

Idris paused, chewing her lip, then retrieved a small wooden box from the shelves. "They will argue for ages about you." She laughed, mostly to herself. "Many won't even train elyir, much less someone of common blood." She pulled open the intricately carved lid. Inside was a pile of trinkets—stones, bits of metal, twigs, sand, charcoal. "This is a testing set. Try it. Does anything call out to you?"

Kura glanced between the box and Idris's face. She wouldn't deny that the thought of obtaining such mystical power was enormously compelling, but her muscles still ached from whatever that sword had done to her.

Idris waited expectantly.

Stifling a sigh, Kura shoved her hand in amongst the trinkets. "Am I supposed to say something?"

Idris shook her head, staring at the box. "Drafting is just a matter of focus."

"But with the sword, you had me—"

"That was in Áclomere—the New Tongue—a few lines from the Forebears' prophecy. Speaking in the original tongue can greatly help with focus. I wasn't sure what you should say, I suppose only Gallian would really know, but true prophecies are powerful things."

"Áclomere?" Kura tentatively removed her hand from the box.

"It is the language of *lumere*, truth, although some translate it as 'light'. They say it is the language in which the Essence spoke when it moved the world into existence. Fidelis learn it as we learn to draft: it connects us both to the material world and to the *temper*—to that of the spirit." She picked the hunk of charcoal from the box and placed it in Kura's open hand. "Maybe you have an affinity for fire."

Kura let out a long breath and clenched her fist around the charcoal.

Idris watched her intensely. "Do hear anything? Do you feel anything? Most describe it as a shiver and then a sudden surge of strength."

Kura shook her head.

Idris sighed and returned the charcoal to the box, mumbling something to herself.

"Idris?" Renard knocked on the door frame, then took a half step into the room. "Trofast is starting everything up again." His grinned at Kura. "Hey, kid, you feeling up to it?"

"Yeah." Kura shoved herself out of the chair. She swayed a little with the sudden change in elevation, but did her best to hide it.

Renard laughed, not unkindly. "Very good." He nodded and gave what almost looked like a salute. "Take your time, I'm sure we're not missing much."

Kura followed at Idris's side as the girl wandered down the shadowy cave hallway. Her first few steps had been embarrassingly shaky, but she'd gradually regained her balance. It felt like she'd run for a half a dayride, but at least she could stand on her own.

Absently, Kura ran her fingers along the silver leaf embroidery on her black cloak. Idris's final insistence—besides leaving the guards behind at the door—had been this change of clothes. The grey tunic was worn at the elbows and the riding pants were dusty, but Kura couldn't remember ever wearing any clothes as fine as these. She'd hastily braided her hair in an attempt to match.

A lone tongue of flame burned in the empty hallway, and Kura motioned to it as they walked past. "Idris, how…?"

The girl glanced up, blinking as though she'd been pulled from thought. "It's just air, really. Although not the kind you can breathe. It seeps up sometimes from deep within the ground, and so Fidelis have harnessed it into channels to make fire. That flame should burn for years without ever having to be refueled or relit."

Fascinated, although not altogether convinced, Kura watched the flame until Idris led her around the next bend. In this hallway, paintings—of the sky, animals, people, centaurs, and strange creatures—covered the smooth walls and tall ceiling. Some were cracked with age, while others stood out with bright colors and intricate designs.

Kura slowed her pace to gingerly touch one of the images. It was a large, scaly, winged beast flying over a mountain-top, spewing fire on the trees painted below. "What is this place?"

Idris glanced up at the walls with a smile, as if she had forgotten until that moment the paintings were there. "This is Ven'yn, or 'place of the remembering'."

Some images were beautiful—noble ladies lounging on flower-speckled hillsides, the night sky lit with a thousand stars; some were simple depictions of farming or house-building, while others were bloody, with armies of men and centaurs and monsters clashing across wide battlefields. Far above Kura's head a centaur, his paint faded with age, stood on a pile of human bodies, a man's severed head in one hand and Ìsendorál in the other.

Her stomach twisted. That centaur looked too much like Trofast.

"They'll be waiting for us," Idris said quietly as she glanced down the hallway. Kura nodded, ignored the remaining artistry, and quickened her pace.

The glow of lenêre stone lit the end of the hallway, and one final turn brought them back to the wide, open doors of the council chambers. Angry voices echoed from the room, but Trofast's voice carried over the rest.

"Silence!"

The group fell silent even before his command finished reverberating in the hallway.

Tentatively, Kura stepped into the chambers, followed closely by Idris. Books and parchments that had been neatly stacked on the table were now mostly scattered about—on the floor, against the wall—as if the argument had been even more heated than she'd heard. Aethan stood at the front of the table, on display, as it were. He was still dressed in his wet and tattered clothing and wore a brave expression—although Kura knew him well enough at this point to see the fear hiding in his green eyes. His gaze met hers, and he smiled in relief.

"Quite an ally you've made," Erryl mused, folding his hands across his stomach. "He wouldn't speak without you. Perhaps you need to corroborate your stories?"

Kura frowned and stepped forward to stand at Aethan's side. "You—"

"Enough." Trofast sighed. "Do any of you wonder where we would be today if we were all not such petty, bickering creatures?" He fixed his dark eyes on Aethan. "Tell us, who are you and what brought you here?"

"I'm Aethan, of Arléast, and I came here following the sword."

Grenja's face twisted in a snarl. "What do Feldlanders care for the sword? Don't think I wouldn't recognize your smell from a half-dayride away."

Aethan glanced down at his boots as he shuffled them on the dirt floor. "The call of freedom is not bound by race or homeland."

Erryl chuckled, but his eyes narrowed. "A Feldlander wouldn't know freedom any more than he's able to steal it."

"If he wants to follow the sword, let him," Renard piped up. He sat with his elbows on the table and his head in his hands. Until he'd spoken, Kura had assumed he was asleep. "We're short on fighting men as it is."

"I..." Aethan took a hesitant step back.

Kura looked at him in surprise. He still wanted to leave.

In the back of the room, Idris mumbled something to herself. Trofast looked to her, his eyes soft, and motioned for her to return to the empty seat at his side. With flushed cheeks and slumped shoulders, she reluctantly obeyed.

"You're from House Bryfoc?" she asked.

Aethan's eyes widened. He glanced, almost in accusation, at Kura, but the look gave way to a stubborn frown. "House Singan, actually. *L'Cenóris n'obleri gemeye, dí l'Fidelis átou nian.*"

Those words echoed in the room. Erryl straightened in his seat, pensive. Idris folded her hands, lowering her head to press her lips against them.

"My people do not forget, do they?" Trofast smiled, but it was a look devoid of mirth and entirely out of place on an otherwise stoic face. "And yours are right to remember. But in your remembering of the past, you neglect the present, and despite our efforts my people have forgotten what we were."

Aethan stiffened, but remained silent.

"I will not lie," Trofast said. "I have shed Fidelis blood for the merit of its nature, and I have fought in the Reconquest as is my place as firstborn among my father's sons. But there came a day when I limped back to my mother's house, covered in both my own blood and that of your kind, and it struck me that I could not determine the difference. I have paid dearly for that realization, but so do all those who seek the truth in this world of darkness, and I accept that for what it is. Some things are never forgotten, and perhaps it should be so. But I swear to you now, whatever it was that your people did against mine, I have forgotten it."

Aethan clenched and unclenched his fists. "Do you think that because I'm elyir I won't know?" He motioned to Grenja and Trofast. "Your kind slaughtered each other for centuries over this land, before any human ever traveled across the sea, but the Fidelis strove to move beyond all of it. The Cenóri couldn't accept that, could they? Gallian sought only peace, but your people struck him down rather than let refugees live alongside you."

Trofast straightened, his eyes narrowed—though not in anger. "So the long past is bitter still, young one?"

"That's the way it was," Idris whispered, "not the way it is, or has to be."

Aethan studied her, and the anger drained from his face. He glanced between the others seated around the table, then raked his fingers through his hair.

"We hold nothing against the elyir," Erryl explained, his tone incredibly polite—almost grandfatherly. "We can honor the houses of our forebears without denying those born outside our confines the right to train. We may bicker and throw petty insults when we shouldn't, but..." He pointed at Trofast. "I would die for that man if it came to it, and he would do the same for me."

Aethan surveyed Erryl for a moment, then glanced back at Kura. "Well, like I said." He smiled only when he met her gaze. "I'm following her."

Kura blinked in surprise. *Gods, he means it.*

Trofast snorted—he might have intended it as a laugh—and eyed Kura. "So, child, you already have a following?"

She had no idea how to answer that.

Renard looked up, scrunching his cheeks as he rested his head in his hands. "Have we got this all figured out, then?"

"Unless you want to add something of value," Grenja muttered.

"Oh no," Renard said. "We've all said quite enough. Save it for the war, I say, save it for the war, but does anyone listen to me?" He stood up, stretching his arms with a yawn. "Ahh, I'm still not sure why y'all wanted me here anyway."

"Sit back down, Renard, we're not finished yet," Erryl said with an exasperated sigh. He motioned to Kura and Aethan. "Come, take a seat. If you're willing to join us, of course. Perhaps you can help us figure out why either of you would consider keeping the acquaintance of Triston, son of Dradge, heir to the throne of Avaron."

Chapter Twenty-Eight

A Good Man

"Go on, you!" Triston stumbled, catching himself with a grunt on the rough-hewn cave wall. "I'm going, alright?"

That was the third time this senseless little man had jammed the blunt end of a spear into his ribs, and Triston was beginning to forget what was stopping him from taking that weapon and whacking the man across his chubby face with it.

"Hey, ease up," the other rebel said to his companion. Both were older men with grizzled beards and weathered hands, but the second carried himself with a gentler confidence than the first. Their weapons were ages old and half-rusted, their plate armor dented and dulled—alone, they were far from intimidating. But he would respect this process—for now—even if they wouldn't do the same for him.

He straightened, smoothing out his shirt in a vain attempt to preserve whatever dignity he had left, and let out his breath as the rebels continued to urge him down the long, dimly lit hallway. He thought he'd read about massive caverns like this, though he couldn't be sure it hadn't been in a children's story instead of a history book. Two turns ago he'd had a sense of the path back to the holding cell. They were leading him in circles on purpose.

"Make a left up here," the second rebel said, pointing his spear toward the wide doorway at the end of the hall.

Grudgingly, Triston did as he was told. It was a small room, covered in gaudy abstract art and lit with the strange glowing stone. There was one exit—the doorway in which he stood.

A single stone table dominated the space. A centaur, armed with a large broadsword on his belt, stood at the head. Two men—the first carrying a sword, the second weaponless—sat on bench seats across from one another. The dog from the river sat on the bench as well, grinning at him, and a petite girl sat at the centaur's side, flanked by two others.

Triston took a step back. It was the Feldlander, looking rather miserable, seated beside Kura. They must have given her that black cloak to replace his tattered soldier's cape, and there she sat, above him as if she belonged with all the rest. As if she were his judge, and he was now *her* prisoner.

Had she planned this all along? That didn't seem possible or likely, but he'd heard her by the river—and again in their shared prison cell. She knew these people and wanted to strike a deal.

"Go on!" the first rebel called out, and Triston leapt forward before the man sent that spear into his ribs again.

"Some decorum, please." The centaur frowned at the man.

Triston stayed out of reach of the rebel's spear anyway and straightened his shoulders. The room's company seemed more animal than human, and he couldn't decide whether he'd stepped into some sort of comedic painting or the heart of a bear's den.

"I am Trofast," the centaur said finally, "son of Gundehar, commander of Nansûr, once known as the chieftain of all Cenóri. I have heard much about you, son of Dradge, although I must say in meeting you my questions only multiply."

Triston nodded cordially. Looking the centaur in the eye, he could almost imagine him as a man. "If it's ransom you seek, then I promise you will get it. It has been paid before."

Trofast laughed, his smile like a flash of lightning—fearsome, and gone in an instant. "The Prince of Avaron, begging, in my presence?"

So much for diplomacy. "You misunderstand me, sir. I offer ransom because it is what my father requests, and because you have yet to do me any serious harm. Personally, I would be glad to settle this in a more admirable way."

"Ah," the centaur said. "You threaten me. That is more of what I expected."

"No, sir, I—"

"There is no need for that. This is a gathering of careworn souls, not a place of posturing like your father's hall." He turned to Kura, tilting his head as he lifted his chin. "You championed him, Kura of Wynshire. Why?"

She championed me?

Kura squirmed in her seat. Clearly the centaur's words were some kind of exaggeration.

"He's..." She glanced between the faces surrounding her, but ultimately looked down at her lap. "He's a good man."

Triston had to run her words through his mind again to believe she'd really said them. Dumbfounded, he studied Kura's face. He'd never been sure she didn't hate him.

"A good man..." Trofast repeated, tilting his head. "Do you agree?"

Triston straightened. "I don't suppose it's my place to say, sir. Though I'd like to think so."

"Hmm," the centaur grunted. "I expect we all would."

"Well," the heavy-set man said, "you're certainly your father's son." He was dressed in garish robes and spoke with an easy confidence—he obviously thought himself to be someone of importance.

Triston nodded to him respectfully. "Sir, you speak as though you intend to insult me."

Trofast chuckled. "A good son is loyal to his father, is he not? But fathers are men, the same as all of us. I have walked this land for more than two hundred of your years and I have yet to meet a truly good man."

"Good or not, my father will hear your grievances, if you care to speak with him. There's no reason for this to come to bloodshed."

The man at the end of the table suddenly perked up, lifting his head from his hand. "You really mean that?"

Triston eyed him, confused. It was Renard, whom he'd met at the river, but he had thought the man was asleep. "I do."

"Can you prove it?"

"Renard," the heavy-set man scolded, "what are you—"

"Come on, Erryl, at least let him offer something!"

Erryl grumbled some sort of reply, and Renard met Triston's gaze with an expectant grin.

"Well," Triston started. What did he have to offer? It would have to be something that both satisfied the rebellion's interest and kept him from turning traitor. *Seren's facility.* He nearly grinned. "There's a place in Shalford that's holding centaurs. These I am willing to turn over to you in exchange for myself."

The dog made some horrible hacking sound as though she were going to be sick, but after a moment Triston realized she was probably laughing. Renard glanced at Trofast.

The centaur sighed. "We also want weapons, and armor—two sets for each man that accompanies you. And ten times your weight in grain." He gave a wry grin. "You are a prince, after all—don't undersell your worth."

Triston couldn't hold back a frown this time. "And what of my soldier your men killed by the river?"

"What of him?"

"I want him buried."

The centaur nodded, respectfully enough. "It will be done."

Erryl scoffed. "This would be a trap, a suicide mission. Who would ever go with you?"

"I'll go." Kura almost jumped up from her seat. She was trying to hide her excitement, but failed horribly. Of course—he'd told her the other prisoners from the Waste had passed through Shalford. They'd probably already gone on to Avtalyon by now, but there was no killing hope.

"Nice!" Renard grinned and pointed at Kura. "I knew I liked you." He turned to Erryl. "Well, I've got the fonfyr. Who else do I need?"

"She's not the fonfyr," Erryl scowled. "She's not even elyir, much less a Fidelis, and she has made no claim to the sword. In fact..." He frowned as he gave Kura a quick once-over. "I'm not sure she and her friend have any further place at this council or its proceedings."

Kura turned on the man with something nearing a glare.

"The fonfyr..." Trofast lifted a beautifully crafted sword that lay on the table before him. "Long have we awaited his return, myself with dread well-earned..."

Despite the coat of rust, the blade flashed gold in the light, and red flickered like embers in the runes inlaid along the fuller. Triston drew in a startled breath. He recognized this sword. At least, he'd seen a shadow of it: the blade that hung in his father's council chambers. He'd always known that one was a fake—both his parents and Seren had told him as much—but maybe he hadn't quite believed his mother when she'd said he should someday expect to see the real one.

The centaur turned to Kura. "I do not know the lore as well as the abbot here, nor do I care to. The prophecy was not written for or by my people, but all the same I believe it will ultimately come to pass. Possibly for our benefit. Kura of Wynshire, you found this sword. Do you lay claim to it?"

"Trofast!" Erryl sputtered, his cheeks flushing red. "She has no ability and no right! She cannot—!"

The centaur did not even glance in Erryl's direction. "Kura of Wynshire." His voice was as calm as a summer morning, but it echoed in the room with the strength of a hurricane. "Do you claim this sword?"

Kura stared at that glimmering blade, and her face tightened in either a grimace or fear. Judging by that look Triston thought she'd refuse, but she glanced sideways at Erryl and drew in a breath.

"I claim it."

Erryl gave some exclamation of shock, but Renard drowned him out as he leapt to his feet. "Alright!" He turned to Trofast. "What do you say now?"

A grin tugged at the centaur's lip as he looked over the sword, then nodded and held the hilt toward Kura. "May Ìsendorál serve you well."

Erryl smothered a groan, but everyone else—including the dog and the girl, neither of whom had spoken a word—appeared pleased enough. Kura attempted some kind of formal bow, which might have been comical were she not so earnest, then stared at that blade in her hands. The rusty steel shone gold in her hazel eyes but her expression remained hollow, blank—a look that oddly reminded Triston of those he'd seen in battle, on the faces of mortally wounded soldiers coming to terms with their own impending demise.

The centaur sighed and turned to Renard. "You can leave in the morning, but only take a few men with you. And if anything—and I mean anything—goes wrong, Renard, call it off."

"Yes!" Renard socked the dog on the shoulder as one might a drinking buddy. "This didn't turn out to be a total waste after all." He pointed at Kura and Aethan before turning to Triston, all with an almost stupid grin. "Y'all be ready bright and early!"

"Trofast..." Erryl whined through clenched teeth, but one stern glance from the centaur and he fell silent.

"Idris, show our guests to where they'll be staying tonight." Trofast motioned to the two rebels standing behind Triston. "And take him back to the holding cell. Gently, if you will. We don't want to damage our wares, now, do we?"

Triston nodded, attempting to maintain the proper air of respect, and stepped to the side as the council members filed out of the room. He'd hoped they'd provide him decent lodging for the night —possibly a bed, ideally some supper—but he hadn't really been expecting it. This arrangement should get him home by tomorrow, and that would have to be enough.

Then Kura stepped toward him. Well, not toward *him* really, but toward the doorway he stood beside. She looked almost regal in that cloak. Of course, her braid was disheveled, her lips pale from the cold, her cheeks sunken from lack of sleep, but all he saw were those hazel eyes—those eyes that didn't hate him.

"Kura." Triston took a step forward.

His old rebel pal stepped between them, lifting his spear—aiming with the pointy end this time—but their eyes had already met.

"I..." Gods, what was he going to say? He glanced down at his hands. "Thank you."

"Oh, get on," the rebel said with a grimace.

And then Kura was gone, just a flash of auburn hair over a black cape as she and the others disappeared down the hallway.

PART THREE

ELUCIDATE

Chapter Twenty-Nine

Lingering Enigma

The man strode down the empty hallway, his grey cloak—grey as his eyes—billowing from his shoulders as he surveyed the marble floor with misplaced intensity. The sunrise shone warm and bright beyond the windows, but thick curtains, drawn tight, allowed for only a sliver of light and a chill more befitting a mausoleum than a castle.

Kura stiffened as Vahleda appeared at his side, her arms folded across her chest and her expression an overzealous frown. She floated at his side as easily as a leaf on a current, and she matched the grey-eyed man's pace without taking a step. Kura froze where she was, tense, unable to flee, unwilling to accept that for certain. But the woman's self-assurance was intoxicating, and through her eyes the world was neither warm nor cold—it was simply there for the taking.

"Darling, I think you've forgotten what I said."

The grey-eyed man came to a sudden stop as he met her gaze. "Oh." He let out a breath, and his face twisted into a scowl. "What are you doing here? What if someone were to overhear? They'd think I'd gone mad!"

She smiled, and let her arms fall lazily to her sides. If nothing else, he remained remarkably entertaining to tease. "I only wanted to see this for myself."

His frown deepened and he muttered something as he started down the hallway again. "I don't need you checking up on me."

Oh, pet, but of course you do.

The grey-eyed man came to the end of the hallway and stopped at the small, lone door. A single torch burned beside it, struggling dutifully to fight back the gloom. He drew in a deep breath, as if steeling himself against the inevitable, and reached for the doorknob.

She re-folded her arms and glowered at the back of his head.

The grey-eyed man shook himself, then pushed open the door. The heavy wood swung back on its hinges to slam against the stone wall, the sound reverberating in the small room beyond. It was nearly empty, except for a rectangular stone slab in the center—the final resting place of a young man covered in an off-white blanket. A dark-haired man knelt beside the slab, his head bowed. He didn't even flinch at the noise.

Her frown deepened as the grey-eyed man hesitated in the doorway, but he finally took a step forward. "Dradge... I'm sorry."

The dark-haired man said nothing at first. The tattered green cloak draping his limp figure made him look more like a mossy statue than a king. Then, with a snarl, he was on his feet. He grabbed the grey-eyed man's tunic and shoved him against the wall. Tears stained the king's cheeks, but none remained in his bloodshot eyes as he shoved his forearm against the grey-eyed man's neck.

"This is your fault." He spoke softly, his voice rich in anger. "You took him with you. You let him die, and you came back without so much as a *scratch*."

Her smile widened as she took a delicate seat on the stone slab, beside the charred body that sheet could not entirely hide. *Well?*

The grey-eyed man glanced at her, then beyond her. "You're right," he choked, his voice hardly more than a whisper. He didn't fight back; he didn't struggle. "It is my fault. I'm sorry."

She bared her teeth in disgust.

The king's clenched fist shook as his face contorted in pain and anger. With a sob, he stumbled back—rippling through her image—and only kept his balance as he fell against the slab. The grey-eyed man slid to the ground, gasping.

"I'm—" the king began, but tears caught his voice. He covered his face with his hand.

The grey-eyed man coughed, then took in a shaky breath. "No need."

She stomped toward him. "You cowardly, tender-hearted ingrate!" The grey-eyed man pushed himself to his feet, his eyes fixed on the ground. "That is how you let him treat you? He who you would—" She grasped at the grey-eyed man's sleeve, but he walked past her, then *through* her.

She shivered. For an instant their bodies were one—him pulsing flesh, her... cold, dead. Nothing. Her rage burned hot, and she whirled around. "You *dare*—!"

The grey-eyed man placed his hand on the king's shoulder. "I can't bring him back, though the gods know how much I want to. But I can offer you one thing."

The king didn't even look up. He clutched that charred body like a mother might a sleeping infant. "What is that?"

"Justice."

Kura's eyes blinked open and she waited there, snuggled under the warmth of her blanket as the room came into focus. It was one of many, just a small cavern with a single port window and a bundle of blankets tossed in the corner to make a bed. Lazily, she rolled onto her back. In the morning light the dream was just a hazy recollection of a king and a burned body, but that sense of fear and brokenness clung to her—like mud—and dampened her spirit.

She sat up, pushing the blankets aside, and grimaced at the effort as a dull pain radiated through her arm. Pulling up her sleeve, she drew in a breath. A deep purple bruise ran along the pale underside of her arm from her wrist to her elbow, the shape twisted like a vein, or lightning—exactly like Aethan's arm the day before. The mark the Essence left on someone who wasn't supposed to be drafting at all.

She sighed and tried again to rub the sleep from her eyes. Breakfast first. She could figure out this mess after breakfast.

A scrap of paper lay on the ground beside the balled-up blanket she had used as a pillow, and she picked it up as she climbed to her feet. Of course—Skellor's note. The letters were smudged from her dip in the river, but she could still make out Gallian's sigil in the top corner. *The withering tree...* Kura shoved the paper back into her pocket, then slipped on the grey tunic Idris had given her. Someone around here had to know where that was.

She reached for her sword, where she'd left it leaning against the wall, then stopped. *'My'* sword. She scoffed. Delicately, she took the weapon into her hands. She thought about drawing it, but instead smothered another sigh, belted it around her waist, and started toward the hallway.

She didn't want it, but after that man Erryl had tried to send her away, she'd done what she'd had to do. If it meant rescuing her family, she could be their fonfyr for one day. She traced her finger along the hilt hanging at her side—cautiously, as if merely touching it would cause the blade to burst into flames. This wasn't the arrangement she'd planned on making.

Hastily pulling her messy hair back into a ponytail, she followed the echo of voices to the archway at the end of the hall. She took a step through the door, then paused beside it. The courtyard was filled with people—centaurs, humans, and nostkynna, some milling about, others seated on benches beside one of many wooden tables. Natural sunlight shone through small windows in the tall, vine-covered rafters. Large stone columns dotted the open space, and Kura couldn't tell if the ceiling had been placed on the pillars or if the whole room had been carved from the mountainside.

"It's you!"

Kura drew back as an old woman latched onto her hand. "I—"

"Bless you." Smiling, the woman patted the back of Kura's hand and didn't let go. "Bless you."

Many more eyes turned to look, and the roar of conversation fell to a murmur as the whisper of *fonfyr* carried through the crowd.

"I'm not…" Kura began, struggling to smile as her cheeks flushed with heat. The woman released her, but more turned to stare—each with sunken eyes in skinny faces.

Every eye was a stranger's, but Kura knew them. She'd grown up among them; in some sense she'd been one of them every year in the Wynshire. But there was something else in their stares—something beyond the dirt and the grime… something dangerously like hope. And she realized maybe it was all that had brought her to this point in the first place.

"What are you doing?"

Kura flinched to find Trofast towering over her, his arms folded across his bare chest.

"I—" she stammered, struggling to find her voice. "I just wanted breakfast..."

The centaur's gaze was stern, but amusement flashed in his eyes. "Very well." He turned, motioning to her with his hand. "Your friends are this way." Trofast placed himself between Kura and the crowd as he led her around the edge of the courtyard.

"They..." she started. "They think I'm the fonfyr."

Trofast snorted. "Rumors travel quickly, especially those of hope—or disaster—in times like this."

"Do you think I'm the fonfyr?"

Trofast slowed his pace. "I look up at the stars, as they are mine to watch. In their dance they speak of a burden, once forsaken, and of the coming trials, but they do not say who will wield the sword through all of it. Perhaps they do not know, or perhaps I can no longer read them." He stopped, his piercing black eyes boring a hole through Kura's. "I do not know if you are *fonfyr*, Kura of Wynshire. But I pray you are not, for your own sake."

Kura had to look away. *Gods, it'd be so much easier if he just said no.*

"There are your friends." Trofast motioned to a nearby table at the edge of the courtyard, where Idris and Aethan already sat, both with their own plate of food.

"Thank y—" Kura began, but the centaur had already turned away, his blue roan horse's half disappearing among the crowd.

Idris was facing away from her. The embroidered hem of an indigo riding dress poked out from beneath her purple cloak, and she'd even done her hair in dozens of intricate braids, tying them back with a matching indigo ribbon. Aethan, on the other hand, looked like he'd just woken up—his brown hair was a tangled mess, and he wasn't wearing anything more than his worn trousers and a baggy shirt.

He noticed Kura standing by the wall and waved. "Hey, you hungry?"

Kura plastered a smile on her face as she joined them at the table, taking the open bench seat beside Idris and across from Aethan.

He slid her a wooden plate, mostly empty except for a dollop of scrambled eggs and oatmeal. "I saved some for you."

"You were talking to Trofast?" Idris asked as she placed a mug of fresh water beside Kura's plate.

"Thanks, yeah. There are a lot of people here, I couldn't find you guys."

Idris nodded and turned back to her own food, but she clearly suspected what Kura left unsaid.

Slowly, Kura took a bite of her eggs, the knots in her stomach working against her appetite. In her mind, she could still see those hopeful faces, all watching her, expecting her to be something—expecting her to... to *save* them.

She sighed and reached for the cup, raising it to her lips, then stopped as she caught a glimpse of her own reflection in the glistening water. Her hair was disheveled, her eyes rimmed with dark bags, her rough, sunburned cheeks marked with small cuts and a bruise. *What on* Ehlis *do they see?*

"Kura." Aethan's voice tore her from her thoughts. "You good?"

"Yeah." Kura set her cup on the table and gave him another forced smile—maybe the last one wasn't convincing enough. "Yeah, I'm fine."

He inspected her face with a sort-of frown, then shrugged and turned back to his meal. "Idris was telling me you woke the sword." There was that excitement—that hope—in his eyes again. It was nearly more than she could stand.

"I suppose I did." Kura spun her spoon in the oatmeal. Her arms ached every time she moved them, and she was grateful for her long sleeves. "Have either of you ever heard of a place called the withering tree?"

Aethan's eyebrows rose, warily.

"The withering tree?" Idris asked. "Maybe you mean *L'Dwinan*? It's a giant old tree, about a quarter dayride west of here." She met Kura's gaze for a second, as though asking permission to continue speaking. "The nostkynna have a story about that tree. They believe that it—"

A sharp whistle carried through the room over the murmur of voices, and the general conversation slowed as heads turned to look for the source. Kura glanced over Aethan's shoulder and spotted Renard standing in one of the open arches leading from the room and into the mess of caverns beyond. He whistled again, then grinned and waved a hand over his head.

Aethan turned back, then chuckled. "Looks like breakfast is over."

Kura shoveled a few more mouthfuls of egg into her mouth as Aethan and Idris rose from their seats, then followed them. A few cheers burst from the crowd as they walked past, and Kura fought to keep from ducking behind Aethan for cover. It was a relief to finally join Renard in the relative anonymity of the hallway.

He eyed the sword hanging from Kura's belt with a nod, then tossed Aethan a long staff.

"What—?" Aethan jumped forward to catch it. The weapon resembled a spear, but the single blade was the size of a dagger. "A real Singan swordstaff? This thing must be ancient!"

Renard laughed. "Like just about everything else in this place. I trust that if you recognize it, you're also able to use it?"

Aethan stepped back and swung the blade in a few sweeping stances. "I used to have one. It was the only thing my father ever gave me." He grinned at her. "Well, that and my green eyes. Mum always said I had my father's eyes."

Kura returned the grin. "I'd say that thing beats a pine branch."

"Captain." A cleanshaven man came to attention in the doorway. He was about Renard's age, possibly younger, but with his well-tended gambeson and tight stances he reminded Kura more of a soldier than a rebel.

"Ah, Chagan." Renard beckoned him forward. "Bring him."

The rebel continued down the hallway, tugging another man behind him. Triston.

They'd bound his hands with rope and taken away his armor, leaving him with his baggy white undershirt—now stained and dusty—his leather riding pants, torn on one knee, and his mud-caked boots. Despite all that he held his shoulders back, calm and proud. Those light blue eyes peeked out from his mop of disheveled black hair, studying the room with such a natural regality that Kura had to see him as what he was: the Prince of Avaron.

He'd thanked her last night, and like an idiot she'd stumbled over her feet and said nothing. She opened her mouth to speak, but the words didn't come. Triston's eyes met hers as Chagan brought him to a stop beside Renard. She cringed and her gaze darted to the floor. They'd been through too much for her to hate him any longer, but that emotion was certainly easier to process than however she felt now.

"Mornin'." Renard grinned as he gave Triston a once-over, then laughed and smacked him on the shoulder. "Lighten up, kid. This is a ransom exchange, not an execution."

Triston recoiled from him but managed a moderately cordial smile.

Idris timidly stepped toward Renard. "I'm coming with you."

"Really?" He blinked at her. "Devna's already gathering some of her people, and my group is just back-up. We don't expect trouble."

Idris nodded. "I still have to do this."

Renard inspected her a moment longer, then shrugged. "As I've always said, six is a company."

Chapter Thirty

BARGAINING

Triston fought the urge to scratch at his blindfold. Fading sounds of metal striking stone told him they'd passed the stone quarries and into Shalford. The city he couldn't see bustled with the murmur of voices, the creaking of wagons, the shouts of children, and the bleating of sheep and goats. That cool, though humid, fall breeze brought with it the delectable scent of fresh-baked bread and the grungy odor of horses.

The rebels riding at his side hadn't given him more than the occasional command, and that was more than enough for his tastes. This whole ransom process was incredibly demeaning. Triston had been ransomed once before, when he'd been maybe nine years old. Some up-and-coming trader had thought it the best means to buy himself a council seat. What *was* that man's name?

Triston's horse came to a stop, the rebels muttering to one another. He stiffened. There was no real reason for him to be nervous, but something ate at him anyway. Kura and the Feldlander —the only two rebels with whom he had any familiarity—weren't among this group, and he wasn't exactly comforted by the blindfold. He lifted a hand to tug at it and received a slap on the arm.

"Quit that." It was a woman's voice, harsh and commanding, and Triston stifled a sigh. She was, unfortunately, the only person throughout this trip who had paid him any mind.

"Hoah!" the woman called out, her horse's hooves crunching against the gravel road. "We've come to speak to the captain of this tower, for an exchange of prisoners."

Triston shook his head. His father's men would neither respect nor be intimidated by a greeting such as that—not from a bannerless band of nobodies—but perhaps curiosity would get the best of the tower's captain and they'd at least give an answer.

They waited in silence, Triston's horse pawing the ground, before something rattled on the gate.

"State your name." The soldier's voice was calm, bordering on disinterested. Triston sighed again and fidgeted with the bonds on his wrists.

"There'll be no names," the rebel woman answered. "But we will get what we've been promised—that is, if you want your prince back."

The soldier laughed. "Our prince, eh? What, did you just return from a trip to Brennsumar? He's dead."

Triston would have laughed himself, had a chill not run down his spine. *Why on Ehlis does this man think I'm dead?*

The rebel woman muttered something, then a hand yanked the blindfold off Triston's face. He squinted, blinking in the sun, until his eyes adjusted to the light. This was Shalford alright. The tower was not particularly tall—the pine trees beyond the city stood taller —but it was built from thick grey stones and stood a good three or four stories high.

The rebel band huddled near the front gates, each of them peering with a frown into the small opening in the solid iron gate through which the soldier was speaking.

The soldier's eyes widened when they fell on Triston's face. "Sir, I..."

Triston forced a tight smile. "I have promised them a few things, if you wouldn't mind cooperating..."

The soldier blinked, then jumped to attention. "Of course, sir."

The rebel woman flashed a sharp smile that ended far from her eyes. "Thank you."

She outlined the agreement Triston had made with Trofast, and the soldier slipped farther behind the gate to speak in a low voice with another man Triston couldn't see. He watched the open panel with a frown. It was his father's policy to give ransom without deception or question—misguided, probably, though material goods could always be re-collected later—but he had the distinct impression these men were not planning on doing what he instructed.

One of the rebels leaned over and whispered to the woman, who then fixed a scowl on Triston. Grey streaked her brown hair, and wrinkles marked the rough skin at the corners of her eyes and lips, but Triston wasn't sure those were a tribute to her true age or the kind of life she'd lived. Her deep green, angular eyes shone bright as a child's.

"You set us up, did you?" Her tone implied a question but her expression said otherwise.

"No, ma'am." Although he was not responsible for what these men might decide to do on their own.

Finally, the soldier returned. "We have the weapons, armor, and grain, but it will take us some time to gather the prisoners for the exchange, and we will have to open the gate."

Triston's eyes narrowed. This had to be some kind of set-up. Judging by the woman's frown, she was thinking the same thing.

She sighed. "They better be unarmed."

The soldier slammed the peephole shut, then pushed the gate open. Two soldiers emerged first, carrying between them a stretcher full of the armor and weapons as agreed. A third man followed, carrying four sacks of grain, two by two over his shoulders. Each man wore his chestplate and chain mail, but none of them had so much as a dagger visible on their belts.

Arrows darted from the tower windows above.

The rebel woman screamed, grabbing at her arm, and her band broke formation. Triston muttered a curse and tried, despite his bound hands, to get a grip on his horse's reins. The two nearest soldiers tossed their load of armor aside and latched on to Triston's upper arms.

"Hey—" he started, but they undid only the rope that held him to the saddle and then pulled him from his horse. "Hey!" Triston struggled as the soldiers dragged him through the open gate, before another man slammed the gate shut.

One of the rebels called for a retreat. When the pounding of hooves faded, silence settled on the other side of the wall.

"I arranged the ransom," Triston said. "It was fair enough..."

The soldiers towed him silently out of the sunlight and into the shadow of the open door leading into the tower. With each step they took, this felt less like a rescue and more like a kidnapping.

They were pulling him toward the side staircase—the one that led to the basement. He hesitated a moment—one precious moment—then let his gut instincts take over.

Triston slammed one man into the wall, wrenching his arm out of the soldier's grip, then leapt at the second. The man drew a dagger from under his tunic and slashed at Triston's face, but Triston caught his hand between his bound wrists. The soldier grunted and tried to pull back—Triston let him, and used the motion to force the soldier's blades through the bonds at his wrists. The ropes fell at his feet.

With a shout, the first soldier leapt at Triston's back. Still running on instinct, Triston caught the man by the arm and threw him over his shoulder, sending him clattering to the ground in a heap of limbs and armor. The second soldier charged again, slashing at Triston's neck. Triston side-stepped the strike, blocking the soldier's arm. He caught hold of the man's wrist, then wrenched his arm behind him. The soldier struggled, but finally cried out in pain and dropped his dagger.

Triston kicked the man in the back, sending him sprawling against the floor, then snatched up the dagger. The first soldier was nearly to his feet. Triston lunged at him and sliced the man's throat. The second soldier screamed in anger, but Triston met his advance, blocking a haphazard punch with one hand as he drove his dagger into the man's throat with the other. The soldier gave a few gurgling last breaths, then fell to the floor.

Deafening silence washed over Triston like a wave. He stumbled back, staring wide-eyed at those bodies at his feet as the soldiers' hot blood dried cold on his hands. The burst of adrenaline that had fueled his fight crashed over him and set his legs shaking.

He'd just killed his own men.

"Alright," Renard murmured as he peered through his contraption. It was an old and tattered thing he called a spyglass. When Kura had asked, he hadn't been willing to give any more answers than that. "Looks like they're going to open the gates..."

Kura, Renard, Aethan, Idris, and that other man, Chagan, had taken up position along the hillside above Shalford, a perch among the towering pine trees that gave them a clear sight of the entire valley. It was a sprawling town, populated by houses built of log and stone, and it filled in the winding flat space between the snow-capped mountains and the river.

Kura nudged her horse to move closer to Renard's.

"Alright, alright," the stallion grunted. He took one begrudging step forward before turning back to scowl at her with one of his big brown eyes.

"Sorry, Akachi," Kura said sheepishly.

The horse shook his mane. "You two-legs, you have no respect."

Kura took in a shuddering breath and let it out. It seemed her nerves had wound tighter and tighter with every step they'd taken toward Shalford, and now she only wished she could see what Renard saw. She squinted at the distant city. There was something strange about this town, something she couldn't quite—

"Aethan!" She turned to him in shock. "Where are the walls?"

He glanced over at her with a grin. "Walls?"

"Yeah! How do they keep the forest out without walls?"

Aethan laughed. "Not everywhere is out to kill you like the Wynshire is, Kura."

"You're from the Waste, eh?" Akachi said with a snort that sounded a lot like a laugh. "Well, that explains it, then."

Kura turned back to the city, shaking her head in disbelief. *A town without walls...* With the mountains and the forests it almost felt like home, although the trees were the tallest, straightest pines she'd ever seen and the mountains far steeper and rockier.

"Shit," Renard muttered. "Devna's group's pulling back. The soldiers in the tower took the prince."

Anger and fear shot through Kura's veins. "What?"

"Augh." Renard shook his head and collapsed his spyglass. "It's over. Everybody got out, but we've got nothin'."

Kura clenched her fists around her reins until her knuckles turned white. "We came to—we can't just—"

"I'm sorry, kid." Renard met her gaze with resigned sympathy. "I know what you're feelin', and I agree, but Devna will be back here in a few minutes and she'll call it off."

Kura shook her head, her jaw set and her glare fixed on that city far below. *What's all this been for if I don't...?* The sword on her hip suddenly felt like a weight. She tore it from its scabbard and held it out. The rusty blade shone red in the sunlight, and strength settled in the very marrow of her bones.

Renard eyed her, curious. "What're you—?"

"I don't care who comes with me or not." Kura stared at Renard first, then turned to lock eyes with each of the others. "I'm getting my family out of that tower."

Aethan's brow creased in concern. "You don't even know if they're—"

She let out a breath, unable to keep looking at him. "If I have to, I'll die trying."

Renard let out a whoop of a laugh. "Well, I'm sold!" He pulled open his spyglass and studied the city again. "We've got two minutes until Devna gets here and puts an end to all this. What's your plan, kid?"

Kura glanced down at the sword in her hands, her flood of emotions grinding to a halt. *My plan...*

"I..." Idris began quietly, as she peered at the mountainside beneath them, toward the stone quarry. Every eye turned to her; it was the first word she'd spoken the whole trip. Seated primly on her grey mare, her small figure draped in regal purple, she better resembled a wayward princess than a plotting rebel. "I may have an idea."

Chapter Thirty-One

Reciprocity

"Quit struggling!" Kura hissed.

Akachi snorted, stomping his hoof as he continued at a casual pace. "Someone of my stature, pulling a cart... This thing is too heavy, and it's chafing my back—oh, let's—"

"Quiet back there!" Renard called out with a grunt as he shifted his grip on the stretcher of stones that he, Aethan, and Chagan carried between them.

Idris peeked out from behind the head of her mare, who quietly towed her little cart of rocks. "Shh, we're almost at the gates."

Akachi swished his tail. "I don't see why I didn't get to stay behind with the horses. They need constant looking after, you know. The fools."

"Shh," Kura repeated as she adjusted the cloth scarf tied across her face. Several of the quarrymen had been more than glad to hand over their loads of stones in exchange for a handful of firri, which Renard said would keep them drinking in the tavern until late tonight.

Kura glanced up at Shalford Tower, her heartbeat pounding in her ears. The structure stood out from the rest of the simple wood-and-stone houses like a mink among a flock of songbirds. Narrow archer's windows dotted every floor of the tower, and sunlight glinted on the polished steel armor of the soldiers hiding in each of those dark openings. Not wanting one of them to catch her staring, she looked back down at the street.

Idris led their procession, her small, unassuming frame nearly hidden behind the bulk of stones her mare carried in the cart. Renard had said they'd have the best chance of slipping in if the most unobtrusive in their group came first and last in their lineup. Idris had dutifully taken up her role, to the point of tattering the edges of her beautiful cloak before covering it in dust, but she couldn't hide the panic in her eyes.

The tower widened along the right side, making room for a metal gate, which currently stood open. Kura drew in a nervous breath. Several soldiers patrolled the rear entrance. They each wore blued chestplates nestled beneath cascading indigo cloaks, their faces shrouded in shadow no matter how they turned.

"Hey, stop there!" a second soldier called out, walking briskly to Idris's side. He sported the same rust-treated chestplate and indigo cloak as the first soldier, but this man had no hood. Idris stopped immediately, and the rest of them behind her did the same.

Kura caught herself biting her inner lip.

A third soldier ambled toward Idris, his spear resting casually on his shoulder. "What is this, shift change already?" He was a rather portly fellow, dressed in the familiar silver chestplate and red cloak, and he leaned over and spit on the ground beside Idris's cart. "Shipment number?"

"Five two six," Idris said, so quietly Kura almost didn't hear her.

"Of course there's another shift change," the first soldier called out from beside the wall, his voice emanating from the shadow of his hood. "Just keep the line moving."

"Bring 'em in," the second soldier agreed, then pointed across the open space. "Put it all along the wall with the rest."

Kura kept her gaze trained on her own boots as she plodded through the gates. Akachi finally embraced his role as a pack animal and walked barely lifting his feet, his head bent low.

The cobblestone courtyard within the walls was mostly empty except for the several piles of stones along the walls, and Kura was a little surprised to find these soldiers so zealously guarding it. Idris continued forward, and Kura discreetly glanced over her shoulder at the tower. A single metal door led into the heart of the structure—and it was open.

"Come on, boys," Renard said with a grunt as he, Aethan, and Chagan struggled to haul their stretcher of stones to the space along the wall. "Just a few more loads of this stuff and we're done for the day."

Kura led Akachi to the side so that both his tall frame and their cart full of stones obscured the soldiers' view of the rest of her group. She checked to see if any soldiers were watching, then unfastened the straps that held the cart against Akachi's back.

She looked to Renard. *Are you ready?*

The man nodded, then let the boulder slip from his hands to the ground. He screamed as the crash of that stone against the cobblestone echoed across the courtyard. "Ah, my leg! My leg!"

Akachi whinnied, rearing up as if in panic. Kura jumped out of the way as the cart fell from his back, the load of stones tumbling to the ground.

"He's loose!" She ducked behind one of the larger stones in the pile as Akachi took off toward the open gate they'd come through. "Catch him, he's loose!"

The soldiers motioned to one another, calling out commands. They didn't sound particularly concerned, but they did move away from the tower and into the courtyard. Idris's mare began to buck and kick as well, and then the two horses bolted for the open gates. The soldiers jogged after the horses, one of them laughing.

"Now!" Renard shouted, and with that they took off—Kura, Aethan, Chagan, Renard, and Idris as well, all five of them sprinting toward the open doorway. The cool air stung Kura's throat, but she pushed herself to run faster.

A blast of fire shot past her arm.

She yelped and jumped aside, clutching her singed sleeve. Most of the soldiers had gone after the horses but one of them—the hooded one from the gates—had broken from his companions and charged after her. He flung his hands before him and another burst of flame shot from his fingertips. Kura yanked her cloak up to shield her face and kept running. The heat scalded her cheeks and her nose stung with the putrid odor of singed clothing—but she didn't stop until she had charged into the tower, and Aethan and Chagan slammed the doors shut behind her.

The metal doors echoed with a dull clang in the darkness and Kura coughed, fighting to catch her breath. Small flames flickered on her cloak, so she tore it from her shoulders to stomp it into the ground.

"What was that?" she asked between gasps.

Renard gave a wry grin, face barely lit by the sliver of sunlight that slipped through the seam between the two closed doors. "Vojak."

She shivered, heart clenching in her chest as she couldn't help but run through all the hints of stories about vojaks her mother had refused to tell. These past weeks had forced her to accept as reality many things she'd once thought myth, but even now some stubborn part of her struggled to believe this. These were the sorts of legends she didn't *want* to be real.

A fist pounded against the metal door from outside. Everyone jumped, and Idris let out a startled squeak.

Gradually, Kura's eyes adjusted to the darkness inside. They stood crowded at one end of a small hallway; a large stairway spiraled upwards at the other end.

"Come on." Renard drew his sword, then motioned to the closed doors lining the hallway. "Everybody pick one."

Voices sounded outside the door. Triston flinched, dropping the arm of the body he'd been dragging to the side of the room, and drew the dagger from where he'd temporarily secured it on his belt. He let out a breath. *Pull yourself together.*

He was jumpy, and he actually had to consciously keep his hands from shaking. He was better than this—at least he had been, before he'd nearly become a prisoner to his own army. Triston looked to the two bodies he'd piled inside the nearer door. He hoped to the gods he'd made the right choice in killing them. Remembering Colmac eased his conscience—some.

What now? If his title had any sway, he ought to simply confront the captain of this tower, but if some faction of his father's soldiers had turned on him, it would be a matter of minutes before someone found him here and finished their mission. Whatever that was.

A man's voice, still muffled, neared the door. A woman answered him, but Triston couldn't hear them well enough to understand what they said. He crept toward the door, dagger raised and his heartbeat steadying.

He had purpose now. He was going to get out of this tower.

The door swung open and Triston lunged, brandishing his dagger. "Hold—"

The newcomer leapt back, raising a sword blade to either parry his strike or cut his throat, and then they both hesitated. It was Kura.

"What are—?" She looked first at his bloodied dagger, then the bodies he'd left along the wall. "You, um...?"

He lowered his weapon. "Uh, yeah, they..."

"The other one's just storage." Renard's voice carried from the hallway, then his figure appeared in the doorway. He looked first at Kura in curiosity, then met Triston's gaze. He grinned. "I take it the exchange didn't work out."

"Not really, no."

Renard tossed Triston one of the two swords he held in his hands. "We're here to bust out some prisoners. Where should we start?"

Triston hesitated, glancing between Renard's expectant grin and the sword in his hand. Should he side with the rebellion set on ousting his father, or the soldiers who may or may not have already betrayed him? He swallowed and found himself looking at Kura's face. "All these towers are built basically the same. The first floor is storage, the second floor is barracks. We can sneak through the basement and take the back stairwell to bypass them. Prisoners should be housed on floors three and four."

"Wait," Chagan said from the hallway. "Renard, we're not seriously..." Idris and Aethan stood at his side, each with similarly displeased expressions.

"Yup." Renard flashed a grin, then nodded toward the open doorway. "Alright, fonfyr, after you."

Chapter Thirty-Two

SHADOW OF SHALFORD TOWER

A narrow staircase, winding in a gradual circle and shrouded in shadow, gave passage to the basement. Kura kept a tight grip on her sword as she felt for the edges of the steps with her feet. Triston had taken the lead, and Kura followed him closely as Aethan, Renard, Idris, and Chagan crept down the stairs behind her.

It was surreal. Her family was locked somewhere in this tower, and the very man who'd put them there was now showing her how to break them out.

They reached the bottom of the staircase and Triston picked up his pace, jogging along the wall in the dark, narrow hallway. Dim firelight flickered at the far end, casting just enough light for Kura to attempt to read his impassive expression.

A voice echoed in the hallway, and she stopped in her tracks. The basement floor was supposed to be empty. It was a woman's voice—distant, but too near for comfort—humming some slow, eerie tune.

Aethan ran into her. "What's wrong?"

"That voice! What—?"

Chagan shoved from the end of the line. "Keep moving!"

Kura stumbled after Triston. Could they not hear it?

Triston stopped, pressing himself up against the wall to keep in the shadows, as they neared the end of the hallway. Wooden crates, stacked in organized rows from floor to ceiling, filled the basement. A narrow passageway led through the center of them to the far wall. There, several overturned and empty crates formed a makeshift table. Two long candles, housed in wrought-iron brackets on the wall on either side, gave off the soft light as they dripped pools of maroon wax on the floor. It appeared to be a shrine of sorts—currently unattended—to the long, double-bladed spear that lay on the crate table.

The woman's song carried among the boxes. Kura searched the shadows for the source as she gripped the sword hilt at her side. She didn't recognize the tune but it felt oddly familiar, like revisiting a nightmare she'd long forgotten upon waking.

Suddenly, the song vanished.

"It's so good to see you again, darling."

Vahleda. Kura leapt away from the wall, tearing her sword from its scabbard. The rest of the group whispered shouts of surprise.

Triston gave her an odd look but raised a finger to his lips and silently pressed onwards into the basement. Vahleda now sat on the corner of the makeshift table, one leg crossed delicately over the other as she rested a gloved hand on the spear. She met Kura's gaze, and her lips twisted into a smile.

"I wasn't expecting you here, pet. This is a pleasant surprise."

Kura froze—both angry and terrified—as she considered trying to run her blade through the apparition again. The candles flickered, then both exploded into roaring flames. Triston stumbled back, reaching for his own sword, and the others didn't bother to whisper this time.

"What in the world...?" Renard muttered, pushing his way to the front.

"Get back!" Idris screamed, latching onto the nearest arm—Chagan's—as she ran for the hallway. "Get back!"

The fire leapt from the candlesticks, growing larger and larger as it spiraled through the room, knocking over stacks of crates and setting others ablaze. Triston retreated to Idris's position, and Kura followed him.

A lone figure emerged from the shadowy doorway at the opposite end of the room. Fire and burning debris swirled around him, but he strode into the center of it unscathed, his indigo cloak billowing from his shoulders. It was the hooded soldier she'd met outside—the vojak.

The man lunged into a fighting stance, throwing his fists forward, one after another. The fire followed him, trailing like massive, flaming serpents across the ceiling to dive toward all of them gathered in the hallway. Kura stumbled back, crashing into Aethan as Triston fell into her, each of them scrambling to protect their faces.

Fire roared through the hallway, hotter than a midsummer day, flinging charred wood fragments in the whirlwind. Splinters pierced Kura's cloak and trousers. She gasped, struggling to breathe in the sweltering heat. Then, as suddenly as it appeared, it vanished.

Coughing, Kura took a step toward the main room. Triston was already two steps ahead of her, and Aethan not far behind. Chagan led Idris by the arm—the girl's eyes were wide in terror, but neither appeared injured beyond some minor burns and scratches—and Renard trailed after them, sputtering curses as he tried to brush the charred marks off his pants.

The vojak stood in the middle of the room, the wreckage of crates and smoldering grain littering the ground at his feet. Fire swirled about him in tongues that leapt from his boots to his cloak hem to his shoulders.

"My lady bids you to depart from this place." His voice sounded like a man's, but only blackness showed beneath his hood.

Triston raised a hand, then pointed to each of them and motioned to a side of the room. Kura stiffened. Who did he think he was, giving them directions? But they all did as he instructed, Kura and Aethan tagging at Triston's heels as Renard and Chagan shuffled to the other side. Idris held back, crouched in the shadows.

The vojak stepped into another stance, punching each fist out from his sides. Fire followed, blocking the way for both groups. Kura charged anyway, raising her cloak as a hasty shield. The soldier turned on her, blasting her with a burst of flame before she got within three steps of him. The fire burned straight through her cloak. She cried out, falling back as it ate through her sleeve, then tore the smoldering cloak from her shoulders to beat out the flame.

Metal clashed against metal. The soldier used his armguards to block the blade Renard swung at his neck. Chagan darted in from the side, sticking the man in the seam of his chestplate. He screamed—more in anger than pain—and every spark in the heap of debris burst into a roaring flame.

Kura stumbled, beating back those flames as well as she could with her cloak. Sweat trickled down her back and forehead; suffocating smoke filled the room with a fog-like haze. Renard and Triston were both shouting something, but she couldn't understand either of them. Aethan, with sweeping strokes from his swordstaff, charged the soldier but was met by a swirling wall of fire.

The ground rumbled and the vojak shrieked. Each flame burst with a flare of white light and disappeared. Blinking in the darkness, Kura pressed her sleeve over her nose to try to keep out the smoke. Smoldering embers provided the slightest light.

Vines had ensnared the vojak. The soil-covered roots wove around his legs, his torso, his neck. He screamed as they tightened, crushing his chestplate, but the sound cut short as a vine sliced through his neck and his head clattered to the floor.

Startled, Kura jumped back. His head rolled on its side—dark blood pooling on the ground—until his empty eyes pointed over her shoulder. It was a man's face, but they were black eyes, black like midnight, like Vahleda's.

Silence, broken only by the snap of burning wood, hung heavy over the room. Aethan picked himself up from a pile of splintered crates, shaking off the hand Triston offered him. Renard dragged Chagan to his feet, beating out the flames on the man's shirt. Slowly, each of them turned to Idris.

She stood in the hallway, shaking hands raised, tears staining her cheeks. Flames had eaten away the hem of her gorgeous dress and her face was smeared with soot. She stared at the man's body, biting her lip to hold back a sob. Eyes wide, Kura took a step toward her. At first Idris didn't move, but her gaze drifted upwards to meet Kura's.

"You alright?" Kura took another step, holding out her hand.

Idris choked back a sob and latched onto Kura's arm. "Let's... let's just go."

The girl clung to Kura's side as she picked her way through the debris. In a matter of minutes, one man had turned the storeroom into a refuse pile. No one said anything, and each of them only tore their focus away from the destruction to ensure nobody had received any grievous injuries. Beyond numerous burns and splinters, they all seemed to be in one piece.

Kura shuddered as she stole a glance at the wall where that weapon had been on display. A crumpled heap of crates lay there now, scattered with dried corncobs. Vahleda was nowhere to be seen, but she could feel the woman's eyes watching her from somewhere in the smoky haze.

Triston took the lead again—Renard, Aethan, and Chagan behind him, Kura and Idris taking up the rear—as they reached the opposite stairway. Kura coughed, pressing her sleeve over her nose, as the rising smoke thickened with their ascent. A loud clang reverberated down the stairwell. Idris gasped and clung tighter to her arm. Triston paused as Renard and Chagan fell into formation behind him, while Aethan stepped back to Kura's side.

The clang echoed again. Triston motioned to the others then continued carefully up the stairs. After rounding the bend, they reached a small landing. Metal bars made the inner wall, forming a narrow cell, and in it a horse beat its rear hooves against the door. A single archer's window on the outer wall provided a semblance of light, and Kura squinted through the shadows. Not a horse, a centaur.

She pushed past the others—inadvertently dragging Idris along—to reach the cell. "N'hadia?"

The centaur spun around, a smile leaping to her face. "Kura!" Her loose shirt was stained with mud and blood, bandages wrapped her arm and two of her legs, and she looked half the weight she'd been before. She grasped at the bars excitedly, eyes as bright as ever. "I thought you were dead!"

Kura returned the smile, sheepishly. *No, but I left you for it.* "Let me get these bars open." A massive beam barred the door, but between her and Renard they lifted it and tossed it aside.

N'hadia burst through the gate, whinnying. "They were planning something terrible for me—every time one of us was sent here, something terrible happened. Come on!" She charged up the remaining stairs, the rest scrambling after her.

A single door blocked the stairway from the first floor, the angry muffled shouts of soldiers carrying on the other side. N'hadia paused, but Renard and Chagan threw it open with a shout and fell on those soldiers with a vengeance. There was a blur of silver and blood, and the next thing Kura knew, a man lay dead at her feet.

The space was a narrow corridor, wide enough for two men to stand shoulder to shoulder, with a point of sunlight illuminating the distant right wall.

"Up those stairs," N'hadia shouted, pointing to another staircase at the end of the hallway.

More soldiers stumbled out of a doorway along the side wall, their armor half-fastened, swords held haphazardly in unprepared hands. Renard lunged at them and with flashing strokes brought a swift end to all three men, one by one, before they'd had a chance to scream. Kura watched in fearful amazement as those lifeless bodies clattered to the floor. Renard turned back toward her with a ghost of a smile, blood splatter staining his cheeks. She wasn't sure she'd ever seen anyone so swift and deadly with a sword in her entire life.

The loud thwack of wood on stone sounded on the opposite wall.

"Archers!" Triston shouted from somewhere behind her.

Figures moved in the open doorway, and a barrage of arrows filled the corridor. Kura bolted for the staircase. Chagan screamed, and the arrows crashed against the stone walls and floor with a patter like rain.

Kura ducked into the hallway of the winding staircase, with Idris before her and N'hadia following behind, grunting. A soldier met them on the staircase, sword drawn. Idris screamed, falling back against the wall, and Kura lunged to meet the soldier's stroke. He stumbled on the stairs, so she caught his shirtsleeve and tugged. He clattered down the stairs, shouting until N'hadia trod him underfoot. Kura squeezed her eyes shut, trying to pretend she couldn't hear his last choking breaths.

Triston and Aethan charged up the stairs behind her. Renard took up the rear, his bloodied sword clenched in one hand as he dragged Chagan's limp form with the other. The man groaned as Renard placed him, gently enough, against the wall. Bright red spots stained his clothing where arrows had pierced his leg and shoulder.

Idris gasped and scrambled to his side. "I've got him," she said, slipping Chagan's arm over her shoulder. "Go on."

Renard ran up the stairs, taking them two by two. Kura ran beside him, and they covered the flight in a matter of seconds. The next landing led to another narrow corridor, this one lit sporadically by narrow slits of white sunlight let in through the narrow archers' windows that ran the length of the right wall. Thick iron bars made the left wall, holding back throngs of shouting people.

Kura's heart lurched.

"Come on!" N'hadia galloped down the corridor. Several arrow shafts protruded from her rear flank, but she didn't seem to notice. "They're this way!"

Kura took off after the centaur girl, with Renard, Triston, and Aethan following not far behind. The prisoners continued to shout and come forward to rattle the bars of their cells. Kura desperately scanned the dozens of grubby faces, hoping to spot those precious few she recognized.

A dark shadow passed over the beams of sunlight, and the shouts of excitement shifted to calls of panic.

"Archers!" N'hadia screamed, sliding to the side, as the two figures stepped into view at the end of the hallway.

Kura threw herself to the ground as several bolts sailed over her head. Two flashes of silver answered them. The archers clattered to the floor, each with a knife in their eye. Kura whirled around. Aethan and Triston had dropped to the ground behind her, but Renard stood at the end of the corridor, his arm outstretched.

The prisoners cheered, and Kura nearly joined them as she met Renard's gaze with a grin. He nodded—then his knees buckled, and he would have fallen had Triston not been at his side to catch him. Blood leaked around the arrow shaft in Renard's side.

"Go on!" he shouted, waving them forward as he tried to brush aside Triston's assistance. Mind a blur, Kura listened to him. She followed N'hadia to the other end of the corridor, then paused to peek around the corner. The hallway was empty.

"We're clear!" she shouted, although she wasn't sure anyone would hear her.

N'hadia charged past to the nearest cell doors, grunting as she lifted the thick wooden beam. With a roar, the prisoners shoved their way out of the cell, knocking N'hadia to the side.

"Over here!" Aethan shouted. He jogged toward the stairway they'd come up, motioning for the others to follow him. "This way!"

Kura hesitated, studying each face that passed her by. *They have to be here, they have to be here.* She realized she was standing, useless, only after Triston ran past her and began struggling to lift the barricade blocking the second prison door. Kura leapt to his side, and between the two of them they raised the beam and tossed it to the floor. This group of prisoners burst out with a cheer like the first and followed Aethan. A few, however, lingered in the doorway.

An old woman frowned at Kura. "Who are you?"

"We're—" Kura started, dumbfounded. "We're breaking you out." She put a hand on the woman's shoulder to usher her forward. "Go on, follow the rest of them."

Still frowning, the woman hobbled toward the stairs, followed by the other few stragglers.

Triston reemerged at Kura's side after the prisoners had their backs turned. "Anyone else?"

N'hadia cantered past both of them. "Yes, come on! Upstairs!"

Triston hesitated as Kura ran off after the centaur girl. He'd been caught up in the moment, but as the shouts of the fleeing prisoners faded into the lower floors he had the sense to question his own actions. This was still a rebellion. And he was still the son of the king.

Renard's pained cry echoed in the hallway, and Triston turned around. The man sat with his back against the wall, his shirt and brigandine armor piled in a heap beside him. Idris knelt before him with a bloodied arrow in her hand.

Triston took a step forward, fascinated. Idris tossed the arrow aside, pressed her hands against the bleeding gash in the man's side, then began whispering strange words too low for Triston to hear. Renard clenched his eyes shut, his face twisted into a grimace, but finally Idris removed her hands and he let out a sigh of relief.

The arrow wound was gone. There was a gash—jagged and dark, which matched the amorphous reminders of many previous wounds on the man's torso—but all that remained of serious injury was the red blood smeared across his ebony skin.

Idris pulled Renard to his feet, and Triston caught the girl by the arm. "How did you do that?"

She glanced up at him, almost fearful, and held his gaze for a long moment. Then she stared at her hands. "The Essence moves by its own intentions."

Triston grinned, nearly laughing. He wanted an *answer*, not nonsensical platitudes. "No, really, how did you do that?"

"Hey." Chagan stepped forward, wedging himself between Triston and Idris—and Triston realized he was still holding the girl's arm. He released her immediately and stepped back. "I'm sorry, I..."

He couldn't help but picture that boy, Darrow, lying dead and mangled on the streets of Pedrida—even after that Feldlander had tried to heal him. And yet here Renard stood with Chagan, weary and limping but very much alive.

Shouts echoed from the upper floor, drawing all their attentions.

Renard nodded in Triston's direction. "Go on." He bent down to retrieve his shirt and chestplate. "I'm already going to catch hell for this whole thing as it is. And you stuck to your end of the bargain."

Triston stared at the man. "You..."

Renard laughed. "Don't argue, kid, just go! And maybe don't be a stranger."

N'hadia took the stairs a handful at a time, Kura two-by-two, until they reached the metal door barring them from the third floor.

"The door's—"

N'hadia whinnied, reared up on her back legs, and smashed her front hooves into the door. The hinges snapped and the sheet of metal dropped with a clang, falling on two unlucky soldiers who stood on the other side.

This hallway was identical to the second floor, and here three more armed men waited. Kura lunged, driving her blade through the neck of the first man—who was too distracted by the screams of his comrade, trapped beneath the door, to bring up his sword. N'hadia pushed forward with a snarl, trampling the next two men in total disregard of their sword and crossbow, and the soldier's metal chestplates cracked and caved under the centaur's weight.

The centaurs cooped up in these prison cells began to shout—commands, it sounded like—and the nearest struck at the iron bars with their hooves. Wood, stone and metal fell to the ground, filling the air with grey dust, and from that cloud emerged the Cenóri. They let out a war cry, which drowned out the final shouts of the remaining guards at the other end of the corridor as they trod them underfoot.

N'hadia shouted in her own language, charging into the cloud of dust. Kura followed, shoulder pressed against the wall, at as safe a distance as she could manage from the centaurs' thundering hooves. They made a loop around the corridor, the prison cells always on their left, as the remaining centaurs busted their cell bars to join the growing stampede.

Their pace slowed when they reached the staircase, pressing together to try to fit down the narrow passage. Kura held back, then trailed behind to rejoin the others on the second floor. Aethan had congregated the group of humans along the left-bound corridor, while N'hadia stood at the head of the herd of centaurs stretching to the right.

Kura pushed herself through the crowd to rejoin Renard, Idris, and Chagan at Aethan's side. She hesitated, looking over their group for a second time. "Where's Triston?"

Renard shook his head dismissively. "Gone." Kura stared at him, baffled to realize she might be disappointed, but the man just motioned to the out-facing wall, catching Idris's attention. "You're up. Again."

Idris stepped forward, clenching her eyes shut, as she pressed her hands against the stone wall. A tentative hush fell over the crowd. Dust from the third floor drifted through the cracks in the floorboards above, highlighting the beams of sun in sharp strips.

With a deafening rumble, the wall gave way. Blinding light streamed into the hallway, forcing Kura to shade her eyes with her hand, and large blocks of stone tumbled onto the street far below. The prisoners pulled back, shouting questions to one another, but Idris continued to work. Her hands moved now in wide, sweeping motions, even as she kept her eyes clenched shut.

Gangly roots shot out of the street below and entangled the mass of rubble from the tower. Idris began to sweat, her movements becoming stiff and jerky, but the roots continued to climb, weaving into one another as they piled the stones into a wide ramp. Finally, they became still. Idris let out a breath and fell to her knees. Before her stretched a steep but smooth pathway of roots and stone, leading down from the second floor of the tower onto the dirt streets of Shalford below.

"Come on!" Kura shouted, waving her arm as she ran forward to Idris's side. She hauled the girl to her feet and pulled her out of the way as the prisoners fled down the ramp.

Panting, Idris clenched Kura's arm and tried to steady herself. "I still have to..."

She pushed herself to stand on her own, and stepped to the edge of the makeshift doorway she'd created. Idris raised her hand, waving it in small, swift motions—as though she were writing in air. A tangle of shoots, marred black with dirt, crawled up the outer wall of the tower, unraveling methodically until they stretched from the ground to the roof. Cautiously leaning over the edge, Kura peered up at the tower wall, stunned. She recognized the image they formed: it was the first symbol inlaid on the blade of Ìsendorál. Gallian's sigil.

She met Idris's gaze, and the girl gave her a weary smile. "So they know who has done all this."

Kura turned back to the symbol, fear mixing with her sense of wonder. *Idris, I'm not—*

"Let's go!" Renard shouted, hobbling down the ramp after the last of the human prisoners as Aethan followed him, supporting Chagan. There was something inherently commanding about Renard's voice, and Kura found herself falling into line beside him —until he tripped.

She darted forward to catch him and slipped his arm over her shoulder even as he grumbled.

"I don't need—"

"I know." She sheathed her sword and held on to Renard's wrist. His arrow wound was gone—likely Idris's work—but by the way he stumbled it seemed he barely had the strength to stand.

The herd of centaurs followed behind them, the echoing thud of their hooves carrying like rolls of thunder as they galloped down the ramp and into the city.

Soldier's shouts rang out from atop the walls of the tower courtyard, answered by the pained, angry cry of a few centaurs. Sunlight flashed on arrow bolts as they sailed into the crowd of prisoners.

Kura grimaced. "They've still got archers in the—"

"I know," Renard muttered.

Minding her footing on the ramp, Kura stole another look at those archers. Silver flashed in the windows above—just a few, but still too many. Beyond the courtyard, a small company of soldiers pulled their horses to a stop. Two men, dressed in the typical silver plate armor and red cloak, flanked another man seated atop a magnificent white gelding. He looked like a king in his silver-hemmed cloak—Kura nearly stumbled.

It was the grey-eyed man.

He frowned at the sigil Idris had left on the side of the tower like it was an inconvenience—as if a servant were late with his breakfast. He was unmistakable—that head of loose brown hair, that sharp, trimmed jawline, those grey eyes... She'd always considered the possibility she was crazy—after all, she was not responsible for what her tired mind made up in her dreams—but this man was very, very real. For some reason that was more frightening than the alternatives.

A centaur's frame passed between Kura and the sun, casting her in shadow. "*Hywn renae*, little one."

Startled, Kura squinted at the light-rimmed face above her, then smiled. "Konik!" Even with the sun at his back she recognized that white stripe in the centaur's hair. She'd left his village as a fugitive, but under the circumstances this felt like a meeting of old friends.

Konik turned to the centaur beside him and spoke a few short words in his own language. The other centaur grunted, then stepped forward to grab hold of Renard and swing the man onto his back.

"Whoa!" Renard blinked, then laughed. "Well, alright then."

Konik offered Kura his hand, and she took it. He hauled her onto his back, and the pair of centaurs cantered forward, bringing Kura and Renard along with them. Kura almost called for Konik to stop, until she turned back to see several other centaurs snatching up Aethan, Chagan, and Idris.

"Where to, *byr'del*?" the other centaur asked, giving Renard a sideways glance. It was Piotr, N'hadia's father.

"Uh, well—" Renard stuttered. "We're going to have to lose these soldiers."

Piotr grinned. "Gladly."

Chapter Thirty-Three

BACKTRACKING

Triston ducked into the shadow of the alleyway, pulling his hood closer to his face as he peered up at Shalford Tower. He'd slipped out unharmed among the prison-break, but the tower itself had not fared well. Guilt ate at him as he watched his father's soldiers picking through the rubble, most of them half-heartedly carrying away stones as the few others stopped, intermittently, to stare and scratch their heads.

But were these his father's soldiers? The few who hadn't given chase looked as true and honest as any, but Triston had seen the *other* soldier for himself. That had not been a sanctioned officer, to say the least.

He lingered in the alley, concerned one of those soldiers might recognize him. He was a traitor now. There wasn't anything else he reasonably could have done, but that didn't change the truth. He'd raised his blade against his own men.

"You are a strange one, aren't you?"

Triston spun around, then suppressed a sigh of relief. It was an older woman, with a hunched frame that barely reached his chest. She was dressed in a long blue cloak with colorfully embroidered edges, and her deep hood hid all of her face except for the strands of wiry grey hair which hung across her chest.

"Afternoon, ma'am."

The woman gave a cackling laugh. "Oh, so polite for so young a man." She tottered to his side and lifted a crooked finger to point at the tower. "A harrowing sight, is it?"

Triston glanced where the woman was pointing—the farther side of the tower—and pulled back in surprise. A symbol in flowing script, adhered to the stone wall like age-old ivy, wound the full height of the tower. He recognized that sigil: it was the very same one on the sword hanging in his father's council chambers, and on that ancient sword Kura had claimed in Nansûr.

"The forebears' mark," the old woman mused. "It has been a long time since I have seen it." Her voice fell to a whisper. "...A long time."

Triston ran his eyes over the symbol again. His father had always laughed at the idea of a fonfyr, calling it one of Seren's old stories, and silenced any rumors that he himself had any claim to the title. But his mother...

"The fonfyr is real." It'd been over a decade but he could almost still hear her, speaking in excited, hushed tones as she pulled him aside to counter his father's jokes and Seren's trivia. *"Your father fought in the memory of such things, and someday so will you."*

Triston flinched as the old woman rested a hand on his arm and motioned to the crowd gathering a stone's throw from the base of the tower. "It has been longer for them."

He'd already seen the crowd—they were half the reason he'd taken refuge in this alleyway in the first place—but as the woman drew his attention to them again, he noticed their faces: they were staring up at the forebears' mark in awe. The people here had feared him and his company when they'd ridden through a week ago, but now they watched the soldiers in almost amusement, whispering behind their backs as a small child attempted to pelt them with pebbles.

Triston let out a slow breath. This was the work of the rebellion, and the people knew it. In a matter of days, the word would spread to Edras and across Avaron. He and Seren had set out intending to squelch the rebellion. Now, it appeared all they'd done was kindle it.

The old woman shook her head. "Prophecies are dangerous things, especially on the eve of fulfillment. But the harvester stands at the winnowing floor, the chaff separated from the wheat and ready for the burning." She looked up, a hint of yellow light glinting in her eyes. "She chose peace, but she lied. Will you still follow her?"

Triston held the woman's gaze with a curious frown. Was she so old her mind had started to wander? "Do you live nearby?" He placed a hand on her arm. "I can walk you home if you'd like."

The woman laughed, her happy cackle ending with a wheeze. "Oh yes." She motioned a way down the alley, to a small tent made of colorful blankets and large, abstract tapestries that hung between the houses on either side of the street. So she was a fortune teller, a Svaldan spiritualist. Such folk were usually driven off from anywhere near Edras—their reputation as thieves and swindlers preceded them.

"Come, come." The woman latched onto Triston's arm with surprising strength. "I have supper. You must join me."

"I—" Triston began, but he caught a glimpse of the face beneath her hood's shadow.

The creature was grotesque, wrinkled far beyond her age, with thin lips curled back against sharp, grinning teeth. He ripped his arm from her grip as a childish shudder of fear prickled down his spine. Was she not human? Was she one of those monsters, those... saja? For one sudden, horrible moment he considered running his sword through her stomach.

"I have to go," he managed to say, giving his best attempt at a gracious bow, and then—without waiting for a response—jogged out of the alleyway and onto the main street. Maybe he caught a few curious glances; he didn't care. He pulled his hood tighter against his face and strode onwards with a renewed sense of urgency.

He had to get home. His father possibly thought he was dead, or else that he was working with the rebellion, and Triston wasn't entirely sure which would be worse.

Dol was the next closest military outpost. He might be able to reach it before news of what happened in Shalford did, if he found a horse. From there, only a morning's ride separated him and Avtalyon—almost as fast as a riverboat, although Triston was not about to try that route again.

He did, however, stop at the post to send a letter to his father. It took some bargaining, as the rebellion had confiscated all his money, but he convinced the short, surly man to give him a scrap of parchment and a bird in exchange for the chestplate he'd stolen from the soldiers he'd killed. The paper was small and the inkwell nearly dry, so all Triston managed to write was:

Alive. Coming home, will explain.
Triston

He sighed, looking over the letter as it dried. It would have to be good enough. He hoped, dearly, that his father somehow hadn't heard the lie about his death. He knew what would follow: war, just like the one his father had waged against the Fidelis after the death of his mother. And now only Seren stood at his father's side, ready to direct that anger as he saw fit.

Seren. Triston ground his teeth. This whole situation stank of something, but he wasn't entirely sure he wanted to find out what. Ignorance might be more palatable than the truth.

He rolled the parchment and then secured it to the pigeon's leg. He held the bird, his hands covering its wings, and looked into its piercing red eye. He laughed softly. This was a fight against myth and monsters; what made him think this little creature had a chance?

With a gentle toss, he let the bird go. It flapped its blue-grey wings in panic for a few beats, then gathered its balance and speed to sail over the slate-covered rooftops toward the horizon. He watched its dark shadow disappear in the golden brightness of the sunset, feeling oddly jealous somehow.

"You wantin' to buy somethin' else?" the scrawny post manager asked, poking his head up from the bottom of the narrow staircase that led to the window. Triston straightened and found the man eyeing his leather boots.

"No, that will be all for me. Thank you."

The man scowled. "A man with no money, tradin' his good stuff away, an' still knowin' how to write?" He shook his head, muttering as he turned away. "Unlucky, I say, unlucky since the day I was born."

Triston left the post and made his way to the market street, where he procured an old farm horse in exchange for his shoulder guards and cuisses. He pulled the animal into an alley as the group of soldiers returned, marching—empty-handed and splattered with mud—down the main road. In groups of two they spread through the city, barring gates and pounding on doors in search of any straggling prisoners, but Triston used the commotion to slip out of town unnoticed. For the first time he was grateful the garrison had spent their funds on a tower rather than a city wall.

Seated on a half-dead plow horse, the setting sun before him, the Prince of Avaron left Shalford, a dead man and a fugitive both.

It took some maneuvering, but Renard guided the company of freed prisoners past the stone quarry, across several streams, and through the densest parts of the pine forest until the pursuing soldiers fell far behind. Anxiety ate at Kura's stomach—she could only hope her family was among these refugees—but at last Renard directed Piotr to a stop in a narrow, stone-lined basin.

Centaurs and humans poured into the clearing, most flopping down to rest in the ample shade provided by the towering evergreens that lined the space. Rocky cliffs corralled most of the field and the trees took care of the rest, forming a natural fence against prying eyes. Kura's heart leapt in her chest when she caught sight of the humans—maybe forty in all—gathering to the side near the steepest cliff, and she flung herself from Konik's back before he even came to a stop.

"Thank you!" she shouted, throwing a wave in passing, and sprinted toward the crowd. If Konik replied, she didn't hear him.

She pushed herself in among the collective of grubby human prisoners. "Father?" The stench of unwashed bodies stifled the air, and she coughed. "Mother?" Several eyes turned to catch her gaze—each unfamiliar, though the proper age to be her parents. "Faron? Elli?"

She stopped, the nebulous mass of humanity churning around her as she inspected each person who passed her by. Most shied away from her, if they even noticed her—they were all strangers, all unknown faces, but she was too desperate now to do anything but hope.

Had someone called her name? She spun around. "I..." she started, not sure what to say. "I'm here!" It came out nearly as a scream.

"Kura?"

She was sure she'd heard it this time. She took off toward the voice, shoving herself through the crowd with reckless abandon.

"Kura?" A second voice this time.

It was her father's face she saw first, his tall, auburn head shining like a beacon over the masses around her. Kura shoved herself toward him, the crowd parting before her, and then she saw her mother, her brown hair cut short and her dirty face tear-stained. She held Rowley in her arms, his skinny face pressed against her chest. Faron stood at her side, lankier than he had been, although his smile shone brighter than the bruise on his cheek. Elli was before him, sobbing, but as her eyes met Kura's, she gave a cry of excitement and bolted forward.

Kura hardly knew what she was doing, but her legs carried her and she found herself smothered in a hug. Her family's voices surrounded her, asking a thousand questions, but she barely heard. She held on to them, tears welling up in her eyes as her chest shook with sobs of joy. They all reeked, but in that moment she had everything she ever wanted in the world and she couldn't remember the last time she'd seen anything so beautiful.

As soon as her family released her, Kura took a step back, struggling to wipe away the tears as she looked up into her parents' faces. What had they gone through? Another sob wracked her chest. They came to her side again, with words of concern and comfort, and that only made it worse.

"I'm sorry," Kura managed to say, the words catching in her throat. "I'm sorry..."

The whole story spilled from her in an incomprehensible jumble; she couldn't hold it back any longer. She told them about the rebellion, her secret meetings, and the more she spoke the more she found she couldn't bear to look at any of them.

"Kura, I..." Jisela took a step back, her face scrunched up in conflict. Faron and Elli stood off to the side, holding hands.

"Oh, Kura," Spiridon said finally, his tone so unexpectedly calm she had to look up at his face. There was a smile in his eyes—not a hint of anger—and he wrapped her in a hug. "I don't care," he said softly, his chin resting against her head as he held her close. "I don't care. Not anymore."

Chapter Thirty-Four

PATCHWORK

"They kept asking for information about the rebels," Jisela said, bouncing Rowley on her knee. Kura sat on the grass beside her mother—her family at her sides—and while she didn't hold her mother's gaze, she couldn't feel the proper shame. *They're alive.* The thought echoed, over and over again. *I found them, they're alive!*

"We got water and bread to share once a day," Spiridon said. "But aside from that, those soldiers seemed to view us as nothing more than a burden." There was an icy edge to her father's tone as he spoke, and she hesitantly examined his face. His eyes were distant, but in them burned an anger she had not seen for a long, long time.

Rowley smiled and laughed, entirely unaware of the conversation, as he reached his tiny hands toward her. She grinned and took him into her arms. His smile only widened, and he babbled something that surely made sense to him as, with some deliberation, he placed his hands on her cheeks.

"I missed you too," Kura whispered, and kissed his nose.

"Sounds like you're the one who's been on an adventure," Faron said with a grin, glancing—almost shyly—in Kura's direction.

She chuckled as Rowley decided to grasp and then try to eat her hair. "You have no idea."

"Can we go home now?" Elli called out, impatiently ripping handfuls of grass from the ground.

Spiridon and Jisela shared a quizzical glance, although neither of them spoke.

Home. Kura pictured her house as it had been, before she remembered how she'd left it. That burned wreck was several dayrides across the country and what felt like a lifetime away. She looked down at Rowley's smiling face, unable to keep from smiling herself. They'd never return to that place. They could make a life here, somewhere, maybe in—

"What's that?" Faron asked, glancing back over his shoulder.

Kura looked up, her thoughts of the future crumbling as the distant shouts pulled her back into the present. She caught only glimpses of it through the crowd, but it appeared a small commotion was brewing between a group of humans and centaurs. A pillar of fire burst into the air. The crowd shouted in surprise and clambered for the relative safety of their own familiar groups.

Anxiety caught in Kura's chest, and she returned Rowley to her mother's arms as she scrambled to her feet. She had to pry his little fingers from her hair before straightening. "I'll—I'll come right back."

"What is it?" Spiridon asked, more concerned than curious.

Kura took a step away from them, trying to figure out how she should explain.

"Kura!" Jisela said, both commanding and distraught. "Don't go, where are you going?"

"I'll be right back, Mother," Kura called out over her shoulder as she jogged toward the commotion, forcing her way through the crowd. She recoiled as another burst of fire carried over her head, and she ran right into Renard.

"Oh, what—?"

"Come on," he said, placing a hand on her shoulder as he tried to direct her to follow the fleeing crowd. "You don't want to get in their way."

She held her ground and peered over Renard's shoulder. Most people had pulled away, leaving a span of grass empty. On the other side stood a small band of humans in threadbare clothes, little more than a dozen in all, each of them with gaunt cheeks and thin wrists—they'd been starved, more than the other prisoners, and while they took strong stances, Kura recognized the desperation in their eyes. Still, they stood in formation, hands raised as though they were armor-adorned warriors.

She drew in a breath. They all had green eyes. They were Fidelis.

Across from them churned a line of centaurs. Most of them stomped and snorted, like horses champing at the bit, but one stood in front of them, between the Fidelis and the centaur line, barking orders to hold them back. Konik.

"Begone, beast," one of the Fidelis said. He was a shorter man, with a bulbous face marked on the temples by dark splotches of skin beneath his wispy silver hair. "I won't ask again."

Konik snorted. "There will be no posturing here, Cynwrig. I know how your kind was kept in that tower. You lack the strength to fight. Go your way."

Cynwrig. Kura remembered that name from something Idris had told her. He was the one who'd made the fake sword, the one who'd helped Dradge become king.

"And let you alone with these innocent people? How many of my kind have you slain, Cenóri?" Cynwrig raised his clenched fists. Droplets of water rose from the ground and formed thin tendrils that circled his trembling arms.

"Hey!" Kura stepped forward, not into the space between the Fidelis and centaurs—she wasn't that stupid—but close enough that they would have to notice her. "Stop it!"

Konik turned to her with curious amusement, but Cynwrig scowled. "This does not concern you, girl. Go back to your mother."

Kura returned the look. "What's there left to fight over, huh? The same man just locked the both of you in the same prison."

"Shut up, girl." Cynwrig didn't even look in Kura's direction; he had his green eyes trained on Konik's chest. "Yours is a faithless generation. I should expect you wouldn't care."

Kura watched the man in utter disbelief. She was already inclined to hate him, knowing what he'd done, and meeting him didn't help a thing.

Cynwrig jabbed a finger at Konik. "Trofast, whom you exiled, proved to be wisest among your kind, but even when I—"

Kura stomped into the open space between the two companies, drew Ìsendorál from its scabbard, and jammed the blade into the ground.

"What are you—?" Cynwrig began, ready to chew her out, but the other Fidelis behind him gasped and pulled back. Wonder rippled through the crowd, leaving a silence broken by whispers of *fonfyr.*

Konik stepped back in surprise, and even Cynwrig fell silent. For a moment.

"It can't..." He looked from the blade to Kura's face. "You aren't..." He reached for the sword. "You aren't prepared for it: the drafting will kill you. Let me study it, keep it safe—"

"No." Kura pulled the blade from the ground and held it in a loose half-guard. She would gladly give up the sword, but not to those over-eager hands. "I found it." *Gods, I sound like a child.* "I... claim it."

Whispers rose again among the Fidelis, and Cynwrig alone held his defensive stance.

"You're welcome to come with us to Nansûr." Kura turned to Konik's company, then toward the rest of the freed prisoners on the opposite side of the clearing. "Anyone who is willing to join us in the fight against Dradge is welcome!"

Cynwrig lowered his hands, the tendrils of water turning to mist, but he shook his head. "I cannot allow you—"

"Then go!" Kura waved her hand at Cynwrig. She knew she was letting anger drive her, but she didn't care. "Anyone, any of you who can't stomach the real fight, just go! My fight is with him." She pointed in the direction she desperately hoped was Avtalyon. "Dradge has taken our homes, our loved ones, our harvests—now's our chance to take something back!"

A wavering cheer rose from somewhere in the back of the clearing, and the Fidelis shared nervous glances. Finally, Cynwrig bowed, the gesture stiff and exaggerated.

"We will go." He strode briskly toward the tree line, and the other Fidelis fell into line behind him without a word.

Kura frowned as she stepped out of his way, but couldn't say she was disappointed to see him leave. Cynwrig paused only a moment and leaned close to her shoulder.

"You aren't ready," he whispered. "Everyone has designs, even the best of us. They will chew you up and spit you out, like the gristle you are."

She opened her mouth to speak, but the man continued on his way, his face impassive—as though he hadn't spoken at all. The other Fidelis followed dutifully at his heels, and she watched them with disgust until their tattered brown cloaks disappeared among the evergreens.

Renard jogged up to Kura's side, laughing, and clasped her on the shoulder. "Well done! I still might catch hell for this when we get back, but well done!"

Kura tried to look up at him with a smile, but her gaze fell instead on Konik. He nodded, gratefully, and she believed he really meant it. She lifted the sword to return it to its sheath, and then the weight of what she'd done came crashing down on her.

Oh gods.

She stumbled back, searching the crowd as fear churned in her stomach. The few that dared to look her way beheld her with either excitement or reverence, and the air hummed with eager energy—a readiness to fight.

They think I'm the fonfyr. Oh gods, I didn't...

All she'd wanted was to keep the Fidelis and the Cenóri from tearing each other apart—and shockingly, she'd managed that. Fonfyr or not, she'd served as the thread that had brought this patchwork of peoples together.

"Alright, kid." Renard placed his hand on her shoulder again, as a gesture of comfort this time. "We're both crowd control now."

"Kura!" Her father pushed against the line of rebels Renard had set up to separate the humans from the centaurs.

Chagan, Idris, and Aethan were among them, along with several others—each of them newly liberated prisoners Renard knew. There weren't many weapons to go around, so the weary band was attempting to reason with two equally weary—and agitated—groups of once mortal enemies.

"Sir," Renard sighed, "you need to stay here, please."

"Are you saying I can't speak to my daughter?"

Kura pushed through the crowd. Two rebel scouts had set out for Nansûr; everyone else was only waiting here for Trofast to arrive. But naturally, everyone had questions—most of them varieties of the same one: where are we going? Unfortunately, *how the hell should I know?* was not an appropriate response.

"I'm here," Kura called out, coming to a stop at Renard's side. The man gave her an exasperated look, but Spiridon smiled in relief.

"Come." He latched onto her arm. One rebel stepped forward defensively, but Kura cut him off.

"It's alright." She forced herself through the rebel line, allowing her father to drag her along behind him, and the group of prisoners muttered amongst themselves. Some of them—all strangers—looked at her with a sense of wonder, but the neighbors she knew from back home gave her disapproving scowls or sidelong glances.

"Kura..." Renard started, a sense of warning in his tone. He had a sort of desperation in his eyes that suggested he expected her to run off and disappear the moment she left his sight.

She gave him a smile, but was surprised to find how relevant his suspicions really were. "I'll be right back."

Renard nodded, reluctantly, and Kura followed her father into the center of the crowd.

"You know," Spiridon said, "that's just what you told us a half-hour ago."

Kura fixed her eyes on her feet. "I know."

Spiridon placed his large hands on Kura's shoulders and turned her to face him. "They say you're the fonfyr. Are you?"

He held her gaze so calmly, so earnestly. She couldn't be certain if he believed 'them' or not, but he would believe her. She nearly said no—right there, without a second thought—but each passing moment drew her attention to the crowd. She couldn't lie, but all the same she couldn't speak the truth.

She gave the barest shake of her head and glanced down at her feet again.

Spiridon sighed deeply. "Look at me."

She did.

"You want out of this? Tell me, and we'll be on the other side of Avaron by tomorrow night."

Kura laughed softly. She could no more accept that offer than her father could really give it, but it felt good to hear him say it. She flung her arms around his waist and pressed her face against his chest. He held her there, his arms a comforting weight draped over her shoulders.

"I always knew you'd do great things, Kura." He chuckled. "Great things, or dangerous things, and damn me but I can't figure out which one this is."

"Kura?" Jisela's voice rose over the murmur of the crowd. Kura leaned out of her father's embrace to meet her mother's gaze. "There you are!" Her worry melted away to joy, and she squeezed Kura into a hug. "You can't just go running away like that..."

Faron and Elli stood nearby—Rowley asleep in Faron's arms—and they watched Kura with curious anticipation as Jisela held her tight.

"I remember..." Jisela continued. "I remember a girl who said the forebears' tales were only children's stories."

Kura clenched her eyes shut. "I think she got lost somewhere between here and the Wynshire."

Jisela stepped back, cupping Kura's cheek in her hand as tears welled up in her eyes. "Don't you dare get yourself killed after I've just got you back from the dead."

Kura winced, but tried to pretend she hadn't. "If the Wynshire couldn't kill me, then how can this?"

Shouts rang out in the clearing, the voices carrying a mix of excitement and panic that spread through the group of humans like wildfire. Kura turned toward the road, squinting against the setting sun, but she didn't have to see through the billowing cloud of dust to know what it was. Trofast's company.

"Is he going to kill us?" a man at Kura's side asked. It was the Horse Thief's husband, from the Wynshire. He'd hardly given her a second glance back home, but now he was watching her expectantly—as if she were the one in charge.

"Yeah!" the Horse Thief shouted, pressing up against her husband's side. "Have you sprung us just to get us slaughtered by those monsters?"

Kura straightened her shoulders, fighting back a grimace.

"Kura..." Jisela said, catching her by the arm with such strength that Kura doubted her mother had any intention of ever letting go.

"You always believed the fonfyr would come, Mother. You've got to let me keep them from tearing each other apart until he gets here."

Those tears welled up in Jisela's eyes again, but she nodded and reluctantly loosed her grip. Spiridon came to his wife's side, wrapping his arm around her, and he nodded. "Go. Do what you have to."

Kura straightened, fear and appreciation welling up all at once, then pushed through the crowd to jog to the edge of the clearing. Renard, Aethan, and Idris already stood there, waiting, as Trofast and his company cantered into view. Aethan gave her a warm smile —one she tried to return—then Idris squeaked and ran to her side.

"Oh, don't leave!" She latched onto Kura's arm.

Kura jumped, then chuckled. "I'm not going anywhere. What's the matter?"

Idris let out a shuddering sigh, and released Kura's arm. "I'm sorry." She took a step back, pressing her hands against her chest. "It's just... do you know how long it's been since they've seen each other?"

Kura hesitated, glancing between Idris's face and Trofast's incoming company.

"Sixty years." Idris tugged at the edge of her hood, the sunlight glistening in the tears on her cheeks. "Trofast became chieftain and he tried to change things—tried to end the slaughter of my kind, end the Reconquest. But Konik and the others exiled him under *Fahsang*, extradition of blood. Trofast was no longer to be seen as Cenóri, but as a stranger. He and Konik nearly came to blows, and vowed to never see or speak with one another again."

Kura nodded, thoughtfully. That would certainly explain why, when she'd met them in the Wynshire, the centaurs had been so upset to find her token from Trofast's rebellion. "You... you think Trofast will try to kill them?"

Idris shook her head, too warily to be reassuring. "He's a kind man. He has been so generous with my mother and me for all these years when no one else would welcome us. But he's been hurt and driven away, and an animal once beaten fights hardest." She let out a shuddering sigh.

"Hey." Kura placed a hand on Idris's shoulder. "It will be alright."

The girl almost laughed. "Oh, I know it will. Eventually. But I'm just so worried about right now."

Hoofbeats pounded on the thick, dry grass then came to a gradual pause at the edge of the basin. Trofast strode first among his company, his proud, lean figure dwarfing the rest at his sides. There was Erryl, seated on a horse, with Grenja following at his heels. Rusket the bear loped along in the rear, with several others Kura did not recognize.

Trofast and his fellow centaurs broke away from the rest of their group, and Konik's followers moved to intercept them, Konik in front. The two factions of centaurs approached one another and formed a sort of ring with Trofast and Konik in the center. Kura couldn't help but see their resemblance now, in their long, strong-featured faces anyway. But where Trofast was lean, Konik was bulky, and while both were adorned with intricate tattoos, Trofast had barely any unmarked skin.

Trofast broke the silence, his voice deadly calm. "I demand *sabot'lian*, as is my right under *Fahsang*."

Those among Konik's people murmured in surprise, but Konik only nodded. "It is granted."

Idris stifled a cry, and Kura glanced between her and Renard, who only shook his head gravely. Kura swallowed her rising fear and stepped toward the gathering centaurs.

"Hey." Aethan caught her by the arm. She almost wanted to be mad at him, but she could see the concern in his eyes. "You can't get involved. The sword might have been enough to sway Cynwrig, but the Cenóri won't care. Trust me."

Kura peered into his green eyes. She didn't want him to be right, but she knew he probably was. At the very least, she wasn't ready to stake her life on a bet against him.

The centaurs pulled back, widening the circle, while the humans moved farther toward the other side of the clearing, their nervous murmurs hovering with the tension in the air.

The two brothers circled one another, no more than an arm's width apart, their ears pinned back against their necks. Trofast struck first, kicking out with his back legs to hit Konik on the side with his hooves. Kura cringed. Who was she rooting for here?

Konik snorted and wheeled around, striking back with his own rear hooves. They kept side by side, pummeling and kicking at one another with their rear legs. Kura thought she'd come to see the centaurs as people—as human-*like* at least—but now they fought like two wild stallions at a watering hole. Fists flew, hooves flashed, and horse's cries echoed through the clearing.

Idris screamed and Kura wrinkled her nose as red blood shone in the sunlight, but Kura wasn't certain who'd drawn it—both of the centaurs' chests and flanks glistened with it. The other Cenóri rallied at the sight of blood, and both sides shouted either encouragements or insults, all in their own tongue.

Then Konik stumbled. Kura took in a breath—for an instant she thought he was dead—but he knelt at Trofast's feet, crossing his fists over his heart as he drew in a shuddering breath. "I yield."

Konik's followers murmured in surprise, which quickly turned to anger. Trofast towered over his brother, blood marring his bare chest and dripping down the side of his mouth.

He stared at Konik, his gaze stern, then a smile broke across his face. And he laughed.

Kura cringed, bracing herself for whatever was to come, but Trofast offered Konik his hand and hauled him to his feet. "Brother!" He pulled Konik into a hug. "It has been too long!"

Konik winced, but when Trofast released him, he too was smiling. "Or perhaps not long enough."

Those among Trofast's company let out a hearty cheer as Konik's followers stepped back—not silently, but with relaxed shoulders and open hands.

Idris breathed a pained sigh of relief, and Kura looked to her in surprise. "That's it?"

"Well..." Idris wiped the tears from her cheeks. "In Cenóri tradition, the victor has the right to kill the loser, but—"

"Where will you lead us, Trofast, son of Gundehar?" The woman's voice was tremulous with age, but it carried over the falling applause and the rising murmur of conversation.

Trofast stepped forward, a deep frown creasing his brow as he scoured the centaur company.

"Where will you lead us?" the woman repeated, louder this time, as she pushed her way to the front. It was the white-haired centaur —the one who'd thought she could read the future with her sack of trinkets, the one Kura had met before in the village by the Everard.

Trofast stepped forward, bowing respectfully. "Mèrora."

Kura didn't know whether that was the woman's name or her title, but either way the old centaur stiffened to hear it.

"Where will you lead us, Trofast, son of Gundehar? Konik listened to the wind. Your father followed the stars. But you—you are not your brother's keeper, and you are not your father's son."

Trofast straightened. "Mèrora, I am not my father's son, nor do I aspire to be. But I do follow the stars. They led me here, before they became still." Anger flashed in the woman's eyes, but Trofast continued. "Tell me, does the Temper still speak, and you understand it?"

"Yes," she said sternly. Idris shivered and moved closer to Kura's side. "Yes, for two of your lifetimes I have asked of the Temper and received the answer. My blood is steeped in the tradition of our ancestors, my eyes are opened to the mysteries of the sky, my ears are tuned to the whispers of the wind. That is why I am Mèrora, and have been since I was but a foal." She strode forward, her dark eyes narrowing. "But you, Trofast, son of Gundehar, your blood is cut from the trail of our ancestors, your eyes are blinded to the celestial dance, your ears are deaf to—"

"Enough, Mèrora," Konik whispered harshly, stepping between Trofast and the old centaur.

She fixed her gaze, stern and cold, on Konik. "You have no more right to command me than I have the right to command the Temper. It is my place to read the truth—of the past, of the present, of the future—and it is my solemn duty to speak that truth when our chieftain stands to lead our people astray."

Konik took a step back with a genuine look of hurt and surprise as the rest of the centaurs murmured among themselves.

"Astray?" Trofast wiped his bloody nose on the back of his hand —he was smiling. "Woman, we have been astray, and only now catch sight of the path again through the trees. Ìsendorál has been found."

The woman scoffed. "The sword is Fidelis legend. It means nothing to us."

"But should it?" Trofast turned from the woman to eye the rest of Konik's followers. "We feel the flow and pull of the Temper on this world in the very marrow of our bones. They cannot, but in their prophecy they catch a clouded glimpse of it anyway. Why shouldn't that mean something to us?" He motioned to Kura, and she felt as though her heart froze in her chest. "We have one among us who found the sword, and who is willing to carry it. How can we not follow?"

The centaurs murmured with one another, in what might be agreement—they weren't angry enough for Kura to think they meant to take up arms.

"No!" The woman stomped forward, ears pinned back, her frail fists clenched at her sides. "This will not be!"

Trofast met her gaze easily. "Then, Mèrora, show me. Show all of us. Cast for it."

The woman's face contorted into a frown. She swung her pack from her shoulder, methodically unpacked her belongings, then cast her handful of trinkets onto the cloth tabletop. The human crowd waited in silence, and only a few centaurs dared to swish their tails or shift their stances.

Her eyes flashed. "Bone of man touches river stone..." She faltered, a shock of fear breaking through her calm exterior. "But the blood ruby lies alone." Her eyes widened, and she muttered to herself as she smoothed a wrinkled hand over the collection of trinkets. "The—the goat sinew..."

The trees above the surrounding basin began to sway in a light breeze, and then a gust of wind blew through the space between the two companies. The old centaur cried out as the air caught her table, overturning it. Most of her trinkets fell onto the grassy clearing, but one caught in the gust—the flashing gold-and-black wing feather of a flicker. It tumbled over itself in the breeze, and the centaur woman watched, her mouth hanging open, as the wind carried the feather above her head, toward the trees, and out of sight.

A stunned silence came over the company of centaurs, and the humans whispered among themselves in curiosity. Kura stood there, Ìsendorál's sheathed hilt clenched in her fist, her heartbeat quickening with each passing second. This meant something, didn't it? But she had no idea what that could be, and some part of her was terrified to find out.

"Did you understand the wind's whisper, Mèrora?" Trofast gave her a reserved smile. "Did the Temper reveal the truth through your casting?"

The woman stared at her fallen trinkets, her mouth agape. "I, I..."

"Surely the wind spoke. Surely, the Temper—as Truth—revealed the truth. But you did not understand, did you?"

The old centaur drew in a shuddering breath and pressed her hands against her temples. She didn't look up.

"I cannot promise you safety," Trofast called out, turning to hold any gaze—human or Cenóri—who dared to meet his. "I cannot promise you comfort, or revenge, or whatever else your wavering hearts might seek. But I can promise you Ìsendorál, and one willing to wield it. And I can share with you a sanctuary for the promise our forebears extended to us all: a promise that each and every one of you will have a fighting chance at freedom."

A cheer rang out among the company, the voices of the humans and centaurs rising together as one excited shout. Kura felt as though she were going to be sick. She took a shaking step back, then collapsed to a seat on the grass.

"Hey!" Aethan knelt at her side. "What—?"

"I'm fine." Kura laughed, though she couldn't conjure up the proper mirth. "I'm fine. I just might have made the biggest mistake of my life."

Chapter Thirty-Five

Rih Hill

Kura breathed a tired sigh as she watched the second-to-last group of refugees amble from the stone basin and toward Nansûr.

The process had been a struggle. They had to vet each person, or at least ask probing questions about their intentions, and then send those interested enough to the stronghold in small groups, both to avoid arousing suspicion and to keep the population at a manageable level for the rebels escorting them. Kura understood the danger—for all of them here, anyway, as even a royal spy wouldn't make it out of Nansûr without permission—but at this point the sun was sinking behind the mountain range in the distance and she wanted nothing more than to find somewhere to fall asleep.

Renard had insisted she follow him through the camp as he arbitrarily stopped to talk to any small group of humans or centaurs. It was engaging at first, but grew tedious. She must have shown off Ìsendorál a dozen times, and avoided explaining just how she'd found it a few more times than that. Gradually, however, she came to understand Renard's intentions: the fonfyr was a distraction, a lone unifying symbol, and her presence served as a buffer between the clash of frayed nerves.

Kura rubbed a hand against her face and smothered a yawn. *The fonfyr.* A dozen times she was a second away from telling Renard everything, from exposing the lie—tearing the sword from her hip, shoving it into his hands to save for whoever really had a claim to it—but each time something stopped her. This crowd *needed* somebody to carry this sword. At least for now.

She chuckled grimly. Wasn't this what she had always wanted? For someone to take up arms against Dradge?

Renard clasped her on the shoulder. "Almost there, kid. This should be the last group. You wanna spread the word?"

She nodded, covering her mouth as she stifled another yawn. These last folks would be no trouble: it was her family, among a few others, with Aethan and Idris for escort. She trudged toward the center of the clearing where her family waited, leaving Renard to have a few words with Idris. Aethan was perched on one of the large stones that poked out of the long grass, her family seated in a vague circle around him. He was finishing a story with a dramatic flourish, and they all laughed as Kura walked up.

Faron leaned back to meet her gaze. "Did you really help him steal some guy's cows?"

She gave a bit of a smile and sank to a seat beside him in the grass. "Is that really what you're all laughing about?" She caught Aethan's eye with a curious glance, and he shrugged.

"I may have embellished a little."

Jisela laughed. "Oh, but that's how it's done! You have a talent for this, young man. Do you play?"

"No, ma'am. Although my mother did her best to try and teach me the flute."

"Ah." Jisela sighed. "And I left my fiddle at home…"

The mention of home immediately dampened their moods—but not Elli's. She jumped up and placed her hands on Aethan's knee. "Tell us another story! Tell us what you and Kura did next!"

Aethan grinned, sheepishly. "Well, I think we're going to leave here soon…"

Kura nodded, leaning back on her elbows in the grass. "Give it about five minutes, and we'll be heading after that last group."

Spiridon appeared to be only half listening. He had Rowley's little hands clasped around his index fingers as he helped the boy stand on the grass, and he nodded in Aethan's direction. "Where do you call home, boy?"

Aethan gave Spiridon a smile, one stiff around the edges. He glanced down, raking his fingers through his hair. "I suppose 'nowhere' would be the simplest answer."

Spiridon grunted. "You make a habit of keeping the company of criminals?"

"Father," Kura said with a frown. Aethan's smile faltered, and he seemed grateful to not have to answer the question.

Spiridon gave her the slightest hint of a grin. "I'd ask you the same thing, girl, but I already know your answer."

Kura shook her head. She knew if she told them what Aethan really was—a Fidelis—her mother would put an immediate end to her father's interrogation. But she also knew that Elli, and possibly even her mother, would then ask for some kind of demonstration, and she couldn't put Aethan in that position.

Soft footfalls crunched the dry grass and Kura turned back to find Idris picking her way across the field, two nostkynna horses—they carried their heads too high and walked with too much verve to be regular horses—following behind her. Kura scrambled to her feet, her sore limbs protesting. "We ready?"

Idris nodded, glancing shyly at Kura's family. "Mejdan and Akachi will take us on ahead of the group, and the others will follow behind after they've answered those questions like everyone else."

Kura frowned. "I thought—"

"They want you back at Nansûr." Idris winced as she realized she'd interrupted. "I think you were supposed to have joined one of the earlier groups. Trofast has already gathered the council—"

"*Another* council meeting? What do they want me for?"

"Well, you are the fonfyr."

Kura's smile faded. *But of course I am.*

Aethan took a step forward. "I'll stay with them, take up the rear. I'm sure we won't be far behind."

Kura shot him a grateful look. "Thanks."

"Where are we going?" Elli asked.

"Oh, we told you already," Faron said, rolling his eyes as he offered the girl his hand.

Spiridon braced Rowley against his shoulder, Jisela retrieved Elli's discarded cloak, and with Aethan tagging along at their side, Kura's family strolled toward the rest of the group that stood at the edge of the basin, beside the horses. Leaving her behind.

"Are you ready?"

Kura jumped, meeting Idris's gaze—she was already in the saddle and waiting. "Yeah." She shook herself, then swung herself up onto Akachi's back.

"Hoo, you ready to go home?" The horse laughed as he started toward the forest, Idris and Mejdan following at his side. "I am. I'm starving! I can't wait to get myself a fresh flake of hay."

Kura nodded, distractedly, as she picked at her tangle of thoughts. She was almost too tired to think, but her mind kept racing anyway. The grey-eyed man. The image of him, seated there on his white gelding, flashed in her memory as though it'd never left.

"Idris," she began slowly. "You said you see things sometimes, right?"

Idris nodded reluctantly, and was suddenly very interested in the stitching on her leather reins.

"How does that work? Is it... dreams?"

Idris shrugged and ran her fingers over her thick braid. "I... I wouldn't say that, no. Dreams are an expression of our souls, not the Essence. Though some believe dreams can touch the *Temper,* the place where the spirits of all things—us, the plants, the animals, the Essence, the Crux—intertwine."

"The Temper is a place?"

Idris tilted her head. "Yes and no. The Temper is a place in so much as it is the part of the *Elaedoni* that we here, as physical beings, are able to touch and understand. I suppose the Cenóri would consider it a state of being, but Fidelis tradition calls it a place."

Kura frowned, chewing her inner lip. None of that was particularly helpful, but she didn't know what to ask. "How, um, how do you know if a dream is, you know, a *dream* dream or something else?"

"Kura, what are you asking?"

She chuckled sheepishly, then shook her head. "I don't know."

Mejdan muttered something under her breath, a long string of words that sounded far more like a horse's whinny than human speech. Akachi burst out in a wheezing laugh, then stole a guilty glance in Kura's direction.

She gave him a half-amused frown. "What?"

The horse shook his head. "I'm not going to repeat it. It wasn't very nice."

"But you laughed."

Akachi arched his neck. "I didn't say it wasn't funny."

Kura frowned at Mejdan. *I think that horse is making fun of me...*

"Here we are." Mejdan snorted. "Rih Hill."

Kura couldn't decide whether it was a mountain that had been worn down through time, or a mound of dirt and stone that had been piled up by peoples in ages past. There was a subtle majesty about it, with the pink sunset emblazoning the silhouettes of trees as it cast the rocky slope in shadow.

Mejdan trotted into the lead, and Akachi followed her around the base of the hill, away from the sunset. Kura shivered in the cool shade, her attention still fixed on the mound—only, she found that without the sun the site lost its beauty. Rih Hill was nothing more than a hill.

"Alright," Idris said after a moment, as Mejdan came to a stop. "We're here."

Akachi stopped as well. Kura frowned, studying the forest around her. Slender birch trunks surrounded them, and the gurgle of the distant Beauduras filled the silence.

Idris dismounted and, catching Kura's gaze, couldn't hold back a grin.

Akachi shook his back. "Go on."

Kura climbed down from the saddle. Idris knocked twice on a tree trunk beside her, the hollow sounds of her fistfalls reverberating into the ground below. A moment passed, then with the creak of timbers and rumble of stone, a dark opening widened in the hillside.

Idris nodded toward the door, then made her way toward it, Mejdan following at her heels. Kura tagged along behind, nearly stumbling over her own feet as she kept staring up at the edges of that opening in wonder. It was a sliding door made of dirt and stone, hiding the mouth of a narrow cave.

She passed through the threshold, Akachi close behind her. The creaking began again, and beyond Akachi's large frame, the hillside slowly moved back together. The door shut with an echoing thump, leaving everything in darkness.

Akachi poked his nose into Kura's back and she jumped.

"Go on," the horse said with a laugh.

Kura edged forward, stretching her empty hand out before her until she brushed against Mejdan's tail. A fist rapped three times against what sounded like thick wood.

"Business?" a muffled, high-pitched voice asked.

"Gathering stores for the winter," Idris replied.

Wood slid against stone, then a beam of warm firelight pierced the darkness as a doorway opened on the other side.

"Welcome back again," the voice said cordially. Kura glanced around, looking for whoever had spoken, and finally spotted the large squirrel perched on a shelf just inside the door.

"Hello, Pattsen." Idris continued forward into the lit room, Mejdan following after her.

Akachi laughed and nudged Kura again. "If I hadn't spent the day with you already, I would think you were dim-witted. Go on!"

"Oh," the squirrel gasped, sitting up as his large, bushy brown tail beat against his back. He wore a smart little vest and hat, and his eyes grew wide as they fell on Kura. "This is her, isn't it?"

Kura smiled, embarrassed, and glanced down at her feet as she stepped into the room. Akachi pushed past her, following Mejdan through the door on the other side of the room.

It was not a large space, and Kura seriously doubted a centaur would fit through comfortably. Most of the Nansûr she'd seen resembled a cavern, but wood panels lined this room and gave it a more homely feel. Thick ropes ran out of the ceiling to the floor and around the walls—she couldn't trace where each began and ended. Wooden wheels and weighted platforms connected the strands together, and in those wheels ran small, furry creatures, each dressed in some dapper outfit much like Pattsen's.

Upon seeing Kura, a squeaky cheer rang out among the nostkynna.

"That's right, tunnel six!" The badger stepped off his wheel to give a high-five to a groundhog standing beside him. "You can tell that to tunnels eight and eleven: the fonfyr has chosen us!"

Kura glanced around the room, looking to each bright-eyed face —there were raccoons and even an opossum among them as well. This level of cooperation was absolutely unheard of in the

Wynshire, and she couldn't be certain she hadn't somehow stepped out of reality.

"This is our security," Idris explained. "We haven't had a breach in twenty and a half years, not since Trofast took the job of security from the Cenóri and gave it to the tunnel guilds. There are fourteen tunnel entrances all around Rih Hill, each sized just a little differently." She motioned to the mass of ropes and pulleys along the wall. "The guilds have developed these. Don't ask me how they work, but with them they manage to open and close the outer entrances."

Kura nodded, still trying to piece the contraption together. "Impressive."

"Well thank you," Pattsen said, lifting his chin. "My great-grandfather designed all these, and I'm the third generation of chief engineers in my family."

Third generation? In twenty years? She could already see the grey in the squirrel's muzzle; it was so easy to forget how quickly time passed for them.

"Come on," Idris said, motioning to Kura as she quickened her pace toward the end of the tunnel. "The council is still waiting."

The groundhog pulled open the human-sized door with a small, rodent-height rope handle, then gave them both an exaggerated bow. "M'ladies."

Kura drew in a steady breath to calm her nerves. Idris had—almost gleefully—left her standing alone at the threshold of the council chambers. Trofast stood at the head of the table, flanked by Erryl and Grenja, poring over a pile of parchments. He'd cleaned himself up after his fight with Konik. Renard sat near the center of the table, his attention divided between the conversation and his plate of food.

"Hey." He grinned at her when he noticed her watching, then slid a second plate of food down the table. "Don't worry, you haven't missed anything. This here is always the best part anyway."

Kura slipped into the empty seat across from him, her mouth watering as she inspected her plate. Fresh bread, three strips of jerky, and a whole carrot.

Trofast frowned slightly at Renard, but the look disappeared as he met Kura's gaze. "What we have been discussing for the last hour is the technical logistics of feeding these sixty-seven new, hungry stomachs you've brought back with you. Don't get me wrong, we need all the able bodies we can find, but it has already been a struggle to feed and clothe the numbers we currently have."

Erryl motioned toward one of the parchments on the table. His robes were shades of blue and white today, with more intricate layers, and he held his hair back in one thin braid. "There are several farming towns in the Au'dal Plains we have not yet contacted for aid."

Grenja's fur bristled. "Is that how you're phrasing it?"

Erryl gave her a long look. "We're at *war*, Grenja. If we don't procure this food, people will die."

"Wait," Kura said with a frown, "you're stealing from people?"

Erryl shifted uncomfortably in his seat before clearing his throat. "It's not ideal, but if aid is refused we have, on occasion, resorted to less than honorable methods. We do not take from homes, mind you, but merchants with excess they are unwilling to part with charitably."

Kura shook her head in disbelief. "The taxes are half the reason most of us hate Dradge. Why in the world...?"

"Well then, *fonfyr*, what do you propose we do?"

Kura took a bite of her jerky, then shrugged. "Steal it from Dradge. The trade guilds collect the taxes for him. In these parts that's mostly a percentage of what people bring to market, right?"

Erryl rolled his eyes. "The ingenuity of youth never fails to astound. Our aim here is to *avoid* royal entanglement, and preferably any other forms as well."

Grenja chuckled. "Because, as we all know, uncharitable merchants are ever so kind to *damned thieves*."

Trofast shifted his stance. "I'm afraid our current needs are greater than what our previous methods will likely sustain. We are capable of more aggressive excursions, if managed prudently. Is there a local target?"

"Lâroe," Renard said. "Small town, strong spirit. The crown's storing the taxes collected from this region in a new tower there.

And it's also one of the supply stations along the river shipping routes that we haven't been able to hit yet. I'll bet they have weapons, too. And armor."

Trofast nodded thoughtfully as he fiddled with the stack of parchments before him. "Do we have the numbers?"

"Trofast," Grenja laughed, "you're always worried about the numbers."

Kura glanced up from her meal. "What about the Varian?"

Four sets of eyes turned to her in accusation.

Erryl frowned. "Aren't they just a legend?"

"Some of my pack have seen them," Grenja said with a shrug.

"I have as well." Trofast's eyes narrowed as he studied Kura's face. "How did you learn of those creatures, Kura of Wynshire?"

"Just rumors," she said, in her best attempt to sound casual. She hadn't expected her mention of the Varian to get quite this reaction, but maybe she should have known better. "But they are fighting against Dradge, right? Just like us?"

Renard snorted. "What looks like saja probably *is* saja, I say."

Kura shrugged and turned back to her food. She wasn't going to push this, but that didn't mean she could let the idea fall to the wayside. She'd seen what the Varian were capable of first hand.

The meeting wound to a gradual close, and while the others tried to encourage her further participation—even when she had nothing valuable to add—Kura found her attention drawn less to the matters of discussion in the council chambers and more toward the map Trofast had before him on the table. The withering tree. It didn't appear to be labeled anywhere—not that Kura could read most of the words—but she did see, drawn not too far from the inky outline of Rih Hill, the shape of a scraggly tree.

Finally, the other council members said their goodnights and filed out of the room. Kura lingered at the table, kneeling on the bench so she could reach the map and orient it to herself.

"Studying the land, eh?" Grenja paused in the doorway with a toothy grin.

"Oh," Kura said with what she hoped didn't sound like a nervous laugh. "Yes."

"Good," the dog said as she continued on her way. "It seems to me that most of your kind could use the practice."

Kura watched until Grenja's fluffy black tail disappeared around the corner, and then reached for the quill pen and inkwell that had been left behind with the map. Renard had pointed out a few other targets of interest as well, and she began painstakingly copying those town names from the map and onto her arm.

She could read better than she could write, but after making a few illegible ink stains on the back of her hand she managed to control the quill enough to replicate the words onto her inner arm—over the bruises Ìsendorál's magic had left behind. Satisfied with her handiwork, Kura set the quill pen aside and blew on her skin until the black ink dried.

What was she going to do, sneak away from Nansûr like a fugitive? She didn't want to imagine the reaction if someone caught the fonfyr fleeing in the dark of night. Maybe she shouldn't trust the Varian. Aethan didn't, Trofast didn't—in fact, it seemed like nobody did. She shook her head, trying to resettle her resolve.

Those Varian in Tarr Fianin had given their lives for her before she had been anything. She laughed under her breath. She still *wasn't* anything, but that was of little consequence now. She pulled her sleeve down over her arm and, one hand resting on the hilt of Ìsendorál, made her way from the council chambers.

Nansûr remained a mess of winding, twisting tunnels, but as she walked, Kura stumbled upon the turns and corners she recognized and eventually found her way back to the narrower hallways where she'd been given a place to stay the night before. These were filled with doorways, each of which looked exactly the same, and she tried to glance in them—discreetly—to find the one that was hers.

In one she found Aethan, kneeling on the ground beside the pile of blankets that constituted his bed, oriented toward the wall with his head hanging down on his chest. She stopped, then stood there grinning at him. "Aethan?"

His head shot up, and he looked around frantically. "What—what?" He sighed, then laughed as he stretched his arms. "Oh, hey, Kura."

She stepped into the doorway and leaned against the frame. "What are you doing?"

"Sleeping, it would seem." He rubbed his eyes with his hand, then transitioned quickly from his knees to his feet. "I was trying to catch up on my invocations. I'm more out of practice than I thought."

"Invocations?"

"They're what keep a Fidelis in tune with the Essence's movements. We're supposed to do them twice a day, at least."

"Really? What do you say?"

Aethan shrugged. "There are a couple scripted prayers, although I prefer to improvise. Whatever works best for you, I guess. It's supposed to be a personal thing." He grinned slightly. "Being in a place like this, and seeing what Idris did yesterday... it makes me want to be that man again, you know?"

She offered an understanding smile. There was longing in his eyes—perhaps that had always been there—but now it came with determination. "Wait, is it tomorrow already?"

"I don't know, it sure feels like it. Makes me wish they had put some windows in this place. Oh." Aethan pointed down the hall, where she had been going. "I sent your family a few rooms down."

"Thank you so much."

He nodded, silent as he glanced at his feet. "I can see why you wanted to find them so badly. If I'd had people like that behind me all my life..." He chuckled, then dug one of his cigarettes out of his pocket. "I don't think I'd be here, now, would I?"

Kura grinned, wanting to mention what had driven her to the rebels and started her whole misadventure in the first place, but she sensed Aethan wasn't talking about where they now stood in Nansûr.

Aethan looked to the intricately embossed scabbard hanging at her side. "You're still carrying the sword, huh?"

"Oh, yeah, I..." She was about to launch into her explanation of how it was only temporary, but with a sinking heart she realized perhaps even he couldn't be her confidant.

Aethan studied her, quizzically. "You convince yourself with your own speech?"

"I guess you could say that."

The silence hung in the air, and she traced her finger along Ìsendorál's leather-wrapped hilt.

"I believe in you, Kura. I always have."

She laughed softly. "You shouldn't, you know."

"Maybe." Aethan shrugged, and placed the unlit cigarette in his mouth to chew on it. "But, no matter how this ends, I won't regret it. I don't think."

She held Aethan's gaze. "Thanks."

In that moment—just for that moment—she almost believed she could do it, that she could be all they hoped she would, all the fonfyr should be.

"Well..." She took a step back toward the doorway with a quiet laugh. "My mother's probably worried sick about me at this point."

He chuckled. "She came here looking for you three times at least."

Of course she did. "Goodnight, Aethan."

"Night."

She stepped out into the hallway and wandered past the last few doorways until she reached her room. It was dark, lit only by the light of the flickering torch in the hallway, and her family had settled in the stillness. The space was small, smaller even than their kitchen area back home, but the air was warm and draft-free, and there was room for all of them to fit comfortably enough.

"Shh," Jisela whispered from her seat by the door. She was rocking Rowley's sleeping form in her arms, and Faron and Elli were already on the bed, curled up under the blankets and asleep. Kura's father was seated at her mother's side, leaning against the wall, head back and snoring softly.

Kura quietly took a seat on the floor next to her mother.

Jisela frowned at her through the shadows. "What were you doing, out so late?"

Kura chuckled to herself as all those fleeting thoughts of grandeur faded under her mother's scorn. "Council meeting," she whispered as she unfastened the buckle that held her sword around her waist. She placed the scabbard in her lap, and Jisela let out a gasp.

"Ìsendorál?"

Kura nodded, running her hand over the scabbard's engravings, which sparkled gold in the firelight. The bundle of blankets on the bed moved, and Elli's face, surrounded by a mane of disheveled brown hair, emerged from beneath the covers.

"Kura!"

"Hey, Elli."

The girl slipped out of bed, dragging her small, thick-weave blanket behind her, and ran over to take a seat next to Kura on the ground.

"Is that the sword?" she asked, her eyes widening.

Kura tucked the blanket around her sister's shoulders as the girl pressed herself against her side. "Do you want to see?"

"Oh, yes, yes!"

Kura leaned forward to give herself some space, and then carefully drew the sword from its scabbard. The rusty blade shone like the sunset in the flickering light, and for a moment she almost thought she saw the inlaid letters flash a deep red.

Elli let out a soft gasp. She was mesmerized by the blade—for a moment. Her face scrunched into a frown. "Ìsendorál should be bigger than that."

"A soldier's sword is bigger, isn't it? That's because this is older, see?" Kura ran her finger across the fuller of the blade. "Modern swords are longer, with a narrower blade, and you have to use both hands to fight with them. This one has a wider blade, it's a bit shorter too, but I can move a lot more quickly and I can use one or two hands as I like."

Elli nodded, politely enough, as she yawned and leaned her head on Kura's arm. "Don't leave again, Kura," she murmured. "We've just got you back from the dead after all."

Kura smiled and shared a knowing glance with her mother.

"It is true, you know," Jisela said, a sparkle in her eyes.

Kura slipped her sword back into its scabbard, and then placed the weapon across her lap as she leaned against the wall with a contented sigh. "I won't have to go anywhere." She slung her arm over Elli's shoulders as she gently brushed her sister's unruly hair from her face. Then she remembered the Varian, and her heart sank. "Not for a while, anyway."

Chapter Thirty-Six

Under Cover of Darkness

Icy rain pattered the ground with the driving wind, and Triston pulled his cloak tight to try to keep from getting any wetter than he already was. It wasn't a big storm, breaks of moonlight shone through the patchy clouds, but it almost seemed to be following him on his way to Dol. The horse stumbled, its hoof catching in a puddle, and grunted as it regained its footing.

"Almost there, old boy," Triston said with a sigh as he patted the animal's neck.

It hurt him to have to use the horse like this, but the rain had begun falling after turning back to Shalford was already out of the question. There should be fresh horses in Dol, and that was most of the reason he'd come here in the first place. The little town stood in the valley between the peaks, marking the only semi-passable section of the mountains for dayrides in any direction. The few gruff fur trappers who made their living out here had attempted to turn it into a proper town, but almost anything in the outpost should be available to the Prince of Avaron if he asked for it.

Triston peered through the rain at the dim outline of the city walls rising at the end of the road. Lightning flashed in the mass of dark clouds behind the distant mountains, outlining the sorry ramparts in white light. He frowned, the thunder rumbling softly in the distance. This outpost looked long abandoned.

The old horse plodded the final few strides to the city gates. The small, wooden wicket gate hung loose on its hinges and flapped in the breeze, smacking loudly in uneven intervals against the door frame. Uneasy, Triston pulled back on the reins.

"Hello?" There was no answer besides the creaking and slamming of the loose door. He dismounted, splashing mud over his shoes, and with one hand on his sword hilt led the horse to the gate. "Hello?"

The narrow streets were empty, and of the many windows in the houses that lined the alleyways, only a few contained warm firelight behind their closed shutters. He nudged the horse through the wicket gate, then shut it behind them, bracing it properly with the board that had been discarded on the side of the street.

"Who're you?" a gruff voice shouted.

Startled, Triston found himself standing eye to eye with a skinny older man. Only fur-lined boots, a pointed nose, and a patchy blond beard peeked out from beneath his cloak.

"Are you the night guard?" Triston asked, although he really meant it as more of a statement.

The man nodded, still eyeing Triston with that same skepticism. "Who're you?"

He was used to his uniform giving his identity away. "Triston."

The man's countenance relaxed, and he squinted at Triston's face in the darkness. "Are ye now?"

"I've come to see Captain Julian," Triston continued. The man stared blankly. "He's in charge of the tower here."

"Is that what his name is, eh?" The man tilted his head and shoved a thick finger under his hood to scratch his ear. "Well, you be getting on yer business now, sir." He stepped back on unsteady feet toward the small gatehouse built against the wall behind him. "And know I ain't been getting in nobody's way, no sir."

Triston nodded, trying somewhat to be cordial. "Thank you."

The man grunted as he scurried back through the open gatehouse door, slamming it behind him.

Triston continued down the street, the old horse plodding along at his heels. Aside from the man in the gatehouse, he passed no other living soul. If these had been normal circumstances he would have stormed through the barracks, waking every sleeping man to give them a lecture on the importance of their diligence, but as it was—and after everything he'd seen already—he suspected something more was at work here than just the natural laziness of undisciplined soldiers.

The guard tower rose in the center of the outpost, a story taller than any other building in town. It was a reflection of Shalford's: same quarry-stone walls, same narrow archer's windows, but half the height and width. At least this gate was closed tight, and light flickered in a few of the windows above.

Thunder rumbled again in the distance, louder this time, as Triston rapped his fist against the iron gate. He waited—rain pelting the stone walls and muddy streets—then pounded on the door again. Another moment passed before feet shuffled on the opposite side of the door.

The small peep door swung open with a clang. A man's face peered out, his features obscured by the contrast of light and shadow cast by the torch in his hand. He said nothing, just stared, his dark eyes unblinking.

Triston cleared his throat. "I've come to speak to the captain."

A grin slowly spread across the man's face. "Triston!" He laughed softly. "Fancy that." His face disappeared—Triston heard the drawbar being removed from across the door—and the gate swung open, just enough for him and his horse to pass through.

With a sigh of relief, Triston led his horse out of the rain and into the tower. "Thank you, this poor horse wasn't made for this kind of travel."

The iron gate shut behind him with an echoing clang. The man said nothing as he placed the drawbar back across the door. He retrieved the torch he'd left on a hook on the wall, then turned back with amusement shining in his eyes.

Triston stopped, that unease in his gut threatening to turn to fear. This man was pale, even in the torchlight, but his eyes stood out most of all. They were sunken and dark-rimmed, with blue irises as natural and clear as any other man, but the rest—the part that should have been white—was a deep black, blacker even than the shadows that filled the hallway. Triston thought that he recognized the face, and it was with dismay that he recalled the name.

"Merric?"

The man laughed, an odd light reflecting in his eyes. "You remember me? I'm rather touched, actually."

Triston stepped away as he looked the man over again, and backed into the old horse. "You're..." To say the words out loud would mean he'd have to accept what he saw. "You're... dead."

"Dead? Hmm..." Merric pursed his lips as he glanced at the ceiling. "I guess you can say I was dead once. I guess I lived a life once. But it isn't my fault that death, just as life, is such a temporary thing."

Triston tried discreetly to push the old horse out of his way, but the animal only grunted. "How?"

"After all this time, you start asking questions?" Merric's smile remained, stiff and unrelenting. "I'm not going to tell you."

Triston drew his sword—its weight a comfort—and drove it toward Merric's heart. The man leapt back, unsheathing his own weapon, and the two blades clashed with a flash of sparks in the darkness. Triston pressed forward. A cool rage drove him, and he parried each of Merric's blows with ease. The man stumbled and dropped his torch. The fire sputtered, casting long dark shadows on the distant wall.

With two quick strokes Triston sent Merric's sword hurtling to the other side of the room. The man cried out in surprise as Triston transitioned his momentum into a backswing aimed at Merric's neck.

A brick flew from the opposite side of the room and smashed into Triston's chest, sending him sprawling against the wall. He scrambled back into his stance—his body bruised, his heart pounding—but kept his sword in hand.

Merric laughed, the sound entirely too joyful for the circumstances. "You held me back. But now I've been set free."

The soldier flung his hands forward, and several more bricks hurtled from the back of the room. Triston dodged, slicing at any that came too close, and his blade shattered in his hands, the silver shards falling like rain against the dusty ground.

"You know, all I wanted was a good word from you." Merric twirled the fingers of his raised hand and a loose brick rose, revolving as though on a string. "Not because I needed it, but because the others thought I did." He laughed again, the sound wild—inhuman. "Can you believe that? A man like me needing a man like you?"

Triston lunged, punching Merric in the face. The soldier stumbled back and Triston pressed his advantage, driving his fists into Merric's ribs and sternum. Growling, the man pulled his hands toward his chest. The left wall began to shake, and Triston dove out of the way as several large bricks came loose and hurtled past his head.

Anger burned like blue flame in Merric's eyes but Triston kept striking—a punch to the nose, to the ribs, a kick to the stomach to keep him at arm's length—and that proved to be more than a match for Merric's poor footwork. The man screamed through clenched teeth and sent every free brick hurtling through the room. Triston leapt aside, but stone debris pummeled the arms he threw up to shield his face.

He found himself on his hands and knees, his pulse beating in the knot on his head. His vision blurred; as he blinked it clear, Merric approached leisurely, his dark figure outlined in orange by the dim light of the fallen torch. Something bright and silver caught the torchlight and flashed it in Triston's eyes, making him squint. The hilt of his broken sword.

Snatching up his fallen weapon, Triston leapt to his feet and slashed his shattered blade at Merric's face. The man shrieked, stumbling back, and flung his arms forward. Stones scraped and rattled in the hallway, and Triston threw himself to the ground. Something dark came from his side, there was a flash of white, and then everything went black.

Kura stiffened as the bundle of covers moved.

She stood in the middle of the room, halfway through taking a step, grimacing as she waited for someone to wake up. It didn't feel right sneaking off under the cover of darkness in the first place, and the very last thing she wanted was a family member catching her in the act.

Among the blankets, Faron mumbled something, but he was still asleep. Kura breathed a sigh of relief. She tiptoed the rest of the way to the door, her boots silent against the stone floor. Of course she couldn't actually tell if it was dark outside or not, but the relative calm of the outer hallways seemed to indicate that everyone else had gone to bed.

Lingering a moment in the doorway, Kura turned back. Elli was where she'd left her on the floor, snuggled in her blanket with her head on her mother's lap, while her mother rested her head on her father's shoulder. He was still snoring. Rowley stirred, then nuzzled his face out from his cocoon of blankets. His big, brown eyes blinked as they held Kura's gaze.

She expected him to start crying, but instead he just watched her, as if pleading with her to stay. The look nearly broke her heart, and she tore herself away before she could be convinced to do otherwise. She'd be back before anyone else noticed, anyway.

She forced a confidence to her step as she jogged along the wall, Aethan's advice from days ago echoing in the back of her mind. *"Strangers will assume you belong until you act like you don't."* Still, she remained prepared to duck into a doorway or around the next turn should she come across someone else. Akachi had mentioned there were stables somewhere at the far end of Nansûr, so she figured she'd be able to borrow a horse (not a *talking* horse, obviously) and head out to the withering tree and back before anyone missed her.

After taking a few wrong turns, she managed to locate the massive, hand-etched wooden gates that separated the stable area from the rest of the compound. This hallway was darker than the rest, lit only by the flickering light of one of those strange torches built into a wall in the back. As silently as she could, Kura worked the latch on the gate and slunk into the stables. Hay crunched under her feet, and a faint breeze brought with it the scent of stable litter.

"What are you doing?" a voice boomed.

She jumped and spun around to find herself looking up at the long face of a horse. "Akachi?"

"Oh, Kura, it's you." He took a step back, relaxing his neck. Slowly, his ears turned back. "What *are* you doing?"

"I... There are regular horses here, aren't there?"

"Sure. But they usually go out grazing at this time of night." Akachi lowered his head to squint at her. "Why are you asking?"

She straightened her shoulders, hoping the darkness hid the panic in her eyes. "I've been sent to gather more troops. From the

Varian."

"Really?"

"Yeah." She pulled the scrap of parchment from her shirt. "See, they sent me this, asking me to meet them at the withering tree."

Akachi snorted. "I can't read it."

She shrugged, folding the paper as she shoved it back in her shirt. "Look, I know a lot of people around here have their doubts, but this is for the best."

Akachi swished his tail, and she couldn't see through the shadows covering his face to guess what he was thinking. "Alright," he said finally. "I'll have to leave my tack behind, or Mejdan is sure to notice, but I think I can get you to this tree you're talking about."

Kura blinked. "You?"

"Yes, me," Akachi said, with an indignant stomp of his rear hoof. "You think those horses could even find their way back here after you got them lost? Hop up." He swung his head toward his bare back. "After the tunnel guilds let us out of this gate, we're going to have to wade through the Helm a ways, and I wouldn't want you to have to get your precious little feet wet."

She laughed. "You're so noble, sir. Lead the way."

Chapter Thirty-Seven

Ghosts

The cold world of light and darkness came into shaky focus. A harsh, irritating smell filled Triston's nose and he pulled back. He blinked, hard, as the throbbing pain in his head threatened to overtake his other senses. Details flooded in all at once. He was kneeling on the stone floor of a holding cell, chained and held up by his wrists, the wall at his back.

"Eh, I didn't kill you after all." Merric loomed over him, arms folded across his chest. A short, burly man dressed in a leather-and-fur cloak stood at Merric's side, holding a flask of amber crystals in one hand and a lit torch in the other. "You can go," Merric said, nodding toward the door.

Without a word, the man did as he was told, taking the light with him.

"So, this is what's become of the Prince of Avaron?"

The pale moonlight shone through the narrow window on the far wall, silhouetting Merric's dark frame, but Triston couldn't hear him well over the ringing in his ears. His stomach churned, and before he could hold it back, he threw up at Merric's feet.

"Have some respect for yourself!" Merric jabbed Triston in the ribs with the point of his shoe.

Triston flinched, groaning, but didn't lift his head. He had blurry memories of riding into a nearly empty town, of finding Merric in the tower... He grimaced as his head throbbed, but a hazy recollection of their fight gradually returned. He realized Merric was still trying to talk to him only after the man drove that boot into his ribs again.

"You're a failure! A coward, a fool! Every day under your charge was one more I endured in suffering!" Merric spat in his face. "You don't deserve to be prince any more than your father deserves to be king!"

Triston let the man's petty taunts ring in the silence.

Merric sighed and squatted down to Triston's level. "Well," he whispered, a grin spreading across his face, "things have changed now, haven't they?"

The brightness of the moons chased the shadows away from Merric's features. There was a large, bloodied gash on the man's face: a deep, oozing scab that ran from his temple, across his cheek to his chin.

Triston grinned bitterly. At least he'd left a mark.

Merric scowled. "Smile, then. Enjoy these last breaths. To the rest of the kingdom you are already dead. Your father sent out the proclamation himself after the rebels left your charred body by the gates of Edras." His face twisted into another smile. "Those savages didn't even attempt a ransom."

Rage surged through Triston's limbs, and he clenched his eyes shut to try to keep from doing anything foolish.

Merric rose to his feet. "Your father will take care of that rebellion, and then we'll kill him, and you, and any other fool who has the notion to stand with you." He started toward the door. "I don't imagine there will be many."

"Who's 'we'?" Merric paused, hand on the doorknob. "I said already, I'm not going to tell you."

"And what about the fonfyr?"

Merric glanced back. His irises glowed like two bright blue orbs mounted in the shadow of a man. "What of him?"

"What of him? You mean you haven't heard the rumors? It isn't just Seren's meddling this time. The fonfyr's come, I've seen him."

"You're lying."

"Then do what you like. Just know, in the end, your fate is the same as mine."

Merric spun on his heels and slammed the metal door closed behind him. The sound reverberated in the room, leaving only silence in its wake. Triston sighed and let his head fall back against the stone wall behind him. The chains strained his wrists, though that was a minor irritation compared to his aching head and upset stomach.

"...*and then we'll kill him, and you...*" That wasn't just a taunt, it had been a promise. He didn't know why Merric had kept him alive—he wasn't going to question it, and for the time being it didn't really matter. Anger surged through his veins. Was he going to sit here and let his father die?

With a shout, Triston yanked at the chains on his wrists, ignoring the pain as the metal shackles dug into his flesh. He pounded again and again, the chains snapping taut and then falling slack, but neither the latch holding them closed nor the mount securing them to the stone wall budged.

Defeated, he let his chin drop to his chest. His own heartbeat pounded in his ears, throbbing with the knots on his head, and warm blood trickled down his arms where the shackles tore his wrists. A part of him was tempted to despair, but he couldn't manage that—not yet. He found himself thinking instead about what he wouldn't give to take back his choice to come to Dol in the first place.

"You weren't going to escape that way, anyway."

Triston jerked upright. His head spun from the sudden movement, but as he blinked, the shifting, swirling shadows beside him took the form of a man. This man crept closer, jangling chains following him, then took a seat cross-legged an armsbreadth away.

"So you're Prince Triston."

Triston laughed bitterly and let his head fall again.

"Did you really mean it?" A tremor of either fear or excitement carried in his voice. "About the fonfyr?"

Triston looked up at the man's shadow-covered face, his heart softening a little. Of course anyone else locked up in this damp prison would have to be some sort of enemy to Merric and his kind. He opened his mouth to answer, to explain what he'd seen, but a wave of nausea came over him again and he threw up whatever was still left in his stomach.

Dizziness muddled Triston's senses, his thoughts slipping into a fog, but somewhere in the back of his mind he heard the man's chains sliding on the floor. Cold fingers gripped his chin and tilted his head up toward the beam of pale light that shone through the window. He grimaced as the light passed over his eyes.

"He hit you pretty good there, huh?"

For an instant, in his blurred vision, he could almost believe the person seated beside him was his father. This was a somewhat younger, skinnier man, but like Dradge, he had deep green eyes, a head of long black hair and a short, greying beard on his cheeks.

"I'm not sure I can help you much," the man said, but he placed his hand over the welt growing on the side of Triston's head and began whispering something. Triston cringed as the man touched him, but he didn't care enough to stop him.

Gradually, a warm, bluish light began to emanate from the man's hand—Triston saw the glow even through his closed eyelids. Then the light flickered, the man muttered under his breath, and darkness overtook the room as he pulled back.

Triston lifted his head slowly. The pain was still there, but it had lessened enough for him to think clearly. "You're Fidelis, aren't you?"

The man chuckled. "Now I see how I sounded, asking who you were." He shifted in his seat with some difficulty, then heaved a sigh. "I am Féderyc of the fifth branch, born of House Gallian and House Evêtra."

Triston searched for his face in the shadows. "The fonfyr. I don't really know a lot about it, but—"

"Shh!" Féderyc hissed, shaking his head. "I shouldn't have asked. You don't know who's listening."

Triston nodded, ashamed for not recognizing that himself. He leaned back against the wall, trying in vain to find a more comfortable position. Now that the pain in his head had lessened a little, he regretted the cuts and bruises he'd foolishly inflicted on his own wrists.

"Your father will come for you?"

Triston's heart sank, and he shook his head. Not unless his pigeon reached Edras without being intercepted, but he had little hope in that. This was it. No one knew where he was, and his father thought he was already dead. There would be no ransom exchange; there would be no rescue mission.

He glanced over at Féderyc. "What's keeping you here?"

"Oh," the man laughed, not entirely amused, "ghosts of the past, I guess. I should be a dead man. I suppose in some ways I am, but Seren took me and brought me back somehow. I don't know what he thought I'd know... what he still thinks I know."

"Brought you back... from the dead? Like Merric out there?"

The man's shadowy silhouette nodded. "But I'm not like him. I think that's what's made Seren so frustrated, he—"

"Seren?" Triston had hoped he'd misheard the first time.

Féderyc nodded. "Seren and his Grey Lady thought they could make an army of people like me. But there was something they didn't understand. I don't understand it quite all the way, but the last thing I remember thinking about—the real me, that is, not whatever I've become now—was how I was ready to die, if I had to... that I'd die a thousand more deaths just the same as that one, even if it only meant getting in his way one more time..."

Triston studied the man's shadow, not entirely sure what to make of his story. Maybe, for the moment, that was the less pressing issue. "How many are in this city? There's supposed to be a platoon stationed here."

Féderyc sat there as if he hadn't heard, then shrugged. "Not many, I don't think. There's Merric, of course, and a few other soldiers, and then just some fur traders who stayed on for one reason or another."

That would explain the man at the gate, and the man Merric had had with him. Triston glanced up again at the window, squinting through the pain—it wasn't of any consequence anymore. "You think a man would fit through there?"

Féderyc shielded his eyes with his hand as he glanced at the window. "Oh, probably a young one like you, anyway."

Triston grabbed two fistfuls of the chains that held him to the wall and, with some effort, hauled himself to his feet.

"Woah." Féderyc pulled back, as though he thought Triston might topple onto him. "Careful there."

Stomach churning and legs swaying, Triston clenched his teeth, fought the urge to throw up, and found his balance. He released his grip on one of the chains, and then tried with his free hand to mess with the latch on his other wrist. The length of chain went taut before he could reach.

He sighed and braced himself against the wall to keep his feet. He released the second chain as well and barely managed to bring his hands together in front of him.

"It won't work," Féderyc said, aggravatingly apathetic. "I've already tried."

"What'd Merric want from you?"

The man sighed. "Merric's pretty new here. Seren was the one stopping by every so often to ask questions."

"What kind of questions?"

"A lot of them, I guess. Numbers and positions, names of allies. Oh, the location of Nansûr, if it really existed." He laughed. "Too bad for him that nobody told me anything. The rebellion's pretty hung up on certain rules. Ironically."

With a frustrated sigh, Triston gave up on the latch and turned instead to the mount of one of the chains above him. It was hard to reach, and even a quick feel of it showed it was far sturdier than the manacles around his wrists. "Is anybody going to feed us in here?"

"Sure, around noon every day, usually. Oh." His chains rattled as he rummaged on the floor. "I might have some old jerky crumbs left if you're hungry."

"No, thanks." Triston sagged back against the wall, clenching and unclenching his jaw. He glanced down at Féderyc. "What's beside you? Anything? I can't see."

"You don't give up, do you?"

Triston ignored the comment and began feeling his way along the wall, searching for a loose stone. He found only a chunk of brittle mortar that hadn't been set properly, which crumbled to dust in his hand as he picked it from the wall.

He gave a heavy sigh and looked up at the moonlit window. It would seem his freedom was just out of reach. Well, there would still be whoever came tomorrow. He tried to pick back through his foggy memories, and he didn't recall the burly man having a weapon, or even the keys to his shackles. Then again, he wasn't in any state to have noticed.

"You really should get some rest," Féderyc said. "You're not going to be able to do much tonight, anyway, not with your head like that."

Reluctantly, Triston lowered himself back down to the floor. He certainly didn't agree with the man, but for the moment he'd run out of ideas. He shifted in his seat, trying to find a position where the chains wouldn't make his hands and arms go numb. His tingling fingers said his efforts were in vain.

Of course, in the silence, he could no longer ignore the questions he didn't entirely want to ask. Seren was a guarded man, yes—calculated and driven—but all of this? He glanced over at Féderyc.

"I don't mean to doubt you, but Seren, he—"

Féderyc laughed softly. "I don't blame you for being skeptical. That man can keep a secret—from you best of all, I'd imagine." His eyes grew distant. "Seren was to be king, we all knew that. Even from the first day Cynwrig brought that young noble's boy tagging at his heels into the University. Seren is, after all, the kingly type: sophisticated, calm, unwaveringly calculated... but it was Dradge we fought for."

"You knew my father?"

"Knew him? I saved his life in the Battle of Fox Run, but of course that was after he'd saved mine."

Triston held Féderyc's gaze, fully interested now.

"Every Fidelis fought for him, just like all the rest in the coup against Hilderic. He was why we won. Seren cooked up all that nonsense with the sword, but no one really listened. It got us talking, sure, but *Dradge* was what we believed in. For all his efforts, Seren was never one for reaching people, touching their hearts. And that's where a rebellion's truly won, you know, in the heart." He nodded thoughtfully. "Your father knew that. There was something about the way he led... recklessly, without regard for his own life. Something in his eyes, I guess."

Féderyc peered at Triston through the darkness. "You look like him."

Chapter Thirty-Eight
The Withering Tree

"This is it," Akachi said in a low voice.

Kura looked up, blinking the sleep from her eyes. Dark clouds had obscured the moons for most of their travels, but now a few pale streaks of light shone through onto a small clearing. Akachi stopped, lingering in the dense tree line that surrounded the open space around the withering tree.

A withering tree indeed. Kura had to crane her neck to see the top of it, but not a single one of its long, scraggly branches bore a bud or a leaf, making its silhouette against the cloudy night sky indistinguishable from the long, dark shadow that stretched toward the forest beyond. Although she couldn't have explained why, the site made her uneasy. It might have had something to do with the way no plant taller than the field grass at Akachi's knees grew within the tree's reach. It was a dead space, guarded by a dead tree.

"So," Akachi snorted, breaking the silence, "where are your friends?"

"I'm not sure," Kura whispered. Skellor *had* sent the note days ago; perhaps she'd already missed him? No, Skellor would be able to find her here, no matter the time. "Let's go wait by the tree."

Akachi muttered something under his breath, but reluctantly made his way into the clearing. Aside from his soft footfalls on the dry grass, only the chatter of night creatures joined with the whisper of the wind through the tree's withered branches.

"There," he said, stopping beside the base of the tree. "Now what?"

Kura scanned the shadowy forest around her. She didn't have a clue. "They'll be here," she said, throwing her legs to one side as she slipped off Akachi's back. The rough field grass crunched beneath her feet, and she traced her finger along Ìsendorál's hilt as she kept her gaze on the tree line. Hesitantly, she leaned a hand against the tree's rough bark.

"What took you so long?"

She jumped back, and Akachi snorted, his flat hooves sliding on the smooth grass as he tried to turn and run away.

"Skellor!" she said with a laugh as his figure emerged from the tree's wide shadow. "Have you been waiting there this whole time?"

Moonlight glinted off his fangs as he smiled, his strangely human, strangely wolfish face outlined in silver. "No, scouts spotted you riding in about half an hour ago." He glanced up, nodding toward Akachi. The horse snorted again, stomping his hoof, as he kept his distance. "Who's your friend?"

"Akachi," Kura said, turning back toward the horse to beckon him forward. "Come on, it's fine."

Warily, Akachi came forward, shaking his mane. He stood behind her, eyeing Skellor suspiciously.

"So," Skellor started, "they say you're the fonfyr."

She grinned. "They say a lot of things."

Skellor nodded, tilting his head as he eyed the scabbard hanging at Kura's side. Her grin turned into a sheepish smile, and she carefully drew her weapon. The rusty blade shone white in the moonlight as she held it out toward him. She wished he could have seen it as it was in the council chambers, with the mirror sheen and muted red-gold color, but a hint of that transformation lingered beneath the tarnish.

The light was reflected in Skellor's eyes. "I knew it..." He ran his gloved hand across the blade as if it were a flame about to burn him, but he didn't hesitate. "I knew it..."

"Right, right," Akachi muttered under his breath. "What'd you want her for, Mister Varian, sir? This place has something off about it, and I for one would like to get home."

"Right you are, Master Horse." Skellor pulled his hand away, and Kura shoved the sword back into its scabbard. "This tree bloomed first at the beginning of the world, and it will not bloom again until time has come to an end."

Akachi swished his tail. "Your time, or ours?"

Skellor grinned. "That is the question, isn't it?" He turned to Kura with a sigh, the grin fading. "You've been a lot of trouble, you know that? Taking your good old time to cross the plains, saja on your tail the whole time—which we held off, by the way—and then you go and get yourself captured, take a leisurely boat ride..." His gaze was stern, but he almost sounded proud. Then he frowned. "Why'd you save the prince?"

"That saja in the woods, was that—?"

"Yes, that was Savis—he's a Varian, not a saja—and you about scared him half to death."

Kura glanced down at her hands. "Triston... he's not what you'd think. He saved my life in the river—oh, and he helped us break prisoners out of Shalford Tower."

"Yeah, I heard about that."

She couldn't tell what he really thought about it.

"So, why'd you come? The folks at Nansûr seem to have taken to you. What do you need me for?"

"Well..." She pulled up her sleeve to reveal the words she'd scrawled on her arm. "We're going to hit these cities in the next few days. It's a start, they want to move on to bigger things if we can pull these off, but we need more fighting men."

Skellor glanced down, tilting his head to study the city names. "Trofast sent you here, did he?"

"No."

Skellor gave a short laugh. "Still doesn't trust us?"

"I tried to talk to them about it, but a lot is going on. I'm sure he'll come around."

"Right." Skellor nodded, and Kura knew he didn't believe a word she said. "Where you going to hit first?"

"Lâroe. Tomorrow. It's just a test, really. More of a heist than an assault. Trofast says he wants to see what we're capable of, and if the people will follow us or not."

Skellor nodded again, taking one last look at the list on her arm. "Very sensible." His lip quirked. "You really want us there, though? We'd scare the shirts off those people, and scared people poke scary things full of arrow holes."

She chuckled. "I didn't come to talk about Lâroe. We still need more fighting men, and I think you know where to find them."

"What makes you think that?"

"Call it a hunch."

Skellor glanced to the side, failing to hold back a smile. "I'll see what I can do. No promises, but I can at least get the word out." He rubbed his chin thoughtfully. "I'll send them here and signal you if someone shows up. But still, no promises."

Kura grinned as she pulled her sleeve back down over her arm. "Thank you."

Skellor inspected her face. "You were a good gamble, Kura. A good gamble." His nose wrinkled, then his smile vanished. "Get down."

The intensity in his tone spurred her into action, and she dropped to the ground as Akachi snorted and backed up into the shadow of the tree. Skellor slunk forward, then dropped down onto all fours. One moment he was a man, and the next he was some strange, cloaked animal moving and swaying with the field grass.

Voices sounded from the edge of the clearing—human shouting, mixed with the growls and calls of animals. Skellor sprang to his feet and let out a mournful howl. The voices became quiet, and Kura waited, steadying her breath.

One voice, not human, called out in some deep, guttural language. Several figures emerged from the shadows of the tree line. It was more Varian; she could tell that even in the moonlight by the strange, hunched shapes hidden beneath their cloaks. But with them were several men and women, all of them bound at the wrist by rope.

Skellor replied in the same gravelly tongue.

The group of Varian brought their prisoners to the base of the tree, and Kura sucked in a breath as she recognized the faces. It was Cynwrig, and several others of his group she'd seen earlier that day. She got to her feet, smoothing her shirt as she brushed the bits of dried grass from her pants.

"I knew it," Cynwrig said, his bulbous face contorting into a frown. He had his hands bound behind his back, and a Varian prodded him with a spear tip to get him to stand beside the tree, but he looked up at Kura as though he were a king and she the servant who'd forgotten to empty his chamber pot. "A traitor to the core. You've sold out the rebellion, have you?" He scoffed. "Fonfyr."

"I haven't sold out anything."

"We caught him snooping around," the Varian at Cynwrig's side explained. Kura recognized the voice, but it took her a good, long look into the shadow of his hood to recognize his bearish face. It was Faeng. "They say they were trying to set up a perimeter and scout for incoming and outgoing travelers."

Skellor laughed.

Cynwrig turned back to Kura. "Conspiring with saja? See, that is why our work is necessary, we—"

"We're not saja," Skellor growled. He stepped forward, his lanky frame dwarfing Cynwrig's short, round shape. Still, that did not dissuade the man.

"And just who are you?"

Skellor folded his arms across his chest. "I suppose you don't remember me, although you may remember my father. I have no space in my heart for Fidelis, and you, sir, I have already cast out."

Cynwrig stiffened. "We are the guardians of Avaron. We always have been. It is our duty, passed down through the generations. It is our responsibility to maintain order, to promote peace."

"You're sloppy, whatever your responsibilities might be. I honestly thought you would have given this whole charade up by now, considering how many of you have fallen to the king's patrols along the way."

Cynwrig's frown deepened, and Kura was surprised to find he had no reply to that. Apparently Skellor's words stung, and she had to wonder how many Fidelis had died under Cynwrig's watch.

"What do you want done with them?" Faeng asked.

Skellor sighed, scratching his chin. He glanced over at Kura. "You want him?"

She held his gaze, surprised by the question. "I'm not sure he's welcome in Nansûr, not after what he's done."

"I didn't stab Trofast—" Cynwrig burst out, then stopped. His followers shared a few whispers, and it struck Kura that this was perhaps the first time she'd heard any of them speak.

"Oh, alright," Cynwrig said with a frustrated glance back at his followers. He shook his shoulders, shooting a glare in Faeng's direction. "Get off me." He sighed again. "It was a student of mine, the son of a rich lord sent to Drosala to study history, to learn literature and the other academic arts. He brought Ìsendorál to me and I—"

"This Ìsendorál?" Kura placed her hand on the sword hilt at her side.

"No," Cynwrig said, as if that should have been painfully obvious. "He'd had it made somewhere. Oh, don't look at me like that. He meant well by it. This was a good student, a wise man, and he had only the best of intentions."

Kura's frown deepened. "What was his name?"

"Is that really necessary?"

She stared him down.

Cynwrig drew in a breath, then let it out in defeat. "Seren. His name is Seren, last of his line in the house of Margel. There, does that mean anything to you?"

The name was familiar, but she couldn't place it. "Go on."

"Well, the student and I took the sword to Trofast, because of course we wanted him to be a part of it, but he would have nothing to do with us. See..." Cynwrig shifted his stance to turn a critical eye on Kura. "The thing Trofast—and you, I might add—doesn't understand about a prophecy is that it doesn't really have to *be* true, just so long as the people, the culture, *believes* it to be true. The Essence moves through us, not for us, after all, and..." Cynwrig's gaze fell on the sword hanging at Kura's side.

She smiled. He must have said those words a hundred times before in that same smug tone, but this was the first time he felt foolish doing it. "So, this Seren stabbed Trofast?"

"It was in self-defense! Trofast wouldn't let us leave with the false sword, and we weren't about to give up on our chance to—to set Avaron right again. Hilderic was a terrible man—you of course wouldn't remember that—but we did what we had to do, the right thing to do. You're all caught up in your ideas of heroes and saviors, but—and you may not believe this—sometimes the *right* thing is not the *easy* thing."

Kura bristled. *I wouldn't remember? I don't know?* She took a step back to keep herself from leaping into an argument that would certainly prove fruitless. "Seren carried the sword?"

A few laughs came from Cynwrig's followers, but he shot them a glare and they fell silent. "He was meant for it, born for it, as nary a king before him. I saw it in him, I knew he was capable of it. It should have been him."

Her eyes widened. "So Dradge really did carry the sword."

Cynwrig scowled. "Seren gave it to him as a last resort, to rally the people. He thought he could still maneuver his way to the throne after the coup, but the soldiers and the people were so enamored with Dradge…"

Skellor chuckled. "This is old history. Are you going to finish, or should I?" Cynwrig's scowl deepened, and Skellor grinned. "Your order fell apart after Dradge became king. You put him on the throne, but you couldn't control him. What do you call it?" He looked dramatically to the sky. "Ah, yes, the Severance—seven years ago now, wasn't it? Your order split from you, elected their own leadership, and then moved in with the one man who probably hates your guts more than I do. You're the outcast now, cut off from your own people. The people you would have ostracized are now ostracizing you. And good riddance."

Kura sighed. Maybe she understood Cynwrig's bitterness now, and she couldn't help but feel a little bit sorry for him—a little bit. She studied him, the shadows on his wide face making him resemble some large toad. She didn't want to fight beside this man; she wanted to send him away the same as Skellor did. But somewhere, in the back of her mind, she heard herself arguing to Trofast about the Varian…

"Old history…" she repeated, looking Cynwrig in the eye. "Are you willing to make it that way? You have the chance here to do that."

The group of Fidelis whispered amongst themselves again. Cynwrig's expression didn't change, but he looked her in the eye. "I'm listening."

She grinned slightly. "The rebellion is growing—we're making our move soon." She glanced up at Skellor. "The Varian know the details. I want you to go with them." Two sets of eyes turned on her in accusation, one from Cynwrig and one from Skellor. "Skellor, I know you can handle it."

He tilted his head to the side, as though he agreed with her latter assertion but disagreed with the former.

"I refuse," Cynwrig said with a frown.

Kura gritted her teeth and turned to the rest of Cynwrig's followers. "Do you all agree with him? Are you going to throw away your opportunity so he can hang on to his grudges?"

The group shared a few uncertain glances between them, but in the end they said nothing.

"Fine," Kura said, throwing up her hands. "I'll take you all back to Nansûr and have Trofast deal with you."

Cynwrig shifted uncomfortably on his feet. "Alright," he said quietly.

"What?"

"Alright," he said, a bit louder. "You'll have it your way, fonfyr." He spoke that last word slowly, as if it pained him to have to try to say it without malice.

Kura held Cynwrig's gaze, although he turned away. "Well, alright then." She grinned, then looked up at Skellor. "We're done here?"

He nodded, a similar amusement shining in his eyes. "Yep, I think so."

"Alright." She took a step back toward Akachi as she played the conversation over again in her mind. Had she really pulled this off? She nodded to Skellor, and then to Cynwrig. "I'll be seeing you soon."

Skellor bowed dramatically. "Until then, fonfyr."

Akachi snorted, swishing his tail, as Kura grabbed a fistful of his mane to haul herself onto his back. They'd crossed the clearing before he turned to weigh her with one of his large, dark eyes. "You trust that man?"

She laughed. "Who, Skellor or Cynwrig?"

"Both, I suppose, but I already know your answer for the first one. Not all Fidelis are the same, Kura. There's a reason the fonfyr hasn't come before, and I'd bet hoof and tail that it's got something to do with that Cynwrig."

A jolt of fear shot through her chest. "You... you think he's a part of the Crux or something?"

"Oh no," Akachi said quickly. "I'd know a vojak to see him—you can always see it in their eyes—but there's more than one way to move with the darkness." He nodded, thoughtfully, as though he'd surprised himself by saying something profound. "More than one way…"

Chapter Thirty-Nine

ERRANT THOUGHTS

Warm, white sunlight lured Triston out of a deep sleep. For a moment he couldn't see anything other than the light, and he winced as it brought back his familiar headache. He blinked his dry eyes hard, and gradually forced them to adjust.

"There you are." It was Féderyc's voice.

Triston straightened. His shoulders ached from how the chains had pulled them back all night, and his fingers were fat, tingling masses he could barely move.

"I was getting a little worried about you," Féderyc said, and while his tone hardly sounded worried, Triston was inclined to believe him. He felt awful—how did he not look it as well?

He turned, still blinking in the morning light, and winced as he saw Féderyc clearly for the first time. The man was half the weight he should have been; only his rib cage gave definition to his torn tunic. He was also filthy, his scraggly beard missing in patches, and his sunken cheeks highlighted the wrinkles around his eyes. His eyes themselves, though, were a deep green and seemed to outshine the rest of him, like the windows to a soul undamaged by the hardships of the body.

"I know," Féderyc said with a laugh as he caught Triston's stare. "Not a pretty sight."

Triston grinned ruefully, his gaze falling on his own legs stretched out before him. "The view is mutual, I'm sure."

He took in a deep breath, then gagged before he could let it out. The place smelled terrible, and it was from more than just his own stink and the piles of dried vomit on the floor. He glanced up, scanning down the hallway. It was a narrow dungeon without cells, and there were several empty shackles mounted along the walls. A second archer's window, at least a story above him, followed the first, and they were the room's only sources of light.

His idea of making a climbing rope out of sets of chains to reach the window didn't seem so viable now, although he couldn't rule it out until he'd tried it. "Anybody come with food yet?"

Féderyc shook his head. "I'd say it's only around ten in the morning, anyway."

Triston nodded, then frowned as he ran different ideas through his head. The ache was still there, not as strong as the day before but still distracting.

"You know," Féderyc said, breaking the silence, "I was sitting here earlier and something occurred to me... You don't hate me, do you?"

"No," Triston laughed. "Should I?"

"Well... the Fidelis killed your mother, didn't we?"

He frowned. "I never really believed that, only because she wouldn't have believed it. Are you confessing to something?"

"No," Féderyc said, with a genuine look of horror. "No, absolutely not." He paused again, still studying Triston's expression. "But isn't that what your father believes?"

"He does. It's all everyone's said my whole life."

Féderyc nodded, lips pursed, and his eyes grew distant. "I'd always had half a mind to think Cynwrig really did do it. The murderer could draft, after all. Then I had a run-in with a vojak..."

Triston frowned. "Where?"

"Feldland plains." He gave a heavy sigh. "I couldn't lead a rebellion against Dradge—so few of us who knew him ever could. But those vojaks... I killed them with a vengeance. Until they began moving with your father's soldiers, see, and that's when I had to wonder..."

Triston looked over at Féderyc's. Wasn't that what he'd seen for himself in Shalford—a vojak working alongside soldiers?

"Think about it," Féderyc said. "Who'd have authority enough to move troops like that unnoticed? You ought to know."

Triston turned away and stared absently at the wall across from him. These were precisely the thoughts he was trying to avoid, but this answer was too easy to find. There were only two men in Avaron with that sort of influence: his father, and Seren.

The sloshing of hooves in the mud and men's voices echoed in through the windows, drawing their attention.

Triston caught Féderyc's gaze. "Is this normal?"

The man shook his head.

Triston strained his ears to listen, but he couldn't quite make out what the voices were saying. "Maybe lunch has arrived early."

Féderyc tilted his head, as if he disagreed. "If you've been plotting something, now's the time to do it."

He grinned slightly. "Are you willing to play along?"

"Oh, am I ever."

Kura knew she was asleep, but it was that strange, hazy place between slumber and waking, and so she lingered there. She was—what was she doing? It was the council room, the bright light of the lenêre stone glaring white in the corner of her eyes. She was copying down the city names from Trofast's map; the words were a blur of black ink on her pale underarm.

What were those other cities? She didn't remember all the names, only Lâroe because that was where they were going next. Frustration overwhelmed her, although she wasn't sure why she should be so irked by this, and she saw herself going over those city names again, the image just as muddled and blurry as it was before.

"Kura," a voice sounded somewhere in the distance. "Wake up!"

She gasped, eyes flying open, and her whole body jerked as Elli landed on her stomach.

"Oh, hey, I'm up!" She sat up, pushing Elli onto the floor. Her sister laughed, scrambling to her knees as she threw her shoulder into Kura's chest. "Elli!" Kura wrapped her arm around her sister's shoulders and forcefully sat her down.

"Elli, let her up," Jisela scolded. She was sitting in the corner, a blanket draped over her shoulder as she fed Rowley. Spiridon and Faron were seated on the bed, putting on their shoes and talking about... something.

Faron turned to grin at her. "Well, it's about time you got up."

Kura rolled her eyes as she hauled herself to her feet. With a grimace and a sigh, she stretched her back. Sleeping on the hard floor like that was proving to be a bad decision.

"You don't even look rested," Spiridon said, catching her gaze. "You sleep alright?"

She paused, fear shooting through her as she wondered if he'd seen where she'd gone. But there was only innocent concern in her father's eyes. She nodded.

"We want breakfast!" Elli took Kura's hand in hers and pulled her toward the doorway. "Mother and Father said they don't know where it is but I can smell it and they said that you would know but they wouldn't let me wake you up until I finally did an—"

"Alright!" Kura said with a laugh. She wrenched her hand from Elli's grip and stretched again, stifling a yawn. "Alright, I can take you…"

A bustle of humans, nostkynna, and centaurs strode down the hallway. Apprehension turned her stomach, and she stepped into the doorway. There were people, dozens of them, with armor—a mix of brigandine, plate, and gambeson—on their shoulders and bundles of weapons in their hands, all jogging down the corridor. For a moment fear caught hold of her thoughts—Nansûr was being invaded—and then she remembered, and the fear matured and remained.

It was today. They were going to Lâroe.

"Kura!" The voice sounded—barely—over the crowd, and she spotted Aethan where he stood in the next doorway over. He was already dressed in his own set of brigandine armor, and he smiled, giving her a cheery wave. "Morning!"

She tried to return the smile.

He took a step into the hallway, but the flow of the crowd forced him back. He held up a large cloth sack. "I was told to give this to you!"

Kura held up her open hands. Aethan swung the sack into the air and she had to leap out into the hallway to get under it, catching it against her chest.

A gruff voice came from behind her. "Watch it!"

Kura jumped back into the safety of her doorway. "Sorry," she said, her voice lost in the crowd.

Aethan gave her another wave, this one in passing. "I'll meet you wherever all these folks are going."

She managed a smile this time, although she couldn't maintain it as Aethan stepped out into and disappeared among the crowd. They were going to Lâroe. She clutched that lopsided sack against her chest. She was the fonfyr and the rebellion was going to pull a heist in Lâroe. It'd all seemed simple the night before, but now the knowledge sank like a weight in her gut as she turned back into her family's room.

"What's that?" Elli asked excitedly, pulling at the cloth in Kura's arms. Kura set the bundle at her feet, then pulled out a brigandine chestplate. She'd already known what she was going to find, but Elli gave a squeal of excitement and Spiridon's face darkened.

"Armor, Kura?" Jisela's voice came weakly from the back of the room. It was a fearful exclamation, almost a rebuke, and not at all a question.

Kura drew in a shuddering breath, her focus jumping between her parents' faces. "We're raiding Lâroe today. Just a small town. They say we're—"

"No," Spiridon said sternly, his fist clenched at his sides as if he were ready to strike someone. "No, not you. They can find someone else."

She gave a desperate laugh. "Father, there is no one else. Not yet, anyway."

Spiridon scowled, his cheeks flushing red in anger. "Everyone knows it, *a gallant heart overflows*. I'm not going to just let you go off and die—"

He stopped, his words echoing in the stuffy cave. Elli stepped closer to Kura's leg while Jisela covered her mouth with her hand, tears welling up in her eyes.

"I thought..." Faron said softly. There were tears in his eyes, too. "I thought we were finally a family again."

In that moment Kura would have felt better had someone just punched her in the stomach. Her mistakes had led to her family being torn apart before; was she doing the same thing all over again? That couldn't true—she knew it wasn't true. So why did it *feel* true?

"I..." She swallowed the lump in her throat. "I should be back before nightfall."

Spiridon shoved himself up from the bed, grimacing as he put weight on his injured leg. "I'm coming with you."

"Father, no. I'm not going to die, but you would. Please." She held his gaze desperately. "Just rest. You spent the last week in *prison*."

"And you, Kura?" Jisela whispered. "You spent that time in comfort?"

She couldn't keep looking her mother in the eye. Of course she hadn't, and her mother knew it. But in the end it really didn't matter.

She fished the rest of the armor out of the sack. There was a helmet, studded with rusting sheets of plate metal, along with the chestplate, gloves, and covers for her arms and legs. Most of it she slipped over her hands and feet easily, but she struggled to tighten the chestplate properly around her waist.

"Let me," Spiridon said, walking to her side. She stood still as her father—calm and silent—cinched the lacings.

"Here, Kura." Elli held up her black cloak.

"Thanks," she said, her voice hardly more than a whisper. She flung the thick cloth over her shoulders, emotion welling up in her throat. "I—I promise I'll come back." She couldn't look at any of them. "But if I don't, know that I've done everything I can to make a better life for all of us."

She stepped out into the hallway before they saw her cry.

Walking among the waning crowd, she still didn't want anyone to see her tears, but her eyes stung anyway and she hoped her leather helmet cast enough shadow over her face. She let out a frustrated, shuddering sigh. *What is* wrong *with me?*

She stood on the precipice of triumph, one leap away from catching hold of all she had ever wanted—freedom from Dradge and a home, a real home, outside the Wynshire—and yet she didn't want to risk giving up what she had in order to get it. She was being petty, and selfish, and short-sighted—and she almost didn't care. She had her family back; couldn't that be enough? She'd already done more for this rebellion than she, rightly, had the responsibility to do.

The crowd came to a gradual stop, and only when she nearly ran into the person in front of her did she give a glance to see where they'd all ended up. It was a large room—nothing more than a cavern at the end of one of Nansûr's countless hallways—made small by the people crammed into it. Trofast stood at the front of the group, towering over the humans, nostkynna, and most of the centaurs gathered before him, but she really wasn't listening to what he said.

Finally, a cheer rang out from the crowd, the sound deafening in that stuffy room, and that was enough to draw her out of her own thoughts. She stiffened as she found all the nearby faces turned and watching her. *Why did I do this?*

Her fingers tightened around the belt holding Ìsendorál's scabbard to her waist, and she had to fight the urge to tear it off and toss it away. She wasn't the fonfyr, and maybe she'd half expected someone else to have noticed by now, but they hadn't. They believed her and they *kept* believing her. So what would happen when she failed, when they inevitably discovered the truth?

"There you are!" Aethan's cheery voice carried over the crowd, although Kura didn't truly notice him until he placed his hand on her shoulder, making her jump. He laughed and flashed a dimpled grin. "What, are you still asleep?"

She looked up into his green eyes—they were alight with excitement, with hope. "I guess you could say that."

Hope. Gods, that was why she'd done it. Except now she had everything she'd ever hoped to gain: her family was free from the Wynshire. They weren't free from Dradge, of course, but—and she felt guilty to even think it—maybe they were free enough?

"Come on," Aethan said gently, taking hold of her elbow as he nodded toward the far right wall. There was a sort of sympathy in his gaze now, and she wondered how dazed she must have looked to subdue his grin so quickly. "They've got you riding up front, but I can come too."

She let him lead her, the crowd parting before them, but she shook herself all the same. She was walking toward a *battle,* and yet she was letting her errant thoughts run rampant over her resolve. She set her jaw. She couldn't change what she'd done now. She would go to Lâroe, she would fight soldiers, and she would win—

that was it, and that was enough. Or rather, it *should* be enough. For now.

"Wmm, gnnd mmhgnn," a muffled voice called out. Akachi nosed his way through the crowd, dragging along a lean, white-speckled black stallion by the lead rope he carried in his mouth. He stopped at Kura's side, then spit out the lead with a snort.

"Ah, the indignity of it," he muttered, shaking his mane. "This uncooperative animal is yours," he continued, as he turned one eye on Aethan. The other horse pinned his ears against his neck as Aethan reached forward—timidly—to grab hold of the lead rope.

"Uh, thanks."

Akachi stared at her, ears flicking and neck arched. "You look awful—didn't you catch any sleep last night? I slept like a foal."

Kura grinned despite herself. "Good morning, Akachi."

The horse swung his head toward his saddle. "Well, come on! They tried to give you just one of the horses, but I said if you're going to have a parade, it's better the fonfyr is carried by a nostkynna or her own silly legs before one of those simple creatures."

Her smile lingered, and she hauled herself up into the saddle. "Thank you."

Akachi trudged forward, and the growing band of rebels parted to make way for him and Aethan, who rode behind. Guardedly, Kura surveyed the faces looking up at her. She tried to sit tall in the saddle, proud and confident like the real fonfyr would have, all while fighting to keep a sickened grimace from her face. If she failed, the crowds didn't seem to notice.

Then, among the strangers, she spotted a familiar face: Elli, waving with both hands from her perch above the crowd. Emotion caught in Kura's throat again, and maybe it felt a little like hope.

Her sister sat on her mother's shoulders, cheering and waving as Jisela gave a small smile, Rowley tucked up against her chest. It might hurt to see her go, but they still had hope in her, too. This time Kura didn't care who saw the tear that slid down her cheek. But where was her father, and Faron?

"Kura!" Her father's voice carried over the crowd, and she turned back to find him shoving himself into the parade line, Faron tagging at his heels. They wore brigandine chestplates and had scabbards hastily slung over their shoulders, helmets tucked under their arms. Spiridon ran to Kura's side and kept a quick pace beside Akachi.

A mix of gratitude and concern twisted in her chest. "Father, you shouldn't—"

"I'm going."

She wiped the tear from her cheek, hopefully before he noticed it. She knew that look; there was no changing his mind. She wasn't entirely sure she wanted to.

He gave her a wide smile, then came to a stop as he placed his right fist over his heart in a proper soldier's salute. "I'll see you there."

She turned in the saddle to watch as her father and brother faded in among the throng of rebels following behind her. Heart pounding in her chest, she drew Ìsendorál from its scabbard and held the rusty blade aloft. The crowd screamed in excitement, but Kura searched them until she found her mother's gaze.

She'd done everything for them, and given the choice she'd do it all again.

Chapter Forty

Veracity

Footsteps echoed in the hallway. Triston slumped forward against his chains, gritting his teeth as it wrenched his shoulders and drove the shackles into his bruised wrists.

"Hey!" Féderyc shouted—quiet and uninterested at first, but increasing in intensity. "Hey, I think this guy needs help in here!"

Triston remained motionless, keeping his eyes shut. The latch rattled, then the metal door flung open with a clang.

"What's going on?" That was Merric.

"He hasn't moved since you left him in here," Féderyc said. "I think he's dead."

Leather boots slid against the stone floor, and cloth shuffled as a person knelt before him. A warm hand pressed against his neck, then a head leaned toward his chest to listen for a heartbeat.

Triston leapt to his feet. He tossed a chain over the man's head and yanked it tight. "You'll do as—"

The man gasped, trying to speak despite the chains digging into this neck—he was on the taller side and skinny, not the burly fellow from yesterday—and threw a sharp elbow into Triston's ribs. Triston grunted, the pain forcing him to loosen his grip, and the next thing he knew the man had placed the point of a cold blade beneath his ear.

"Triston, let me go."

Shock coursed through Triston's veins. The voice was so calm, so commanding—he recognized it instantly, and he didn't know how he hadn't realized sooner.

It was Seren.

Triston let his arms fall limply at his sides, as far as the chains would allow.

"Thank you." Seren stepped back, shoving his knife into its sheath on his belt, and smoothed out his shirt with a dignified sigh. Triston could only stare at him.

The man studied him sympathetically, but the expression faded as he noticed the bloody gash on Triston's head. "What's he done to you?" He turned on Merric with a scowl, muttering something in a strange, guttural tongue.

Merric glanced down at his feet, folding his arms behind his back, and answered in the same language.

Seren shook his head in disgust. "I'm sorry about him," he said with a nod in Merric's direction.

Féderyc laughed, and Seren frowned at the man. "What's he still doing here?"

"Sir, you—" Merric began.

"I know, just get him out of here," Seren said, tossing his hand in the direction of the door. "Keep him... somewhere... until I'm finished here."

Merric stepped forward, digging a bundle of keys from a pouch on his belt, and then knelt down to unlock the chains on Féderyc's wrists.

Féderyc grinned. "Can't I stay? I promise I'll be good."

Anger flashed across Seren's face, but he didn't reply.

Merric hauled Féderyc to his feet, then threw the Fidelis's arm over his shoulder as he dragged the man toward the door. Féderyc's eyes met Triston's with a look of encouragement. Triston nodded, slightly, feeling anything but encouraged.

Just what does he think Seren's going to do to me?

Seren watched as Merric disappeared down the hallway, then turned back to Triston. "I swear, I didn't want you to get mixed up in all this."

"You care to explain what that means?"

Seren clasped his hands before him. "I'll try to explain everything, in time, but—"

"We have time." Triston lifted his shackled wrists, jangling his chains.

Seren just stared at those chains, eyes vacant. "Yes, I suppose we do."

"Aren't you going to let me go?"

Seren slowly shook his head. "See, I know what she'd want me to do... But she doesn't know you're here, and I have no intention of changing that."

"Who's 'she'? Your Grey Lady?"

"Is that what they say?" Seren chuckled. "I would be the *last* to call her a lady."

"Alright, why aren't you back in Avtalyon right now like you agreed, to meet me?"

"Well now"—Seren grinned, that same familiar expression the man had given in jest so many times before—"that's something I should be asking you, isn't it?"

"Why'd the soldiers in Shalford think I was dead?"

Surprise flashed across Seren's face. "I... look, Triston." He took a hesitant step forward. "I may have used unorthodox methods, but the both of us ultimately have the same goal here: the preservation of Avaron. That's all I've ever worked for, from my days studying her history to the years standing at your father's side. But somewhere along the line he stopped listening to me—"

"And you decided to just do what you wanted anyway?"

Seren's jaw tightened. "He was never supposed to be king—ask him yourself, he'll say the same. This isn't about what I want or don't want, this is simply what must be done. They're coming, Triston, from Lovaria first. I don't know when, but I do know—"

Triston laughed. "Is this more of your talk about shadow-men? There's always rumors coming out of Lovaria. It never turns out to be anything more than a misguided raid. We've driven them back a dozen times."

Seren shook his head, his expression grave. "That's just what your father said, too, and when I tried to explain he laughed at me, same as you just did. But I know what I know." His gaze fell. "And I've done what I had to do."

This was the talk of a crazy man, but of all things Seren was not crazy. "What have you done?"

Slowly, Seren's gaze met his again. It seemed he wanted to explain, but he didn't speak. Finally, he sighed and raked a hand through his hair. "Triston, you're like a son to me. Please understand that. A son I didn't raise and didn't ask for…"

"Seren, what have you done?"

The man didn't appear to be listening. "I never intended to hurt you, but I can't change the past, no matter how much I want to. I wish I could have presented this under better circumstances, but here we are. There are some things I desperately need to know, and I have reason to believe you know them." He gave a friendly, although desperate, smile. "We can arrange that, can't we? You tell me what I need to know, and I'll let you go."

Triston could only laugh. "It's easier to *blackmail* me than just give me an explanation? What do you even want to know?"

"Where is Nansûr?" Seren didn't look away, even as those words echoed into silence, and gradually Triston's grin faded.

"Where is what?"

"Triston…" Seren massaged his temples. "I know where you've been. I've heard about everything you've done. This is so much bigger than you. All of this, it's bigger than me, it's bigger than Avaron, it's bigger than…" He stopped, and Triston wasn't sure whether Seren couldn't think of something bigger than Avaron, or had realized he shouldn't say whatever it was he had in mind. "Every member of the council has pledged troops. You know how your father is when he's set his mind to something."

"Then let me go home, let me talk to him. I can end this. You know that."

Seren nodded, solemn, a strange look in his eyes. "Can't you see what he will do, though? The rebellion—and the Fidelis, the last *real* threat in this country—will be crushed. Believe me, he wouldn't do that for anyone other than you…"

Apologetic: that was the look. It was so unlike Seren to apologize that Triston hadn't even recognized the expression on the man's face.

"Do you really mean to—"

"You can't go home, Triston." Seren spoke too quickly to maintain the facade of calm. "There's already a dozen men posted, waiting to make sure you don't get in, and I won't be able to stop them from using whatever force they have to."

"You'd really let them harm me?"

Wrinkles creased beside Seren's eyes, making him look a decade older. "Please. Just tell me what I need to know and we can put this behind us."

"I already told you, I don't know anything."

"Numbers, then?" Seren rubbed his face in frustration, then folded his arms across his chest. "Can you give me some numbers, Triston? How about who's in charge?"

"I still don't know what you're talking about."

Seren clenched his hand into a fist and pressed it against his forehead. "Triston, please." He looked up with a desperate laugh. "Can't you give me something—anything? I don't want to have to do this." He threw his open hands to his sides in defeat. "Here, just give me the fonfyr's name. Just his name, and I'll let you go."

"What's a fonfyr?"

Seren turned away, shoulders tense. Rage burned in his eyes—that was not uncommon, but Triston couldn't remember it ever being directed at him. Seren paused in the doorway, leaning one hand against the frame. Triston thought he was going to say something, but the man straightened and strode into the hallway.

"Hey," Triston called after him, "you're not seriously going to leave me here—"

Merric stepped into the cell, and the door slammed shut behind him. The soldier smiled, his unnerving blue eyes glinting with sick satisfaction. Heart thudding in his chest, Triston steeled himself for the worst. He wouldn't take anything without a fight.

As soon as Merric was in range, Triston kicked his stomach. The soldier stumbled back, gasping for breath. There was a rage in those black eyes now—deep, animalistic, and unpredictable. Triston steadied his breathing as Merric came forward again. He lashed out with another kick, but Merric brushed it aside.

Triston stumbled, grabbing fistfuls of chain to catch his balance, and lifted himself off the ground, striking with both feet this time. Merric grunted as Triston's feet met his hands, but he redirected the blow. Triston's feet dropped to the ground. His head spun with the exertion but he sent another kick in Merric's direction—anything to keep the man at a distance.

It wasn't enough. He tried to cover his face, but the chain went taut and Merric's fist crashed into his face. There was a flash of white and a surge of pain as the blow tossed his head to the side. Triston's legs crumbled beneath him, and he landed, hard, against the wall.

He opened his eyes. The world spun, a mass of grey stone broken only by Merric's dark figure leering over him. Another punch landed on his cheek. The darkness lasted longer this time, and when Triston finally became aware of himself again all he heard was Merric's voice, shouting in his ear.

"Where is Nansûr?"

Triston shook his head. His mouth tasted like blood, and he leaned forward to spit on the ground. Merric kicked him in the stomach. He clamped his jaw shut to keep the man from having the satisfaction of hearing him scream.

The question came again, louder. "Where is Nansûr?"

Triston didn't answer.

Merric punched him in the face again, and out of instinct Triston lashed out. The chains went taunt, digging into his wrists before he could reach. Merric shoved him back against the wall, a hand on his neck.

"Where is Nansûr?"

"Give it up!" Triston kicked Merric's knee. The man cursed and stumbled back, clutching at his leg.

He snarled and returned with a vengeance. He asked no more questions, but the blows kept coming, one after another, with a power born from a deep, uncontrollable rage. Triston squirmed, fighting with all the strength he had to try to block the strikes, but even as every other blow landed on his calf or his shins, he couldn't keep himself in the moment, and his mind began to drift.

"That's enough!"

Triston tried to open his eyes, but his head hurt and his face hurt and he could see only the shifting shadows of figures before him. The voice was Seren's.

"He is a soldier!" He almost sounded proud. "I told you not to hurt him! What did you think this was going to get you?"

"Sir, he—"

"Go!"

Triston tried to open his eyes again, but the light felt like daggers, so he let his head hang limp, content for the moment with his efforts to keep his chest heaving for air.

"Triston." It was still Seren's voice, calmer and closer this time.

Triston felt a hand on his shoulder, but his head hurt and his chest hurt and in the end he didn't care what Seren did.

"Triston," Seren said again, with urgency this time. A hand grabbed a mass of hair from the top of his head and tilted his face upwards. Triston groaned, blinking, as he forced his eyes open.

Seren was kneeling before him, a relieved smile on his face. He released his handful of Triston's hair and instead gingerly held his hand under Triston's chin to keep his face from falling forward.

"I'm sorry about him," he said softly.

Triston laughed, but winced as the movement triggered a sharp pain in his side. He continued to blink, trying to clear his blurred vision. His left eye was tight, and it didn't open all the way.

"He wasn't supposed to..." Seren gave a shuddering sigh, and muttered something under his breath. "It's just that ever since the rejoining he's been so unpredictable." He had a cloth in his hand, and he wiped away the blood that flowed from Triston's nose. "Here." He pushed Triston back against the wall to keep his chin elevated.

Triston let his eyes fall shut. Who did Seren think he was, having him beaten one minute and then binding his wounds the next? Faintly he heard the jingling of metal, and a moment later his arms dropped, one after the other.

"Merric!" Seren shouted, somewhere in the distance, but Triston let the sound drift away as he settled into the comfort of the darkness.

A cold, wet cloth passed over his forehead.

He had to force his eyes open again, and once the blurry image became clear, he found Seren kneeling before him, trying to wash his wounds with the bucket of water on the ground beside him. Triston met Seren's gaze. There was a look of familial concern—a genuine care for his wellbeing. It was enough to make him sick. If he'd had any strength left, he probably would have wrung Seren's sorry neck right there.

"I don't want to leave you here," Seren was saying as he placed the cool cloth over Triston's forehead. He had an old, wool blanket in his hands, which he draped across Triston's lap. "But I can't stay any longer or she'll notice I'm gone, and even this is better than anything she'd..."

Either his voice trailed off, or Triston found himself no longer listening. Seren said something else, something he didn't hear, and in the end Triston only became aware of himself again as the metal door to the prison slammed shut.

"You didn't tell him anything, did you." It was Féderyc, on his hands and knees in front of the closed door, as if someone had just tossed him in. And he wasn't asking a question.

Triston laughed despite the pain it caused him. "I didn't tell him anything."

It hurt to sit there propped up against the wall, it hurt to take in each deep, shuddering breath, but he didn't have the strength to do anything else. He let his eyes fall shut, a grin still on his face. He knew the truth now, didn't he?

And surely for that, all this was a small price to pay.

Chapter Forty-One

THE RECKONING

The line of boats drifted through the fog, the company as quiet as the morning. Kura tried to hide her grimace as she adjusted her helmet with a shaking hand. Had they talked about boats in the council meeting?

These river vessels were twice the size of the one she'd ridden in with Triston, but it still took four of them to hold all the rebels as they made their way toward Lâroe. She sat toward the helm of the lead boat, with Faron beside her, her father beside him, Aethan across from her, and Renard at the front. Her brother kept turning in his seat to watch the water stream by the hull, and then looking to her with a grin.

At least he's *enjoying himself.*

Renard sat back down in his seat, shaking the boat so violently Kura couldn't keep herself from latching on to the side.

"Quiet now," he hissed, his voice echoing in the silence. "We're almost there."

The boats glided toward the bend in the river, and as Chagan—who sat in the back with the rudder—made the turn, Kura caught her first glimpse of Lâroe Tower. Compared to Shalford, it looked like a hut.

The structure was only two stories tall—the flat roof barely peeked over the short trees that grew beside the water—and roughhewn logs and bark-covered panels made its frame and walls. It jutted out beyond the shore, creating an overhang, which sheltered a single dock that stretched out toward the center of the river. The town of Lâroe lay behind it, smoke from its cookfires drifting lazily over the blazon of autumn branches that blocked all but the first few log houses from view.

A red sunrise shone bright behind the tower, as if to spite the dark clouds that hung about the horizon, rumbling with thunder. Kura shaded her eyes with her hand until the boats passed into the tower's shadow. It was deathly quiet, a stillness that bred fear instead of comfort, but she tried to pretend she didn't notice.

Something splashed in the water and she turned to look, expecting to find a fish. A second splash followed the first, closer, and this time she caught a glimpse of arrow fletching as it sunk into the water.

She flinched and pointed. "Ar—"

"Shields up!" Renard's command broke the remaining peace of the morning.

Spiridon lifted his shield to cover the front quarter of the boat— the other shield-bearers jumping up alongside him—as arrows pattered the wood and the water. The tower loomed over them as the boats continued to glide toward the docks. Its windows more resembled those of a house than the archer's turrets at Shalford, but archers stood in those openings all the same, shooting at the boats below.

Renard muttered something under his breath as he shrank behind the shield. "There are twice as many men up there than the scouts reported. We're supposed to be pulling a heist, not waging a proper battle. We ought to scrap this—"

"What?" That escaped before Kura could hold it back. She let out a breath, and an arrow sank into the shield above her head. "You want to come back to Nansûr emptyhanded, without even trying? After that send-off?"

Renard eyed her for a long moment. "No."

He spun back around to the front of the boat and pointed at the tower. The boat listed toward it, the others following through the barrage. Faron yelped as an arrow passed between the shields and sank into the seat beside him.

Renard laughed. "Don't worry, kid. We'll have something better than arrows here soon enough."

Chagan paddled the boat up against the dock, and the patter of arrows faded as they floated beneath the tower's overhang. The shield-bearers jumped onto the docks first, forming a barricade between the boats and the door that led into the tower, and then the rest of the rebels filed behind them.

Kura found herself the last one standing in the boat, her stomach lurching every time someone stepped onto the dock, shaking the vessel. She clenched her fists, trying to muster some semblance of courage, but all she saw was the depths of the river sparkling between the dock and the boat.

"Come on." Aethan extended his hand with a sympathetic smile. Kura swallowed whatever remained of her pride, then grasped his arm and let him haul her onto the dock.

Voices sounded from within the tower, and Renard took off toward the door, several of the shield-bearers tromping at his side. Kura followed, Aethan and her father at her shoulders, as Faron pulled their boat farther down the line to make room for the other incoming parties. He—fortunately—had agreed to watch the boat, while her father had insisted on accompanying her into the tower.

She glanced up at her father's face. His eyes were distant—cold, even—and he gripped the sword hilt at his side with a white-knuckled fist. He was almost a different man, except she recognized the expression: the same one had overcome him every time she'd made the mistake of asking about his time as a soldier.

They passed through the doorway with no resistance, then took the stairs two-by-two. Kura shook herself and let out a shuddering sigh. That boat ride had rattled the sense of focus she thought she'd found leaving Nansûr, and without it she felt dangerous—unprepared and unbalanced.

Halfway up the stairs, her head cleared the top of the floor. The room was wide and open, divided only by the stout pillars that ran through from the floor to the ceiling, but it was not empty. Piles of grain, leather, armor, weapons, and other materials filled the room—along with a dozen soldiers, armed and ready.

The shield-bearers charged with a shout, and the rest of the rebel company followed them. The two lines met with a clash of metal and wood, and the soldiers broke past the shields. A man ran toward Kura with sword drawn. Her thoughts fell to silence, her world narrowing to just that one soldier. She lunged, and after a few short parries and a thrust, he lay dead at her feet.

She let out her breath, the rest of the rebel company rushing by in a blur as she stared at the dead man's bloody face. One moment she'd been struggling with a thousand emotions, the next she'd harnessed only one—resolve—and with it killed a man. She'd killed before, but this was the first time she had realized it was *easy*. Terrifyingly easy.

A cry sounded behind her, followed by a flash of sunlight on polished steel. She ducked, the soldier's blade carrying over her head, then spun around to shove her blade into his unprotected gut. That quickly, a second man was dead, and she forced his final screams from her mind. This was what she'd come to do, after all. Kill.

The room shook with a cacophony of clashing swords and shouting fighters, but silver chestplates clearly marked enemy from friend. She threw herself into the battle, her lingering frustrations lending strength to her sword arm as she kept her feet light and her thrusts swift. She didn't count the number of men who fell to her bloodstained blade—she didn't want to know—and she did her best to keep from glimpsing any other dead man's face.

A deafening shout filled the room and Kura spun around, brandishing Ìsendorál with a pounding heart—then realized the skirmish was over. The cry was that of victory, and it came from her own companions.

Taking a gulp of air, she lowered her weapon and haltingly turned an eye to the carnage at her feet. There wasn't a soldier left standing, and those that remained were marred corpses, silent or groaning, lying in puddles of their own blood, excrement, or entrails.

Kura gagged. *I did this.*

She'd brought a band of rebels here and she'd done this. She'd blindly hated all the king's soldiers before, but then she'd met Triston, and...

Had these all been bad men? Did they deserve to die like this?

"Hey!" Renard slapped her on the back. She flinched and met his gaze. His expression was almost gentle, his eyes almost understanding. "Keep your head together."

At first, all she did was stare at him. Then she swallowed, and nodded, and the rest of the world came rushing back. Her father stood an armsbreadth away, looking her up and down as though he was trying to determine which—if any—splatters of blood on her arms and face belonged to her. He didn't have a scratch on him—not that she had expected anything less. He looked both younger and older somehow, thanks to his armored poise and haggard expression.

Kura managed to give him a shaky smile. Her father tried, but he couldn't return it.

"Let's go!" Renard's voice carried—he spoke to everyone and no one at once—and he passed her by, a sack of grain slung over each shoulder. "Get this stuff to the boats!"

She cleaned her sword on her pant leg before sheathing it, then jumped to work beside Aethan. The other rebels had already cleared most of the floor, but he picked up a stack of cured leather, and Kura an armload of spears, before following Spiridon in the procession toward the door.

She breathed a sigh of relief as they started down the stairs. They'd almost done it. But Aethan watched the ground with a pensive frown.

"What is it?"

"Hmm?" He looked up. "Oh. Do you think this was too easy?"

Dread sank in Kura's gut. How hard was it supposed to be?

She stepped onto the dock, only to be met by a scream. More than half of the rebels had returned to their boats, but there were too many boats.

Aethan jumped back as she hesitated, a caustic mix of anger and fear surging through her limbs. There were soldier's vessels, in number at least equal to her own group's—most filled with archers, who loosed on the docks.

A wave of water rippled out from the tower, overturning the nearest soldier's boats, but it lost momentum and only jostled the remaining watercraft. Aethan grimaced and lifted his shaking hands. A thin wall of water rose between the docks and the open river, providing meager cover from the archers.

Another shout split the air—a man's this time—and Kura turned in horror to find Faron pulling back from the edge of the dock, leaving his boat behind as a shaggy beast climbed out of the river. It was as big as a bear and covered in black fur, but had a decidedly human-like face and massive claws on its front paws.

The beast shook its wet, mangy fur, then stood tall on its rear legs and roared. Faron stumbled as the saja swatted at the nearest rebels. Spiridon dropped his sack of grain, drawing his sword, and charged through the crowd toward the beast. He hadn't taken three steps before arrows struck him, in the gut and shoulder. He fell.

Kura screamed and ran after him, fumbling with the bundle of spears in her arms. She took one into her hand and chucked it at the saja. It flew past and splashed into the river. Nearly blind with tears and rage, she continued hurling spears. One stuck in the beast's shoulder—it might have grunted, but continued to lumber down the dock as sure and strong as ever.

Faron pushed himself to his feet and scrambled to his father's side as other rebels jumped into boats or dove into the river to avoid the saja's advance. The beast eyed Faron as he struggled to tug Spiridon to his feet.

One arrow shot past Kura's neck and another glanced off her chestplate, but she didn't care. "Hey!"

The saja raised its greying muzzle to look at her, and she threw another spear at its chest. This one sank into the thing's thick fur, drawing blood, and the beast growled. It stepped away from Faron, then swatted at the log supporting the tower overhang.

The beam splintered; the saja's unnaturally strong claws bit through the wood like a machete through field grass. The tower creaked, and in a heap of timbers the corner broke from the structure and collapsed onto the dock.

"No!" Kura's voice rang in her own ears. She couldn't see her brother or father but she ran toward the tangle of debris anyway—until something latched onto her arm.

It was Aethan, pulling her back. "Come on!"

She fought to wrench her wrist out of his iron grip, but the severed beam had broken through the dock at her feet, exposing the river, and bits of log and wood paneling toppled into the water. It cut her off from the rest of the rebels, from the boats—from her family. The wall of water shielding her from the archers trembled, then splashed into the river.

Numb, she let Aethan drag her back into the tower.

At the top of the stairs, they found several other rebels waiting—Chagan's was the only face she recognized. Once they saw her, they gave a cheer and began asking questions, but echoing snarls burst in from the other side of the room.

Saja had breached the tower walls.

The far corner, over the river, lay crumbled—exposing the darkened horizon—but the beasts had broken through the opposite door and streamed in from the streets of Lâroe.

This *had* been too easy. All along, this had been—

Rage and fear boiled over in Kura's chest, and it all came out in a shout as she drew her sword and charged the incoming saja. They were strange beasts, hunched and covered in stringy brown fur, and they looked something like apes. If apes had massive, muscular arms with talons for fingers.

She struck at them as though Ìsendorál were a scythe and the saja wheat. All she saw was blood, all she heard were the saja's yelps—carrying in that stuffy room like music—and all she thought of was her father and brother, lying beneath that beam in the river.

The rebels let out a hearty cry, which she only noticed ringing in the back of her mind when two figures moved toward her. On one side was a stranger, on the other Aethan. The saja snarled and pulled back, so she pressed her advantage, striking at legs, tails, anything her blade could reach.

Then horrifying clarity washed over her and pulled her to a stop. She wasn't thinking—about what she was doing, about anything. She raised her sword and paused to survey the room. The saja hadn't pulled back; they'd split to try to encircle her group.

Two soldiers charged through the doorway, with more following behind.

"Fall back!" she shrieked.

The rebels tried to react. Aethan leapt to Kura's side. The rebel beside her fell, the saja tearing out her throat. Eyes stinging, Kura continued the retreat, hacking at any beast that came too close. Another rebel fell with a scream, the mass of saja swallowing him as they circled around from behind. The soldiers pressed forward, the monsters parting before them. One parried a few strikes from Chagan before thrusting his sword through the rebel's chest.

Tears blurred Kura's vision, but she planted her feet and met the soldier's advance. His blade slid across her defense, then sliced her ribs. She gasped and pulled back, bracing herself for the pain, but her brigandine chestplate took the blow.

Aethan lunged forward with a shout and drove the blade of his swordstaff through the soldier's neck. The soldier jolted, his eyes wide, then Aethan pulled out his blade and ran—even before the man's body hit the ground. Kura followed him, saja tagging at her heels. But where was there to go?

They reached the far wall. Aethan slung his staff over his back, then leapt onto the windowsill and hauled himself up and out of sight. Kura sheathed her sword and jumped up into the window after him, but she couldn't tear her gaze from the snarling saja that barreled toward her.

"Grab my hand!" Aethan hung over the edge of the roof above her, his hands outstretched. Kura grasped his wrists, and with a grunt he hauled her up onto the roof.

He fell back, and she clambered to her feet. Saja's muffled snarls murmured in the floor below them, joining in with the cries from the river. Thunder rumbled, closer now, and the scent of rain hung heavy in the damp air.

Kura spun around as the clatter of stones carried up from the city streets below—a section of ground rippled like water, throwing saja off their feet. Nearby, tendrils of water materialized into spear-like shafts and tore through the next street with an arrow's precision.

Hope, long lost and much welcomed, caught in her chest. It was the Fidelis—Cynwrig's band, moving in from the forest to catch the soldiers and saja at the tower. Cloaked figures darted between buildings, attacking and defending in some sort of synchronized pattern. Dark shapes shifted in the trees, and then streaks of black rained down on the farthest soldiers. The Varian at work.

Saja still swarmed the tower—the nearest of them attempting to use their large front talons to climb out the window after her and Aethan—but the rest pulled back, right into the Fidelis and Varian's waiting arms. Kura wiped the tears from her cheeks as the ray of hope brought her enough calm to think. She still saw rebel boats—manned by rebel fighters—floating on the river below her. There was someone left.

There was still something to salvage from all this.

A Fidelis sent a burst of flame through a narrow alleyway, and she drew her sword. The rusty blade glinted red, even as the nearing storm darkened the sun, and a maybe foolish, maybe terrible idea came to her mind. She ran to the center of the tower.

"Kura!" Aethan glanced over his shoulder as he struck at a saja with his staff. The beast had climbed the wall, but he slashed it across the chest and sent it toppling to the ground below. "What...?"

She took in a deep breath, then let it out as she sank the tip of Ìsendorál into the wooden planks at her feet. The growing storm winds swirled around her, whipping her hair back from her shoulders and billowing her black cloak. "I—I've got to light the tower." She'd drafted before, setting Ìsendorál's blade on fire in the council chambers, and now the entire structure was full of saja.

"You..." He wanted to argue and she didn't fault that. All the same, she ignored him.

She opened her mouth to speak, then realized she didn't know what to say. What had Idris made her repeat? Strange, flowing words... she couldn't remember them, so it didn't matter.

"Come on!" Kura shouted, to herself as much as anyone. She tightened every muscle she had; she focused with all the strength she could muster. Nothing came—nothing beyond the whipping winds that pelted her with cold droplets of rain as the distant, rumbling thunder crept ever nearer.

"Kura..." Aethan hesitantly walked to her side. She saw it in his face: he was going to argue this time, and she was ready to give in. She was about to turn away, about to shove that stupid sword back into its scabbard where it belonged, but a guttural, raspy voice sounded above.

She turned, the wind tossing the strands of her hair across her face, and watched as a large flicker landed on the wooden beam jutting out over the river. The golden color of its inner wing feathers flashed as it settled on its perch. This was quite an old bird, with speckles of white marring the patch of bright red feathers at its throat, but it still carried itself with pride.

The flicker opened its long, wide beak to give another squawk. Somehow, Kura found herself captivated by the sound, and as she looked into the animal's watching, grey-green eye, she felt in her heart that it was speaking to her. Not in words, not even in any sort of language that could be conventionally understood, but she knew what it was saying. It was a warning.

She shoved Ìsendorál into its scabbard and latched onto Aethan's wrist. He stumbled as she pulled him forward, quite confused.

"What—?"

She didn't answer. To try to put it all into words would have kept her from acting.

When they reached the ledge, Kura stopped, feet sliding against the wood panels, and involuntarily tightened her grip on Aethan's arm. She had been about to jump off. *Why on Ehlis was I going to dive off?*

The flicker squawked and flapped its wings—flashes of gold on black—before taking flight. Its warning came again, just as strong and clear as it had the first time, but she'd had time to think about it now. The bird sailed through the air, swooping amid the currents as if it had been born among the winds.

Then it dove at Kura's face.

She yelped and threw her hands up as she tried to swat the bird away. The smooth sole of her boot slipped, and with a lurch, she was standing on nothing. She lashed out for the ledge, but in a second it was out of reach—she was falling.

"Kura!" Aethan lunged after her.

A blinding light shot from the clouds. The cool autumn air flared hot, the force of it reverberating in her chest as the wind rushed past her, and every hair on her arms and neck stood up. For that instant there was nothing but the light. Then it disappeared, crackling thunder booming in its wake. The sound echoed in her soul.

She was still falling. She knew that, some part of her was screaming, but the rest was captivated by what she saw. It was lightning, and it had struck the tower on the lower level. Fire—bright, dancing, red-and-yellow fire—sprang up from the sides even as the wall fell to splinters.

Aethan.

There was time enough for that one thought, and in vague relief she found his figure framed as a dark silhouette against the flames engulfing the tower. Then reality set in—they were falling, both of them. She turned, the wind rushing past her face, whistling in her ears and making her eyes water.

The smooth surface of the river rose toward her like a great, lopsided hand. Kura screamed, covering her face with her arms, and crashed through the water.

It was deathly cold, and dark, and she couldn't hear over the roar of the river and the gasping, pathetic sounds of her own fight to swim, to breathe. Still, she was moving—to where, she didn't have time to wonder—and then it was over.

She gasped, throwing her eyes open as she struggled to her knees. Her cold, wet clothes clung to her and the wind sent a chill to her bones, but she was alive, the air stinging her lungs attested to that. She was on the shore; she was kneeling in the mud on the banks of the river.

Aethan lay on his back in the mud next to her, raking his fingers through his wet hair. He was laughing.

She met his gaze. Nothing was at all funny, but she found herself laughing along with him.

Footsteps crunched on the shoreline pebbles and she bolted upright, clutching at her sword.

"Hey." It was a woman—a little past middle age, dressed in a simple shirt and trousers—and she approached with hands raised. "I'm here to help. We've pulled some others from the river."

Kura heaved a sigh of relief, then pushed herself to her feet as heavy droplets of rain began to pelt her shoulders. Debris littered the shoreline, along with the occasional body. She grimaced and hoped to the gods the dead were all soldiers.

The woman laughed. "I thought y'all were crazy, coming in here against the king's men as you did, but you didn't back down, even after those beasts came to slaughter you, and we couldn't just stand by after that." Her eyes widened when they fell on Kura's sword. "I heard the rumors, but... you're the fonfyr, aren't you?"

Kura was completely unprepared to give any sort of reply.

The woman grinned and pointed over Kura's shoulder. "Foolish question, I already know!"

Kura turned, her wet hair sticking to her cheeks, to look at the river.

Thick, black smoke billowed from the burning hull of what had been Lâroe Tower. Dying saja screamed from within the listing structure as the rest ran from the flames and the heat; townsfolk from Lâroe met them on the streets and struck them down with rakes, logs, stones, anything within reach. A cheer rose in the distance, and she squinted through the flames to see rebels standing in the few boats that remained, throwing their fists over their heads.

Her shoulders sagged and she turned back toward the tower. She wanted to feel relieved, happy—anything—but she was unable to process any of it. The tower let out a shuddering creak, and then with slow, inevitable movement, the whole wooden frame crashed into the river. The smooth waters churned, sending long waves, which slowly rippled out from the wreckage to lap against the shore.

Aethan slipped in the mud, and both the woman and Kura jumped to catch him by the arms. His hands shook, and his knees buckled under his own weight. He smiled, embarrassed, but he didn't try to brush either of them aside.

"I..." He swallowed. "I did too much, I think. With... with the river."

"No trouble." The woman slung Aethan's arm over her shoulder and pulled him toward the log cabin that stood nearest the shore. "We've opened the house there for the wounded."

Hope leapt in Kura's chest, making her hands shake so badly she struggled to sheath her sword. Somehow she met Aethan's gaze, and he nodded.

She bolted toward Lâroe, and even though she was gasping for air after running up the slight slope from the shore, she didn't stop until she stumbled—weak and breathless—through the doorway of the house. It seemed to be someone's home, with a small kitchen in the corner and a fireplace on the opposite wall, but all the furnishings—tables, chairs, cots—had been pushed aside to leave the space open.

Figures lay on the dirt floor, most of them wrapped in blankets, all of them packed together so that the few standing individuals had to tread lightly to move between them. Kura stared at those faces, her gut clenched. The wounded were all rebels, each of them marred by claws, arrows, or swords, some missing limbs. A few lay still, completely covered in sheets.

She staggered back and only caught herself against the doorframe. Her breath wouldn't come. There were so few left. Renard had wanted to turn back, but she... she'd...

"Kura!" A voice rang out from the other side of the room, splitting through her jumble of thoughts like a ray of sunshine through storm clouds. It was Faron, standing beside the fireplace, leaning on a crutch.

Relief set her arms shaking, and she gingerly made her way around the other wounded to reach her brother's side. His clothes were soaked, his lips blue with cold, and his left leg splinted, but he laughed all the same and wrapped his free arm around her neck.

"I knew you'd make it! Father was worried, but I wasn't."

She pulled out of Faron's embrace and found her father lying on the ground at her feet, propped up on a pile of blankets by the wall. His face was pale, startlingly so, and his wet tunic stained through with blood from where he'd been struck by the arrows. But the arrows were gone, and a cloaked figure knelt beside him, whispering flowing words under his breath as he tended to the wounds.

A Fidelis.

"Father?" Kura knelt at his side and placed a hand on his arm. His eyes blinked open and found her face with a weary smile.

"There you are, girl." His voice was weak and hoarse, and he struggled to keep his eyes open. "I shouldn't have worried. I saw you fight..."

The Fidelis pulled back, wiping his bloody hands on a clean cloth. "He needs to rest, I—" Kura looked him in the eye, and he stopped speaking.

"Cynwrig?"

The man's bulbous face grew tight, his green eyes widened—and then all expression vanished. "Hmm," he grunted, and pushed himself to his feet. "You're lucky we came, fonfyr."

Kura rose, at a complete loss for words. A cloaked figure brushed past her shoulder: another Fidelis, moving among the wounded. There were four of them in all, tending to at least ten men and women. "...Thank you."

Cynwrig grunted again and took a step away from her. "I can't do anything more for him now. He'll need rest, and then another healer to see him once he's a little stronger."

Kura nodded, tears catching in the back of her throat as she stared at her father's sleeping face. *So pale.*

Without another word, Cynwrig strode toward the door. She watched him go, then slowly turned to look over the room again. Was this everyone? All she saw were the broken limbs, the bloody bandages—her family alive, while so many others lay dead.

But every face that turned toward hers *smiled*. Like she was their heroic leader, like she was—

Kura ran to the door and stumbled out into the rain. *I did this. They followed me.* She fell to her knees in the mud, clutching at her stomach as the raindrops mingled with her tears, but her mouth tasted like bile. *They followed me, on a lie, and I killed them.*

"Kura!" Faron's frantic cry carried loudly enough in the deluge.

She was angry at first—couldn't he leave her alone for one moment?—but when she turned to find him standing in the fire-lit doorway, leaning on his crutch, her heart broke.

"What's wrong?" He hobbled a step into the rain, and she scrambled to her feet.

"Faron—" She tried to brush aside the tears before he could see, but his gaze met hers and his face fell.

"We did it, Kura." He pointed toward the river with his free hand and struggled to give her a smile. "We got the supplies—two boatloads of armor and weapons, and grain that would be more than enough to feed our family for a year. Renard and a few of the others stole the soldiers' boats, and then picked Father and me and others out of the river. Don't you see? We did it."

She laughed, then pressed her hand to her mouth as it came out as a sob. Was this what victory was supposed to feel like?

"Hey," Faron said gently. He hobbled another step away from the doorway—farther into the rain—and pulled her into an embrace that was more a headlock than a hug. "It's fine. It will all be fine."

Chapter Forty-Two
Mortal Severance

Through the darkness, Triston heard water wrung into the bucket beside him, and then felt the comfort of a cool cloth pressed against his face. He groaned, taking the cloth into his hand, and forced his eyes open.

"Sorry, I wasn't trying to wake you," Féderyc said, sympathetically enough.

Triston shook his head, blinking until his vision cleared. The man was kneeling beside him with a look of worry that had become a fixed part of his regular expression.

It was evening; deep orange sunlight beamed through the narrow archer's windows. He'd sat here all afternoon, then, somewhere between slumber and waking, as though he could simply sleep away what Merric had done to him. He let the cloth fall from his face. It had seemed like a good idea at the time, but the pounding in his head and the stiff ache in the rest of his body indicated that his rest hadn't solved anything.

Triston tossed the old cloth over the edge of the wooden bucket. He'd sat still long enough.

"Wait," Féderyc said, almost scoldingly, "what are you doing?"

Triston gritted his teeth and, grasping the chains beside him, tried to haul himself to his feet. His arms ached and shook with the exertion—he ignored that, but pain tore through his side. He grimaced and fell back to the floor.

Each ragged breath triggered a sharp, radiating pain that came from somewhere deep within his torso. Carefully, he tried to evaluate the extent of his injury, and had to smother a cry as he felt his left side. That rib was broken, and a few others were probably bruised as well. He let out a frustrated sigh, wheezing as even that motion hurt.

"Take it easy," Féderyc said gently. "You've earned that much today."

Triston shook his head, clenching his eyes shut as he prepared himself to try to stand again. "I've got to get out of here, Féderyc. He's going to kill my father, he's going to, to—I can't just let him..."

"I know." The man's expression held both respect and apology, but Triston couldn't help but notice how Féderyc stared at his swollen bruises, not his eyes. "I should be able to—I'm supposed to be able to..."

Shouts carried from beyond the window. They were men's voices, rich with desperation and courage, and Triston recognized them in an instant: it was a battle. Metal clashed against metal, the sound echoing in sporadic intervals against the stone tower. Strength surged through his veins. Out there it could be the rebels, or his father's own company, or—

He reached again for the chains. His fists clenched those cold metal links and, grunting against the pain, he pulled with all his strength. The ache coursed through him again before he'd gotten very far, but he gritted his teeth harder, pushing against it. It was agony, radiating into his core as if his whole body was on fire, and he couldn't hold back his cry this time. He collapsed to the floor, pressing his arm against his side in some vain effort to quiet the pain.

"Triston."

With some effort, he met the man's gaze.

"I don't know what's happened to my connection with the Essence—I know it doesn't always express in the same ways—but we've both still got Gallian's blood flowing through our veins..."

Surprised, Triston was about to ask for more of an explanation, but Féderyc gripped his hand.

"It's been done before," he said, as though still trying to convince himself. "If things can conduct, then why not people? Just say this with me: *Elaedoni, diau brýte nnan jema.*"

Triston gave an exasperated grin. "Féderyc, I don't know what you're—"

"Oh, it shouldn't really matter how you say it, anyway. Just so long as you believe it, deep down in the core of you, and don't fight it." He gripped Triston's fist in his own. "'Essence, move in me, make what is broken whole.'"

Triston opened his mouth to speak, amused and frustrated by this situation all at once. Féderyc's green eyes didn't waver. "Essence, move in me, make what is broken whole."

Reluctantly, Triston began to repeat the phrase along with him. He didn't see the use—the Essence was a powerful thing, for other people—but Féderyc was so insistent.

Suddenly, a spark of energy flowed from Féderyc's hand into his. Triston looked up, startled, as the words fell from his lips. Féderyc didn't seem to notice; his eyes were clenched shut and he still muttered under his breath, although now he'd reverted back to the New Tounge like he'd spoken the first time.

The energy flickered again, more than a spark this time—it was a power, flowing from Féderyc's hand into Triston's. It permeated every part of him, seeped into him like the warmth from a late winter sun on a cold day. But that strength wasn't his, wasn't Féderyc's—it was something else, something deeper, something beyond him reaching down for him as he reached out for it.

But gradually, he began to feel something else. It was subtle, so much so that he almost didn't notice, but there all the same: darkness, creeping into his soul like cold seeped into a warm room through an open window. He couldn't name this, but he recognized it—like he was reading, for the first time, a word he'd only heard. And in some ways it felt right, like a part of himself he'd never properly understood until that moment.

Féderyc ripped his hand from Triston's grip. Triston gasped, the tangle of sensations in his core tearing from him. He realized that Féderyc had been trying to take his hand away for some time, but only now succeeded.

"What was that?"

Féderyc shook his head, refusing to look Triston in the eye. "I shouldn't have... I'm sorry, it was a mistake."

Triston studied the man. Féderyc was ashamed—almost distraught. Because of the darkness? It hadn't done anything to him, and he knew even from that brief moment that the light was stronger. He looked down, running a hand over his ribs. They still hurt, but nowhere near the way they had before.

He grinned, amazed. "Gallian's blood, you said?"

A smile pierced Féderyc's haggard expression. "Your father never told you, did he?"

Triston shook his head. "What should he have told me?"

Féderyc shrugged. "About his green eyes," he said, motioning to his own. "It's the mark the *Elaedoni* leaves on a Fidelis. Well, *potential* Fidelis, I should say. Not everyone is trained, and Cynwrig and three generations of abbots before him refused to train anyone not directly descended from the six Fidelis houses."

Triston shook his head in disbelief. This was far more than he was prepared to consider right now, but he found himself asking the question anyway. "What does that make me?"

Féderyc held Triston's gaze, then shook his head. "You'll have to figure that out for yourself."

A loud crash sounded outside, drawing their attention back to the window.

Féderyc grinned. "Later."

With renewed strength, Triston grasped the chains beside him and hauled himself to his feet. His side still hurt—his face, his head, his everything still hurt—but the pain didn't stop him this time. He scanned the narrow dungeon as he let his shifting vision clear.

Snatching up the wooden bucket, he discarded the water inside it, and then smashed the thing against the wall.

Féderyc pulled back, startled. "What are you doing?"

Triston rummaged through the bucket's debris to pick out the metal handle. He tore off the few bits of wood that still clung to it, then used the stiff metal to unscrew the bolts holding his chains to the wall. It took some fine, precise motions—exactly the sort he didn't have the patience for—but he managed to loosen the bolts and finagle the length of chain.

Grinning, he made quick work of the next few chains down the line. It had been Seren's mistake, leaving him and Féderyc free like this. After he'd harvested four or five lengths, he tore strips from the old blanket Seren had left him and used those to tie the chains end-to-end. The bundle was heavy as he gathered it in his hand, but he carried it to the wall, ignoring his sore muscles.

He took the end of the chain in one hand, eyeing the narrow window above him, and tossed it. The motion wrenched his ribs, the pain so sharp and sudden he couldn't help but cry out, and the chain clattered into a lopsided pile beneath the window.

"You alright?" Féderyc had pushed himself to his feet.

Triston nodded as he gathered up the chain again. He swung it a few times to gain momentum, then tossed the links toward the window. He held his tongue this time, but pain cut his range of motion short and the chain clattered to the floor.

Féderyc said nothing, but Triston felt the man's crestfallen eyes fixed on him. Seething with frustration, he kept staring at that window as he collected the chain to throw it again.

"Try this." Féderyc tossed him the bucket handle, now bent into the shape of a hook.

Triston nodded, renewed hope surging through him, and secured the handle to the end of the chain. He threw the links again, pushing through the pain. It made it to the window's ledge before falling.

Triston clenched his jaw tighter as he collected the chain one more time. It was possible, he'd seen it now—it was possible. He threw the links with all his strength, groaning as pain burned in his side, but none of that mattered as the end of the chain disappeared beyond the bars and the hook caught on the ledge.

He turned to Féderyc with a grin, nodding toward the window. "Come on!"

"You go." There was a look of content resignation on his face.

With a sinking heart, Triston realized what the man intended. He was so frail he struggled to stand; his arms were no wider than a young boy's. There was no way he'd be able to climb up to the window.

"I'll carry you." Triston doubted his own strength at this point, but he wouldn't leave the man behind.

"No." Féderyc shook his head with such a stubborn frown that Triston knew there'd be no convincing him to do anything else.

Unwillingly, he turned away from the man. With a deep, shuddering breath, he began hauling himself upwards, one hand over the other, his feet braced against the stone wall. His ribs ached, his limbs trembled with the pain, and he'd hardly made it anywhere before his boot slipped and he came crashing back down to the floor.

He leaned against the wall, head resting on his arm. Each breath came as a short gasp; his body demanded more but his ribs said otherwise. He clenched his fists until they shook, angry at the pain, angry at his failure—angry at everything—and channeled that anger deep into his gut.

I have to do this. I have to.

The dungeon door swung open, clanging against the wall. Triston jumped, reaching instinctively for the sword he didn't have.

A man stood in the threshold—the burly man who'd been assisting Merric earlier. This time he was alone, holding a bloodied sword in one hand and a bloodied dagger in the other, and he scanned the dungeon, frantic but determined. His eyes locked with Triston's and he stepped forward, sinking clumsily onto one knee.

"Sir." He fixed his gaze on the ground. "I'm sorry. I shouldn't've let 'em do that to you, sir. It's just we didn't think there was anythin' left for us, see, with the way Lord Seren came in an' he had evr'body with him, he said—" The man paused, taking one long, nervous breath, and didn't raise his eyes. "But I've been hearin' things about the fonfyr comin' back, and I seen what you done, and, and that's when I knowed we had somethin' left to be fightin' for."

Triston grinned, grateful in more ways than he could express, and stepped forward to offer the man his hand. "It's alright. Your timing is perfect."

The man looked up slowly. His eyes widened as he saw Triston's smile, and they widened further as they came to rest on the cuts and bruises marking Triston's face. In the end, he took Triston's hand and let the Prince of Avaron haul him to his feet.

"It's your men fighting out there?" Triston asked.

The burly man nodded, the motion pushing his full, curly beard against his chest. "We've taken the tower, but Merric and some other soldiers've got to the gates first."

Not bad. "Can I get a sword?"

The burly man was still staring at the wounds on his face. He jumped when he realized he was hesitating, then shoved his bloodied sword into Triston's hand.

Triston hadn't intended to take the man's weapon, but he wasn't going to argue. "Help him," he said, nodding toward Féderyc, then took off through the open dungeon door.

Each pounding footfall sent a shock of pain through his bruised ribs, but he hardly noticed now. He charged down the hallway, pausing only to get his bearings, then ducked through an open doorway to reach the tower's main courtyard. It was empty, the iron gate torn from its hinges and tossed aside so that the bright evening sunlight shone into what had once been shrouded in shadow.

Triston ran onto the street, squinting into the sunset as he scanned the silhouette of the town walls in the distance. Dark figures bobbed along the top of the log structure, their movement followed by the sharp whistle of flying arrows. Triston muttered a curse and ducked behind the nearest cabin as the bolts sank with a splash into the muddy street.

In the shadow of the alley, he stopped to catch his breath. The town was in shambles. Many of the cabins had been destroyed, some with large stones which seemed to have rolled or fallen into the structures, while smoldering fires ate at the sides of others. Several dead men lay in the alleyways, while others—still living—darted this way and that among the wreckage.

"Triston!" Merric's voice rang out in the alleyway, taunting him, beckoning him to come forward.

Triston peered around the corner of the building, readjusting his grip on his sword. Smoke billowed from one of the other nearby buildings, drifting across the open street, and obscured Merric's figure. He walked casually—almost carelessly—down the center of the road. The tip of his sword dragged in the mud, his cloak whipped back from his shoulders in the wind, and his matted brown hair fell in a tangled mess across his face.

"What do you want?" Triston called out from his hiding place. Two arrows sank into the street before him, and he pulled back farther into the cabin's shadow.

Merric sloshed through the mud, drawing lazily closer. Triston glanced up and down the alley, trying to figure out a way to move unseen by those archers on the wall. The house's door was beside him—he pushed it open, ducked through, then shoved it closed.

The space contained only a table and a few chairs, and dim streaks of light shone through barred shutters on the far wall. Triston ran for the window, then waited. Merric's footsteps came ever closer, carrying from the street beyond. The man's dark shadow passed over the streaks of orange sunlight.

Triston threw open the shutters, latched hold of Merric's tunic, and dragged him into the house.

He didn't feel the pain in his side, or in his head, or even in his fist as he repeatedly punched Merric in the face and tossed him to the ground. What he did feel was a rage—calm, calculated—which drove him with strength and precision. Merric struggled on his back, lashing out with his sword, but Triston stomped on the flat blade and thrust his own sword through the soldier's throat.

Merric screamed—a sound of fury as pure as only a dying man could make—but thick, dark blood oozed from the wound and cut it short. Triston removed his sword, then lunged toward the window to pull the shutters closed before the archers could take another shot at him.

Merric kept screaming.

Triston turned to finish him off, then stumbled back in shock. The man was on his feet, unsteady but with sword in hand. On instinct, Triston thrust his sword into Merric's stomach. The man's cry became a guttural moan—strangely human and yet strongly animal—and then a great force knocked the wind from Triston's chest and sent him flying backward.

Timbers creaked, stones shook, and the house exploded around him. Triston was in the air, tossed by some invisible hand like the wind of a great storm, and then he landed with a jarring lurch on a pile of rubble in the center of the street.

He groaned, trying to shake the fog from his head, and struggled to his feet. Everything around him was destroyed—house after house, building after building—all the way to the town walls. It was like a tornado had touched down in Dol, just for a second, and left nothing but debris in its wake. What had happened to the archers,

Triston didn't know, but the wall now lay in broken pieces on the ground. Rubble surrounded him; he was half-buried in the bits of wood and stone from the building, and he realized he'd lost his sword.

Somehow, Merric was still screaming—that screech trembled in the cool air—but the sound finally ended. Triston shoved himself backwards, his soldier's heart pounding with something far too close to fear, and searched the rubble for Merric. The man stood in the middle of the house's foundation. He was at the heart of the destruction, and yet unscathed by it. He was the *source* of it. Stones and logs and bits of the table and chairs had scattered from him in all directions, like the wreckage was a hurricane and he was the eye.

Even at this distance, Triston could see the light in Merric's black eyes, fierce like the raging of a dead fire. Blood, a deeper and darker red than it ever should have been, flowed from the gash in his neck, staining his white tunic, but even that fatal wound did not stop him. Anywhere he had been marked—from the old gash across his face to the fresh, gaping hole in his neck—burned with a blackness darker than midnight. It was so dark it seemed to glow.

The air rang and trembled with the power of it—power, that was what it was. Raw, unchecked power. It had been unleashed, and it was tearing the man apart.

Merric flung his hands to his sides, then snarled as he clenched his fists. Every bit of rubble within arm's reach rose into the air, slowly. He fixed those rage-filled eyes on Triston, who struggled to his feet, grimacing through the pain. Forget the sword—what was he supposed to do with it?

"Merric!" a man shouted on the other side of the street.

Both Merric and Triston turned to look. Féderyc stood alone in the open tower doorway, the rest of the men cowering behind the stone walls. Triston opened his mouth to tell the man to stand down, but then he saw Féderyc's eyes. His irises were still that same deep green, but the rest of his eyes had turned black. Like Merric's.

Triston tore through the rubble, looking for his sword. He still didn't know what good it was going to do him, but he had to have it. The smoky air tensed. Triston felt it, somewhere deep in his soul, and the hair on the back of his neck stood up.

"You!" Merric let the bits of rubble he'd collected fall to the ground, the stones tumbling in a cloud of grey dust. "You wouldn't dare!"

Féderyc set his jaw, face radiant with peace and determination, then stepped toward Merric, flinging his arms before him in sharp, flowing strokes. The water in the muddy streets sprang up, crystalized into thousands of pointed ice shards, and hurtled at the soldier like a barrage of arrows.

Triston dove behind one of the large piles of rubble, still curious—or scared, or foolish—enough to keep his face exposed and his sight unobstructed. The ice fell with a patter like hail against a rooftop; Merric stood in the middle of it, white fluff piling up around the rubble he'd raised to form a makeshift shield.

With an angry cry, he let the stones fall and lashed out with a vengeance, hurtling a pile of debris at Féderyc. The Fidelis leapt to the side with ease, nimble on his feet—far more than Triston had expected from someone more corpse than man—and drew large spikes of ice from the ground to drive them through Merric's back.

Merric shrieked, this one louder and more animalistic than the first. Dark blood leaked from his side and formed tendrils of color against the icy spikes, but the rubble rose and began to circle his position. The debris Triston knelt on shifted, and he tumbled to the ground as it rose into the air. His sword sat in the dirt, just out of his reach.

Features twisting into either a grin or a snarl, Merric hurtled his swirling collection of stones at Féderyc. The valley echoed with the clatter of stones. Triston jumped to his feet, scooped up his sword, then charged Merric from behind, swinging that blade clean through the soldier's neck.

The air quivered, and then the stones fell. Triston jumped back as Merric's body collapsed, head dropping into the mud at his feet. He was dead now. Triston covered his nose. This was the look and stench of a body dead seven or eight days—just as Merric should have been.

Destruction surrounded him, marring the mountain valley with the smoldering rubble of what had once been a growing town. If Triston had come across Dol as it was now, he would have assumed it'd been undone by fire or some great storm or at least a small army, but he knew the improbable truth. All this had been the work of one man.

"Help!" The voices came softly at first, then repeatedly and with greater urgency.

Triston turned, and his heart sank. A massive pile of rocks stood where Féderyc had been, and while the burly man and several others had ventured beyond the tower walls to begin digging, Triston knew it wouldn't be any use. Still, he stuffed his sword behind his belt and ran to help.

Something rumbled deep within the pile, and the rubble shifted. Triston stumbled back, dropping the stone in his hands, as the other men shouted and pulled away. A voice emanated from somewhere beneath the debris, and then Féderyc burst from the rubble. The man was screaming, that same inhuman sound Merric had quit making only moments before. Dark gashes marked Féderyc's body where the stones had fallen on him—his chest was caved in, one of his arms hung limply from his shoulder, and yet he stood, clinging to a life his body had no place to hold.

One man stepped forward, a sword in his hand.

"Get back—" Triston shouted, but Féderyc whirled around and flung hundreds of shards of ice in the man's direction. Triston drew his sword and ducked behind a large stone as the man sank to the ground, his weapon falling from his hand with a clatter. Dozens of ice shards had pierced his face and chest.

Triston was not accustomed to fear. It was a dangerous emotion, a thing that threatened to make even the best of soldiers either thoughtlessly impulsive or quivering cowards, and he'd trained for years to silence it, to block it out. Now, however, as he looked into Féderyc's burning black and green eyes, he was afraid.

"Féderyc!" he called out, adjusting his grip on his sword.

For a moment the man stopped, his black eyes widening in horror. He stumbled and pressed his only good hand against his face.

Two mountain men burst out from behind what was left of the tower walls: one with a hatchet, the other a bow and arrow.

"Wait!" Triston called out, but the men had both let their weapons fly.

Féderyc howled in pain as the arrow sank into his side and the hatchet stuck into his back, then fell to his knees, his fists clenched at his side. That inhuman sound hummed deep in his throat, fighting to be let loose.

"No!" he shouted, waving his hand back as he shook his head. "Get back—stay back!" The man's eyes were bloodshot now, but the white was again in the right place.

The archer let out two more shots, each arrow sinking with a sickening thud into Féderyc's back.

"Hold!" Triston stepped into the open space between Féderyc and the other men. Féderyc shook his head, coughing as he struggled to speak, then sank forward onto the surrounding debris. Triston ran to his side.

The man's body was broken. It almost hurt Triston to look at it, with the numerous, bloody marks from stones, arrows, and the man's hatchet. Féderyc coughed again, the sound wet and raspy, as each successive breath came with a rattling shudder. As delicately as he could, Triston rolled the man onto his side.

"They did right..." Féderyc whispered, holding Triston's gaze before his face contorted with a spasm of pain. "I couldn't control it."

Triston's stomach sank. What was he supposed to do?

A grin spread across Féderyc's face, his teeth stained red by his own blood. "I prefer this death over the first one." He laughed, the sound cut short by another choking cough. "It was an honor to serve you, my king." His features faded into a look of utter relief as his rattling breaths fell silent.

Triston rose to his feet.

"Is he dead?" one man called out, hopeful, from behind the wall. He was the one who'd thrown the hatchet.

The cold wind whipped through the town, carrying with it the smell of smoke, the thickness of the settling dust, and the stench of death. It tugged strands of Triston's black hair back from his face. He nodded solemnly, and didn't look away from the broken, dried corpse at his feet. "He's dead."

Just as Merric's body had decayed, so had Féderyc's; he looked like a man dead for a good three months at least. It was a terrible sight—his dried and sunken eyes staring out of a shriveled, wrinkled face—but all the same Triston couldn't tear his eyes from it. He was disgusted, not so much by what he saw, but by the fact that this, whatever it was, had been done to someone at all.

"Sir?" The burly man stood a few paces away, quaking in his boots, and he was the only one who dared venture even that close.

Triston stepped back to jam his sword into the soft ground. "We'll bury him with the others."

And so the group got to work, silently and efficiently erecting a mass grave for all their dead where Féderyc had fallen. They were men of few words, and for the moment so was he. The battle's adrenaline wore off quickly, and left each ache screaming louder than before, but Triston didn't let that slow him, even as he hauled stone after stone.

In the end, their grave became a tower of rubble nearly a story high: a memorial, as it were, and a fitting remembrance of those who had been lost. The mountain men gathered around the grave, sharing a few words for their fallen comrades, and then sang together in a cacophony of low voices. Through this, Triston stood respectfully to the side with his head bowed and his arms folded across his chest.

"Peaceful rest now, the day is won..."

These men sang as though this was the end of their struggle—as though the final battle had already ended in victory—but Triston knew better. These mountain dirges served not as closure, but as a forewarning.

Surely, this was only the beginning.

Chapter Forty-Three

JUNCTURE

Kura sat on a log beside the fire, her damp cloak wrapped tight around her shoulders. The people of Lâroe bustled about the clearing, moving from house to cooking fire and back again as they handed out fresh food to anyone who appeared hungry or empty-handed. She had a plate of it sitting on her lap herself —an ear of roasted corn, a hunk of flatbread, and several strips of fried meat— but as delicious as it smelled, she hadn't managed to eat more than a few bites.

All those who were able had spent the evening burying dead, clearing debris, and sinking barricades into the roads leading into Lâroe. The people of the city never seemed to tire, and working beside them had kept her torrent of thoughts at bay, but now in the stillness she didn't have the strength to hold them back.

Her father and brother had already left for Nansûr, with the rest of the wounded who were well enough to travel. She longed to have gone with them, but also wished there was more she could do here. The townspeople had dead, too. Five, all of them run down by saja fleeing the tower.

Of the thirty rebels who'd left Nansûr, only nine remained. Twenty-six good people had lost their lives because of her. Because this was supposed to have been a heist—something covert—and she'd kept them going even when it turned into an outright battle they never would have planned to fight with so few men.

Ìsendorál's scabbard pressed against her side, and she let out a shuddering sigh. No one seemed to blame her, though—if anything, after the tower had fallen, the rebels and townspeople alike looked at her with *more* reverence.

"Mind if I join you?"

Kura jumped before she recognized Aethan's voice. He wandered up to the fire with a dimpled grin, a blanket draped over his shoulders.

"Hey." Kura set aside her tray of food and scrambled to her feet to offer him her hand. "You shouldn't—"

He brushed her aside and took a seat on the log. "I'm perfectly fine." He shivered, even under the blanket, but tried to hide it. "Honestly, it's like none of you have ever seen someone get a little wet in the rain before."

Kura knew that was a lie as well as he did, but she couldn't help but smile anyway. For a moment.

"Besides…" There was a mischievous gleam in his eyes. "I couldn't let you sit and brood out here all by yourself."

"I'm not…" *I am.* She sighed and leaned forward to rest her head in her hands. "Aethan, they think I took down the tower."

"Yeah. They do."

Tears caught in her throat. "It's a lie—you know it's a lie. But they followed me, and they… and they *died*…"

"We all knew when we left we might never come back."

"We *should* have gone back, but I—" She realized she'd raised her voice, and stole a timid glance around the courtyard to see if anyone had overheard. A few of the townspeople met her gaze with that same hopeful smile, and she tried not to look away too quickly. "They would have been better off here without me."

Aethan studied her face. She thought he was going to scold her, but his expression was too gentle. "You're not thinking of running, are you?"

She glanced down at her hands. She wasn't—not seriously enough, anyway, to think she had to answer yes—but the thought had flittered through her mind. It certainly seemed the easiest solution. She could give the sword to Renard, or somebody…

Aethan gave a heavy sigh. "I don't blame you. Gods, I don't blame you. But once you start running, you can never stop." He stared aimlessly into the darkness. "You'll be a thousand dayrides away from where you were, but not one step farther from what made you run in the first place."

She met his gaze. There was a tiredness in his face, and it reminded her of what she'd seen in his eyes when they'd first met.

After a moment he noticed her staring, then gave most of a grin. "Maybe someone else would have done this better, but who's to say? You've got us this far. Maybe there *isn't* someone else..."

Kura clenched her teeth and pulled up her sleeve to reveal the twisted bruise on her underarm. "That's what happened when I woke the sword."

Aethan's face fell as he took her arm in his hand. He ran his fingers over the bruise, then let go of her arm. "Kura, all this means is you're not in tune with the Essence's movement."

Is that all, then? She didn't know whether to laugh at him or believe every word.

"Here." Aethan swung his leg over the log so he faced her. "I'll teach you the Riht—it's fairly simple." He took both her hands into his, and she opened her mouth to protest, but he closed his eyes and bowed his head as though he hadn't noticed.

"Essence, speak to me, that my thoughts may be true

Essence, call to me, that I may seek what is true

Essence, strengthen me, to uphold what is true

Essence, move in me, that I may always be true."

The words echoed in her soul so loudly she almost forgot to repeat them. But Aethan waited, and line by line she recited after him. She didn't remember her mother's *andojé*, but she wanted with all her heart to at least be able to remember this.

Finally, Aethan released her hands and she folded her arms back under her cloak.

"Thanks." In the long run, she didn't think any of it would make a difference, but somehow, in that moment, it had. She managed a laugh. "I don't know what convinced you to follow me halfway across the country, but I'm really glad you did."

"You know, to be perfectly honest, in the beginning I was just curious. But now..."

The soft crunch of footfalls against the fine, sandy soil of the riverside drew her attention as Renard wandered up to the campfire, a tray of food in his hands.

"Well," he said with a laugh as he took a seat on a log across from the fire, "this all looks quite good."

Aethan stood. "I'm going to see about finding some of my own."

Kura sat in silence as he headed back toward one of the cooking fires, the gentle crunch of his boots against the loose dirt disappearing as it became part of the sounds of the night.

Renard gnawed on his ear of corn, then jabbed it in Kura's direction. "Something's bothering me about this whole thing."

Her heart froze in her chest. "Oh?"

"They knew we were coming here today. I mean, it's the only explanation for all of this."

She had to catch herself before she breathed a sigh of relief. Unfortunately, Renard's musings made that easy. "How could they have known?"

"Someone must have told them. Someone from Nansûr who listened in on our councils."

"Who would do that?"

Renard shrugged. "Folks have done it before." He took one last bite from his ear of corn before tossing the cob into the fire. "I just wanted you to know. 'Cause, well, I know it wasn't you, and I've got to start getting the warning out somewhere."

The dark road stretched out before them, narrow and winding as it traversed the ever-steepening mountainside. Kura took in a deep breath of the cool night air as she gazed up at the silhouettes of the thin pine trees that surrounded her. She and the remaining rebels had left Lâroe at least an hour before, but she'd only just shaken the lingering smell of smoke from her nose.

They'd paraded out of town amid fanfare and cheering, and even now she could almost hear them. Renard had insisted she walk at the front for their procession and that was where she remained—Aethan beside her, Renard and the others behind. At first she'd resented Renard for it—she was altogether too tired to play as their savior any longer today—but gradually she'd come to understand.

When the people looked at her, they didn't see *her*. They saw what they wanted, they saw Ìsendorál, they saw everything it stood for. She didn't deserve their honor—now less than ever—but she didn't have the heart to take away their hope.

Something snorted in the darkness not far beyond them. She froze, peering down the road. The rebel company came to a jumbled halt behind her, and Renard's voice rang over the others. "What is that?"

The dark shape came closer, and instinctively, she reached for her sword hilt. It was a horse, riderless, with stirrups jangling against its sides and loose reins dragging on the ground. She went to step out of the way, but Renard cut in front of her and caught hold of the horse's halter as it neared their group.

"Looks like soldier's tack." He stroked the horse's nose. "But it doesn't look like a soldier's horse."

Kura frowned and peered down the empty roadway. She ought to have been concerned, but one soldier didn't seem like a threat anymore. "Where's the rider?"

Renard grunted in reply and stepped past her, leading the horse. "Keep watch, everybody."

Kura followed, fist clenched around the sword hilt at her side. The animal might belong to a vojak. That would be reason enough for concern, if they did in fact ride horses. The rebel band continued in silence, but as they rounded a bend another shape materialized in the darkness.

It appeared to be a man, leaning against the bank beside the road. Renard kept walking, waving for the rest of them to stay back as the man drew his own sword and struggled to his feet. He stumbled and ended up on one knee.

"Hey!" Renard called out. "Who's out there?"

"Who's asking?"

Kura let go of her sword hilt. "Triston?"

The man on the road laughed—in relief? "Ah, it's just you." With a grunt, he fell back against the hillside and let his sword clatter to the ground beside him.

Kura brushed past Renard. "What are you...?" She knelt down beside Triston, then grimaced when she got a better look at his face through the shadows. He'd been beaten terribly—his lip was busted, the left side of his face swollen, and by the way he sat hunched against the hill behind him, he had to be hurting elsewhere. "I thought you went home?"

Triston laughed again, then winced. "I tried."

Aethan came to Kura's side and silently handed her a water skin, which she passed on to Triston. He nodded gratefully, and took a long drink.

"What are you doing here?" she asked.

Triston pointed over her shoulder. "I spent the evening trying to find Nansûr—by the gods, that place is hidden impossibly well—but more specifically, I was trying to follow that smoke when my stupid horse dumped me."

She nodded back toward Renard. "That horse?"

"Yeah. You all can keep it."

She caught herself staring at his swollen cheek. "You run into some trouble?"

He chuckled. "A little. But more's coming." His eyes locked with hers. "I don't want war. I promise you, I can stop it if you're willing to give me the chance."

Kura leaned back, studying his gaze. She'd been prepared to be skeptical, but he seemed so earnest. In fact, she'd never seen him anything *but* earnest.

"Um," Aethan started, "are we really buying this?"

She grabbed hold of Triston's arm to help him to his feet. "We are."

PART FOUR

ERELONG

Chapter Forty-Four
Traitor Among Renegades

Kura pushed through the crowd, past the other rebels streaming into the entrance to Nansûr. The narrow passages here were mostly empty—a perk of this side entrance; most of the company trickled in via one of the main ones. Renard had thought it best to keep Triston away from the masses for the time being and—guiltily—Kura was happy to avoid the crowd's prying eyes as long as she could.

Her job: find Idris. And she let her tangle of thoughts rest on that.

She rounded the corner and stepped into a hallway of barracks, the walls smooth and painted with elaborate, colorful patterns. She stopped, glancing over each open, closed, and half-open door, hoping to spot Idris, or at least someone she knew.

A closed door near Kura creaked open, casting a beam of bright light into the dim corridor. Devna stepped into the light, humming a tune to herself as she swept the floor. At the sound of Kura's footsteps, she stopped, and frowned when their gazes met. Wrinkles collected around her piercing green eyes, showing her age more than her stance or expression.

"You looking for someone?"

Kura swallowed, then nodded. "Yes, Idris. Is she…?"

Devna inclined her head toward a half-open door, three rooms down the right wall. "Over there."

"Thank you." Kura scurried along, if only to escape the woman's ire, but she could feel Devna's eyes on the back of her head.

She stopped in front of the door the woman had indicated, then knocked, the sound echoing dully. The door creaked open slightly under the weight of her hand and she glimpsed two figures—one seated in a chair, the other standing.

"Coming!" Idris called, and a moment later she appeared at the door. She was wearing a loose-fitting cotton shirt, belted around the waist, and a flowing patterned skirt that ended at her bare feet. "Kura!" she said with a bright smile. "You're back!" The smile disappeared. "What is it? Something's wrong, isn't it?"

Kura shrugged helplessly and quickly explained her finding of Triston on the road. "He needs a healer."

"Kura, I…"

A woman's voice came from within the room, soft but strong, speaking in the flowing Fidelis tongue—Áclomere, the New Tongue. Idris turned back over her shoulder, muttering a quick reply in the same language.

"Idris," the voice came again, scoldingly. "Let her in. She is welcome here."

Idris gave a heavy sigh, and without looking up, she pulled the door back and motioned for Kura to follow her. Tentatively, Kura did. It was a small room, made cozy by the worn, colorful rugs on the floor and the bright tapestries hanging on the walls. A large table took up most of the space on one side, with two wooden bedframes filling up the wall on the other. A great, glowing crystal of lenêre stone protruded from the ceiling, bathing the room in light.

"I'm sorry," Kura started, "I didn't—" Then she caught sight of the woman in the chair beside the table.

To judge by her lack of wrinkles, she couldn't have been older than Kura's own mother, but with her frail arms and the way she sat hunched in her seat, her legs wrapped in blankets, she looked decades older. She had long, curly hair, like Idris, but it was tied back in a thin, greying braid and her dark skin was marred with white, oblong scars that spattered her face and bare hands. And then there were her eyes. Perhaps they'd been a bright green once, but now they were covered with an opaque, bluish film.

The woman brushed the few loose strands of her hair back behind her ear and straightened as much as she could. "Idris," she whispered. "Introduce us."

"Kura," Idris said, shyly, "of Wynshire. This is my mother, Celene, of the sixth branch, born of House Appris."

The woman smiled brightly, reaching out in Kura's direction. "Do not be ashamed. I have earned these scars in the hope of the prophecy and in the service of my king, and so I wear them proudly."

Kura stepped forward to shake the woman's cold, thin hand. She tried not to stare, but the impulse was hard to fight. Celene's face—her whole figure—was a testament to great, terrible suffering, and she was humbled by the consideration of it.

"Courage, dear one," Celene said, looking up in the general direction of Kura's face. There was a kindness in her expression, a deep gentleness that outshone the rest of her. "Though fearful, don't fear it. Though doubtful, don't doubt it. While the fire burns it also cleanses. Two paths diverge, yes, but many are the routes between them."

Kura held the woman's blind gaze as she ran through those words again. She knew better than to think of them as nonsensical, and they seemed too familiar to do that anyway, but whatever meaning they had escaped her and she didn't know what to say.

Celene released her hand, then waved in Idris's direction. "Go on. I'll be fine here on my own for a little while. They need you."

Triston tried not to grimace as Idris gripped his chin between her fingers and tilted his head back to study the bruises on his face.

He was glad to see the long ride to Nansûr finished—at least he had been until, in a mass of spears and voices, the rebels had shoved him down one of the narrow side tunnels to force him into a rickety chair in this little room. He hadn't figured out where he was any better than that—their intention, no doubt—and he had to squint against the achingly bright firelight from the torches along the wall.

"Hold still," Idris muttered under her breath.

Triston caught glimpses of the girl's green eyes behind her mane of curly black hair, but he couldn't tell what she thought of him at this point. She refused to meet his gaze, out of fear or hatred—or both, maybe—and continued to poke and prod him as though he were a market steer and she was considering him as a purchase.

Kura watched Idris work with a frown of concentration. She was leaning against the wall beside the door, her arms folded and her auburn hair pulled back in a messy bun.

"Will he be alright?" Her tone didn't clarify how she meant her question: as his friend, or as his master.

"I don't like to make promises." Idris finally let go of Triston's chin and stepped back. "Pull up your shirt."

With a stifled sigh, he tugged his shirt over his head and balled it up on his lap. Small bruises the size of Merric's foot dotted his torso, but it was the large, purplish mark running nearly the entire length of his left side that caused Idris to let out a gasp. Triston stiffened as she ran her small, cold hands over his ribs.

"You broke them?" She managed to meet his gaze this time.

Triston clenched his teeth against the discomfort. "I think so."

Idris analyzed his injury for a moment longer before stepping away, wringing her hands. "Well, I should be able to help. But fresh wounds take time to heal." She hurried past him and across the room to rummage through the clay jars set on a shelf hollowed out from the wall.

"So." Aethan adjusted his stance beside Kura—and the guard at the door. "You said this Seren guy did this to you?" He'd had a quiet, stern expression on his face ever since they'd met on the road, like he expected Triston to transform into some kind of monster—and he was ready to beat him down when it happened. Kura, however, suddenly appeared to be looking in every direction but his, and her cheeks had turned a shade of red.

"He wanted to find this place," Triston said.

"And you didn't tell him, did you?"

Triston chuckled, but the motion triggered a stab of pain in his side. "I can't tell him the location of something I can't even find myself."

Idris returned with two small clay jars and a metal tuning fork. The jars she set on the ground beside his chair, but the tuning fork she held toward him. "This will be uncomfortable for you, but I need to know precisely where the fracture is located to be able to heal it."

Triston watched her quizzically. Idris quietly rang the tuning fork by pinching the ends between her fingers—the sound was low, and barely audible—then placed the end against the rib nearest his armpit. The metal was cold against his skin, and he could feel the vibration emanating across his bone.

Methodically, Idris rang the tuning fork and placed it on his next rib, then the next. The moment the metal touched the rib in the center of his side, Triston cried out and pulled away from her hands. "Gods! Why...?" The low vibration of the tuning fork had made the broken edges of his bone grind together.

"I'm sorry," Idris muttered, tracing her fingers along that rib until she located the most tender spot. She left one hand there, then set the tuning fork aside and scooped a glob of white salve from her clay jar to smear on his skin. The ointment smelled faintly of peppermint, and while it was colder than her hands, against his injury the chill was a comfort.

Idris closed her eyes, then began to whisper to herself. Triston listened to those words intently, as though after all he had seen with Féderyc he would be able to understand them. He couldn't.

Warmth radiated through his side. It wasn't the tight, throbbing heat which came from the swelling of his injury, but a soft, encompassing sensation that unstiffened his muscles and chased away the sharpest pains. But the progress was slow, and before the pain had quite disappeared, Idris pulled her hands away.

Without a word, she retrieved the tuning fork and began the searching process again. His next two ribs were just as painful as the first. She didn't stop prodding him until she'd inspected all his ribs—both right and left—and when she'd finished tending to him, she stepped back to wipe her sweaty brow on her sleeve.

"I don't want to do too much today."

Triston shoved his arms back into his shirt sleeves. "For your sake or mine?"

"Both, really. An injury healed too quickly or a healer who drafts the Essence for too long develops *l'malde*, a terrible sickness, much like a fever for the injured party and something much worse for a Fidelis."

"What happens to a Fidelis?" Kura asked. She spoke as plainly as she had before, but there was an intense curiosity in her eyes—not fear, but close to it. Triston tugged his shirt back over his head.

Idris glanced over her shoulder. "You've seen my mother."

Kura looked down at her feet, and the room settled into an uncomfortable silence.

Expressionless, Idris scooped some salve from one of the other jars. This was thick and rather yellowish, with a faint scent of flowers. Idris smeared some of it on his face.

"Hey," Triston muttered, pulling back from her hand. He wiped a glop of salve from his cheek and rubbed it between his fingers. "Just what is this stuff?"

"It will quicken the healing," Idris said as she picked at the abstract etchings on the side of her jar.

Triston heaved a sigh. It wasn't really his place to question her, was it? If he'd been able to make it home, the castle physician would've just washed his wounds and sent him to bed with the hopes he'd still wake up in the morning.

Hesitant this time, Idris applied the salve to Triston's face. "You were hit in the head?"

He sighed again. "Yes."

"Any loss of consciousness?" Idris worked over his swollen cheek as though she was a sculptor and he a statue.

"Yes."

Her forehead creased in concern. "Have you been having any headaches, or blurry vision, or sensitivity to—?"

"Yes, all of it."

Idris set aside her jar. "I don't mean to pry. I just have to understand. The *Elaedoni* flows through me; it heals, but I must guide it where it should go."

Triston nodded. At this point, he didn't much care how it all worked, so long as it could get rid of this nagging headache.

Idris placed her hands on either side of Triston's head, squeezed her eyes shut, and began to murmur under her breath. He waited, stiff and uncomfortable, as he tried not to feel the others' gazes so harshly. Gradually, the headache throbbing in his temple began to subside—the pain didn't go away entirely, but the stiffness, the ache, did.

Idris released him. She was again out of breath, but there was a timid curiosity in her eyes as she searched his face. "You've been healed already. Not very well, but someone tried. How?"

Triston stared up at Idris, this petite girl suddenly seeming to tower over him. What was he going to say? He hadn't had the time to process everything for himself yet, and the last thing he wanted to do was try to explain it to someone else. But he had to say *something*. "Seren had taken a Fidelis as prisoner before me."

"Really?" Idris asked.

"Who?" Aethan added, almost interrupting, as he took a step forward. His eyes said he was curious, but his frown remained skeptical.

Triston shook his head. "He didn't make it out."

Aethan scoffed. "I'm supposed to believe that? How do we know you didn't make him up? Or maybe you killed him."

"Aethan..." Kura started.

Aethan turned back to her, his expression apologetic but his shoulders stiff. "You know who he is."

"I do, but—look at him. He—"

"What better ruse is there than this to find a way back in here?"

"If he wanted to be here so badly, why did he leave in the first place?"

Aethan shook his head. "You're too trusting—"

"Well..." Renard's booming voice echoed in the small room, and he stepped through the doorway, followed by Erryl. While the latter wore a handsomely embroidered tunic, Renard hadn't even taken the time to wash the grime from his face, much less change of out of his worn and sullied armor. That didn't seem to faze him, however, and he eyed Triston with a wry grin. "You had your chance to get out of this place, and you blew it."

Triston gave a bit of a laugh, feeling the sticky paste on his face more acutely. He used a baggy sleeve to gingerly wipe off most of it.

Erryl's eyes narrowed. "Do you think us fools? You see to it that you've won some place in her heart," he said, jabbing a finger at Kura, "and then intend to use that advantage to worm your way in among us?"

Kura's eyes narrowed and she took a step forward. "He—"

"Let him answer," Erryl said.

Triston glanced between each face in a sort of disbelief. With the possible exception of Kura and Renard, they all watched him as though he was some kind of criminal. It might have been his mistake for expecting something different.

"I could have given you up," he said, focusing most of all on Erryl. "To your credit, this place was not as easy to find as I thought it would be, but I'm damn sure I could have got Seren close enough."

Erryl continued to glower at him, but seemed to relax his stance—slightly. "Why didn't you do that?"

Triston drew in a breath. That was a simple question with anything but a simple answer. As succinctly as he could manage, he launched into an explanation of what he'd witnessed in Dol—Merric, Seren, all of it except for Féderyc. They listened, quiet and attentive, aside from Erryl, who asked a few clarifying questions. Skeptical expressions faded, but Triston didn't find that as comforting as he'd thought he would.

"Bringing men back from the dead like that," Renard muttered in disgust. "Is it possible?"

Erryl sighed. "It is an ancient craft, a long-forbidden and even longer ago forgotten ritual which re-binds a person's spirit to the material world. Most often the person's spirit is returned to their body, but it is said that a spirit can be bound to any material thing..." The man nearly shuddered as he spoke. "*Nezjir*, developed by those of our forebears who pledged themselves to the Crux. Where could Seren have learned this?" He sounded skeptical. "All of those with the knowledge died generations ago, taking the method of the craft with them."

"He..." Triston ran through what Féderyc had told him. "He said Seren had a lady—"

"His wife?" Renard said, wrinkling his nose.

"Seren never married. They called this woman 'the Grey Lady'. Seren didn't tell me her name, and neither did Merric, but she was the one who knew the nez-j... the reanimating the dead thing."

Erryl shook his head. "You're going to have to give me more than just vague rumors. Those are not in short supply in a place such as this."

"Vahleda," Kura said softly.

Her voice barely carried over the rest of the conversation, but her interjection was so out of place the attention turned to her anyway. Triston looked up at her in surprise. Her face was pale, her eyes wide, and she seemed to be on the verge of crying.

"Vahleda," she repeated, louder this time.

"Yes," Erryl said with a placating nod, "she was one of the forebears I just mentioned. What about her?"

Kura began to speak, first in short, broken sentences but gaining in momentum. A stunned silence settled over the group as she told of saja and helry, and of meeting this woman somewhere in a strange, stone forest. Kura's voice shook, and she didn't look at any of them. Triston wished someone would comfort her, but under the circumstances he didn't dare, and in the end he wasn't all too sure she'd want it.

"I'm sorry, Kura," Erryl said softly after she had finished speaking. Triston couldn't tell if the man really meant it, but it seemed to be the only appropriate thing to say. "I don't mean to disbelieve you, but none survive the poisoning of a helry."

Aethan folded his arms across his chest. "My mentor did."

"Who was he?" Erryl asked.

"Féderyc, of the fifth branch, born of House Gallian and House Evêtra."

"Ah." Erryl rolled his eyes, as though now he understood entirely.

Surprise coursed through Triston's veins, and he found himself staring at Aethan.

Aethan noticed and scowled. "What do you know of it?"

"I..." Triston only held his gaze for a moment before he had to glance down at his feet.

"You recognize that name?" Aethan stepped toward Triston, ferocious, like a son set on avenging his father.

Triston started to shake his head, but the last thing he needed right now was to be caught in a lie.

"Maybe you killed him, huh?" Aethan spat. "It was your father's soldiers who killed the Blackembers, three months ago on the Feldland plains. I was there."

Triston turned aside, clenching his teeth as he fought to keep his temper from speaking for him. "I know the name Féderyc... Because I met him. Yesterday."

Four sets of quizzical eyes turned on him, and Triston started the story he'd resolved not to tell. As he spoke, the whole event began to feel distant, as though he was just making up some elaborate ruse—surely that was what this sort of tale should be. But he knew the truth—the weight of it settled in his gut—and above all else he regretted having to tell the story at all.

Aethan shook his head adamantly when Triston concluded. "Impossible." He held shaking fists clenched at his side. "He was dead. I saw him die."

Triston made a point of looking him in the eye. "I'm sorry." Those words came easily—they were the truth, after all, and he meant it.

"No." Aethan ran his fingers through his loose hair, then took a step back. "No, I don't believe it."

"Aethan..." Kura said softly, placing a hand on his arm.

Aethan shook out of her grip and stepped away from the crowd, raking his fingers through his hair again as he turned away from all of them.

Renard let out a loud sigh. "Well, this here's a mess, now, isn't it?"

The words lingered in the room.

"If..." Idris started, stepping forward from where she had been standing against the wall. "If the Grey Lady is alive..." She folded one arm across her chest and raised the other hand to twirl her finger around a strand of her curly hair. "Is it possible she was bound to the world by *nezjir* ages ago? She was found dead, after all. She wasn't killed by any Fidelis."

"I suppose it is possible," Erryl said, his eyes distant. "And if a man had been poisoned by her magics in the past, then it may leave a soul more susceptible to the *nezjir*..."

Renard frowned. "Sure, well, but how does that explain anything about what this Seren's been doin' up in the Rohgens?"

"The helry's poison is a powerful thing..." Aethan said quietly, turning back toward the group. "Féderyc told me it is like having your will beaten from you, and having hers put in its place. If you don't die, you become linked to her, linked to the Crux, and by extension linked to all her vojaks which have come before."

"Linked?" Erryl rubbed his chin thoughtfully. "That could explain it, then, how we seem to have a mole among us. Vahleda's beasts could have deluded any of these poor souls..."

Kura yelped, and slowly every eye turned back to her. She had her hands pressed against her temples, and great tears welled up in her wide eyes.

"Oh gods..." she breathed, her words barely audible. "Oh gods, it was me."

Chapter Forty-Five

BOUNDEN

Kura sat cross-legged in the corner, elbows resting on her knees, head in her hands. She wasn't sure if she felt like crying or punching something, and somehow the compromise was doing neither. Why hadn't she realized sooner? The strange dreams about the grey-eyed man had been dismissible enough before she'd met him, but she should have known better after she'd dreamt about trying to read those town names she'd written on her arm.

Lâroe *had* been her fault. She was the leak who'd warned the enemy of their plans, and the fool who'd led the charge into the waiting forces anyway.

People were still milling about—they hadn't even left the small room in which the guards had placed Triston earlier—and they spoke in hushed voices. Erryl had called together a few of his fellow Fidelis and they, along with Aethan and Renard, hoped to figure out a way to sever the link between her and Vahleda. Kura had tried to listen, tried to offer her own suggestions, but they'd sent her away out of concern the Grey Lady would somehow overhear.

Maybe she really should have run when she'd had the chance. She had tried now, but Renard had physically held her back. *"The fonfyr can't run,"* he'd said.

Kura let out a desperate sigh, which ended in a wheeze as tears tightened her throat. Erryl had already questioned her on every little thing she'd heard or overheard, and everywhere she had been in Nansûr. Of course, she'd heard almost everything and been almost everywhere.

And now Vahleda had as well.

Footsteps echoed toward her, and Kura glanced up as Idris sank to the floor beside her. Kura waited, expecting to receive some sort of update, but Idris didn't even look at her. They sat in silence for what felt like a long, long time, then Idris placed a hand on Kura's arm.

"They'll find a way." Her face was stern, her focus fixed on an invisible horizon. "You bear the sword, after all."

Kura smothered a laugh. "Like Dradge did?"

Idris met her gaze, then looked away.

Kura sighed and leaned back, tears stinging her eyes. For some reason, all she could picture was Idris's mother, the woman scarred and broken by the movement that had followed the last pretender to wield the sword she now carried at her side.

"How can you believe in me, Idris, even after everything that's come before me has ended in disaster?"

"Because..." The girl nodded, as though to complete her thoughts. "Because happy endings are real, too. And they're the ones worth fighting for."

Kura stared into the girl's green eyes as tears welled up and blurred her vision. That was ridiculously hopeful, and yet she latched on to it with everything she had.

Erryl cleared his throat, catching their attention. He stood before them—almost timidly—with his hands clasped against his round stomach.

"I believe we have an idea..." He cocked his head to the side, reluctant to look her in the eye. "If Vahleda's connection with you was strong, she would have found this place by now, and so that gives us a chance. But if this does work, it will not be easy."

Kura drew in a breath, smearing the tears across her cheeks with her open hand. "Let's do it."

"Alright." Erryl breathed a sigh. "You may look."

Pulling down her blindfold, Kura had to stop and stare. Erryl hadn't told her where he was leading her, of course, but based on the hushed and heated discussion he'd had with the other Fidelis, it was somewhere of importance.

She took a step forward, craning her neck to study the ceiling. It hung less than an armsbreadth above her head—no centaur could walk here—and lenêre stone wove across it, snaking through the obsidian cave like bolts of lightning frozen in time.

Gingerly, Kura reached out to trace a finger over her own reflection. Her face stared back at her from a thousand distorted mirrors of rough-hewn stone, illuminated in soft blue. The cut angle made her appear small and disheveled—or maybe that was just the truth.

Erryl took only a single step to follow her, one hand resting on the iron doorframe. "This is not a place most would bring even an elyir, much less one of the common blood, but I suppose times have called for it." He spoke easily—he'd clearly said the same to others before—but paused as though still struggling to convince himself. "Appris herself had this tunnel dug when our forebears still walked the land. She and her house have always been sensitive to this sort of thing, you see. Lenêre stone outdates us but its glow stems, ultimately, from the same power source as our abilities. This is called E'shân. It is a place for meditation."

Kura nodded. "What do you want me to do?"

Erryl took another step into the cavern. His face didn't show it, but he seemed hesitant. "Traditionally, this is a personal experience, one you would venture alone, but I have always said I would not allow tradition to become a chain on my wrist." His tone implied he wished to take that back now. "I will guide you into the Temper, where—"

"The Temper?"

"The Essence touches all things, is in all things, in its own way. The Temper is where all those different shades of spirit unite to the One. Fidelis make that venture for self-reflection, but it seems Vahleda dragged you there with her helry's poison and bound your spirits together."

"Then why do I want to go back there?"

"So I can sever the link. I don't think she meant to bind herself to you in this way. Likely she was careless, not expecting you to break free before her machinations were complete." By the way he spoke, Kura thought he might believe her story now, though his eyes betrayed nothing further. "Nothing, physically, that occurs in the Temper holds in reality, but that does not mean the effects cannot last." He stifled a sigh—or maybe tried to hide a shudder. "We must tread carefully."

Another face appeared in the doorway: Devna's. Kura apprehensively met her gaze but the woman ignored her, looking only to Erryl. The man nodded, and she shut the heavy metal door with an ominous thud. Kura drew in a shaking breath.

"This way." Erryl led her to the far end of the cave—the space wasn't large; only two more adults could have joined them—then motioned for her to take a seat beside him.

Kura complied, shifting uncomfortably on the polished ground. Dusty footprints led to her seat. Should she have removed her shoes? Erryl reached out and placed both hands on a vein of lenêre stone, and she copied him. He shut his eyes and she halfway followed, keeping them barely open to glance sideways at his face.

"Breathe in," he said.

She did.

"Breathe out."

Erryl continued, the intervals increasing with each repetition. For the first minute Kura's heart pounded in anticipation, but gradually her eyelids grew heavy and fell shut.

She awoke with a jolt to the moan of the wind. Startled, she scrambled to her feet.

"Erryl?" Her voice—horribly meek—carried into the shadows. No one answered. Maybe she had to come alone? Darkness hung all around her but, squinting, she could make out the terrain. This was the last place she wanted to see again.

It was just as she remembered: the jagged stone spires reaching up toward a black sky, the dying embers of a fire on the ground before her, the thin fingers of the dead tree reaching out of the encompassing grey fog. Except... the space beyond the fire was empty. Vahleda wasn't there.

Kura's very bones ached with the desire to leave, but she had to finish what she'd come to do. "Vahleda!" she screamed into the darkness.

For one, long, agonizing moment her voice was the only sound, reverberating endlessly among the spires. And then the woman was there.

Vahleda smiled, a thin, taunting gesture, but her eyes were fixed on something beyond. "Hello, darling." Her image flashed forward. She was standing closer to the fire now, still smiling as she rested one hand on her hip. "Fight, yes. I find it amusing!"

Kura stared at the woman's face. Vahleda wasn't even looking at her; it was as if Kura were observing someone else's conversation.

Burning pain shot through her veins and she found herself writhing on the ground, looking up at the dark night sky far above as her own cry reverberated in the stone forest. She had felt this before—she had lived this all before. Vahleda laughed as Kura fought to keep from screaming. How had she got away?

The flicker.

Kura looked up at the tree, but the black bird was nowhere to be found. She growled and dragged herself to her knees. "I don't belong to you!"

Vahleda's self-assured laugh echoed in her ears. With a flash of red light, the image changed. It was like a dream; Kura both watched from a distance and acted in the moment. Vahleda charged with her bladed spear, and Kura slashed wildly with her sword. Then, as before, the woman sent Ìsendoràl flying and knocked her to the ground.

Vahleda sank her blade into Kura's chest. Kura tried to scream, but the sound caught in her throat as her mouth filled with blood. Vahleda's breath tickled her cheek and her body spasmed with pain as the woman twisted the weapon in her chest.

"Despair, pet. It's all you have left. This is my domain."

It was agony; she was dying all over again. But none of it was real —she knew that this time. With a desperate, gurgling shout, Kura grasped a fistful of Vahleda's dreadlocks. The woman's smile vanished, her black eyes widened, and then all of it disappeared.

Faintly, Kura saw the image of soldiers. Each had a bright red cloak thrown over their shoulder, the black bird overlying the red, pointed cross adorning their polished armor. They were in boats, dozens of them, which filled the winding river for as long as she could see. There was a multitude, and they were coming.

Triston let out a deep breath as he slid to a seat at the base of the wall.

At least an hour had passed since Erryl had called his friends together and dumped him, Renard, Aethan, and Idris into the hallway. Renard and Idris both stood beside the door, the first leaning against the frame with his thumbs tucked into his belt, and the second perched with her hands folded and pressed against her mouth. The Feldlander had taken to pacing the hallway and was starting into his second cigarette, the smoke from the first still lingering in a thick cloud.

Triston adjusted his seat, keeping his arm pressed against his side to hold back the dull pain. This was not the turn of events he had expected. But despite everything, what he felt most of all was relief. Relief that he'd made it here instead of anywhere else.

A muffled scream echoed down the hallway, making everyone jump. Triston stiffened, his heart catching in his chest. Was that Kura's voice? The sound came from the direction in which she and Erryl had disappeared.

The scream sounded again, longer this time, and something inside Triston snapped. He leapt to his feet—grimacing against pain and ready to charge down the hallway—but Renard stepped forward to stop him.

"Didn't you hear her?" Triston glanced between the three of them in dismay. Renard seemed apathetic—just a soldier taking orders, albeit reluctantly—while Idris solemnly bowed her head, and Aethan spared him only a glance and another scowl. "We've got to stop this—"

Renard shook his head. "We can't."

"Why not?"

Aethan took a long drag on his cigarette, then let the smoke blow out his nose. "That's what's got her into this in the first place, breaking the thing off too early." He spoke carefully, as though still fighting to convince himself. "This isn't like healing some wound on the surface. These are things no one ever should have been messing with."

Triston took a step back and let the angry strength seep from his limbs. He supposed that explanation made sense enough. For now.

Kura's chest heaved with each labored breath, but gradually the world came back into focus. She was on her hands and knees on the cavern floor, her fists clenched and her shirt stuck to her back with sweat.

"Kura!" It was Erryl's voice, and it must have been at least the third time he'd said her name. He gripped her arm and pulled her to her knees. Sweat beaded on his temples, and the haggard face that turned to inspect hers was filled with worry.

Any hope she'd had that he'd succeeded died in that moment.

Erryl opened his mouth as if he was going to say something, but he simply climbed to his feet, then pulled Kura up to hers. Her legs swayed beneath her, but Erryl kept his grip on her arm and gently led her to the iron door. He knocked once, and Devna threw it open.

The light in her eyes faded as they came to rest on Erryl.

He simply shook his head. "The bond is stronger than we thought."

"I..." Kura sucked in a breath, then wriggled out of Erryl's grip. "I just saw the same thing over again, everything Vahleda did to me before." Those words came out far more calmly than they sounded in her head. "But, this time, I—I saw soldiers..."

"Soldiers?" Erryl said. "What were they doing?"

Kura quickly explained what she had seen.

"Is it possible," Erryl started carefully, as he glanced to Devna, "that she has seen something of the Grey Lady's memory?"

The woman eyed Kura with an all-too-familiar frown. "We could try again."

"No," Erryl said sternly. He gave a heavy sigh and wiped his glistening forehead on his sleeve. "We have stepped into a world which we do not fully comprehend, and I will not do so blindly again."

Devna shrugged. "The texts may speak of different remedies. If you'd given me more time I would have consulted them."

"Alright, do it. We should, tonight at least, put something together to serve as interference."

Kura's heart sank. Even after all of this, they were no closer to a solution.

"Well..." She swallowed. "I... I suppose everyone should keep away from me... Don't tell me anything, or let me near anything of value..."

"I'm sorry," Erryl said, and there was something in his eyes now that made Kura think he really meant it. "But I believe you are right."

Chapter Forty-Six
REPERCUSSIONS

Kura glanced at the distant sunrise as she wiped her sweaty brow on her arm.

The warm, pink rays shot across an indigo sky and filtered through the leafy, vine-covered skylights of the main dining hall. She hadn't slept a wink, but morning was still a welcome sight. For about an hour and half she'd tried to relax, but despite the protection Erryl had tried to arrange for her, she hadn't been comfortable falling asleep. Vahleda would be waiting.

Taking in a deep breath, Kura bounced on the balls of her feet then sprinted down the longer wall. She was heading into her fourth set; she'd already worn her knuckles bloody with strength exercises and exhausted her core with every workout she'd ever learned, but stopping meant sitting still with her own thoughts. She'd done more than enough of that.

She came to a loping stop beside the far wall, then leaned against it as she fought to catch her breath. In the Wynshire, she'd done exercises almost every morning before the sunrise, honing her physical strength and sword skills as she waited for the time she would inevitably need to use them. It was oddly comforting to have some sense of normalcy—even as she flopped to a seat on the dusty floor, drenched in sweat.

Leaning back against the stone, Kura pressed the small pouch hanging around her neck between her fingers. Erryl rightly wouldn't tell her what was in it, but she thought she felt bits of metal, dirt, and a few other objects she couldn't discern through the burlap. Devna and several other Fidelis had pored through their texts for hours and then returned with the necklace, but in all honesty Kura doubted its effectiveness. It was just a talisman to ward off evil spirits; she'd seen so many Svaldans make the same for themselves and their children. But the Fidelis had done what they could, and the best she could do was attempt the same.

"There you are, girl." Her father's voice echoed in through an archway along the wall to her side.

Kura forced her eyes open, then pushed herself to her feet to jog to his side. Spiridon had a blanket draped over his shoulders, and his face was still a shade too white.

"Father, you shouldn't—"

He laughed and waved her hand aside. "And what is it that you're doing now? If you aren't going to sleep, at least try to pretend at resting."

Kura shrugged. "You were looking for me?"

"I am, actually." Grenja stepped out of Spiridon's shadow, then nodded toward the skylights with a toothy grin. "Did you see it?"

Kura frowned and glanced at the sky. She'd seen the sunrise, of course, but—

A single band of smoke rose from beneath the horizon, faint enough to fade in the morning light but too precise to be from a campfire. The Varian's signal.

Kura met Grenja's gaze in surprise. "I don't—"

The dog laughed, the sound somewhere between a yip and a bark. "I know what Skellor's told you. In fact, he told me to keep watch for you three days before you even showed up. I've been trying for years to get Trofast to work with the Varian, but like all Cenóri he takes his good long time. He's sent scouts out after that, though, and they'll be back within the hour with whoever's showed up. I thought you ought to be there." She looked Kura over, wrinkling her nose. "But maybe not smelling like that."

The small room at the end of the hall teemed with people and Kura trudged toward it, tugging at her collar. Grenja had found her a bath and then a change of clothes fit for some kind of lord, and while both were appreciated, the latter was far from comfortable.

"You're the one who brought the Varian and Fidelis to Lâroe?" Aethan tagged at Kura's heels. He was not so enthusiastic about the signal, but had graciously agreed to accompany her anyway.

She nodded, not sure she wanted to face his scorn. It was quite possibly the only thing she'd done so far that wasn't a mistake.

Aethan looked as though he was going to be angry, but then he laughed and shook his head. "Alright then."

They continued toward the open doorway, and a hush settled over the room. Its inhabitants were a rag-tag band, dressed in patchworked garments with only a few possessions. Murmuring to one another, they stared at Kura as she struggled to find her voice. Several of them looked familiar.

Aethan followed her into the room. "Sygus?"

"Aethan!" The man was cleanshaven with round features, dusted in road dirt like the rest of them. He broke into a grin. "Then we have made it!"

Sygus. Kura recognized that name, and gradually she matched it with the face. The group's long leather capes alone should have given it away: they were Feldlanders.

The mass parted as a figure made her way toward the doorway. She was a shorter woman with light brown skin and flowing black hair, which showed only where her large, hooded cloak did not cover her. The rest of the gang seemed to treat her with reverence, but the woman carried her shoulders low and her steps were far from confident. A delicate smile spread across her face when she looked up.

"Serika?" Kura said with a surprised laugh.

The woman nodded quickly, then sank down on one knee. The others began to follow her lead.

"Oh, get up," Kura muttered, latching on to Serika's arm and dragging her to her feet.

"I had to come." Serika hesitated to look Kura in the eye but managed it, her voice shaking and her cheeks flushed red with excitement. "I didn't mean to tell Baza that you were leaving, but I overheard, and when he started questioning all of us after you and Aethan had disappeared, he made me..." Her smile broke, and she covered her mouth with her hand as tears pooled in her eyes.

"It's alright." Kura gently rubbed Serika's arm. After everything else, she'd nearly forgotten about Baza and their exchange on the road. "Serika, I don't blame you for anything."

Serika took in a deep, shuddering breath. "So, the next night, we ran. All of us here." She gave a small, reassuring look to the rest of the group. "We kept to the mountains, staying clear of the roads, until we entered the Deorwynn Forest and we heard rumors of the fonfyr..."

The group murmured in agreement, and a few began adding details of their own. They spoke in low voices, all at once, and Kura couldn't understand any of them.

"So," Aethan asked, "why'd you come here?" He was trying not to show it, but Kura knew him well enough now to tell he was pleased.

"We were wandering the roads," Serika explained, "searching for the nearest town, when a hooded man came across us. I was afraid he might be a robber or a brigand at first—I never saw his face—but he said if we were looking for the rebellion then we should wait under the tree and they would find us." She hesitated, then set her jaw and nodded. "We've come to fight." She laughed sheepishly, and glanced down at her feet. "Well, we've come to do what we can, anyway."

Kura surveyed the dozen faces. They stared at her as the folks in Lâroe had, and somehow that made a big, dumb smile spread across her face as she tried to swallow the lump in her throat.

Serika hadn't seen Ìsendorál. She hadn't struck out to find a rumored savior. Her journey had started with a spark of courage, kindled by whatever foolish—though heartfelt—ideas about freedom Kura'd shouted at Baza in passing. And neither the Grey Lady nor anything else could change that.

She placed her fist over her heart in salute. "We would be honored to fight beside you."

Chapter Forty-Seven

Duty and Dereliction

Triston strode down the hallway, adjusting the fit of his shirt, hoping his half-hearted efforts had left him presentable enough.

Renard had fetched him before the sun rose with a curt 'good morning' and an unceremonial toss of the bundle of clothing he was now wearing. They were heading toward the council chambers, presumably, and he wasn't sure whether he should be concerned or relieved. Renard kept his narrowed eyes fixed on the hallway before them; breaking into a short jog to keep up with the man's quick pace, Triston decided against asking questions.

"This way," Renard said with a nod as he turned down a side passage that led to the council chamber doors. They were closed, but muffled voices carried from the other side. A huge bear stood guard, a long spear in his paws. Triston stopped and caught himself staring at the animal—the bear itself was threatening enough, without the large weapon.

Renard motioned toward the doors. "They're expecting us."

The bear eyed Renard, then huffed as he pushed open one of the large doors. Renard trod lightly under the bear's gaze, and Triston followed him closely as they passed into the council room.

Glowing veins of stone made the room bright as the midday sun. The group gathered around the table—Trofast, Erryl, Grenja, and another centaur Triston didn't know—had been in a heated discussion, but they fell quiet as they glanced toward the door.

The other centaur's ears were pinned back against his neck. "You've brought him anyway."

Renard slid into his empty seat, grinning at the others' sour faces. "For a second there I thought y'all were talking about me."

The other centaur snorted and stepped away from the table. "I have fulfilled my station."

Trofast sighed deeply. "Konik..."

"*Mursol, aldor*," Konik said, crossing his arms in an X over his bare chest to bow at the waist. "I will fight for you, but I cannot in good conscience advise you any longer."

Trofast frowned, but returned the salute. "*Solme*, brother."

Triston stepped to the side, but the centaur brushed past him to get to the door. Their eyes met. Konik's were narrow, piercing—filled with caution, not animosity—and he nodded before disappearing into the hallway.

Folding his hands before him, Triston fought to keep from appearing overly tense. He was accustomed to meetings—Seren had seen to that—but here his rank and title had no pull or authority, and that made this council something else entirely.

"What we need from you," Erryl started, glancing up at Triston as he rearranged the stack of parchments on the table before him, "are numbers. Troop counts."

So, they wanted an informant. He should have expected that, but he had left Dol imagining an arrangement where, naturally, he explained his plans and they then assisted in the execution. Triston stole a glance in Trofast's direction. Of course that wasn't how this was going to work.

The centaur sighed. "Well? Have you misplaced your tongue between last night and this morning?"

"No, sir." How difficult could be before they simply threw him back in the prison cell from his last visit? "With all due respect, I must make it clear to all of you that I am not here to wage a war against my father."

Grenja growled, her hackles raised. "He's not ready to do what has to be done. This is a waste of time."

"Hey," Renard said. "You're asking a lot of him here, give him a break."

Trofast shook his head. "Forgive me, Renard, if that does not sway me. All here have already given more than we had to lose."

Renard turned to the centaur, squaring his shoulders, and held his ground. "Sir, there's no honor in merely losing something. The honor comes in what you do afterwards, or what you do despite the loss. He's risking everything he has to stand here before us today, and I think that should earn him a bit of damned respect."

Renard's words netted a moment of silence from the council; even Trofast eyed the man with a quiet frown.

"Look..." Triston stepped forward. "I don't plan on losing anything, and if we can work this right, then neither will any of you."

The council members turned to him with a curious eye, and Trofast nodded. "Explain."

"My father does not want war. I—"

Grenja laughed. "The rebel king doesn't want war?" She fell into what sounded like a fit of yips. "Go on, tell us another lie, Prince! It's with them he won the throne—I should have known the pup wouldn't stray far from the den."

Lies? Every face eyed him with stern, though reluctant, agreement, and suddenly he remembered Kura's sword—and the mirror of it that hung in his father's council chambers. He laughed in disbelief.

"Is that what this is all about—the prophecy? My father carried some sword, yes, but he never claimed to be the fonfyr. In fact, it was Seren..." Triston's smile faded. "It was always Seren."

Trofast grunted, and if Triston hadn't known better he would have thought the centaur was surprised. His ear twitched, his tail swished, and he stomped a rear leg as though trying to chase off flies. Finally, he nodded to Triston—the motion almost a bow. "I will listen, son of Dradge. I cannot promise your father will not end up dead with the rest of us at the end of this, but share what you will."

Triston took a step back, straightening as he deliberately studied each face at the table. This stuffy cave might not match the subtle grandeur of his father's council chambers, but those faces—expectant, judgmental... those he was used to. "If you don't want to speak with my father, then speak with me. Name your grievances."

Grenja wrinkled her nose; Erryl's expression didn't change, but Renard's eyebrows rose and he glanced at Trofast. The centaur's ear flicked. He said nothing.

Triston jerked his chin at Renard—likely the most amicable of the group. "I can tell you served. Under my father, or before that?"

The man straightened in his seat with what must have been the remnants of a soldier's pride. "Both. Served with some private groups, too. I guess that's my grievance: I want to be able to follow my conscience. I don't want to kill unarmed civilians or confiscate stuff from poor folks."

Triston nodded. "I can get you a pardon—doesn't matter if you were court-martialed or deserted. I can get you your rank back, too, if you want it. At its core, my father's troops are comprised of men like you—good men. That doesn't excuse the rot, and I won't try to apologize for what should never have happened in the first place, but that's not how my father and I want this country to be. Work with me and we can fix it."

Chuckling, Erryl lifted his chin. "With whose tongue do you speak, boy? It can't be your father's."

Triston bristled, holding back the true—although unhelpful—reply of *My own.*

"Maybe your mother's, then? Except she was kinder than this cruel world deserved, and by my recollection softer-spoken than this. So, that leaves Seren." The man smiled delicately, altogether too pleased with himself. "I watched you grow up, toddling at his side, drinking in every instruction he had to give you. He hides them well, but his claws are sharp, and he sinks them into anything that may prove suitably susceptible or useful."

Triston hoped his face hadn't twisted entirely into a scowl, and he looked to Trofast instead. "What's your grievance? I know my father was not kind to your people. In exchange for a cessation of hostilities, I offer you sovereignty and an allotment of land—a square, or thereabouts, a dayride in each direction—in any low-populated area of your choosing between Edras and the Waste. I can even guarantee you a waterway and access to the coast, if you value that."

The light of genuine amusement sprang in the centaur's eyes, deepening the wrinkles on his cheeks. "You are not the first of your blood to stand before me and make such offers. I suspect I was a young fool to believe them then, and that would make me an old fool to entertain them now. I admire your intentions, son of Dradge, but you are a youth—even by your people's standards. What can a sprout, growing amongst the roots of a great tree, do beyond ask for permission to remain growing? That much I have granted you. Be grateful."

Triston blew out a breath and turned back to Erryl. "Your grievance is with Seren? So is mine. Form a party, of no more than three hundred to avoid the appearance of aggression, and let me ride at the front. I'll even go unarmed if you insist on it. I'll get you into Edras, I'll get you before my father and the council, and we can all testify against that man and have him sanctioned, imprisoned, or hanged as the evidence sees fit."

Renard perked up a little, but Erryl just chuckled again, shaking his head, as though there was anything amusing to be found in that offer.

Triston ground his teeth and glanced in the dog's direction. What would she want? Probably to tear this throat out if she discovered his instinctive answer to that question was 'scraps of meat.' "Do your people seek land or sovereignty? I make you the same offer as I did the Cenóri."

"Nah," the dog grunted. "That sounds like work."

Triston waited for her to explain further, but she didn't. She actually bent over and began licking the fur on her stomach, oblivious to the quizzical looks the others shot her.

He scratched angrily at the back of his head, then examined each face at the table again. There was a man, a Fidelis, a centaur, and a nostkynna, and each of them had dismissed him entirely. *Maybe I should have just gone home.* Seren could have been bluffing about those guards... Of course, all this was easier to consider now that his ribs weren't screaming at him every time he took in a breath.

"Renard," he said, "since you were in the service for that long, we must have served together? At least in passing?"

The man nodded, thoughtfully, chewing his inner lip.

"Then you and I understand this more clearly than they do. Tell them. My father—"

Erryl laughed outright. "What, now you'll have *him* vouch for you? I've heard enough." He peered up at Trofast. "I think it's fair to call this a failed experiment?"

The centaur shifted his stance, but Renard frowned.

"I've served with a lot of guys," the man said, staring at the table before him, "good ones and bad ones. I wish that was all it took to put an army in the wrong or in the right." Guiltily, he glanced up. "Sorry, kid, this fight's gonna happen. Your father never seemed like so bad a guy to me, but I think you've seen it for yourself: there's something bigger going on here. Something twisted. I won't tell you my side's any more right than yours is, but you'll have to pick one."

Triston sighed, then clenched the belt around his waist—at least that wasn't a totally obvious display of frustration. "Fine. Let me go home. Give me my horse back and I'll head for Edras myself. I've been told there are guards waiting on the roads to kill me—guards a group of us could easily handle, together—but so be it. That's a risk I'm willing to take. If there *are* sides to be drawn up, it's not me against you: it's all of us against Seren."

"Let you go?" Erryl rolled his eyes dramatically toward the ceiling. "Now you must think we're stupid as well as gullible."

"Rash," Trofast said softly, dark eyes hollow. "We're rash—all of us. As hasty as we are headstrong. It is the one trait that unites our races, the same singular quality that drives us apart. Words may tame that rashness—they may buy peace, for a time—but freedom is paid for in blood. I would rather you not lose your life, son of Dradge, but I am glad you are willing to spend it. Would that we were all so willing. Fortunate is the soul that gives itself freely."

Renard scoffed. "I don't plan on dying any time soon. Assuming we actually decide something here, and I don't just keel over out of sheer boredom." Sighing, he stretched his back. "Us against Seren... I can stomach that." He reached for the large, faded map spread open on the table and shoved the parchment towards Triston. "How many men is he good for? Where are they stationed?"

Triston peered down at the map, leaning his palms against the table as he surveyed it. Couldn't hurt to give that information up, right? "Seren's a strategist, so he could call up men from any outpost within a day's ride of Edras," he said, tracing a ring around the small triangle that marked the capital city, "totaling about a thousand. Give him more time and he could double or triple that, but he'd need several weeks' time and authorization from my father."

No one replied; they all just stared at the map. Well, maybe that was a good thing—fear was a powerful motivator. He still didn't want to hand over troop numbers, but if they understood what they were up against they might realize how much they still needed him.

"That's just who will answer to Seren directly. He's also convinced the entire council to pledge troops to the cause. I'd count Tanith for another thousand, Lavern for twelve hundred, Therburn for nine hundred, Hamlyn maybe for seven hundred, and Rigan for about three hundred. And then of course there are two thousand standing at the ready in Edras to answer my father's call, so that's a total of seven thousand one hundred men Seren could have marching your way in under two days."

Those four faces stared at him this time, pale and just about slack-jawed, and he nearly laughed.

"That's your worst-case scenario. Five thousand one hundred of those men will pull out at my father's command, and if you can get me the chance to speak with him, I'm sure a fair number of them will fight with you. Best-case, you're facing about two thousand soldiers and however many of those beast things Seren's pulled out of the Waste."

The council members shared sidelong glances—Erryl squirmed in his seat—and still they all said nothing. Well, they were certainly afraid...

"How many are you here?" Triston asked.

Grenja gave Trofast a cautionary look.

"Eight hundred?" Renard offered with a shrug, turning to the others for help. "Possibly nine-fifty if you count those idle hands we can shove a spear into."

"Oh." Triston breathed a sigh. Eight hundred, dressed in decades-old armor, armed with rusty weapons, and fed for months on half rations... He hadn't just scared them; they were probably terrified.

Trofast snorted, the sound oddly animalistic from such a human face. "We were never meant for this. I planned for small heists and skirmishes, like what we were supposed to have done yesterday in Lâroe. We could have sustained our momentum for years going that way, chipping at the legs until the throne fell right out from beneath him. But I need Nansûr for that, and it's only a matter of days before those monsters come clawing at *our* walls."

Grenja bared her teeth. "Not all of us have your years anyway, Cenóri."

Trofast beheld the dog for a moment with something akin to sympathy. "I suppose you're right."

"Good riddance," Renard said, waving his hand. "Sorry, Trofast, but your plan sounds boring anyway. And besides, when it comes down to it, numbers aren't going to mean shit if we can control the time and the terrain."

The centaur gave a bitter laugh. "Eloquently put, Master Soldier, but how do you suggest we do that when over seven thousand men are soon to be standing on our doorstep?"

Renard didn't answer, and Triston joined him in letting the silence linger. He might still be able to swing an arrangement where he left here with a small company for Edras, but he'd have to be gentler when asking for it.

Erryl rubbed his nose. "Well, while it is the cause of our disadvantage, we may still determine the time if—"

"No," Trofast said sternly. "We'll have asked too much of the girl by the end of this as it is."

Renard stiffened. "Kura will be fine."

Erryl's eyebrows rose, and he stared up at Trofast with a taunting sense of surprise. "So, you do believe in the finality of the prophecy? *Un bryhte medla debordyur*—a gallant heart overflows?"

"As I've told you," Trofast said, tersely, "I do not know what to believe."

Shock caught in Triston's chest, and he looked around the council table in disbelief. "You would let her die for you?"

Renard shook his head vehemently. "Absolutely not."

"But it is what the prophecy says," Grenja said, jostling the fur that bristled on her back. "All lives end in death. Your years only lull you into thinking it will never catch up to you. Kura is deserving of an honorable death more than many I know. She should be honored to face it."

"The interpretation is not settled," Erryl said, eyeing the dog with a frown. "The seventh stanza could refer to self-sacrifice, not necessarily death, and that she has already done. And besides, while I will admit I am less skeptical than before, I am not yet convinced she is the fonfyr."

"Not the fonfyr?" Renard laughed. "Didn't you see what she did in Lâroe?"

Erryl fell silent.

Trofast let out a heavy sigh. "She knows what she's chosen."

"No one's gonna die," Renard said dismissively, and Triston was surprised to see in the seasoned warrior's face how much he meant it.

A large fist pounded on the council doors, and then one door creaked open. It was the bear, poking his large nose into the room.

Trofast stepped forward. "What is it, Rusket?"

"There's a group of refugees here for vetting. Feldlanders."

"I'll go," Renard said, rising from his seat. He glanced over at Grenja. "Fill me in?"

The dog nodded, and Renard followed the bear out the door.

"Feldlanders..." Erryl mused as the door fell shut. "Do you suppose any of them practice Pokalfr?"

Trofast's eyes widened just a bit. "It would be risky. She would have to agree to it."

"You said Pokalfr?" Grenja tilted her head to the side. "That weird thing the Svaldans do?"

Erryl nodded, solemnly. "It is a strange ritual art—some perversion of my people's invocations, no doubt. But if done properly, it can bring about a powerful, although temporary, trance. The Grey Lady has likely already seen enough to know our general location, but we might fool her into thinking Nansûr was somewhere else nearby. If Kura was willing, of course."

Triston frowned. Tactically, the idea seemed viable, but his skin crawled to hear them all speak of Kura so callously, as a tool instead of a person. His father did the same in battle—war turned humanity into weakness—but this felt... different.

"It doesn't seem right," Grenja said, tail bristling.

"But if it could be done," Erryl said, "we would have our advantage."

Triston shook his head. "That's not much of an advantage, facing down seven thousand royal soldiers. Get me into Edras, and I'll triple your numbers while cutting your enemy's in half."

Grenja barked a laugh. "Exactly how fast do you think we can run? We'd never make it to Edras before your soldiers made it here."

Triston took a step back and muttered a curse under his breath. This whole time he'd been measuring the distance with the speed of a royal charger, but a rag-tag group like this wouldn't make good time. He breathed out, running a hand through his hair to scratch the back of his head. "Then, when those troops do come close enough, find my father's company—or Lavern's or Therburn's—and get me there. If I can speak with any of them I can still end this before it begins."

Erryl laughed. "Do you really think we'd—"

"We will consider it," Trofast said. He didn't raise his voice—didn't even glance in Erryl's direction—but the man fell silent anyway. The centaur looked Triston in the eye, then bowed slightly at the waist. "Thank you for your counsel. You are dismissed."

Triston nodded, ready to offer some kind of similar thanks, before he processed the second part of the statement. Even then he nearly questioned it, but under the centaur's stern gaze he found better sense than that. As cordially as he could, he returned the bow and then half-stumbled back through the door to wander into the hallway.

The shadowy corridor sat empty, aside from the voices echoing at the far end, and Triston stood there as the door fell shut, clenching his fists at his sides, as his veins still coursed with the urge to do something—anything. They would *consider* his offer? Given the circumstances he should probably be grateful for that, but at the very least he was not accustomed to being dismissed from a meeting before it reached its conclusion.

The conversation played over again in his mind, but instead of fixating on what he could have done differently, his thoughts settled on a separate problem. Maybe one he could actually solve, while he waited for them to come to their senses. He turned and jogged down the hallway, glancing up only to confirm that he was headed in the right direction. He knew Kura would do whatever she had to do to win this fight, and he wasn't about to let her die—no matter how honorable the reason.

Chapter Forty-Eight
Invocations

Kura took a seat in the dusty corner of the training room. The small space, lit by a vein of lenêre stone, was empty except for a rack of training weapons on the opposite wall. She didn't want to disturb her father's rest in her own room, but she didn't feel comfortable wandering the halls of Nansûr, either. Not with Vahleda waiting.

Drawing in a deep breath, she shut her eyes and savored the fleeting moment of solitude. It couldn't hurt for the Grey Lady to see this room. The silence made her tangle of thoughts resurface, but this time the knot had unraveled. She wasn't the fonfyr, but she would carry the sword anyway. Somehow.

She unbuckled the scabbard at her hip, then shifted to her knees to place Ìsendorál on the floor before her. What was she doing? Making an offering? She examined the engravings on the leather scabbard. How did Aethan do this?

She placed her hands on her knees and looked out at the stone wall above her. "Essence, speak to me…" Her voice sounded weak and empty as it echoed in the room. "That, that my thoughts may be true." She glanced down at her hands, feeling ridiculous. "Essence… move in me, so that I…"

Already, she'd forgotten nearly all of it.

With a frustrated sigh, she fell back to sit cross-legged on the floor. That worn scabbard at her knees loomed before her, like a tribute to all that she should be and all that she wasn't. But that didn't matter anymore.

She clenched her eyes shut. *Essence, I need to do this right.* Did that sound pretentious? She set her jaw. *Give me the strength.*

She wanted to imagine she felt something, she wanted to believe this made a bit of difference, but in the end she found only a foreboding sense of calm. That was going to have to be enough.

Footsteps pattered in the hallway and Kura started to her feet before she saw the silhouette in the doorway. Elli paused, one hand resting on the wall while the other clutched a hunk of bread, and a big smile spread across her face. "Kura!"

"Hey, Elli," Kura said with a laugh. She buckled her scabbard back around her waist as her sister wandered into the room. "What're you doing here?"

"Mother said I had to go, 'cause Father needs to sleep." She peered with wide eyes up at the weapons, raining crumbs on her shirt as she chomped at her bread. "I wanted to look for you."

"Well, you found me."

Elli nodded. "Somebody always notices where you went."

Kura chuckled, but wasn't entirely sure she found that amusing.

"Father says you have to go to war." Elli didn't look up; she kept nibbling at her bread. "Mother says she doesn't want you to go."

Kura let out a heavy sigh and joined her sister beside the weapons rack. "Well, I don't really want to go, either. But I have to."

"I know." Elli spoke simply—so confidently—Kura had to laugh.

"You know?"

"Sure. You've got the fonfyr's sword!"

Kura grinned and glanced down at the sword on her hip. "Yeah, I guess I do."

Elli peered up at her, look as stern and piercing as only a child's could be. "You promised to float bark boats with me."

Huh? I don't think I— "Oh." Kura laughed. How her sister remembered *that*, after all that had happened, was beyond her. "We didn't get to do that back home, did we?"

Elli shook her head. "Father says there's a stream nearby."

"How about after all of this, you and me can check it out." Kura's smile faded. There was no guarantee there would be anything for her after this.

Still, Elli's big grin returned. "I'mma make a sailboat."

Kura nodded, forcing the proper veneer of interest, and she traced her finger along the sword hilt at her side. She had been about Elli's age when Benger died. Elli didn't even remember

Benger—she'd been younger than Rowley was now. Kura shuddered. If she died tomorrow, would Rowley remember her? Would Elli spend the rest of her life trying to forget the night she'd lost her?

Elli reached into her pocket and pulled out a wooden medallion hung on a hemp cord. "I think you lost this."

Kura squinted at the trinket for a moment before realizing what it was. "Oh, that's a necklace I bought in Tarr Fianin. It's got a flicker on it, see?"

Elli ran her hand over the crude image. "I like it."

Kura took the necklace by its cord, chuckling at the circumstances that had led to her buying it. "Here." She knelt down in front of Elli. "Let me put it on you."

Elli straightened, proudly, but fidgeted as Kura brushed back her tangled brown hair to tie the cord behind her neck. "It's very pretty."

Kura planted a kiss on the top of her sister's head. "Well, it is now."

Another set of footsteps carried from beyond the door, heavier this time, and a dark shadow passed over the light from the hallway. Kura rose, expecting to see either another family member or Aethan, but the black boots in the doorway didn't belong to anyone she knew. She lifted her gaze, then froze as it fell on Triston's face. Elli let out a startled cry and pressed herself against Kura's leg.

Triston took a step back. "I'm sorry, I—"

"It's alright, Elli," Kura said, placing a hand on her sister's shoulder. Elli clung to her leg, peering up at Triston with wide eyes.

"I..." Triston began to take a step back as he stared at Elli, but stopped when he looked at Kura. "I was hoping I could talk to you?"

Kura studied him for a moment. He was dressed in new clothes—new for him, at least; as almost anything else in Nansûr, they were certainly years old—and the bruises on his face were now a sickly yellow instead of a harsh purple. Idris worked quickly. Some silly part of her had to point out that he'd looked better before, in his riding clothes, even if they had been a bit muddy. This indigo tunic had ornate stitching at the hem, but in the end it was still masquerading as noble when he was the real thing.

"Sure," she said finally, with a shrug.

Elli tightened her grip. "Kura!"

"It's alright, Elli." Kura pried her sister's cold hands from her pant leg, then knelt down to look Elli eye-to-eye. "He's a friend." There she was, using that word so flippantly again. "You can wait in the hall if you want, or I can come find you this time."

Elli nodded, and Kura got to her feet as her sister reluctantly made her way through the door—darting past Triston—and out into the crowd in the hallway.

Kura tucked a lock of hair behind her ear, then met Triston's gaze again. His eyes flicked to the weapons rack on the wall, and he gave a hint of a smile.

"Well, it might be easier if I just showed you. Is that alright?"

Kura shrugged. He picked two wooden training swords and tossed one of them to her. She caught the hilt—it felt odd to hold a blade while another sat sheathed on her hip—and he stepped back into a guard stance.

"This is, um..." He gave her an apologetic glance. "Just something I noticed after you—well, I mean, after we met in the Deorwynn." Kura watched him quizzically, but he beckoned her forward with his free hand. "You move first."

She fought back a scowl as she adjusted her grip on the training sword. She didn't like to remember how their last fight had ended, but what was she supposed to do, back down from this one?

She lunged with a sweeping strike from the side. Triston stepped back, blocking her advance, then shifted his weight forward. With a flick of his sword, he caught Kura's blade in a spiral and sent the wooden blade flopping to the ground.

Those all-too-familiar emotions of inadequacy welled up in Kura's chest, and she muttered a curse under her breath.

"Sorry." Triston stepped forward to retrieve her fallen sword. He was smothering a grin—apparently all of this was incredibly amusing—but she appreciated his effort to *pretend* he wasn't laughing at her. "You practiced a lot on your own, didn't you? Maybe on a dummy or something?"

That was surprisingly accurate. "What makes you say that?"

Triston held out the training sword's hilt and Kura begrudgingly took it. "You're fast, and quick on your feet, too. Most people are going to be done in by that. But you've got bad form." He adjusted his grip. "Come at me again, choose something different."

Frowning, Kura complied—with as much strength and precision as she could muster. Still, Triston side-stepped her strike, as though he already knew what she was going to do. Mercifully, he stopped short of sweeping the sword from her hand this time.

Kura smothered a sigh, feeling absolutely foolish—both for losing, and for taking that loss so poorly.

"You've got a tell," Triston said. "You're stomping your lead foot before you make a move. Even the best swordsmen develop quirks like that, although it comes easier when you're training on something that can't fight back and call you out on it."

Kura started to shake her head, so Triston grinned and took a step back, raising his sword. She grimaced, then lashed out with a succession of quick strokes. Although she managed to back Triston toward the wall, he blocked each strike with ease.

With a grunt of frustration, she turned away, clenching her fists. She felt like a child getting so angry over this, but it hadn't been since she was a child that she'd lost a sword fight so decidedly. "Is this what you've come to tell me, that once the real battle comes, I'm dead?"

Triston laughed. "No, of course not. But I can show you a few things. You know, if you want. Bad habits like these are very difficult to undo, but I'm sure we could make some progress."

She ran those words again in her mind again until she appreciated the weight of them. Was she too good to pass up free lessons from possibly the best swordsman in Avaron? "I…" Pride still made the words difficult to say. "I would appreciate that. Thanks."

Triston visibly relaxed. "Here." He retrieved a wooden shield from the weapon's rack and tossed it to her. "Let's start you with this. Hopefully it will get you out of what you're used to doing, and maybe make it easier for some of this to stick."

Kura fumbled with the shield as she cinched the straps on her left arm. It wasn't particularly heavy, but its bulk felt awkward in her hand as she stepped back into a fighting stance. And like that, the training began.

It was painful—psychologically far more than physically—but Triston continued to patiently repeat the same few drills with her over and over again. He was a skilled fighter, as if she didn't know that already, but he was a fine teacher as well: quiet, for the most part, unless he had something to say about her stance or form.

Finally, and long after her shield arm began to ache, he called for a break. Kura let her shield and wooden sword clatter to the ground as she sank to a seat against the far wall. She wasn't sure how much of this would stick, but she was certainly more confident. Triston returned his training blade to the weapon's rack, then lowered himself down beside her.

The silence lingered between them, broken only by the sound of Kura struggling to catch her breath.

"For, um," Triston began, then swallowed. "For whatever it's worth, I'm sorry."

Kura looked over at him, but he was inspecting his hands as he picked at his fingernail.

"For everything in the Wynshire, I mean. I'd take it all back if I could."

Kura let out a long sigh. Gods, she'd hated him so much before, but now—even when she tried—she only found an odd memory of that animosity. "I wouldn't." Those words were a shock to hear herself say, but when Triston turned to her, she grinned. "Life in the Wynshire was one step away from hell. I was trying to barter passage out, but it seems a royal escort worked just as well."

Triston stared at her. "Didn't... didn't one of my men shoot you?"

She shrugged.

"Well." His face broke into a smile, and he leaned back against the wall as his gaze drifted to the center of the room. "...Thank you."

The silence overtook them again, and Kura found herself fidgeting with the hem of her shirt. She wasn't used to being at a loss for words, and she didn't recall ever wanting so desperately to say something while being unable to find anything at all. Maybe it was that smile. She'd spent enough time with him by now to know he didn't just give them away, and maybe she liked knowing this one was for her.

"Do you, um," Triston began, then scratched the back of his head as the tips of his ears flushed a bright shade of red.

Kura bit her lip to hold back a grin. Was all Avaronian nobility this inarticulate?

"Kura?" The voice came from the hall. Erryl appeared in the doorway.

Triston's face darkened, but he rose to his feet and offered a hand to pull Kura to hers.

Erryl glanced between them and the discarded training weapons with a curious frown, before clearing his throat. "The council has been in discussion, and we believe we've come to a solution."

Both fear and hope caught hold in Kura's chest. "What kind of solution?"

"Are you familiar with Pokalfr?"

Kura thought back to that patchwork tent she'd seen in Davka'vara, then nodded.

"Well..." Erryl smoothed the sash he wore as a belt. "There may be a way to use it to exploit your connection with Vahleda, to give us the advantage."

Kura grinned, even as she knew it was premature. "Really?"

"Yes." Pride broke through his composure, but it didn't last. "I will not lie. This has never been done before. I want to promise that no harm will come to you, but I cannot do that. All I can say is that, should we be successful, we will have gained a great chance to rout the king's forces and dismantle the Grey Lady's scheming. A chance only."

"Kura," Triston said softly. There was a warning in his eyes, as though he'd heard all of the risks and none of the rewards. "You still don't have to do this."

She held his gaze. He didn't turn away, and even with the heat creeping into her cheeks, she didn't either. So that was what he was doing here: trying to look out for her. Which was very sweet, actually. But it didn't change her answer.

"Yes I do."

Chapter Forty-Nine

BANISHED TEARS

"Watch your step."

Kura stumbled, but caught herself on Aethan's arm, which was wrapped around hers. The scratchy blindfold over her eyes gave her nothing but darkness to look into, and while she tried to laugh at Aethan's terrible ability to guide her, anxiety ate away at her gut.

"I want to promise that no harm will come to you, but I cannot do that."

An entire evening and night passed since Erryl had spoken those words to her, but they still echoed in her mind. Now that it had come to it, she almost wished she hadn't agreed to this. Almost.

A rush of cool morning air blew across her face, tugging her loose hair back from her shoulders. It brought the rich aroma of wet dirt, and dew-laden pine needles crunched beneath her feet.

"Almost there," Aethan said. He was trying to sound casual—confident, even—but she heard the nervous edge in his voice, and his clothes reeked of the tobacco he must have smoked before they left.

Finally, he pulled her to a stop. Horse's hooves stomped across the forest floor, then a familiar voice spoke.

"She can remove the blindfold."

Kura pulled that scratchy bit of cloth from her face and looked up, blinking against the rising sun. Konik towered above her, his stern expression and the dark shadows cast across his face by the light at his back making him look very much like Trofast. A quilted gambeson covered the chest and shoulders of his human half and stretched across the back of his horse's half, but Kura noticed most of all the massive pair of broadswords that hung from his sides. He was ready for war.

"Courage, little one." Konik smiled, and that easily he no longer resembled his brother. "This day is burdened with great promise of victory."

She managed to smile back.

"This is it, then?" Aethan asked, glancing past the centaur's enormous frame to frown at the short, domed structure behind him. It was built of wood and bark and covered in colorful, although faded, blankets. A Svaldan hothouse.

Kura grimaced. *Mother would kill me for this if she knew.*

A woman pushed back the cloth opening, a cloud of white steam pouring out around her figure, and Konik stepped aside with a swish of his tail.

Kura took a step back in surprise. "Serika!"

The woman's curly black hair had been pulled up over her head in a bun, and she wore nothing more than a short, sleeveless dress that more closely resembled a child's blanket—or the misshapen tent behind her—than any true article of clothing.

Serika laughed. "This is how all *khra'vörs* dress." She ran a hand across her stomach, looking over the bits of cloth. "Each piece comes from a cover blanket from each ceremony I've conducted under my teacher's guidance. Only after I'd collected enough to make this was I allowed to conduct the ceremony on my own." She gave Kura a mischievous grin. "I brought a proper outfit for you, but I suppose you won't be wanting it?"

Kura shook her head and tried not to frown. She'd never considered herself a prude, but that outfit was simply indecent. *Gods, I can see almost all of her legs!*

"Well..." Serika stepped back to push aside the flap door. "We can begin, if you're ready."

Kura let out her breath. She was ready; she had to be ready. She didn't feel ready.

Aethan offered a little wave—as though she were merely taking a trip to the next town over. "Good luck."

Kura nodded, then followed Serika into the Pokalfr house.

It was a small space, hot and humid, lit only by the glow of the bed of coals in the center of the dirt floor and the sunlight that barely seeped through the covering. Serika made her way across the room, crouching to avoid hitting her head on the domed roof.

"You can take a seat," she said, motioning to the empty space across from her.

Haltingly, Kura sat cross-legged on the damp floor, leaving the bed of coals between her and Serika. The thick air caught in her throat as she tried to take in a deep breath and calm her nerves.

Serika retrieved a small wooden bowl and shook a dusting of its contents on the bed of coals. Yellow flames sprang up as the substance fell upon the embers with a crackle, and then tendrils of smoke rose to fill the tent with a pungent scent.

"The purpose of Pokalfr," Serika began, looking up at her, "is in the journey. The body is but the vessel. It must be forgotten for the mind to be free."

Kura nodded placatingly and did her best to keep from frowning. The room was stiflingly hot; she wiped the sweat from her brow before rolling up her sleeves. Serika picked up a small evergreen branch from the ground beside her and placed it delicately on the coals, whispering something under her breath. Harsh grey smoke emanated from the smoldering branch. Kura pressed her sleeve against her nose.

"You must be open to the experience for Pokalfr to work," Serika said. "An open mind is free, but a closed one is trapped and stifled within the body."

Kura sighed and reluctantly lowered her hand. She still tried to keep from breathing in too deeply, but the air was so heavy with steam and smoke she struggled to breathe in the first place. Sweat trickled down her spine and stuck her shirt to her chest—maybe Serika had a good reason for wearing so little.

"First, we must give our offerings to the gods." Serika pulled a handful of dark, rich soil from a pouch beside her. "Ehlis, in honor of Jameu."

Kura nodded, trying to at least appear grateful for Serika's efforts. She couldn't help but picture her mother staring her down with that irksome, matronly scowl.

"The youngest crops, watered by Arakt." Serika pulled out a few green sprouts and placed them on the glowing bed of embers. "Fire, in honor of Réleil." She sprinkled a handful of small, opaque crystals on the coals, and as each fell a bright blue or green flame flared up. "And finally..." She pulled a silver blade from her satchel. "We seek the protection of Tácnere, the guardian, who once shed his blood for us."

Kura flinched as Serika pierced her own finger and let a few drops of her blood fall onto the embers. She held out the blade.

"I can't. I mean, I shouldn't. I don't think I believe in a Tácnere."

"Kura," Serika whispered harshly. "You have to—that is how the ceremony works. We always seek the intercession of Four. And you, of all people, need a guardian."

Kura wrinkled her nose as she stared at the bloody blade, Ìsendorál a weight on her hip. At this point, what was another lie? Gingerly, she took the knife and held it over her index finger. Then, with a deep breath, she pricked her own skin. The cut wasn't deep, but it hurt more than it should, considering she'd done it to herself. A few drops of her own blood, black in the dim light, fell and landed with a sizzle on the burning embers.

Serika took back her blade, handing Kura a thin bandage. Kura wrapped it around her bleeding finger, and Serika retrieved a small drum from behind her. Softly, she eased from it a slow, steady beat, and began to whisper. It seemed nonsensical at first, but gradually Kura came to understand she was repeating a single word.

Nansûr.

Time dragged on, as slow and steady as the beat of that drum. Kura took in another deep breath—for whatever little good it did— as the heat and incense surrounded her, enveloped her, until it muddled and confused all her other senses.

"We are going on a journey now," Serika said as she continued to beat her drum. "Close your eyes, and do not open them until the journey is complete."

Kura looked up. That... was a command? Serika glanced in her direction, and Kura pressed her eyes shut.

"All journeys have their destinations. We must get there quickly."

The drumbeat quickened, and Kura's heartbeat quickened with it.

"We are running through the forest. Trees tower above us, the sunrise shines over the hillside before us."

Kura drew in a breath. She heard crunching leaves, and she had to fight the impulse to open her eyes.

"There is a stream running beside us. A bird calls above."

The noises came again, this time gently flowing water and the loud call of a bird. Kura's heart pounded in her chest now. The room was stifling her; she grew lightheaded no matter how many breaths she took.

"We are running away." Serika's voice was smooth and calm, and now seemed to come from all directions. "We don't belong where we were, we must run away. Where are we running to?"

It took Kura a moment to realize she was supposed to answer the question. "I..." Her voice came as a whisper. "I don't know."

"This is not about the destination, then, this is about the journey. The journey is the destination." The drumbeat sped up again, and Kura wiped away the sweat that trickled down her face. "Picture a place. Secluded, secret. In the forest, surrounded by tall trees."

The image came to Kura's mind, and it was almost as though she was there, like a dream.

"There is a bright sunrise above the mountaintop which is shining down on you. Everyone is waiting for you there. Can you see them? Who is waiting for you?"

The faces of Kura's family came into her mind, distant and immaterial but just as precious as they ever could have been.

"But you left them?" Serika's question came as calmly as those that had come before, but a shock of pain pierced Kura's heart. She *had* left them. "You're running away. Where are you running from?"

"Nansûr," Kura whispered. The answer came automatically.

"Nansûr," Serika repeated. The drumbeat slowed. "Where is Nansûr?"

"I don't..." Kura started, but then there came the rustling of leaves and suddenly the image came to her mind. She didn't mean for it to be there, but it came all the same: a place with tall trees by a babbling creek, lit up by the rising sun. *Nansûr.*

And suddenly the Grey Lady was there too, standing in the shadows of the trees like a phantom. Her cold, black eyes met Kura's, and the woman smiled. Kura froze. She hadn't run far enough. The Grey Lady had found her anyway.

"Darling, I knew it was only a matter of time."

Kura swallowed, her throat dry. "Until what?"

"Until you gave me what I wanted." Vahleda grinned. "It was a lot more work than I expected, though. And since you've been rooting around in my memories, it's only fair I get to take a peek through yours." She sauntered forward, her hips swaying beneath her colorfully embroidered brigandine armor.

Kura turned and ran, but it didn't do any good. The Grey Lady stood before her no matter where she turned. The woman reached out and grabbed her face—fingernails digging into her cheeks—and held on with forceful precision. The sunlit forest churned into a swirling mass of colors and darkness, and Kura screamed.

It didn't hurt—not physically—but the woman was in her head, rooting through her memories as though they were pages in a book. Short, bright images flashed across her eyes—her home, her favorite possessions, the face of each and every person she had ever loved—and then it was over.

Kura found herself alone in darkness, chest heaving. Her limbs trembled with relief. It was over. But then she noticed the points of starlight, outlining the silhouette of the leafy trees towering above her. And, with sinking horror, she realized where she was.

Among the trees, a boy screamed.

"Benger!" Kura heard herself calling out at the top of her lungs. Fear surged through her like she had never felt before or since this night. She was running, her legs powering beneath her as she tried to push aside the tall brush growing up around her. It blocked her path and tore her hands and cheeks. "Benger!"

In the light of the moons she saw him: his tall, lean frame seated on the ground beside a dark creature. Kura stopped, her feet skidding on the dew-wet grass. The creature looked up, the moonlight glinting off its curved horns and the silver drool that dripped from its bared fangs.

It was a saja. Her younger self would have had no way to know, but she recognized it now.

"Kura, take Faron!" Benger's voice was rich with adrenaline, enough to make him sound angry, but she knew better. He never got angry. Kura ran forward, and the dark outline of Faron's little shape separated from Benger's shadow as she fell to her knees at his side. Faron was still, his hands pressed together, his limbs trembling and his eyes wide—he was too shocked to even cry.

The creature lunged with a growl, and Benger screamed again.

"Go!" Pain elevated the pitch of his voice. "Go!"

And then she was running, Faron's little body locked tightly in her arms. The shadowy darkness around her blurred into a wash of black and grey, but she could still hear Benger screaming. Tears streamed down her face, but she kept running. She just kept running, and she didn't look back. She didn't even look back.

A shock of cold yanked Kura from the memory and she gasped, falling forward to brace herself against the dirt. She was back in the Pokalfr tent—she recognized the heat, the smell, the sticky sweat covering her body. Only now the embers burnt low, and she was soaked with cold water. Serika stood before her, an empty wooden bucket in her hands, and while fear still showed on her face, she managed a smile.

"Are you back with me? Are you alright?"

Kura froze, eyes wide, too numb to answer. And then it all came flooding back: the vivid images of a memory she thought she'd so long ago forgotten. A sob caught in her throat, and she covered her eyes with her arm. She was too ashamed to let Serika see her cry, but she couldn't hold back the tears.

"It's alright," Serika said softly. Kura felt a hand come to rest awkwardly on her shoulder. "I'm so sorry. It's alright. Do you want to talk about it?"

Kura shook her head, swallowing. Gods, she thought she'd banished these tears, beat them down into some forgotten corner of her heart where she wouldn't have to dwell on them. But maybe she had dwelt on them anyway. Why did she get up before the sun every day to train? Why had she been so set on leaving the Wynshire? A thousand decisions made a life, but hers as it was now could in some ways be traced back to that one horrible night.

She drew in a shaking breath and wiped the lingering tears from her cheeks. She wasn't that helpless child anymore. "I saw Vahleda," she whispered. She looked up at Serika. "I think she believed me."

Serika rummaged through the satchel beside her and pulled from it the talisman necklace Erryl had made, slipping it over Kura's head. "I expect she did." Serika smiled shyly. "You achieved *kalfr*. It is supposed to bring about a sense of clarity and peace."

Kura wiped the sweat from her upper lip. That memory had left her dazed, and she struggled to think in the oppressive environment of the room, but all the same she found herself laughing. *Clarity and peace.* Well, she'd found clarity at least.

Serika frowned. "Are you feeling alright?"

Kura just let her smile fade. "How do we know if it worked?"

"I suppose we will have to wait."

Chapter Fifty

Arbitration

Triston woke with a start to someone shaking his shoulder. He sat up, fumbling for the sword he ought to have had at his side, and instead found the shadow of a figure standing at his shoulder, firelight from the open door behind her illuminating her silhouette.

"Shh," the figure whispered harshly. "It's alright."

"Idris?"

The figure nodded. She wore a riding dress, the skirt sewn up the center like pant legs, with sleeves that cinched at the wrists. "I need you to come with me. I mean, would you come with me?"

Triston pulled himself up to sit on the bundle of blankets that made this sorry excuse of a bed. "What is this about?"

"Don't you want to go to Edras? Didn't you ask to intercept the soldiers before they arrived?"

"You're sending me to Edras?"

The girl tugged on her braid. "No—I mean, possibly. Just come with me?"

Triston studied the shadows of her face under her hood. She was being awfully insistent. "Alright."

Idris latched on to his shirt sleeve. "Hurry."

Triston let the girl drag him from his bed, then followed her at a jog down the hallway. He brushed back his hair with his hand and tried to tuck his baggy shirt into his pants—at least when Renard had hauled him up for that council meeting he'd been given a chance to look presentable.

They rounded the corner, and Trofast's echoing voice met them. "That is beside the point!"

Triston came to a stop. A small crowd had gathered in the narrow hallway—Trofast, Renard, and two Fidelis he thought he might recognize, all huddled in a semicircle around a single, cloaked figure. A figure who was clearly not welcome.

Idris continued forward, then turned back when Triston didn't follow. She peered up at him in desperation. "Please?"

Tentatively, Triston stepped after her.

"I brought him," Idris called out, her soft voice struggling to carry over the rest of the noise, but every gaze turned to look at her anyway.

Trofast stomped his hoof. Anger flashed in his eyes, and everyone except Idris pulled back. "Girl, I said I did not want—"

"Please." Idris placed a hand on Trofast's arm—she looked like a child about to beg for sweets from her father. "Just hear him out?"

Trofast snorted, but did take a step back.

The cloaked figure nodded to him and gave something that was more akin to a curtsey than a bow. "My liege." The man righted himself and his hood fell back, exposing his face.

Triston recoiled from him. This was not a man at all, this was—this was a saja? One without horns and who walked like a man and dressed like a man... "You...?"

The creature flashed him a toothy grin. "Skellor. We've met before, actually. Oh, though maybe you don't know that." He pulled his hood over his head and let the deep shadows hide his face again. "Recognize me now?"

Triston inspected the creature with a frown, then his eyes widened. "Wait, you were the guard? Outside Tarr Fianin?"

"Hey!" The creature laughed, and threw back his hood. He sent a meaningful glance in Trofast's direction. "See, me and him go way back."

The centaur scowled. "And why am I supposed to find that comforting?"

Skellor tilted his head, but Idris stepped forward to stand between him and Trofast. "Please—you said you'd come here in good faith. You've already broken through our security, and now you antagonize us?"

"That's a fair point." He sighed, then pulled a folded bit of parchment out of a pocket on his cloak. "I wanted to speak with

Kura, actually—I sent her here, you know. You're welcome for that."

The group remained silent, and Idris looked up at him with pleading eyes.

"Right. Sorry. Anyways..." Skellor placed the parchment in Triston's hand. "Since she's not here, I'll give this to you. Might be more your thing, anyway." He leaned closer to Triston's ear. "I kind of saved your life, by the way. Just saying."

Triston continued to frown, but unfolded the parchment. He had to read it twice before he believed what he saw. "This... this is a request for negotiations."

Skellor nodded. "And signed by your father, right?"

"Seren, actually."

"Hmm. That's not what it says at the bottom, see?"

"True enough, but Seren wrote that signature."

Skellor raised a shaggy eyebrow, maybe more intrigued than anything else. "How do you know?"

"You can read it."

Skellor smothered a laugh. "Well, very good. I knew that already, though."

Triston examined the note again. It appeared official—it had the proper seal. "How did you get this?"

Skellor held his hands up at his sides. "Some soldiers tried to pass through, we tried to stop them. They shot at us, we shot at them—it was a whole thing. Point is, they gave up first and left that behind." He looked to the rest of the group. "I had the area scouted. This Seren's waiting at Renann. He's got about two hundred men backing him, but he appears to be holding to the traditional neutral-zone restrictions."

Trofast grunted. "It's obviously a trap."

Skellor shrugged. "Probably."

Each of them slowly turned to face Triston, clearly expecting something but apparently too timid to ask.

Seren wasn't exactly the person with whom he wanted an audience, but it didn't seem like the leadership here was willing to consider his more than decent proposals, and this might be the only chance he'd get to leave *before* a battle began. He took one last look at that parchment, then shoved it back into Skellor's hand. "I'll go."

Renard stepped forward, with a bit of a laugh. "Kid, we both know he'll kill you—"

"Maybe not." Triston turned to each of them with a bitter grin. "What have you all got to lose? Me? But if I can get word to my father, we'll win this thing."

Silence settled over the group.

"Damn," Skellor whispered. "How did that girl...?" He looked Triston in the eye, serious now. "I can get you some cover, for when he tries to pull something."

Triston nodded his thanks.

"I'm coming." Renard stood at Triston's side, almost like a guard at attention.

Trofast narrowed his eyes at the man. "This is where you'll stake your life?"

Renard's shoulders sank, but he didn't look away. "I've not sworn any oaths to you. You said that here, I was free to follow and refuse orders where I saw fit."

The centaur nodded solemnly. "I did say that. If only this were the first time you made me regret it."

A grin flashed across Renard's face, and he stood tall again as he surveyed the rest of the group. "The traditional restrictions say three of us can show up, right? So we get one more?"

"I'll do it." Idris spoke so quietly Triston barely heard her, but Trofast stepped back in surprise.

"You will?"

Idris managed to smile at him. "I will."

The centaur let out a low, rumbling sigh. His ears were pinned back against his neck—by his stance, Triston figured he'd protest—but the centaur's dark eyes were vacant, like a man watching a funeral procession.

"Then so be it." He scowled at Skellor. "I thank you for this information, Varian. And now I never want to see you again."

Triston's horse came to a lumbering stop at the side of the cliff. Renard and Idris had taken the lead, but while they both dismounted Triston had to stare at the rocks overhead. *So this is Renann?*

The jagged cave entrance looked as though had it split from the mountainside a millennium ago. The edge rose above the dense forest, rocky slopes spotted with pine trees wherever it wasn't too steep for them to take root. At a glance, the shadows beneath the swaying branches hid the entrance altogether.

Triston would have liked to think he'd remember a place like this from his history lessons, but considering all those stories had involved—at their best—intense trade agreements and treaty negotiations, he hadn't been paying much attention. Given the circumstances, that might have been a mistake.

"Go on," the horse said, shaking his back. "Get off."

Triston did as he was told, peering up at the gaping cave mouth. Light emanated from the center of the darkness—it seemed to flicker, as though cast by flames. He heard no voices.

"You're heavier than you look," the horse grumbled. He'd said his name was Akachi. "They should have chosen someone else for this. I grew up on a farm—I pulled a plow to earn my keep. I'm no warhorse and I don't want to be."

Triston patted the animal's neck. "Few do." He followed Renard and Idris, who came to a stop beside the cavern.

"One person stays here," Renard said, nodding toward Idris, then met Triston's gaze. "I'll follow you inside."

Triston nodded. That was simple enough.

Renard had a hand clenched on the sword hilt at his side, and Idris alternated between pacing and muttering what must have been prayers under her breath. The horse spared them one last glance then trotted off into the forest, back the way they had come. They were afraid. Triston didn't blame any of them, and yet he didn't share the sentiment. What had life in Edras prepared him for if not this? He grinned. Not life in Edras—*Seren* had prepared him for this.

He glanced into the forest behind them. The dark shapes of Varian archers shifted amongst the gently swaying branches. If he hadn't known to look, he might have missed the fact they were there at all. Not a comforting realization, but soon enough he'd likely appreciate the backup. He didn't expect they'd listen to him, but they'd probably help him out of this should things take a turn for the worse.

He strode into the cavern, Renard following a step behind. The narrow walls and low ceiling crowded around him, but he could walk without stooping or brushing his shoulders on the sides. Daylight faded into shadow, and when he rounded the corner, shadow became firelight.

The cave widened here, creating a small natural room. Torches hung on the walls and a single beam of sunlight streamed through an opening in the ceiling to illuminate a large stone slab.

"Well, I've been wondering if anyone would show up."

Seren stood at the opposite side of the stone. His helmet sat on the slab before him, but the etched plate armor he wore sparkled in the torchlight—because of course the suit had spent far more time on its display frame than actually doing anything useful.

Triston didn't bother to reply, studying the soldier standing a few steps behind Seren's right shoulder. Colmac. His armor was respectably worn, and he stood with a hand resting on his sword hilt, watching the room with something close to an amused grin.

He had black eyes. Like Merric's.

Seren's brows creased in some semblance of sympathy. "Are you alright? I told him not to hurt you."

Triston grunted and placed a hand on his belt, near enough to his sword so he was ready to draw it. "Just present your terms. You and I both know you don't have to negotiate right now. What's your secondary gain?"

Seren measured him, then managed a likeness of a smile. "You're serious about this, aren't you?"

Triston let the words linger, and finally Seren shook his head.

"I... I guess I just had to see it for myself. I suppose I don't have terms, really—I exaggerated in that letter. I just wanted to talk with you."

"What about?"

Seren slumped forward to lean against the table, losing all pretense of formality. "Triston, this is useless. The rebellion has no chance here: you about admitted that much yourself already. I didn't set out wanting to make an enemy of you. I swear, I wanted to explain all of this. Why do you think I asked you to come along with me to the Wynshire? I thought if you saw for yourself—I thought this trip would present the opportune moment to..."

Triston took a step back. The man was serious—he felt like a fool to believe it, but he knew Seren too well. He meant every word.

"...but you began asking questions I wasn't prepared to answer, and I had no opportune moment."

Triston smothered a laugh. "It's my fault then, is it?"

Seren almost smirked. "I didn't say that. Still..." He straightened. "I made a mistake, Triston. I'll admit that. But I'm asking that you put that behind us."

Triston nodded placatingly. "So you're calling the whole thing off? You're sending the troops home? You'll let me speak with my father?"

"No." Seren laughed, frustration tainting his expression. "I intend—"

"You intend what? To lie to me all my life, to leave me beaten half to death in some prison cell, and still expect me to just—?"

"You forced my hand!" Seren's voice echoed in the cavern. He sighed and rubbed his temple. "Triston, you don't have to fight and die for the likes of them. Work with me, and I can get you out of this."

"No you can't."

Seren raised an eyebrow.

"No one can. I couldn't see it before, but I've always been in this. Nature of my heritage, I guess. And it's about time I started making my own choices."

"You don't know what you're saying."

"I know enough."

Seren shook his head slowly. "No, you don't." He looked down at his hands, and Triston tried to ignore the unease twisting in his gut. Seren looked... nervous. "I went to the forebears' legends first, Triston, honestly I did. That prophecy sat unfulfilled for nearly two hundred years, and yet there were still so many waiting to see it come to pass. So we tried to fulfill it for them." He scowled and shook his head. "For whatever good that did anyone. The Fidelis had their chance, and they squandered it on a man whose life would have been better spent working the fields than sitting on the throne of Avaron."

Triston clenched his fists. "So you're going to draw my father out on a false pretense, and then make sure he dies somewhere along the way? That leaves you with the throne, doesn't it? As long as you get rid of me."

Seren's expression hardened. "Let the sword fall where it may. I have done enough already. Just know I never meant for you and—" A hint of sorrow pierced his composure. "I never meant for you to be caught up in any of it."

Triston laughed incredulously. "Well, I am caught up in it. Does that change anything?"

Seren watched him for a long moment, then turned to look up at the cavern walls. "When the *Elaedoni* failed me, I turned to the *Myrk'aviet*. The Svaldans and their gods are a waste of time, merely some misguided shadow of that which our forebears brought with them from across the sea. But nearly all the texts agree that the Essence and the Crux are powers that shaped this land for thousands of years before any of our kind set foot on it. They are powerful remnants of ages dominated by monsters and beasts." He gave the trace of a smile, although it didn't linger. "And that was when I found her."

Triston flinched and stole a glance around the cavern, as though he expected the Grey Lady to suddenly be there.

"Her soul's still human, I think. But she's undeniably powerful. And demanding." He looked Triston in the eye. "You do have a choice, Triston. You'll tell me where Nansûr is willingly, or I'll be forced to let her drag it out of you."

Triston began to laugh, but he knew first-hand how serious Seren really was. "This is neutral ground. If we can't come to some sort of agreement, then we both walk out of here, unharmed, and take this fight to the battlefield."

Seren scowled again and placed a hand on his helmet. "I—"

"Get down!"

The voice echoed in the cavern, then four arrows shot over Triston's head. At least one struck with a clang against Seren's chestplate, and another grazed the man's ear. Triston ducked behind the table, drawing his sword, and Seren cursed as he shoved on his helmet.

Triston whirled around. Renard pressed against the cave wall as two cloaked figures ran down the corridor, each of them with bows in hand. The nearest nocked another arrow and loosed it, but Seren leapt to the side.

"Hey, this is—" Triston started, rising from his place behind the table, then realized whatever law of chivalry he was trying to uphold had already been irrevocably broken.

"Guards!" Seren flung his hand out to his side. Darkness seeped from the shadows, then a staff appeared in his hand.

Triston stumbled back in surprise, but Seren pressed forward, spinning the weapon with impressive speed to knock aside the next two arrows the Varian loosed at him. The shaft was longer than a spear, and had a straight-edged blade on one end and a curved one on the other.

Cries echoed from the other end of the cave as soldiers flooded the room. The Varian took a step back behind the table for cover, but Triston lunged, thrusting his blade at Seren's neck. The man parried—not well, as the opposite end of his staff struck against the low ceiling, but it was more than enough to knock Triston's blade aside.

The double-bladed weapon would have been cumbersome despite the cave, but Seren maneuvered it with ease. They used to spar with one another—infrequently—when Triston was younger, but after he'd beaten the man squarely in a match at age thirteen, Seren had found enough excuses to ensure they never crossed blades again. It was a shock to find himself stumbling back to keep from being struck by one of Seren's strikes.

He lunged to the side and thrust his sword at Seren's guts, but the man caught his weapon in the crook of the staff's curved blade. With a flick of his wrist, he wrenched Triston's weapon from his hand and sent it clattering into the center of the room. Triston pulled back—bashing his shoulder against the cave wall—and met Seren's gaze.

The man hesitated, eyes wide. This was the precipice of one step too far, and he knew it.

He thrust his blade at Triston's heart.

With a shout, Triston blocked the strike with what he had—his bare hands. The blade slipped along the top of his arm, then sank through the plates in his brigandine armor and into his shoulder. Triston bit back a scream and wrenched the weapon out of his flesh. Seren still held on to the pole, but he wasn't moving—he was just staring at the blood on that blade.

"*You idiot!*" A woman's voice echoed in the cavern, ringing in Triston's ears over the cries of the surrounding men. "*Just pull back! The girl's already given me what I need!*"

Seren did pull back, ripping his weapon out of Triston's grip, but he stared at the red stain seeping from Triston's shoulder. Triston clamped his jaw shut, pressing his hand over his bleeding wound, then froze.

He could see the woman—the Grey Lady.

She was nothing more than an opaque image, shifting in quality, like some sort of hallucination. She wore ancient brigandine armor, similar to that which Avaronian princes had worn generations before him. Her pale blonde hair was done up in dreadlocks and tied behind her head in a thick braid. A smile tugged at her rosebud lips, and she stood with her hand on her hip as though she belonged there—as though she had been there the whole time.

"*Stare if you have to, darling.*"

A soldier's cry wrenched Triston back into the moment. Men had flooded the cave, each fighter charging with sword drawn as Seren slipped back behind their line. Triston leapt forward to follow, but ducked as the nearest soldier swung a sword at his head.

He jumped to his feet, about to draw his dagger, when the soldier hesitated.

"Triston?"

"Garan?"

A dumbfounded grin spread across the man's face, which twisted into a snarl as he spun back to face his own company. "All of you! Stand down!"

The soldiers paused, but Seren's voice rang out from the rear and they pushed forward again.

Triston caught hold of Garan's arm, knowing the old captain would obey him over Seren any day. "Come on!"

He followed the retreating Varian, grimacing as the motion aggravated his wounded shoulder, and Garan tagged at his heels. It was chaos, but Triston counted four Varian plus Renard fleeing from the incoming band of soldiers, so it seemed they were all in one piece.

The ground shook and stone cracked deep in the ground, the sickening sound echoing through the cave. Rocks fell in the center of the cavern as thick vines shot out of the ceiling and wove together to form a barricade between the rebels and soldiers. Idris's work, without a doubt. Men screamed as they fell among the wreckage, but it didn't stop everyone.

"You!"

Triston ducked as Colmac lunged, swinging a sword at his head. Both Garan and Renard broke from the retreat to fend off the few other soldiers who'd made it through the barricade—the former parried, avoiding any killing strokes, but the latter didn't hold back. Triston drew his dagger, then lunged as Colmac came at him with another sweeping strike. He used his small blade to deflect the soldier's larger, then stepped within the man's reach and grabbed hold of his arm. Triston yanked the man forward and slammed his face into the cave wall.

Colmac screamed, then whirled around, his blade striking rock in the process. Triston tucked into a roll and slipped under the attack, then jumped to his feet behind Colmac and slit his throat. Hot blood stained his hand; in disgust, he kicked Colmac's body to the floor. The soldier's limp form clattered into a crumpled heap against the cave walls, but then he rolled to the side, slashing his sword at Triston's ankles.

Triston leapt back, muttering a curse.

Unnaturally thick blood oozed from the gaping wound in Colmac's neck, but his black eyes seethed with unquenchable anger. Triston scrambled backward as Colmac struggled to his feet, and with growing horror he recalled what he had so foolishly forgotten he'd witnessed in Dol.

A maniacal grin twisted across the soldier's bloodstained face, and he raised his broken sword. "Justice is the tool... of the righteous when..."

Triston kicked Colmac in the face, the force throwing the man's head back against the cave wall. That slowed him a little, and Triston had time to jump away as Colmac swung at him again.

Sunlight flashed on a bare blade. Colmac froze, and then the man's head toppled from his shoulders, his helmet ringing against the stone floor. Renard stood in the man's place, sword in hand. He was splattered in blood—possibly some of it his own—but he grinned.

"You've got to cut their heads all the way off."

Triston snorted. "Why?"

Renard shrugged, then began jogging back toward the rest of the retreat. "Talk to Erryl or somebody if you want to know the whys. I'm just here to kill 'em!"

Triston took off after him, keeping a hand pressed against the bleeding wound in his shoulder, and after a few strides emerged into the sunlight outside the cave. The Varian were already gathered there, along with Garan. Idris leapt from her hiding place behind a rock outcropping and flung her arms down, drafting a mess of thick, tangled vines over the entrance, which temporarily sealed them off from the other side.

Triston breathed a sigh of relief and leaned against the hillside to steal a few precious moments of rest. The jagged slopes provided a natural barrier between them and whatever troops Seren had brought with him. They had maybe two minutes before someone peeked over the ridge.

"Sir!" Garan jumped to attention. The man was nearly trembling, and struggled to look at him directly. "They said you were dead, sir! And after I let you leave Pedrida in that boat? Sir, I've just been sick to my stomach about it. Didn't I tell you, sir, these were strange times? We all came out to fight, but then I saw you, sir, and—"

Triston laughed. "At ease, soldier."

Skellor stepped forward, slinging his bow over his shoulder. "That went well. You all ought to scurry back to your little mountain—"

"No." Triston pushed himself to stand up straight, turning to Garan. "My father's here, right?" He really didn't need to ask. His father always fought on the front lines—every self-respecting

Avaronian king had, as far as he knew. They swore to do as much in their coronation oaths.

"Yes, sir, with General Lavern's and Lord Therburn's companies, over the hill a ways."

"Then that's where I'm going."

Chapter Fifty-One

Among the Fallen

Kura let out a slow, methodical breath as she fought to steady her pounding heart.

The rhythm thundered in her ears, and might have drowned out the silent forest had the cool dirt at her hands or the other rebels' shoulders pressed up against hers not kept her in the moment. Erryl knelt at her left and Aethan stretched prone at her right, but all of them watched the basin clearing through the branches.

It was a gorgeous morning, one of those sunny, cloudless days that was warmer than autumn should be, but still cooler than the typical summer day. A gentle breeze blew through the treetops, making the sunlight cascading through the branches dance on the forest floor.

She still felt her mother's fingers in her hair as she tied it back, heard Elli's soft crying; she saw her father and Faron—dressed in their worn and battered armor—looking up at her with an impossible blend of pride and fear and hope. Her father wasn't well enough to fight, but Faron had been sent off into one of the side companies. The fonfyr had been given a position of prominence.

A stick snapped in the valley, jerking her back to the present. She clenched her fists and peered over the cliff's edge to the bottom of the basin. It remained empty as it had been before, patchy sunlight beaming down on the boulders strewn about the grassy clearing. But Vahleda was supposed to come here.

Aethan let out a muffled sigh beside her and shifted his position. Kura glanced over at him, but his narrowed eyes stayed fixed on the ravine before them. She set her jaw. She should have been watching the field, too. Why was it so difficult?

She traced her finger along the embossed edge of the quilted gambeson Erryl had given her that morning. It fit better than that cumbersome plate armor they wanted her to wear. But even this and the chain mail shirt felt bulky compared to her homemade gambeson. If Aethan hadn't come knocking on her door, she might have left it behind.

He'd given her another prayer, shorter this time, which she forced herself to remember. He said Gallian had written it, so what better prayer could there be for this moment? *Essence, shield me from the blade, guard me from the arrow, and keep me from destruction. But if I should die, let it be with my sword in hand and my face toward home, on the field of victory.*

Leaves rustled in the tree over Kura's head. She stiffened, but it was just a bird—no, a flicker—which landed unceremoniously on a branch. Kura sighed again, but the bird squawked and suddenly she remembered Lâroe. She glanced up again, giving the bird a second look. It simply started to preen its wing.

A shadow passed over the trees, then the dark silhouette of a creature crossed between them and the sun. Another bird, maybe, but its huge wings didn't appear long enough to support its stocky body. It opened its jagged mouth and let out a shrill cry.

A black dart shot up from the ravine. The saja howled and plummeted to the ground, its wings limp.

"Erryl!" Kura grasped the man's arm. *Some twitchy archer just gave away our position!*

"It's alright," Erryl said, wrenching free of her grip. "We want her to know we're here."

The weight of those words sank into the pit of Kura's stomach. This was it, then. This was what they'd all come for. She clenched the hilt of the sword at her side, heart pounding.

I'm ready. I'm ready.

Saja charged into the valley, their figures tall and twisted even while obscured by the trees. Their fur was shaved in odd patterns, arms and chests marked with colored paint, and horns decorated with bits of bone, hair, and skin—trinkets collected from past victims. The horde let out a battle cry, an eerie sound animalistic enough to remind anyone listening of the gruesome death that waited.

Kura balled her shaking hands into fists.

Rebel bowstrings twanged along the ridge, raining arrows into the basin. Many saja howled in pain, but any who didn't fall continued to advance. The rebels let loose a second barrage and more saja fell—among them a bear, a dozen bolts protruding from his chest. Adrenaline surged through Kura's veins. She knew it already, but it was a comfort to see it again: even monsters could die.

A sharp horn blasted from somewhere beyond the ravine, and growls, shouts, and footfalls thundered in answer. More saja of all shapes and sizes—wolves, bears, large cats, four-legged creatures with antlers, and strange figures she didn't recognize—charged into the ravine to replace those who had fallen. She was about to jump to her feet when Erryl placed a hand on her shoulder.

"Hold."

She met his gaze, opening her mouth to ask why, when the archers began to loose at random. Saja along the front line fell, one after another, creating mounds of bodies, which the others had to vault over, though that did not stop them. Erryl rose to his feet, flinging his arms out to his sides, and a gust of wind circled the ravine. The tree branches swayed, but the saja gave no sign they had even noticed.

Suddenly, the ground shook. Kura scrambled to her knees and shoved her round wooden shield into place on her left arm. With a deafening crack, the steep, rocky cliffs lining the basin fell into the clearing. Dust rose from the valley, obscuring her view, but she heard the boulders rolling to a stop in the grassy plain and the dying screams of saja crushed underneath.

The trap had *worked*.

She leapt to her feet, a cry already on her lips as she yanked Ìsendorál from its scabbard—and the rebel company answered. She charged toward the edge of the basin, Aethan at her side, as the dust continued to rise from the valley, bringing with it the monsters' howls and the clash of metal against metal.

Erryl waved his hand, and the dust whipped back from the edge to reveal a misshapen mass of debris that would serve well enough as a staircase. "Go!"

Kura didn't hesitate, and a dozen rebels followed as she leapt from one large fallen stone to the next until her feet landed on the soft grass of the valley. With a snarl, a saja met her at the bottom; it had a bleeding gash across its face and it limped toward her, dragging its back leg. There was a look of death in its one good eye. She fell upon the creature with a shout, severing its head from its body.

Every second after that was utter chaos.

Boulders filled the valley, some four times her size, some only half, and around most of them a monster waited. The first was some sort of enormous cat, curling tusks protruding from its lower jaw, and she felled it with two quick thrusts. The second was a smaller creature—a fox?—nipping at her ankles. A downward slice severed its head from its shoulders. The third was a wolf...

Each sword stroke blended into the next as Kura pressed through the mess of boulders. She weaved between the stones, using some for cover and others as a vantage point as the saja closed in around her. Some she deflected with her shield, the rest she brought down with a flash from Ìsendorál. The dust caught in her throat and the air stung her lungs, but each gasping breath declared she was still alive. Gloriously, temporarily alive.

At last it seemed the final saja lay dead at her feet. Kura sagged against a boulder as every cut and bruise on her body throbbed at once. The sounds hit her like a wave—the shouts of man and beast, the clashing of swords and the twanging of bowstrings, and the cries of pain and rage and joy all merged together into an incongruous roar that hung over the valley like the rising cloud of dust.

A figure charged toward her, and Kura would have run her blade through him had she not finally registered that it was Aethan, calling her name. She lowered her sword, fear seizing her as she realized what she'd nearly done.

"Take out as many as you can—Trofast will bring in the second wave." Aethan's face was dirty and splattered with drops of blood—she hoped it wasn't his own—but he still held his swordstaff in hand, and only paused long enough for her to nod in reply.

A horn sounded from somewhere in the forest, low and long, reverberating through the trees. It stirred something in Kura's chest, and even though she'd never heard that tune before, she knew without a doubt what it was. Both she and Aethan ran to scale the large boulder in front of them.

Her breath caught in her throat. The lingering cloud of dust obscured some of the battleground, but the other rebel fighters, most in groups of two or three, were darting between the rocks to take out the saja that trickled in from the forest beyond. Bright light flashed in the corner of her eye, and she turned as a man sent a burst of fire through one of the crooked stone alleyways. It was a Fidelis. Of course it was a Fidelis.

A woman stood beside the boulder, coaxing tendrils of water up from the ground, which she used to pull the saja to pieces. There was a man near the edge of the forest, waving his arms above his head as one tree reached down and plucked several saja from the ground. The creatures screamed as the branches twisted around them and tore them apart.

It was surreal. Kura knew what she was seeing, but her mind struggled to accept it. It was more incredible and terrible than she could have ever imagined.

A large spear smashed into the boulder at her feet, pattering bits of stone against her leg. Both she and Aethan stumbled back as a large saja—a bear—a few paces away hefted another spear.

Kura caught hold of Aethan's arm, then dropped to her knees and dragged them both to slide over the edge of the boulder. The ride was jarring and the landing rough, but she picked herself up, locking eyes with Aethan. "Go right!"

She darted around one side of the boulder while Aethan ran to the other. The saja lumbered toward them, then stretched toward the sky to let out a roar that shook the ground. That roar echoed in the marrow of Kura's bones, but she was too high on adrenaline and too set on living to feel anything beyond brash courage.

She ducked behind her shield as the beast swatted at her, taking the blow without losing her balance, but even after Aethan jabbed the thing in the chest with his blade, the saja kept advancing. Snarling, it dropped onto all fours and swung its head from side to side, fangs bared—taunting them.

A second roar shook the boulders. Kura scrambled back, Aethan with her, her gut clenching at the thought of facing a second beast, but a mass of fur barreled into the saja's side, pinning it to the ground. It was Rusket. Clumps of his thick fur stuck out between the spaces of his shining shoulder guards and chestplate, his muzzle already stained red with blood. The saja writhed beneath his paws —its claws slid across his armor with an earsplitting screech—but Rusket bent low, roared in the monster's face, then tore out the creature's throat.

Stunned, Kura stood useless as Rusket lifted his head to stare her down. Fresh blood splattered his face and dripped from his teeth, and the animalistic gleam in those black eyes was hauntingly familiar.

He turned and spat on the grass. "Humans."

Panicked rebel cries carried from the forest, along with the yips and howls of beasts. Kura set her jaw as a fearful resolution tightened in her gut. A second wave of saja streamed into the ravine, fur sleek and eyes alight from the scent of blood. Without a word or even a glance between them, Kura and Aethan—Rusket behind—charged the front lines.

Vaguely aware of the bodies by her feet, Kura ran through the maze of stones. In the back of her mind, she knew that with one true look at the horror around her she'd lose her nerve—and under no circumstances could she afford to do that. So she pretended she didn't see.

Rebel fighters trickled in from amongst the boulders, another face joining the group each time she looked. Most of them—both human and nostkynna—appeared to be congregating at the forest's edge, lining up shoulder to shoulder, brandishing weapons or baring fangs, and so she followed. She let that be her symbol of hope, a sign that everyone else wasn't as lost as she was.

She fell into one of the open spaces in the rebel line as the wave of saja charged from the forest. She couldn't begin to count how many fell by her blade, but she fought, with Aethan on her left and another woman on her right, until her shield arm shook and her shoulders burned with each swing of her sword. Still, she didn't stop. She couldn't stop.

Shadows—strange, shifting masses that grew and shrank like flashes of darkness—drifted in the forest. It was as if small clouds were passing overhead, intermittently blotting out the brightness of the sun, but the sky remained blue as ever. Kura suppressed a shudder. This wasn't right.

A man charged from the forest, among the saja. He wore a soldier's uniform, except that across his polished chestplate he'd painted garish symbols in something red enough to be blood. He brandished a sword, and Erryl broke from the line to meet him.

Kura struck down the saja at her feet, then joined Erryl in the charge. The Fidelis whipped his hands in front of him, catching the wind in the small clearing between the boulders and the forest in a whirling gust. The soldier leapt aside, stumbling as the cyclone knocked him off balance, but he threw an open hand forward then clenched his fist shut.

Kura screamed. Erryl's body just seemed to... implode. His chest folded in on itself, wrinkling flat like a bit of meat left to dry in the sun. The man toppled over, blood oozing from his mouth as his eyes bulged in a blank look of surprise.

Another Fidelis charged, pulling a dirty root from the ground and impaling the soldier on it before one of the other rebel fighters sliced off the man's head. Kura swallowed, blinking hard, as she forced herself back into the moment. Her hands shook—not from exertion this time—as she ran, but Aethan and the other woman were already a few steps ahead of her. Sheer panic gnawed at the hardened confidence that had held her together so far. But she couldn't give in to that. Not yet.

A second man—a second vojak—emerged from the forest, following one of the saja. He carried no weapon. He needed no weapon. Panicking, Kura ducked behind her shield and charged at him.

She juked to the side, then leapt over a diving saja to swing at his neck. He jumped back, bringing his arms into guard in front of him as every tiny vein in his hands began to radiate darkness. The air around Kura tensed, as though it could weigh her down, but with a shout she severed the man's outstretched hand from his arm.

The man yelled, and the air burst into flames. Kura turned away, ducking behind her shield as the wave of fire passed over her and disappeared. Pungent smoke rose from her singed shield and tunic but she lunged, plunging her sword into the man's chest.

His mouth dropped open, and his eyes went wide. The irises were a deep brown, but where his eyes should have been white they were black—blacker than black, as black as a cloud-filled sky on a night with no moons. He began to scream. The man's mouth was open, but the scream emanated from somewhere deeper, somewhere within his chest.

Kura leapt back, yanking her sword from the man's body, her knees trembling. *He's dying, isn't he?* That, of course, was what she wanted, but she hadn't expected this. The pitch of the man's scream rose as thick, black-red blood oozed from the mark in his chest. And then the sound cut out entirely, and he crumpled into a heap at her feet.

This was not the man she'd killed. This body was a time-withered corpse held together by garish armor.

Rock crackled against soil. Kura threw up her shield to block a large stone that hurtled from the forest. The impact shoved her arm against her body, knocking her to the ground. She struggled back to her feet, wincing as she moved her arm—her shield had crumpled into three pieces, one of which dangled off her arm by the strap.

Another vojak, bright emblems emblazoned on his chestplate, shouted something, and Kura dove out of his path, still shaking the remains of her shield off her arm, as a second stone crashed into the ground where she had been standing.

She lunged at him, slashing wildly. With her shield gone, the new habits Triston had tried to teach her melded with the old she was supposed to forget, and in the end she found herself moving with no sensible direction or style, and barely kept from tripping over her own feet.

The vojak pulled back, eyes wide as he stared at her blade. "It can't—"

Kura plunged her blade into his guts. The man began to scream, but—clenching her eyes shut—she removed her sword and turned her back to the spectacle. She couldn't see it again.

Bodies of her fellow fighters lay in broken heaps all along the clearing between the trees and the boulders. Sorrow and nausea mixed in her throat, but there were still voices—figures fought back the saja among the flashes of darkness a stone's throw away from her in every direction. They hadn't lost; the enemy had pulled away from her. And only her.

A lone soldier seated on a white gelding emerged from behind the trees. He wore the most handsome set of silver armor Kura had ever seen, and a flowing grey cape settled around his shoulders like fog might around a snowy mountain peak at sunrise. She thought he was the king, until she really noticed his face and realized she knew him. It was the grey-eyed man.

Shit.

He had something in his hands, a staff something like Aethan's, but on both ends there was fixed a blade—the first straight, the second split and curved, like a cupped hand. A word echoed back to her from somewhere deep in dreams or memory: the *atgár*. The man himself, however, appeared a bit disheveled. His right shoulder was stained from a bandaged but bloody gash on his ear, and his horse wheezed like they'd just finished a gallop.

The saja who'd pulled away from her in fear gathered at the grey-eyed man's feet. They strode forward with him, their heads held high with renewed purpose. The rebel company gave shouts of dismay and scattered, breaking formation as they ran for cover among the rocks. Kura turned to follow them, but caught a glimpse of her own reflection, tinted red on Ìsendorál's rusty, blood-soaked blade.

No. It echoed in her mind like a command. *The fonfyr can't run.*

Drawing in a shuddering breath, she jogged after them, trying to peer over the massive boulders and through the lingering dust. They kept going—they were running for the hill and they weren't looking back. She skidded to a stop, then put her fingers under her tongue to produce a sharp whistle. More than a few faces turned to look at her, and she raised her sword.

"We hold them at the rocks!"

"Come on!" A hand caught hold of her arm, and Kura spun around to find Aethan dragging her farther in among the boulders.

She almost tried to plant her feet in the dirt, to refuse to follow him, but shouts carried between the other rebel fighters. Most of them—at least those she could see—weren't running any longer. They ducked for cover, brandishing weapons, and it seemed Aethan was only trying to do the same. Relieved, she stumbled after him into the cool shadows of the nearby boulder, stealing a glance over her shoulder.

The grey-eyed man still advanced, saja flanking him on each side. He was too calm as he surveyed the battlefield; his grey eyes scanned bodies of rebels and saja alike, and he didn't so much as blink. How a man found such ease among the dead, she didn't want to know. His beasts charged in among the boulders to engage with the re-forming rebel line, but he continued his leisurely stroll. He was searching for something.

Saja—short, doglike things with rounded little ears—circled around their boulder from both sides. Aethan struck at the nearest snarling face with his staff, but they crept forward, nipping at their ankles. Kura jumped up onto the boulder, boots finding purchase enough for her to climb the sheer slope, and Aethan followed her, whacking aside any saja that tried to do the same.

"Back!" Kura shouted, slashing the nearest across the face. It wasn't the most creative thing to say, but the beasts listened, whimpering as they bared their fangs at the blade.

A cry carried from beyond them, and a rabble of rebel fighters charged the pack from behind. The saja snarled and split into two masses, attempting to fight on both fronts, which gave her and Aethan the chance to beat them away from their boulder and reclaim their hiding space.

Kura slid to the ground, falling into a fighting stance with the stone at her back and Aethan at her side. He took a step closer to her, holding his weapon in guard, as the saja warily eyed her sword. Her heart pounded so loud in her ears it was a wonder she could hear anything else, but they had a chance like this—a slim chance, if there were still more rebel fighters willing to aid them.

The saja retreated. Kura watched them, shocked, until they circled around a certain white gelding to regroup. The grey-eyed man sat in his saddle, watching her through narrowed eyes—it seemed he'd found what he was looking for. He snapped his fingers then pointed towards the heart of the valley. The saja bounded off in that direction, screams echoing after them.

The grey-eyed man dismounted slowly, *atgár* slung casually over his shoulder. Kura thought about running, but there was nowhere to go, so she tightened her grip on her sword.

"He's the leader," she said softly.

Aethan grunted, swordstaff gripped in white-knuckled fists. "I figured that."

The grey-eyed man strolled towards them, gaze weighing her. She and Aethan shared a glance—his wide eyes said he didn't know how to handle this any more than she did—and they lunged forward together, weapons raised.

The grey-eyed man knocked her strike aside easily—she wasn't even in range of touching him—but Aethan pressed onwards, his single-bladed swordstaff glancing off the grey-eyed man's weapon, and the two began some sort of deadly, balanced dance.

The air hummed with the spinning of staffs, the sound interrupted only by the repetitive thwack of wood against wood as the grey-eyed man forced Aethan toward the boulder. Kura hesitated, spinning the hilt of her sword in her grip.

Finally, she found an opening.

She lunged to thrust her sword into the grey-eyed man's exposed side. The blade caught against his shoulder guard and he leapt back, parrying her strike before it became lethal. Then, with two impossibly swift motions, he sank one end of his weapon into Aethan's gut and then sent the other end upside Kura's head.

There was a flash of white and a moment of darkness, then she found herself on the ground, ears ringing. A voice screamed in her mind for her to get back to her feet, to rejoin the fight, and her fingertips brushed against Ìsendorál's hilt on the ground beside her.

A shadow passed over her face. The grey-eyed man stood over her. Kura grasped her sword and thrust it at his guts, but he drove his blade through her arm. She screamed, pain surging through her, then lashed out with a kick.

She missed.

The grey-eyed man knelt down, driving his knee into her stomach, then plucked the talisman necklace from her neck. She struggled beneath his weight, air catching in her throat as his sharp knee drove the breath from her, but he didn't even look her in the eye.

The grey-eyed man rose slowly, crushing the pouch in his hand with a curious frown, and Kura gasped for air as soon as his weight left her stomach. But his staff's blade was still in her arm, pinning her to the ground.

A sound like rain pattered against the grey-eyed man's plate armor. He gave a frustrated cry and stumbled back, yanking his blade from Kura's arm. She bit down on a scream as the blade caught against her bones—but an instant later she was free, struggling to her knees as she cradled her bleeding arm against her chest.

Tendrils of water flashed over her head. Aethan was on his feet, his swordstaff gripped in trembling hands, and he pressed forward, a thin sheet of water swirling around his arms and his weapon. The grey-eyed man scowled then strode toward Aethan, his staff whirring as he spun it before him.

Kura grabbed her sword with her good hand then forced herself backward, scooting across the grass. Aethan walked past her, meeting the grey-eyed man's jabs stroke-for-stroke. Water lashed through the air, striking the man wherever his blocks left him exposed. He parried most of Aethan's strikes, but not all—and soon points of bright red blood marked his silver tunic. But Aethan's stomach was redder still, and the stain widened as each successive swing of his swordstaff grew weaker.

Kura gritted her teeth, braced against the boulder behind her with her good arm, then hauled herself to her feet. She adjusted her grip on the sword—she'd fought left-handed before, enough to be good enough. But then she froze.

There was a second outline following the grey-eyed man's. Another person made each of his movements with him. She blinked hard, wondering if the battle had broken her mind, but she only saw it more clearly. It was Vahleda, her hands gripping that weapon, moving as it moved.

A low chant issued from the forest. It was an eerie sound—rhythmic, almost melodic—a harsh cacophony of voices punctuated by the snap of metal on stone as arrows flew from the trees.

The grey-eyed man muttered a curse, then took a step back as he sent a few final, hasty blocks in Aethan's direction. A second barrage of arrows rained in from the forest, joined this time by a thundering of hooves. Centaurs, dozens of them—each adorned in quilted gambesons and carrying bows and pikes and longswords—

charged into the valley with such an air of confidence that Kura had to cheer. And she didn't cheer alone.

The remaining saja pulled back to the grey-eyed man's flanks, and they slipped away among the boulders as Kura ran to Aethan's side. He collapsed to his knees; the water hanging in the air fell around them with a muffled splash.

Kura slipped her shoulder under Aethan's arm as the thundering of hooves came ever closer. He smothered a wince as she pulled him to his feet, and he kept his hand pressed against the gash in his stomach. Fear caught in her chest. The blood had already soaked through his shirt.

There came a sharp whinny, and Kura turned around—N'hadia galloped to a stop at her side, followed by her father, Piotr.

"Trofast's called the retreat, we were supposed to be part of the battle here but we were ambushed by soldiers—" N'hadia's eyes widened. "Kura! You're—"

Kura sheathed her sword. "Help him."

Aethan grunted and muttered some sort of disagreement under his breath, but N'hadia had already grabbed him under his arms, as if he were a child, and set him down on Piotr's back. She offered Kura her hand. "We're here to get you out."

Gratefully, Kura grasped the centaur girl's arm. N'hadia swung her up onto her back, then galloped through the boulders.

Kura took in a breath with each of N'hadia's thundering footfalls. *Are we winning?* It didn't feel like it, but they had killed *so many* saja. She cringed as Aethan yelped and held his side, pain contorting his face as he struggled to stay on the centaur's back.

N'hadia whinnied, her hooves sliding on the grass as she slowed to join the rest of the centaurs on the other side of the valley. The company charged uphill, most of them carrying riders or nursing some sort of injury. There were hundreds—surely there were hundreds? She started to count, then stopped herself. Maybe it would be better for her—for all of them—if she didn't know.

Shouts carried from the rear. Soldiers kept the pursuit, shooting at the centaur herd with crossbows.

"Duck!" N'hadia shouted, and Kura leaned to the side as the centaur girl swung around, bow in hand, and loosed a few quick shots behind them without changing pace or direction.

Trofast charged past at a gallop. "Keep going!"

N'hadia let out a frustrated snort, but she swung around and picked up her speed. In little time Rih Hill loomed before them, the sunlight shining gold on the tree-covered slope. Trofast veered right, cutting down toward the river, and the rest of the company followed him.

Shouts rang out from the rear—the soldiers were gaining on them, but the centaurs charged into the river. Cold water kicked up by N'hadia splashed against Kura's legs, and the slosh of hooves in the river roared like a waterfall. The soldiers maintained their pace, and an occasional arrow smacked against the rocky river cliff sides.

"Go!" Trofast took a few jogging steps past the open tunnel entrance, then turned around, snatching a few arrows from his belt quiver. The lead centaur ducked into the tunnel, and the company pressed together to charge into Nansûr.

Trofast loosed arrows, dropping each nearest soldier with a single shot to the right eye. His motions were fluid and calculated—as natural as a blink or a breath—and Kura watched in awe. He didn't miss once, nor did she expect anything less. N'hadia gave a frustrated snort, pulling up her own bow as she began to veer toward Trofast.

"N'hadia!" Piotr scolded, and the centaur girl reluctantly fell back into line.

They passed through the tunnel opening; the air shifted from warm sunlight to cool darkness. The echo of voices and hoofbeats was deafening, but N'hadia charged into the stable area at a near canter and came to a jarring halt along the far wall. The space was already filled with people, nostkynna, and centaurs, and more poured in from the outside.

Kura drew in a shaky breath. *Faron.* She turned, frantically scanning the surrounding faces, hoping against hope to find him easily. Every eye she caught was a stranger's.

Trofast's shout carried from the end of the tunnel, although Kura didn't understand what he said, and then came a shuddering boom. The light within disappeared and Trofast charged out of the darkness, dust billowing at his heels.

The entrance had been sealed. Permanently.

"Regroup!" Trofast shouted as he galloped past. Mud and blood splattered his blue-roan coat, but he wasn't even winded. "Regroup!"

"Why are we retreating?" Kura whispered. She wasn't sure she should be told, but she had to ask.

N'hadia swished her tail, stomping her rear hoof. "They're trying to split us up into small factions they can pick off one by one. This might give up Nansûr, but we need to regroup—we need somewhere we can take a stand together!"

So, this was their last-ditch effort. Somehow the girl made that sound like an exciting challenge.

Kura slid down from her back, wishing she could find even a modicum of that enthusiasm, but at this point all she felt was numb. Aethan gave a grunt as he struggled to climb off Piotr's back, and Kura rushed to catch him before he toppled to the floor. His face looked pale, even in the dim torchlight, and a large red splotch now stained the front of his tunic and trousers.

"I'll find a healer," N'hadia said quickly, and before Kura could respond, the centaur girl had taken off into the crowd.

Carefully, Kura helped Aethan to the wall and lowered him down beside it. He grimaced at the effort, clamping his jaw shut to keep from vocalizing the pain. *Is this my fault?* Tears stung her eyes. *He wouldn't be here if it wasn't for me.* If he hadn't believed she was something she wasn't.

Aethan looked up, catching her gaze. "Hey." He gave a valiant attempt at a smile. "This isn't over yet."

Chapter Fifty-Two

PRETENSE

"Just a bit farther, sir. Up this way I think," Garan said, for the third time.

Nodding, Triston tried not to scowl. The captain meant well, of course, but his little remaining patience was wearing thin. Over the course of this mostly uphill trek, the cool of the morning had given way to the increasing warmth of the midday sun—plenty of time for battle to have broken and turned, all before he even got there.

He winced as he rubbed absently at his injured shoulder. Idris had done what she could, which was far better than nothing, but in the end Garan had bandaged the wound and they'd headed on their way.

Figures moved among the trees ahead, and both Triston and Garan stopped. It was four men, each dressed in polished chestplates and short red cloaks. They shouted to one another, and the nearest pointed in Triston and Garan's direction. They could be anything from friends to allies to abject enemies, and he didn't have the luxury right now of asking.

"Disarm them," he said to Garan, before drawing his sword and charging.

The nearest man stumbled back, drawing his weapon, but with one quick sweep Triston disarmed him and moved on to the next man. The two of them parried one another for a few strokes, but in a matter of three more Triston had disarmed him, too, and lunged for the next man.

"Wait!"

Triston froze, then stared at the man's face in surprise. "Dylen?"

"It can't be..." Dylen's eyes grew wide, and he stepped back, pointing his blade at Triston's chest. The two disarmed men scrambled back behind their captain, staring with similar shock. "You, you..."

"It was a lie, all of it," Garan said, stepping up to Triston's side. "Seren—"

Dylen waved Garan aside but didn't break from Triston's gaze. "What's your mother's name?"

"Lyara. But anyone would know that."

"Right." Dylen glanced down at his feet, scratching his chin. "What's your horse's name?"

Triston smirked. "Ash. And you made fun of me for not choosing something more original."

"Triston!" A wide smile spread across Dylen's face, but it didn't last long. He smacked Triston on the arm with the flat of his sword. "How do I know you're not, I don't know, a ghost or something? I saw the body myself, the seal ring..."

Triston sighed and knocked the sword away. "Dylen, I need to find my father. Whose camp is nearby?"

"My father's, Therburn's, Lady Rigan's..." Dylen straightened. "My father left me in charge, actually. Of the reinforcements." He looked Triston over, then laughed. "Gods, what are you wearing?" He squinted at the red stain on Triston's shoulder. "Wait, have you been stabbed?"

Triston brushed past him. "Come on, where's the camp?"

"This way." Dylen took the lead, his strides long and face serious. Those two other soldiers fished their swords out of the pine needles and fell into line behind Garan.

A loud horn blasted somewhere deep within in the forest.

"Shit," Dylen muttered. "Seren's calling for reinforcements."

Triston caught him by the arm. "Don't answer him. He just tried to kill me."

"What?"

Garan struck off on his own. "The horses should be back here, sir."

"Yeah." Dylen picked up his pace. "Come on."

After a quick jog, the trees lessened enough for Triston to spot the thin plumes of campfire smoke rising from the clearing. The company had chosen a defensible position for the camp, a small field nestled in among a ring of large boulders. But the smoke... no soldier would be careless enough to give away the position of his camp like that unless he'd already left it.

"Over here." Dylen motioned toward one of the nearest boulders, beside which dozens of footprints had worn a muddy path. Triston followed, Garan and the other two soldiers falling into single file behind him.

The place was nearly deserted; just a mass of short white tents remained, lined up among the few smoldering embers of campfires. A temporary corral hedged the far side, with some rope strung between a few stones and some scraggly pine trees. Most of the horses were already gone, except for several who belonged to the few lingering soldiers.

"Hey!" Dylen ran up to the edge of the corral. One soldier turned back, halfway in the saddle, standing in one of the stirrups. "I need those horses. Um, General Lavern's orders."

Confused but obedient, the soldier dismounted, and he and the other two men handed their horses' reins to Triston, Dylen, and Garan. The man eyed Triston rather strangely, then gasped as Triston swung himself up into the saddle.

"Triston, sir?"

Triston drove his heels into the charger's side, and the animal took off like an arrow from a bow. He pressed the horse between his knees, grinning at the burst of speed. This was how an animal was supposed to run. He nudged the reins to direct his mount through camp, scanning the tree line in the distance as he followed the departed company's prints.

"This way!" Dylen's voice rang out over the hoofbeats, and he steered his bay stallion to the left. Beyond him, between two large boulders, the forest thinned; among the sparse branches Triston caught glimpses of the main troop.

He yanked the reins to the side, his horse's hooves sliding on the grass, but they held the turn and were soon charging neck and neck beside Dylen. Sunlight flashed off the soldiers' silver armor and Triston used that glimmer as a beacon. He smacked the horse's shoulders with the ends of the reins. The stallion shook his mane, ears pressed flat against his neck, but responded with a second burst of speed anyway, thundering past Dylen and leaving Garan far behind.

The soldier line loomed before him, creeping ever closer. Triston muttered a curse under his breath and eased back on the reins. He was charging into a battle between royal soldiers and a rebel army—dressed as a rebel. His horse continued forward at a loping trot as Triston debated his options. He was going to have to risk it.

He drew his sword, then dug in his heels.

A short horn blasted from the front of the company, and the soldiers scattered in all directions, responding to whatever was happening at the front lines, where he couldn't see. If the captain had already called a formation break that wasn't a good sign, but Triston set his jaw and directed his horse to the center of the fray. The nearest rider came at him with a shout, brandishing a spear. Triston deflected the strike and charged past him without breaking stride.

Calls echoed from among the men behind him, warning the next as he galloped past. He couldn't help that. He juked around the trees, keeping his body low against the horse's neck. With any luck, he wouldn't wind up with an arrow in the back.

Breaking through the scattered soldiers' formation, he stumbled into a narrow field where the air was thick with the heat of battle. Huge, muscular centaurs—dressed in quilted gambesons, wielding swords and pikes three times larger than any regular man of their stature could—formed the opposing line. Their formation was crude and disorganized, but the piles of dead and dying men and horses testified to their proficiency. Triston yanked back on the reins, muttering a string of curses as he fought to keep his horse secluded among the trees.

He was caught between two armies, and at the moment he didn't rightly belong to either of them.

"Triston!" Dylen's voice managed to carry over the sound of everything else. Triston turned back and found his friend standing in his saddle, approaching with at least six other soldiers in tow.

"Get them out of here!" Triston shouted, waving back toward the forest. "They're going to get slaughtered! Regroup back at camp."

"What about you?"

Triston gathered the reins tighter in his grip as his horse fidgeted beneath him. "I'll..." He didn't have a good answer. "I'll meet you." He nudged his horse forward, then held on as best he could as the charger lurched down the small embankment and took off through the narrow path between the evergreens.

A horse whinnied behind him, and Triston turned back to find a centaur tagging at his heels. He was running out of curses, but he sputtered some anyway and drove his horse forward.

The centaur juked beside him, then swung a massive broadsword at his head. Triston blocked the strike, yanking his horse around to better face him for the next one. The centaur raised his blade again, then hesitated.

It was Konik, Trofast's brother, from the council. His eyes narrowed, but he lowered his sword. "What are you doing here, little one?"

"My father!" Triston shouted over the battle. "I find him, I end this war!"

The centaur grunted, studying him. Finally, he lifted a burly arm and pointed to Triston's left.

Triston nodded in thanks and took off.

He turned his horse downhill, and the animal gained speed with each thundering footfall. The fighting diminished, quiet in sections where the bodies of men and centaurs—mostly men—littered the ground, half-buried in twigs and pine needles. Triston had seen the dead similarly mangled dozens of times before, but this time it haunted him. This time he might have been able to prevent all of it.

Shouts ahead drew his attention. While there may have been men's among them, man was not the source. They were animalistic cries, deep and loud and rumbling, and Triston easily recalled the first time he'd heard them. *Saja.*

He drove the horse harder, whether the animal had any more speed to give or not.

A monster snarled somewhere below and his mount brayed, jerking away as it reared up on its hind legs. Triston held himself in the saddle with his knees and pulled the horse's reins to the side to get the animal turning in a circle. Reluctantly, the horse listened, but continued to wheeze nervously as the creature growled again.

It was definitely a saja—some twisted, grey creature that looked something like a wolf—and it lunged, nipping at the horse's back legs. He wouldn't be able to both keep his seat and reach the saja with his sword, not with his mount this agitated. Triston let out a frustrated sigh, then drove the horse onwards. If the two of them couldn't fight together, they could at least run together.

The charger left the saja behind in a matter of seconds. Triston juked the horse right, cutting uphill and behind a dense grove of trees. And stumbled into the heart of the battle.

Centaurs lined the right side, half of them charging at the advancing saja with pikes as the rest shot them down from a distance with arrows. Triston pulled back on the reins and paused a moment to find his bearings. There were saja here, yes, but very few—and each time one fell, a soldier replaced it. So, that would have to be Seren or Tanith's company. That at least made them a clear enemy.

Triston nudged his charger on, but the horse hesitated, snorting —one of the saja carcasses along the soldier's line had spooked it. He forced it to keep its pace and allowed it to veer off to the side.

"Hey!" One rider broke from the soldiers' line and charged after him.

I don't have time for this!

Triston smacked the horse's shoulders with the reins—he had seen the thing's speed before, he could rely on that. The charger darted forward, leaping over a fallen log. They sailed through the air, then landed with an awkward lurch on the uneven ground. The force threw him forward in the saddle, but he held on.

The soldier shouted again, then something sharp struck Triston's arm. The blow stung, but miraculously the rusty chain mail he'd received in Nansûr took the brunt of it. He spun his horse to the side and brought up his sword to meet the soldier's second strike. He couldn't be sure whether this rider recognized him, but after a few parries he caught the soldier's gloved hand and flicked his weapon from his grip by the crossbar.

Triston yanked his horse to the side, goading it toward the increasing density of soldiers. They neared a second clearing, this one wider and full of large boulders, but he needed to find the center of the battle. His father always fought somewhere toward the center. Cries and the crash of metal rang in the basin at his side, but he veered away, charging against the flow of soldiers.

There—a dense group of fighters he could just see through the trees. A ring of saja packed them in a circle; they were the only soldiers clearly working against the monsters instead of with them. Triston dug in his heels, and the horse met his request with the expected burst of speed until it caught sight of the saja. The animal snorted, turning off course as it tried to come to a galloping stop.

Triston leapt from the saddle, landed on his hands and knees on the forest floor, then picked himself up and charged toward the battle on foot.

The first saja he felled from behind, along with the second, but he caught a glimpse of the third's shining yellow eyes before he lopped off its head. Adrenaline pounded through his veins. His silver blade was an extension of himself, and he fought with a calculated ferocity that left no room for thought or error.

He broke through the saja line, then hesitated as he found himself face-to-face with a soldier. The man shouted and charged. Triston side-stepped the strike and kept running.

The soldiers called out warnings to one another, but Triston hardly heard them. He found his father's cloak—that short red one he always wore in battle—pressed with the other men in the front of the line, fighting back saja. A hand grasped Triston's shoulder; he shook it off. A sword swung at his neck, but he parried the stroke in stride.

"Father!"

The sounds of battle swallowed his voice, and he might as well have not spoken at all. Triston leapt forward and caught hold of his father's cloak.

Dradge spun around, his sword aimed at Triston's neck. Triston parried and Dradge lunged forward with a thrust. Triston caught his blade, spinning it upwards until their swords locked between them.

"Look at me!"

There were dark circles under Dradge's eyes, an unkempt beard on his cheeks, and it hurt to see the wrinkles on his father's face—it was like the past week had aged him a year. Rage burned in Dradge's eyes, but as they fell on Triston's face, the emotion drained from him. He was like a man frozen in time, caught between impossible hope and stoic disbelief.

"Father, it's me."

Dradge stumbled back. "Triston?"

"Yes, Seren—" A saja launched itself at his father's shoulder. "Get down!"

His father ducked, and with one wide swing, Triston sliced the creature's throat with the tip of his sword. Dradge glanced down at the writhing carcass, then spun back around to fell the next twisted creature that made its way through the line.

"Call the retreat!"

Dradge turned to him. "Why? We've almost got all these damned things—"

"Call the retreat!" Triston didn't have time to explain it all here.

Finally, his father nodded. Dradge picked up the horn slung over his shoulders and pressed it to his lips. Triston plugged the ear nearest the horn and listened with a sinking heart as that melancholy tune echoed out among the trees. Very few times had he ever heard that played in earnest.

"Come on!" Dradge motioned for Triston to follow as he made a break for a tree line not far away. The soldiers fell back as commanded, and Triston jogged at his father's heels until they reached the herd of horses the king's company had left among the trees. Dradge swung himself up into the saddle, Triston followed close behind, and together they led the charge back to camp.

As soon as his father's horse passed into the courtyard, Triston dismounted and moved to the edge to allow the other men who had followed to pass him by. Dradge circled his horse around to Triston's side then leapt from the saddle as the others rode in behind him.

Dradge stepped forward, slowly, as he studied every curve of Triston's face. He lifted a hand to touch his cheek. "How...?"

Triston tried to go back to the beginning. "Last week, at the edge of the Deorwynn—"

Dradge pulled him close and smothered him in a hug.

Triston grimaced as his father's arms crushed his injured shoulder, but relief overwhelmed the pain. It didn't seem possible, but for just that moment it felt as though he'd set everything in the world right.

"There were so many endless, dark days I can't even count them, and I thought I'd never see your face again..." Dradge pushed Triston back, gripping him by the shoulders. His eyes were red—only once before had Triston seen his father cry—but Dradge managed a smile anyway. "I have half a mind to never let you out of my sight again, boy." His eyes fixed on Triston's bloodied shoulder. "Look at you! What happened? Gods, what am I..." He took a step forward, waving a hand toward the rest of the company. "Hey! I need—"

"It's alright." Triston caught his father by the arm. "It's as good as it'll get for now."

Dradge frowned, but he let it go. "Did those rebels lie, then? Sending me that charred body, to do what?"

As succinctly as he could manage, Triston explained everything that had happened to him since Colmac deserted. At first his father was naturally skeptical, but all the pieces fit too well—Triston knew that himself—and as the story unfolded, Dradge's hesitance gave way to anger.

"Seren," he growled as Triston finished the story. The fire was in his father's eyes now, and Triston knew that nothing but blood would quench it. He'd seen that look once before, when his mother's body lay in his father's arms. It had scared him then. Not anymore.

"Those were Seren's beasts you were fighting out there, not the rebels'. This is what Seren wanted all along—to get you and those loyal to you to fight his battles."

Dradge met Triston's gaze. "Oh, we have come to fight."

Chapter Fifty-Three

FIRE

Kura sat against the wall in the dim, damp stable. Time streamed past and she made no effort to catch hold of it or slow it down. Her mind wanted to run through all she had seen, hoping to make sense of it, but her heart refused. Living it once had been enough; she didn't want to do it all over again. Voices droned around her, but she might as well have been dayrides away—she saw and heard everything, but felt nothing.

Aethan sat beside her. N'hadia had found a healer; she'd dragged the Fidelis over by her elbow despite the woman's protests. Kura had tried to apologize, but couldn't find the words—any words. Something about the woman's face made her think she might understand. Hopefully she did.

Her arm felt alright now. There was still a gash under her bandages, but given the circumstances she didn't really care. Aethan said he felt better, but he was just as pale, sitting there with his eyes shut and his head leaning against the wall. Kura watched him through sideways glances, obsessively checking to see if his chest continued to rise and fall.

Some part of her was begging to go in search of Faron, but her legs wouldn't move. She'd spent so many long nights struggling through his loss before; she didn't want to feel that pain again. So she didn't search. He simply had to be alive.

Absently, Kura's gaze came to rest on the mass of people wandering through the open space before her. There were centaurs, humans, and nostkynna. Almost everyone nursed an injury, some obviously more wounded than others. The company that had left Nansûr had been a people with a spirit of fire and unquenchable courage, but the company that returned—she drew in a breath. What were they now? Every face was despondent, and it startled her to realize she probably looked the same.

Was this what she had thought war was going to be? She'd never been foolish enough to expect a gallant quest for glory, and Lâroe had crushed any sense of that idea besides. But... had she imagined this? Death—that was what she saw around her, death in every face and around every turn.

Kura shivered, then frowned. She'd seen death before. She'd grown up in its midst, she'd both seen it and given it; the threat of death had been what drove her from the Wynshire in the first place.

Pulse quickening, she became acutely aware of the warmth of the blood that coursed through her veins. What right did she have to lose hope now? If she'd stayed in the Wynshire, or if she stayed where she sat, death awaited her either way. Was she going to die sitting, or die on her feet?

She pushed herself up and ran into the crowd, hands shaking with a newfound rush of courage. Many an eye turned to look at her, and she accepted it—relished it—and let it fuel her pounding heart. Stretches of wooden fence sporadically divided the stable. She jumped up onto one beam and climbed to the uppermost rung, steadying herself with a grip on the post that ran into the ceiling.

"Friends!" she began, her voice echoing farther than she had expected.

The buzz of conversation faded as those forlorn faces turned to look up at her.

"Do you remember what brought you here?" A silence lingered over the crowd, and most of them shared bemused glances. Kura chuckled under her breath. "I don't mean right here, but here at all. What drove you to this place?"

A murmur rippled through the crowd. Some of them must have had answers, but weren't sure how to share.

"I came from the Wynshire. I watched those I love suffer and die around me as I dreamed of the chance to change it." She held any gaze that met hers. "How many days did you spend in squalor, dreaming of that same chance? I probably spent a lifetime, hoping for the future but never really believing in it. Well, I tell you now—friends, we are living it!"

A few excited shouts rose from the crowd.

"A thousand moments we wasted away before this, and maybe a thousand we'll waste again afterward, but *this* moment—this moment of death and blood and courage—is the one that stands to make the rest of them worth living!"

A cheer rang out from the crowd, and Kura couldn't hold back a smile. They were a thousand mixed and broken people, but the cacophony of voices called out together in hope. She pulled Ìsendorál from the scabbard at her side and held it aloft. The rusty blade was nicked in places now, but still it caught the light of the torches, the inlaid lettering flickering red like fire.

"With this sword I promise, by my living or dying..." Kura gripped the post in her hand all the more tightly. "I promise by my living. I swear by the very life beating in my chest that I will not give up this fight until every last king's man stands in surrender, or lies dead on the battlefield. What do you say?"

The crowd roared. There were shouts and cheers and the pounding of hands and feet and paws against the walls and floor. A chant started somewhere in the back, although Kura didn't understand the words. She didn't *have* to understand the words. She almost felt like crying, but not out of sadness, and she found herself searching the faces gathered at her feet with the hope of catching Faron's eye.

"Kura!"

She turned back as Trofast cantered to a stop beside the stable fence. He studied her for a long moment, his black eyes holding hers with a stoic sense of wonder, then let out a deep sigh. "Come here."

Obediently, Kura jumped down to land noiselessly on the dirt floor. She shoved her sword into its scabbard before tentatively looking the centaur in the eye.

"You killed two vojaks," Trofast said.

"Yes, sir."

"How?"

"I... I don't know. Same way I'd kill anyone, I guess."

Trofast's eyes narrowed. "What do you know of vojaks?"

"Not much."

The centaur straightened. "The Essence works by giving energy—giving life, giving strength. But a vojak, he feeds on energy. You must have seen the darkness. The Crux takes what is and perverts it for its own purposes: a vojak pulls the life from what's around him to preserve his own. A Fidelis, properly trained, can heal injuries, where a vojak endlessly prolongs only his own life." He glanced down at the scabbard hanging from Kura's belt. "For a vojak to die, his head must be fully severed from his body—the heart separated from the mind, severing the soul. Anything less, the Crux keeps him fighting."

"But I didn't, and they still—"

"I know." Trofast placed a fist over his heart, and Kura swore she saw a smile in his eyes. "Keep up the fight, child. We all stand with you."

A loud, echoing boom shook the stable. She jumped, turning to the ceiling as thin columns of dust drifted down onto the crowd. She thought it was thunder, but Trofast's face said otherwise.

"Be ready." He reared up on his back legs and charged toward the open archway on the opposite side of the stable.

Kura watched him go, clenching her fist around Ìsendorál's hilt. The walls shook with another distant crash, silencing the crowd to a nervous murmur, and she snaked her way back to where she'd been sitting. Aethan had pulled himself to his feet, balancing with one hand pressed against the wall and the other arm wrapped around his stomach. He looked to her as another boom rattled the cavern.

"What is that?"

She shook her head.

Frenzied shouts—some fearful, some yearning to return to the battle—carried through the cavern. She swallowed, trying to hang on to the fighting spirit she'd found mere minutes before.

"Topside!" The voice rang out from the other end of the stable, and the message passed along until those gathered around her repeated it to one another. "Topside!"

The crowd flowed toward the archway. Kura took a few steps after them before she realized Aethan was not following her. "Come on, we've—"

He was still leaning against the wall, his hand pressed against the wound in his stomach. "Go on." He tried to give her a smile, but it was still far from convincing. "I'm just going to slow you down."

She closed the distance between them with a few strides. Even if that was true, she didn't care—she wasn't leaving him down here to be forgotten or buried in a cave-in. She retrieved Aethan's swordstaff, slung his arm over her shoulder, and together the two of them merged in among the moving crowd.

They crossed the flat plane of the stables easily enough, but when they reached the sloping path which led to the upper levels, Aethan began to struggle. His chest heaved against her side as he took each short step, but she kept a tight grip on his arm. Another boom shook the cavern, followed by a sharp crack from somewhere within the walls. She stared at the solid stone around her—it didn't seem possible for it to break.

Gradually the path leveled and the majority of the crowd stopped there, at the landing. Light, bright and natural from the sun, shone in from a few narrow windows along the top edge of the wall, carrying the fresh scent of the outdoor air.

Kura took another step forward, but Aethan didn't try to follow.

"I've..." A mix of pain and shame caught in his voice. "I've got to stop."

Kura met his gaze in concern, but he didn't lift his head. She took the few more steps needed to reach the wall and gently helped him take a seat beside it.

Shouts carried among the crowd—figures rushed back and forth in the cramped space, pressing against one another—before another crash sounded from the outside. Kura stumbled as the ground shook, and she frowned as she tried to catch a glimpse out of the nearby window. Someone must have launched something at the hill.

"I won't make it out there," Aethan said quietly.

Kura stared at him, even after he'd looked away. She didn't want to leave him, but she couldn't stay here.

Slowly, she handed Aethan his staff. "I'll—"

The ground shook, the air rang, the crowd screamed. A blast of fire billowed down the hallway, carrying with it shards of stone. Before she even blinked, it all hit her—the force of the sound, the heat of the air, the sting of debris. It threw her backward, and then everything went black.

She became aware of herself as a voice echoed in her ears. *"You lied to me."*

Vahleda. Kura cried out in surprise. She saw nothing and felt nothing, but the woman's voice carried out into the oblivion.

"What do you want?" she screamed. "Why me?"

Vahleda laughed, her voice fading as a distant point of light broke through the darkness. *"Darling, I don't give a damn about you. You just happened to make yourself useful."*

Kura could feel everything.

It was smothering her—the sharp stones digging into her body, the very air she tried to breathe. She coughed, her nose filling with dust. A single point of light, bright and blinding, pierced the cracks above her. Panicked, she squirmed toward it. The surrounding weight shifted, and with a gasp of fresh air, she hauled herself out into the open.

Limbs shaking and chest heaving, she pushed herself to her knees. The bright blue sky hung above her. She knelt on stones—stretching beyond her was nothing but stones, all the way to the forest at the bottom of the slope. She spun around. A jagged cliff that she'd never seen before towered over her head. And the sobering realization hit: this was Nansûr. She was kneeling on the rubble of Nansûr.

"Aethan!" Kura scrambled to her feet.

All across the hillside, humans, centaurs, and nostkynna were pulling themselves from the rubble. That wasn't a cliff behind her, it was a labyrinth of caves: Nansûr's tunnels were now exposed to the sunlight, and figures still moved in the shadows.

Voices cried out in the forest beyond the rubble, and a barrage of arrows rained down on the stones. A company of soldiers—riders mostly, with crossbows—charged toward the remains of Rih Hill.

Kura covered her head and ran, but where was she supposed to go? Her foot caught on something, and she fell onto her hands and knees.

It was a tree. She'd just tripped on an entire tree that had been buried in the rockslide.

"Hold the line!" That was Trofast's voice, bellowing over the rest of the noise. "Hold the line!"

Kura pushed herself to her feet on the unsteady ground, the breeze catching loose strands of her hair as Trofast—a great sword in each hand—charged past her, down the hill, to meet the incoming soldiers alone.

"Kura, come on!" N'hadia's voice this time; she came galloping down the hill with her bow in one hand and the other outstretched.

Hardly aware of what she was doing, Kura caught hold of N'hadia's arm, then jumped as the centaur swung her onto her back. Kura held on with her knees and stole a glance to either side. All across the hillside, rebels pulled together and followed Trofast to form a line.

N'hadia leapt from the final boulder and landed on the grassy ground below with a lurch. Kura toppled forward but managed to hang on to the quilted gambeson N'hadia had strapped to her horse's back. Still in stride, the centaur girl nocked an arrow to her bow and loosed it. She got off three shots before Kura even drew her sword.

Two charging soldiers fell from their saddles and N'hadia veered off, circling around the enemy line as she loosed several more shots. A few soldiers fell, but others quickly took their place. With a wild shout and the clash of bared steel, the two lines crashed together. N'hadia lunged to the side, still firing her bow, as Kura gripped the gambeson with her free hand, just hoping to keep her seat.

A soldier looped around from behind, his sword drawn. Kura swung back, meeting his strike. The look in his eyes was amazement and fear, all rolled into one. He pulled around behind N'hadia, so Kura turned to sit backwards to keep parrying his strokes. He pulled back on the reins, he and his horse falling in among the crowd.

And then the battle truly began.

A second soldier charged, sword drawn. Kura hopped onto her knees, balancing precariously on the centaur's back to beat away attacks without inflicting collateral damage as N'hadia maneuvered through the fray. Kura wasn't certain any of her strikes drew blood, but the soldiers steered clear anyway.

N'hadia pulled out of the clearing, then came to a galloping stop in the shade of the forest as she turned back to Kura with a laugh. "What are you doing?"

Kura spun back around to sit properly. "I don't know, I just—"

"Well, it kind of hurts! We'll have to get this figured out better for next time."

Next time. Kura shuddered. *This is far too early to start talking about a next time.*

Soldiers circled back toward Nansûr with a shout, catching many of the rebel line along them. N'hadia swung around and charged toward the fight, loosing three arrows as she ran. Three soldiers fell before they met the line, and one galloped away in a wide-eyed panic as Kura lashed out with her sword at anyone she could reach. A wake formed around them as the soldiers disappeared—either dead, wounded, or scared—and the enemy line split into two groups.

The smaller of the two groups retreated toward the forest, and N'hadia charged after them with a shout, still loosing arrows. Kura held on, excitement rising in her chest as the soldiers turned and ran. And then, with a jolt of fear, she saw why.

Vojaks, dressed in garishly painted armor, stepped out from among the trees.

The nearest man hurtled a blast of fire in their direction. Something beneath the ground shook, and suddenly the flames burst around them. N'hadia let out a whinny. Kura wasn't sure if the centaur fell or if something pushed them aside, but the next thing she knew she was on the ground, fire raging over her head before it died completely.

Kura tried to get up, aching from how she'd landed on the knobby ground. Beside her, N'hadia lurched back to her feet, swishing her tail and stomping her hooves as she tried to pound out the little flames that had started on her hair and armor. Kura felt incredibly small, sitting on the ground beside a centaur, and with a shout she realized she'd fallen onto the bodies of several dead soldiers.

Hands shaking, she snatched up her sword and scrambled to her feet. Soldiers' mounts churned the ground on one side of her and vojaks slipped between the trees on the other, and she clenched her sword all the harder to hold back the panic.

She noticed a discarded shield lying by one of the bodies—a soldier's shield, small and round with the bird and pointed cross of the Avaronian flag blazoned across it in rich black and red paint. The soldiers shouted and scrambled toward her, each of the nearest raising a loaded crossbow. Kura dove for the shield and hid behind it as several arrows flew over her head, and a few more sank into the wood with a thunk.

She peeked up over the rim. *How many shots was that?*

Kura sprinted for the forest's edge. The cool shadows shifted between light and darkness as though a strong breeze tousled the branches overhead—only there was no breeze. Figures darted between the tree trunks, casting fire or stones or tendrils of water between them.

She nearly laughed. The image was ridiculous—impossible—and yet that magic could kill her at any moment. Weighing her options, she took a few steps back. There were vojaks before her, soldiers behind, and a fractured rebel line scattered in pockets between.

She hesitated too long.

A figure leapt out from behind a nearby tree: a woman, dressed in a vojak's painted armor, who growled and threw her arms forward. Gnarled, dead roots shot up from the ground and tangled around Kura's ankles. She cried out in surprise and hacked at the vines, but the woman charged, drawing from the ground a long, wooden spike, which she wielded like a spear.

Kura brought up her shield and thrust her sword at the woman's neck. The shield caught the woman's arm but missed the spike. Kura bit back a cry as the wooden tip pierced her shoulder pads and stuck into her shoulder. The vojak let out a scream and stumbled, clutching at the gash in her throat. Kura sliced the woman's head from her shoulders.

It gave her some satisfaction to hear the screams this time, but she was more relieved when they finally ended.

A saja's snarl overcame the second of stillness, and Kura braced herself behind her shield as the beast leapt at her throat. The force of the impact knocked her back, but she planted her feet and threw the saja from her shoulder. The animal squirmed and jumped upright; she lunged and thrust her blade through the creature's heart.

Farther ahead a howl split the air, the mournful cry lingering over the relentless roar of the battle. Several more dark figures slunk out of the forest. She gritted her teeth, raised her sword and shield, then ran to meet the first saja. She felled that one, and then the second, and then the next, adrenaline driving her to fight even as her aching muscles begged her to stop. But she couldn't stop. Gods, she couldn't stop.

A saja snapped at Kura's sword arm. It sank its wolf-like fangs into her chain mail, then dragged her down onto one knee. She smashed the edge of her shield into the back of the saja's head and it yipped, pulling back—so she sliced through its neck.

Panting, Kura rose to her feet. The saja circled away—for the moment—as another figure joined her among the trees. He looked familiar, although blood marked his temple and cheek, and the shadow of his hood shrouded his bulbous face.

It was Cynwrig.

He swung his hands toward each other and she ducked, involuntarily, as droplets of water seeped out of the tree trunks around her. The water flew past and melded together into a long, thin strand that wrapped around the neck of the saja behind her and severed its head.

She recoiled as the saja's bloody corpse fell to the ground at her feet, but there were more behind it. She fell back into the motion, her shield the only thing separating her from the beasts before she ran them through. She swung her sword until her shoulder ached, held up her shield until her arm shook, but still the saja kept coming, forcing her to retreat—out of the forest and toward the line of soldiers.

They were overrun.

A man's scream shook the trees. Cynwrig fell, a pack of saja at his feet. Kura started to his side, but a saja caught hold of her ankle. She cried out—in frustration as much as pain, as its fangs didn't make it through her boots—and slashed the beast across the back until it let go. Fire burst through the shadows as another Fidelis leapt to Cynwrig's side, chasing the saja back, but he was already gone. His body was a mangled and red-stained heap, covered by a tattered green cloak.

Kura pulled away from the forest, emotion catching in her throat. No man deserved to die like that, and all she'd done was watch.

Saja pressed forward, another emerging from the shadows to replace each one she struck down. She let them push her to the edge of the forest, but no farther. A few other rebels—alone or in small bands—fought the monsters just as she did, but any step Kura made toward a companion, a saja lunged to cut her off. Which was better: fighting until she fell—like Cynwrig—among the beasts, or taking her chances in a charge against the soldier's line?

Arrows whistled among the trees. Yipping and howling, the saja pulled back. Kura ducked behind her shield and bolted for cover behind a nearby tree trunk.

"Kura!"

She flinched, then looked to the trees. Cloaked archers perched on the low-hanging branches, their bowstrings humming as they rained arrows on the saja below. The figure on the branch above her grinned and waved. "There you are!"

She nearly laughed in relief. "Skellor!"

"Told you I'd be here." He swiveled to fire an arrow over Kura's head.

She spun around, then ducked behind her shield as a vojak—a short soldier in simple garb painted with flowing blue runes—pelted her with shards of ice.

Hooves thundered beyond the forest and Kura braced herself for the soldier's charge. Instead there was a shout, a flash of sunlight on polished steel, and the vojak's head fell from his body. The figure's shadow passed over her, dwarfing her in darkness—it was Trofast, a bloodied broadsword in each hand.

"Get back to Nansûr!"

Kura bolted for the hill, and several others followed at her side. The rebel line had reformed somewhat, and was pushing the group of soldiers back ever so slightly. An opening might lead her through the skirmish and back to the caverns.

Soldiers shouted, pointing in her direction. Kura muttered a curse and spun around, raising her shield between her and the enemy line. Arrows whooshed past—most flew over her head, but a few stuck into the ground near her feet, and one landed with a solid thump in her shield.

Trofast whinnied. Kura peeked over her shield as he charged the soldiers' company. The men called out in a panic, scrambling to reload their crossbows as their mounts whickered and broke formation. The centaur reared up, striking one man from the saddle with his front hooves as he ran a second and third through with his swords.

Kura's mouth dropped open in awe. Three men down in a matter of seconds. The remaining soldiers retreated, the farthest man getting off a parting shot from his crossbow. Trofast flinched as the arrow sank into his shoulder, but it didn't even slow him down.

Raising her sword, Kura gave a shout and ran after him—and the remaining rebel fighters, who had been trying to flee, charged with her. Trofast pressed onward, cool and calculated, felling any soldier within reach of his blades or his hooves. A few crossbowmen raised their weapons, and Kura ducked behind her shield as the arrows snapped from the string. But they weren't aiming at her.

Trofast grunted, but still didn't slow. Streams of red seeped from where arrows stuck into his chest and flank, but the centaur kept running, so Kura kept following him. The soldiers veered to the side, quickening the pace of their retreat, and as Trofast moved to pursue them, she saw why.

The grey-eyed man rode from the forest and toward the rebel company, mounted on a magnificent white horse with the *atgár* slung over his shoulder. Fear seized in her chest and she slowed her pace, the other rebel fighters passing her.

With a piercing whinny, Trofast charged for the tree line. The grey-eyed man pulled back, his eyes narrowing as he lifted his weapon. The rebel fighters clashed with the group of crossbowmen at the edge of the forest while Kura took a few hesitant steps in Trofast's direction. She couldn't leave them, but she didn't want to die.

Trofast lunged, striking at the white horse with his front hooves, and swung his swords at the grey-eyed man's neck. The horse shrieked in anger, pulling back, while the man spun his weapon to block the centaur's advance. Kura squinted at the patchy shadows shifting across the grey-eyed man's figure. She knew what they were: Vahleda's ghost moving with him as he parried.

That weapon. She ran forward, an urgent sense of purpose overcoming her fear. The Grey Lady was tied to that weapon somehow. If she got rid of it, maybe she'd get rid of Vahleda, too.

The white horse reared up, juking away from Trofast, and with a shout of frustration the grey-eyed man fell from the animal's back. Trofast lunged, sweeping low with his swords, but the man thrust his straight blade upwards, catching the centaur in his horse's chest. Fear clenched Kura's guts, but she couldn't just stop now.

Trofast pulled back with a grunt, limping a little but still wielding his swords. The grey-eyed man scrambled away, pushing himself to his feet with the *atgár* before lashing out at the centaur. Shouts rang in the clearing. Kura turned back as a line of saja advanced toward her, followed by several royal crossbowmen—half the rebels were chasing the other soldiers into the forest, while the rest turned and ran to meet the monsters in stride. Kura ducked behind her shield as a barrage of arrows sailed past her, and she cried out as one grazed her leg. They weren't aimed at her.

Trofast stumbled back, his breath coming in rattling gasps, and Kura cringed to find most of the arrows now protruding from his back and flanks. Still, the centaur bellowed and swung at the grey-eyed man, his strikes sloppy but strong. The man leapt back, blocking the attack with ease. He knocked one sword from Trofast's hand, leaving the centaur's side momentarily unguarded, then drove his blade into the centaur's chest.

Kura cried out. The grey-eyed man removed his blade, and Trofast's legs crumpled beneath him. There was a look of satisfaction on the man's face, and he took a step back as though to admire his handiwork. Trofast, struggling to breathe, swung at the man with his remaining sword.

"Hey!" Kura shouted, only realizing how utterly foolish she sounded as her voice echoed back to her against the trees.

The grey-eyed man looked up and examined her face with an incredulous frown.

It was far too late to turn back.

She ducked behind her shield and jabbed her sword at the man's neck. He jumped back, swinging the *atgár* up to block her strike. But it wasn't just him. For that moment, as the sunlight filtered down on him through the branches above, Kura caught a glimpse of Vahleda's face hovering like a shadow over his.

While the grey-eyed man frowned, Vahleda grinned. *"Darling, I've been waiting for this."*

The grey-eyed man lunged, spinning his weapon before him with grace and ease. Kura leapt back, bracing herself as her shield took blow after blow from those double-edged blades. She'd had Aethan fighting at her side before. How quickly she'd forgotten how that had ended.

With a painful shout, Trofast—still crumpled at the grey-eyed man's feet—thrust his blade at the man's chest. The tip deflected off the grey-eyed man's plate armor, but slid to pierce the space between his shoulder guards and chestplate. He grunted, in both pain and surprise, and pulled back.

Trofast caught Kura's gaze. "I told you to go!" There was anger in his tone, but something else entirely in his eyes.

Kura could only stare mutely at the blood trickling down the side of the centaur's mouth.

The grey-eyed man jabbed his spear and Kura jumped into his path, blocking the strike with her shield. He stepped away, each motion fluid—like a dance, like he anticipated her moves—and swung the second blade around to slice through Trofast's throat.

Kura screamed. Trofast fell forward, his body spasming in the mud before going limp. Hot tears welled up in her eyes, but anger proved more potent. She lunged at the grey-eyed man with a shout, lowering her shield just enough for her to lash out—repeatedly—with Ìsendorál. The man stumbled back under the fury of her blows, but he still blocked them with ease. *Vahleda* blocked them with ease.

"You certainly fight like a fonfyr! They've filled your head with lies long enough that you believe them?"

Anger, two-fold, twisted in Kura's chest, and she pressed forward with renewed strength. The man stepped to the side, catching Ìsendorál with his curved blade, and then with a twist of his wrists wrenched Kura's sword from her hands. That red blade clattered to the forest floor, out of reach.

With a shout of both rage and fear, Kura struck at the grey-eyed man's staff with the edge of her shield. *Without that sword, what am I?*

A horn blasted in the forest, the sound sharp and deafening—and her heart sank. It was the royal army. She pulled away, shrinking behind her shield as she threw a glance into the forest beyond her. Shockingly, the grey-eyed man did the same with a look of concern.

The first rider emerged from the trees.

He sat tall in the saddle—his magnificent armor rivaled only by that of the grey-eyed man—and while he certainly dressed like a soldier, across his chestplate murky charcoal paint formed a large, flowing symbol. Kura's eyes widened. It was a hasty addition to their armor, but every single one of these men, probably a thousand in all, bore it on their chest: the forebears' mark, Gallian's sigil.

The grey-eyed man took a few hesitant steps back, his hands shaking.

"The sword!" Vahleda's voice rang in Kura's head, but she was standing at the man's side, fury burning in her black eyes as she shouted up at him. *"The sword!"*

Kura darted after Ìsendorál, but the grey-eyed man jumped, thrusting his spear into the space that separated them. Kura braced herself, taking the blow on her shield.

"Seren!" The lead rider broke from the group, only one other man following him, while the remaining company charged into the body of the fight with weapons drawn.

The lead rider leapt from the saddle as his horse trotted away. He already had his sword in hand, his fists clenched at his sides. "What has all this been about?"

The grey-eyed man—Seren—opened his mouth as though he was going to try to explain, but his eyes fell on the second rider and he didn't say a word. Kura followed his gaze and took a step back in surprise. It was Triston, jumping down from the back of a bay mare —she hadn't even recognized him; his outfit was a mismatch of a rebel's uniform and soldier's plate armor.

Shock jolted through her chest. If Triston was the second rider, then that would make...

She turned back to the other man. He was younger than she'd imagined him, with color in his cheeks and fire in his eyes. He and Triston looked so alike—the same curling black hair, the same strong chin, the same brow creased in stoic concern—and she wondered how she hadn't noticed it right away.

She'd always imagined Dradge to be some wrinkled old despot; it was easier to spend a lifetime hating someone who looked like that. But the man that stood before her walked with long strides and with his broad shoulders held back—with a natural air of confidence—and she no longer questioned how the people had come to call him king.

Seren lunged after the sword, and Kura jumped to cut him off. She struck him in the shoulder with her shield, throwing her weight into the impact. The man stumbled, but regained his balance and used to his spear to sweep her legs out from under her.

Every muscle ached the second she hit the ground, but she threw her shield over her head and torso and scrambled back to her feet. Seren already had the sword; he held it in his hand, frowning as he inspected the rusty red blade. Kura drew in a raspy breath. Ìsendorál had brought her here—brought them all here—and now she'd lost it just as easily as she'd found it.

Dradge charged Seren, swinging his broadsword with wide, calculated strokes. Triston followed closely behind, matching his father's strides. Seren took a step back only to brace himself. He held Ìsendorál in one hand and the *atgár* in the other, blocking Dradge's strikes with a few sweeping motions from his staff, then moving against Triston, slashing at him with the sword.

Anger surged through Kura's veins to mix dangerously with her fear. *He has no right to use that sword—Vahleda has no right!* Her hands shook with both exertion and frustration, and she tried to get her racing mind to decide on what to do next.

A harsh squawk carried over the roar of battle, and a flicker perched on a nearby branch.

Nervous excitement caught in her chest. That wasn't *a* flicker, it was *the* flicker—the old bird she'd met in Lâroe. The flicker flapped its wings, squawking again, and she understood.

It didn't make sense—it hadn't made sense before—but she ran at Seren, her shield up. The flicker dove from the tree, its pointed beak aimed at the man's shoulder. Vahleda shrieked in frustration, and Seren looked up. Triston lunged, knocking the sword from the grey-eyed man's hand—the bird threw out its wings, claws extended, and caught the hilt before Ìsendorál hit the ground.

Kura slid to a stop as the flicker lifted the sword into the air. For that instant, the bird itself vanished entirely, and the phantom of a man stood in its place. He was tall, with white skin, black hair, and green eyes, and he wore some sort of strange brigandine armor that was fearfully similar to Vahleda's. He held Ìsendorál up in one hand, his eyes locked with Kura's, and somehow she wasn't afraid. She knew him—she didn't know how or from where—but she knew him.

The man threw the sword into the air, and his figure vanished as suddenly as it had appeared. Kura lunged, catching the hilt in her hand as the flicker's wings pumped over her head like a heartbeat.

Dark clouds gathered over the battlefield, and lightning flashed in the sky. She felt someone moving with her, directing her stance and her arms as she crossed her sword and shield in front of her, then whipped the blade at Seren.

A word echoed in her mind—echoed in her soul—and she found it coming from her own lips. "*Al'fayder!*"

Light, like fire, shot down from the clouds.

It engulfed her, but for some reason she wasn't afraid. The surge of heat and energy coursed through her, tightening every muscle, strengthening every limb. She held within her the power of the sun and the storm at once, and it gathered on the sword. Lightning shot from Ìsendorál's blade, closing the distance between her and Seren in an instant, and it shattered the *atgár* into a dozen pieces.

Thunder echoed against the ruins of Nansûr. Vahleda screamed— a horrible, agonizing sound that Kura might have pitied had she not known where it came from—and the whole of the valley burst into flame. The burning wall of fire washed over Kura, too quickly to really hurt, but it left the grass at her feet a crisp black.

She drew in a deep breath. Had she forgotten to do that before? She tried to step forward—tried to charge at Seren while she had the chance—but her limbs trembled with the very effort to keep her standing, and her vision blurred a mix of red flame and green forest. For one instant her veins had flowed with power, but here in the next she was left with nothing.

Ìsendorál fell from her hand, her legs crumpled, and she collapsed on her shield.

Triston had jumped back to block Seren's staff strike when he had noticed the clouds gathering over the battlefield. He paused—too long, any pause was too long—but both his father and Seren stepped back as well, eyeing the sky. The sun shone bright in every other direction except for the space above them. Lightning shot down from the clouds, streaking in a jagged line to the ground —where Kura stood.

Triston cried out, lunging toward her, but it was already over— she was dead.

But she wasn't. Kura stood in the center of the light, her whole figure glowing and sparking with the crackle of fire. It was an impossible image, seemingly plucked from tapestries of the forebears or from the illustrated texts of the Svaldan gods. Lightning shot from her sword with a blinding flash, and brought a wall of fire with it.

Triston dove to the ground, covering his head with his arms as those flames washed over him and burst through the valley. He scrambled to his knees. Seren stood in the center of it all, his staff crumpling in his hands. Dradge knelt on the other side with his sword poised, watching it all unfold with widening eyes.

Then there came the scream. It was deafening, and no matter how Triston pressed his hands to his ears he couldn't drown it out. The fire burned in a misshapen ring around them, filling the air with the smoke of burning grass and a flickering red light—and cutting them off from the rest of the battle. The scream was the woman from the cave: Seren's Grey Lady. She floated above them like a ghost, her fists clenched in anger and agony. Seren stumbled back in utter shock.

The Grey Lady turned her stare on him.

Never in his life had Triston seen Seren afraid—rightly, truly afraid—but he saw fear in the man's eyes now: wide and real and primal. Vahleda lashed out, catching hold of Seren's neck. He squirmed, clawing at her hands, but grasped nothing more than the air she was.

"Get away!" he screamed, the commanding tone of his voice mingling with Vahleda's painful screech until they spoke as one. Seren's face twisted, his limbs convulsed, and then he fell onto his knees.

All became quiet.

A breeze whipped the flames, the roar of their movement the only sound, and fear struck Triston's heart as he caught sight of Kura's crumpled form lying on the charred grass. She wasn't moving. He ran to her side, then knelt beside her to place a hand on her shoulder. "Kura?"

She groaned softly as her eyelids fluttered.

Seren shouted, a horrible, guttural sound that was nothing like his voice—it sounded like the lady's. Triston turned, rising cautiously to his feet as he placed himself between Seren and Kura.

Seren's metal plate armor glowed red, like it was being heated over a flame. Gradually it flexed, splitting down the center as it trickled in large, oozing clumps down Seren's arms to collect at his hands. A fearful smile spread across his face, the expression emphasized by his eyes.

His irises were the same pale grey, but the rest of them had gone black.

Seren flung his hands forward, and globs of that heated metal shot from him like thrown daggers. Triston defended himself with the only means he had—his sword. His blade clashed with one of the daggers and shattered. A piece of that hot metal caught him in the arm.

He fell to one knee, discarding his hilt, and clutched at his burning arm. Dradge charged with a shout, his sword raised. Seren spun around, flinging molten daggers in his direction. Triston flinched, his heart catching in his chest as each dagger struck, some deflecting off his father's plate armor while others slipped into the seams at the shoulder guard.

He snatched up Kura's fallen sword and charged Seren from behind.

Seren laughed as he caught Dradge's sword with his bare hand. The blade cut deep, splitting his index finger from his hand to catch on his wrist bones, but even as bright red blood seeped from the wound, Dradge's sword began to glow orange. He pulled it back, slicing at Seren's neck, but the man caught it with his other hand, bending and then crushing the blade before it struck him.

Triston thrust Kura's sword at Seren's gut, but the man spun, flinging more molten daggers. Most deflected off his plate armor, but one caught in between his chestplate and shoulder guards as another sank into his leg. Triston couldn't help but cry out as he fell back, clutching at his leg. The blade stopped only when it hit bone, singeing flesh all the way.

Dradge knocked Seren's arm aside as he lifted it to send another dagger in Triston's direction. Anger flared in Seren's eyes, and he lashed out with a vengeance. Dradge stifled a shout as molten daggers caught in the arm he had raised to cover his face, but with his free hand he reached for Kura's fallen sword, which Triston had left behind.

Something in the air shifted.

It wasn't a thing Triston could hear or see, but he felt it in the marrow of his bones. Even Seren seemed to notice. He hesitated, scowling. A large black bird with flashing golden wings circled overhead and gave a cry. Dradge stumbled back, gripping Kura's rusty sword with both hands as he stared with wide eyes. The rust seemed to melt away, leaving a glistening mirrored sheen behind.

Lightning flashed in the sky above, then the blade burst into flame.

"No!" the Grey Lady shrieked. Seren's mouth was the one that moved, but Triston only heard the woman's voice ringing in his ears.

Dradge lunged, swinging that flaming sword before him more naturally and easily than Triston had seen him handle a weapon before. The air crackled, and lightning flittered across that blade and around Dradge's arms. The wall of fire surrounding them danced, flaring up with a roar as Seren stumbled back.

The monster Seren had become flung its hands forward, shooting molten daggers at Dradge's chest, but they caught in the trail of fire left by Kura's blade and dissolved to nothing before they reached him. Firelight flashed in Dradge's eyes, and Triston had to stare in wonder at the man—the warrior—before him. While the world had been given a soldier and a king, surely this was what his father had always been meant to be.

The Grey Lady—screaming through Seren's mouth—formed what was left of Seren's plate armor into a crooked spear and charged. Dradge ducked beneath the strike, then thrust Kura's flaming sword through Seren's exposed guts. Lightning struck both of them with a blinding flash—Triston shielded his face with his arms—and the echo of thunder rolled through the valley.

Seren froze, his eyes growing wide with pain and horror. Black scorch marks marred one half of his body as blood, thick and red, oozed from the wound in his chest. Dradge shoved the blade in farther, driving it up until it caught on the man's ribs and sternum. A high-pitched scream emanated from somewhere deep in Seren's throat, and then it cut out entirely.

Seren coughed, blood spewing from his mouth as his limbs grew limp. Dradge pulled the sword from the man's gut with a grimace, and Seren collapsed onto his knees. He stared up at Dradge with a sense of anger and disbelief, before his gaze fell on Triston.

There was a look in those plain, grey eyes. It wasn't of remorse—he didn't seem to have enough clarity to seek any sort of forgiveness—but it haunted Triston all the same. It was the last thing he saw in Seren's eyes before life left him. A look of regret.

Triston forced himself to his feet, wincing as he tried to push through the searing pain in his leg. It proved to be too much, and he ended up half-limping, half-stumbling to his father's side. Dradge attempted to steady himself, leaning on one knee with Kura's sword jammed into the ground before him, and his head fell as he swayed. Triston dropped onto his good knee to catch him.

"Come on." He tried to sling his father's arm over his shoulder as panic scratched at the back of his mind. "It's over. We've done it."

Dradge coughed as he struggled to speak, blood trickling down the side of his mouth. Twisted bits of metal stuck from his arms, his side, his chest. Gently, Triston laid his father on his back on the burnt field and reached for the dagger sticking from his stomach. Dradge cried out as Triston's fingers brushed the end of the shard.

"Hey, I've got to—" Triston began, but Dradge shook his head and caught hold of Triston's wrist with a shaking hand.

"...proud of you," he whispered. The words caught in his throat, and his chest rattled with his efforts to breathe.

Triston tried to smile, but couldn't be sure he managed it as his heart tore to pieces inside his chest. He placed a hand on his father's shoulder, gritting his teeth to keep the tears from welling in his eyes. There was so much he wanted to say, a jumble of words screaming in his head, but in the end he only managed to nod and hold his father's gaze with all the stoic strength he had.

And then he was gone.

Triston clenched his fists at his sides, but he didn't know what to do with them, and he ended up leaning forward, head hanging down with his arms resting on his father's chest. When his mother had died he'd sobbed like the child he was, struggling through a pain he had never thought he'd feel again. He pressed his fingers into his eye sockets, massaging away the few stinging tears that escaped. This didn't feel the same. It would be easier if it did.

He swallowed and made himself look at his father's dead face, swiping at the moisture on his own cheeks, refusing to turn away until at least that image became something he could stomach.

Kura pushed herself to her knees, thoughts whirling in some confusion of excitement, disbelief, and horror. Seren was dead—Vahleda was dead—but so was the king, his body stretched out beneath the sword Ìsendorál, which he'd left upright in the ground. The wall of fire around them was growing. It shone red in that blood-soaked blade, casting a long, black shadow across Dradge's body, and Triston, who knelt beside it.

Wings beat above the roar of the flames, and the flicker descended to land on Ìsendorál's hilt. The bird spread out its golden wings, looked down at Dradge, and let out a mournful cry. The sound echoed dully against the charred ground, and then the flicker took flight, soaring up over the flames to disappear among the trees.

Weakly, Kura dragged herself to her feet and stumbled to Triston's side. He didn't so much as move to acknowledge her presence. Emotion caught in her throat as she couldn't help but stare at Dradge's scratched and bloodied face, his vacant green eyes staring at the sky as if there was something up there she couldn't see. Hesitantly, she placed her hand on Triston's shoulder.

"We've got to go."

The fire roared in the silence between them, and then Triston drew in a breath, wiping the remaining tears from his cheeks with the back of his hand. He nodded, not looking at her, and grunted as he tried to get to his feet. There was a blade sticking out of his leg. Kura slung his arm over her shoulder and, with wobbly knees, managed to pull him to his feet.

The heat from the flames seeped through her clothes and sweat trickled down her back as the walls edged in around them. She pulled Ìsendorál from the ground with her free hand, then she and Triston—each of them braced against the other—limped away from the forest and the growing flames, and toward the ruins of Nansûr.

The fire raged in all directions but one, where a small collection of rubble cut it off from the field below. There, it smoldered in little tongues that flared up bright and orange as it crept toward the few remaining patches of unburnt grass. Kura could peer over the flames, for the moment—the top of Rih Hill loomed beyond, with hazy figures gathered in its shadow—but soon the wall would rise there, too. It would trap both of them, so they would burn to death on what could be their field of victory.

Triston tightened his arm under her shoulders. "Now!"

Kura ran. Triston clung to her side, matching her stride for stride, and suddenly she realized she was glad to have him there. They must have both had the same idea for escaping this, and somehow it was easy to believe they'd succeed, doing it together. The flames danced, burning hot against her cheeks, but as she and Triston neared the edge they jumped in tandem, sailing through the fire to land on their hands and knees on the other side.

Coughing, Kura tried to catch her breath, and then voices screamed around her. She fumbled with her sword in a blind panic, but strong hands caught her by the arms, patted out the flames on her clothing, and dragged both her and Triston to their feet.

Kura blinked. There were faces—so many faces; a crowd filled the clearing. N'hadia loomed above them, asking a thousand questions that she honestly couldn't hear, and it was Renard who stood at her side, his arm under her shoulders, holding her steady. Where had he been this entire time?

"The fonfyr!" Renard shouted—he was repeating it, but Kura only noticed when he wrapped his hand around hers and pulled her arm, and Ìsendorál, over her head. "The fonfyr!"

Cheers rang out among the crowd. There were soldiers with the forebears' mark on their chestplates, the dirty faces of her fellow rebel fighters, the toothy grins of nostkynna, the towering figures of centaurs, the shadow of the Varian among the distant trees. Kura watched it all in a daze.

I'm not... didn't they see Dradge...?

Renard kept talking; she stumbled as he dragged her along. "...the damage isn't as bad as it might look, so with the help of those soldiers we..."

His words faded in and out of her muddled mind, but at last she pieced together what this all meant. She laughed, still grinning as tears welled up in her eyes and streamed down her cheeks. They'd done it—they'd truly done it.

They'd won.

Chapter Fifty-Four

As the Stones Settle

Kura sat in the hallway, her back pressed against the rough, cool stone as she stared up at the wall across from her. Sunlight, along with the murmur of voices, filtered in from the far right end of the cave and served as a quiet reminder that she'd been heading to do something in particular. That had been before she'd found the painting.

This was the hall of remembering—she hadn't recognized it at first, given how Nansûr had changed—and the painting was one of many. He was a tall man, broad-shouldered, with a bushy black beard and curling black hair. His armor, while elegant, was too similar to Vahleda's for her taste, although the green cloak draped dramatically over one shoulder complemented his eyes as he lifted a sword above his head. It was unmistakably Ìsendorál, glittering as the distant sunlight caught the metallic paint in a way torchlight had not.

Kura recognized the man. He was the flicker.

The relative silence of the cavern swaddled her like a blanket, and somehow this moment—as she stared at that age-old image with a thousand questions—was the first she'd had to think. She couldn't remember what she'd done after the battle. Her shoulder was sore where the vojak had pierced her, but a Fidelis healer had soothed most of her injuries and then she'd gratefully fallen asleep. A long, comforting sleep, without dreams.

The morning had brought its own questions.

They kept coming to her—Renard, and Grenja, and even others that she only vaguely remembered meeting before—asking for her opinion, her approval, her blessing. Kura wasn't sure of half the things she'd said, and she only hoped she'd given suggestions that were at least somewhat sensible. But of course Trofast was gone, and so were Erryl, and Dradge.

Although... it might not matter much what she said. The others rarely seemed to take her suggestions seriously, and Devna in particular spent plenty of time giving directions herself. The Fidelis woman was plotting something—if the time she spent whispering behind closed doors was any indication—and while she'd only been elected abbot the night before, she was already taking her job quite seriously. Whenever someone didn't do what she said, she'd pull Kura aside and try and make her say it. Kura had yet to actually do that, but the woman had also yet to quit asking her.

They wanted to split the country. They didn't explain it to her, but she'd gathered that much. Renard and everyone else busied about like that had been their plan all along—and maybe it had been. It certainly seemed to be what Devna wanted, and Kura couldn't help but remember how Cynwrig had tried to do the same thing: control the last fonfyr, and by extension control the kingdom. Apparently Devna was a little less greedy; she didn't want to rule the whole thing, just part of it.

Kura let out a contented sigh as she gazed up at the painted figure looming before her. She'd done what she'd come to do, somehow, and the fact that she sat here—alive and unbroken—was still baffling. She traced her finger along Ìsendorál's hilt where it hung at her side. Yesterday was as far as *she'd* planned. As it stood now, she knew just one thing: she wouldn't be their puppet.

"Hey." Aethan's voice echoed in from the sunlit side of the cavern, his footsteps crunching louder on the pebble-strewn floor as he came to a stop at her side. He tried to hide the little limp he still had as he walked, but his face was a healthy color again. "You alright? I thought you were heading in for something to eat."

Kura motioned to the painting. "Do you know who that is?"

Aethan glanced at the image, then laughed. "Yeah, that's Gallian. Some artist's rendition of him, anyway. Why?"

Kura stared absently into the painting's green eyes, then shrugged. "It's pretty accurate, I think."

Aethan watched her, evidently on the verge of asking for an explanation, but the silence lingered between them and somehow she didn't mind. Silence was better than screams. Silence was better than questions she couldn't answer. Aethan let out a deep sigh, then sat down beside her.

Kura turned to him. "What happened to the hillside?"

"They say a vojak lit the gas tunnels that fed the torches on the wall. It only took the front off the hill." Aethan's forehead creased with a lingering sense of concern. "You got caught in the rockslide, but I just got buried in where I was."

"Oh." Kura glanced at her hands as she rested her elbows on her knees. That was all she could think to say. The emotions of yesterday were still so raw and real, but they had finally settled down in some corner of her heart, and she was content to leave them there.

"How'd you draft the fire?"

Kura stiffened, drawing in a sharp breath. Apparently *everyone* had seen her call that lightning down from the sky. They hadn't seen Gallian moving with her, and—thanks to the wall of fire that'd burned for hours afterwards—they hadn't seen anything Dradge had done, either. Somehow, she had succeeded in living the lie.

"It should have killed you," Aethan continued, his grin widening in amazement. "Fidelis train for *decades* to do *half* of what you did yesterday."

"The flicker..." Kura began, but couldn't find the right words. Bracing herself, she pulled Ìsendorál from the scabbard on her hip. Despite the battle, the blade was now impossibly sharp and held a mirrored sheen of muted gold. She'd made it look this way, for a moment, before the rebel council at Nansûr, but after Dradge had picked it up, it had transformed permanently. She swallowed. "Dradge killed Vahleda."

"What?"

"He did it, Aethan." She stared into his green eyes. Gods, he'd believed in her most of all. "The flicker showed me how to do, I don't know, *something*, but Dradge did the rest. He—he..."

"He was the fonfyr." Aethan didn't shy away from her. He was surprised, confused maybe, but not angry.

She nodded, slowly, and looked back down at that sword.

"Kura!" Elli's sharp voice echoed in from the end of the cave. Kura smiled to see her little sister's sunlit silhouette making its way down the corridor. "Kura!"

"I'm here, Elli," she said with a laugh as she sheathed Ìsendorál and pushed herself to her feet.

"There you are!" Elli gave a dramatic sigh as she ran to Kura's side. She stopped a few strides short, folding her little arms across her chest as she glowered at Aethan. "Mister Aethan, did you get lost?"

"Elli!" Kura exclaimed, but Aethan laughed.

"I got tired." He stretched out his hands. "Help me up?"

Elli latched on to Aethan's big palms with her tiny hands and tugged with all her strength to get him to his feet. "Come on!" Holding Aethan's hand, she reached out to grab Kura's. "They're all waiting for you!"

"Are they?" Kura let Elli drag her down the corridor.

Once they'd reached the mouth of the cave, Elli released her and ran ahead. Many hands had worked many hours since the battle had ended to piece Nansûr back together. The rockslide had been moved aside, with much of the rubble now edging pathways or serving as paver stones to make short staircases and long, sloping ramps that led to the several exposed cave openings.

A large group had gathered in the open space between Nansûr and the forest, and many an eye turned to look as Kura made her way down the path, Aethan tagging along behind. Kura braced herself as she tried to keep her apprehension from showing on her face. They were all longing eyes, seeking guidance as before, but she had nothing left to give them.

Elli ran around the outer edge of the crowd, then came to a fidgety stop at her mother's side. Jisela was leaning against Spiridon, his arm around her shoulders, but she turned back to greet Elli, then Kura, with a smile. Kura returned it and leaned into her mother's embrace as Jisela pulled her close. Both her mother and father had been in the stables when she'd given that speech, just two people among the crowd, and she hadn't even noticed.

"Did you see the fire, Kura?" Faron asked, pointing as he peered around his father's large frame. Faron had fought in the first battle among the boulders, then chased a pack of saja deep into the forest and missed the retreat. His company had made it back for the final stand, and he'd fought to the end with little more than a scratch.

Kura pulled back from her mother's embrace to look over what had brought them all together here in the first place. It was a circular mound of stones, as tall as a man and wider than Kura's entire house in the Wynshire. A flame, a pillar of fire nearly the height of a centaur, burned at the peak of the cairn, hovering over the ground and dancing slightly in the breeze.

"They say the fire sprang up on its own," Faron said. "It stayed, right after you..." He shrugged, as if it was all too much to say out loud.

Kura nodded. She didn't want to face those words, either. She recognized this place, despite how it'd changed. Here, the flicker had shown her how to draft the fire; Vahleda had fallen at the hands of the fonfyr. Now it was a grave.

Idris stood near the edge, a small stringed instrument in her hand, and her soft voice carried among the stones. It was a melancholy tune, the words flowing and beautiful although Kura couldn't understand them. One by one, folks from the crowd stepped forward with an armful of flowers or a trinket of remembrance and placed it on the pile. Gradually, the stones disappeared beneath the collection of offerings. Kura could only imagine how many bodies lay under those stones—soldier, rebel, nostkynna, and centaur alike—and she felt overwhelmingly fortunate to have her family pressed at her sides.

She peered through the burning flame: the remaining soldiers had gathered opposite the rebellion to pay their respects. She'd had to fight to get the others to allow them to stay the night here, but she didn't regret it. She didn't care if Triston was the *heir*, or if his men outnumbered hers, or what his intentions for the rebellion were. He'd done nothing but try to prevent that battle yesterday, and in her heart she knew he'd be the last one to continue it.

Besides, how could she let Devna send him away when he looked like that? The bags under his eyes suggested he'd barely slept, although he carried himself with the same confidence he always did, and any soldier she saw him speak to stepped at his command without question. She'd tried to talk to him—didn't matter that she hadn't yet figured out what she needed to say, she just wanted to talk to him—but slipping away wasn't easy.

"It's unsafe," Devna had told her, and Grenja and Renard and everyone else had reluctantly agreed. Even now, the two groups, rebels and soldiers, didn't mingle, and most eyed one another warily.

She breathed a quiet sigh. Not so long ago she'd have gladly hated those soldiers, too. But she knew better now; things would never again be that simple.

Triston watched as his soldiers placed tokens of remembrance on the gravestones alongside the rebel company. It was a fitting tribute to the men and women who'd made such noble sacrifices. Or so he told himself to smother the nagging emptiness in his heart that called him away. Of course he had nowhere to go —nowhere but Avtalyon, to lonely halls filled with the promise of responsibilities he didn't know how to carry. Responsibilities he wasn't sure he *wanted* to carry.

It didn't matter what he wanted. And so his feet remained where they were planted.

Idris's song faded, and Renard attempted to convince Kura to step forward. They whispered to each other, and she shook her head vigorously even as her family put hands on her shoulders and encouraged her to go. Triston nearly laughed at the innocent look of surprise on Kura's face. Did she really think she could return to anonymity, after all this?

She cleared her throat as she glanced at the crowd. "We owe this victory," she said, her voice quiet at first but gaining in strength, "to those that now lie under these stones." She turned to face the flame, letting the silence stretch a little too long. Finally, she drew that sword from its scabbard, and gently rested the flat of the blade on the stones before her. "This place will now be known as Kiriath. Fire of the forebears."

The crowd murmured in agreement. Triston nodded, placing his fist over his heart, and many of his soldiers did the same. Kura sheathed her sword, but as she tried to fall back in among the crowd, that sharp-eyed Fidelis caught her by the arm. Devna. She was the woman who'd spent that entire ransom attempt scowling at him.

Kura and the Fidelis shared a few quick words, and a look of concern crossed Kura's face. Devna latched onto Kura's wrist and tugged her a step closer to the rebel crowd.

"There was one oath," the Fidelis called out, voice carrying in the clearing, "our forebears swore before all others: here, in the New World, we would be neither conscripts nor kings. And so why is it that, for all our lives, we've been subject to kings?"

The crowd belted out their dissatisfaction, and Triston made no effort to hide his frown. The Lovarians had, almost two centuries ago, split off into their own country to emulate the extreme interpretations of that oath, and it had left them conscripted to their own chaotic lawlessness. The oath was certainly well-intentioned, but a king—or a queen—was necessary to preserve a country, to protect civilians, to maintain order.

"Now," Devna continued, holding up her hand, and the crowd quieted to a murmur. "We've all had enough of the fight, but I don't think a little battle-weariness means we have to simply crown another king—do you?"

A roar of agreement came from the crowd, followed by another, and another, until the response became a chant. Triston stiffened, gripping the sword hilt at his side. But what had he expected? He could have salvaged this had they not needed to fight at all, but as it was...

A hand settled on Triston's shoulder. "I don't like this," Dylen whispered, leaning down to look him in the eye. "We could hold them here, right? Cut off their momentum before this becomes something we can't handle?"

Triston kept frowning as he surveyed the rebel crowd. That would be the sensible thing to do. So why did the idea sit like curdled milk in his stomach?

"I think their fonfyr is all that's really holding them together," Dylen said. "Take her out, and the rest will probably scatter."

A spike of anger rose in his chest, and he glared up at his friend —a harsher response than he intended. "You sound like your father."

Dylen raised his hands with an apologetic grin. "Hey, man, I'm not saying I *like* the idea, I'm just saying it. Whatever you've got in mind, we'll do it."

Devna grinned at the crowd. The look was too sharp for Triston to think she enjoyed the attention, but all the same she seemed pleased with herself. "I propose we—"

Kura stepped in front of her. "March to Avtalyon." She stood with her shoulders drawn up and fist clenched around her sword hilt like she thought she might have to use it, but she held her ground. "And ask for a public airing of grievances."

The crowd offered a confused, although still mostly enthusiastic, cheer to that. Devna scowled and opened her mouth to speak, but Renard grabbed Kura's hand and made her hold Ìsendorál up for all to see.

"All willing to follow the fonfyr to Avtalyon, answer 'aye'!"

The crowd cheered to that, too, and while Devna still stood there sulking, the rebels broke apart, many of them milling back into Nansûr—presumably to prepare for the journey. Triston's wandering eyes came to rest on Kura as she attempted to dutifully navigate the throngs of well-wishers. She was certainly *something*, but with all he'd witnessed, he seriously doubted she was actually the fonfyr. If any such thing existed at all. Kura was playing a role, a role she was unqualified and untrained for—she knew that, he could see it on her face—but he understood the stuff of which she was made.

Despite the crowd, her gaze found his. She smiled—the look bright, if apologetic—and offered him a little wave. He caught himself grinning back, and nodded before the crowd inadvertently moved between them. Was he a fool to think that, if hard lines were drawn, she'd be on his side?

"Shit," Dylen muttered to himself. "You're not thinking straight —gods, who would be?"

Triston realized Dylen must have been staring at him only after his friend grabbed his upper arms and made him look him in the eye. "I'll follow you, you hear me? Plenty of guys here will. *I* don't care who I have to fight. That crown belongs to you."

Triston chuckled, wriggling out of Dylen's grip, although maybe there was a part of him grateful to hear that. He knew Avaron had to have a king. There would be too much uncertainty, otherwise; it was a matter of necessity that he fill the role. But maybe—if he worked this right—none of them would need to fight for it.

Chapter Fifty-Five

Alone

"Come on!" Elli ran toward the river, little bark boat in hand.

Kura chuckled and tried to match her sister's enthusiastic speed. Had she thought about anything but these silly boats since they had left the Wynshire? Though her sore limbs protested, in the end she really didn't mind. It was a relief to get away from the crowd.

Devna was absolutely seething—she'd yet to quit complaining about how Kura had overstepped her bounds, how she'd sown discord among the ranks, how she'd possibly ruined everything they'd been working for...

At first Kura had tried to reason with her, but she eventually gave up and just made sure she nodded intermittently during the woman's rants, not letting her lips upturn in a smug little grin. She still wouldn't be their puppet—not when it came to something like this. Maybe now Devna actually believed that.

They were to go to Avtalyon tomorrow, all lined up in some grand parade, to meet for the negotiations. Renard had her back on that point—he had even jumped in occasionally and steered Devna's attention to what sorts of things they should demand. The Fidelis were still set on splitting the country—forming a West Avaron, or maybe Forebearsland—and after a while Kura had had to stop listening. She knew she wasn't experienced enough to judge the situation properly, but she wasn't sure whose judgement to trust over her own. So, she would make sure they asked for what was most sensible. Fortunately, she still had a day to determine what that was.

"We've got to start them at the same time!" Elli knelt beside the river, her hand outstretched to hover her boat over the water. It was a crude little thing, a curling piece of dried bark with a small stick shoved through the center to make a mast, but she never had been patient enough to craft anything else.

"I'm here." Kura crouched down beside Elli, the clear water sending a shock of cold through her as she placed her boat in the river. She'd put some effort into this one, tying up the sides of a fresh square of bark she'd stripped from a tree to actually make a proper boat shape. She'd also put a small, flat rock in the bottom for balance—Benger had taught her that.

"Ready?" Elli met Kura's gaze with a grin. "Let go!"

They both let go of their boats, and the shallow current swept them away.

"I'm winning!" Elli jumped up and took off downstream. Kura followed her at a jog, the little boats smacking together as the current tossed them about. "Oh, now you're winning, Kura!"

Kura let out a shuddering breath and tried to focus on every little detail—the crunch of the stones under her feet, the cool breeze skirting up from the water, the gleam of sunlight beyond the trees—as though that might drown out the mess of thoughts screaming in her head. The boats traveled much more quickly than either she or Elli could, and finally the current swept them toward the rocky hillside that made up Nansûr.

"Careful," Kura called out, catching hold of Elli's shoulder and pulling her close. Here, there was no longer a shoreline to tread, just a sheer cliff that became the side of Rih Hill. Her sister whined in frustration, but stopped anyway as she took hold of Kura's hand. The two little ships continued downstream and disappeared around the bend.

"Now we won't be able to see who won!"

"That's alright," Kura said, rubbing her sister's shoulder. "We can't always see how things end. We'll just have to make our best guess."

A branch creaked overhead. "Sounds like you went and got wise on me, fonfyr."

Elli yelped and Kura flinched, pulling her sister close to her side, before she noticed the cloaked figure perched above them, braced against the trunk of the tree. "Skellor?"

The figure nodded, leaning forward enough so that the sunlight illuminated half his face.

Kura grinned, letting Elli go, but her sister still clung to her hand. "Where have you been?"

He shrugged. "Around. I hear everyone else is all set on dividing up the spoils. You good with that?"

"...Not really?"

He nodded, then leaned back into the shadows—like he'd gotten what he came for. "Good."

"Where are you going?"

He chuckled. "I'm going to make myself scarce until I see how this goes down. We all are."

Kura frowned, chewing her inner lip. That was probably sensible, but the Varian deserved to be treated better than that.

"Don't worry about us." She could hear the smile in his voice. "We're partial to the shadows, anyway." He lifted his hand to his forehead to give her a wave. "Maybe I'll move to whichever half of the country you pick." He leapt to the next tree, then the next, his shape just a bundle of fur wrapped in a fluttering cape that soon disappeared amongst the branches.

Elli stared after Skellor, then turned to watch the river, the churning water echoing off the cliff side and filling the silence. Finally, she sighed and let go of Kura's hand. "I don't think I like some of your friends, Kura."

Kura snorted, then laughed outright—harder and longer than she should have—and felt a bit guilty when she couldn't find a proper retort.

Elli peered up at her, confused, but gradually a proud little grin spread across her face; she always was proud of making her big sister laugh. "Your boat was better than mine."

Kura sighed contentedly and wiped the laughter-induced tears from her eyes. "I can show you how I made it. Do you want me to?"

"Yes!" Elli jumped, then jogged a few steps away from the river. "I saw you get bark from that big tree!" She bolted ahead, toward Kiriath.

Grimacing, Kura climbed the short bank by the riverside, muscles protesting at every step. *I've got to find that girl a more sedentary hobby.*

An odd splotch of crimson poked between the distant tree trunks. Kura paused, frowning. It was a figure, cloaked in red, kneeling beside a long pile of dirt and stones—man-sized; a grave, probably. Her heart caught in her chest. It was Triston.

She peered through the few thin trees that separated them. His back was mostly toward her, and he just sat there, motionless.

"Kura!" Elli's shrill voice carried through the whole valley. Kura lifted a hand, urging her sister to continue on without her. Elli dropped her arms to her side in a dramatic sigh, then shrugged and ran off.

Kura picked her way into the forest, pine needles crunching loudly under her feet. A short distance away, a few other red-cloaked soldiers stood amongst the trees. Each man watched her, eyes narrowed, hand on his sheathed sword, but they didn't speak or move to intercept her, so she continued. Triston gave no indication he'd noticed her even as she stopped an armsbreadth away.

"Triston?"

He straightened sharply, then turned back and caught her gaze. "Oh." He looked away, smearing the tear on his cheek—as though he could keep her from noticing.

Haltingly, she took a step forward. "You alright?"

"Yeah," he said quickly, but she'd already seen the look on his face.

Kura sank to her knees beside him. This had to be a grave, and if Triston was here... She stared at those stones with a mix of sorrow and anger. Dradge should have been buried with honor with the rest in Kiriath.

"Who did this?" she asked softly. "Did Devna do this? I didn't know—"

Triston shook his head absently, not looking up. "It's alright. He always said the greatest men are the ones buried under the dirt and stone they bled to defend. This is how he honored his troops. He'd expect nothing more or less."

Kura glanced down at her hands. The man she'd spent her life hating had given his life to save hers; at the very least she should say something.

"He never saw himself as a king." Triston wiped his nose on his sleeve. "He was always a soldier first. There's nothing he wouldn't have done for his country." He gave a bit of a laugh. "I suppose that sounds strange, considering how everything was for you... but I'll never be the man he was."

Kura peered into his blue eyes, even though he didn't lift them to meet hers. She wanted to tell him he was already a good man, to tell him he was already everything he needed to be. But what good would that do? Reality would remain as true and potent as it ever had been, those terrible feelings still demanding to be felt. She knew that.

Without a word, she reached over and took Triston's hand in hers. He flinched as her fingers encircled his, but she held on anyway, the warmth of her hand chasing away the cold in his. The silence lingered between them, but maybe—as they sat side by side in the shadow of the trees—it didn't have to be so lonely.

Chapter Fifty-Six

First Impressions

Eyes shut, Kura drew in a deep breath as the cool autumn breeze stung her cheeks and pulled her loose hair back from her shoulders. She caught the rich scent of the pine trees towering above her on either side, the faint whiff of dust kicked up by the company of feet and hooves following behind her, and above all that something else—something new, something distant.

"Akachi, you smell that?"

The nostkynna snorted and swished his tail. "Don't look at me. Only a horse would be so indecent, mucking up one of Avaron's fair roadways—"

"No!" Kura laughed, opening her eyes. "I mean, in the breeze, there's something…"

"Oh." Akachi shook his mane. "You're talking about the sea." He glanced back, looking at Kura with one large eye. "You've never been near the sea before?"

"No, but I've heard of it. Water blue like the sky, shimmering for as far as eyes can see…"

The horse snorted again, then nodded to the right. "You can probably see it for yourself over those trees."

Kura stood in the stirrups, craning her neck to peer over the tops of the fir trees that dotted the steep, rocky bluff sloping down on the right side of the road. The wide path wound along the traversable sections of the jagged mountainside, but beyond that—beyond the trees—the land became a large, flat expanse of dark blue that disappeared at the horizon.

"I see it!" She pointed over the trees and turned to the others riding beside her. "Do you see it?"

Four quizzical stares met hers, each face bearing a placating smile.

She sank back onto her saddle, her cheeks flushing with heat. "The—the ocean, I mean..."

"I grew up by the sea," Renard offered, nodding toward the trees as his scarred warhorse plodded down the road without so much as flicking an ear. "My father was a fisherman. I don't rightly remember the first time I saw the ocean, but she's certainly a majestic thing. That there, though, is just the bay."

"Oh." She didn't want to have to ask him to explain what difference that made.

"What I want to see is Edras!" N'hadia galloped to Kura's side, hooves pounding the dirt. Her sleeveless tunic showed off the intricate black tattoos that now graced her shoulders.

Kura grinned at her. "Yeah, I—"

Devna drove her horse between them. "Let's be careful with that loose tongue of ours, hmm? If you'd given me the chance, I would have waited to take this trip until I made you presentable, but here we are. These people must accept you. Show them you deserve their loyalty."

Kura turned away before Devna saw her frown. The trouble was, she *didn't* deserve their loyalty—she never had. But she'd gone along with it that morning when they'd dressed her up in the most beautiful set of embroidered brigandine armor she'd ever seen—she'd even put on the long, flowing red cloak. Everyone was dressed in their best, from Renard beside her at the front of the company to the very last rebel child at the end of the procession.

One big show, dressed in flashing colors to hide the stains underneath.

Akachi jumped, lurching Kura forward in the saddle. "There it is!"

She drew in a breath. Edras. It towered above even the trees.

The city itself sprawled across the flat stretch of land near the ocean shore, with the different districts built on separate plateaus jutting out from the mountainside. Buildings varied in quality from simple shacks to stone mansions, but the towers of Avtalyon overshadowed them all.

For a moment Kura was tempted to think those towers belonged to the mountain's peak, but lights shone in the windows and brightly colored flags—red and black, with the blackbird and pointed cross—flew on poles atop the shorter roofs. She'd heard tales of this place—she'd heard tales of many things—but where most stories told too much, she wondered if, about this place, she'd heard too little.

"You shouldn't have let the prince go ahead of us," Devna grumbled, not for the first time. "How much do you want to bet he has more friends on the council than you do? They followed Dradge, and Seren. Without the people of Edras on your side, what makes you think they will want to listen to us?"

Not sure I want to make friends with the council. Kura smiled to herself, tracing her fingers across the leather stitching of the sword at her side. Any influence she'd won over the last few days came through her association with inanimate objects, not people.

"We sent scouts yesterday," Renard said with a look of encouragement. "As if rumors of the fonfyr haven't spread from one end of Avaron to the other already. Don't worry, the city will be waiting for you."

Kura nodded, trying to be grateful, as she peered up at the stone towers. They had been built by the forebears' hands, and it was their legacy that gave her any right to be here at all. She'd taken the lie too far to recant now—and she didn't regret it—but that didn't mean she should take it further. Symbols stayed on banners for a reason.

Triston was the rightful heir, for whatever that was worth, and he would make a fine king—if some of the others ever quit looking at him through sideways glances and whispering as he walked by. Grenja seemed willing enough, at least, and possibly Konik as well.

Glancing over her shoulder, she searched the crowd trailing behind her and found the centaur marching near the center. He also had fresh tattoos, and wore a loose, thickly woven shirt covered almost entirely in tiny, colorful beads. N'hadia had called the shirt something special and explained that any Cenóri was free to challenge him, but if he managed to keep it in his possession for the next seven days, he'd be officially instated as chieftain in Trofast's place.

Kura let her gaze drift until she spotted her family, walking with the other refuges toward the rear. Her mother and Faron appeared engrossed in a conversation with Aethan, but Elli—seated on her father's shoulders—grinned and waved. Kura grinned and waved back.

She would've had them riding at her side, but Renard, Grenja, and Devna had all insisted otherwise. With a dozen hands fighting to pull her in a dozen different directions, she had to pick her battles carefully.

In front of the procession, a man and his son struggled to pull their rattling handcart off the road. A woman with a swaddled baby in her arms and a young girl tugging anxiously at her skirt already stood beside the trees, gawking at the band of rebels.

Kura stiffened as Devna nudged her horse close. "This is your moment. Sit up straight!"

Fighting a sigh, Kura squared her shoulders and adjusted her seat in the saddle. With a burst of speed, Renard urged his horse ahead as he unfurled the flag—white, with a simple red stitching of Gallian's sigil in the center—he'd kept rolled up behind his saddle. "Make way for the fonfyr!"

The little girl gave a cry of delight, and after the man had lowered his handcart he looked up with wide eyes from their place on the side of the road. They wore threadbare clothes, their cart overflowed with red potatoes—they were a simple family who would have looked at home in the Wynshire as sure as they belonged here. It was almost a relief to find folk Kura recognized. She smiled at them.

The woman gasped and the man sank down on one knee, pressing a fist against his chest as he gestured to his boy to do the same.

Kura's smile froze on her face. Renard's continued greeting echoed somewhere in the back of her mind, but the image of that family was seared into her memory. Just a few weeks ago she would have belonged with them on the side of the road, not here.

The procession passed under the shadow of the city gates. A multitude of awestruck faces lined the streets beyond the walls. Kura's guts twisted, and no matter how she fought, she couldn't keep her expression pleasant.

Akachi turned one large eye on her, then laughed. "You don't look excited."

Kura grimaced, and he laughed again.

"Come on! You should be excited. I'm excited."

There were shouts, there was applause—flowers were tossed up over the crowd and laid on the cobblestone for the horses to tread underfoot. Kura thought she'd witnessed the full frenzy of humanity in battle, but even the war hadn't been like this. Screams rang in her ears, though the source was excitement and hope.

At least, for most.

All the eyes that met hers near the road were full of joy, but as she peered farther back, she caught more sour expressions. These people stood with arms folded across their chests, not much more than a skeptical frown on their face—they wanted to see what the fuss was about, but they weren't about to join in it themselves.

Suddenly, both Devna's stern hesitance and Renard's over-the-top enthusiasm made sense. Triston still had allies, too. And they numbered far more than any of the rebels would have her believe.

Triston cut his stride short outside the council chambers. It *had* been a relief to finally return home, but the longer he walked those empty halls—the only sound that of his boots echoing on the polished marble floors—the more he remembered all that hadn't returned with him.

He stared at the intricately carved council chamber doors, the loneliness pressing in on him with the silence. Seren had always been the one to call these meetings, and his father the one to lead them. Now, he was doing both.

Bracing himself, he pushed the doors open. The thick wood slid across the frame, then the frustrated murmur of the council overtook the silence of the hallway. Triston let the doors fall shut behind him with an echoing thud, and he strode toward the table without glancing up.

"Triston!" Lady Tanith's voice rang in his ear as she met him at the threshold. "Have you lost your mind? You've been avoiding me, but I will speak with you—"

Triston lifted his hand and motioned toward the table. "Take your seats. Please."

The council members muttered to one another, but they settled into their customary places obediently enough. Triston hesitated as he pulled the chair back from the head of the table. It was his father's chair; never since the day his young mind had realized how princes became kings had he ever dreamed of sitting in it.

He took his seat, stifling a sigh.

The council waited in silence, the hostility in their expressions almost palpable. Therburn sat at Triston's left as the possible exception, but at his right Lady Tanith adjusted her wide-brimmed hat to study him more severely. General Lavern sat at her side, his stern look that of either disappointment or boredom—he was infinitely more difficult to read than Dylen, despite their similar features. Lord Hamlyn and Lady Rigan both sat beside Therburn, Hamlyn's bulbous frame a stark contrast to Lady Rigan's petite and regal air.

Triston drew in a deep breath. "As I'm sure you know, my father is dead. His death is Seren's doing, as was likely much more." He looked Tanith in the eye. "Your company fought at Seren's side. Why?"

"Why?" Tanith smiled gently, brows creased in a visage of concern. "For you, of course. Seren fooled us—"

"Don't. If you're not going to answer honestly, then there's no point in speaking. Therburn's men fought beside me, as did General Lavern's, so this address is not really for either of them. But Hamlyn, you and Lady Rigan fled."

Lady Rigan shrugged and said nothing.

"It was chaos!" Hamlyn started, raising his hands. "You expected me to stay around and—?"

"No. I only expected a level of honesty and integrity befitting men and women of your stature—an expectation that I evidently misplaced."

Silence settled over the council again, and Lady Tanith shifted in her seat. "Well, you've certainly come in here with precisely the attitude to win our respect."

Triston allowed himself a wry grin. "Why do you presume that is something I value? True respect requires a certain maturity, and so for the time being, from you, I would be better off counting on mere obedience. You swore as much to my father. Will this be a peaceful transition of power, or is someone here going to pitch a fit?"

Again, silence, but Triston saw the fear creeping into their faces.

"So you expect us to, what?" Lady Rigan said with a delicate frown. "Roll over and play dead? To a company of animals and cast-outs?"

"No. I expect you—all of you"—Triston looked each of them in the eye—"to get up from these chairs, and to walk to the main gate. I expect you to greet our guests politely, and I expect you to pledge yourself appropriately to the concessions agreed." Hamlyn lifted a hand, opening his mouth to speak, but Triston ignored him. "And if I see you even consider doing anything less, know this: more men fought under my banner this past day than they did yours, and if you should want to start yourselves a war I promise you I will finish it."

His words echoed into silence as five sets of wide eyes stared at him. Therburn shot up from his chair, slapping his fist over his heart. More slowly, Lavern did the same, followed closely by Hamlyn and Rigan.

Lady Tanith rolled her eyes and settled back in her seat, crossing one leg over the other. "Your father wouldn't have negotiated."

Triston held her gaze. "I am not my father."

Chapter Fifty-Seven

By the Power

Kura sucked in her stomach as the woman pulled the sash around her waist tight. "What are you doing?"

"Hmm?" She peered around Kura's shoulder, several pins pressed between her teeth, then turned back to continue fussing with the cloth hanging from Kura's hips.

The woman—she said her name was Madilene—had brought out this long red dress and a bundle of red cloth as soon as Kura had stepped into this massive dressing room, and she hadn't stopped fiddling with it since. In truth, the past hour had flown by in a blur.

Kura had met the royal council at the castle gate. They'd seemed friendly enough; each of them had given her a bow and then their name, which she quickly forgot. Triston had stood off to the side, hands folded, watching them all with furrowed brows, and gradually the truth of the situation became clear. The council members had been cordial with her, but their sideways glances and hesitant steps under his gaze said they respected *him*.

Their eyes had met before Devna shuffled her out of the room, and he'd given her a reassuring smile. Heat rose in her cheeks as she remembered it, but that was when she realized she might have the semblance of a plan after all.

"Well..." Madilene stepped back, taking the pins from her mouth as she looked Kura over with a nod. "That's looking pretty good." Excitement flashed in her brown eyes. "It's been quite a while since we last had another young lady in this court. I was afraid I might be out of practice."

Kura smiled, trying to be friendly. Madilene was about her age, probably a bit older, and she carried herself with a confidence that made her seem older still. The ivory-colored dress she wore, buttoned at the back, looked magnificent—the thing itself was made of both smooth and lacy cloth that clung to her stomach but lay loose around her hips—and her neck and ears glinted with the sparkle of stones and precious metal wherever her cascading brown curls didn't hide them.

"Do you want to see?" Madilene pulled a rolling, full-length mirror away from the stone wall.

Kura gasped. Had she ever even *dreamed* of a dress this beautiful? The red was as deep and bright as blood and fire. It had tight, lacy sleeves, an intricately stitched bodice, and a flowing, floor-length skirt that swept lightly to her ankles along with the billowing sash which Madilene had pinned around her waist.

"I..." Kura wouldn't have believed that image to be her own had the figure's hand not risen to sweep a lock of unruly, auburn hair behind her ear as she did the same. That face was hers—the freckles, the eyes, the fading scrapes and bruises on her cheeks—but above that dress it seemed so out of place.

She'd been content with the outfit gifted to her in Nansûr, but when Madilene had offered to 'make her look more presentable,' Devna had insisted she agree. The Fidelis kept guard at the open door, glancing into the room every so often with a disapproving scowl. *Even when I do what she wants, she's not pleased.*

"Oh, of course we still have to do your hair." Madilene stepped into the reflection, studying Kura's face in the mirror. She gathered a handful of her auburn locks. "What are you thinking? Maybe something done up?"

Kura laughed uncomfortably as she glanced between Madilene's reflection and her own. "I—I don't know. What were you thinking?"

Madilene gripped Kura by the shoulders to turn her away from the mirror. "How about a little of both? Something to bring out your cheekbones and distract from these broad shoulders here."

Kura glanced self-consciously at her hands. What did she know about dresses and hair-doing? Although, as a woman, perhaps she ought to know more than she did.

Madilene began brushing out Kura's hair. "So, fonfyr, what are your intentions with us?"

"My intentions?"

"Yes, your intentions. With the way you rode in, all those people and centaurs and animals following you, I would have thought you wanted to make yourself a queen. Is that a good guess? Do you want to be queen?"

Kura laughed, "No, I—" and then caught herself. There was some sense of malice, or at least mistrust, in Madilene's eyes, and she didn't owe this stranger any sort of truth.

"No? You don't want to be queen? Those folks throwing flowers in the streets were just overcome with a sudden enthusiasm for botany?"

Kura stiffened, studying Madilene with a sidelong glance at the mirror. "Some people are just excited. We've been promised concessions."

Madilene nodded, her focus on whatever she was doing with Kura's hair, but Kura could almost feel the woman's glare boring into the back of her head.

She sighed. "Have you ever seen a crowning before?"

Madilene shook her head. "I've heard of them. The bell in the tower rings, the people gather in the courtyard, the one to be crowned makes some vows, gets crowned, and then the nobles pledge their oaths to the crown. Something like that."

"What sorts of vows?"

Madilene laughed derisively. "Shouldn't our future queen already know?"

Kura didn't try to hide her scowl. "Triston will be there, right?"

"Of course." Madilene stepped back, a taunting edge to her smile. "Does someone maybe have a little crush?"

She bristled. *That is none of your business.* "Do you know him well?"

Madilene scoffed as though that was a ridiculous question. Kura fought a twinge of jealousy until she noticed the thin gold band on the woman's right wrist.

"Do you want me as your queen?"

Madilene gave her a bland look. "Sweetie, I thought I was making it abundantly clear I do not."

"Good. Then please teach me the vows."

Devna pinched Kura's elbow as she dragged her down the long, castle hallway. "Let's run through this again."

Kura grimaced, then nodded, as she didn't trust herself to speak pleasantly. The Fidelis had left her well enough alone in the presence of the other rebels, but as they walked now—their boots clacking against the polished marble floor, with only a select few representatives trailing behind—Devna apparently no longer found a need to hold her tongue.

"Remember, we want the split down the Seln River and then across the Feldlands. Let them keep their mines and shipping routes through the Deorwynn Forest and around the Saligens. The plains and the Waste ought to give us enough to build on for now." She paused for a breath, and to appraise Kura with another scowl. "This is not an opportunity to be taken lightly, I don't know why you won't permit me to write down—"

"I've made my decision." Kura stared Devna down until the woman looked away. That level of hostility seemed to be the only thing she respected.

As they neared the large, wooden doors that led onto the balcony, Devna caught hold of Kura's elbow again and pulled her to a stop. "Let them announce you."

Kura smothered a growl, but stood idle as Renard and then Rusket came forward to push open the doors. The rumble of the crowd drifted in with the autumn breeze, and Kura drew in a startled breath as she tried to keep from staring at the churning mass of humanity far below. An ornate table stretched from one end of the balcony to the other—it clearly didn't belong outdoors, but she had insisted on making the negotiations public.

"...Kura of Wynshire!" Renard's voice carried over the crowd as though he was a born speaker. The people murmured with interest; a few belted hearty cheers.

"Remember," Devna said, leaning close to Kura's ear before releasing her elbow. "We are not *asking* for anything. You are in the position of power here: these are *your* demands. Make him know that."

Kura set her jaw and stepped out into the sunlight. She didn't feel like herself—her hair pinned high on her head, just a few strands sweeping down to brush against her shoulders where that red dress left her skin bare—but Ìsendorál's comforting weight hung at her hip and, despite Madilene's protests that they didn't match the outfit, she'd worn her own riding boots.

The council already sat at one end of the table, and two rose from their chairs as Kura strode toward them. Triston, at the opposite head of the table, was the first. He looked more a king than she'd ever seen him, with that red soldier's jacket edged in black and silver, and his dark curls resting light on his shoulders. He placed his right fist over his heart, stance precise and rigid, but there was a smile in his eyes when they met hers.

Gods, he needs to stop doing that. Cheeks burning, she managed to return the salute.

A white-haired man at Triston's side gave a salute so fervent, Kura had to—shockingly—compare his enthusiasm to Renard's. The general beside him only rose once Kura put a hand on the seat at the head of the table, and she had to imagine that disdain lay behind his impassive, dark eyes. The brown-haired woman beside him stood and gave a half-hearted salute, her eyes flicking over the balcony and toward the crowd, and the remaining members didn't stand at all. The older woman scowled at Kura from beneath the brim of her hat, while the large man gave a shout and pointed at Rusket.

"A bear! That's a… that's, uh…"

Kura waited until Devna, Renard, and Grenja took the open seats beside her before sitting down. The chubby man yelped and pointed again when Konik came to stand at her right shoulder.

"That's a… uh…"

The crowd murmured in anticipation, filling the silence, as Kura drew in a deep breath. She forced herself to look each council member in the eye—Renard had told her that was essential, when they'd workshopped this speech together.

"You may have good reasons to hate us. Some of us are criminals, deserters. We may have despised each other, or stolen from each other, or even tried to kill each other. But just days ago, many of us put that aside and fought together. It's with that spirit I stand before you today. To put into words what we previously sought via the sword. To ask you to listen."

The lady in the hat muttered something under her breath, but Triston nodded. "We will listen."

"We ask for an end to the military draft."

Devna hissed and leaned forward to try to whisper something else in Kura's ear, but Kura ignored her.

Triston nodded again. "Done."

The general shifted uncomfortably in his seat. Kura could've sworn he wanted to whisper something in Triston's ear—like Devna had hers—but decided against it.

"We ask for our own representatives on the council." Several of the council members balked at this, but Kura continued. "Grenja or whoever she should choose for all nostkynna, Konik or whoever he should choose for all Cenóri, and Devna or whoever she should choose for all Fidelis."

Triston glanced between the other rebels gathered before him at the table, more thoughtful than hesitant. "I will, but only if this man," he said, pointing to Renard, "agrees to head the royal garrison."

Conversation rippled through the crowd, and the lady in the hat threw her head back and laughed. "A menagerie! You're building a menagerie!"

The general did lean over to whisper in Triston's ear this time, but Triston waved him aside.

Renard glanced from Triston to Kura, his mouth hanging open. "...Me?"

Kura grinned and shrugged. *It's up to you.*

Renard jumped to his feet and slapped his right fist over his heart. "Until death or release, I swear to uphold—"

Triston laughed and motioned for him to sit back down. "We can hold off on that for now. But thank you."

The lady in the hat sighed dramatically. "Is there anything else?"

Kura gave her a discerning look. "We want an end to all taxes on goods made and sold by non-guild members, and a fifty percent tax cut on goods that are." *Gods, what do I know about taxes?* She'd repeated that sentence to herself over and over again to feel comfortable saying it aloud, and still she wasn't sure she'd gotten it right. This was where she wished she really could trust Devna to write their demands down.

Triston frowned pensively. "We might be able to cut taxes on all basic goods, like wheat and corn, and maybe a fifteen percent drop on everything else."

Devna began to shake her head, but Kura ignored it. Of anyone at this table, she knew she could trust Triston. "Done."

The large man at the end fell into a coughing fit, and the dark-haired lady turned on Triston with a look of scorn akin to that of a wife who'd caught her husband kissing the housemaid.

Devna muttered something under her breath and rose from her seat, but before any others followed, Kura spoke. "I have one final demand, and this is not up for negotiation."

The Fidelis sank back into her chair with eyebrows raised.

Triston didn't waver. "Name it."

Kura rose, stepped into the space between the table and the balcony's railing, and drew her sword. "Kneel."

Gasps rippled out among the crowd and those gathered at the table. The white-haired lord now regarded Kura with a sense of fear, and the general's hand went to his sheathed sword. Some people below began to shout, and when Kura stole a glance over the balcony, her stomach lurched. It was as if the entire world stood watching.

"Kura," Grenja started, "you…"

Stoic and silent, Triston got up from his seat and dropped to one knee at her feet. He stared up at her, uncertain yet unafraid.

Frenzied shouts rang out from the crowd—some excited, some panicked—but they all hushed when she raised Ìsendorál's blade, flashing red in the setting sunlight, and placed it on Triston's shoulder.

"Triston, son of Dradge, do you swear by the right of our forebears and the honor of your name to govern this country of Avaron in justice, wisdom, and prudence?"

Triston's eyes widened in utter astonishment, but he found his voice. "I do."

"Do you promise the people of this nation that you'll place their interests, both in safety and prosperity, above your own?"

"I promise it."

"Will you, in times of trouble, be the first on the battlefield and the last to leave it, so long as your life is yours?"

Triston's gaze had strength now, and it carried over to his voice. "I will."

Grinning, Kura tapped the blade on his left shoulder before lifting it over her head. "Then, by the power vested in me by this sword, I crown you King of Avaron. I pledge my loyalty to you, and ask the rest of my friends and companions to do the same."

The crowd below roared in excitement, a deafening cacophony of clapping, shouting, and cheering. Kura sheathed Ìsendorál, and Triston rose carefully to his feet. He looked as though he intended to say something, but she took a step back and placed her right fist over her heart.

Madilene stepped onto the balcony, the crown of Avaron held in her outstretched hands. At a glance, it was a simple bit of jewelry—woven silver wires marked with silver leaves to resemble a tangle of vines—but precious gemstones sparkled among the strands. Triston regarded her curiously, but she flashed him a smile and placed the crown on his head.

The general stood and saluted, his voice nearly lost to the crowd. "The oath I swore to your father I now pledge to you."

As if responding to an invitation, the other council members stood and offered similar promises. Kura peered over her shoulder, chewing her inner lip. Devna sat at the table, fists clenched and resting on her thighs, scowling. Looming behind her, Konik's face was stern—Kura's heart clenched; was he mad at her now, too?—but slowly he bowed his head to Triston and crossed both his arms in an X over his chest.

"My brother long dreamed of peace between our races. I will not dishonor his memory by seeking otherwise today."

That wasn't exactly a pledge of loyalty, but Kura caught herself grinning anyway. Triston nodded to the centaur and offered an Avaronian salute—right fist over his heart.

Grenja jumped down from her chair, fluffy tail raised as she glanced between her and Triston, then barked a laugh. "Sure, I'll make that pledge. I can't do it for all my kind, but a lot of them still listen to me. Maybe this will be fun."

Muttering under her breath, Devna shoved herself to her feet and stalked back into the castle without a word to any of them. Kura stared after her, but decided against trying to argue. Glancing down at the crowd gathered below, she thought she could pick out some of her fellow rebel fighters—they were somehow dressed both more richly and more simply. A portion—more than she'd like—gathered their families and companions and stormed off too, shaking their heads, but most of them smiled and joined in with the cheer from the Edras folk.

Kura shuddered and slowly let herself feel the relief. They were cheering; they were happy. Surely there was more to come from this, but all she knew right now was the excitement of the crowd, and all she saw was Triston standing, dumbfounded, before the people of Avaron. Exactly where he belonged.

Chapter Fifty-Eight

Will and Prophecy

Triston leaned against the great stone pillar between the hallway and the courtyard as he sipped at a mug of wine. Music, louder and more cheerful than he'd heard in years, echoed in the grand hall and spilled out into the courtyard. The crowd did much the same, dancers stumbling into the night air as the churning mass inside spun and swayed to the stringed instruments and the beat of the drums.

"Come on, then, next song?" Madi asked, leaning against Dylen's side.

He chuckled, pulling her close as he wrapped his arm around her shoulders. "Fine. Next song." Dylen turned to Triston. "You coming? With that crown on your head, you might get one of these girls to dance with you."

Triston laughed. "No, you two go on." As a younger man he'd questioned it, but now he understood why his father had stopped dancing. With the solemn weight in his heart, it was quite enough just to watch the revelry.

Madi grasped Dylen's hand and slipped his arm off her shoulder. "What do you think about that Kura girl?"

Triston took a sip from his mug but couldn't hide his smile. "Are the two of you already plotting something else against me?"

Madi laughed, but her amusement didn't linger. "It wasn't my idea. I mean, I was plotting, but..." She reached under the white sash around her waist and drew a tiny silver dagger.

Dylen gasped, and Triston had to fight down a sudden spike of anger at both his friends. In some abstract sense he was touched by their dedication, but why would the two of them think he'd want anyone to do *that*?

"Hey..." Dylen gently took the knife from her hand. "Love, do you even know how to use this?"

"If you earned Captain with that silly thing," she said, slapping the hilt of the sword hanging on his belt, "how hard could it be?" Still, she shuddered, pulled the concealed dagger sheath from her dress, and handed that to Dylen as well. "I thought I could do it. I thought I *needed* to do it. But..." Her voice fell to a whisper. "I couldn't. I'm glad I didn't." She looked up at Triston in apology. "Perhaps I'm not so into the sport after all."

Triston stared into her dark eyes for a long time before his attention returned to that unassuming dagger resting in Dylen's hands. All the possibilities of what might or could or should have been swirled within him at once, and he didn't know what to say.

"Well..." Dylen sheathed the dagger, then shoved it into his pocket. "I'm going to hang on to this, and if you stay on your best behavior, you might have it back tomorrow."

Madi laughed, her smile weak. "It might be best if you just keep it."

"Well now..." Therburn meandered around the pillar, a mug in his hands, which he rested on his large stomach. "I'd thought I'd find you two dancing."

"I tried, Grandfather." Madi grinned, then turned sweetly to Dylen. "But he said we had to wait for the next song."

"Fine." Dylen stepped back, squaring his shoulders, and took Madi's hand. "Shall we dance then, milady?"

Madi curtsied, then latched on to Dylen's arm and dragged him toward the center of the hall.

Therburn glanced down at Triston with a curious frown. "You're not going?"

"Maybe next time."

Triston's gaze settled on the mass of dancers, and with a smile he found Kura among them. The group was a mix of plainly dressed peasants and rebels, oddly attired nostkynna and centaurs, and noble folks dressed in their very best, yet still Kura stood out among them. Her shimmering auburn hair had mostly fallen loose from that configuration Madi had designed, and nothing looked quite as out of place as that sword and scabbard hanging from her hips along with that flowing red dress. But her smile shone brighter than anything else in that whole room.

Gods, she was beautiful.

He'd known that already, but this was the first time he let himself savor the thought, running it over again in his mind as he watched her keep perfect time with the beat.

"You know," Therburn said after a moment, "I was mighty glad to see you alive at the end of this. I don't think I had the chance to tell you that before, but it's true. It was a dark day in Avaron to think we'd lost you."

Triston nodded gratefully.

Therburn took another swig from his mug. "This council, though —you know the rest are some ambitious folks, don't you?"

Triston held his gaze. "Comes with the job, doesn't it?"

"Ah, I'm too old for this job as it is! But I thought I ought to be letting you know."

"Well, thank you. Although I'm sure the rest would have preferred me to be more diplomatic."

Therburn shook his head, lifting his hand to point a chubby finger at Triston's chest. "Oh no, they needed to hear that. All politics ever has been about is making friends or making enemies, and talk like that is how you know which you're leaving with when the conversation's ended."

Triston grinned. He wasn't particularly inclined to agree with the man's advice, but he had to appreciate the honesty.

The song came to an end, and the crowd filled that moment of silence with cheers and applause. Therburn let out a heavy sigh and placed a hand on Triston's shoulder.

"Know we're rooting for you, boy. And anybody else worth having at your back is doing the same." He nodded, then placed a fist over his heart as he stepped away. "My king."

Triston returned the salute.

King. That word had been echoing in the back of his mind all evening. On hearing it, he pictured his father's face—that was about all his thoughts wanted to dwell on, anyway. But *king*... The weight of the crown pressed down on his head, and that was not something he could easily ignore. He'd taken the vows. He had a responsibility to these people—the same he had always had, maybe, but now he saw it for what it was. He couldn't change the circumstances that had brought him here, but he was responsible for the *next* step. And maybe that was a heartening prospect.

"No, your left foot!" Kura called out over the music and the crowd. The musicians were playing "Autumn Harvest", of all songs—everyone seemed to recognize the tune, but no one knew the proper dance to go with it.

Aethan laughed and stumbled to meet her alongside the other dancing partners. "I told you, I don't know how to dance!"

"Come on, everyone knows how to dance, you just have to be shown the steps." The beat changed, and Kura shifted her stance. "Oh, right foot!"

Aethan jumped back, stepped on the next dancer's toes, then jumped forward again—all out of sync with the music. "I think I might need a better teacher."

Kura laughed. *Won't say I disagree.* The beat quickened, and the pairs merged again. Kura danced forward, catching Aethan by the arms, and dragged him in a circle before pulling in, interlocking his arm around hers as the tune came to an end.

The crowd around the dancers erupted into clapping and cheers.

Kura grinned and nodded toward the girl beside them. "Apologize for squashing her toes, then ask to be her partner next time. She's pretty good."

Aethan laughed, with a shrug, and kept his hand pressed against hers. "If it's all the same to you, I think I'll stay here." He leaned forward, their noses brushing together, and then his lips pressed against hers, soft and warm. She stepped back, startled.

Aethan pulled away, eyes wide. "Oh—I'm sorry, I—"

"It's alright," Kura said with an awkward laugh. She slipped her hand from his to nervously sweep her hair back behind her ear. Her heart pounded in her chest, and a caustic fusion of emotions churned in her stomach. How long had he felt like that? She saw the look in his eyes now—it might have always been there, but somehow she hadn't noticed until this moment.

This horrible, ill-timed moment.

Aethan took a step away, raking his fingers through his hair. "I..."

"I need some fresh air."

Aethan nodded, and Kura turned away before she let herself meet his gaze. The last thing she wanted to do was hurt him, but what in the world was she supposed to say?

The crowd brushed by in a blur. Maybe the music began playing again, maybe it didn't. She only found some sense of peace when she wandered out into the quiet darkness at the edge of the courtyard. She stopped as she reached the stone railing, then let out a deep sigh and leaned against it, looking out into the city.

She didn't love him. She might not even know what love was—not really—but she knew that much. He was the most constant friend she'd found since leaving the Wynshire, probably her best friend. Maybe she should love him? In some way she did, but it wasn't in the same way he'd looked at her.

Kura ran a hand over her face and stared aimlessly at the flickering speckles of light that dotted the black cityscape. *How could I have been this blind?*

The muffled sound of the music echoed out onto the courtyard balcony, along with the footfalls of the dancers. Aethan was probably still back there, just as hurt and confused as she was. *I should go talk to him.* He would understand, right? But her feet wouldn't move, and she gladly soaked in the solitude.

The night was cloudless; the moons had yet to rise over the horizon, and despite everything, the sight was captivating. Thousands of points of light glistened in the deep and never-ending darkness above the horizon. She drew in a breath.

She didn't recognize all of these constellations, but this lonesome sky brought back a memory she'd forgotten of that long night so long ago, where she'd sat alone—an arrow in her shoulder—at the bottom of the Everard Ravine. She'd shouted at that nothingness a desperate plea, one of anguish and despair and unbelief.

Emotion caught in her throat. A potent joy gripped her pounding heart and made it still, even as her eyes stung with tears. She hadn't expected an answer then—she'd bitterly gone on thinking she hadn't been answered at all—and yet, somehow, she stood here now, looking up at that same night sky with more than she ever could have dreamed to ask for.

"You had enough of the party already?"

It was Triston's voice. Kura turned, startled, as he walked out from one of the lighted archways that edged the hall to join her on the balcony.

"Oh, just catching some fresh air. My king," she added, throwing her fist against her chest in her best attempt at a proper salute.

Triston shook his head, embarrassed. "You don't have to do that." He rested his arm against the railing as he delicately took the crown off his head. "I wouldn't even be wearing this thing, except it's kind of the whole reason for this celebration."

Kura shrugged, not sure she disagreed. Triston slowly rotated the crown in his hand, the jewels glinting different shades as they caught the light from within the hall. There was clearly something on his mind, but whatever it was, he didn't seem quite comfortable sharing.

Finally, he turned to look her in the eye. "You didn't ask for anything for yourself."

It took her a moment to realize what he was talking about. "Oh." She tucked a loose strand of her hair behind her ear. Devna and Renard and everyone in between had suggestions for what the fonfyr should demand. She didn't think she deserved anything for somehow proving a good liar, and when it came down it, she already had everything she wanted. "It didn't really seem like something I should—"

"Would you like to be Lady of Edras?"

Kura looked at Triston in surprise, too shocked to let herself speculate too far. *'Lady'... that means a council seat?* Red colored the tips of his ears, but he managed a smile.

"I would have offered earlier today, but I thought for sure you were going to ask for something. Seren was Lord of Edras, the crown's advisor, and while the council stands to grow considerably, that seat is still empty."

Right, a council seat. "And you want me...?" Kura could only stare at him in disbelief. "You know I don't actually know anything about taxes, or council meetings, or..." She turned toward the darkened city as her cheeks flushed with heat. "I can't write, and I can barely read."

Triston grinned wryly. "You might be overestimating the capabilities of the current council. Besides..." He shrugged. "There aren't many people in this city who I know I can trust. My motives are more than a little selfish. It would be my honor to have you sit at my side."

"Well..." She stared into his light blue eyes and was suddenly grateful her cheeks were already red. "I guess I would be honored to accept."

Triston reached out to shake her hand. "Then I guess this is decided."

Kura took his hand in hers. It was rough and warm and enveloped hers easily and gently. Emotion fluttered in her stomach. And then their hands pulled away, and both of them turned to look out across the darkened city. She pressed her arms against her chest, repressing a shiver as a mix of something—part fear, part excitement—quickened the beat of her heart.

She'd had crushes before, when she'd been considerably younger and a bit more foolish. The Wynshire had no shortage of roguishly handsome faces—certainly not for a girl with an imagination yet untamed by responsibility. Discreetly, she studied the shadowy outline of Triston's face. This was something different.

He *was* handsome, to be sure—more handsome than such a remarkable swordsman and soldier had any right to be. But as those light blue eyes held the firelight in their soft smile, she thought she might have glimpsed the soul behind them: a beautiful soul, one earnest and strong and independent.

Was this love, then? Somehow, the answer came back a resounding no. But all the same, she knew she could love him, if given the chance. If, of that soul, she could catch more than a glimpse.

"Oh." Triston glanced up as he picked at one of the jewels in his crown. "Seren had a rather large estate. There's no family to lay claim to it, so it's within the crown's rights to decide where it goes. And I think it ought to go to the next Lady of Edras."

"An *estate*?"

He grinned. "It's quite nice, actually—out a way into the mountains but still within the city walls. Not that he really spent much time there. I can take you out to see it tomorrow if you'd like."

Kura gaped. "I..." She laughed. "Yes. Thank you."

Triston nodded in reply. Again she thought he wanted to say something, but in the end he turned away to look out at the horizon. Maybe she was imagining it—projecting her own emotions into his expressions. She felt as though there was something she should say, at least after everything they'd been through, but whatever it was remained a feeling, a whisper in her heart that she couldn't shape into words.

Triston leaned back from the balcony. "You heading back to the grand hall?"

"In a minute."

Triston took a step away, catching her gaze with a small—almost shy—smile. "Alright."

Kura listened as his footsteps faded into the background noise of the crowd behind her. She sighed contentedly and peered up at the stars as she grasped at the intangible mesh of emotions in her chest. Her father would be happy to know they had a place to stay—no doubt that thought had crossed his mind long before it had hers. She'd left them somewhere near the dining hall, her mother and father talking and rocking Rowley to sleep (that boy would sleep through anything) as Faron and Elli ran off into the crowd.

First, she needed to talk to Aethan. Something about the brightness of the stars made her less hesitant about that prospect.

Turning away from the balcony, Kura lingered with a hand resting on the railing. The soft breeze carried the scent of woodsmoke and the nip of winter's impending chill. A squawk, low and guttural, mingled with the rustling of leaves, as a branch swayed at the edge of the terrace. She recognized the sound but only placed it as the small, dark figure settled on its perch, its black feathers a silhouette against the starlit sky.

It was the flicker.

A Note from the Author

Thank you so much for reading this book!

With my writing, I want to, most of all, offer readers an exciting and emotionally fulfilling escape from day-to-day life—to give a soft, persistent reminder that maybe magic still exists in the world, no matter how much the daily grind tries to convince us otherwise. I hope this story was able to achieve a little something like that today.

As an independent author, the biggest challenge I have is letting the world know this book exists at all. The best method for getting that word out? Ratings and reviews. And those of course come from you.

If you are willing to leave a rating or a review (on any platform) I would be forever grateful! You don't have to *write* something; a star rating alone is still valuable. And, if you do want to write something, it doesn't have to be long-winded or eloquent—it just has to be honest.

Thank you again, and happy reading!

GLOSSARY

A searchable glossary is available on my website:
https://labuckauthor.com/

WANT TO READ MORE?

Join my newsletter for an exclusive short story set 150 years before *Fire of the Forebears:*

Dancing Across the Water

Evêtra deserted the Service to escape the endless wars she waged for the nation she once called her own. But, even after crossing the ocean itself, she finds only further strife.

When her fellow captain's attempt to broker peace with the centaur natives goes awry, it's her own life she'll be fighting for as she's forced to re-examine the world she thought she understood.

Subscribe here: https://sendfox.com/lp/36j252

About the Author

A goat farmer, engineering graduate, first degree black belt, and medical student, the one thing Lauren Buck always knew she wanted to be was an author. The first stories she ever wrote, as a grade-schooler, were about super heroes. But, raised on a steady diet of Lewis, Tolkien, and Sanderson, it was only a matter of time before she set her sights on epic fantasy.

When not writing, working, or studying, she enjoys drawing, playing the guitar, traveling, as well as outdoor activities such as hiking, fishing, and kayaking. Sometimes you can find her hanging out on Twitter, probably with a German shepherd or two sleeping at her side.

According to Myers-Briggs Lauren is an INTJ, and country roads will always take her home to wild and wonderful West Virginia.

FIND ME ONLINE!

Website:
https://labuckauthor.com/

Twitter:
https://twitter.com/LABuckAuthor

Instagram:
https://www.instagram.com/labuckauthor

Facebook:
https://www.facebook.com/LABuckAuthor

Pinterest:
https://www.pinterest.com/labuckauthor

Goodreads:
https://www.goodreads.com/labuckauthor

Bookbub:
https://www.bookbub.com/authors/l-a-buck

Printed in Great Britain
by Amazon